# The Walker

### By Peter Sawyer

The Complete Epic Saga of Daryo the Walker

Including

Dead Moon

and

Eight Years Walking: Seas & Roads and Swords & Stars

- Book 1- The Orphan
- Book 2- Seas & Roads
- Book 3- Swords & Stars
- Book 4- The Warrior
- Book 5- A Wandering Lord
- Book 6- The Smith
- Book 7- Legacy of a Hero
- Addendum and Map

## Prologue

'Move silently. Stay close to the trees. They will not see us coming.'
The group of uniformed soldiers nodded. None were wearing their armour, just their dun-coloured doublets, trousers, boots and a leather skullcap. Each had a short-bladed sword sheathed, a hooked knife that was more tool than weapon and some carried wooden "arm-shields"- small shields barely wider than the carrier's forearm and slightly longer at each end. Their leader carried a slim hatchet on his belt and a square shield. A soldier nearby held the reins of his horse.
'Move.'
The group of nearly a hundred men broke into smaller teams and started picking their way through the forest in the direction of the newly-risen moon. The land sloped upwards gently; the sound of fast-flowing water was audible over the noises of men in the trees. The trunks thinned and the leader raised his free hand. The company straggled to a halt near the edge of the trees. Ahead, not a hundred yards away, was a cluster of tents around a large fire. There was a score of the conical tents, a few horses and goats and several people moving around. Beyond, another five hundred yards, were the houses of a large village with the spire of a temple in the centre.
'Draw swords.'
The soldiers' weapons were in metal-ribbed hide sheaths and made little noise as they were drawn. The leader took his steed's reins and mounted quickly, readying his hatchet.
'Begin.'
The men surged forwards, their mounted captain following at a gentle trot. Someone near the edge of the encampment must have heard a noise or sensed the approach and shouted a warning. The captain spurred his horse on, overtaking his men and swung the blunt side of the hatchet, knocking the helpless man to the ground. A woman screamed as soldiers flung her tent open and hauled her out into the night air. They pushed her roughly towards the fire in the midst of the camp, where already several others were stood closely guarded. A man raised a massive sword to defend himself; a soldier parried his lunge and the captain rode past, striking the man's head clean through with his axe. Someone tried to run from a tent but was tackled by three soldiers and dragged towards the fire by his feet screaming curses and threats. A child sobbed, an old man objected to his treatment and was slapped by the flat of a sword and pushed into the assembly. The captain turned his horse about and had it walk to the fire where about fifty people were now penned by a ring of soldiers. One soldier stood guard over a small pile of confiscated weapons.

'People of the Batribi! You are not welcome here! You steal crops! You take animals! You are to be removed from these lands!'

'Liar!' shouted one woman.

'Where to?' demanded a man.

'Beyond the River Dithithindil.'

'That's Vidmaria! That's death to any Batribi!' The man insisted.

'You are no longer welcome in Yashoun lands. You will be removed by these men tonight. Any man or woman, any elder or infant who resists or returns will be put to the sword!'

The thicket of swords and the axe-wielding captain convinced the captive Batribi that resistance would be a futile endeavour. The Batribi were a nomadic people and peaceable in philosophy. Their difference was what made many fear them. The Yashoun, the Vidmarians, the Jaboen, the Boskinians all ostracised Batribi to a certain degree. The Yashoun soldiers were fair-skinned, many with fair hair and pale features. By contrast, the Batribi were a dark-skinned people, many with characteristic beaked noses and dark eyes, many of the men shaved their scalps but grew their beards. The women tended to wear close-fitting garments and used natural colours to enhance their complexion. The differences had caused even being a Batribi in Vidmaria to be punishable by death.

The captain nodded to a subordinate. 'Round up their baggage. Load it on whatever horses that can carry it and then move them out.'

'Yes, sir. Move!'

The Batribi began to comply reluctantly. Several were crying. The soldiers followed each move closely, weapons ready. A shout from the far side of the camp caught the captain's attention. He pulled the horse around and spurred it on. A soldier was in pursuit of a fleeing figure. A Batribi had hidden or found a weakness in their security and was attempting an escape.

'Where?' he demanded.

The soldier waved with his sword towards the village. A woman was running and she was apparently young and fleet-footed.

'Help in the encampment!' The captain pursued the woman. She was nearly to the village. The captain remembered that the village was called Thiel and built down a series of manmade switchbacks down a steep slope to the river. Unusually for a village so close to the Vidmarian and Yashoun borders it had no wall. Several stone houses were built side by side to form a perimeter but no more than four or five constituted a row, leaving many ways into the village. The woman darted through a gap too narrow for the captain's horse. He urged it on, found another gap a little further on and turned in, ducking beneath a low archway. The narrow street came to a T, the captain guessed left and saw the woman turn to the right down another alley towards the crest of the ridge. He had to pass it again and take the next lane, paved with cobblestones that made the horse skitter. He urged it on again and turned right. The centre of the village was an open square, probably for markets, with the temple on one side at the crest of the ridge. The woman was almost at the steps of the temple, still running. The captain spurred his horse into a full gallop. The woman leaped up the stairs, screaming in terror and threw her spare hand against the closed door, hammering and screaming for help. The captain's horse mounted the steps and she turned to run again. The rider wheeled his horse and the still-rushing animal knocked the woman to the ground. She cried as she rolled down the steps.

'STOP!' shouted a man.

The captain reined in his horse. A man was hurrying around the temple, the cowl of his robe raised but still trying to tie the sash.

'You desecrate the temple of Spinel!'

The captain groaned inwardly. Spinel, Third Goddess, Guardian of Understanding, Respect and...

'The Third Goddess teaches compassion! What are you doing?'

'I am a captain of the Yashoun Guard, my name is Tuvak.'

'I did not ask your name, Captain. I asked your purpose.'

'There was an encampment of Batribi outside the village. We are removing them from these lands, across the Dithithindil River. She ran, I pursued.'

'A grown man, armed and armoured, mounted. Against a woman.' The priest strode down the steps to the prone woman. 'A woman that you killed on the steps of the temple.' The priest rolled her onto her back from her side and the bundle in her arm moved and started to cry.

'Is that a baby?'

The priest opened the blanket. It was a baby boy wrapped in nothing but the blanket. There was a gash on his forehead from the fall. 'You have taken this child's mother from it. There is only one way to redemption. You must care for the child as your own.'

'Impossible,' scoffed the captain. 'I am a man of the Yashoun Guard. I have no way of caring for a child while I'm fighting for the Emperor.' He thought for a minute. Spinel was a Goddess revered in the Guard teaching respect for the enemy, compassion for the prisoner and mercy to the opponent. 'I would fund the child's keep. It could be sent to a School of the Temples.'

The priest nodded slowly. 'Agreed.'

## Book 1- The Orphan
## Chapter 1

### Fifteen summers later

The end of week market was always more crowded than the normal daily one. Carts and barrows were brought into Salifa from many leagues around. The town was the only place for many to sell their wares for over a day's fast ride. The stone-buttressed earth walls encircled the city of some seven thousand people straddling the Riy River, a tributary of the Dithithindil, which ran almost exactly north to south. The east and west gates were where every potential trader was checked by the town's Pickets. Most were well known and passed with a cursory inspection and a friendly word. Anyone new, unfamiliar or not obviously a Jaboen would have their wares searched and their business questioned. Market Street ran along the east bank of the river between the two bridges. The northern bridge was the oldest known in Jaboen, just wide enough for two horses to pass, the Old Bridge was an unwalled wooden-stilted but solid construction. Downriver, nearly two hundred yards along the Market Street was the Stone Bridge, twice as wide and decorated by intricately-carved stone plants and animals on the stonework. Several traders were able to set their wares on the bridge, the rest lined Market Street on both sides, watched over in the centre of the thoroughfare by the Temple of Dule, Fourth God, Bringer of Wealth and Security, a constant fire burned in front of the Temple doors to demonstrate the perpetual nature of commerce and trade.

Backing onto the river, right at the top of the bank and almost midway between the Old and Stone Bridges was a blacksmith's stall. A sizeable forge was set out, and had been for a generation, under a thatched roof, with a wooden wall at the rear. A strongly-built man worked the forge; his hair greying around the fringes, his hands scarred and calloused by his life's work. As he worked, he kept a close eye on the young Batribi that worked with him.

Daryo was tall and lean, his dark Batribi skin disturbed only by a pale scar above his left eye, his curled black hair kept under his habitual red hood. In the manner of many Batribi men, he worked with his short scarlet tunic belted and in black breeches and boots. He was testing the balance of a new sword with wide swings and sharp stabs.

'This is well-balanced, Master,' he said, his voice deep and smooth.

'Then get it sharp.'

'Yes, Master.'

Daryo took the blade to the grindstone at the side of the forge and started to sharpen, his right foot regularly pumping the stirrup to turn the stone wheel as wide as his hand and ten times the distance across. With each push of the stirrup, the wheel turned and sharpened the new sword.
'By the power of Dule... Daryo!'
'Master?'
'The butcher's tools! Fetch them!'
'Yes, Master!' Daryo stood and slid the sword into a bucket before setting off at a run for the Old Bridge. Vehllal was a strict but reasonable master for a School Ward; the cooper beat his boy regularly. Daryo returned to the school lodging every evening tired but having learned something more about the making, honing and use of weapons. The butcher had two sets of his great knives and cleavers and had them sharpened on alternate days. Vehllal normally had Daryo collect from the butcher as soon as the smithy was working.
The butcher's wooden-walled, close-fronted shop, much like the forge, also backed onto the river but was immediately next to the Old Bridge. A huge deer carcass, hung by the neck under the thatched awning at the front of the shop, was being cut down by the butcher's young apprentice; the butcher would not take a School Ward and had a townsman's boy as his apprentice.
'Gods' Watch on you, Daryo.'
'Gods' Watch, Kalif. I'm here for the tools.'
'Of course.' Kalif turned and went into the shop. It was unthinkable for a School Ward to enter the shop of a tradesman not his master so Daryo waited outside. Kalif returned with a thick leather roll the length and breadth of a man's thigh. 'My master asks that they are returned in the new morning.'
Daryo thought for a moment. 'I think my master can do so, although he has the Picket's work too.'
'Gods' Watch.'
'Gods' Watch, Kalif.'

The day ended with the setting of the sun. The stalls and shops along the Market Street closed, except for the inns at either end. As the sun finally disappeared behind the distant hills, Vehllal dismissed his apprentice. On the edge of town, on the west side of the river, was a long, low thatched building with a smaller example of Dule's fire at the door, this was the School of the Temple. Two score boys lived under the care of the elder priests of the Temple, sleeping on straw mattresses, learning to write, read and do simple sums. All but one were apprenticed around the town to traders on Market Street, a cook at the Lord's house and farmer's close to the walls. The last had been dismissed so many times from his apprenticeships that he was now allowed only to clean the Temple under strict supervision. Two Wards, both younger than Daryo, were sparring outside the door with wooden bars.

'Batribi!'

Daryo had an idea of what was about to be said but kept walking to the door.

'Batribi! You seem to have fallen in the dirt! No! My apologies! It is your skin!'

The other boy laughed uproariously. Daryo continued walking into the School. The School was a single room- a long table surrounded by somewhat flimsy chairs filled the centre, the walls were lined by low, narrow beds, a large fire blazed in the stone hearth at the far end.

'Daryo!' Only one other ward addressed him as anything but 'Batribi'.

'Suffayah.' Daryo sat down on a bed alongside Suffayah's. 'A hard day's work with the cattle.'

Suffayah nodded slowly. He was the same age as Daryo but taller and broader with oddly straw-coloured hair, he worked for a cattle and swine farmer a mile's distance from the town. 'Calving, never easy. We are fortunate that we have not lost any cows.'

'The farmer must be pleased.'

'He is. He cannot pay me in coin but...' Suffayah glanced around furtively and withdrew a long cucumber from under his bed's blanket. 'Payment was made.' He produced a knife, cut a few inches from one end and handed the piece to Daryo.

'Thank you.' Daryo ate quickly. 'The butcher's tools were done but the Picket Captain will be unhappy that his work is still not done.'

'At least you cannot be blamed.'

'There is just so much work: the butcher, the carpenter, the sawyer, the Pickets, the farrier...'

Suffayah nodded in understanding. 'This is good.'

'It is.' Daryo yawned. 'I should sleep. Vehllal wants to start early tomorrow.'

'Of course.'

Daryo woke in the darkness. Far too early to head to the forge, the Pickets would arrest him. The first light of sunrise was the cue for the Pickets to withdraw from the town's streets. The room was dark, the Wards were all sleeping, a hound barked somewhere in the town. And Daryo could hear voices. The School was just a couple of feet from the wall, a seven foot earth wall with a line of massive stones along the base each side. In

some places, elderly wooden stakes formed an extra barrier. The wall was slightly lower by the school but had the old wooden spikes across the top. Sound carried well over the wall and Daryo could hear, through the open window space by his bed, low voices.
'Salifa,' said one, a man, his voice gravelly and elderly-sounding. 'They are a tolerant people. The market people.'
'We are too close to Yashoun,' said another, younger-sounding man.
'They are a tolerant people,' repeated the first. 'We will be as welcome here as anywhere. It is dark, we cannot travel any further. The children need to sleep, the ox needs to rest. Build a fire, Laulra.'
Daryo sat up in his bed. Laulra was a Batribi name. The people outside the walls were Batribi. He had seen maybe a finger's numbers of his own people since he had been brought to the School. There was some quiet noise, somewhat muffled by the wall, as the fire was built. After a few minutes, Daryo could smell the smoke from the wood. There was some conversation that he could not clearly hear for a while before a soft tap-tap sound began. It became more regular, as if more people were making the sound. Daryo thought it sounded like the soft clapping of hands or the slapping of thighs or arms. And then the gravelly voice began to speak again:

*'Our people walk and walk again,*
*This fate of ours is each one's bane,*
*To sleep beneath the stars each night,*
*To walk and walk again in flight.'*

A different voice took over, a woman:

*'The night is dark and full of fear,*
*How long may we few linger here?*
*Our children cry for meat and bread,*
*Our elders' hearts cry only dread.'*

Several voices spoke together:

*'Our people walk and walk again,*
*This fate of ours is each one's bane,*
*To sleep beneath the stars each night,*
*To walk and walk again in flight.'*

Another woman:

*'Wolves dog our steps, do they not sleep?*
*The weariness that burns our feet,*
*The sun that burns, the cold of snow,*
*Know but that we must yet now go.'*

*'Our people walk and walk again,*
*This fate of ours is each one's bane,*
*To sleep beneath the stars each night,*
*To walk and walk again in flight.'*

'Peace, my kin,' said the older voice. 'The hour is late. I will go to the Captain of the Guard in the new day to see if we may enter the town and buy some provisions. Halvan, take the first watch.'

'Yes, Stai.'

Daryo heard the sound of a sword being drawn and then silence fell. He did not sleep again.

Sunrise came and Daryo left the School before anyone else even rose, seizing a bread roll from the table as he passed. He knew the Pickets would be withdrawing outside the walls, a procedure known as the Alert Watch guarding against a dawn attack on the town. Daryo hurried to the fifty yards to the West Gate. The wooden gates were slightly taller than the wall either side- the Gates were younger than Daryo, the walls were centuries old. Three Pickets were stood at the Gate, all wearing an iron-banded leather skullcap and light hauberk over their dark purple tunic and leggings. Two carried bows and sheathed daggers, the third had a spetum- a long spear-like shaft with a curved blade, sharp on the outside with two downward-pointing tips- and carried a shield with a snarling, rearing badger device.

'Where are you going, boy?' demanded the shorter of the bowman, a man of many long season's service with a mighty scar down the side of his face.

'I wanted a walk around the wall before I go to the forge,' said Daryo. 'I am Master Vehllal's apprentice.'

'Go to the forge,' ordered the bowman. 'There are some of your people outside the walls, dangerous people.'

'They are not my people,' said Daryo firmly, although not really believing in his own words.

'Batribi are all dangerous, dirty folk,' said the other bowman and his colleagues nodded as if in agreement with some great universal truth.

Daryo turned on his heel and headed for the Stone Bridge. The first job of Daryo's day was to light the fire. The forge rarely went completely cold and it was easy to start a raging blaze in the stone ring at the centre. Next he checked the grindstone and anvil for any damage and then laid out the smith's tools ready. When the bells rang from the temple, the Lord's house and the Picket's Barracks for the second hour from dawn,

Vehllal arrived, greeting his apprentice with a gruff "God's Watch" and a leg of chicken, which Daryo took and ate gratefully. Wards only got meat every other day at the School.
'There are Batribi outside the walls, did you know?'
Daryo feigned ignorance. 'I did not, Master. Many?'
'A score, maybe fewer, an ox and a large cart, they have put up their tents.'
'They will be allowed to stay?'
'Lord Hummat is tolerant of Batribi. They trade what they can, they rarely cause real trouble, we may get some coin out of it if they have weapons or tools that need repair.' Vehllal thought for a moment. 'Go and see.' He took a metal badge from his belt, an anvil and hammer were carved on it. It signified Vehllal's status as master of an apprentice. If the apprentice bore it, it was permission to leave the town. Some apprentices such as Suffayah practically lived with theirs but Daryo had never been handed his master's badge.
'For sure, Master?'
'For sure. I know it has been several seasons since I let you leave the gates but this is a godsent chance to get some extra business. And if you have won the business, I will permit you to do the work.'
Daryo beamed. 'Thank you, Master.'
'Go.'
Daryo took the badge and tried not to hurry across the Stone Bridge to the West Gate. The same bowman confronted him.
'Where do you go, Batribi?'
'Outside the walls,' said Daryo, showing his Master's badge.
The bowman took the badge and studied it carefully before returning it. 'Apprentice passing the gate!' he called.
Daryo strode out of the gate as the Lord of Salifa did. The conical Batribi tents were arranged in a loose circle facing outwards about ten yards from the wall directly across it from the School building. A very large and elderly-looking ox was tethered to a stake on the thin grass nearby. A young man with long braided hair, dressed in loose olive-coloured robes and holding a short, somewhat curved sword in his hand saw Daryo approach from the gate.
'An approach!' he called.
Several other Batribi emerged from their tents, some holding swords, one wielding a short spear with a leaf-shaped blade. One was an elder, his hair a mass of grey reaching almost to his waist, naked from the waist up as if come from washing. He was unarmed and held up a cautionary hand to his compatriots. Daryo guessed that he was Stai.

'Who approaches?' he called as Daryo came within a stone's range. He then noticed Daryo's appearance. 'Are you one? Are you Batribi?'

'In my heritage, elder,' said Daryo, stopping a respectful distance away. 'I am a Ward of the School of the Temple in Salifa. I am the apprentice to Vehllal the smith. He brings you greetings and offers his services to you.'

'Typical Jaboen, wanting money and nothing more,' snorted the young sentry.

'Peace, Halvan.'

Daryo recognised Halvan's voice as that of the man that had argued against staying outside Salifa. 'My Master recognises that Batribi are seldom welcomed and seldom aided. This is all he offers.'

'We do not yet have permission to enter the town.'

Daryo inclined his head. 'And thus my Master puts me at your service.'

'We cannot pay in coin but we have items that your Master may accept in trade,' said Stai, coming closer to Daryo. 'And I would speak to you, if I may, Daryo. Let us see what business and what goods we may offer.'

'Agreed.'

The Batribi were nineteen in number: Stai the elder, six men of youth and middle age, nine women on average younger than the men and three girl children less than six summers old. Eight tents, a cart and an ox made up the travelling party, most of whom were Stai's nephews and their families. A total of four swords and eight spears as well as several tools were deemed by Stai to require attention at the forge. The payment suggested was three flasks of ox milk, a large well-made woollen blanket and one of the spears themselves. Daryo relayed the proposal to Vehllal, who accepted and sent his apprentice back for the items. Daryo had worked with Vehllal for nearly five summers and had learned most of what he needed to know about smithing. He repaired the three damaged mallets and the bent saw and then sharpened the weapons conscientiously. Vehllal then inspected the weapons before Daryo returned them. The master smith let nothing leave his forge unless it was of a sufficient standard.

'Very good, Daryo,' he said after what seemed like an eternal evaluation from the apprentice's place. 'Yes, very good.'

'Thank you, Master.'

'Have you had a chance to speak with any of the Batribi?'

'No, Master. I had work to do.'

'You should speak with them. It would be good for you to know something of their life and your heritage and they would be the best teachers. What is the hour?'

'It is the twelfth, master.'
'Take back the Batribi's items and you are permitted to remain without the walls until sundown.'
'I... my thanks, master.' Daryo had handed back his apprentice badge on returning to the forge and now had it returned to him.
'I can handle the forge. Gods' Guidance, Daryo.'
'Gods' Guidance.' Daryo quickly assembled the Batribi tools and weapons and placed them gently in the two large sacks that they had come in. He gave his smiling master a brief bow and left at a trot for the West Gate.

'Daryo of the School of the Temple!' the young woman standing watch hailed him.
He remembered her name, she was guardian of the tools and equipment, was mother of one of the children, and he addressed her in the Batribi fashion. 'Yiua, kin of Stai. I bring your charges.'
'Thank you!' Yiua was nearly as tall as Daryo and had a ready smile. She took the larger sack from his hand, opened it and withdrew a sword. She ran her thumb across the blade. 'Excellent! You are a skilled smith, Daryo of the School of the Temple.'
'I had a good tutor. Vehllal is the forgemaster and maybe the best in Jaboen.'
'I know Stai wished to speak with you. He is in his *kaff*.'
'*Kaff*?'
'I am sorry, we still sometimes use the words in our own tongue. The *kaffa* are the canvas homes.' She indicated the nearest.
'The Standard Speech says tents.'
'Tents... tents... thank you, Daryo of the School of the Temple.'
Stai was sat on a small stool in his tent, cleaning a piece of harness for the ox with a small knife and a bucket of water. He wore a long hooded woollen robe over leggings and a rather baggy shirt. 'Daryo, welcome. Sit.'
Daryo sat on a large straw-filled cushion. 'My master has given me permission to spend some time with you, elder. He believes it would be good for me.'
'I agree. Tell me what you know of your kin, your parents.'
'I know nothing but that they were Batribi, elder. I grew as a Ward of the School. I have known nothing else. The priests tell me that the Batribi were pirates and brigands long ago.'
'Perhaps. We came from across the sea to the north; a warmer land and one of much sun and almost no rain. Our ancestors landed on the Yashoun coast but were driven out over time. Now we are spread in small kin groups throughout the known lands-

Yashoun, Jaboen, and Boskinia. In some places we are hunted and slaughtered. The Regents of Vidmaria passed laws long ago offering a price on the head, and just the head, of any Batribi bought to him. In some of the whorehouses of Yashoun, Batribi women with nowhere else to turn earn barely a knob of bread in exchange for their bodies. But some places we are permitted. Many market towns permit us, such as Salifa does.'

'Why were our people driven out, elder?'

'Because folk fear the abnormal, the unaccustomed, the different. Our people became known as outcasts, legends and superstitions, myths and lies grew up around us. We are shunned now, as we probably always shall be.'

'Is there anything our people can give? To change opinions?'

'I think our time to do that is long past. We are too scattered, too talked about, and too mistrusted. We have our own ways, our ways of speaking to others, our skill with words and poetry, many Batribi are excellent workers of canvas, wool, leather, linen. My own niece, Diatia, could knit you a sword sharper than your blacksmith's steel.'

Daryo smiled. 'So you have goods to trade and weapons to defend yourselves.'

Stai laughed. 'Indeed. But wool and material are items that we have to barter for as well. The blanket that we gave in exchange for your smithing skills was made by Diatia with wool bought in Three Rivers.'

'Did you walk from Three Rivers here? Along the river?'

'Not directly. We followed the Red Mountain road to Lalbi before coming to Salifa. We are less welcome under the mountains than we are by the rivers. Three Rivers and Salifa are the kindest places for us to visit but we can never stay. Rumours begin, a crime is blamed on one of our number and we are forced away. We walk and walk again.'

'I heard that poem that you spoke when you first made camp. The School of the Temple is just within the wall.'

'It is the Verse. It tells our story. Only the refrain is repeated, our people use their skill with words to create their own lines. All Batribi speak the refrain and all Batribi learn to speak their own words. If nothing else, our people can imagine and speak their thoughts.'

'I think it a fine tradition.'

'It is one of the few parts of our culture that remains and one that even the young can participate in. Speaking of participation, would you eat with us?'

'I would be honoured.'

Stai stood and Daryo did so too. At the entrance to the tent, Stai called to one of the men. 'Burus, is the meal ready?'

'Yes, Stai.'

'Come, Daryo.'

Stai's kin were seated around their fire. A brace of large rabbits had been caught and roasted. Fruits and bread were produced and Daryo sat, ate and listened to the talk of the extended family group. He learned that one man was Stai's son, his wife and all but one of the girl children were theirs. The rest of the adults were Stai's nieces, nephews and their kin. Yiua was a cousin of Stai's, her husband was Burus, their daughter was Impini, named for Stai's late wife. The group had dwindled in number since they had been at Lalbi; Stai's son had taken nine adults southwards again. Smaller groups attracted less attention and those without children could move faster.

A horn was heard and one of the Batribi suggested that it was near sunrise. Daryo looked up. The sky was darkening.

'I should go,' said Daryo. 'I must be within the walls at the close of the gates. I thank you, Stai, and your most gracious kin. I shall return if at all I can.'

He turned for the gate. He was close before he realised that the huge doors were already closing. He broke into a run.

'Hold! Hold! I'm the smith's apprentice! Hold the gate!'

An unfamiliar Picket, holding a long spear and with a horn at his belt, barred the way.

'Stop, Batribi!'

Daryo stopped an inch from the levelled spearpoint. 'Hold your blade! I am Daryo, a Ward of the School of the Temple, apprentice to Vehllal the Smith. I was given permission to come outside the walls.' He handed over his apprentice's badge.

The Picket peered at it in the twilight. One of his colleagues stepped through the almost-closed gate and looked at it too.

'From whom did you take this?'

'My master,' said Daryo, confused.

'I thought Batribi had no masters. Or laws, or decency.' The spearman swung the haft of his weapon and knocked Daryo sideways.

Daryo shouted in surprise and anger and tried to seize the weapon. 'Get Vehllal! Get Uzum of the Temple! They will–'

The spear swung again, Daryo tried to catch it and the second Picket's fist connected with his jaw. Daryo had no memory of crying out but within a moment, six of Stai's clan had appeared.

'Leave him!' snapped Burus. He was carrying a curved Batribi sword. A hand pulled Daryo to his feet, it was Yiua, carrying a leaf-bladed spear in her free hand. Laulra, Halvan, Bori and Drai were also armed and had formed a loose cordon around Daryo.

'To arms!' shouted the spearman. 'Pickets to arms!'

Yiua released Daryo and stepped forwards, lowering her spear. 'Men of Salifa, this man is not one of us! He is an apprentice to your forgemaster. He is Daryo, Ward of the School of the Temple. He came outside the walls to bring us some goods repaired by his master and is now returning to his School. Please allow him passage and we can forget this.'
There was no warning, no order to withdraw, the arrow whistled from a Picket behind the gate and struck Yiua full in the throat. She was dead before she fell.
'YIUA!' screamed , her brother.
'Hold hold hold!' shouted Daryo. The bowman, the one with the scar, had notched another arrow. 'Hold! Kin of Stai, you must withdraw. You must. Strike camp. Walk again.'
The words of the Verse resonated with the Batribi and they lowered their weapons one by one. 'Withdraw,' hissed Burus.
Daryo spread his arms wide. His right arm was stinging from the spear blow and his jaw ached from the clenched fist. 'Picketmen, I am going to remove the dead woman from the road to the camp. The camp will be struck tonight. No Batribi will approach the gate.' He crouched down slowly and pulled Yiua's body over his shoulders, standing up slowly, bearing the weight, trying to ignore her blood running down his back and arms. Resolutely, he turned his back on the gate and stepped slowly to the Batribi encampment. Beside the fire, he gently lowered Yiua to the ground. Stai emerged from his *kaff* and sank to his knees wordlessly.
'Elder, I... she...'
Stai held up a hand. 'You are not to blame, Daryo of the School of the Temple. We protect our own. Yiua followed her blood and now walks with her mother's footsteps.' His voice was strained. Burus came from another tent and drove his sword point-first into the earth by Yiua's head. The rest of the clan did so too; even her young daughter did so, weeping and sobbing as she did so. Daryo found his knife on his belt and was the last to place its point in the dirt. Drai, Yiua's brother, spoke slowly, trying to keep himself from sobbing like his niece:

'*Yiua walked like light through shade,*

*Her voice, her wit, sharpened like blades,*

*Her life now spent, her footsteps fade,*

*Our sister was light, our love she made.*'

Daryo joined the kin group, knowing instinctively what they would say:

'*Our people walk and walk again,*

*This fate of ours is each one's bane,*

*To sleep beneath the stars each night,*

*To walk and walk again in flight.'*
Stai placed a shaking hand on the cooling brow. 'Gods that guard our steps and watch our nights, take care of our sister and niece, daughter and mother, Yiua, daughter of Uli, kin of Stai and Impini. Let her find her road at her mother's side. Let her footsteps light the sky with her mother and all Batribi that have gone before us.' He stood slowly. 'Pack the camp. Drai, care for Niaa and Huryo. Burus, harness the oxen. Temma, I wish you to look to the tools and weapons for this night. About your duties.'
Daryo went to talk but Stai held up a hand again. 'Daryo, you have no need to speak. I am sorry that we have brought this upon you.'
'You have brought nothing on me!' Daryo protested. 'I should have heeded the sun and returned earlier!'
'No. You associated with us, a Batribi kept like you within the walls is tolerated, when you stepped outside to fraternise with us, you became one of us in the eyes of the townsmen.'
'I must get into the town, speak to the priests...'
'They will not allow you to return.'
'I can get into the town.'
'They will not allow it.'
'I am a Ward of the School,' said Daryo. 'There are ways that the Jaboen boys use, boys who would not stand one from another to a Picket in the dark. I can get in.'
'You should stay with us. I would make you my kin.'
Daryo swallowed his next words, stunned by the offer. 'Thank you... thank you, elder. You will go west?'
'South.'
'Walk south to the Crumbled Temple. Wait until the sunrise after tomorrow's. I will join you there. If I do not, my footsteps will be walking with my mother and my father, Yiua and her mother.' He looked down where Yiua lay. Her daughter was laid on the earth beside her, the daughter's head nuzzling in her dead mother's hand. Her husband paced a few steps backwards and forwards in grief.
'Go.'
Daryo seized his knife from the ground and, after a heartbeat's hesitation, a curved sword from where the woman named Temma was collecting the clan's weapons and tools. He ran through the gathering darkness, following the wall north and around to where it joined the river. The river ran through a tunnels dug through the wall's earth foundations. To either side were smaller tunnels, almost sewers, which were overflows in times of flood. They were just large enough for a man to crawl through. Daryo scrambled

into the west-side tunnel, it was cramped and oppressive with a couple of inches of brackish, stagnant water in the bottom. He was glad it was only about fifteen feet before he emerged in a small well-like hole just inside the wall. He crouched, hidden in the hole, hidden by the little wall that prevented people from falling into the open space from anyone that did not look directly down the shaft. He used the muddy water to wash some of Yiua's blood from his arm and neck. The School was about a hundred yards around the wall to his right but it was near the gate. The Pickets would have a heavy presence there to ensure that the Batribi moved on and that none approached the gate. But less than thirty yards along the bank was somewhere else he thought he could go.

'Daryo! Dule's Anvil on you, boy! What are you doing here?' Vehllal lowered the fire poker that he had been about to defend himself with. Daryo had clambered in through a window and knocked a metal kettle off of its stand in the process. The smith's house was simple, he lived alone with frugal possessions.
'I'm sorry, Master. There was... an incident.'
'The Pickets are saying that the Batribi tried to force their way through the gate.'
'No, Master.' Daryo explained the entire story slowly.
Vehllal looked into his eyes for a moment. 'I believe you, Daryo. But the Pickets will be believed. By the lord and council and by the town.'
'I cannot stay.'
Vehllal shook his head slowly. 'I fear you are right. I am sorry, Daryo. You have been a good apprentice, a worthy man. If you remain here, even if I speak for you, you are likely to be thrown in a water cell, or beheaded.'
'I know, Master. I cannot stay.'
Vehllal took a sack from a hook on the wall and put a handful of potatoes, a loaf of bread and some apples in it. 'You might need these. I see you're armed.'
'My... my people gave them to me.'
Vehllal said nothing but handed over the sack and then took a small shield from the back of the door. It was unusually painted- plain wood with a steel rim, then with a black smith's hammer crossed with a gold key. 'I made this shield as my last apprentice piece. It is strong, although I have never had cause to use it. The hammer stands for my craft, the key for it earning me the right to unlock the door to my first forge.' He passed it to Daryo. 'Take it, use it. May it keep you safe.'
'Thank you, Master.'
Vehllal unbolted his door. 'How did you get back inside the wall, Daryo?'

'Through the flood shaft.'
Vehllal nodded. 'Good. You should exit the same way. Gods' Guidance, my friend.' He extended his knurled hand.
Daryo grasped it firmly, trying to put as much feeling into his grip as he could. 'Thank you.'
'Go. Quickly.'

Daryo guessed he had taken about two hours to get from the encampment, into Salifa, to Vehllal and back again. The Batribi were gone. The campfire smouldered and a single curved Batribi sword was still stuck in the soil. He took it and slid it into his belt. There was a dark, damp patch that was the only evidence that Yiua was even there. Daryo laid the sword on the bloodstain and started south.

Once, a long-forgotten Jaboen ancestor had raised a temple not in the centre of a town but on the top of a cliff looking down across the river valley. It had been dedicated to some ancient god and when the religion of the Yashoun Empire had been spread across Jaboen and accepted as truth, the temple had been left to crumble until the very nature of its decline had become its name. Two huge grey columns stuck into the dawn light like bare ashen trees, behind them the walls were head-high piles of rubble, the slates of the roof formed the floor. The Batribi had camped in front of the columns, between them and the edge of the cliff. As Daryo slowly climbed the snaking path up the cliff to the crest, he could see Diatia on watch at the top. She had forgone a bladed weapon for a short bow. She had an arrow ready but relaxed it when she recognised Daryo. He made another about-turn to follow the last stretch of the path to the top. It was nearly a cliff and Daryo had to use his free hand to steady his ascent. Diatia reached down and helped him over the crest.
'Welcome, Daryo of the School of the Temple.'
Daryo hung his head. 'No longer of the School of the Temple, Diatia, kin of Stai.'
'I am sorry. I spoke without thought.'
'No sorry is necessary. I grieve with you for your kin.'
'Thank you.' Diatia looked across the valley from her vantage point. 'We will bury her at sundown of this day. Stai thinks it best to stay here and we will lay Yiua here in the sight of the old god.'
'That is good.'
'My uncle sleeps. You should rest until dawn at least. There is a blanket spare in the *kaff* here.' She indicated the nearest.'

'Thank you.'
Laulra and another man were asleep. Daryo thought he could not do likewise but was asleep within moments.

# Chapter 2

'Hold your position!' barked a voice. 'Hold your position! Do not move!'
Daryo shrugged off his blanket. He was the only one left in the *kaff* and he seized his sword and shield as he ducked out of the flap. The Batribi were lined up along the edge of the cliff. Diatia, Laulra and the youngest of the men, Jui, had arrows drawn on their short bows. Daryo approached but Stai held up a cautionary hand.
'Stay back,' he instructed firmly. 'Household Guards from Salifa.'
Picketmen worked for the Lord to protect the town, the Household Guard was the personal bodyguard of the town's Lord. Their long rectangular shields would be divided across the middle by a white band. Below the band would be the black and white badger on its purple field. Above would be a trio of black crows, the Lord's personal emblem; its presence meant that they had been dispatched for one reason.
'They are looking for me,' said Daryo softly. 'How many?'
'Five. One with the horses on the road, four are about halfway up the cliff.'
'You should not be going through this for me.'
'That is our decision,' said Stai fiercely. He turned away from Daryo and stepped confidently to the edge of the cliff. 'Men of Salifa! Hear me! I am Stai, son of Izai, elder of this clan! You have no business outside the Lord of Salifa's lands!'
'We come for a murdering Ward who has broken his bond!' shouted the leader of the four on the path. 'We believe he is with your clan and your behaviour tells me that we are correct. Yield him now and no blood needs be shed on this ancient site.'
An arrow was loosed. Laulra's shaft stuck a pace in front of the leader. 'Hold there and withdraw and no blood is shed!' he shouted after it.
'Hold your shafts,' ordered Stai but it was too late.
Laulra had fired again, then Jui. One of the Household Guard on the path was hit in the shoulder, his comrades surged forwards. Laulra's next arrow took out his original target. Jui dropped his bow and drew his sword.
'No!' shouted Daryo and burst down the path in front of Jui. The leader of the Household Guard raised his sword but Daryo's blood was pounding through his limbs. He batted the Guard's wide sword away with Vehllal's shield and hacked viciously into the man's neck between his chainmail and his helmet. The blood sprayed, Daryo planted his boot into the newly-made corpse, kicked it backwards against its living comrades and then ran up the body as the two other guards tried to retreat. Laulra's next arrow struck the rear-guard, Daryo's next slash took off the guard's sword hand and Diatia's arrow struck him in the back.

'The horseman escaped,' said Jui, disappointed.

'I asked you to hold your shafts.' Stai was even more disappointed. 'That was unnecessary. The horseman will ride back to Salifa with all speed and return with scores.'

Daryo bowed his head, watching the blood drop from the point of his sword. 'All of this is at my doing. And they will hunt you.' He started back up the path.

'They will fail,' said Diatia. 'We are Batribi. We walk, we change, we are all Batribi and every Batribi. The Jaboen cannot tell one clan from another, one *kaff* from another, one ox from another. We will merge into the other clans that walk.'

Stai nodded. 'Well spoken. If we walk, nobody will see us again. We shall head-'

'It is better that you do not tell me,' said Daryo. 'I must walk alone.'

Stai nodded again. 'It is best. We will give you what we can- the sword, a blanket, whatever we can spare- and we will not ask where you go.'

'My thanks.'

Stai looked at Diatia. 'Get Daryo what he can carry and what we can spare.'

'Yes, my uncle.'

'Daryo of the Road, I would speak with you before you leave us.'

'As you wish.'

Daryo followed Stai into his *kaff* and laid down his sword. The elder turned to him. 'You will be marked from now, Daryo. And a lone Batribi will be easily found, we travel in clans.'

'I cannot stay with you, Elder. It would be dangerous for you all.'

Stai sighed. 'I know. But I have something to help you on your journey.'

He shrugged off his robe. Underneath two straps went around his shoulders with another across his chest. He untied the chest strap and slid the shoulder straps off. Two dark wooden scabbards, inlaid with copper leaves and vines, just over two feet long, were attached to a circular leather panel. Protruding from each was a solidly-made silver hilt, one pommel shaped like a horse's head, the other a bear's. Stai offered the pommels to Daryo and the young man drew them both. The swords were particularly narrow, the points off-centre but the blade double-edged, very well balanced and Daryo could tell just by looking that they were exceptionally sharp.

'I cannot take these.'

'You will need them.'

'I cannot take these.'

'I am giving them to you.'

'I cannot-'

'To refuse a gift is the apogee of rudeness, surely the School of the Temple teaches that. You will take what is offered.' Stai's voice had a startlingly hard note to it.
'I thank you, Elder.' Daryo returned the swords to their sheaths. 'And I am sorry.'

Less than an hour later, Daryo started down the path from the Crumbled Temple. Stai's swords were strapped to his back with a haversack over the top, Vehllal's shield strapped to his left arm. Temma had found an old but well-made Batribi sword: a curved leading edge, a barbed tip and a solid wood hilt wrapped in old leather. It was excellently balanced and superbly sharp. Daryo wore it on his left hip. The haversack contained the food, firesteel and other odd items that Diatia had found for him and a blanket was bound to the back. He had changed from his old clothes into some brown Batribi leggings, vest and a green hooded robe like Stai's. He had not talked to any of the other Batribi as he left; the guilt of Yiua's blood and the mark he had placed on them was like an iron weight on his neck. At the base of the cliff, Daryo paused. North and then east would take him back towards Salifa or north and then west would take him to Taam on the River Yoaeje and the Yashoun border. South would take him along the River Road to Thiel. He decided it was the obvious direction for a fugitive from Salifa but that it was also further from danger. A decision as to his ultimate destination could come later. The stone road was old but smooth. It turned away from the cliff and ran alongside the Huba. The river was quite low but was always fast-flowing this far upriver. Daryo had been along the river slightly further in the past, Vehllal had visited an iron mine over three summers ago and permitted his apprentice to accompany him. He remembered a small hamlet just along the road from the mine and the name Ibaban came to his mind. A small fox darted out of the thick undergrowth to his right, caught sight of Daryo and dashed back into the bushes. *I might need to be eating foxes soon*, Daryo thought and immediately cursed in the name of the First Goddess; he had no bow to hunt with. He stopped walking for a moment and considered returning to the Crumbled Temple. *Stai and his kin have given me too much and earned only death and infamy in return*, he said in his head and began to walk south again. The road climbed away from the edge of the river gently, the bank between them getting steeper as the road sloped uphill. A farmer came down leading a horse and cart, doubtless heading for the market in Salifa. He stared openly at Daryo as he passed.
'Gods' Watch,' Daryo muttered but the farmer remained silent. A Batribi walking the road alone was unusual; Daryo wondered how much attention he would generate. Would the farmer say anything to someone in Salifa? Would he hear a guard talking about the Batribi fugitive? Daryo quickened his pace as the road crested a rise and went

back down towards the riverside. A line of trees separated the now wider road from the still-fast river. After nearly an hour's walking, a small track led up off of the main road. Daryo wondered if this was the mine. The shield was getting heavy after two hours of walking. That suggested that the hamlet was just further along the road. He wondered if the mine was worth going to, they may have supplies to trade, but he decided that the greater the distance from Salifa, the safer he would be. He switched his shield to the right arm and kept walking. A pair of black birds took off from a tree as Daryo passed underneath.

Another figure rounded a bend in the road. Daryo noticed that this was not a farmer, this was a young man slightly older than Daryo himself, broad across the shoulders, walking with a seven-foot staff in one hand. He saw Daryo and slowed his pace. Daryo shifted his shield back to his left arm. The approaching youth was wearing a light leather armour and metal vambraces, a copper-coloured gorget and had a sword at his hip. He raised the staff from the ground and stopped, allowing Daryo to approach. Daryo had been a Ward of the School of the Temple, growing up with other orphans and strays who fought and scrapped. Just a few months ago, Huhlil had almost decapitated little Albahd in an argument over bathing. He knew when there was tension, he recognised threatening behaviour and he also had the feeling in his heart that something was hidden. Daryo was within ten yards when the youth turned his staff to parallel the road.

'Stand, dark one!' he demanded.

Daryo moved his shield aside to show his sword. 'Stand aside, boy.'

'Boy! I have four summers on you! What is a rat like you doing wandering the road in daylight? Rats hide in the shadows.'

Daryo felt his heart rate increase. 'Stand aside. I am walking to Thiel. See this device?' He raised his shield again. 'This device? It is the device of the Smith of Salifa. I am on his business. Stand aside.'

'You are no smith. But you may be a thief. And a thief will carry gold.'

'So you carry gold?'

The youth smiled. His features were hard and square, his brows thick and a scar crossed his chin. 'I do not but he does.'

Daryo turned slowly. A much older man, his short beard grey, his head covered almost completely by a helmet that was surely not his by right. He wielded a vicious poleaxe with both hands.

'And you are welcome to take it from me!'

Daryo dropped his pack and drew his sword, Temma's Sword. 'I have no wish to fight you. I have no need. Allow me to walk again.'

'You will walk across the bridge to the next kingdom!' roared the youth, starting to run. Daryo thought and acted on the spur of the moment. He spun and hurled Temma's Sword at the on-rushing youth. It had mere feet to travel and the surprise of the whirling blade caught the youth unaware and the pommel smashed him in the face. Daryo reached his right hand up quickly and drew one of Stai's swords, The Horse, from his back. He lunged forwards and his wild slash caught the youth across the ribs. The would-be robber screamed and fell to the floor. Daryo turned and just caught the poleaxe as it was swung over its owner's head and down like a plummeting stone. The force of the blow knocked Daryo to his knees. The next blow was almost as fierce and he barely held his shield. The third knocked him onto his face. Just before the fourth could fall, he stabbed The Horse upwards. It caught the bearded one at the joint of leg and groin. His shield forgotten, Daryo, still face-down, drew The Bear with his left hand and slashed at the man's knees. The Gods-given sharp blade sliced muscle and sinew and the axeman fell. Daryo used The Horse's pommel to bring himself to his knees and slashed with The Bear again, opening his fallen foe's throat. The spray of blood and the man's last rattling breath made Daryo's heart surge again. He was on his feet and turning for the youth. Despite his wound, the boy was up. His sword swung down like an axe, two hands behind the swing. Daryo crossed his blade instinctively and caught the swing. There was a moment as they glared at each other and Daryo felt a foot strike his right knee. He pushed upwards with Stai's swords as he fell. The downwards slash missed him by less than a hand's width. Daryo stabbed The Horse forwards and slashed sideways with The Bear. The youth hopped backwards and lashed his sword out. The Bear went flying away but Daryo saw a space for The Horse. It jabbed in just below the boy's ribs inside his free arm, right alongside his first wound. The boy moaned like a beaten dog and sank to his knees slowly, his sword falling from his hand.

Daryo slowly, torturously, vindictively, raised The Horse to the youth's eyes. 'Give me a single word to send you to the next kingdom with.'

'Mercy, sir! Mercy! In the name of Spinel!'

'In the name of the Second God and the Fourth and Darkest Goddess I should spread your blood on the road!'

'Hold your blade, Batribi!' shouted another voice. A woman was running down the road, an arrow notched and drawn on her longbow. 'Hold your blade! I do not preach the Third Goddess but the Fourth is satisfied. I beg you, hold.'

Daryo felt his heart slow, the surge in his head receded. He slowly raised The Horse and slid it back into its sheath above his right shoulder. 'As you will. I shall retake my weapons.'

The woman exhaled slowly and relaxed her arrow. 'Do so. I would see a man with that talent with a blade hold one again.'

Daryo regarded her curiously. She was wearing a light plate cuirass with mail sleeves, her legs were armoured with plate and, as well as her bow, she bore an arm shield and a greatsword hung on her back. Deep, hollow brown eyes regarded him from under thin brows and rather lank brown hair swung in four long braids around her shoulders. She went to look at the youth as Daryo retrieved The Bear from the shoulder of the road, Temma's Sword from at the foot of a riverside tree and Vehllal's shield from the feet of the dead axeman. The poleaxe had left a great fist-sized dent in the shield just below the key's shaft. The bruise of the shield was beginning to throb on Daryo's forearm. The youth sobbed as the woman poured a dark liquid on his slashed ribs.

'Close your jaw and be a man,' she muttered. 'The scars will be proud ones.'

Daryo gingerly reset his shield on his arm. 'Is he mortally wounded?'

'No. Seriously. Are we far from aid?'

'There is a mine, along a track away from the river, about one third of an hour's walk north towards Salifa.'

'He needs a physician, if they have one at a mine he will be treating crushed bones and heads, not sword cuts.'

'The village...'

'I came through? No physician. That leaves Salifa. There was a good young physician when I last passed this road.'

'I cannot go back to Salifa,' admitted Daryo. 'My life would be in danger.'

The woman sighed slightly. 'For sure? Then I shall have to go alone. Can you stand, lad?' The stricken youth moaned pitifully and shook his head. 'A shame. I cannot lift and carry a man your size.'

'What are we to do?' asked Daryo impatiently.

'Well, if your strikes had been truer, this predicament would be avoided,' she said conversationally, the youth sobbed in terror. 'I guess the kindness is to go to the village I passed through and hire a cart. Would you go?'

Daryo snorted. 'A villageman would not lend a Batribi his spit.'

'As you say. I shall go. You will wait for my return?'

'If you wish.'

'My thanks.' The woman turned and trotted away south.

Daryo regarded his former foe for an awkward moment then turned away to find a stone. He then sat and sharpened Temma's Sword, regardless of how intimidated it may make the wounded man feel. He stared fixedly at Temma's Sword until the sound of a horse and cart was heard. The woman had returned with a rather elderly man and an equally elderly horse that towed a flat cart. The villager carried a staff and raised it when he saw Daryo.

'The Batribi killed these men?'

'Yes, but in self-defence,' said the woman placidly. 'And unless something unfortunate has happened and the Fourth and Darkest has claimed her newest acolyte, the younger man lives still. Do you live, boy?' She prodded the youth with the toe of her boot and got a wail of protest in return. 'He lives. As agreed, you take him to Salifa and do not leave him until the physician is satisfied.'

'If you have the coin.'

The woman took a purse from her belt and handed over ten silver halves. 'That should pay for your time and the physician.' She handed over two more. 'And a few drinks in the Olives and Ferret on the riverside.'

'God's Watch on you, milady.'

'And on you, sir.'

Daryo sheathed Temma's Sword and helped lift the wounded man onto the cart. The elder tugged the reins and the horse began to plod south. Daryo picked up his shield and haversack again, glanced at the woman and began to walk to south again. After a few yards, he was aware of the woman walking alongside him.

'Where do you walk, Batribi?' she asked.

'In a different direction to you, woman.'

'Dravin is guiding my legs this day. Do you have a name, or must I refer to you by your tribe?'

'I am of no Batribi clan.'

'Where do you come from then?'

'That is of no business of yours.'

'Where do you go to?'

'And that is of no business of yours.'

'You said that you could not go back, and those were your words, to Salifa as your life would be forfeit. Thus something happened in Salifa that has marked your name. A theft? A murder?' She studied Daryo's face as they walked. 'No... something that you were innocent of but your name or your skin meant was blamed to you.' She smiled slightly. 'I thought so. And now you are fleeing but you have no thought as to where.'

'You are surmising.'

'I think I am correct nonetheless.' She seized his arm and stopped him. Daryo shook her off but she held his gaze. 'I can give you somewhere to go.'

'Where?' Daryo was scornful.

'Somewhere were a talented bladesman such as you can be put to use.'

Daryo unconsciously dropped his hand onto the hilt of Temma's Sword. 'Tell me.'

'Not here,' said the woman. 'Do you know Lalbi?'

'The Town under the Mountain. I am Batribi, I am not welcome there.'

The woman shook her head. 'No matter. This side of the town, below the cliff, is an inn. The Beacon Inn. Tell the innkeeper that your sword is sharp but your eye is sharper.'

'I tell him...'

'My sword is sharp but my eye is sharper.'

'My sword is sharp but my eye is sharper.'

The woman nodded. 'Someone will meet you there.'

'You will not accompany me?'

'You said that you were not walking in the same direction as I am. So I shall ensure that that is right.'

Daryo shrugged. 'As you wish.'

The woman smiled. 'I would suggest that you cross the Huba at Riy Ford and go across country. The roads may be no kinder than this one.'

Riy had once been a town straddling the Huba River like Salifa further upriver. Its bridge had been stone piers and the rest of the structure wooden. A small fort in the old fenced style had stood at the east end. Immemorially long ago, the river had widened and sped up, wiping out the bridge and taking the fort and most of the town. Now Riy's bridge had crumbled into the river causing a shallow ford and the town was a small forest of collapsed walls and overgrown streets. Daryo's skin prickled as he ducked under the branches of a small oak tree that was growing from what had once been a firepit in the centre of a house. Riy felt like the perfect place for an ambush. He drew The Horse. The wind was starting to blow harder from the south, bringing a sharp chill with it. He had struggled to stay warm when he stopped to eat earlier. A roaring fire and a roast leg of pig would have been very welcome to Daryo's growling stomach.

*Cross the ford and eat there*, he told himself, clutching The Horse a little tighter. Around another half-fallen wall and Daryo saw a flag flapping in the southern wind.

There were eight lords of Jaboen, defined by the number of deities. The Lord of Salifa was shown by his rearing badger on purple. The Lord of Thiel had his white pike on blue. The Lord of Three Rivers bore a winding river across a green field. This banner was midnight blue with a single star in one corner. Seven of the eight lords had their own estate, such as Salifa. The Seatless Squire was the eighth, normally a late-born son or cousin of the king, who had no lands but an allotment of men to serve the king. Some Seatless Squires worked for the nation, some for the king, some for paymasters and some simply for their own advancement. Daryo did not know the identity of the current incumbent of the position but his men were apparently at the Ford. He continued to walk; there was no more reason to turn around than to continue. He ducked through a low stone doorway standing alone without its walls and the ford, the start of the old bridge flanked by a crumbling stone tower and a new wooden watchtower, was right ahead. Three archers in navy blue tunics with stars on their right shoulders manned the wooden tower and four men-at-arms stood around a small campfire near its base. One of the bowmen saw Daryo and shouted an alert to his comrades.

Daryo slowed to a stop several yards from the men-at-arms.

'Where are you walking, dog?' demanded one, the only man wearing a helmet.

Daryo swallowed the bile at the slur. 'Hef. I am the apprentice of the smith in Salifa.' He raised his shield slightly.

'Why come this way? Why not simply walk from Salifa?'

'I had to visit the mine on the Thiel road first. Now I go to Hef to take some goods back to my master.'

'Stand. Place your shield and blade on the ground.'

Daryo shook his head. 'I will not. I will keep my shield and sheath my blade.'

'Slowly.'

Daryo opened his left arm away from his body so that his shield no longer covered his body in a gesture of openness. Then he slowly raised The Horse and sheathed it over his shoulder. The men-at-arms came forwards. The helmeted leader studied the device on Daryo's shield and accepted the explanation that it was the smith of Salifa's arms. Three blades were also accepted as being carried by a smith's apprentice as an example of his work and for self-protection on the roads. Nothing in his pack excited comment and it was returned wordlessly.

'The Seatless Squire has ordered a toll on the use of the ford,' said the leader.

'I have little coin,' Daryo told him.

'Goods are acceptable.'

Daryo dug into his pack and came out with a well-made pewter cup that Stai's kin had given. The leader inspected it, pronounced it appropriate and allowed the walker to wade across the ford.

## Chapter 3

Daryo found a convenient ledge of rock to serve as shelter and slept fitfully on the ground, his weapons and kit off but one hand on the hilt of Temma's Sword. Dawn woke him and he started to walk again. The walk was uphill and it took another day and a half of walking up into the foothills of the mountains before Lalbi, the Town Under The Mountain, came into sight; a large sprawl of wood-and-stone houses around an impressive stone tower and a temple of Spellis. A single building stood away from the town on the road to Hef, a long low stone-walled thatched building. As darkness fell, Daryo pushed the door of the Inn of the Beacon. The inn's hall matched the width of the building and was almost as long. A short man with a deep, old scar across his cheek stood behind the bar. A dozen or more patrons looked up as the young Batribi crossed to the bar, farmers, farm hands, cowherds by their mien.

'Get out, dog,' said the barman sharply.

Daryo swallowed sharply, sensing the others in the bar starting to gather. 'I think I will stay, thank you. I require a drink.'

'I do not serve dogs.'

'I am no dog. Dogs do not carry swords.' He drew Temma's Sword, aware he was a boy of few summers surrounded by men but knowing that he could handle his blade, at least against two or three.

'There are nine other swords behind you. Yours had better be sharp.'

'My sword is sharp. But my eye is sharper.'

The barman leaned forward. 'Say that again.'

'My sword is sharp but my eye is sharper.'

He leaned further forward. 'And what does your eye see?'

'A drink.'

The barman stood up straight. 'Not here.' He beckoned Daryo around the bar and through the back door. A small but proportionally long anteroom had a brace of doors either side, the inn's rooms for guests. However the barman opened a wooden ground-door and led the way down a steep flight of stairs into a low cellar. They turned about and walked between casks of ale and wine lining the wooden-walled sides and ceiling. Light came from a series of small lanterns strung along the centre aisle between the casks. The cellar seemed to follow exactly the plan of the inn above, finishing at the far end with a line of huge ale casks standing on their butts that were almost as tall as Daryo. The innkeeper slipped between the cask on the left end and the one next to it and pushed the end cask aside on unseen wheels, revealing a low door. Two keys were needed to unlock it, followed by a barrage of bolts and hasps. The innkeeper was not tall but had to stoop to make it under the lintel and stopped to light two lanterns just inside the door. This next room had a lower floor than the cellar, was stone walled, a comfortable twelve feet square, roofed by thick beams. One wall was an armoury; swords, daggers, maces, lances, spears, javelins, bows, all hung on racks on the left-hand wall. A single bare-metal shield hung in the centre. A clutter of chairs surrounded a small table in the centre of the stone floor. Above a fireplace on the back wall hung a slightly-mildewed and stained banner; olive green with a black device, a circular shield with a simply-drawn sword on top, a series of symbols on the blade with the eight-fold circles of the Pantheon at the point.

'Who's is that sign?' asked Daryo, pointing at the banner.

'You do not know?' responded the barman, going across to light a readied fire. 'It is not my place to tell you. I will get you that drink, and some food. Please stay here.'

Daryo stood aside to let the innkeeper pass. He decided that he was safe enough as the password that he had been given had dispersed the barman's hostility and bought him to this refuge. Lalbi was a town known to be hostile to Batribi. Or Yashoun or anyone else that was different. A concealed room behind a cellar beneath a quiet inn outside of the town limits would be the safest refuge he would find. He sheathed Temma's Sword, propped his shield against the leg of a chair and removed his heavy pack. His shoulders creaked in protest as he put it down. After a moment's thought he removed his robe and Stai's blades from his back before sitting down.

The barman returned with a heavy tankard of ale and a pewter platter with a leg of cold chicken, three boiled-hard eggs, an end of bread and a couple of slightly wrinkled apples.

'The bounty of the First Goddess.'

'Gratefully received,' said Daryo with a smile, accepting the plate and cup. He got a good chance to look at the barman- short but muscular, an axeman rather than a swordsman or an archer, what little hair he had left was turning to snow, a thick moustache and dark eyes. He had a short sword held naked in his belt, partly concealed by his heavy canvas apron. He pulled out the chair opposite Daryo and sat down.

'I left my girl minding the hall,' he told Daryo as the Batribi started to eat. 'I apologise for the... performance upstairs but Lalbi is not welcoming to Batribi.'

'I understand.'

'I haven't asked your name.'

'Daryo.'

'Dar-yo. The Batribi are known as kin of one aren't they?'

Daryo chewed for a moment to give him time to think. 'I am Daryo, kin of Yiua.'

'I am Adil,' said the barman. 'The Beacon is my place, passed to me from my father.'
'And a good recipe for beer was passed too,' said Daryo appreciatively.
'I would ask how you came by the password.'
'A woman. I was attacked by two footpads. I fought them and she prevented me from killing the second one. Then she had him taken to Salifa to see a physician.'
Adil nodded. 'The Ranger. I know her well. You are the first of your people that she has sent back.'
'Sent back?'
'The Ranger looks for new recruits. Those she finds in Jaboen come here.'
'Recruits? For what? Or for whom?'
'That's not my place to tell you.'
'Whose place is it?'
'I have sent word for them. Until then, I think it best if you remain here. Have you your letters? I can send down a manuscript I have.'
'I would rather a bed.'
Adil thought for a moment. 'A bed is difficult. If the town patrols come and find a Batribi in one of the rooms, neither one of us will be given good tidings. I can bring some blankets down.'
'That would be more than sufficient.'
'I shall inform you when someone arrives.'
'Thank you. Gods' Watch.'
'And on you.'

The lanterns were out when Daryo woke. His sleep had completely disrupted his sense of time. The door was closed and Adil had shown Daryo how to lock it from the inside. The door had then been concealed from the outside and a coded knocking pattern arranged so that Daryo knew when Adil returned. The fire was getting low and Daryo got up and put another few pieces of wood in. A cold cooked egg and a piece of bacon remained on his plate and he finished them slowly, enjoying the salty, fatty taste of the bacon. Wards of the Temple rarely got bacon.
*Rap-rap-rap* came on the door. There was the sound of two bolts slid out and home firmly. *Rap-rap-rap* again. Daryo got up quickly and held down the two latches that secured the key-locks from the inside.
'Enter!' he called and the door was immediately pushed from without.
Adil led in a man dressed for battle. He was an elder and built like a fox- slender limbs, eyes like black glass beads, a pointed nose with pointed whiskers and beard below, his

russet-coloured breastplate was textured like fur, his breeches looked like actual fox fur but instead of claws the fox had a single-handed axe, a long dirk and a shield that bore the same device as the banner above the fireplace with a snarling fox head surrounded by oak leaves at the pommel of the sword.

'Daryo, kin of Yiua, this is Kitsun the Shrewd.'

Daryo inclined his head. Kitsun drew his dirk and held it, point down, high in front of him. 'My sword and my service,' he said in a gravelly tone. His features crinkled in a broad smile. 'A Batribi. The Ranger has never sent me one of your people, Daryo.'

'And this concerns you?' Daryo allowed some anger into his voice.

'Not at all! The Batribi people are a noble and resilient people, misunderstood and misrepresented by the ignorant and fearful. Perhaps she has just never seen one of your people at the right time. May I ask how she found you? Adil said she had you spare a life.'

'I was attacked. They attempted to rob me. I have grown up around weapons and know how to use them. I killed one who attacked me but your... Ranger had me spare the second, a boy of my own age, in the name of the Third Goddess.'

'Our Order teaches that the blade must be tempered with wisdom.'

'Order?'

'The Order. The Order of the Shield and Sword, for we shield the just, the righteous, the innocent, the weak and the shieldless. That the Ranger has sent you here to The Beacon suggests that she believes that you have the right qualities of heart, mind or hand to join our fellowship.'

'Qualities? How can I have these qualities? I'm an apprentice, a dismissed apprentice, a Ward of the School of the Temple who has fled for his life! A Batribi!'

'And a warrior, a warrior's whose hand is tempered by reason and thought.'

'A street swordsman...'

'A survivor.'

'A fugitive...'

'A traveller.' Kitsun smiled again. 'Come, I can teach you.'

'Teach me?'

'I will take you to our Towers. You can decide with all the details before you. If you decide not to join us, I will bring you back here. Or to anywhere you command.'

Daryo thought frantically. 'I am not safe in Jaboen.'

'Fear not. We must cross the mountains. East of the mountains we reach Aslon.

Daryo nodded. 'I consent.'

Kitsun clapped him on the shoulder and turned to the innkeeper. 'Adil, if you could spare some provisions, some blankets, a small flask of flame oil? I shall pay when I return. If not, tell the Ranger and she will pay.'

Adil snorted in amusement. 'The day the Ranger pays your dues, Kitsun, that is the day my butter knife becomes a broadsword.'

Kitsun laughed. 'And so it shall, my friend. And so it shall.'

'I will give what I can. But you will pay, not the Ranger. The Bright no longer comes this way,' said Adil as he led the way out of the room.

'He has taken up duties at the Tower, he was grievously wounded by a crossbow bolt, he nearly lost his foot.'

'Awful, truly awful...'

And Daryo was alone again. He began to collect his belongings; they had not had more than a few hours to be spread. He repacked his haversack, buckled on his swordbelt and Stai's harness and put his robe over the top. After a moment's thought he extinguished the fire, blew out the lamps and he closed up room as he left, disguising the door with its specially-adapted cask of ale. He made his way through the cellar, up through the trapdoor and into the main hall. It was empty except for Kitsun, who had just taken a small pack from the innkeeper and grasped his hand in gratitude. 'I shall pay when I return.'

'Be sure that you do.'

Kitsun's smile grew. He drew his dagger again and held it high by the hilt, point down. 'My sword and my service, Adil. Daryo, we should start out.'

'Thank you for your hospitality,' said Daryo to the innkeeper. 'Gods' Watch.'

'Gods' Guidance, young man. Walk well and keep your eye sharp.'

Kitsun led the way out of the inn and around the town. The sun was only just up. The road led up from Lalbi and into the mountains. Kitsun seemed happy to shoulder the bulk of the load and to walk in companionable silence. After a few miles, Daryo decided to break his silence.

'I heard you talking to the innkeeper about the Ranger.'

'Aye.'

'That was the woman that I encountered on the road. She stopped me from killing me the footpad.'

'Yes. A blade is nothing if it is not tempered by both water and wisdom.'

'Tell me of your Order. Please.'

'The Order is ancient. The Empire of Yashoun is three centuries old. The nation of Jaboen is nearly five centuries old. Our Order is older than the sum of both of their ages. We are the Order of the Shield and Sword, as you see on my shield and on the old banner in the Buried Room beneath the Beacon Inn. We do not fight for a nation, or a king, or a lord, or the Second God Thiney. We fight for what is right, for the meek, the defenceless, the oppressed and the wronged.'

'Who decides who is worthy?'

'We are led by a council known as the Aides, as long ago they were aides to the Captain-General, who is now the leader of the Council. Below the Aides are two bodies- the Blades choose where and when our Members work, the Trenchers look after our buildings, provisions and arms.'

'Which are you?'

'Neither in these late days. Most of our Members are not Blades or Trenchers but follow their command. I was a Blade as a younger man but now I follow the direction of the Aides to conduct new recruits from Jaboen and Yashoun to the Five Towers, our home near Aslon.'

'Are they all sent here by the Ranger? The woman I met?'

'Not all of them but many. The Ranger is something different to all of us. She works alone, travelling long distances, mostly on foot, fighting her own fights and sending new apprentices to us as she finds them.'

'And the innkeeper mentioned... the Bright.'

'Solie. He did a lot of work around Lalbi some summers ago.'

'Why is he called the Bright?'

'His sun-like hair and bright face, a truly bright and radiant person. He was wounded and now works at the Five Towers with new recruits and the Tower guards.'

'And you are called the Shrewd.'

'I am.'

'Why is that?'

'A name that was given to me as a young man. It also made a good fit with the fox that I chose as my sign. So I took Shrewd as my sword name.'

'Sword name?'

'Each of the Order who take up commitment to the Order and speak their Promise before the Aides takes a sword name and choose a badge for their shield's pommel. I chose the Shrewd, Solie chose the Bright and a radiant sun. I have not seen Vilya the Ranger for several seasons but she has a lit beacon as her badge. The Vanguard has a wall of shields, the Swift a bird in flight, the Greensward a cluster of trees.'

'Is it all personal choice? Can you choose any name and badge?'

'It is choice but the wise listen to counsel from friends and comrades. The only rule that the Order keeps is that no Member of the Order can take a name or badge that has been used. So no Member may be named the Shrewd or have a fox's head as his badge until every comrade that knew me has consented although there is only objection on very rare occasions.'

The road began to get steeper and Daryo could see ahead the road began to twist and turn back and forth into the mountain pass. A single hawk was patrolling the road ahead.

'How long have you been in the Order?'

'So many questions! Nearly forty summers, I had seen fourteen when I was found on the streets of Three Rivers by the Ranger's predecessor.'

'You have had a long life.'

'Long and stimulating. I have travelled far and eaten strange foods. I have made many brothers and sisters and met with many foes in battle.'

'How many have you killed?'

'I have never counted. Some do. The Ranger's predecessor, the Hammerfist, used to cut the symbol of the Fourth Goddess into the handle of his warhammer after he went to battle for every soul he had sent to her. When he died, his warhammer had sent one hundred and sixty-nine to her.'

'I have killed one.' Daryo felt his feet stop walking.

Kitsun noticed this and turned, smiling kindly. 'Death is the next step to life as your left foot is the next step to the road. If you had not killed him, he may well have killed you. You did so, he did not. You sent him, if he was faithful and true, to the care of the Fourth Goddess. If you join our Order, if you choose to and are chosen, you will kill many more.' He reached out and touched Daryo's arm. 'Come, Daryo.'

Daryo nodded slowly and allowed Kitsun to guide him back into step. The road was getting steeper with each turn of a corner and the quality of the stone paving was deteriorating. Kitsun seemed to know the road well, pointing out a small cave and a fox den. Nearly an hour's walk further and they came to a small shack set back from the road. Kitsun held up a hand to stop Daryo and went to push open the door, peering inside.

'She is away.'

'She?'

'There's a woodswoman who lives sometimes here and sometimes in another hut further up the mountain side.' He pointed up and to the left and Daryo could just see a short chimney visible through the evergreen branches. 'There's no fire here and no smoke from the other so I assume she is away and hunting.'

'Do you know her?'

'I have travelled this road many times. I know her and have hunted with her more than once.'

They resumed walking.

# Chapter 4

Sleep came under a low outcropping of rock just away from the road. Kitsun built three small but hot fires across the entrance and settled down to sleep. Daryo struggled to sleep but did so eventually, his feet pressed against the close wall of the little cave. He was woken by Kitsun shaking him.

'Awake, Daryo. I need you awake.' Kitsun's voice was low and urgent. The fires were out and dawn just broken.

'I am.'

'Stay quiet. Are you better using your twin blades or the single with a shield?'

'I don't know.'

'Take the twins. Follow me. Stay very quiet.'

Now more awake, Daryo could detect the note of concern in Kitsun's voice. He quickly drew the Horse and Bear from their sheathes and followed Kitsun out of their shelter at a trot. The older man scurried across the road and into the undergrowth on the opposite side. They were scrambling down the slope through the dense trunks of the evergreen trees, Kitsun holding his axe and shield with one hand and using his free hand to steady himself. After a hundred yards he stopped. Daryo crashed to a halt alongside. Kitsun held his fingertips to his lips for silence.

'Very, very quietly.' He switched his axe to his right hand and eased his way around a tree, slowly down the slope and in behind a larger trunk about twenty yards ahead. He beckoned Daryo to join him and then pointed forwards. Another sixty or so yards ahead, in a small clearing caused by a fallen tree, were a quartet of skin tents around a good fire. Tied to a stake beyond the fire was a woman of about Kitsun's age. She had been stripped down to her skin and her chest, breasts and arms were covered in bruises and welts. A huge man dressed in roughspun and animal skin was roasting a rabbit over the fire.

'Peak tribesmen,' growled Kitsun. 'Savage men, animals. They take women to breed, like cattle. If they can't breed, or they resist, they die horribly and over many days.'

'Is that the woodswoman?'

'Aye. And we are going to liberate her.' Kitsun glanced at Daryo. 'Can you help me?'

Daryo gripped his swords tighter. 'I can and I will.'

'Good. Four tents, no tribesman would ever share a tent so four of them. One by the fire, one in the smallest tent on the left.' He pointed and indeed a pair of shod feet was visible. 'Two others are probably in their tents but I don't trust the Second God that far.

I want you to go straight to the prisoner. Cut her loose and bring her back here. No more. Fight only what you have to do to fulfil that. Will you do this?'

'I will.'

'Then we will succeed. Move.'

Kitsun scampered away to the right. Daryo did as he had been told and went straight forwards towards the fire. The noise of his approach alerted the man by the fire, who shouted an alarm in his own staccato tongue, flailing to reach for a roughly-made broadsword. The sleeping man was rousing himself, repeating the alarm.

Daryo reached the fire at a run and stabbed the man there through the gut before he had armed himself. A glut of blood came out and the tribesman fell back gurgling as he died. Daryo withdrew his sword and was quickly at the stake. The woman was barely sensible and her skin was ice-cold to the touch. Daryo cut the bonds on her wrists, ribs and the noose around her neck with the unbloodied Horse. The noose had cut into the flesh of her neck leaving a vicious gouge. The sleeping tribesman was now astride his fallen comrade, armed with an oddly short spear and the fallen man's sword. He bellowed furiously and started forwards but was distracted by Kitsun's battlecry. Daryo turned away, wrapping his cloak around the bare woman, putting his arm around her and getting hers over his shoulders. She moaned in distress as Daryo half-dragged half-carried her past Kitsun, who had quickly dispatched the tribesman, trying not to injure her with the Bear's blade.

'Move!' Kitsun barked. 'I have not found the other two!' He banged the haft of his axe on his shield. '*Ha dack ro dack yo vo ro!*' he shouted to the woods. 'Faster, Daryo!' Daryo continued to drag the woman towards the trees as Kitsun bellowed again: '*Ha dack ro dack yo vo ro! Ha so mo darr!* Daryo, keep moving! *Ha so mo darr!*'

Daryo reached the treeline. 'Come, please, I'm trying to help,' he muttered to the half-dead woman. And then the two tribesmen were blocking his path. 'Kitsun!'

The older man turned and rushed to Daryo's side. '*Ha dack ro dack yo vo ro,*' he told the wild-looking pair firmly. '*Zo dack yo mo han ran so.* Daryo, lay her down.'

Daryo carefully eased the woman to the earth, making sure his cloak covered her and then stood up quickly, bringing his swords to guard.

'*Zack do maj,*' the tribesman closest said. They were large men, with wild hair, long beards and both were carrying the rough-made swords. The closest had a kind of maul made of a large stone bound to a piece of wood with rope.

'*Han ran so.*'

'*Han hav so!*'

'Take the one with only the sword, Daryo,' said Kitsun. 'Now!'

Daryo darted in front of Kitsun and swung the Bear wildly in his left hand. Kitsun had already caught a blow from the maul on his shield. Daryo's opponent was a foot taller than him and much broader. His sword was much wider than Stai's blades and significantly longer. Daryo knew immediately that his enemy was intimately acquainted with his weapon. He was using it to both fend off Daryo's attacks and fight forwards, pushing Daryo back into the clearing. Daryo blocked three, four, five overhead slashes with his swords crossed. Another, a seventh, an eighth and Daryo stumbled, tripping and almost falling.

'To your god with you!' roared Kitsun, his axe cleaving into Daryo's foe's throat. He pulled it out as the wildman fell, spun and blocked his original adversary's blow on his shield, swept his attacker's sword aside with his shield and hacked into the tribesman's chest nearly to the backbone. He kicked the body away to free his axe and sprayed the woman and Daryo's cloak with blood.

'Well fought, Daryo,' he said between heaving breaths of air.

'I was almost killed,' said Daryo dully.

'You were not,' said Kitsun bluntly. 'Come, help me take our friend back to some shelter.'

Between the older man and the youth they managed to safely get the woman, more awake and sobbing, back into the shallow cave. Kitsun dug a tunic and breeches from his kit and helped her into them, talking softly in the Peak language while Daryo started a new fire. Gradually his words had an effect and the woman was able to tell Kitsun what had happened. He gave her a wineskin and an apple and helped her into his bedroll before guiding Daryo outside to the shoulder of the road.

'The Peak Tribes have been moving into the passes and lower down the hills,' Kitsun told him. 'She was going to leave, to head north, but was caught by that group of raiders. They were going to take her back to their village at dusk. We arrived just in time.'

'How did you know where the camp was? That there was even a camp there?'

'I saw tracks by the road and smelt the smoke of the fire. I was curious and the spirit of the hunt came to me. I found their camp and thought that you would benefit from aiding me. It also made my friend's survival more likely as you could guard her. You did very well, Daryo. You will make a fine addition to the Order.'

Daryo smiled, feeling flattered by the older man's comment. 'How did you come to speak their language?'

'It is more startling that I have the Common Speech. I was born in the Peaks.'

They left the woodswoman with Kitsun's clothing, the wineskin, a dagger and a few kindly words in her own speech. Then the Peak man and the Batribi youth started up the road again.

The road got narrower, steeper yet and poorer as it approached its highest point. Daryo was panting for breath and sweating despite the cold headwind. His pack felt as if it had been loaded with stones and the straps of Stai's swords bit into his chest. Kitsun was barely breathing hard, pointing out problems with the road, observing birds and animals and keeping up a steady flow of talk. It transpired that the warrior knew almost nothing of smithing and saw Daryo's company as an opportunity to learn. Daryo found himself having to think hard to find the answers to Kitsun's difficult questions about almost every weapon and piece of armour imaginable then public ironmongery and household items such as keys and pans. By the time they reached the mouth of the pass, even Kitsun's curiosity was sated.

'Tember Pass,' announced Kitsun grandly, pointing down the narrow valley. The all-but-bare rock walls of the mountains rose no more than thirteen or fourteen fee to either side of the road. After just thirteen hundred feet, the road kinked left and the rock walls hid the progression from view.

'And beyond?'

'A whole new country,' said Kitsun enigmatically. 'And the Five Towers.'

'How far?'

'Another two days' walk. Three perhaps.'

'Can we break here? Just a pause?'

Kitsun nodded and found a rock to sit on. Daryo took off as much of his equipment as he could before collapsing to the ground in an undignified heap.

The older man chuckled. 'Smiths! All upper strength, big arms, lots of power, but no endurance, no distance in the legs.'

'My haversack is heavy, cutting into the skin of my shoulders.'

'Find some whitebane, crush the leaves against your skin and use you pack to hold them there. It will stop the soreness.'

Daryo sighed and pulled back one side of his collar. There was a broad stripe, rubbed and raw, where the strap had dug into his skin. 'When I am rested.'

'Do not rest too long. Tember Pass is dangerous. Peak tribesman roam here, lowland bandits, rock falls, snow falls, I want to be through by sundown.'

'Do many people use the Pass?'

'The lords of Jaboen trade across the Pass and several traders pass the other way, mostly to Lalbi and Three Rivers. Jaboen scholars also visit Allesbury, the Archive there is a great seat of learning.'

'Have you been there?'

'Twice. It is truly spectacular. It is time, find some whitebane and put your gear back on. We need to be through the Pass and into the Tember Vale by sundown and time is getting onwards.'

# Chapter 5

The smell came first- that of putrefying flesh and death. Kitsun held up a hand and scouted forwards for a few yards alone. He crouched beside a shallow silt puddle, examining the spread of mud around it.

'More footsteps away than towards,' he announced, standing up. 'Should be safe but keep your sword arm free anyway.'

Rounding the next turn in the winding pass, the source of the stench became very clear. Seven bodies of people and two mules were deposited on the left of the road, the debris of a two-wheeled cart, a large trunk and the shreds of bags and sacks lay to the right.

'Peak Tribes' work,' Kitsun stated. 'They separate the dead from any potential plunder.'

The dead had been so for several days. The blood on their wounds was dry but flies and maggots were doing their works. Kitsun picked up a whip from the road, examined it for usability and cast it aside. Daryo nudged the split trunk, now a rough assembly of wood and iron, with his toe.

'Keep moving,' said Kitsun. 'The Fourth Goddess is in communion with these men, we have no need to disturb her.'

Daryo took the lead as they left the scene of death behind them. It was impossible to take a wrong turning as the walls of the ravine were rarely even twenty yards apart; for most of the way they had been barely ten yards apart with the irregularly-paved road at the centre and sometimes reaching both sides. The winding path had still been gently ascending; it then descended sharply for nearly a mile and then began to climb again. As it reached the next crest, the road was flanked by two statues evidently carved from the very rock of the mountains to either side. Facing away and to the east on both sides was the winged boars of Jaboen. Facing the two walkers were launching birds of prey, wings spread in take-off, talons spread across the rocks and mighty beaks open in screams of challenge. The carved statues were unknowably old but looked hardly touched. Kitsun paused and put a small morsel of bread in the snarling jaws of one of the boars.

'A thanks for my safe journey in Jaboen once more. My four-times-fourth, the Fourth Goddess has favoured me as my servant every time but never her companion. And for the four-times-fourth time, I am back in Gourmin. Welcome to the Land of the Red Hawk, Daryo of the Batribi.'

The sun had passed its zenith before Kitsun permitted a pause to rest and eat. Daryo had done his best to continue, to keep up his pace but tiredness and weight of load had taken their toll. The whitebane leaves had worked for a few hours but afterwards had become a damp mess providing little cushioning or relief. Now sitting on a long-stumped tree, divested of baggage, Daryo removed the pulp from under his clothes, dropping it on the ground. His companion was studying the slopes to either side of the pass.

'I don't want to stop here for long,' he said. 'Eat swiftly.'

Daryo chose to simply obey and found a roll of bread, a small square of cheese and a rather bruised pear in his bag. Kitsun had a breast of rabbit and his own piece of bread and he ate standing, one hand on the head of his axe. A lone bird flapped across the ravine, squawking angrily. A gust of wind rustled the few plants and bushes that adorned the otherwise bare rock walls. The bird took off from its new perch, squawking again and flew upwards and away from the path towards the north.

'Up.' Kitsun's voice was sharp. 'Up, get your things ready. Come quickly, quickly.'

Daryo stooped to pick up his bags and found them rising to meet him as Kitsun picked them up. 'My thanks.'

'Don't thank. Be ready. Quick. Quick, now!' Daryo had all done up but slinging his shield when Kitsun held up a hand to stop him. 'Don't, keep your shield ready. We are not alone.'

Daryo seized his shield and quickly looked around. 'I see nothing.'

'Not on the road, up in the rocks.'

Daryo looked in the direction indicated. 'I still see nothing.'

'Believe my words.' Kitsun unhitched his axe. 'Start walking.'

Daryo complied. After a few dozen steps, he felt that he would walk the swifter with a sword in his hand. He drew Temma's Sword. Kitsun was walking sideways, trying to watch forwards and behind on the road at the same time.

'How many?' whispered Daryo, afraid to raise his voice.

'Seven. Perhaps eight.' Daryo clutched Temma's Sword all the tighter, quickening his step, but Kitsun hissed urgently at him. 'Slowly. Walk. Running will make them attack.'

'Why don't they?'

'Pushing us into a trap. Maybe massing more forces. Or maybe simply watching us through their lands. That last thought is probably just the Fourth Goddess testing my old mind. Oh, she still wants this old warrior alongside her in her halls.' He stopped. 'And she may yet have me.'

Rounding an elbow in the Pass, three brawny Peak Tribesmen blocked the road. Each carried one of the long, two-handed rough swords. One also had a nastily-spiked metal mace that looked too fine not to have been taken from a fallen previous owner. Daryo squared his shield, suddenly aware that he had fought a battle only twice in his life. One by one, more of the wildmen were appearing from behind boulders and from within hidden clefts- seven, eight, nine of them.

Kitsun hammered the haft of his axe on his shield. '*Kro ha da see! Yo vanna ho da!*' he barked in challenge.

The tribesman with the mace laughed. '*Va ha vanna ki reet? Kra ha!*'

'*Yo vanna ho da...*'

The Peak chief scoffed and pointed his sword lazily at Kitsun and Daryo. '*Hev.*'

And the man fell forwards, a small blade embedded in the base of his neck. The stunned tribesmen had no time to react before the man to the felled leader's right hand was struck by another blade just below the ear. In a blur of Kitsun's axe, a flurry of arrows and another thrown knife, the few remaining tribesmen had melted like snow back into the crevices in the mountain side.

Kitsun lowered his axe, panting. 'Obscua.'

'Indeed.' A striking woman, dressed in a queer patchwork of grey, green and brown, much like the walls of the Pass, seemingly appeared from within the rock, a bow in her hand. 'Kitsun the Shrewd.'

'Obscua the Unseen. And?'

'Hannick. To be called the Veiled.' A small but strong-looking young man came into being where Daryo had thought a rock had been. He seemed to be only a few seasons older than Daryo. 'He makes his Promise at the death of the moon.'

'A tail soon to be docked.'

'Indeed. And your tail?'

'Not grown yet. Daryo, kin of Yuai. Daryo, you stand before Obscua the Unseen.'

Obscua was taller than Daryo or Kitsun, her hair shorn very short and coloured to make it a dull green. Her skin also appeared stained in a motley of browns and blacks. Her very flesh resembled a patchwork blanket and her hardened leather jerkin was barely distinguishable from the skin. Daryo could see no metal on her armour and her boots were soft and flexible. She carried a double-curved bow and had quivers on her back and at her waist as well as a narrow sword. The ensign of the Order was painted beige on her jerkin with the symbol of the Fourth Goddess, the dead moon, as her badge.

'A new recruit for the Order.' Her voice was low, quiet and soft.

'I hope so, ma'am,' said Daryo, feeling rather awed by the woman. Kitsun was an old, smoked warrior, the woman was something different entirely.

'A respectful recruit,' she said with a hint of a smile. 'If only you had been so, Hannick.' The oaken young man in moss green wool and dark brown leather nodded and smiled obligingly but stayed silent.

'I'm taking Daryo to the Five Towers,' said Kitsun.

'You would want to be heading to there too. Muster is called.'

'Muster? You would not give this as sport to an old man, Obscua?'

'On my dead moon.' She drew a line with her finger across the dead moon on her jerkin. 'At the first glimpse of the new moon.'

'Muster. There has been no Muster in thirty autumns.'

'Thirty-two. I walk to Lalbi with Hannick to bring you, the Ranger and the Thrice-Killed. The Bright rides south, the Swift rides east.'

Kitsun shook his head, returning his axe to his belt. 'Muster. Why?'

The Unseen unstrung her bow, coiling the string carefully before replying. 'I think that all of us know, we just do not speak that which we know.' Hannick nodded slowly in agreement.

'We may be wrong.'

'Indeed.' Obscua checked her quivers. Her apprentice had already become one with the rocks. 'At the first glimpse of the moon's light. In the Sanctuary.'

'As it should be.'

Daryo heard noise behind him and glanced back nervously. When he looked forwards again, Obscua the Unseen had gone.

Kitsun checked his shield for damage and then slung it over his back. 'Come, Daryo.' He began to walk, his pace brisk.

Daryo hurried to catch up. 'Who is mustering?'

'The Order of the Shield and Sword. Muster summons every Member and apprentice to the Sanctuary.'

'How many is that?'

'At my own guess... six hundred and maybe two hundred apprentices.'

'What did Obscua mean that you know why the Muster has been called but cannot speak it?'

Kitsun stopped and turned sharply on Daryo. 'Obscua says little and most of it more hidden than her true skin. Pay it no mind.'

'She sounded-'

'Come. We must clear the Pass by sundown.'

'But-'

'Move.'

## Chapter 6

They were halfway down the slope on the eastern side of the Pass when the light failed. The pair slept in the shelter of a fir tree and was thoroughly bathed by a considerable downpour of first rain and then sleet. At the earliest opportunity, as soon as the light was enough to see by, Kitsun commanded a restart to the march. He rejected or ignored any attempts at conversation. He strode along the road in stolid silence. The clouds hid the landscape and the sleet was unrelenting. Visible was Kitsun, the road and about twenty yards beyond. The sleet was cold and wet and had made Daryo the same. He trudged on, trying to ignore the aching shivering that coursed through his body.
The road levelled out after the descent, still downhill but less markedly so. At first a few trees begin to dot along the road and after another mile the forest was a dense mix of sweet-smelling pines and firs. The densely-packed trees shielded them from the worst of the downpour. The road had become much better, fully paved with even grey stones. Daryo found himself muttering the Verse under his breath in time with his steps.
'What is that you keep repeating?' demanded Kitsun, sounding exasperated.
'The Verse,' said Daryo, relieved to hear words after so many miles of silent walking. 'It is something my people use to share stories, their knowledge and their view of life.'
'I have never heard it before. A fine tradition.' Kitsun stopped and studied their surroundings for a long moment. 'This way.' He led the way off the road to the left. After a few steps, a track just wide enough for a horse became evident through the woods. 'Stay on the trail. There are a few traps in the trees to keep out the uninitiated and the uninvited.'
'Are we near the Five Towers?'
'Very near. It was the stronghold of an ancient lord or a king, according to some. It was at the hub of a large town which has long since crumbled. Many centuries ago, the Order found the empty, crumbling edifice and made it our home. There has only ever been one Constable, the Constable made the Five Towers our sanctuary and it has been so ever since.'
Daryo thought he heard footsteps. 'I can hear someone.'
'One of the Brethren. They are all descendants of a family who served the Order centuries ago as guards and servants. Now grandsons, cousins and nephews of the family continue the role.'
Daryo peered through the tree trunks and saw a lone figure in the gloom, a longbow in hand and a longsword on the belt, a yellow badge on his arm and a matching hood. 'Brethren?'

'Brethren. A guard, he wears the yellow of our soldiers, servants wear blue.'
The path dipped and within fifty yards they were out of the trees. On either side of the path were random piles of stone that were once a town. The Five Towers stood above the ruins against a cliff, the cliffs curved around like open arms, the outer wall of the fortress was stone and built straight across to enclose the space between the arms. The wall was nearly fifty feet high and inside the walls was the Towers themselves. They were each at least three times the height of the wall. The two on the left of the line were shorter than the others and joined at the waist by a bridge that also ran to the wall. On the right, the towers were taller and wider, one off-square with a crenelated roof like a castle, one domed and shining like silver. The largest, tallest and widest was at the centre and appeared to be wooden.
'The First- and Secondborn Twins, the Castle Tower, the Temple Tower and the Wooden Fortress Tower.'
'Kitsun the Shrewd!'
Kitsun turned towards the voice. Strolling out of stone ruins was a Member of the Brethren in a yellow hood with a scarlet fringe to it. He lowered his hood revealing straw-like hair and rheumy eyes. He looked to be of an age with Kitsun and obviously new the Shrewd well.
'Downe! Good to see you!' He grasped the Brethren's wrist.
'You have been gone a long time.'
'Indeed. But now I return with a new aspirant. And Muster is called.'
'It is. Who is the boy?'
'Daryo, kin of Yuai of the Batribi. Daryo, Herren Downe, Command of the Brethren, third-great grandson of Yarron Downe, first of the Brethren.'
'A Batribi apprentice! My Brethren and ancestors have never seen a Batribi apprentice.' He extended his open hand to Daryo. 'Long awaited, well met.'
Daryo grasped it. 'Well met.'
'Welcome to the Five Towers. My Brethren and I are at your service.'
Kitsun beckoned Daryo on. The gate was almost half the height of the wall and instead of an exotically-carved example, the gates were simple iron-banded wood in a simple archway. Daryo looked up and saw a lifted portcullis in front of the massive gate. The sally port was open and two of the Brethren stood sentry, both with drawn two handed swords resting on chainmail-clad shoulders.
'Welcome, Kitsun,' said one. 'The third word?'
'Heart,' said Kitsun and the Brethren ushered him and Daryo over the high threshold of the gate-within-the-gate and under the inside portcullis. 'This is the Compound.'

The Compound was the courtyard around the bases of the towers formed by the half-circle of the cliffs and the straight line of the wall. A dairy and bakery were built against the base of one of the Twins' Towers, a fruit press stood a short distance away. The stables were behind the Twins' Towers, the smithy was a long building between them and the Wooden Tower at the centre. Between the wall and the Temple Tower were a cluster of actual temples. The Order apparently welcomed many beliefs in its Compound. A group of youngsters, younger than Daryo, were fighting with wooden swords under the supervision of one of the Brethren in the drizzling rain. A short distance from them, a woman with the Order's badge on her shield and dressed in a startling number of colours, was deflecting a barrage of axe blows from a youth and encouraging him to vary his strikes as he pushed forwards, a small group watching them.
'Kym the Harlequin,' Kitsun told Daryo, seeing where he was looking. 'She trains many novice Members of the Order; although she is not perhaps our most skilful she is a keen teacher.'
The young woman called her attacker off and smiled at Kitsun. 'Good morning, Shrewd. Fancy your axe against my shield?'
'Your shield is too well-made, Harlequin.'
'Or you axe is too poor. A friend?'
'Apprentice, courtesy of the Ranger.'
'Is she still alive?'
'So I believe.'
'Oh. Shame.' Her smile suggested it was a joke.
'A great pity. Is Olvar still in charge of new apprentices?'
'He is but your recruit is a little old to start from there.'
'Then he goes straight to be a tail. Sorrell the Greensward?'
'I should say so.'
'Firstborn?'
'Isn't he always? I don't think he remembers the sun.'
'My thanks,' said Kitsun and beckoned Daryo away towards the Twins' Towers.
'Why are they the Firstborn and Secondborn?' asked Daryo.
'They were the first and second towers to be built and named for the twin sons of the first of the Brethren.'
The Firstborn was the furthest of the two towers, slightly taller and with several more arrow-slit-like windows. Kitsun ducked in the low doorway. The lower floor was apparently an armoury. Racks upon racks of blades from daggers up to two-handed broadswords lined the walls. Pikes, spears and axes were lined up in the centre of the

room and an entire wall was hung with shields- arm shields, boss shields, even a few huge Yashoun-style line shields.

'Impressive,' said Daryo, stopping to admire a trident. 'These are very difficult to make well.'

'Our blacksmith is truly expert. Only one of the Order uses a weapon like that but the smith likes to try his skills. Come.'

The staircase followed the curve of the inside of the tower wall. Up the first flight was the armour store- helmets, breastplates, gauntlets, codpieces, greaves and myriad others. A second round and they were in a fully-equipped bowyer's and fletcher's workshop- short bows, long bows, double-curved bows, crossbows and barrels of bolts and arrows of dozens of designs. A small man with very little of his nose was affixing metal heads to a stock of unfletched arrows. He nodded to Kitsun and looked curiously at Daryo as they passed by on the stairs. At the next level, the stairs finished following the curve of the tower wall and instead became a tighter construction around a metal core. The rest of the floor of the tower was walled off. Kitsun knocked on the door in the centre and pushed it open.

Sat behind a large table was a man of immense proportions, Daryo guessed he would be over two yards high when he stood but his girth was as large as his height. On a green silk doublet was the Order's badge in gold thread. His skin was milk-white, his eyes small and close-set, russet hair was turning white and his moustache was down below his chin. A boy of about twelve summers was stood nearby with the blue badge of the Brethren on his arm.

'Kitsun the Shrewd, bringer of apprentices, thief of my time,' grumbled the leviathan, barely glancing up from his parchment.

'Sorrell the Greensward, guardian of the table. I bought you a task rather than luncheon. Daryo, kin of Yuai with the greetings and salutations of the Ranger.'

'Hm. The Ranger. The renegade, the thoughtless, the witless.'

Kitsun breathed slowly to calm himself. 'The Renegade was killed two winters ago, Sorrell. The Ranger is walking through Jaboen somewhere. It is her calling to send back apprentices to me. This one is her latest.'

The Greensward looked up at Daryo, then down. He studied his parchment for a moment and then his head rose. 'What is this?'

'Daryo, kin of Yuai. The Ranger's latest.'

'He's blacker than the Ranger's feet.'

'He's a keen fighter. He aided me against the Peak Tribesmen as we crossed the Tember Pass.'

'Nate here could fight a band of Peak Tribesmen with a butter knife,' said the Greensward, jerking a ham-like thumb towards the boy.
'He'd die in the attempt but a brave gesture. Daryo is too old to go to Olvar as an apprentice. He will need to be a tail. That's your job, Sorrell, giving tails.'
'I will not.'
'Because you don't like the bearer?'
'Because you bring me a shaved boar not a recruit for our noble Order.'
Kitsun leaned on the table with both hands, lowering his head to the height of the flabby one of Sorrell the Greensward. 'That is not a matter. There is no law or statute or code that says of what origin our Members are. We have Yashoun, Jaboen, Gourmini, Boskinian, Vidmarian, we have a Silver Islander in our ranks.'
'Not a Batribi, not a thief and a traitor and a child-stealer.'
'How dare you, sir!' Daryo had fought to stay quiet but gave into his anger, marching fully into the room. 'If you know none of my people, how dare you presume to know my people? I fought for my life and the life of a total stranger alongside your comrade the Shrewd and then again for my life in the Pass along the same man. He and your comrade the Ranger has judged me worthy and you, who have seen me only these last few breaths, presume that I am not capable or not deserving simply as my skin is darker than yours! Your skin is paler than mine, sir, and therefore do I judge you unworthy? I judge you by your words, your character and actions and only so do I judge you unworthy, sir!'
The tirade made the Greensward's face turn purple, Kitsun's face crease in a silent laugh and the boy's jaw drop open in astonishment.
'I will take him to the Aides if I must, Sorrell,' said Kitsun, when his composure returned. 'And they ruled aye on a Boskinian and a Silver Islander. They will rule aye on a Batribi. Why not save their time and my breath and simply accept what you will be forced to accept anyway?'
The Greensward muttered several base oaths under his breath. 'Nate! Take the... tail to quarters.'
'Yes, sir,' said the boy, hurrying forwards.
'My most humble and profuse thanks, Sorrell,' said Kitsun, his voice dripping sarcasm like new honey as he turned to leave.
'Boy!' barked the huge man. 'Note these words in whatever fine words you care to use: one single mistake, a slip, a trip, a wasted meal and I shall see you chased from here by dogs. Get out.'

'Such a charming man,' said Kitsun when they reached the outdoor air again. 'I always thoroughly enjoy speaking with my comrade and brother the Greensward.' He raised a finger. 'Be warned though, Daryo. The Greensward rarely makes threats in air. He makes them in steel. Be cautious.'

'I shall be.'

Kitsun nodded and smiled. 'Good. I should go and see Novar of the Brethren and find myself a room in the Castle Tower. Nate Downe will look after you.'

Kitsun strode away leaving Daryo with the young boy. Daryo had taken in lots of new names and facts but the name was definite in his mind.

'Nate Downe, you are related to Herren Downe?'

The young boy nodded. 'His second son. I assist the Greensward- run his errands, fetch his food, see to his cleaning and toilet.'

Daryo shuddered at the thought. 'Lead on.'

The boy led the way across the Compound, aware several stopped to look if not to stare at perhaps the first Batribi they had ever seen. Daryo took the approach that he had always used in Salifa; he kept walking as if there was no-one else in sight. The Harlequin waved her hand to Daryo as he passed. The Temple Tower was closer to the wall than the Castle Tower and slightly shorter, its shining dome catching the midday light. To get to the entrance, they had to pass between the tower and the wall where there were a cluster of various temples and shrines: the domed stone building was a temple to the Pantheon of Eight Gods and Goddess, the dome supported by columns without walls with the statue of woman in the centre was for devotees of the White Lady, another building was for followers of the Great Shepherd, the other six buildings were foreign to Daryo's eyes.

'Do all new recruits live in the Temple Tower?' he asked Nate, who was trotting slightly ahead.

'Yes they do. The Members in the Castle Tower, my Brethren in the Secondborn Tower. The Aides have the privilege to live in quarters in the Wooden Tower if they so wish but most choose to stay in the Castle Tower as it is where most have always lived as Members of the Order.'

The Temple Tower's base was a single hall, lined with table and with a huge fire at one end. The stairs led up following the wall as in the Firstborn tower but every floor's stairwell gave onto corridors between small rooms. The Tower was a warren of stone walls, wooden doors and a steady bustle of people.

'This one,' said Nate. They were on the seventeenth level, not far from the top. Nate pushed open the first door on the left from the stairs. The room was small but there was everything needed- a low bed, a wooden chair, a chest, a small wooden weapons rack and a stand with a bowl of water.

'This is your room,' said Nate. 'It there is any need you have, my Brethren are at your service. If you are to become a tail, you will be asked to attend to meet your lead.'

'The Member I will be with?'

'Yes.'

'Do you know who it is?'

'No. Normally an apprentice builds up a record, his Paper Shield, and those who are going to take on a tail will choose their tail based on the Paper Shield. I do not know what they will do with a tail with no Paper Shield.'

'How old are apprentices normally?'

'Thirteen summers. You must be sixteen summers; this will be your seventeenth winter.'

Daryo shrugged. 'I do not know.'

'I am well-practised at judging apprentices working for the Greensward. If you have no further need of me...'

'No. Thank you, Nate Downe.'

The boy put his hand on the badge on his arm. 'My service is my name.' He departed.

Daryo was glad to finally remove his pack, throwing it onto the bed. He drew Temma's Sword from its scabbard and hung it on the sword pegs on the wall before removing his belt, dropping that next to his pack. Then he removed the straps of Stai's swords and looped them over the peg meant for a bow. Vehllal's shield went on the correct hook below Temma's Sword. Next he pulled off his outer robe and then the loose shirt beneath, bathing his face and strap-eaten shoulders with the cold water from the basin. The water stung the welts on his skin and he winced.

'You get used to the cold water,' said a woman's voice.

The door was still open and a young woman of an age with Daryo was stood in the doorway. She was dressed in a short tunic, breeches and with a light mail shirt over the top. A long and slim sword, a longer version of the Horse or Bear, hung at her hip. Round brown eyes regarded him from under razor-thin brows while hair of a colour with her eyes lay in a thick braid down her back almost to her belt.

Daryo wiped his face on a strip of towelling nailed to the basin stand. 'I was raised in a School of the Temple in Salifa. Until I started with the blacksmith, I had never had anything but cold water.'

'I have never seen a man with your skin and bearing.'

'I am of the Batribi people.'

'The Walkers.'

'Indeed. My name is Daryo.'
'I am Lana, soon to be called the Cocksure.'
'You are going to make your Promise?'
'In two moons' time. And if Tronn the Jade passes, as he remembers Un the Cocksure.'
'Is Tronn the Jade likely to pass?'
'He will within the week, so the Brethren Healer says. It will be an honour to take the name of the Cocksure. You are new to the Five Towers?'
'I was brought here this morning by Kitsun the Shrewd.'
'And you would be the biggest duckling in the Compound,' said the girl with a grin. 'Straight up to tail.'
'So I was told.'
Lana stepped in through the door and perched herself on the edge of the bed, bringing her sword across her lap. 'Have you a lead yet?'
'No.' Daryo had been listening to her voice as well as looking at her. 'You are Jaboen.'
'I was born in Lalbi.'
'And you don't think that Batribi are thieves and liars.'
Lana smiled. 'No. The Brethren will be serving midday meal. Come with me?'
'I could do with some food.'
'It's a long walk.'
As they walked down the stairs, Lana told Daryo about her lead, Ayiyz the White Hand. The hall at the base of the tower was filling with tails. Some were wearing tunics and breeches, some were in elaborate robes, most were in leather or mail, Daryo had never seen so many people in one space and almost all of them were armed. Kitsun had said that there were two hundred apprentices and Daryo guessed that over half were in the hall. He estimated that maybe a third of them were younger than he- fourteen summers or a few less. Only a few seemed to be more than a couple of summers older. If Nate Downe was right about Daryo's age, it would make everyone in the room less than nineteen summers. At the back of the hall, two Members of the Brethren were rapidly ladling out huge wooden bowls of vegetable stew. The apprentices were moving through collecting bowls and chunks of corn bread.
'Come,' said Lana. 'We should get in before the ducklings.'
'Ducklings?'
Lana nodded towards a group of the youngest apprentices. 'Those still learning in the Compound, not ready to come out yet. They stay near the nest and their mother duck. Ducklings. Then you become a tail, following a Member of the Order around until you

are ready to make your Promise.' She tugged Daryo by the arm into the line of apprentices slowly trudging forwards for their meal.

The stew was thick and tasty, full of lentils and carrot. Daryo was sopping the last of the gravy from the bowl when a towering man strode into the room.

Lana looked up, as did many other apprentices. 'That's Fayd the Vanguard. He's the leader of the Blades Group, they control who goes where and what jobs the Members take on.'

Fayd the Vanguard had needed to duck under the lintel of the door. He was broad and powerful. His arms were thick, his legs thicker, a dense brown beard reached to his mid-chest and a thick braid of hair was nearly as long. From the neck to the waist he was in battered plate armour, mail breeches reached to plate boots and a huge rectangular shield was slung on his back. 'I'm looking for the Batribi!' he barked.

Silence fell. Several hands willingly pointed out Daryo. He rose to his feet slowly and walked halfway across the hall, aware that every eye was on him.

'I... I am Daryo,' he said quietly.

'The only Batribi in the Compound so I would guess so,' boomed the giant. He was even taller when seen closely and the sword on his belt looked more like a battle axe. 'Follow me.'

He turned and stomped out of the tower hall, Daryo hurrying to keep up. The huge strides of the Vanguard meant that for every five steps he took, Daryo had to take eight or nine. There were several apprentices and Brethren in the Compound and they parted like grasses as the Vanguard strode from the Temple Tower across the centre of the space to the immense doors of the Wooden Fortress Tower. They were lighter than the wood of the Tower itself and not much smaller than the gates to the Compound. One stood open and the Vanguard strode through. Inside was an atrium with a staircase on one side. The Vanguard went straight up the stairs, ignoring the first floor and continuing to the second. He came off the stairs, pushed two doors open and led the way into a small hall with a C-shaped table, points towards the door, surrounded by Members of the Order. Each had their shield hooked to the table facing into the centre of the C, where three large swords were painted on the floors. The centre seat was vacant. The Vanguard held up a hand to stop Daryo and then strode to the centre of the table. He unslung his shield and placed it in front of the vacant seat before walking all the way around the table to sit down. Daryo counted eleven seated people, seven men and four women, then saw Kitsun the Shrewd, Kym the Harlequin and Nate Downe standing to one side. He felt like the accused before the lord's justice.

'Daryo of the Batribi,' said the woman to the Vanguard's right. Her shield had a small figure with an arrow in its hand as its badge. 'I am Allistrora the Arrow Nymph. We are the Council of Advice and Direction of the Aides of the Captain-General, known as the Blades. We have been informed that you were sent to Kitsun the Shrewd by Vilya the Ranger as a potential apprentice. We have no apparent issues with this. However the Order has never had a Batribi apprentice and we are aware that this may cause trouble with some. I am sure that you are aware of the reactions some people have to those with your heritage.'

Daryo nodded quickly but could not find his voice.

'There are some who think that a Batribi apprentice could be divisive,' said an older man, on the left end of the table, with three green jewels on his shield. 'If there are those among our Members who mistrust and dislike Batribi, this could create division. The Order could not permit this.' There was a silent chorus of nods around the table.

Daryo's stomach dropped.

'Nonetheless, the Order has no reason to refuse you,' said the Vanguard. 'The Order has many people from many lands and creeds. We have admitted strangers from all of these before and someone must have been the first Jaboen and but three springs ago we permitted a Silver Islander to join us and soon he is to take his Promise. The Batribi are a people with a long and fine tradition. They will add to our own. As you are too old to become a junior, you will be made up to an apprentice.'

'Thank you,' breathed Daryo.

'Normally,' said the Arrow Nymph, 'Sorrell the Greensward would assign you a Member to follow and learn from. However a Member has already come forwards and volunteered herself as your tutor.' She pointed to the Harlequin, who had been leaning nonchalantly against the wall but now stepped forwards.

'We've been introduced,' said the Harlequin with a broad smile.

'Kym the Harlequin has been training some of our youngest apprentices and wanted to get back to operations. You will be her apprentice. You will follow her instructions and learn from her.'

Daryo nodded and the Harlequin winked at him.

'Kym the Harlequin,' boomed the Vanguard. 'Do you pledge to guide, protect and teach this apprentice until he is deemed ready to make his Promise?'

'I pledge.' The Harlequin drew a line with her finger across the figure on her shield. 'I pledge on my Promise and my harlequin.'

'Kitsun the Shrewd,' said the older man. 'Our thanks. You will return to Lalbi?'

'After Muster.'

'Of course. Our thanks, Shrewd.'
'My sword and my service.'
'Our swords and our service,' said the Vanguard. 'Thank you, Harlequin.'
'My sword and my service, Blades.'
'Our swords and our service.'
Kym turned to leave and jerked her head. 'Come along, tail. Let's get you some real clothes.'

The Firstborn Tower had a cellar and it was apparently a tailor's, rows upon rows of high shelves covered in clothes. The Harlequin led Daryo through a selection of new clothing, some with the Order's sign on it that she said was forbidden until he had made his Promise, some without, some with other insignia on them.
'It's a bazaar for the vain warrior,' said the Harlequin, studying a green robe with a red hood. 'A bit unremarkable, this one. I wonder where Salli is.'
'Salli?'
'Our master tailor, Herren Downe's younger daughter. Maybe she can find me something.'
'I thought you bought me in here to find me some clothes.'
'Oh, I did. But while I'm here, this is getting dull.' The Harlequin used her hands to show that she was referring to her clothes. She was wearing a halved blue and violet tunic, scarlet leggings and high brown boots with a green cuff around the top. 'I've had a long thing with halved tunics; maybe I need to go back to quarters. Let me go and find Salli. Pick whatever you want.' The Harlequin disappeared into the rows of shelves. When she returned, sporting a new tunic with two sky-coloured quarters, one scarlet and one green, Daryo was in black breeches and his well-worn boots, over a hooded vest he had an identically-coloured rust-coloured leather cuirass with thin steel armour plates in the chest and back and sleeves. The Harlequin nodded in approval.
'Most handsome,' she said with a grin. 'Somewhat plain but... Here, I have something for you.'
She had been carrying a shield, slightly smaller than Vehllal's. 'You need an Order shield and I thought that you would be loath to repaint your existing one. '
Daryo took the shield by the rim to look at it. The metal banded shield was wooden and painted dark brown with a crimson Order symbol on it with no badge at the pommel. On the reverse, above the two leather straps, was a small carved figure. 'Is that...'
'A harlequin. A rather younger Kym cut that with an arrowhead. This was my apprentice shield.'

'I am very grateful.'
'No trouble. Have this night and I shall talk to the Vanguard. I think we should get out of the Compound as soon as we can.'

The sun had set below the western arm of the cliffs when Daryo emerged from the Firstborn Tower. The Harlequin had decided to remain in the cellar with the seamstress talking about clothing. Daryo diverted to his right and the smithy. A small but leanly-muscular woman was sharpening a small axe on the grindstone. She looked up as Daryo approached.
'Gods' Watch,' she said pleasantly.
'Gods' Guidance. I used to be apprentice to a smith. This is pleasant. Like home.'
'Are you new to the Five Towers?'
'I am. I walked in with Kitsun the Shrewd this morning.'
'Very new. Do you have a name?'
'Daryo.'
'I am Siva the Fuller.' She held up the axe end-on to check its edge. 'What do you think?'
Daryo took the axe and checked the edge, the haft and the joins. 'Good. I would be proud to have made this weapon. Are you the blacksmith?'
'I am one of them. We have three. The Master Smith is Dibat the Trident, there is also Solv the Strike. Have you a lead yet?'
'The Harlequin.'
Siva paused. 'How interesting.'
'You dislike the Harlequin.'
'Nobody dislikes the Harlequin. It is said, by some, that perhaps she is more interested in appearance and reputation than in her bladesmanship.'
Daryo frowned. 'Really?'
'Only by some,' said Siva quickly. 'Only by some.'
'Thank you, Siva the Fuller. Gods' Guidance.'
'Gods' Guidance.'
Daryo walked across in front of the Wooden Fortress and towards the Castle and Temple Towers. The moon had risen; it was waning towards the dead moon in three days. A dozen Members of yellow-badged and hooded Brethren were walking back towards the Twin Towers. Herren Downe was at the rear of the group and inclined his head respectfully to Daryo as he passed although several of the Brethren stared openly. Daryo kept walking and decided to visit the temple before going inside. As the sun set, a small cymbal was being beaten outside the shrine to the White Lady by a barefoot female

duckling in a traditional gown almost fine enough to see through to her skin. She stared as Daryo passed and then resumed tapping her cymbal with a small wooden hammer. Daryo had thought that perhaps the Temple would be to the Second God, or perhaps the Fourth Goddess. Instead it was a Temple of the Second Goddess, her flames painted above the door in bright orange and red. The door was ajar and Daryo slipped through. Inside the stone-walled temple, the air was cool and light came from a series of iron candelabras hung from the arched ceiling. The rows of bolsters were neat and compact as the nave was narrow. At the top of the nave, the altar was the eightfold circle with both a glass flame and a lit fire representing the Second Goddess, the teacher of duty, responsibility and passion. Above the altar, the dome rose nearly fifty feet. Daryo knelt on the closest bolster to the altar, crossed his hands onto their opposite knees and allowed himself the peace of the temple.

An hour's quiet in the Temple, alone as far as he had been aware, gave Daryo time to think through everything his one day had bought him: the amiability of Herren Downe, the hatred from Sorrell the Greensward, meeting Lana and Siva and Nate, being summoned by the Vanguard, his interview in front of the Blades, the Harlequin volunteering herself as his lead, the few whispers he had heard against the Harlequin, the mixture of welcome and antipathy. When he left the sanctuary, the sun was gone. Lanterns were being hung outside the Towers and along the wall by the Brethren. A single Brethren sentry, carrying one of their long swords against his shoulder, had taken up post at the door of the Temple Tower.
'Am I breaking curfew?' asked Daryo.
'There is no curfew for tails,' said the Brethren. 'Only the ducklings are restricted, two hours after sunset.'
'My thanks. Gods' Watch.' Daryo slid through the door and started up the stairs to his quarters. It was a long climb and he was panting for breath at the top. The door opposite his was open and Lana was sat cross-legged on her bed.
'Daryo, is everything well?'
'It is. I was taken to meet my lead.'
'The Harlequin.'
'You knew?'
'I think the whole Tower knew as soon as you came out of the Blades' Chamber. Nate Downe is our wellspring of all knowledge. She then took me to the Firstborn Tower as apparently I was inappropriately dressed. I then returned through the smithy and the Temple of the Second Goddess.'

'You follow the Second Goddess?'

'I follow the Faith. You?'

Lana rocked her head from side to side. 'I was raised by Faithful Parents but... I am not sure. The Faith doesn't burn in my heart as it does in my parents'. Did you meet Dibat at the forge?'

'No, Siva the Fuller.'

'Do not trust all you hear from her. She speaks more than she should.' Lana indicated the stool by the narrow window of her chamber. Daryo entered the room and sat down. Her sword was in its sheath hanging on the wall alongside an oval shield. A stuffed white bear's paw was on the table alongside a carved wooden totem, a jug full of purple flowers and a large chunk of cheese with a small knife stuck in it. Lana cut herself a piece and ate from the knife. 'But she's a skilled smith. She made my sword.'

'I keep hearing negativity about the Harlequin. Should I be worried that she's my lead?'

'You don't get a choice of your lead but if you really do not live well together, the Blades may change your lead. The Harlequin has been training ducklings for three autumns. It is said she was bought back to do the teaching because she ignored orders while in the field.'

'Why?'

'I would say if I knew. It is just what was said in this Tower. She had no tail so there is no witness. Perhaps only the Blades and the Harlequin know for sure.' Lana had another piece of cheese. 'Tell me about the Batribi Daryo.'

'What about?'

'Your parents?'

'I know nothing of them. The only life I knew until a few days ago was as a Ward of the School of the Temple in Salifa. When I was old enough, the priest found me an apprenticeship with the smith because he was the only tradesman in the town that would have a Batribi apprentice. He taught me to smith and to use what I made as well. He had no kin, no children, and he had said that when I was of age and he was too old to continue, he would pass his forge on to me.' Daryo then recounted the events that had led to his exile- the arrival of the Batribi, Vehllal's trade with them, the Pickets, Yiua's death, the events at the Crumbled Temple, the footpads on the south road and the Ranger's intervention.

Lana nodded. 'Sometimes it is more courageous to stay your blade than slash with it. The White Hand has said that to me.'

Daryo then talked about the trip to Lalbi and then across the Tember Pass with Kitsun.

'You seem to have had quite a journey.'

'I feel as if I have been walking since last autumn.'
'You should get some rest.'
'I think so.' Daryo stood up. 'A pleasure to have met you, Lana.'
'My pleasure.' She smiled widely and Daryo was still picturing that smile when he fell asleep.

## Chapter 7

The morning reveille was given by a Member of the Brethren walking the staircase of the Temple Tower with a large hand-bell. Daryo found that someone, presumably the Brethren, had refilled his bowl with fresh and clean water and brought a fresh roll of bread, a few thick slices of ham, a small pot of blackberries and a mug of the juice of apples. He ate and dressed before leaving his room for the hall at the base of the tower. Several apprentices were in the hall, some eating, one sharpening a quiver of arrows, a single female apprentice was using a section of the staircase wall as a target and hurling a knife at it.

'Pillca, no weapon practice in the Towers,' said a tall Member of the Order as he entered.

'Sorry, Snake.' She retrieved her dagger and sheathed it.

He strode past her and stopped in front of Daryo. 'You are the boy that Kitsun the Shrewd bought in from Jaboen.'

'Yes, I am.'

The Member studied Daryo for a moment. He was much taller than Daryo, neatly groomed with a short beard and beady black eyes. As he talked, Daryo noticed his tongue was oddly shaped and it gave him a somewhat lisping and phlegmy tone. 'I am Natis the Snake. I am great friends with the Shrewd. He says you have exceptional skills with those two blades of yours.'

'Kitsun is a better judge of such matters than I.'

'Very intelligent answer, young Batribi.' The Snake drew his sword, holding it by the hilt, blade down in front of his body. 'My sword, my service, Daryo of the Batribi.'

'My thanks. Do you know where I might find the Harlequin?'

'I have not seen her this morning. Gods' Watch, Daryo.'

'Gods' Guidance, Natis the Snake.'

The Snake hailed an apprentice who Daryo assumed was the Snake's tail. Daryo avoided a group of ducklings complaining about one of the Brethren and stepped outside. The sky was grey, the colour of cheap pewter, threatening snow. Daryo walked around the Temple Tower and towards the Castle Tower. A Brethren sentry was at the door and held up a hand.

'No apprentices in the Castle Tower,' said the sentry bluntly.

'I'm looking for Kym the Harlequin.'

'Fortress Tower.'

'My thanks.'

Daryo turned about and headed for the Wooden Fortress Tower. In the better light, Daryo could see a magnificent banner, olive-green with the Order's badge in gold, hung from the battlements and fully half the length of the Tower. The Vanguard came strolling out and nodded formally to Daryo, followed by the older man from the Blades.
'Ah, our new Batribi tail,' he said stopping. 'I think we were not introduced. Dava the Three Crystals.'
'Crystals of the Third Goddess?'
'Indeed. I am the... spiritual of the Blades. We have a priest but he confines himself to the Temple of the Second Goddess Brokea. What think you of the Five Towers?'
'Most spectacular. It is a town in its own right.'
'Indeed. The highest town in Gourmin, the most memorable and the best-defended.'
'A fortress.'
'Eight fortresses.'
'Eight?'
'The Fallen Town, The Gatehouse, The Firstborn, The Secondborn, The Temple, The Castle, The Wooden Fortress and the Caverns.'
'Caverns?'
'You have not seen them?'
'No, I have not.'
'Come, I will show you.'
'I have to meet with the Harlequin...'
'She is with her old lead; she will be some time still. Come.'
Dava led the way around to the rear of the Fortress and to the very foot of the cliffs. In the walls was a deep recess with a heavy wooden and iron door. As they crossed the threshold, Daryo saw that there was a portcullis hung up in the rock itself. The door led through into a tunnel that sloped downwards, lit by wall-mounted braziers backed with polished mirrored bronze to reflect the light.
'The legends of our Order tell us that when the first of our number came to the Five Towers, they found the rubble of the town, the foundations of the Castle and the Temple Towers, the Wooden Fortress in ruins and the sealed gates of the caves. It took the Constable many days to get through and he found the maze of tunnels behind the gates. The portcullis is much newer. Now the caves would be our last resort if ever we should be attacked. It is also the home of some of our most treasured places.'
They reached a fork in the tunnels. Dava turned left and the tunnel became a flight of stone steps. Dava took a torch from the wall and lit it from the next brazier. The steps continued for nearly thirty yards before stopping. Suddenly they were in a huge cave.

The lit torch barely illuminated any distance. Daryo could see straight lines of cairns of stones with a wooden shield and sword laid on top of them stretching off into the darkness. He shivered without meaning to.

'The dead.'

'Our honoured and lamented fellows,' said Dava. 'From the dawn of the Order. Ten thousand, maybe more, an army of those who fought for what is right. Every one that we can is brought back here to be laid with their brothers and sisters here. Come.' He started forwards through the avenues of the dead. There was just enough space to walk between the knee-high cairns. After twenty rows he turned left and started along a row. After nearly thirty yards, he stopped at a cairn. 'My tail.'

'Your...?'

'He was my tail. I taught him as the Harlequin will tutor you. Ofavxo the Water, he was slain while we were defending a village against an immense pack of wolves in Boskinia. He sleeps with illustrious company here.'

He turned suddenly and strode away towards the entrance, Daryo hurried after. Back up the stairs to the main tunnel and Dava turned to head deeper into the cave system. The walls were now more regimented, more even, the height of the ceiling was closer to level.

'This tunnel was made by hands,' said Daryo.

'It was expanded by hand,' Dava clarified. 'The tunnel is natural but it was made more useable by the work of our earliest Members nearly eight hundred winters ago. The tunnel began to slope upwards and after nearly fifty yards, they came to another open door, this one over a foot thick but with several archers' slits cut through it. After five spaces was another identical door and then a third.

'This is a fortress,' said Daryo.

'Indeed. As I said, if ever we were overrun by an attacker, the caves would be our last stronghold. This is the Threefold Door. Between each are traps that can be set and the doors can be barred and braced. The arrow notches are in lines and progressing larger so that an archer behind the third can fire at a foe before the first.'

The tunnel sloped upwards once more, steel gates at intervals and ending after a further fifty yards at a firmly closed wooden door, no arrow notches but steel bars and locks were much in evidence.

'We go no further,' said Dava. 'Beyond this door is our greatest sanctuary. It is opened only for Muster and in the event that we would need to retreat here.'

'So it will be open at the dead of the moon?'

'It will but not one moment before. There are only two keys for this door, the Final Door: the Captain-General's and the Commander of the Brethren's.'

'Daryo! Dava!' They both turned, it was the Harlequin, carrying her own torch. 'I was told that the Three Crystals was showing my tail our caves.'
'Indeed. Forgive me, Harlequin.'
'No apology needed, Three Crystals. I was planning this same walk myself.'
'We should find the light again.'
The three turned about and walked back out of the caves to the Compound where the Three Crystals took his leave.
'I've got us a job,' the Harlequin told Daryo. 'The nearest town to here is Aslon, where the lord has very carelessly lost a woman.'
'Lost?'
'From his dungeon. Very careless. She's apparently hidden in a shack along the river.'
'What did she do?'
'Killed a couple of men, a known thief... was going to be executed anyway so if we can't bring drag her back to Aslon or she puts up a fight...'
'I understand.'
'Go and get your gear, I'll meet you by the gate.'
'At once!'
Daryo hurried across the Compound and bounded up the stairs to his room, gasping for breath by the time he got there. He seized his Batribi robe, buckled his sword belt and grabbed Stai's swords, fumbling for the straps. Lana was sat on her bed, sharpening a knife with a whetstone. Daryo was flapping for the loose straps and she walked across quickly.
'Let me help you.' She reached out and took the free strap, looping over Daryo's arm and tying the one across his chest. Then she took the Harlequin's shield down and handed it to him, helping him slide his hand through the loops. 'There. A warrior of the Order of the Shield and Sword.'
'My thanks.'
'My pleasure.' Lana smiled shyly, kissed him lightly on the cheek and before Daryo had realised, she was back in her own chamber with the door closed.

The Harlequin was waiting by the gates with two haversacks at her feet. Daryo had not seen her with a weapon before, just a shield, and now had a slightly-curved sword at her hip and a quiver of arrows and a longbow over her back.
'Are you well?' asked the Harlequin.
Daryo nodded eagerly. 'Very.'
'You look very happy.'

'Oh! Excitement...'

The Harlequin nodded. 'Good. You've got a lot of gear.'

'I have?'

'Three swords, a knife, a shield...'

'They were gifts.'

'So were many weapons I have but one doesn't need all of them for every journey.'

Daryo nodded slowly. 'I understand. Should I...?'

'No, no worry. Take them this time, we aren't going far and we will be returning within a day or so.' She picked up the haversacks. One was black canvas, the other red and green patchwork and she handed the former to Daryo. 'More gifts. Some clean underclothes, a skin of water, another of small beer, some food and a blanket.'

'My thanks.'

'We can collect packs like this from the Firstborn Tower when going on a job. Ready?'

'I am.'

'Forwards then.'

The Harlequin led the way out of the gate, past the Brethren sentries and through the ruined town. She kept a brisk pace, one hand holding her pack out of the way, the other flicking the string of her bow absent-mindedly in time with her steps. 'This must have been a lovely town ages past,' she said, stopping plucking her bowstring for a moment to wave at the ruins.

'Many ages past.'

'My old lead, my first lead, Jun the Village was named for the town.'

'Named for it?'

'As an apprentice, he used to spend days exploring these ruins. When he made his Promise he took the name the Village.'

'He was your first lead?'

'He was.'

'You had another?'

'Two. Jun the Village died of a fever. Ukbal the Frost asked that his... troublesome apprentice be given to another Member. I finished my training with Nubar the Red Pike.'

'Given to another Member?'

'We did not get along well. I was young, enthusiastic, a touch... flamboyant. He was a fool.'

Daryo laughed and they passed the rest of the walk to the road in companionable silence. The Harlequin pointed east and they started downhill. The sun was pale and the clouds slow-moving and heavy on a southern wind.

'Could be snow,' said the Harlequin, studying the sky as she walked.

'I saw a real fall of snow several winters ago. I was still a child,' said Daryo. 'It turned Salifa white for some days.'

'We are higher in the hills than Salifa. Some of the snows later in the season will last for weeks and reach to your knees. When I first made my Promise, the snows were even deeper. The Brethren and the Members of the Order had to dig to keep the doors open and the stables clear. The roof of the Castle Tower sagged from the weight of the snow.'

'I have heard several speak of the Promise.'

'Indeed. It is central to whom we are in the Order and it is our pledge to do our duty.'

'What is the Promise? The words?'

'With my heart, my mind and my honour, I promise to do my duty as a Member of the Order of the Shield and Sword and to follow orders as given on the authority of the Captain-General and his Aides. I swear my Shield and Sword to the defence of the just, the righteous, the innocent and the weak. By this oath, I pledge my sword and my service until I am discharged by death.'

Daryo listened intently. 'It pledges much.'

'But gives back threefold. A Member of the Order gets to walk and ride the lands, to do good by those who need it. This job is poor reasoning on that theme as we are aiding a man of power and influence but we are doing right by the laws of decency and virtue. You will gain skill with a blade and bow; you can see wonderful lands and fascinating people. I have seen creatures and sights that I could never have dreamed of as a girl in Allesbury.'

'How did you come to the Order?'

Kym laughed. 'I applied to join the town guard. Five times. I even offered to duel the captain of the guard to prove I was worth it. He declined but sent me to a fletcher friend of his in Aslon who supplied the Order. I ran away from home to meet him. He arranged for me to meet a Member of the Brethren, who brought me to the Five Towers, and after challenging Niddir the Barricade to a fight, I was a duckling.'

'What of your parents?'

'My mother was killed in a fire when I was a babe. My father raised me and wanted me to be his wife- cooking, watching the house. I would have done better being his son. I tried to live up to both roles; that is why I tried to join the town guard, to be the strong son as well as his daughter. When I told him I was leaving for Aslon, he forbade me to leave. So

I snuck out at midnight during a dead moon. After I made my Promise, I went back and made my peace with my father. He joined the Fourth Goddess two winters ago.'

'Peacefully?'

'Very. What of your parents?'

'I was a Ward of the School of the Temple. I know my parents were Batribi and the priests told me that they would be either dead or simply uncaring to have left me to the Temple. I was sent as a babe from Thiel to the School in Salifa.'

As they walked, the road sloped down more steeply and they came to a ford of the river. About two hundred yards further down, the water roared over a precipice.

'Don't fall in the water,' warned the Harlequin, skipping lightly through the ankle-deep ford. Daryo followed more carefully. The water was shallow but the current was strong and Daryo had to be careful not to lose his footing.

The road curved down to follow the river over its short fall and down to the valley floor. The forest was less dense than further up and the wind less keen. A cart laden with possessions, hauled by a pair of oxen was inching up the incline towards them, a woman leading the oxen with a child sat on the cart and three men were walking alongside, one clearly the son of another. All three men carried staves and the son, a boy of about thirteen summers, wore a short sword.

'Gods' Watch,' said the Harlequin cheerfully and Daryo echoed her.

'Stay away!' snarled the woman.

The Harlequin stepped aside and spread her arms wide to show that she was not holding her weapon. 'My apologies. I merely meant to greet you.'

'You mean to take what little we have left!' the woman snapped, drawing a dirk from beneath her tattered robe. The men hurried to her side. Closer to them, Daryo saw that both the older men were missing their right hands and had badly-welted faces, the boy was painfully thin and looked terrified of the sword he had drawn.

'We are merely travelling east,' said the Harlequin. 'My comrade and I will gladly lay on the ground until you pass, if that makes you feel safer.'

'And what of your comrades waiting for you to do that as signal to attack?'

The Harlequin sighed. 'There are no comrades in the trees. I am a Member of the Order of the Shield and Sword, I am sworn to protect the vulnerable, not to rob them. If I can aid you in any way, I shall. If I cannot, my apprentice and I shall be on our way.' The Harlequin beckoned. 'Come, Daryo.' She resumed walking down the slope, Daryo following quickly.

'Wait! Wait!' The boy had dropped his sword and run after them. 'Help us, help us!'

The Harlequin turned and smiled kindly. 'In any way I can.'

'We had a farm. There were always tribesmen nearby but they let us be. Then two days ago they came and told us if we did not leave, they would kill us and take the farm. And they came while we were loading our cart. They...' He started to cry.

The Harlequin knelt next to him. 'Tell me. You can tell me.'

'They cut the hands off my father and my uncle and cut their tongues out! They did things to my mother in the barn! I heard her scream!' He dissolved into hopeless sobs.

The Harlequin nodded. 'We will take your farm back.' She stood up and turned to Daryo. 'Are we agreed?'

'Indeed.' Daryo felt his heart quicken.

The Harlequin took the boy by the shoulder and guided him back to his mother. 'We will take back your farm. Everything you lost will be restored to you.' She drew her sword, holding it by the handle, point down. 'My sword and my service are yours, my lady.'

The woman still glared at her. 'You are saying that you will put your lives at risk to fight an entire clan of tribesmen just to hand our farm back to us.'

'I am.'

'I do not believe you.'

'Mother!' The boy pushed her slightly. 'I can help.'

The Harlequin smiled. 'I'm sure that you can.'

'No, I really can.' He drew the sword. 'I can use this.'

'Let us see about that later,' said the Harlequin. 'How far is your farm?'

'We left at dawn,' said the mother.

The Harlequin took a piece of cloth from her belt, olive green with the Order badge embroidered on it, and handed it to the mother 'Carry on up the path with your men. When you are a league into the forest, shout for aid as loudly as you can. A man in a sun-coloured hood will join you. Give him this and he will take you to safety.' When the woman agreed, the Harlequin patted the youngster on the shoulder. 'Come along; show me where your home is.'

They walked for several hours, past midday. They stopped to eat at the side of the road just out of the trees and the Harlequin shared her bread, cheese and beer with the lad, who was named Voy. Another half of an hour's walk and they reached a dirt track leading off across the grasslands and down a steep incline. At the bottom was a small orchard, some hedged fields and a cluster of thatched buildings.

'That's the longhouse in the centre,' said the boy. 'The barn is the big one at the back. Sheds for the chickens...' He pointed to a cluster of wooden sheds on the right 'The

burning one was the vegetable store.' The building on the very right was still
smouldering. A figure was walking around it.

'How many tribesmen did you see?' asked the Harlequin.

The boy shook his head. 'I never learned my numbers.'

Daryo held up both hands, fingers stretched. 'One for all of my fingers?'

'No. No. I don't think so.'

Daryo closed one hand. 'That many?'

'Maybe some more. A hand and a half.'

'Six or seven,' Daryo suggested to the Harlequin, who nodded, grinning.

'If we can take away two or three of those, this gets easier.' She took the bow from her back and nocked an arrow. 'Can you defend yourself with that blade, Voy?'

'I can.'

'Take this too,' said Daryo, giving him his shield before drawing both the Horse and the Bear.

'Reverse your left hand blade,' the Harlequin told him. 'Use that to defend yourself.'

Daryo turned the sword so that it was point-down. 'Correct. We can get closer, there is the orchard which I can use for cover, use the shadows of the trees. Daryo, take Voy around to the side of the burning building.' She pointed. 'Stay in the crops, stay with your hearts to the ground as much as you can. When the time is right, I can shoot the man by the fire. If he screams, it will bring the others. I will try and take down as many as I can.'

'What if he does not scream?' asked Voy.

'Then we make noise,' said the Harlequin. 'Rap your shields and swords together and shout to the Second God. They will come.'

'They will have longswords, short spears, possibly mauls,' said Daryo. 'I fought several in the Pass with Kitsun the Shrewd. They are large and strong.'

'So we must be quick and clever,' said the Harlequin. 'Go.' The boy was already scuttling down the slope when the Harlequin hissed: 'Daryo! Protect him with your life.'

'I will.' Daryo chased after Voy, who was already darting through the cornfield. 'Voy, slow down,' he rasped. 'We have to let the Harlequin into her shooting position. Slowly, quietly.'

Voy allowed Daryo to reach him before continuing at a slower pace. The shield was a little big for him but the sword was a good length and weight. They reached the edge of the field, Daryo looking for the Harlequin in the orchard across the track. He realised suddenly that her multi-coloured clothing made it difficult to identify the shape of a woman among the trees. The smoking wooden shed was about fifty yards away from

Daryo and Voy. He pointed to a plough furrow and Voy slid into it. Daryo could see the tribesman walking around the ruins, poking things with the edge of his spear, apparently foraging. Daryo glanced aside for the Harlequin but still no person was visible.

The first arrow struck the tribesman in the chest and he roared in surprise and pain. The second arrow struck his throat and he fell. There was a commotion in the longhouse and a pair of tribesmen came out of the door, one carrying a sword and one with a spear. The Harlequin fired another arrow, just missing the swordsman. One saw the flight of the arrow and shouted a warning.

'NOW!' shouted Daryo, rushing out of the field.

The tribesmen turned to face this new threat. The Harlequin's arrow took the spearman as another three tribesmen boiled out of the door. The first swordsman was almost to Voy. Daryo stepped in front of the lad, blocked the tribesman's slash with his downward blade, the Bear, and opened the savage's throat with the Horse. Another arrow hit a tribesman. Voy had found himself face to face with a man twice his size. He blocked a slash with a rough sword and was thrown to the ground by a brawny, hairy arm. Daryo barely managed to intercept a blow that would have severed Voy's head. The Harlequin fired a last arrow to kill Voy's attacker, dropped her bow and raced into combat with her sword. She blocked a rash lunge, ducked under the successor and decapitated the source. She broke into a sprint and slid along the ground with both feet into the next tribesman, taking him to the ground. She slashed through his chest as they both lay on the ground and sprang up. There was one tribesman left, one about the age of Daryo, clutching his spear defensively across his chest, tight enough to turn his knuckles white. He was talking quickly in his own language and shaking his head. He looked down at his spear, went silent for a moment and then dropped his spear quickly.

'Run!' The Harlequin shouted at him. 'RUN!'

The tribesman turned and did just that. The Harlequin hurried back to where she had left her bow and drew an arrow.

'Voy! Your choice!'

Voy looked from the Harlequin to the dead tribesmen to Daryo and the fleeing survivor. He bit his lip and nodded briskly. The Harlequin released the arrow and the fleeing tribesman fell dead, the shaft buried in his back. She sighed. 'I disagree but I understand. Daryo, help me clear the bodies to the burnt shed and we can burn them. Then we'll go and finish our first job and take Voy back to the Five Towers.'

Daryo and the Harlequin stacked the bodies, Daryo found a small pile of scrap wood and some straw and the Harlequin started a blaze again in the ruins of the vegetable shed.

'We have a task to complete for our Order,' Kym told Voy. 'It is probably best that you come with us and then we'll take you back to your family and someone will escort you home.'

Voy nodded. 'My thanks for all you are doing.' He swallowed hard.

Kym put her hand on his shoulder. 'It is the least we can do. We are sworn to serve. Your family are being cared for and you will be sorting out your home again soon.'

Voy smiled. 'My thanks.'

They walked back up the farm track together. Back on the road, the Harlequin thought for a moment and turned left, back towards the Five Towers. It took nearly an hour's walk before they came to another track that they had bypassed before. It was barely a game trail, a rough slightly bare patchwork through the grassland that led towards the river.

'Slowly,' said the Harlequin. 'The woman is dangerous.'

'So is the woman with us,' said Voy mischievously.

The Harlequin chuckled quietly. 'Very much so.' She drew her sword. Daryo and Voy did the same. The Harlequin led the way up the track. It descended to run right alongside the river, almost at a level with the fast-running water. Perched amidst a small stand of willow trees was a small shack, a cabin made of wood almost on the waterline. A small fire had been in front of it but now was just charred wood and drifting smoke. The Harlequin paused for a moment.

'Voy, stay here.'

The youngster nodded and the Harlequin beckoned Daryo forwards. 'Go around the back of the hut, just in case there is a hidden exit.'

Daryo complied, circling around away from the river bank, up a low bank and in behind the willows as the Harlequin reached the door-less entrance. She looked in cautiously and lowered her sword. 'Too late.'

Daryo came around the little shelter and looked inside. The woman was in the corner, her dead hand still on the hilt of the knife in her chest. 'She will not find favour with the Fourth Goddess.'

The Harlequin nodded in agreement. 'It is not for us to choose when to join her. We know she is no further threat to the honest people. We should return to the Five Towers and reunite Voy with his parents.'

Voy's family had been found temporary lodgings in the Secondborn Tower, where the Brethren occupied most of the accommodation. A young woman in the blue of a Brethren attendant was bustling around the chambers, Voy's father and uncle had been tended to by physicians and his mother had been cared for. Their possessions were safely stored and guarded as valued treasures. A Member of the Trenchers Council, Nura the Guarded, had come to see that they were well cared-for and had promised that a Member of the Order, their apprentice and two ducklings who were old enough to become tails would accompany the family back to their farm and remain there for four nights to ensure their safety. The family would also be provided with two pigeons with which assistance could be summoned.

'I think a very successful day,' said the Harlequin as the pair left the Secondborn Tower and the sun set over the cliff. 'Our first task was without fruit but we found ourselves a worthy deed nonetheless. That is the joy of our service.'

A horn blew from the gatehouse, a long mournful wail, and the gates themselves began to open. The horn sounded two more notes and there was a rush of Brethren towards the gates.

'What is it?' asked Daryo.

The Harlequin's face had gone pale. 'Members of the Order have been killed. The Brethren give them a guard of honour into their home. Ready your sword and shield.'

Daryo complied as a horse and cart plodded through the gate and between the lines of the Brethren. Three further carts followed in line. The Harlequin gasped in shock. As the grim procession reached them, Members of the Order, tails and ducklings were holding their shields in front of their chests and their swords in front of the shield to make the sign of the Order. Daryo did the same and the Harlequin, without a shield, held the pommel of her sword in front of her face. Each cart had two bodies, covered in blankets, grasses and herbs and their shields on the top.

The carts passed, followed by the ranks of the Brethren from the guard of honour as the gates closed again, the Harlequin lowered her sword.

'Did you know them?' asked Daryo.

'The first cart bore two Members. Liane the Ash and Huw the Glade. They were married, a great pairing of minds and skills. The third cart was Muhllali the Lone Peak and his tail. The fourth bore a Member whose name I forget but who was the Four Spears. Eight Members and tails slain. They must have been slain near each other and brought home together. I must go and speak with someone. Rest, eat, we will find a task for the morrow.'

The hall of the Temple Tower was in sombre mood. The tail of the Lone Peak had been named Sîomera, a well-liked and vivacious woman from the Jaboen port of Nalb. The tail of the Four Spears had been named Hamanapt, a Yashoun man known for his prowess with an axe, expected to make his Promise at the dark of the moon and to take the name of the Tree-Feller. Their customary seats at table had been left empty, a single unlit candle at their place. Lana had known Hamanapt well and was unable to eat; tears ran down her face as several other apprentices attempted to console her. Daryo ate but through necessity, the fight over the farm had drained him and his rations had been shared with Voy. After eating he went across to the smith and spoke with Solv the Strike, a bear-like man with a greying beard and a voice like a falling rock. When convinced that the Batribi tail was capable, he permitted Daryo to clean, polish and sharpen his swords and knife.

# Chapter 8

The next day dawned dull and grey. Heavy black clouds drifted across from the Peaks and threatened rain or snow. The shields of the dead Members and apprentices had been hung above the doors of the Wooden Tower. Five of the eight were Members- the Ash, the Glade, the Four Spears, the Lone Peak and the Furious- along with the tails of the latter three- Siomera, Hamanapt and Heeyivan- with their shields hung alongside that of their lead. Daryo was studying the display of honour when five mounted men rode up to the base of the Wooden Tower. Two were Brethren soldiers, the other three were unfamiliar to Daryo- apparently Gourmini, two in russet-coloured mail and helmets, the third in russet robes with a spectacular plumed helmet and bearing a large and sharply-curved sword with a dome-shaped hand-guard. He was escorted swiftly into the Tower by a Brethren servant and the doors shut rapidly behind him.
'Who was that?' Daryo asked of the Brethren who had escorted the men in.
The Brethren, possibly a very close relative of Herren Downe by his face, shrugged. 'A guest of the Captain-General.'
'Daryo!' The Harlequin was approaching. 'I spoke to the Vanguard last evening. No Members are leaving the Compound now. We are a night and a day away from the death of the moon when the apprentices to become Members make their Promise and the day afterwards is Muster. The Blades are asking us to stay within an hours' walk of the Five Towers.'
'How disappointing.'
'I think it is dangerous for us to roam too far at the moment. We can do some training around here.'
'If you wish.'
'Can you shoot a bow?'
'No.'
'We can work on that then. Go to the Firstborn Tower and I'll meet you at the archery range behind it when you're ready.'

'Is anybody here?' called Daryo.
A lean man with a broken nose appeared from behind a barrel. 'Yes. Yes, good morning, good morning.'
'The Harlequin sent me up to get a bow and some arrows for some archery practise.'
'Ah, archery, yes, yes, that's what I do. I am the bowyer. Are you a bowman?'
'No, the Harlequin wishes me to learn.'

'Yes, yes, very good, yes. Something simple, something easy to use then, yes, yes.' He looked around the tower room for suitable bows. He took a bow from a rack, held it up towards Daryo, took it away and swapped for a slightly larger one. 'This one, yes, I think, this one will do fine.' He handed it to Daryo. 'How is this?'
Daryo studied it. 'I would imagine so. I know little about them.'
'Take some quivers with the red fletching. They are training shafts, no tips.'
'My thanks.'
'Not a problem, not a problem.'

The archery practise took hours. The Harlequin was a harsh tutor- constantly correcting Daryo's errors. By midday, his fingers and hand ached with the constant drawing, holding and release. But from one arrow in the centre ring in the first hour, he was hitting the centre ring with eight from every ten by midday. He rotated his shoulder several times as the Harlequin announced that she was satisfied with his progress and sent him away for some food. The afternoon was spent with riding and then more archery practice. By nightfall, Daryo retired to bed exhausted.

Tronn the Jade died during the night. Lana went to the temple to honour his memory. At first light, one of the Brethren, an exceptionally tall blond woman, came and took Lana's shield.
'I have to have my badge painted on it for this evening,' she told Daryo.
'You take your Promise.'
'I do. I have to assemble my things. As soon as I am a Member I cannot stay in the Temple Tower, I have to move to the Castle.'
'Will you get a tail?'
'Not necessarily. Only one in three Members have tails. Most work with other Members or alone, some work at the Towers of course.'
'Sorrell the Greensward.'
'Precisely. Would you like to come?'
'Come?'
'My Promise ceremony. There are five of us and we are allowed to invite guests. Maufana, Didax and Sourirz are coming. You are very welcome.'
'My thanks; this is most generous of you.'
Lana smiled. 'My pleasure. Meet at the Fortress doors at sundown.'
'I will be there.'

There was a small crowd outside the doors of the Wooden Fortress Tower. Daryo recognised Hannick, Obscua the Unseen's apprentice. A somewhat elderly Member was stood in front of the closed doors, a broken bow in a white cloud on her shield, flanked by Herren Downe and a man that was undoubtedly his brother.

'Gentlemen and gentlewomen, welcome,' he said. 'I recognise most of the faces before me. For those of you unfamiliar, I am Smalli the Black Bowyer, one of the Aides to the Captain-General. I am to administer the Promise ceremony for the five of you making your Promise tonight. Please come forwards.'

The five stepped forwards. They were all in simple olive robes with the Order sign on the chests and each carried a wooden sword and face-sized shield.

'You are about to enter the Wooden Fortress Tower for the last time as apprentices of the Order. After this night, you are sworn to the Order. You are sworn to defend those who cannot defend themselves. You are sworn to obey the orders you are given and to give your life in the pursuit of right and truth. If any of you wishes to decline, simply lay down your sword. You will be welcome to remain at the Five Towers and may choose to join the Brethren.' There was a pause and nobody moved. The Black Bowyer nodded, turned to the door and drew his sword. He hammered three times on the door with the pommel.

'Who goes there?' demanded a voice inside.

'Smalli the Black Bowyer, Aide to the Captain-General. I bring five new Members of the Order of the Shield and Sword.'

The doors opened slowly, four Members raised their swords in the Order's salute. Smalli led the way inside, the new Members behind, their guests following. The procession wound its way to the first floor. The doors of the chamber were closed. Smalli knocked with his sword again.

'Who goes there?'

'Smalli the Black Bowyer, Aide to the Captain-General. I bring five new Members of the Order of the Shield and Sword.'

The doors opened. It was a duplicate of the Blades' Chamber above but with a wooden plate with a hammer and pickaxe crossed painted on the floor. The Trenchers Council was assembled.

'Five new Members of the Order,' announced the woman at the centre of the table. 'We, the Council of Trenchers, welcome you. We accept you as defenders of the Five Towers, of the meek, the just and the righteous.'

The new Members saluted with their wooden swords and the procession moved on to the Blades Chamber where the process was repeated by Smalli and the Vanguard. They then continued up the stairs, to the very top. On the roof of the tower, ten Members were waiting in two groups, their shields held in front of them, surrounded by a circle of burning torches.

Smalli walked away from the new Members and joined one group. A Member stepped forward- he was of an age with Kitsun, smaller in height but stronger in build with a neat black beard.

'I am Hoyuz the Calm, Captain-General of the Order of the Sword and Shield. Who comes before me and my Aides?'

'Cazus. To be called the New Morning.'

'Hannick. To be called the Veiled.'

'Kibbe. To be called the Clay.'

'Lana. To be called the Cocksure.'

'Yi. To be called the Islander.' As each spoke, they stepped forwards and raised their wooden sword.

'And who speaks for their worthiness to join this ancient Order?'

A Member from the other group stepped forwards. 'Tamur the Hunter.'

'Obscua the Unseen.'

'Rockinha the Quarrel.'

'Ayiyz the White Hand.'

'Delyaya the Swift.'

'Does anyone else vouch for them?'

'Aye!' shouted the guests.

The Captain-General drew his sword and so did the other Members. 'If you are no longer apprentices, if you are truly Members of the Order of the Shield and Sword, you require shields and swords.'

The leads came forwards, taking the wooden weapons and handing over the individual's own sword and shield.

'Which leaves one requirement.'

The five new Members recited with one voice: 'With my heart, my mind and my honour, I promise to do my duty as a Member of the Order of the Shield and Sword and to follow orders as given on the authority of the Captain-General and his Aides. I swear my Shield and Sword to the defence of the just, the righteous, the innocent and the weak. By this oath, I pledge my sword and my service until I am discharged by death.' On the last sentence, they raised their swords by the hilt in salute.

'Cazus the New Morning, Hannick the Veiled, Kibbe the Clay, Lana the Cocksure, Yi the Islander, welcome to the Order. Especially welcome to the Islander as the first Silver

Islander to join our ranks.' He gave a short bow to Yi the Islander, a boyish-looking figure with sallow skin, a flattened nose and uncommonly narrow eyes, who returned the bow. 'The Brethren will have moved your belongings to the Castle Tower. You are now fully Members of the Order. My congratulations and profuse welcome to you, my newest brothers and sister.'

He came forwards, the Aides flanking him to congratulate the new Members, followed by their old leads and their guests. The Islander came across to Daryo.

'Daryo of the Batribi. I am Yi to be call... the Islander. Yi the Islander.'

'My congratulations, Islander.'

'Thank you. Great honour it is to be first Silver Islander to make Promise. You will be first Batribi, yes?'

'One day, I hope so.'

'Great honour. You know Silver Island?'

'I have never been. I know it is far to the west, off the furthest coast of Yashoun.'

'Deserts and plains and mighty rivers. A great and good people as yours are. It is privilege that I say this first to you, Daryo of the Batribi.' He lifted his sword by the pommel, point down. 'My sword and my service.'

'My thanks, Islander.'

He sought Lana, now bearing her shield with a golden cockerel wielding a sword as her badge. 'Cocksure. Congratulations.'

'I feel so excited, it really is wonderful! A lot of hard work but most rewarding. A Member of the Order. The ninth Member with the sword name of Cocksure.'

'You should be most proud.'

'I am! I am!'

A duckling had replaced Lana in the room opposite Daryo's. He was rather slender and lacked any sort of maturity. His apprentice's shield was rather too large and he took off and put down his sword as if he feared it. Daryo paid him little mind as he hung up his equipment and retired to bed in preparation for another day of the Harlequin's training.

# Chapter 9

The preparations had begun early. The pathway into the caves had been covered with straw and lined by tall torches. A large bell was hung by five of the Brethren outside. As the sun set, the apprentices streamed out of the Temple Tower to watch as the Brethren soldiery, nearly a hundred of them, paraded from the Secondborn Tower to the Wooden Fortress and then to the gate and walls. A steady stream of Members had been arriving through the day and into the evening. Daryo had been enjoying a conversation about swords with Herren Downe when he saw a familiar face pass through the gate.

'Ranger!'

'Daryo, warrior of the road. You made it safely.'

'Indeed. I have already been at work with the Harlequin.'

'Kym the Harlèquin? She is your lead?'

'She is.'

'An interesting choice by the Blades.'

'It was not their choice but hers. She asked to be assigned me.'

Vilya the Ranger considered this. 'Interesting.'

'You will attend Muster?'

'There are only a very few who will not. I will attend. I shall see you inside the Sanctuary. Herren.'

'Ranger.' As she headed for the Castle Tower, Herren Downe cocked his head and frowned in thought. 'I am trying to remember when I last saw the Ranger going to her room in the Castle. It must be nine autumns and a summer before that. The Ranger lives a life very separate from the Five Towers but she is a Member of the Order and is always welcome home. It is a privilege of being a Member.'

'What do you do during Muster?' asked Daryo.

'The Brethren deploy on the walls and at the gate. All of the Order's fighting force is in the Sanctuary so we must be alert to any threat to the Five Towers. We are approaching time to lock down.'

'Lock down?'

'You will see.' Herren looked up at the sky. 'It is time.' He had a horn on a cord around his neck. He lifted it to his lips and blew a long note. 'I blow that note only to lock down.'

The two sentries outside the postern stepped inside quickly and closed the gate-within-the-gate behind them with heavy bars and bolts. A loud rattle and roar was the outer

portcullis falling. Ten feet behind the gate, the inner portcullis lowered with an equally-loud crash. The Brethren along the walls came to alert.
Herren Downe raised an arm to his brother on the wall who called out at the loudest possible: 'The Brethren were born to guard and to serve the Order! Tonight we must do so once more! Who stands with me?'
'HURRAH!' Every Member of the Brethren on the wall or in the Compound roared their support, Herren Downe included.
'I feel very safe,' said Daryo honestly.
'We shall keep you so, Daryo of the Batribi, my Brethren and I.' The great bell sounded. 'Muster is called. Muster is called!'
The shout was taken up by the rest of the Brethren. 'Muster is called! Muster is called!' Members and apprentices began to drift towards the entrance to the caves. The Ranger was still visible, marching resolutely in the opposite direction towards the Castle Tower, being hailed by several people as they passed her. She was obviously well-known and liked.
'Daryo! There you are!' The Harlequin strode up. 'Come, we should get in and find a good position.'
'Of course.'
Herren Downe clapped him on the shoulder and moved away towards the wall. Daryo and the Harlequin followed the straw path into the caves along with a throng of others, rightwards at the fork, through the Threefold Door and to the Last Door, which had been unlocked and thrown open. Daryo felt his breath stop as he passed through. In front of him, the Sanctuary Cave stretched for nearly a hundred yards and maybe twice that high. The cave floor had been carved into tiers leading down to the most incredible sight- a tall, spreading tree growing from the cave floor beneath a cleft in the cave roof.
'Unbelievable...' breathed the Harlequin. 'Spectacular.'
'I could look on this every day and never tire,' said Kitsun, arriving behind them. 'We should get near the front.'
Some Members were contenting themselves with staying at the rear close to the door, most were clambering down the three-foot ledges towards the tree. As they got closer, Daryo could see a wooden platform in front of the tree.
'How can a tree grow in a cave?' asked the Harlequin.
'The gap in the rock gives light and water,' said Kitsun, breathing hard as he scrambled down the ledges. About ten levels from the front, out of about fifty, he stopped. 'Close enough, close enough. These legs are not as keen as they used to be.'

The Aides were assembling on the platform- the Arrow Nymph, the Vanguard, the Trident, the Black Bowyer and two others with the Captain General.

'Who are the two Aides?' asked Daryo, naming the ones that he knew.

'Samm the Planner and Zerro the Scout,' said the Harlequin. 'The Planner is the senior Trencher, Zerro the Scout is the newest of the Blades.'

The noise in the Sanctuary was growing as it filled up. Daryo noted that about eight hundred, as Kitsun had estimated the total of Members and apprentices at, would perhaps half-fill the space. The sheer size of the cave was difficult to comprehend. Hoyuz the Calm made his way down the levels to the platform. A post with a hook on it stood at the front of the dais and he carefully hung his shield on it, his badge a coiled green snake. He looked around the Sanctuary and spoke briefly to Smalli, who shook his head.

'Not everyone is in,' said Kitsun as if agreeing with Smalli or answering the Captain-General's question. There was still a flood of Members and apprentices through from the tunnel. 'I was a new Member when last I saw this sight.'

'Thirty-two autumns and the spring and summer before,' said the Harlequin. 'I was not even born.'

'Barely more than a duckling,' scoffed Kitsun. 'Vilya!'

The Ranger had appeared. She had changed from plate and mail into a light-armour jerkin and breeches, her greatsword on her back, her wild hair had been tamed by a wooden comb behind her head. 'Kitsun the Shrewd, Kym the Harlequin, Daryo kin of Yuai.'

'Do not give me that,' snapped Kitsun but then he smiled and embraced the Ranger. 'How are you?'

'Well. Glad to come home to my chamber. I could do with a few days of rest. I have been on the road for nearly five seasons. A few skin blisters and aches that need tending and resting.'

Kitsun squeezed her hand keenly. 'Good.'

'Was the Ranger your tail?' Daryo asked and they all laughed.

'Tail? Perish the thought! Vilya the Ranger is my daughter!'

'Daughter? Why did you not say so on the road?'

'You never asked.' Kitsun chuckled. 'As if I could stand my own daughter being my tail!'

'As if could walk beside my father with my head high!'

The Harlequin laughed. 'Family are too much difficulty. Lovers too.'

'You have enough lovers, Harlequin,' said the Ranger. 'You simply keep them for a day and then move on.'

'Less difficulty. Means not having to remember their name.'

They all laughed although Daryo felt somewhat excluded from a conversation about lovers.
'Vodyony the Pickerel,' Kitsun told Daryo, pointing to a Member with a leaping pike on his shield. 'Hyldemoer the Fallen Leaf. Geier the Scavenger. Rote the Lyre. Eme the Verdigris. Mobi the Seafarer. Many Members of our Order that I have not seen in a long time.'
'You rarely come to the Towers anyway, Shrewd,' said the Harlequin with a grin.
'I rarely stay,' corrected Kitsun. 'I visit frequently with those like our young Batribi friend.'
'I rarely come at all,' said the Ranger dismissively.
The Sanctuary was nearly half full. The Black Bowyer got the Captain-General's attention and said something affirmative. The Vanguard lifted a large sword that appeared to be crystal or glass above his head. A ripple of noise went around the Sanctuary as the assembly began to sit on the stone ledges. Kitsun carefully removed his cloak and folded it to make a cushion before sitting. One by one the Members fell silent. The Vanguard lowered the sword into a socket in front of the Captain-General's shield. Hoyuz the Calm stepped forwards. 'Gentlemen and gentlewomen, thank you. I thought when I first became Captain-General that this was a sight that I would never have to see. Muster is something that has not happened in over a hundred seasons but this situation means that we have no other choice. This Order is in danger.' He paused and looked around the cave. 'This Order is facing an abyss. No doubt most of those present are familiar with the fact that eight of our Members were returned dead to their Five Towers in these past days. They join four dozen fellows slain since midsummer's day. Never before in such a short period of time have so many of our brothers and sisters been hunted in this way.' There were mutters of concern around the Sanctuary. 'We are being hunted. In the last few days, I received an envoy. They offer an exchange to halt the hunting of our Members. That this Order disbands.' The Sanctuary was filled with a roar of noise of dissent that echoed off of the stone walls in a cacophony of sound. The Calm, true to his sword name, waited for silence to return, encouraged by hisses from the quieter members. 'I assume from the reaction of my brothers and sisters that you dissent from this view.'
Someone near the front shouted something. The Calm nodded. 'Solv the Strike suggests that we are the Order of the Shield and the Sword and can defend ourselves.' There was a quiet wave of agreement. 'I agree.' The roar returned, this one of approval, Daryo found himself joining it and saw the Harlequin raise her fist. 'Our Order has made enemies, it is undeniable. We defend the defenceless and the oppressed, it therefore

stands to reason that the aggressive and the oppressors resent us. There are those that believe that we are doing this for financial gain, that we hoard vast quantities of metals and gems beneath our towers. There are those who believe we exact tributes, taxes, even slaves from those that we aid. We fight for the knowledge that we have aided those without the ability to aid themselves. That is the truth but there are those that are deaf to the truth. I submit to the Muster that we shall continue to help those who need us.'

The approval was overwhelming and took several minutes to quieten. As the noise faded, the Vanguard stepped forwards. 'We are not only going to defend the weak, we must defend ourselves as well. Some will be needed for this purpose and the Trenchers will be organising volunteers to supplement the Brethren in defending the Five Towers. The Blades will be continuing with giving assignments to those following our normal cause of protecting others. The Aides will be summoning some to pursue assignments towards an offensive against those who threaten this Order.' This received a ragged cheer that grew in intensity. 'I ask all those here for Muster to remember their Promise and to continue to perform their duty as instructed.'

'Promise! Promise!' someone shouted and it was taken up by others.

The Vanguard looked at the Calm and received a nod of assent. 'Promise. Draw... SWORDS!'

Muster sprang to its feet; swords, daggers, axes and other weapons were raised in the salute. 'With my heart, my mind and my honour, I promise to do my duty as a Member of the Order of the Shield and Sword and to follow orders as given on the authority of the Captain-General and his Aides. I swear my Shield and Sword to the defence of the just, the righteous, the innocent and the weak. By this oath, I pledge my sword and my service until I am discharged by death!' The last assertion rang around the cave.

The Calm spoke in the sudden quiet. 'Muster is dismissed.'

Most of the Order seemed to congregate in front of the Wooden Tower after Muster. The night was mild and still and the Compound lit mostly by the torches leading to the caves. The Brethren had lifted the lock down and the Ranger and Kitsun headed straight out of the reopened postern. The Harlequin gestured for Daryo to wait and disappeared into the throng. Lana came out of the caves and Daryo hailed her.

'Good evening, Cocksure.'

'Good evening, Daryo. What did you think of Muster?'

'Worrying.'

'I thought so too. The Sanctuary is beautiful but beautiful surroundings only soften bad tidings. They are still bad tidings. What do you think of what the Captain-General said?'

'I think he is right. We should stand up against any threat to ourselves as well as to others.'
'I agree.'
'Batribi! We have not met.' Hoyuz the Calm was standing behind Daryo. Lana stepped back swiftly. 'I am Hoyuz the Calm, the Captain-General of the Order.'
'Yes sir. I saw you at the Promise ceremony and at Muster,' managed Daryo. Close to, Hoyuz was slightly taller than Daryo had originally thought and had very eerily grey eyes.
'I make it my duty to greet every newcomer to the Five Towers. Any new apprentice is welcome but you especially. As you saw at the Promise Ceremony, we have the first Silver Islander to take their Promise. One day, I keenly hope that you will be our first Batribi Member. What is your name?'
'Daryo, sir.'
'Have you a lead yet?'
'Yes sir. Kym the Harlequin.'
The Calm nodded. 'A fine Member of the Order and a fine tutor. She will guide you well.' He drew a short dagger from his belt and saluted with it. 'My sword and my service.'
'Thank you, sir.'
'Cocksure.'
'Captain-General, sir.' The Calm walked away and Lana seized Daryo's arm. 'The Captain-General! He had never spoken to me before my Promise Ceremony! And he came and found you!'
'That was... intimidating.'
'Intimidating? Unbelievable!'
'Daryo!' The Harlequin had returned. 'Was that the Captain-General?'
'Yes... welcoming me...'
The Harlequin looked impressed. 'How unusual. We have an early start. I spoke with the Scout; the Blades want us to go to Allesbury.'
'Allesbury?'
'That's right. As an escort for a friend of the Order. Can you ride?'
'I can.'
'Good. We leave at sunrise.'

The morning dawned clear, breezy and freezing cold. Frost gave the world a crisp white coating. The two horses, one pale brown and one dappled grey; were tied up outside the stables and tended by a Brethren attendant. Daryo, having obtained a heavy woollen cloak from the tailor in the Firstborn Tower, was offered the grey, slightly larger and leaner than the dun. Packed saddlebags were already in place. Mindful of the Harlequin's advice last time, Daryo had left Temma's Sword and his shield on the wall of his room and bought just Stai's Swords and his knife. The Harlequin had her curved sword, a buckler and a short bow and a quiver full of long arrows that hung from the saddle. The saddle bore the Harlequin's badge on the pommel. The horse was well-behaved and responsive and trotted obediently behind the Harlequin's as they went to the road and in the same direction as they had before. The horses trotted well for over three hours and reached the grass city of Aslon well before midday.

Aslon was like an island in a sea of grass and fields. The road entered the walls immediately beside the river, the walls then extended in a wide semicircle with the river itself forming a barrier. The walls were high, much higher than Salifa's, but thin, buttressed by half-moon towers at intervals. The town banner over the gate was a half moon rising from the river. Inside a sturdy wooden gate a guard stepped out of the gatehouse, the Harlequin showed her shield and was waved onwards. Most of the houses were stone, presumably brought down the river, with thatched roofs and many had glazed windows, suggesting a prosperous city. There were wharfs and riverboats along the water's edge and a large, open marketplace next to the waterside, much like Salifa.

'The river goes through Allesbury,' the Harlequin told Daryo as they guided their horses through the streets. 'Seafaring ships can get all the way up from the sea to the port in Allesbury at high tide and this allows the people here to trade beyond Gourmin. It is also the closest town to Jaboen so it gets much of the trade through the Tember Pass too. The one weakness of the town is that it is small, restricted by the river and the wall, so it cannot grow too large. The town guard is small and mostly concerned with theft and crime within the wall. That is why we had to chase down the woman that escaped the gaol- there is no manpower here for the town guard. No child in Aslon wants to be a warrior; they want to be a rich merchant or farmer.' She pointed out a conical roof above the others. 'That is the home of the Lord of Aslon, Meyidaro. He is a great friend of the Order and we aid him whenever appropriate. In return, he gives the Order produce and horses. His second son is a Member and his first daughter is Barran Downe's wife and therefore Nate Downe's aunt.'

A young woman came through the crowd carrying a basket and casually walked between the Harlequin's horse and Daryo's despite being completely naked. Daryo's jaw dropped in astonishment.

'An acolyte of the White Lady,' the Harlequin explained with a laugh. 'There is a House of Devotion in one of the bastion towers. About three dozen young women who give literally everything they have away and serve the White Lady. I always think they must sometimes rethink their enthusiasm when the weather gets so cold.'

Daryo shook his head in wonder. Such a bold display of any belief other than the Faith would not have been permitted in Jaboen, where those who followed other beliefs had to do so clandestinely. He was somewhat reassured by the presence of a priest of the Second God preaching the Writs.

'Maybe he should preach the Fourth God surrounded by a market and the river,' said Daryo.

The Harlequin laughed. 'Not in Aslon. The river rises and floods the town. The grassland burns in summer. The fields freeze. The world around makes the city rich but also worries the population. Thiney preaches conflict and strife, that's Aslon: conflict with the world around and fighting for profit.'

The road moved away from the riverside and came to the town's eastern gate. The fields were more regimented on this side of the town; people were harvesting a crop of potatoes and, further on, an orchard of apples was being picked.

'They make apple cider from some of the crop,' said the Harlequin. 'Very good apple cider too.'

'Cider?'

The Harlequin laughed again. 'I will find you some.'

About two hour's ride, they came to a village. It was again on the river and opposite a swathe of trees. Alongside the river on the far bank was a sawmill and a wharf. On the village side was another wharf, a smithy, an inn and a cluster of nearly three dozen houses.

'Riverhelm,' announced the Harlequin. 'Home of most of the timber in Gourmin. Almost everyone here works across the river felling, cutting and shipping timber.' She pointed to the wharf across the now wide and slow river where a large section of tree trunk was being loaded onto a barge. 'That barge might go up to Aslon or downriver to Allesbury. We should stop.' She steered her horse towards the inn and a girl of about twelve summers hurried out from behind.

'Good day to you, honoured travellers,' she said, sounding as if she was reciting a learned piece. 'The Inn of the Wooden Heart is honoured to honour you.'

Daryo tried to stifle a laugh. The Harlequin smiled indulgently. 'Thank you, fair maid.' She dismounted. 'Might I leave my steed with you?'

'You may. He will be well cared for.' The girl took the halter and stroked the horse's nose affectionately.

Daryo dismounted and handed over his horse's reins. The girl clicked her tongue and the horses followed her. The Inn itself was on a wooden frame held up above the ground, Daryo guessed for if the river flooded, and the Harlequin led the way up the steps and inside. The interior was much like any other inn that Daryo had been in- two long tables led away from the door to the bar at the top. To one side of the bar were a couple of lodging rooms, the other side had storerooms.

The Harlequin hailed the innkeeper and showed her shield. 'Meat and bread please, sir.' The barman went to comply and the Harlequin sat down on the closest bench. Daryo strode up and down a little to exercise his legs. A small group of men in one corner eyed him with suspicion but Daryo ignored them. Four good legs of roasted chicken and a small loaf were produced along with a pitcher of golden liquid.

'Apple cider.' The Harlequin poured a beaker for Daryo and raised her own cup in salute.

Daryo drank. It tasted of apples but something of wine as well. 'Pleasant.'

'Very good in the warm summers,' said the Harlequin. 'Sit, eat. We need to get closer to Allesbury if we can tonight. The sooner we arrive, the sooner we can head home.'

'I am quite content to explore.'

The Harlequin smiled. 'I forget you have not been riding the country with me for many seasons. You do it so well. If I could, I would take you all across Gourmin finding people who need our shields but we have an important contact to meet in Allesbury, a good friend of the Order. One day we can travel as we will, like the Ranger. I swear on my harlequin.'

'I would enjoy that.'

They ate in companionable silence. The chicken was moist and tasty, the bread still warm. The cider was thirst-quenching and gave Daryo a content feeling. The Harlequin burped in satisfaction and went to pay the innkeeper, requesting the horses. At the front of the inn, the young girl was holding the horses and rubbing her nose against the dun horse's.

'I think you have a friend,' said the Harlequin, taking her horse's reins.

'He is very nice.'

'When he retires, I shall leave him here for you,' said the Harlequin.

The girl surrendered Daryo's horse and waved them away. The road left the river immediately and led on to moorland beyond. The road was elevated about the swampy, brownish land around. Every hundred yards or thereabouts small streams passed through tunnels under the roadway. A few times, they had to slow the horses to a walk and pass farm carts. A small flock of sheep took some careful negotiation.

'Harlequin?'
'Daryo, my name is Kym.'
'Kym.'
'Yes, how can I help?' She kicked her horse on slightly to come alongside and slowed it to a walk.
'What do think about what the Captain-General said at Muster?'
'What do I think? I think he said that the Order is under threat.'
'Do you agree that we should carry on with our purpose?'
'I do. We have responsibilities. If you were a father and you had a wounded arm, would you still take up your sword against a wolf or would you let your children fight the wolf?'
'I would fight the wolf.'
'Exactly. If the Order is the father, we cannot leave our children to fight the wolf whatever afflicts us.'
'You speak of a father, I did not know that Members could father children, raise a family.'
Kym nodded. 'There are not many. But when men and women live together as the Order does, fornication happens and children can result. They are raised at a School in Allesbury, much like the School of the Temple, but the parents are quite welcome to see them as much as their duties allow. Some Members have children with those outside our Order, who of course can remain with the other parent while the Member is away.' She thought for a moment. 'The Hunter has a wife and two fine sons living in Lalbi. The Ranger is, as you learnt, the Shrewd's daughter. The Frayed and the Ascent have a child at the School.'
'Do many of them come into the Order?'
'Several do: The Ranger, the Bright, I think.'
The road turned north-east and began to ascend. The moor was giving way to a wilder, rockier landscape. Outcrops of grey rock were scattered across the wilderness. A single kite patrolled the road ahead, riding the increasingly icy wind.
'Hold your horse,' said Kym. A large crag of rock was right alongside the road and a fall of boulders had come down on the road. 'Most likely the frost.'
'Can we go around?'
'Let's look.'
The Harlequin dismounted but stopped a pace away from it. She looked up and back at Daryo and put her finger to her lips to request quiet. She jerked her head to indicate he should dismount and Daryo did so as quietly as possible, tying the horses' reins together and tying them to a handy bracken spear. She mouthed the word 'sword' and 'slowly'.

Daryo reached up, drew the Horse and the Bear and reversed the Bear in his left hand. The Harlequin walked towards the twenty-foot rock outcrop by the right hand side of the road. She repeated her gesture for silence.

'No, I don't think we can go around,' she said loudly. 'Let me just go across and see how bad it is.' She beckoned for Daryo to follow. Several large pieces of rock almost blocked the road, the two were just able to pick between them; the horses would need the road cleared. The outcrop ran alongside the road for nearly ten yards. As the Harlequin came to the end of the outcrop, an ageing, heavy man with a leer and a yawning gap in his cheek stepped forwards. His leer disappeared as he almost walked onto the Harlequin's sword point.

'This would be a poor ambush with only one man,' said the Harlequin with a lightly casual tone to her voice. 'Call out your comrades and I shall leave you a throat with which to call them.' The man growled. He had a cudgel in one hand but it was at his side. He saw Daryo with two blades and the last defiance in his eyes died.

'Gord! Huggir!' His speech was oddly piping caused by his open cheek wall.

A woman came from behind him bearing a sharpened wooden stake as a crude spear, a younger man scrambled down the rock with a poorly-made short sword. The woman, possibly of an age with Kitsun, looked angry; the younger man looked perplexed.

'Throw your weapons away,' commanded the Harlequin. The cudgel was dropped on her foot but she ignored it, the woman threw the spear down, the younger man crouched and slid his sword across the road towards Daryo. 'A good site for ambush but rather too obvious. I am sure that you have ensnared many a farmer or merchant. I am no trader and my comrade is certainly no crop-raiser.'

'You are no trader,' agreed the woman. 'You are one of the fools who walks for miles to exercise their dog. You even taught yours to ride.'

The Harlequin's victorious smile and calm demeanour vanished like mist on glass as she glared at the woman. 'I would have no trouble watching my comrade make you sorry for that remark. That *dog* shits more worthy beings than you shall ever be. That man is my comrade and at this moment has the power to send you and your miserable companions to the Fourth Goddess in small pieces. How many people you have unfairly sent to her is no business of mine as one would be too many. You will clear every single rock from this roadway, bury your weapons and we will allow you to leave. Resist, defy and you may join the Fourth Goddess with those of your victims who resisted or defied you.'

Daryo supervised the three would-be robbers with the Harlequin's bow and a notched arrow while the Harlequin explored the area for anything suspicious or otherwise of interest. She found a knapsack with a small collection of silver coins, a jewelled ring, a glass lens and other sundry trinkets and miscellany.

'This will be given to the School of the Temple of the First God in Allesbury,' the Harlequin told the angry but helpless group of bandits. 'I will give no oath as you would not trust it, oath breakers and thieves have no use for promises, but it shall be given to the School.'

She decided to dispose of the weapons herself. The wooden spear was snapped across the Harlequin's knee, the cudgel hurled across the moor by Daryo's arm and the low sword was so poor that it shattered when the flat was struck on the rocks.

It took two hours for the rocks to be cleared. The Harlequin thanked the furious and ragged trio for their efforts, bid them a safe and productive evening and kicked her horse on.

# Chapter 10

The delay meant that they had to ride hard to reach Allesbury before dark. They seemed to ride straight off of the moors into the town. The darkness had fallen and the only light came from lanterns outside some of the houses.

'Is there no wall?' asked Daryo.

'We have not reached it yet,' said Kym. 'There is a lot of the town that has grown outside the wall. This is the Town Without. It is a less... refined place than the Old Town. The trading docks are here Without, the Seawards Dock is for ferries and the like. I was brought up in the Town Without, although there was much less of it when I was a child.' She reined in her horse outside a large house with two floors. 'This is the Order's School. As so many go on to become ducklings, a lot of Members call it the Nest.'

They dismounted and the Harlequin led the way around the building to the courtyard at the rear. One of the Brethren was lighting an oil lamp under a horn hood at the gate. He looked curiously at the Harlequin and more suspiciously at Daryo.

'Who goes there?'

'Kym the Harlequin and a tail.'

'The tenth word.'

'The tenth word is promise.'

'Correct.' As he opened the gate in the high stone wall, he took a long look at the Harlequin's shield as well. 'Allow me to take your horses, Harlequin.'

'Thank you. I assume there are a couple of rooms that we can use?'

'There is only one spare room but I am sure that some arrangement can be made.'

'I should see the Blind.'

'She will likely be in the hall.'

'The Blind?' asked Daryo as they went inside.

'Leroyfa has been in charge of the Nest for many, many years. Her sight is excellent; her sword name is some reference to her character as an apprentice.'

The rear door of the house gave into a small anteroom with several doors and an open arched passage to the hall, a large space that occupied most of the floor. A narrow stair led up from one corner of the hall, which seemed to be a combination of dining hall, kitchen and library; large tables and benches occupied the area nearest the stairs, at the rear of the hall was a good-sized kitchen and the walls flanking the front door were lined with shelves laden with books. On the wall above the massive fireplace, an Order shield hung with a blindfolded girl child as the badge, behind it was an old guard-less sword and a staff with bronze ends. On the fire was a large copper pot; a very slender, almost

frail looking woman of at least fifty winters was stirring vigorously. A dozen children, some just three or four summers, some three times that, were engaged with their evening meal and a stout woman of the Brethren, wearing a blue hood, was attending to them. The woman at the pot straightened up.
'Good evening.'
'Gods' Watch,' said the Harlequin. 'I am Kym the Harlequin, this is Daryo, my tail. We've been sent to Allesbury to escort someone to the Five Towers. Is it convenient for us to stay?'
'You are welcome although we have many children at the moment. The Five Towers, some say, is not safe so we have some of the younger ducklings with us. However, we shall do what we can. I am Leroyfa the Blind, housemistress. Can I interest you in some fish stew?'
'Very much so!' said the Harlequin.
'Have a seat by the stairs,' said the Blind. 'I will bring over some bowls. Please do remove your boots, do whatever needs must to make yourselves comfortable, we have no ceremony here.'
Daryo and Kym found that the table closest to the stairs was larger than the others, the chairs larger and higher than the benches, suggesting that they were clearly manufactured for adults and not for the young. The Harlequin had barely sat down before she was untying her boots and allowing her stocking-clad feet freedom. Daryo removed his cloak, robe and Stai's swords before sitting down. A few of the children glanced at him nervously but most were equally interested in the Harlequin. The Blind brought two huge wooden bowls full of a rich white fish stew. It was creamy, thick with potato and peppery and Daryo ate hungrily. A trapdoor under the stairs opened and three members of the Brethren soldiery emerged.
'The night watch,' said Leroyfa, sitting down opposite Kym. 'We have two during the day, three at night and three attendants here.'
'Are you the only Member of the Order?' asked Daryo.
Leroyfa inclined her head. 'I am. The children are taught by a docent from the Archive. I am rather old to be doing what you both are doing but I can be of use here. My own child was raised here by my predecessor.'
'Is your child in the Order?' asked Daryo.
'No, he is a docent at the Archive.'
One by one the younger children were leaving the table and making their way upstairs. The older ones, of about nine summers and older, were staying talking at table or going

for book and games from the shelves. One of the older girls came across to the group of adults.

'Leroyfa, may I do some training with you?'

Leroyfa shook her head tiredly. 'Not tonight, Jenni.'

'What did you want to do, young one?' asked Kym.

'I want to make my sword better.' The girl looked at Kym with direct blue eyes.

'Daryo, you have skill with a blade,' said Kym. 'Perhaps you would give young Jenni a challenge?'

'Of course,' said Daryo, getting up immediately.

The girl smiled widely, went away and came back with two wooden swords and a buckler painted crudely with pink and blue bands. 'We need to practise in the courtyard,' she told Daryo and led him outside. The courtyard was now lit by several lamps and torches and they gave enough light to see by. The girl was lean but strong for her age and struck hard but precisely. Daryo found himself rarely having to test her skills with her shield, instead allowing her to attack and parrying her blows. On occasions that he was able to counter, she was agile and tended to avoid his attacks rather than block or parry them. After half an hour of practise, she discarded her shield and began to wield her sword with two hands. Her blows became harder but less accurate. Daryo found it easier to block her attacks and respond. He drove her back against the wall several times before allowing her away and to resume her attacks. It was almost two hours of hard work; Daryo was sweating despite the cold and panting hard. Jenni had reached the point of exhaustion and she had just told Daryo that she was ready to stop when Leroyfa came out of the house.

'Jenni, it is time you retired to bed. The hour is late, more than four hours from sunset.'

'Yes, Leroyfa.' She raised her wooden sword by the handle, point down, in imitation of the Order salute.

Daryo smiled and imitated the gesture. 'Well fought, Jenni. You were a worthy opponent.'

'My thanks, apprentice Daryo. A restful night to you.'

'And to you.'

Jenni took the swords and shield and hurried inside. Daryo followed Leroyfa.

'She shows promise,' the housemistress said.

'A lot of promise,' Daryo agreed. 'She is much stronger than she first appears.'

'I am far too old to compete with her. And with Oban but he has gone to the Five Towers as a duckling. I am afraid that we have only a single free bed.'

'The Harlequin has greater need of it than I.'

Leroyfa chuckled. 'She said that you would say so. However the Brethren are preparing cushions and a straw mattress for her in my chamber.'

The chamber was in the cellar, a room made by wooden sheets with a curtain across, but the bed was long enough and the bolster presented was comfortable and Daryo slept soundly. He was woken an hour after daybreak by one of the Brethren guards.

'Your lead has gone to meet with the one you are to escort,' he told Daryo. 'She said that you may enjoy the freedom of the town and left a bag with Leroyfa the Blind that she said you may find helpful.'

'My thanks.'

Daryo ate some oatmeal and fruit with Leroyfa and she handed over a small pouch from the Harlequin.

'Can you recommend where I should go within the town?' he asked.

'The Archive is the place most wish to see,' said Leroyfa. 'There is also a great temple to the First God and one to the Great Shepherd. The Dock Without is a sight for any who are unfamiliar with other nations and peoples. The market of the old city is a repository of great things also.'

'My thanks.'

'Be mindful of the City Watch especially within the walls. And be aware of those around you.'

'I was a ward of the School of the Temple, the Blind. I will be most aware.'

'Of course. The Harlequin will return here at noon. She would have you return then.'

'I will return then.'

The bag contained a handful of silver coins and a small doll of a harlequin. Daryo decided it wise to take a weapon and put on Stai's swords, hidden under his cloak, before stepping out into the bright, cold day. The streets were busy. Above the Town Without, towering grey-white walls almost as high as those of the Five Towers loomed. Daryo followed his nose down the narrow, unpaved streets to the waterside. The docks reached out from the riverbank as a network of wooden platforms. Close in to the bank were the little coracles, rowboats and canoes of the local fishermen, then the skiffs and sloops of traders and, furthest out, the large ocean-going trading ships, some with two decks and three masts, larger than houses. Smells and sounds, strange and seductive assaulted him. A woman at the top of one of the pontoons was selling brightly-coloured spices from jars. A barrel of vinegar had been dropped from a ship's winch and smashed covering the wood with pungent brown liquid. A catch of fish was being gutted by the bank. A pair of spotted dog-like animals in a cage chattered excitedly as people passed and bared their teeth. Daryo followed along the bank. Where the riverbank met the city

wall, there was a huge tower, taller than the walls and very wide. On the top, Daryo could see the arm of a catapult. The walls were rounded, made of huge stones and there was a huge number of arrow slits suggesting it had been built to protect both the town within the walls and the river. A few yards along the wall from the tower was the gate, monitored by three of the City Watch in fur-crested steel helmets, red-painted breastplates and bronze-coloured breeches. They all carried pikes with red pennants hung from the shaft and short swords. They barely glanced at Daryo as he passed through the gate, under a portcullis and through a thicker inner gate. The town within the wall was a closer, more suffocating but tidier place. The streets were paved, the houses seemed to be built to the same pattern with stone walls, wooden roofs and three levels above the street. And towering over all of them was the Archive. It had the appearance of a giant flight of steps, reaching from the street level to the top of the wall. It started in, as much as Daryo could tell, the centre of the town and reached out from there for at least half a mile, supported at intervals by immense columns from beneath. Someone collided with Daryo and scolded him for blocking the road; it was then that Daryo realised he had stopped in the middle of the roadway to stare at the sight of the Archive. He resumed walking, following his own judgement to where the Archive met the ground in a large square in the centre of the town. The bottom step of the Archive was nearly a hundred yards wide and built of a much darker stone than the rest of the town. The doors looked like beaten silver and were flanked by white banners showing a black staircase ascending to a shining golden sun. On the opposite side of the square was a stone palace, topped by a trio of small turrets and guarded by the City Watch. The third side of the square was the Temple of the First God, a spreading plane tree in front of it, and opposite the temple was the shrine to the Good Shepherd. The square itself was full of carts, barrows and stalls of a small but bustling market. Daryo found a man selling hand-sized carved wooden Archives and bought one. He had a several carved animals, one a cockerel and Daryo bought it on impulse as a gift for Lana. A woman further along the row was selling items of jewellery, including a sword-and-shield belt clasp studded with chips of colours. Daryo purchased it for the Harlequin and one without the colour for himself. Another woman, who looked like a Silver Islander, was selling small hot pastries, cooking them in a big pan full of oil. Daryo purchased a handful wrapped in paper and ate them as he walked the market. The vegetables in them were unfamiliar but there were small pieces of bacon and fish too and he went back and bought more. The bell in front of the palace tolled midday and Daryo hurried back through the town towards the Nest.
The front door was open so Daryo walked straight inside. The Harlequin was demonstrating a technique with a sword to some of the older children. Every time she

attempted it, she was hitting herself on the forehead with the hilt of the wooden sword provoking gales of laughter. The more laughter it provoked, the more determined she stated that she was to get it right and the harder she was hitting her own forehead. Daryo joined in the laughter as the Harlequin hit herself on the head for the eighth time and feigned a swoon. She laughed too, handed the sword to Jenni and greeted Daryo.
'Did you enjoy your walk?'
'I did. And my thanks for the coin.' He presented her with the belt clasp.
'Thanks indeed, my apprentice. That is most generous of you. I have met our friend, he will not be able to leave until morning so we can stay here tonight and leave when he is ready.'
Daryo nodded. 'As you say. We could do some work with the young ones here and give Leroyfa and the Brethren a rest?'
'A good idea. We should eat and then we can put these young people to work.'

Kym took charge of archery and Daryo of sword and they kept the older children, nine of them, working until sundown. The children enjoyed it immensely. Jenni proved herself the most skilled with the sword and a rather heavy boy, Lamber, the best with bow. The Harlequin promoted them to the adult table and waited on them through the evening meal. The younger children were retiring to bed when there was a firm knock on the door. Leroyfa and the Brethren, all were still in the hall from the meal, exchanged puzzled looks. Leroyfa got up and answered the door. Daryo could not see who was there but heard the words 'City Watch' and 'important'. Leroyfa denied something but stepped aside. There were three men of the City Watch, they came in, divided and spent several minutes looking around the house before departing with apologies.
'What happened?' asked Kym.
'Looking for a fugitive,' said Leroyfa. 'There was a rumour that he had hidden here.'
'Looks like they caught up with you, Daryo,' Kym chuckled.
Daryo grinned. 'They would never have tracked me. Kym the Harlequin taught me too well.'
The evening passed pleasantly. Daryo helped Lamber with learning his letters, the Harlequin tried to show some of the young ones how to carve with a knife with many comedic drops of her knife and her piece of wood and one drop of her breeches before they all retired.

'Daryo! *Daryo!* Wake up!'
Daryo was aware that Kym was shaking him vigorously. 'I am awake! I am!'

'Get up, dress, arm yourself!'

'What? Why?' Daryo scrambled out of bed, reaching for his clothes. The Harlequin was dressed and carrying her unsheathed sword.

'The Nest is surrounded by a mob. The fugitive the Watch were hunting, the Town is convinced we are hiding them and have threatened to burn us out!'

'Where are the Watch?'

'Who can say? I think there is something behind all this, perhaps the reason the Muster was called.'

'You think so?'

'I wish I could say. Hurry!' She was already leaving the cellar.

Daryo finished dressing, pulled on Stai's swords and wrapped his cloak around his waist, tying it like a belt. He hurried upstairs and suddenly realised just how serious the situation was. Two of the Brethren soldiers were barricading the front door with the tables. The children were clustered under the stairs, twenty-one of them with the Harlequin and the Brethren servants with them. Leroyfa came down the stairs with a bundle of cloaks and began handing them out around the children. From outside, Daryo could hear the shouts of the crowd.

'I've sent a pigeon to the Five Towers,' she hissed to the Harlequin. 'But they will take a day at least to reach us!'

'We have to get the children out,' said Kym in a low voice, beckoning Leroyfa and Daryo away from the youngsters. 'I do not believe that crowd outside is bluffing. And an angry mob is not above slaughtering children.'

'What can we do?' asked Leroyfa, a note of panic in her voice.

'We have to treat this like an illusion,' said Kym. 'Distract attention while the switch happens.' There was a bang on the door.

'This is the time!' shouted one of the Brethren, drawing his sword.

'This is the time,' repeated Kym. She turned to Daryo 'Take the children into the back room. When the mob breaks through the door, the Brethren and I will hold them here. When there's a breach, the army floods in. The crowd at the back will come around the front. Climb on to the woodshed and over the wall into the smith's yard behind. Break out of the smith yard and follow out of the town eastwards. You'll come to a stream outside town, follow it back to the road and head back to the rock where were ambushed. The Brethren servants will come with you. The other Brethren, Leroyfa and I will hold the mob as long as we can. If we can, we will try and hide out, meet our contact tomorrow and join you. If we do not join you by the next dawn, head for Riverhelm and you should meet the party from the Five Towers coming here.'

'You'll be killed!' protested Daryo. 'Leroyfa, you should go and stay with the children.'
'No, I'm too old to run,' said Leroyfa sadly. 'Take care of them.'
The Brethren servants were already pushing the children into the back room as the door was hammered again. Most were crying. Jenni had somehow obtained a short sword, Lamber as well, some of the other older children bore the wooden weapons that they trained with. The Harlequin drew her knife and gave it to one of the Brethren servants as she passed. Leroyfa, tears streaming from her eyes, stood on a stool to take down her shield and weapons. She considered the staff and sword for a moment and handed her sword and shield to Jenni. Daryo went to protest but the Harlequin shook her head sharply before laying her hand on Daryo's shoulder.
'Say it,' she said.
'Say what?'
'Speak your Promise.'
'I'm... I'm not ready. I have no sword name. I am not ready.'
'You are. I say that you are. Speak.'
Daryo drew the Horse. 'With my heart, my mind and my honour, I promise to do my duty as a Member of the Order of the Shield and Sword and to follow orders as given on the authority of the Captain-General and his Aides. I swear my Shield and Sword to the defence of the just, the righteous, the innocent and the weak. By this oath, I pledge my sword and my service until I am discharged by death.' He finished in tears, raising the Horse in salute as another smash came on the door.
The Harlequin clapped him on the shoulder again. 'Choose your sword name wisely. By dawn, there will be two new names. I had Leroyfa put on the pigeon message that you had taken your Promise on my word. You are a Member of the Order of the Shield and Sword. Now do your duty.'
Daryo raised his sword again by the pommel. 'My sword and my service.'
'Until I am discharged by death,' said the Harlequin. 'Go. Please.'
Daryo stepped into the crowded back room. Twenty-one children and five Brethren servants made it hard to get the door closed behind them. The Brethren were doing their best to quiet the children. Then there was the smash of the front door and the baying of the mob. The Harlequin roared a challenge and there was a scream of pain. One of the Brethren cursed and the Harlequin shouted again.
'Go,' Daryo hissed at the Brethren at the door.
She pushed the back door open. The back gate had not been attacked yet and the compound was empty. The horses whinnied nervously at the shouts from the street. The woodshed was against the wall furthest from the house.

'Quick! Onto the shed and over the wall!' Daryo hissed, still aware of the tears on his face. He saw two metal troughs nearby used for the horses. 'Here, help me!' he asked the only male Brethren with them and the only one armed. Together they lifted the first trough and used it to brace the door shut. They used the other to brace the gate as the children scrambled up onto the woodshed and over. The older ones helped the Brethren pass the younger ones over; Lamber was perched astride the wall, his small sword stuck in his belt. Lamber and Jenni were the last two children over the wall, followed by the four female Brethren, then the man and Daryo was last.

They were in another courtyard, smaller and without a house but with a smithy in the centre, contained by another gate. Daryo smashed the lock with a large hammer, drew both of his swords, reversing the Bear, and shouldered the door open. Already now a street away from the mob assaulting the Nest, he led the children and the Brethren eastwards through the otherwise empty streets, trying to ignore that there was a glow of fire behind.

'How far is it?' asked one of the younger children, a girl with black hair wearing a cloak that was far too big for her.

'A long way, little one,' said Daryo shortly.

'Will Leroyfa be there?'

'I hope so.'

They hurried onwards. As they passed a meeting of streets, a City Watch patrol was approaching and shouted a challenge.

'Run!' barked Daryo, turning to face the threat. The children and Brethren began to run. The three members of the watch spread out, levelling their pikes. Daryo recognised the threat of the long weapons and closed immediately, parrying the first thrust with the bear and slashing across the wielder's chest with the Horse. This aggression surprised the Watch and the other two stepped back quickly, shouting nervous warnings to Daryo to surrender. Daryo ignored them, parried the next awkward thrusting attack and swung the Horse down. It was sharp enough to slice through the shaft of the pike and its owner ran. The last Watch-man, deciding that he was no immediate hero, threw down his pike and followed his comrade. Daryo sprinted to catch his charges as they left the Town Without at an awkward run. He glanced back; there was a definite glow of fire in the town.

There was a call from the front of the group and everyone stumbled to a halt. Daryo hurried past the children to where the Brethren had reached a narrow but deep stream. 'Follow it downstream, south,' said Daryo, looking back again. 'Follow it until we join the road. I will walk at the rear.'

After an hour's walking, one of the women suggested that they stop to allow the children to rest. Most of them were whimpering and crying from tiredness and cold.

'Daryo?' The Brethren man had come across. 'We have not met. Fletche.'

'My thanks for coming.'

The man sighed deeply. 'I have served Leroyfa for eight autumns and nine summers. I hope that she has been taken into His care.'

'His?'

'She was a follower of the Good Shepherd. I am not but she was pious.'

'The Harlequin... the Harlequin followed the faith. She will be communing with the Fourth Goddess.'

'Fletche, I'm cold,' said one of the younger children.

Daryo undid his cloak from around his waist. 'Here, child. Wear this.'

'Thanks.' The cloak was far too big but folded in half and tied at the corners it served its purpose.

'We should build a fire,' said one of the women.

'We are much too close to the city,' said Daryo. 'We may be seen. We do not want a City Watch patrol coming out to investigate us. We must keep walking to the road and then get as far from the city as possible before daybreak.'

'The children are tired.'

'I am tired too but we have no alternative.'

'I really think we should stay here.'

'I have told you what we are going to do. I was told that the Brethren served the Members of the Order.'

'We do,' said Fletche. 'Be still, Gali, we make for the road.'

The children were all but asleep by the time they reached the road. They were walking with their eyes open but their little minds were asleep, instinctively following the one in front. The youngest three were in the arms of Daryo, Gali and Fletche and well asleep.

'The pigeon should have reached the Secondborn Tower by now,' said Fletche, a sleeping boy in his right arm and holding the hand of a girl only slightly older. 'The Order will know that we need aid.'

'What will they do?'

'We are the most important asset that the Order has, its greatest treasure to be held out of the sanctuary of the Five Towers. A lot of Members will want to come to our aid. They will ride out hard.'

'What about the City Watch? Will they come after us? Or the crowd?'

'I doubt that. The Watch were not protecting us and will not care if we left the city. The cowards in the mob will have homes and jobs to go to.'

By daybreak, even talking seemed hard work. Daryo left them to find somewhere to conceal themselves for a few hours. A natural depression with a rock wall on one side was the best he could find. The children all slept where they dropped, the Brethren and Daryo around the edges. Daryo had intended to keep watch but was asleep within heartbeats.

It was past midday when Daryo was woken by one of the youngest children crying for Leroyfa. The Brethren had brought as much food with them as they had been able to assemble but it was all cold and the children were sobbing and shivering. Someone had gathered some bracken and started a small fire. Only two people were nowhere near the fire: Lamber and Jenni were stood on the edge of the hollow, swords drawn, Jenni had the Blind's shield across her body as protection against the wind. Daryo clambered up. They were about fifty feet from the road.

'Anything concerning?'

'Nothing,' said Lamber. 'Some farmers.'

'You should go down and warm up by the fire.'

'Yes, Daryo.'

Lamber scrambled down into the hollow. Jenni stayed. 'I am warm,' she said defiantly. Daryo stretched his arms and back. Jenni was clutching the hilt of the Blind's sword tight enough to turn her fingers white. Daryo was familiar with the old style swords- effectively a single piece of iron, shaped and sharpened but left round at the base to make the handle, which was completed with some fabric wrapped around and tied.

'May I see your sword, Jenni?'

'This is not my sword. It is Leroyfa the Blind's sword.' Her voice quavered.

'May I see it?' Jenni handed over the sword. 'My thanks. Go and warm up by the fire.'

Jenni started to argue but then gave up and slid down the edge of the hollow to the fire. Daryo turned towards the distant town. There was a column of smoke rising against the blue sky.

'There was a fire in the Town Without last night,' said Fletche, joining Daryo. 'I think they burned the Nest.'

Daryo nodded sadly. 'I think so. Along with your Brethren, the Blind and the Harlequin.'

'Leroyfa the Blind and Kym the Harlequin died fulfilling their Promise to defend the defenceless. My Brethren died fulfilling their pledge to defend Members of the Order.'

'Do the Brethren have a Promise?'

'We have an inheritance. An unbroken line of fidelity, bravery and commitment.'
Daryo studied the road. 'We should get the children moving.'
'We should.' Fletche made his way back into the hollow, spoke to the other Brethren and they started cajoling the youngsters into movement. Within a third of an hour, the children were on the road and moving, some being carried by the older ones and the Brethren, only Daryo had empty hands as the Brethren had decided that he needed both hands free to defend them if necessary. He was also carrying the Blind's shield to allow Jenni to carry the smallest child. They were walking for a couple of hours before Daryo suggested they stop for a rest. The children sat down along the side of the road. One of them started crying again as a horse rode up. The man on its back was tall, with a beaked nose, a longbow on his back and the Order's badge on his chest. The horse he was on was panting for breath as the rider dismounted.
'Daryo? You must be Daryo.'
'Yes!'
'I am Moded the Archer. I was the fastest rider. I was with the Lord of Aslon and had a pigeon from the Five Towers. I came as fast as I could.'
Daryo took the Archer a short distance from the children and told the story in full. The Archer stayed silent until Daryo had finished.
'The Harlequin and the Blind will be greatly missed,' he said with feeling. 'But the children are safe, that is the most important. My congratulations on taking your Promise. A Promise taken in the face of battle is a true one indeed. Do you have a sword name?'
'My people have a Verse, a song of what is done and what is known. It speaks of the need to walk and walk again. That is all I seem to have done of use to the Order. Is there such a Member as the Walker?'
'Not to my mind. Daryo the Walker, it is well chosen. The Aides will confirm it but I think it is well chosen. We should put the smallest of the children on my horse and we can continue. There is a bigger force coming from the Five Towers and they will hire a cart or carriage when they reach Riverhelm to carry the children properly.'

The bigger force, which met them by sundown, was eight Members led by Lana's former lead the White Hand, three apprentices, five Brethren attendants and twelve Brethren soldiers. A wagon had been procured and was loaded with blankets and provisions. At Daryo's insistence, one of the Members and her apprentice went to the rock where the ambush had been to wait against hope that the Harlequin and the Blind would escape. Daryo was given an escort of three of the Brethren and the Archer and requested to ride hard for the Five Towers.

They rode through the day and reached the Five Towers on exhausted horses by midnight. Daryo was directed straight to the Wooden Fortress Tower by the Archer, up five flights of steps and into a small room. A cluster of candles in a metal candelabrum on the table gave light. Three people were sat around the circular table- Hoyuz the Calm, Fayd the Vanguard and Smalli the Black Bowyer.

'Please sit, Daryo,' said the Calm in his measured voice. 'You must be tired and I apologise for having you brought straight here.' One of the Brethren appeared with a beaker of ale and a large end of bread before retiring. 'I am sure you told the Archer all of what has happened but I would beg the tale again.'

Daryo complied, trying to talk slowly and provide as much detail and information as he could. When he mentioned the City Watch's search, the Vanguard muttered a curse under his breath but did not interrupt. Smalli's head dropped when Daryo spoke of Leroyfa and Kym's sacrifice. When Daryo finished the story with the arrival of the Archer, Hoyuz the Calm managed a smile.

'Our thanks, Daryo. The Harlequin was quite correct in having you speak your Promise in battle. Many Members have done so. You are therefore as much a Member as any other. Do you have a sword name?'

'I would take the Walker,' said Daryo tiredly.

Smalli nodded in assent. 'That name has not been taken in a century.'

'Daryo the Walker, the first Batribi to be a Member of the Order of the Shield and Sword,' said Hoyuz. 'I do not believe that this attack on the Nest was a mere act of an outraged mob. However we cannot deal with such issues at this hour. Daryo the Walker, under the circumstances, I think it best that you sleep in your old chamber in the Temple Tower tonight, where you are familiar. We shall find your berth in the Castle Tower with the dawn. Get your sleep, Walker.'

Daryo was too tired to do anything more than nod. He walked back down the stairs and out into the Compound. The cold air hit him and suddenly the impact of the previous two days struck him. He stopped still for a moment and tried to stop himself from crying. He walked vaguely forwards towards the gate, was seized by a sudden impulse and strode towards the gatehouse. A member of the Brethren had a cup of soup and was standing by the door to the gatehouse itself.

'Are Members permitted on the wall?' Daryo asked.

The Brethren smiled. 'Members are permitted anywhere. I thought you were the new Batribi apprentice.'

'I made my Promise this night past.'

'Congratulations.' The Brethren stepped aside. 'The stairs immediately inside the door will take you straight to the parapet.'
Daryo climbed the stairs. The steps were narrow, damp and worn and he had to tread carefully until he emerged on the top of the wall. The wind was keen and piercing, Daryo wrapped his cloak around himself tighter. Not his cloak, he reminded himself, Jenni was wearing his cloak. And carrying Leroyfa's sword.

*'Leroyfa, Kym as brave as brave*
*They fought through fire to find their graves,*
*The young and sweet and I still breathe,*
*Our saviours' names and lives we grieve.*
*My people walk and walk again,*
*This fate of ours is each one's bane,*
*To sleep beneath the stars each night,*
*To walk and walk again in flight.'*

'Very poetic,' said a familiar voice.
'Ranger.'
'Walker.'
'You heard.'
'It's a small Compound. The Archer came straight into the Castle Tower. Congratulations. Very few Members are battle-born.'
'Battle-born?'
'As you did, making their Promise in the face of their enemy. I know only the Bright who was battle-born. What was that you were speaking?'
'The Verse. It is a tradition in my people to share their experiences and their thoughts with each other.'
'A fine thought. A fitting tribute to the Harlequin and to the Blind. I was raised in the Nest by Leroyfa. She was a good woman, a good and caring person who loved those she cared for. She gave her life for the children in the full spirit of her Promise and her life.'
'It does not make it easier to lose her. Or Kym. Kym was my lead for only days but I got to know her in just that time.'
The Ranger nodded. 'I know. I have lost several comrades, many beside me.'
'I found myself thinking on the ride. I was thinking as to how my father and mother died.'
'You were a Ward of the Temple?'
'I was.'

'Then it could have been any way. I would hope that they were with your people, that they had a verse said over them as you did for Leroyfa and Kym.'
'I hope so.'
'If you should need an ear to listen or just an arm to grasp, I offer myself.' She drew her blade 'my sword and my service, Daryo the Walker.'
Daryo drew the Horse and responded. 'My sword and my service, Vilya the Ranger.'
'You should get some sleep, Daryo. You look exhausted.'

Daryo woke to the ringing of the bell on the staircase. His shield been moved, he noticed. The Harlequin's shield. It had been repainted with the Order's badge. At the pommel was a milepost with a harlequin and a blindfolded girl joining hands across it. The Horse, the Bear and Temma's Sword had been cleaned and sharpened. As well as these swords, there was a primitive sword that he recognised as Leroyfa's. A note had been left under it that read simply '*Thank you, Walker*' in a childish hand. Daryo realised that it meant that the children had reached the Five Towers safely and sprang out of bed like an excited child. He ran down the stairs and found one of the Brethren.
'The children? Where are they?'
'The children? From the Nest? They were found a large room in the Wooden Fortress Tower to serve as a dormitory.'
'Would I be permitted to see them?'
'I am sure you would, Walker.'
Daryo found them and he received a tight, joyful embrace from Jenni and a more restrained one from Lamber. Daryo offered to return Leroyfa's sword but Jenni refused, saying that he would get more use from it and that she would accept it back when she took her Promise and not before.

Daryo was just leaving the Wooden Fortress when he was almost knocked down by a young woman running in. She failed to do so much as apologise and went running up the stairs. Daryo wondered at her rudeness but found Herren Downe outside the tower. At the Brethren leader's request, he recounted an abridged version of the occurrences in Allesbury. Herren Downe shook his head and lamented the threat to the Order.
'I fear that the Blind and the Harlequin will not be the last that we lose.'
'Is there nothing that can be done?'
'We are trying. I mean that the Aides are trying. A dozen Members are out across Gourmin to help and bring in our friends, another dozen in Boskinia and some in

Jaboen. Twenty Members are out investigating the threat to us in more detail. I think that the young woman that nearly ran me down was one of them: Nila the Sharpened.'
'She seemed to have some haste.'
'Perhaps it is news. I fear that if she finds it necessary to move so quickly then the news is particularly bad.'
'What is the threat?'
'As the Captain-General said, there are those who mistrust the Order, that fear its power and its arms, they believe it works for profit and monetary gain or for prestige. And they are moving against the Order. The riot in Allesbury, the slaying of those eight, many more have died suspiciously. The Members of the Order are being hunted and killed like deer.'
Hoyuz the Calm emerged from the tower, saw Herren Downe and strode briskly up to him. The face of the Captain-General was pale and he looked truly scared. 'Commander of the Brethren, I as Captain-General of the Order of the Shield and Sword have called Muster. Immediately.'
'Muster?!'
'You heard me, Herren. Get your key and meet me at the Last Door. Walker, start to spread the word. Muster is called for Members of the Order only, no apprentices, immediately. All Brethren are to man the wall. All Members are congregate in the Sanctuary. Apprentices are confined to the Temple Tower.'

It took until midday for the message to have got around. Very quickly the Sanctuary filled up with Members, many somewhat disgruntled having been separated from their apprentices for Muster, all absolutely bewildered by two Musters in three days after two in the intervening thirty-five winters. The Aides were already in the Sanctuary when Daryo arrived and found the Ranger, the Shrewd and a young fair-haired woman. The Vanguard lifted the crystal sword and slid it into its slot in front of the Captain-General's shield. Silence was almost instant.
'My brothers and sisters, I shall be brief and to the point,' said Hoyuz. 'The threat to which I referred in this very Sanctuary is growing. My aides and I believe we have no choice but to tell you exactly who it is that threatens us. There are those of you standing here that will know that there is one name that was struck from our lists in seasons past and that no Member may ever take that name again. The bearer of that name tried to betray the Order and to deliver this fortress to a known enemy.'
'Sevant,' Kitsun whispered.

'Sevant the Stone,' Hoyuz told Muster. 'Sevant was a Member, he was a Blade, he was an Aide, he was expected to be Captain-General. And he sold himself. He approached the Vidmarian King, who has long desired territory in Gourmin, and offered him the Five Towers and the Order as his servants when he became Captain-General. The plot was discovered and Sevant was cast out. Now with the aid of the new Vidmarian king, the son of the one he bargained with, he is coming. He has reached Tiverta with an army. An army of over ten thousand.' A surge of concern and anger filled the Sanctuary and the Vanguard had to bang his fist on his shield for silence and eventually bawled: 'The Order is not just being hunted, we are about to be destroyed!' He stepped forwards, taking the floor from the Calm. 'The Aides have narrowed our options to two possibilities and we have decided that it is only reasonable to tell you the options. We ask only for silence until we have made the cases. The Aides making the cases were chosen by lot, so we beg you not to persecute the speaker for the view they put forth.'
Smalli the Black Bowyer stepped forwards. 'The Order could flee. We are from many lands and tongues. We have skills to do jobs from town guards to rangers, smiths, hunters, we could survive as individuals and small communities scattered to the eight winds. We would abandon the Five Towers to the attackers, taking what we could and burning the rest. Our Order would survive as groups of devoted and selfless people all across the known lands.'
The Black Bowyer stepped aside and Zerro the Scout stepped forwards.
'The Order could fight. We are an ancient Order of those fighting for the defenceless. We have always defended those who need us, now the Order needs us, the Brethren needs us, the Five Towers needs us. We may be victorious in a glorious battle, we may be left as legend in the memories of those that we helped. We may all be slaughtered. But we would go proudly.'
The Vanguard took precedence again. 'It is very simple, Members.' He pointed to his left side, where the Black Bowyer was stood. 'If you believe we must disperse, move to this side.' He indicated the opposite side where the Scout was. 'If you believe we must fight, move to this side. Please do so with thought.'
Daryo was quickly on his feet and moved to the side of the Sanctuary where the Scout was. He looked around earnestly, trying to see how many were going to each side, fight or flee? There seemed to be more on his side, most of the Members wanted to fight surely?
The Aides looked around, each seemingly counting a small section. The Vanguard stepped forwards. 'Firstly, I must say that either decision takes immense courage. There

are five hundred and ninety Members present. Of those, four hundred and three have voted to fight. The Order will fight!'

Muster continued as a briefing of troops and opportunity for question. It was announced that any Member that wished to leave would be permitted to do so. It was also decided that any apprentice of less than fourteen winters should be moved and the others given a choice of whether to stay or not.

'We could remove them to Sinsebil,' said one older Member with a white dog on his shield. 'It would be long journey but it would be to safety.'

The Calm inclined his head. 'Agreed. I am sure many who would leave anyway would agree to escort our youngest to safety.'

'The Brethren?' asked someone else. 'Would they join the escort?'

'They will want to remain here,' said the Arrow Nymph. 'Perhaps the older apprentices.'

The Calm nodded. 'It is a good suggestion. I will tell Sorrell the Greensward.'

'How will we defend the Five Towers?' asked Daryo.

There was a pause. Several people looked at Daryo.

'Who are you?' asked the Member with the white dog.

'Daryo the Walker.'

'We have several days to prepare the Five Towers,' said the Calm. 'Sevant is not ready to advance. We can prepare the town, the wall and the Towers.'

# Chapter 11

Rumour was quick to circulate but the only one to be proved true with any despatch was that the Vanguard would take command of the defence of the Five Towers, coordinating the gathering of supplies and provisions with the Trenchers, the assignment of Members with the Blades and the reinforcement of the Order's defences with the Brethren. Over the next two days, foodstuffs were brought into the Compound by carts and wagons along with wood and iron. The swinery against the outside of the Wall was emptied of its pigs and burned. Halfway through the second day, nearly seventy youngsters including those from the Nest and eighteen young Brethren, were put on a series of wagons and started out on their long journey north accompanied by twenty-nine Members and thirty older apprentices. Daryo heard Herren Downe talking with some of his Brethren: some Members had come and gone but Herren was expecting a handful more than six hundred Members, about a hundred apprentices and just under two hundred Brethren to be able to defend the Five Towers. Daryo had been initially put with the forest teams but had reminded Kitsun the Shrewd, now a member of the new fifteen Blades, that he had been a skilled smith and joined Dibat the Trident and his juniors in the forge, creating as many new weapons as they could manage. In breaks in their forging, the younger smiths were assisting some of the Brethren to make rope and nets. The ropes were being gathered in the gatehouse, the nets were being carried away into the forest. The Ranger came and went, often with one of the Brethren servants, but the third morning found Daryo.
'Walker, I would have you join me.'
'Me?'
'If you would. I need some assistance in the forest. Will you come?'
'Certainly.'
'Meet me by the gatehouse after the morning meal.'
Daryo did so and was nearly knocked down by a figure that ran out of the gatehouse to meet him. 'Jenni!'
'Walker! Are you coming with us?'
'Us?'
'I am assisting Vilya the Ranger. Nate Downe, Lamber and I.'
'Do you know with what purpose we are assisting?'
'Checking traps.'
The traps proved to be pits, some nearly twelve feet deep, that had been dug by the Brethren at random spots around the forest. They were now preparing nets and

sharpened wooden stakes for the bottom of each pit and then the hole was to be covered by sackcloth and disguised with leaves and soil. Daryo was warned that any tree with a yellow flag on it was five feet in front of a pit or other trap and to be aware. Nate Downe had taught Lamber to make rope snares and he enthusiastically taught Daryo. The Brethren had a number of bear traps and the Trident had constructed some more. These were then concealed under the debris on the forest floor. Nate explained that, close to the road, the trees would be felled when the enemy approached to try and block their path before the Brethren withdrew. Only the pathway would be safe by that time, he predicted, and this would be trapped as the Brethren fell back.

The plan for the defence of the Wall and Compound had been disseminated by the Aides. Working in relays, the Members and the Brethren would defend the Wall for as long as possible. When a breach inevitably happened, the defenders would split. The apprentices and an assigned group of Members would withdraw to the caves, most Members would hold the Castle Tower, the Brethren would retreat to the Twin Towers. The Wooden Fortress would be abandoned. When the attackers breached the walls and attacked, they would be distracted by the closest force to them while the other remained clandestine. When enough of the attackers were in position, the other force would counter attack and the besieged force would break out along with the third group from the caves. The Order would then retreat to the caves and hold out for as long as possible before going to join the ranks in service of the Fourth Goddess.

Most of the inhabitants of the Five Towers were trying hard to concentrate on their duties and not on the undeniably hopeless cause before them. A scout team had returned, Obscua the Unseen in command, and confirmed that the army gathering in the southern Gourmin town of Tiverta was carrying burgundy banners with a statue of a swordsman on them. The statue had been Sevant the Stone's badge as a Member of the Order. Between the Unseen, Hannick the Veiled and Lassai the Whisper they had counted ten thousand and eight hundred. Large teams of oxen were hauling catapults, the bases were ready for siege towers and the Whisper had seen at least two large battering rams. That night, Daryo found himself assigned as a sentry at the head of the concealed pathway near the road. The Ranger had been sent on some distant errand and he found that he inherited the young triumvirate of Lamber, Jenni and Nate, so he stood guard with these companions instead of another Member; Nate with one of the Brethren's pikes, Lamber with a borrowed greatsword and Jenni with Leroyfa the Blind's sword that she had eventually accepted and Vehllal's shield.

As the sun set, the trap-setters withdrew and the young foursome were alone, sat on logs by the pathway about ten yards from the road with a small fire for warmth and a horn to sound the alarm. Lamber was trying to grow a beard to give the impression of being older and sat with the five-foot sword across his knees; Nate held his pike with both hands with the haft between his feet; Jenni had her sword sheathed and shield by her side; Daryo bore Stai's blades and Temma's Sword and had his shield on his back. The talk had mostly been of the upcoming battle, mostly the three youngest talking softly among them with Daryo feeling much older than his companions: Jenni of about fourteen autumns, Lamber of maybe thirteen and Nate the same. Daryo found himself wondering if any of them would see the spring.

'What do you think, Walker?' asked Lamber.

Daryo had not been listening to the conversation and had not entirely got used to been referred to as the Walker. 'My apologies, I was not listening.'

'Nate believes that the Members would be better served to defend the Wooden Tower. I believe the Castle is better. What is your thought?'

Daryo considered his answer. 'I think whichever the Blades chose is correct; they would have chosen the best location.'

'Ha!' said Lamber with a snap of his fingers. 'I was right, Nate.'

'My Brethren have been guarding the Five Towers since there was but one tower,' Nate retorted. 'We know best.'

Lamber went to argue some more but Jenni laid a hand on his arm. 'Quiet. You will not change anything. The Members will be in the Castle and your arguing will not change anything.'

'Have you thought of your name?' Lamber asked, as if this was a continuation of his discussion with Nate.

'My name?'

'Your sword name.'

'Why should I?'

'We will all be battleborn, like the Walker. I want a strong sword name.'

'We will have no time to be battleborn! We will be dead!' snarled Jenni. She got up and stalked away towards the road. Lamber tried to defend himself but Daryo stopped him. 'Stay here,' he warned and followed Jenni.

She had walked out to the road and stood in the lee of a tree that the Brethren had marked for felling.

'Jenni…'

'I am right. Tell me that I am. We will all be dead.' She determinedly did not look at Daryo but instead stared out at the sky. 'In nine days it will be my born-day, my fourteenth. My mother died as a result of my being born. The summer before me ninth

my father, Perse the Snowfall, was killed by Vidmarians in the Peaks. I was raised in the Nest by Leroyfa the Blind. Leroyfa was killed to save my life. My father died doing what he thought right. Now I am going to die.'
Daryo sighed. 'Perhaps.'
'You say *perhaps* but what you mean is *surely*. How can we possibly survive?'
'You could leave. You could take a horse and go to Sinsebil or Spiert, Lalbi, Salifa...'
'I cannot. I was born into the Order. Ever since I was able to talk I was being taught the Promise. The only family I have is... Lamber. And you.'
'Me?'
'I thought all Members were brothers and sisters of all other Members.'
'True.'
'So you are my brother as a Member of the Order. And I grew up alongside Lamber. He is like a brother in kin. Have you fought in a battle like this?'
'No. The Order is not an army, is it? And I was an apprentice smith before.'
'I think we are all going to die.'
Daryo heard Jenni's voice waver. He put his hand on her shoulder in what he hoped was the manner of an elder brother. 'I cannot say what is going to happen. Maybe the Second God could say, or perhaps the Fourth Goddess knows who she wants to join her in the next kingdom. What I can say is that if I am going to join the Fourth Goddess, I will go with my sword in my hand and shouting defiance at her forces. Nobody should choose when they join the Fourth Goddess, we must go when it is chosen for us. This may be our time, this may not.' He grasped Jenni's hand. 'I promise that I shall be alongside you whichever.' With his free hand, he drew Temma's Sword and raised it in salute to her. 'My sword and my service, Jenni, daughter of the Snowfall, until I am discharged by death.'
'My thanks. Thanks.' She put her head in his chest and cried softly.

'Is Jenni upset?' asked Lamber when Daryo returned to the fire.
'She calmed down. She had to find a privy.'
'Out here, that could be difficult,' said Lamber, smiling thinly.
Daryo sat back on a log.
'The Walker.'
The three jumped up at the strange voice. Obscua the Unseen stepped into the firelight.
'The Unseen. Are you our relief?'
'I am.'

'I must bring my other sentry in.' Daryo turned towards the road but Jenni had returned with her face rearranged into a picture of normality. 'Our thanks, Obscua.'
'Sleep well, Daryo.'

Daryo's chamber in the Castle was on a low level, immediately over the kitchen which made it pleasantly warm. It was no different to his room in the Temple Tower but for a chest and a well-made stand for cloaks and capes. He undressed and, with a blanket around his shoulders, polished his blades before extinguishing the candle and lying down in bed. He was on the brink of sleep when he heard the soft creak of the door opening. Daryo was worried that he was about to be murdered in his bed. He reached for Temma's Sword when the figure used a taper to light a candle. The flame flared, illuminating the figure.
'Jenni!' Daryo sat up.
She put the candle on the desk. 'I had to see you.'
'Jenni, this is the Castle Tower. Apprentices should not be in here.'
'I had to see you,' she repeated. 'I had to thank you for what you said and for what you have done.' She slipped off her robe. She was completely bare beneath it. On her chest, she had the start of breasts, the teats were hard with the chill, between her legs was a puff of blond hair.
'Jenni! Put that robe back on!' Daryo could scarcely believe what was before him. He lunged forwards for the robe on the floor.
'I am fourteen almost. Girls in Vidmaria and Boskinia get married and have children at fourteen,' she protested. 'I thought you would... like me. Girls can... do things to men, for them. I could do them... I could... could do them for you.'
'Jenni.' Daryo got out of bed, trying to control his racing mind and a feeling of tightness in his groin. 'Jenni... no... this isn't right. A brother, you called me. Brothers and sisters must not... a brother who lies with his sister in Jaboen would be beheaded.'
Jenni looked hurt. 'You... do not like me.'
Daryo sighed. 'Of course. You like Lamber. I like Lamber. But a woman should not give her body to a man in thanks.' He picked up her robe, put it around her shoulders, pulled it together and tied the cord around her middle. 'Your... offer is not one I could ever accept. Because you are my sister. And I love you as a sister.' He kissed her softly on the forehead. 'Can you get out the same way that you got in?' She nodded quickly. 'Then be careful. I will see you in the morning.'
She gave him a long look and then slid noiselessly out of the door.

'Walker!'
Daryo raised his hand in greeting. Jenni was blocking Lamber's sword thrusts with a staff. She gave him a meaningful smile and returned to her work. The Compound was becoming more and more fortified. A wooden palisade of very many spiked wooden stakes had been built in front of the Wooden Fortress and around the Temple Tower to give the impression that they were defended. A scattering of trap pits had been built between the two Twin Towers and the Wall as well as along the outside of the wall, disguised similarly to the ones in the forest. A Member was working with some apprentices to build a catapult alongside the stables. A pile of stakes to build fortifications was being assembled by the entrance to the caves. Daryo made his way to the forge; he was due to be aiding Dibat the Trident in the smithy. Siva the Fuller was stoking the fire. Solv the Strike was sharpening an axe. The forge was beginning to run out of essential material. The pace had slackened considerably as supplies became shorter. Daryo found a sword lacking an edge and took it up.
'Walker!'
Daryo looked up and saw the Vanguard striding towards him. 'Vanguard.'
'Come with me, Walker. The Blades have an assignment for you.'
Daryo put the sword down, nodded a farewell to the smiths and followed the Vanguard to the Secondborn Tower. Herren Downe was there along with two women- one of the Brethren who was about Daryo's age and the other a dark-haired Member who Daryo recognised as one who had been a scout.
'Daryo the Walker, this is Carma the Ibex. She has been in Jaboen, watching for us and she has discovered something that we may be able to make use of. It is a very small chance but we may have found a small slice of hope. There is a gathering in the peaks. We need you to attend.'
'Why choose me?'
'Because you are a Batribi. It is the Batribi who are gathering.'
'The Batribi?'
'The Ibex saw hundreds of Batribi assembling. They have found a place of safety in the peaks. More are expected. The Aides would like to propose to the Batribi that they come to our aid. We are sending Helli Downe to negotiate.' The young Brethren girl smiled charmingly. 'We think that sending our only Batribi Member is the best representation we could have.'
Daryo nodded. 'I hope so. I will go.'
'We are departing now,' said the Ibex.
'Of course, I will get my gear.'

Daryo turned and hurried across the Compound. He saw Jenni and Lamber still practising and diverted hurriedly. 'Jenni, Lamber, I have to go. The Vanguard has given me an assignment. I have to leave.'

'Where?' asked Lamber.

'Why?' demanded Jenni.

'I am sorry, I have to be quick. I shall return.'

'Can I accompany you?' asked Jenni.

'You would have to ask the Vanguard. He was by the Secondborn Tower.'

Jenni dropped her staff and sprinted away across the Compound. Daryo continued to his room and gathered his weapons and clothing, stuffing them into a small bag, before rushing back to the Secondborn Tower. Jenni was there but looking downcast.

'Good,' said the Vanguard. 'I appreciate that the apprentice here wishes to accompany you but this task requires speed and stealth, both of which will be aided by a smaller group. Fare well.'

Daryo clasped Jenni's hand before following the Ibex towards the gate.

## Chapter 12

At the end of the pathway and on the road, the Ibex turned right.
'We are going through the Tember Pass,' said Daryo.
'Into, not through,' said the Ibex cryptically. She was older than the Harlequin had been, leaner and somewhat cervine in her appearance with large, dark eyes, a long face and small, leaf-like ears. She was carrying a small buckler on her back, a small pickaxe the size of a dagger and a small, curved blade. Around her body like a sash was a long, thin rope. The ibex on her shield was perched atop a rock.
'I have never been to the Pass,' said Helli. She was compact and solid, her hair the colour of dark straw with soft blue eyes. She had a charismatic, bold attitude that Daryo enjoyed.
'Dangerous,' said the Ibex flatly.
'I came through with Kitsun the Shrewd,' Daryo told Helli. 'We were attacked by Peak Tribesmen and only saved by Obscua the Unseen. The Pass is very narrow.'
'And snow-covered at this time of autumn,' said the Ibex. 'This is why the Batribi are hiding in the mountains. The snow makes it hard for anyone to reach them.'
'You are the first Batribi that I have seen,' Helli said to Daryo. 'Are all your people so...'
'Dark?'
'Hale.'
Daryo felt complimented. 'We are a strong and resilient people, we have to be. In Vidmaria, my people are treated like game.'
'Sevant's men will treat you like the rest of us, have no fear,' said the Ibex.
'May I ask why you are the negotiator?' Daryo asked Helli.
'I am Helli Downe, I am the daughter of the Commander of the Brethren and thus speak with his voice. I am a woman, so I am a symbol of honesty. I am a skilled barterer, I arrange the prices of almost everything that that is bought for the Order. A Member may be more known but one of the Brethren shows that we are all part of a whole and all are asking for aid. This is also why a Batribi is the best companion that I could have. So, what is likely to appeal to a Batribi?'
Daryo smiled. 'We value tradition, the passage of knowledge and experience and kin above all.'
'So the Brethren being kin and the Members being a family of comrades is likely to be heeded?'

'I would hope so. My people can be generous and tolerant but I am sure they will want something in return for this. There is no purpose to them coming to the Order's aid for no recompense.'

Helli nodded. 'What I am required to do is to find out what recompense they would accept.'

The road began to climb uphill as it left the forest. The sky was blue studded with balls of white cloud. Over the peaks, the clouds were thicker and darker. From the road, the summits looked white. Helli shivered and dug in her shoulder bag for a fur hood. She was dressed warmly, an iron-blue Brethren tunic and matching cloak with furred boots and thick leggings. Daryo had seen a long, thin sword under her cloak earlier. The Ibex had got a dozen yards ahead and froze. She glanced back and motioned for quiet then led the way into the shelter of a nearby fallen tree. At the first turn, towards the mouth of the Pass and about eight hundred yards ahead of them, was a wooden barricade and alongside it was a cluster of troops. A halved banner was hung on the barrier- a white statue on a midnight-blue field and two black wolves rearing against each other on a gold field.

'A white statue,' said the Ibex. 'Sevant.'

'We should go around,' said Helli.

'We cannot. There is no way around. Those rocks are too steep for you to climb and we would be seen.'

'They have a horse,' said Daryo. 'To ride for help?'

'Undoubtedly. In case the Order tries to flee through the Pass. We must stop a rider escaping.'

'We need a bow,' said Helli.

'We need Obscua,' said Daryo.

'We need to be fast,' the Ibex told them. 'We cross the road. That gives us the most cover. We must stay close to the ground. When we break out, we must be very fast. I will go for the horse, regardless. You both must guard me until the horse is slain. Then we kill every man there and dispose of whatever we can. Take any supplies or useful weapons and burn the rest.'

'There may be another choice,' said Daryo. 'We can use our Batribi.'

'Use our Batribi?'

The post was isolated, cold and windy. An icy blast seemed to roar down the mountainside and chill any man there to the bone. The barricade was improvised- a wooden trestle with bundles of branches tied to it to make an improvised roadblock, a couple of tents alongside the road, a stake pounded into the ground to tether the horse and seven men. The men were Vidmarians all, part of the New King's army with his wolves on their chests but under the combined flag of the New King and the Stone. Most of the army joined for the security of a wage and regular food. The New King was ambitious and aggressive and his army had been blooded in the west and the south and now had marched boldly into Gourmin in the north-east. Soon the main force would be striking at the Order of the Shield and Sword, the secretive and dangerous hoarders of wealth and menace. But some inevitably were out in the wilds, in case the Tower-dwellers decided to flee. There were blocks on the road to Aslon and another by a river leading north. The one at the mouth of the Pass was considered the least likely to be used and therefore the most lightly-defended. Anyone who was palpably not connected with the Order had a toll of coin, or goods, extorted and then was allowed to pass. Anyone who the sentries suspected of aiding the Order was robbed and turned back. They had orders to slay anyone who looked to be a sworn Member of the Order or one of the incestuous clan who served them.

Thille Ledeur was the captain of the detachment, his rank showed by his black cloak instead of brown, which most of the army wore, and his carrying a long-handled small-axe instead of a spear. He pulled his cloak a little closer around him, the wind was piercingly cold. One of the men had not worn gloves and was not unable to move his right hand after it froze around the haft of his spear. He had found the duty incredibly dull. The passage of traders through the Pass had been slowed as the snow had fallen and made traversing the narrow pathway more difficult. They had seen nobody since dawn the previous day until Cabecou saw the single figure walking up the road towards the block. It was hard to determine anything under a russet cloak until he got closer.

'Is that a black dog?' Ledeur asked Cabecou, using the normal derogatory term for one of the nomadic Batribi.

'I think so, Captain.'

'Well he won't have anything to do with the Order. They don't have dogs. He won't be one of the family-fuckers either.'

'He may have coin.'

The figure was a hundred yards away. Ledeur strolled out to meet it. It was a young man with the short, curly dog hair and a pale scar over his eye. When he got closer, Ledeur saw that he had his arm wrapped in cloth.

'Stop, dog!' Ledeur commanded, bringing his axe to a two-hand grip.

The Batribi complied. 'I did not know this was a toll, sir.'

'Dogs have to pay double.'

'I left my hound with my kin, sir.'

This reminded Ledeur of something. 'Where is your kin? Don't dogs travel in packs?'

'They went on ahead, sir. I was hurt working on a farm.' He showed his left arm, wrapped in cloth. There was some blood showing through the bandages. 'The farmer cared for me until I was well enough to join my kin, sir. I know they crossed the mountains to go to Salifa in Jaboen.'

'This Pass is now property of King Vrie Masson of Vidmaria and a toll is demanded.' At least the dog was a respectful dog.

'I have little to pay with. My people trade rather than carry coin. The best I can offer is this.' He took a skin from under his cloak. 'It is a Gourmin wine, sir. I got it as a gift for my father but if I cannot join him unless I pay, it is better that you have it.' Ledeur took the wineskin cautiously and opened the stopper. 'It is spiced. It will be good against the cold.'

Ledeur sniffed. The wine did smell good. He nodded. 'It is enough. Do you plan to return?'

'No, sir. We were heading west.'

Ledeur jerked his thumb up the road. 'Pass.'

'Thank you, sir.' The young Batribi smiled, showing very white teeth, and started his climb up the road again. He reached the barricade and stepped through the small gap between the end and the rock face and reached where the horse was tethered before stopping. 'Oh, sir. May I ask?'

'What?'

'Why are four of the king's men here?' He fondled the horse's nose.

'Can't you count, stupid dog?' scoffed Cabecou.

'Seven of the king's men are stopping the king's enemies escaping an entrapment,' Ledeur told Batribi.

'Oh, I see. Well the king will be... disappointed.'

'Disappointed?'

The Batribi threw his cloak off. He was armed, a sword at his side, two more over his shoulders and on his back a shield with the Shield and Sword. 'Because the king's enemy just escaped!'

He drew his sword and pulled his shield around as Cabecou, the nearest to him, lunged with his spear. He kicked the spear aside and turned away, his sword slashing into the horse's throat. The animal screamed in pain and reared. The Batribi darted away from the dying animal as Cabecou drew his sword. Ledeur ran to join his man but was distracted by the sound of pounding feet behind him. He turned, shouting 'To arms! To arms!' to rouse his other men and saw the flash of a blade coming towards his face. He felt a searing pain and then oblivion.

Daryo finished off the first man with the back of Temma's Sword's blade and turned to confront the next man, who was impaled almost immediately as the Ibex seized the first man's spear and hurled it. The horse was down but screaming and kicking in its death throes. Daryo gave it a wide berth as he ran to Helli's aid. She was holding off a spearman with her blade but was unable to counter. Daryo got between them, shoved the spearman back with his shield and Helli darted around Daryo to aim a precise backslash into the Vidmarian's unguarded nape of the neck. The Ibex had meanwhile fought off two Vidmarians and sent a third running up the road towards the Pass. The last man had been kicked by the dying horse, his face was a blooded hole and he was trying to cry out but was choking on his own blood. Daryo took a deep breath and drove Temma's Sword into the man's chest.
'Fourth Goddess receive you,' he muttered.
In moments it was all over and silent. The horse had died.
'One escaped,' said Helli, breathless.
'He is going in the wrong direction to warn anyone,' said the Ibex. 'If he turns, he will have to pass us anyway. Let him go, the coward.' She looked into one of the tents and found a sack with some bread and cheese in it, which she appropriated, and a simple wooden shield that she offered to Helli.
'My thanks but no, I fight better with a single blade and no shield.'
'There is some gold and trinkets,' said the Ibex. 'Nothing else of value. We need to go.'
Daryo ripped a piece of cloth from one of the Vidmarian's cloaks, wiped Temma's Sword clean and sheathed it. Then he had retreat down the hill a little to retrieve his cloak. He put it on quickly, the wind was harsh. The trio started up the road. After a few yards, at the next bend, were three mounds of earth that looked suspiciously like graves. One had a shield laid on it; face down in what Daryo imagined was an insult. Out of curiosity, he stopped and turned it over. It was an Order shield- a sword and lute crossed at the pommel.
'Ibex! Do you know this badge?'
The Ibex came back to him. She looked at the shield and sighed. 'The Lyre Hunter. Hessiz the Lyre Hunter. Used to joke that he could fight a foe and play a ballad at the same time. I was a duckling with him. A maverick, an eccentric, a great friend of the Harlequin. He would play in the hall of the Temple Tower and she would dance.' She

took the shield and reverently laid it face up at the head of the grave. 'Another lamb for the Good Shepherd to tend.'
'Who could the other two be?' asked Helli.
'Innocents, perhaps. Members that do not carry shields. We do not have time to exhume them and discover the truth.'

The Tember Pass was white with crisp snow. It gave slightly underfoot allowing the traveller to step carefully but to keep a good pace. The wind was less pronounced in the Pass. The snow crunched underfoot. The Ibex led, Helli close behind, Daryo stayed a few yards behind but keeping the distance constant. They climbed steadily towards the border and reached the statues on the border with Jaboen by midday. They stopped to eat and then carried on, the Ibex setting a fast pace despite the ankle-deep snow. She stopped after a mile, checked an undercroft on the left, carried on for another few hundred yards and checked another one.
'This is it.'
'What is it?' asked Helli, crouching down.
'A hidden tunnel. Used by the Peak tribesmen. We can use to get where we are going.' The Ibex unwound the road from her waist, tied it around a spit of rock and threw the other end into the hole. 'This may be a tight fit.' She took off her bag and cloak and threw them into the hole, then took Helli's and Daryo's and sent them after hers. 'The drop is about thirty feet.' She got into a crawl position, gripped the rope and slid her feet into the darkness. 'Keep a tight grip on the rope or you will come down on my head. Do not come down until I say.' She disappeared into the hole.
'Interesting,' said Helli with a brave grin. 'Like the caves at the Five Towers.'
'I think it may be a little smaller in there,' said Daryo, checking over his shoulder.
'Quite permissible, I am a little small.'
The Ibex's call came up and Helli squirmed down the rope, leaving Daryo alone in the Pass. He waited a few minutes before Helli called up. He got his feet into the hole, flattened his hips to the rock and pushed himself backwards with his elbows, gripping the rope with both hands. He got his feet over the edge and shuffled backwards until he was holding his entire weight and then began to work down the rope. He could feel the rock of the tunnel against his back as he slowly edged down. It felt like a long descent before he felt rock under his feet.
'I can feel the bottom, I think,' he told the darkness.
A hand tapped his ankle. 'Yes, the bottom,' said Helli. 'Well done, you managed to not fall on my head.'

Daryo released the rope and turned around, standing up. He heard someone scrabbling around. 'What is that?'
'The Ibex left some torches down here. She's trying to-' Helli cut off as the light of a torch flared. 'There.'
The tunnel lit up. It was about four feet high and a little wider. Helli carefully passed a lit torch to Daryo. The Ibex had lit another torch from the first.
'Are you upstanding, Daryo?' asked the Ibex.
'I am.'
'Can you light the end of the rope? We cannot leave the rope there.'
Daryo stepped forwards, ducking down to get into the tunnel, reached back and held the lit torch to the end of the rope. The rope began to burn. He stepped forwards another pace and Helli handed his bag and cloak. The Ibex, holding the other torch, began forwards, bent almost double, the torch out to her side so as to not ignite her hair. Helli was significantly smaller and was just hunched slightly. Daryo was bent over like the Ibex. After a few hundred yards, which seemed a longer distance to Daryo's strained back and legs, the tunnel got narrower and then taller. He was able to stand up straight although at a slight angle to edge between the walls of the tunnel.
'How long is the tunnel?' asked Helli.
'About three miles,' said the Ibex, her voice echoing slightly.
'Is it all at this height?' asked Daryo.
'Until the end,' came the reply. 'Then it is like the start of the drop- somewhat narrow.'
'Do animals live in the tunnel?' Helli sounded nervous.
'Sometimes perhaps. But I would be more concerned about the Peak tribesmen coming through. Probably more dangerous than any bear. The Walker should be safe from them though.'
'I burned the rope, remember? I have no escape.'
'My corpse might block the tunnel and you may have time to climb the rocks,' said the Ibex.
'Stop it!' snapped Helli.
'My apologies, Helli Downe.'
After about a mile and a half, the Ibex suggested they stop for a rest. They sat on the floor of the tunnel by the light of the torches and drank and ate quickly before proceeding. The pace was slow due to the confines of the tunnel. A junction offered itself to the right but the Ibex ignored it, saying it went nowhere. The tunnel got wider and higher for half a mile and then narrower again. Gradually the ceiling got lower. The

Ibex and Daryo ended up bent over again and then reached an apparent blank wall. To the right was a low space, hip-high but wide.

'We have to crawl,' said the Ibex. 'Slowly. We are not able to take the torches. Crawl slowly and feel in front. Try and keep your hand near the feet of the person in front.'

The crawl was slow and a form of torture. The ceiling was uneven and they hit their heads; the floor was rough and uneven and cut their hands; the air was thick and foul and the tunnel descended sharply after a hundred yards which made it difficult to maintain their level. Ahead a bright spot was occasionally visible and it got gradually brighter and larger. Eventually the Ibex scrambled out of the hole and pulled Helli after her. Daryo threw his bag ahead and found Helli's small but strong hand grasp his and she helped him out. They were at the top of a ravine, narrower and steeper than the Tember Pass with a trickle of water down the centre. The snow was lighter and they were out of the wind.

Daryo looked at his hands; he was bleeding from several cuts. This was actually his blood, unlike the pigeon blood on the rags on his arm that he had used to fool the Vidmarian sentries. Helli had a long ragged cut on the back of her sword hand and a scuff above her eye.

'I might have a scar like yours,' she said to Daryo as they began to descend.

'That will look very attractive,' said Daryo.

'I think I am anyway.'

'I think so,' said Daryo and suddenly felt embarrassed. Helli glanced back at him and grinned. To cover his embarrassment, he called forwards: 'Carma! Where are we?'

'This is the Stannia Ravine. It leads down to the Stannia Lake. The Batribi are gathering alongside the lake. It is sheltered, it can be fished, it is defensible if anyone should attack and it is secluded- well away from anywhere.'

The ravine was steeply downhill. Daryo used his hands on the rock walls to steady himself as they scrambled down. The sky had cleared in the time they had been underground and it was colder but brighter. The sun was well past its highest and was starting to descend. The walls got further apart as the stream at the centre of the ravine got deeper and wider, recognisable as a young river now and not just a trickle of water, it started to tumble over short step-like drops. The Ibex was walking in the water, using the steps to make the descent easier. The ravine twisted to the right and the lake was in view- a patch of blue in the white, a kidney-shaped blue expanse with the young river running into it at the inside of the curve. By the banks, where the river joined the lake, was a small forest of the cone-shaped Batribi tents.

'There are more than when last I was here,' said the Ibex. 'I hope that this is a good sign.'

'More opinions, more ideas,' said Helli. 'It may work against us. It may just be dependent on the Walker's ability to speak.'
'My ability?'
'Why do you think the Blades sent our only Batribi?' asked Carma. 'I am no speaker, I simply knew the fastest way to get from the Five Towers to Stannia Lake.'
'I am a commodity trader,' said Helli. 'I can speak *for* the Brethren but not *to* the Batribi.'
'What am I supposed to say?'
'Whatever is effective,' suggested Carma, unhelpfully.
The descent was steeper and at times they had to turn to face the ground and climb down. It took several hours to reach the bottom of the ravine and they approached the Batribi camp as the sun set. They were seen by a sentry and Daryo heard a warning that he had heard before under the walls of Salifa: 'An approach! An approach!'
He spoke softly to the other two. 'Stay quiet. Stop here. Wait for them to come to us.'
He lowered his hood.
A small crowd of Batribi had assembled very quickly. The sentry came forwards with his sword drawn. 'Who approaches?'
'Daryo, kin of Stai! The Walker of the Order of the Shield and Sword!'
'You are one of us?'
'I am.'
The sentry studied him closely. 'Whose kin did you say you are?'
'Stai, husband of Impini.'
The sentry shook his head. 'There is no-one here of that name.'
'Laulra, Halvan, Diatia.'
Someone in the crowd said: 'Laulra is brother of Dostan!'
The sentry lowered his sword. 'You are kin of Dostan, you are my kin. Come, I will take you to him.'

'DARYO!' A man came out of a *kaff*.
'Drai!'
'We thought you dead!' Yiua's brother embraced Daryo.
'I feared you dead. Is Stai with you?'
Drai lowered his head. 'Stai walks with Yiua and Impini. His age...'
Daryo felt his throat thicken. 'I will mourn him.'

'Dostan, Laulra's brother, leads our clan. Laulra's wife is newly with child.' He looked past Daryo to the Ibex and Helli, who looked distinctly out of place. 'Who are your pale friends?'

'Carma the Ibex, Member of the Order of the Shield and Sword, and Helli Downe of the Brethren.'

'Order of the Shield and Sword? You found *them*?'

'They found me. I am a Member too. The Walker.'

Drai laughed. 'The Gods and Goddesses have a sense of intrigue!' He took Daryo by the arm and guided him to a *kaff* a short distance away. 'Dostan! Laulra!'

Laulra embraced him warmly, Dostan was equally pleased when Laulra recounted the story of Daryo's involvement with the clan.

'Any man that Stai named kin is my kin and my clan,' said Dostan. He was smaller and slimmer than his brother with a shaved scalp and a long beard. 'You are welcome but I must ask why you are here.'

'I come seeking aid for my new clan. Is there a leader here?'

'No, we are independent clans.'

'Is there any council?'

'There is an assembly of clan leaders, if it is needed.'

'Can it be called?'

'Why is it needed?'

'Because many, many lives depend on it and there is a chance for our people to make a great gesture and to gain many friends.'

Dostan frowned and glanced at his brother, who nodded. 'Very well. I shall call for the assembly at dawn.'

'This cannot wait, Dostan. I swear I would not ask if it were not crucial.'

'As you wish.'

The assembly met by the lake. A large fire was burning by the bank, nearly fifty yards from the nearest of the *kaffa* and about thirty assembled, most of them male elders but some younger like Dostan and three women. The only other ones present were Daryo, Helli and Carma.

'Speak, Daryo, kin of Dostan,' said one of the elders. Daryo noticed that one younger man was talking softly to a few of the older ones, presumably those who spoke only the old Batribi tongue.

'I am Daryo the Walker of the Order of the Shield and Sword,' he announced. 'Many of you may know of our Order. We are sworn to defend those who are unable to defend themselves. We fight for the righteous, for the meek and for the just. We are not interested in personal glory or wealth but in shielding those without shields of their own. I am the son of the Batribi but I am also a Member of the Order. My adopted clan is in danger. A traitor has bought an army against the Order. They outnumber us by ten to one. We have a plan to defend ourselves but, against such numbers, we have little chance without something that our attackers are not expecting.'

Helli touched his arm and stepped forwards. 'I am Helli Downe, daughter of the Commander of the Brethren. The Brethren have served the Order since time immemorial. I have accompanied these two Members of the Order as a representative of the Brethren and to offer whatever incentive or reward you wish in return for aiding us.'

'I am Carma the Ibex of the Order. I am here as a Member of the Order. I was bought up by the Order, my parents both fought for the Order, I was raised by the Order and learned to defend the helpless. My life and the lives of many others may depend on your intervention.'

'What incentive could you possibly offer?' asked one of the women.

'We have weapons, food, a safe refuge,' said Helli. 'We have ways of making and improving steel that is not practiced anywhere else. You could even settle on our lands, should you wish.'

One of the elders needing translation said something to Dostan. Dostan nodded. 'We are a travelling people. We have no need for somewhere to settle.'

'Some among us may,' countered another man.

'Some may not.'

'This is not an argument as to what we want in payment,' said another man, his scalp shaved but for a strip in the centre of his skull. 'We are people that helps those who need it.'

'As I was helped by Dostan's clan,' said Daryo. 'An outcast taken in; clothed and aided by strangers.'

'We are not a warlike people,' said a woman.

'We are,' argued another, rubbing her hand on the hilt of her sword and suddenly the air was full of argument and counter-argument.

'These people are nothing that affects us.'

'We can get supplies and arms for aiding those in need.'

'We are not fighters!'

'You must have fighters.'

'Not that I would sacrifice in a lost hope.'

'Sacrifice is all our people do.'

'We do not spend our lives like coin!'
'A plot of land would ensure my clan survives.'
'How many could be lost?'
'How many could be saved?'
'What would we get in return? Graves?'
'Weapons?'
'Horses, my clan needs horses.'
'A life is precious, any life!'
'The Second God is careless with lives.'
'The Second God protects us!'
Dostan sidled around the circle to Daryo. 'This debate could last a long time. Go back to Laulra and he will feed you and find you somewhere to sleep.'
'My thanks.'
Daryo motioned to Helli and Carma and they left the still-arguing clan leaders. Laulra provided fried fish and yam and an empty *kaff* that had been a store was put at the three's disposal along with blankets.
'What do you think they will decide?' asked Helli, finishing the last of the yam.
'I do not know,' said Daryo honestly.
'If they cannot decide, we must leave on the morrow,' Carma declared. 'The Order will need every sword possible when Sevant's army arrive.'
Daryo nodded. 'It is a shame that we cannot stay here. It feels... right here.'
'One day perhaps the Batribi will have their own lands.'
'As you heard, many would not want lands. We have walked for so long... if you have only ever slept with woollen blankets, a fur blanket will render you awake all night. So many Batribi are happy to continue the life that they have always known.'
'You could lead them,' said Helli with a mischievous grin. 'The Walker leading his people into their kingdom.'
'I think not.'
Daryo looked outside. The sky was clear and star-studded. He could hear the rhythm and words of some people nearby reciting the Verse. The cold was not deterring the younger Batribi in particular. Several of around ten and twelve winters were playing a game with a carved wooden ball between two small fires. It seemed to have few rules, there was lots of pushing and pulling of bodies, jumping into piles, throwing the ball and running in packs. After some time, one team dropped the ball into one of the fires and celebrated with a short dance around the blaze. One of the other team tried to retrieve the ball but

his chosen stick was too short. Daryo was only ten yards from the little fire. He stood up, took Temma's Sword from its sheath and used the tip to flick the ball out of flames.
'My thanks, warrior,' said the boy.
Daryo raised the sword, point down. 'My sword and my service, young one.'
'You are the warrior, yes?'
'I am a warrior.'
'You came across the mountains.'
'I did. I came under the mountains.'
'Under?!'
'I did. We came through a small tunnel about the size of a fat snake.'
The boy laughed. 'Why do you not walk with our clan?'
'You are of my clan?'
'Dostan is my clan leader.'
'I walk with another clan. Let me show you.' Daryo retrieved his shield. 'This sign, the shield and the sword together, are the sign of our Order. The two figures at the bottom, the blindfolded girl and the harlequin, are representatives of two of my sisters from the Order who gave their lives to save me and a group of children. They walk together past the milepost to show my chosen name: the Walker.'
'You choose your name?'
'To tell my comrades and my enemies who I am and what I do.'
'I would be a wolf!'
'And a fearsome wolf you would be! I saw you playing, go, you should finish the game.'
The boy smiled and turned back to the game, diving onto a pile of players. Laulra came past.
'I would suggest that you sleep. The assembly could take until dawn!'
Carma groaned. 'Will there be a decision by dawn?'
'I cannot say.'
'We must leave by midday tomorrow.'
'I will tell my brother. My *kaff* is at your pleasure, Daryo. The ladies will doubtless enjoy the privacy.'
'My thanks, Laulra. Carma, Helli, good rest to you.'

Dawn was shockingly brutal. The walls of the *kaffa* were translucent and, as soon as the sun came up, the light lit up the interiors waking all but the most ardent sleepers. The sky was still clear and the ground, the laying snow and the skins of the *kaffa* with a thin coating of ice. The fires had been tended overnight and the overnight sentries had stoked them at dawn so that the fires in their circles of stones were bright and hot as newly-wakened people emerged from their *kaffa*. A woman had an iron skillet full of apples that she put straight on the fire. Groups of children had chunks of bread on sticks and daggers and were toasting the bread over the smaller fires. By the lakeside, the assembly fire had been built up and the assembly slowly reconvened after its overnight recess. Dostan, feeling slightly ill, took his place by the fire. The young woman from the Order's servants, the Brethren, returned to listen but much of the talk was in the Old Tongue. He had expected Daryo to attend but he did not. He had Laulra summoned and sent his brother looking for the young man.

Laulra had grown to like Daryo. He seemed like a worthy, dependable and passionate young man and, most importantly, Stai had trusted him. Dostan had chosen to as well and the blessings of his late and his current clan leader was enough for Laulra. He asked after Daryo and was eventually pointed to the outer edges of the encampment. It became evident that Daryo was on sentry duty by the lakeside.

'My friend, I thought you would be at the assembly!'

'Helli told me that most of the talk was in a strange tongue. I do not know the old language of our people so I thought that it would be best if I put my skills to best use.' Daryo's sword, the one that he had been given by Temma, was drawn, he was carrying his shield and the twin blades gifted to him by Stai were on his back under his cloak; the hilts just protruded over his shoulders. 'I am a Member of the Order but I am still one of our people.'

'I am glad that you are not brooding.'

'I am in my heart.'

'To be busy is the best remedy. Stay alert, guard. I will tell Dostan that you are well and aiding our people.'

'I will stay here if I am needed.'

Daryo had relieved another young sentry just after dawn and found himself as the last in the line surrounding the camp, closest to the bank of the lake, just north of where the small river joined the body of water. Someone had produced a bridge from the base of a cart. The Batribi sentries were about a hundred yards apart and all had their weapons drawn so Daryo had done the same. He had seen little to excite his interest but nonetheless tried to stay alert and ready. He tried some of the sword play that he had seen apprentices in the Compound practising, repeated patterns of cuts and parries against an invisible opponent. He sheathed Temma's Sword, drew the Horse and repeated his invented exercise.

'Daryo!'

'Drai.'

'You should be resting.'

'I have no need to rest. I am waiting for the assembly to decide.'

'The assembly may take days. Our people have been walking longer than anyone could remember. It is longer than I can remember since so many Batribi gathered together. It is that long since an assembly and the last one, deciding if the Batribi should settle around a lake in Yashoun lasted for nine nights.'

'Nine? And what did they decide.'

Drai smiled thinly. 'They did not decide.'

'Most comforting.'

Drai nodded sadly and then brightened slightly. 'Niaa asked after you.'

'Your sister's daughter.'

'Yes. She was very... impressed with your respect for Yiua. When she heard that Stai had called you our kin, she has been referring to her absent brother.'

Daryo laughed. 'I should speak with her.'

'She would like that.'

'May I ask as to how Stai passed?'

'Very peacefully. We had walked here, the gathering had been rumoured, and the first morning after our arrival he did not wake. It was cold, Stai had seen more than seventy winters, it was time for him to join the Fourth Goddess. She will have received him graciously. And I think perhaps he was glad to join her. Dostan will make a fine leader of our clan.'

'Why was it not Laulra? Is he not the older brother?'

'Age is not only the consideration for leading the clan. Capability is also and desire. Laulra did not desire leadership.'

Daryo nodded. 'I understand.' He showed his shield. 'I did not desire this but it has happened.'

'You have found a clan to walk with, of a sort,' said Drai. 'This is good for you. It is good work too, helping those who need you.' He grasped Daryo's arm. 'Stai would be proud.'

'My thanks, Drai.'

'I am at your service, my brother. Your friend is coming.' He pointed back towards the camp; a very cold-looking Helli Downe was tramping through the snow towards them.

'Hail, Helli of the Brethren.'

'I do not believe we have met,' said Helli, puzzled.

'I am Drai, kin of Dostan. You are one of only two women in the encampment who is not Batribi. Your presence is well-known.'

'I understand. Walker, your kinsman in the assembly says that the discussions will not be concluded this day. Some of the others present wish to consult with their kinsmen outside of the assembly. They have adjourned until the next dawn.'

'Next dawn?' gasped Daryo. Drai groaned.

'Next dawn. Carma the Ibex suggests that we leave. One of the clans has offered us horses and the Ibex suggests that we proceed as soon as we can.'

Daryo shrugged. 'I think that prudent. We should be at the Five Towers.'

The horses were loaded and ready when Dostan strode up. 'Daryo! My apologies.'

'You are doing all that we could have asked, Dostan.'

'If, and I do say if, the assembly decides to aid your Order, we will come with all speed. It would be a death march to come as just one or two clans.'

'Of course. My thanks for all you have done.'

Dostan looked grave. 'Stai never had a chance to do this but I this now.' He produced a knife. 'Give me your hand.'

Daryo presented his left hand. Dostan turned it palm up and made a short cut in the palm. He then cut his own hand and laid it palm-down on Daryo's. 'Our blood is one. This makes us kin. Walk in the light, my kin.'

Daryo drew Temma's Sword and held it up by the hilt. 'My sword and my service are yours, my kin.'

# Chapter 13

The horses were good and fast. The Ibex followed a depression in the hills out of the area around the lake and after a hard ride reached the road from Lalbi into the Tember Pass. They turned eastwards and into the Pass. The sky had stayed clear but the road was covered in a thin layer of snow.

'Ibex!' called Helli as the rode. 'Why is Sevant attacking now? Don't armies normally campaign in the fairer weather?'

'I believe the Aides have had this discussion!' the Ibex called back. 'The only conclusions that they came to was that either the Vidmarian king wants his army back or that Sevant believes that the Order has something valuable or secret that could be removed in fair weather!'

'Such as what?!'

'Since we have nothing of value and nothing secret, I could not say!'

The Pass was traversed in a blur of white and grey and they had to slow the horses to negotiate the turns in the road down from the mountains towards the forest. The Vidmarian roadblock was still there, it had been given a light dusting of new snow that almost obscured the corpses. Brown stains marked the snow around the recumbent forms. The barrier had been moved aside by unknown hands and an incomplete attempt had been made to burn it along with the Vidmarian tents. The Ibex muttered something unpleasant as the horses picked their way through the debris before she kicked her steed on. The forest was quickly upon them and the horses were blowing and panting by the time they reached the hidden pathway. A Member of the Order stepped out of the trees.

'HALT!' he bellowed.

The Ibex's horse reared slightly but she bought it under control. 'Whoa! Whoa! Lobrin, it is I, Carma the Ibex.'

The Member lowered his axe, which was mirrored in a glowing, newly-forged form on his shield. 'Carma!' He looked past her. 'Walker. Helli Downe.'

'Indeed.'

Lobrin the Harsh regarded them all for a moment. 'You are allowed to enter if you are Members or Brethren.'

'We know, Lobrin.' The Ibex dismounted as did the other two.

'Not Sevant the Stone. I am allowed to kill him.'

'You are. May we pass?'

'If you are Members or Brethren.'

'Our thanks, Lobrin.'

Carma led her horse past the sentry and onto the pathway. Daryo brought his house alongside. 'Is he quite well?' he asked softly.

'Lobrin? As well as he gets. Lobrin was hurt training as an apprentice, a bad blow to the head. He is a fierce warrior and a good companion but he is sometimes a little slow to understand things. He takes some time to work information into a form he can understand. There are some Members who keep a gentle watch on him.' She pointed backwards slightly into the trees. Another Member, a leaping hart on her shield, was sat by a fire. She smiled and waved a hand in greeting, which Carma and Daryo returned. As the small group entered the ruins of the town, a dozen Brethren were working on a trap pit along with a group of apprentices. Herren Downe detached himself from the party.

'Ibex, Walker. Helli!' He embraced his daughter.

'Father.'

'Herren, the Batribi may not come,' said the Ibex flatly. 'They are holding an assembly of their clans but many are very averse to doing anything.'

Herren shrugged. 'We thought that that may be the case.'

'They did not deny us completely,' said Daryo quickly. 'My kin are there. They will do everything that they can.'

'Then there may be a hope. Go inside, rest, east. We believe that Sevant's army has begun to move. We sent more scouts but the ones that were to be closest to the army's encampment have not returned when they should. We believe that they have been killed as Vodyony the Pickerel would have returned.'

Daryo remembered the Pickerel as an acquaintance of the Shrewd. He could only find it in himself to sigh sadly and to follow the Ibex and Helli into the Compound. The catapult by the stables was finished and a hive of activity around it was assembling ammunition- rocks, bales of wood that were being soaked in oil, a large box nearby was buzzing angrily suggesting bees were contained within. The Batribi horses were happily taken by the Brethren in charge of the stables although she did say that there were now plans that the horses by taken to Aslon and given away. Helli gave Daryo a friendly hug around the shoulders and headed for the Secondborn Tower. The Ibex said that she had to report to the Vanguard and went towards the Wooden Fortress. Daryo felt somewhat useless so he wandered across the Compound towards the Castle Tower. The sky had clouded over during the morning and it began to snow.

Daryo had found some food around midday and, as the hall of the Castle Tower was rather full, sat in the lee of the Castle to eat a rich vegetable stew. The snow had stopped but the sky was still dark. The air seemed somehow full, as if there was an unseen presence in a small room. Daryo ate without appetite, his thoughts his own. The Compound was busy; the Five Towers had constant streams of people in and out. He was aware that a large group of Brethren poured in through the open gates as he finished his meal, led by Herren Downe. Herren went straight for the Secondborn Tower while his Brethren dispersed. A few moments later, one of the Brethren mounted the gatehouse and blew a horn, a long mournful note. The gates began to close. This was accompanied by a scurry of people getting inside the gates. A surge of Members, apprentices and Brethren began to take up positions. Daryo suddenly realised that this was the sign. The portcullises rattled down. The army approached.

All Members and apprentices had been given assignments to certain companies. Each had been given the name of its leader and a pennant improvised. Daryo hurried across to near the White Lady's temple where a grey and black halved pennant flew from a stake and Toxiz the Coalfire, one of the Blades, was rallying his force. Forty members and twenty apprentices were in his company and they were all quickly assembled. Daryo recognised Yi the Islander and Moded the Archer among them. Toxiz the Coalfire was particularly tall and very dark haired with a pile of disfiguring black lumps on his cheek and neck.
'This is it!' he announced. 'Sevant's scouts have crossed the road and the first of the traps has been tripped! Stay calm, stay courageous and stay true! Your comrades, your brothers and sisters in arms are behind you! The Brethren will be loyal to the death! We will fight to victory or we will be remembered with honour! For honour and glory!'
'Honour and glory!' echoed his assembled company, Daryo among them.
'Those of you without bows need to retrieve one quickly from the Firstborn Tower and meet us on the wall. Go now.'
The Brethren, all now in yellow armbands and hoods, had hauled bins of weapons outside and were passing out weapons to those who needed them. Daryo secured a longbow and two quivers of white-fletched arrows before using the gatehouse steps to reach the top of the wall. The Coalfire's company were manning part of the wall in front of the Temple Tower. As he hurried into position, Daryo passed a green and red pennant with the Shrewd stationed beside it.
'Kitsun!'
'Daryo.'
'This may be the last chance I get to speak with you. I want to thank you.'
'Thank me?'

'If you had not brought me through the Pass and spoken my case to the Blades, I may not be here.'

'And you may have lived for many more winters.'

'I would rather have lived a life of worth for days than a life of seasons in malaise. My thanks, Kitsun. My most sincere thanks.'

'You are very welcome, Daryo.'

'Is the Ranger with you?'

'No, she is leading her own company.'

'I hope I see her again.'

'As do I.'

'If you do, and I do not, please thank her as well on my behalf.'

'I will. Fight well, Daryo the Walker.'

'And you, Kitsun the Shrewd. And my thanks again.'

The nervous talk of the defenders died as the hours passed. A muting silence fell across the Five Towers. The quiet was broken only by unpredictably irregular screams and moans from the trees as the attackers fell victim to the traps. A dull thump was a rigged tree trunk dropping. A snap and a visceral scream was a line of set crossbows being loosed when a wire was broken. Short shouts and gurgles were the trap pits. And then a single Vidmarian soldier broke the tree line.

'Hold your arrows!' came the order along the wall.

The single soldier was quickly joined by a dozen more, then another score, another hundred. Two score of the Brethren rushed out from the gatehouse with flaming arrows readied, Helli Downe amongst them. Her uncle gave the fire command and the burning arrows struck barrels concealed in the branches of the trees. The barrels were filled with flame oil; the barrels ignited, exploded and showered the trees, ground and Vidmarian soldiery around with burning oil. The screams of the Vidmarian soldiers rose over the crackling of burning wood.

'One volley!' echoed down the wall. 'Draw!' Over four hundred bows were drawn along the wall and their bearers leaned out around the crenulations. 'LOOSE!'

A shower of arrows buried themselves in the attackers, the ground and the trees. Quiet fell again, broken only by the roar and crackle of the now-burning forest.

'That should deter them for a short while,' said the Coalfire with satisfaction.

'They will face more traps as they withdraw from fire,' said the Islander to Daryo.

'And the melted snow will make the ground harder to pass,' the Coalfire said, having heard. 'That will have killed scores as well- the fire and the arrows. Hundreds if the Second God is with us.'

The fire burned more fiercely until just before sunset when the snow returned. After a while the snow dampened the smouldering branches. The fire had cleared some more space beyond the ruined town. As darkness fell, there were definite noises out in the town and soon after nightfall a series of fires sprang up across the ruins.

'To obscure our view,' the Coalfire told his company. 'The bright flames make it hard to see beyond the line of fires so the enemy can begin his preparations without being seen. If we do not fire into darkness, they can work unmolested. If we do, we are wasting arrows. Fortunately we have a third option.' He pointed to where a group of apprentices and younger Brethren were gathered on the gatehouse, holding long lengths of leather. One by one they started hurling pebbles and chunks of rock with these slingshots into the darkness. Occasional screams and yelps came from the enemy as stones found their marks. And then the retaliation began; arrows from random spots began to fly in response, sending the slingshot-users into cover. When the arrows finished, the slingshots resumed. The duel continued well into the night and the Coalfire's company were relieved by one led by the Arrow Nymph by midnight. Daryo retreated to his room and managed some sleep.

Just after dawn, Daryo was back on the wall, right on the top of the gatehouse. The Vidmarians had been busy. Out of bow range, the forest had new clearings, closer to the ruins of the town most of the charred trees had also been removed and wooden archers' screens had been erected. Large halved banners with Sevant the Stone's statue and the Vidmarian king's wolves were flying from several places, a shield with the wolves had been attached to the face of most of the screens. In one of the clearings further back in the forest, Daryo could see a catapult being assembled. In the middle of the morning, the Order's catapult began launching burning bales of wood towards the Vidmarian launcher to try to burn it. The double crash of the catapult's launch began echoing around the Five Towers at regular intervals, at the command of Samm the Planner. By midday, after no success, the Vidmarian catapult began to respond. The first few shots hit the cliffs behind the Towers, showering the ground below with rock. A particularly huge boulder smashed a chunk from the top of the wall and the falling debris destroyed the Gods Temple and the chapel of the Good Shepherd. Another shot smashed the roof of the Firstborn Tower and killed several Members at the base of the tower. The Temple Tower was struck near the top, raining debris on the White Lady's temple and the assembling members of the Arrow Nymph's company, injuring almost all of them. The Wooden Fortress had two huge holes smashed in its front wall by hurled rocks. The Vidmarian archers began firing, most at the wall but many simply fired randomly into the Compound, meaning that anyone moving in the open had to carry their shield over their head to protect themselves. The companies had to form up behind the Wooden Fortress Tower or in the caves and then dash across the Compound with their shields raised. Only the catapult team and the companies on the wall remained in the open. By sundown, the Aides declared the Towers too dangerous to sleep in and all Members and Brethren gradually moved their bedding to the Sanctuary. Overnight the Vidmarian archers finished their work and there was a rush of movement to move the stores into the caves as well. The next morning brought a second Vidmarian catapult and midday brought the first ram.

A four-wheeled cart on each corner supported a short leg. On the top, a roof of treated wood and walls covered in tempered hides. Slung on ropes beneath, a thick and dense trunk. The slingshots and bows rained rocks, steel and fire down on it but, protected by the roof and walls, the men beneath pushed it forwards until it reached the first portcullis. The slam of the ram against the portcullis shook the whole gatehouse. Daryo felt his heart quicken, lit another arrow, drew and loosed it towards the ram. The arrow stuck into the roof of the contraption, burned out and then remained; a pinprick alongside a thousand others.

'How do we fight something like that?' he snarled, ducking down behind the wall as a scattering of arrows struck nearby.

'With cunning,' said the Coalfire. 'But also with patience.'

The sun set and Obscua the Unseen mounted the wall. 'Daryo the Walker, I would have your aid.'

Daryo nodded. 'Of course.'

'Come.'

The Unseen led the way along the wall past the neck that joined it to the Twin Towers and to the very end of the wall where it joined the cliffs. Hannick the Veiled and Lassai the Whisper were there along with one of the Brethren and a large pile of rope.

'We are going to go down the wall,' the Unseen said quietly. 'We will attack the ram and stop it from working.'

Daryo, Hannick and Lassai all nodded. Daryo left his shield and bow at the top with Hannick's bow. The Brethren peered over the wall and then threw the rope bundle over the top. It was anchored at one end and proved to be a long ladder made entirely of rope and cunningly tied together. It reached to the very foot of the wall.

'Be calm and careful,' the Brethren said. 'A fall from the wall would be the last thing you did in this life. The ladder will remain here. Be sure to say if you are killed so we do not leave it here for you.'

Hannick clambered over, found the first rungs of the ladder and began to climb. Obscua indicated that Daryo should go next. He climbed the edge of the battlements and felt Hannick's hand guide his feet to the rungs. Slowly he climbed down, his eyes focused on the rope ladder. Above him was Lassai. Every move of all four climbers shook the ladder but they remained silent. Hannick must have reached the ground, Daryo decided, as the ladder suddenly was pulled and held downwards. He reached down with his foot and Hannick hissed. 'Towards the gate, Walker. That is my gut.'

Daryo moved his foot to his right and put it down on solid ground. Hannick was hanging from the bottom rung, using his weight to hold the ladder down. Daryo drew the Horse and the Bear, reversing the Bear to defend himself.

Lassai jumped from the third or fourth rung and landed beside him. The Unseen slid up next to him as Hannick released the ladder. Hannick drew a sword, the Unseen had a pair of daggers held as Daryo held his swords, the Whisper had a long but narrow blade. The Unseen led the way, crawling with her shoulder against the wall. The ram slammed into the portcullis again. With every blow there was the cracking and splintering of wood.

'Now!' hissed the Unseen, already sliding into the shadows.

The Whisper tugged Daryo's arm and they ran for the front of the ram. A dozen men stood on either side of the trunk, swinging it with rope handles looped around the shaft. The first two never even saw the Whisper and the Walker before they died. Then the roars of anger came from the other end of the ram as the Unseen and the Veiled attacked from the other end. Daryo quickly realised that none of the soldiers manning the ram were armed. The slaughter took moments but the attack was attracting attention from the other attackers.

'Back to the ladder!' ordered Obscua.

The Whisper was fastest, racing back along the wall to the dangling rope ladder with Daryo close behind. Vidmarian soldiers were closing in on the ram. There was a sudden heavy thud as the ram fell from its slings. Hannick the Veiled ran out from the ram shelter as the first Vidmarians reached the ram. An arrow struck his back just as Daryo reached the ladder.

'Hannick!'

'Climb!' ordered the Whisper. Daryo paused and she shoved him. 'Climb! They did their job!'

Daryo screamed in anger and began to climb. Hannick had reached the ladder but another arrow struck him and he fell. The shouts of combat came from the ram, then silence. The dozens of Vidmarians surrounding the ram began to search the area. Daryo reached the top of the battlements and scrambled over. The Whisper followed, grabbed a torch and set fire to the rope ladder.

'Well done,' said the Brethren. 'The Unseen and the Veiled...'

'Are hiding under a rock so that the Fourth Goddess can't find them,' said the Whisper flatly. 'I need to get some rest.'

Daryo slumped to the floor, his back against the battlements. 'They were killed.'

'I am sorry,' said the man. 'Many of my Brethren have been killed too.'

'How many?'

'Eleven thus far.'

'Do you know how many Members?'

'I think more than forty now. And about the same apprentices.'

Daryo sighed. 'And more will die.'

'I fear you are right, Walker.' He pulled Daryo onto his feet. 'When did you last sleep?' Daryo shook his head. 'Come, you should get some sleep. I'll take you back to the Sanctuary.'

## Chapter 14

'To arms! To arms! Everyone to arms!'
Daryo was shaken awake by an apprentice. In nine days since the siege had started he had carved out his own part of one of the levels in the Sanctuary alongside the Ranger and the Shrewd. He seized the Horse and the Bear and joined the race out of the caves. The wall was breached. There was no time to put the plan into action. The Vidmarians were pouring over the collapsed wall. A stone from a Vidmarian catapult had hit the Temple Tower and it had come down like a tree, smashing down the section of wall that it had hit. Company after company of Vidmarians were scrambling over the rubble and into the Compound. Daryo joined the line of the Order assembling in front of the Wooden Fortress. At the very front, the Vanguard raised his axe.
'UNTIL I AM DISCHARGED BY DEATH!' he roared.
'Until I am discharged by death!' echoed the ranks.
'CHARGE!'
Daryo joined the charge. The Vidmarians were trying to form ranks but the Order's charge caught them unprepared. Daryo ducked a sword thrust, blocked the riposte with the Bear and slit the Vidmarian's throat with the Horse. He spun to counter the next attacker, kicked him in the stomach and the Brethren behind him finished him. A long spear nicked his side and Daryo turned, knocking it aside with the Horse and stabbing with the Bear. The spearman swiped sideways and Daryo blocked it. An arrow struck the spearman in the throat. The Member beside Daryo was cut down but the vanquisher walked straight onto the Horse's point. Daryo pulled his sword out and saw the Vanguard getting run down by a whole group of Vidmarians. The Order ranks were crumbling. Many people were being killed, the Order was being overwhelmed.
'Pull back! Pull back!' someone shouted.
The Order began to stream back towards the caves. A large group of Members had been cut off by the Vidmarians and they were retreating into the Castle Tower. Daryo cut down another Vidmarian as he backed towards the caves. The Order's catapult fired once more and then someone set a fire beneath it. Daryo was one of the last through the cave door before Herren Downe and two of his Brethren closed it, locking the door and then lowering the portcullis. Daryo followed the dispirited forces back into the Sanctuary. Behind them, Herren Downe was setting the traps in the cave tunnels. Daryo passed through the Threefold Door; the Brethren were silently setting the traps in the spaces between.

Daryo reached the Sanctuary and laid down his swords, checking the cut in his side. A Brethren healer came up.

'Let me see, Walker.' He complied, lifting his tunic to allow the woman to see it. The cut was several inches long but not deep. 'This will be fine.' She poured some wine on it and Daryo winced as she then bound it with a bandage and moved on. Daryo looked around. He counted less than a hundred. Most had been caught outside when the door shut. The thudding of blows on the outer door began to echo down the tunnels as the Vidmarians began trying to gain access. Several people were sobbing. Many were injured. Daryo gathered his swords, sheathed them and moved to help an apprentice lying nearby. She had taken a slash across the chest but again it was not deep. Daryo made a pad of cloth from a discarded tunic and pressed it against the wound to stem the blood.

'I am going to die,' she moaned as Daryo propped her head against his legs.

'Not this day,' he said, managing a smile. 'Not this day.'

'I am. We all are.'

'We have to believe that we will live.'

The girl started sobbing and Daryo could only hold her as the hammering on the outer door continued. Herren and Helli Downe came into the Sanctuary as a few went to man the archery slits in the Threefold Door for when the breakthrough came. Daryo noticed that Helli's hands were covered in blood. She saw him and clambered down to where Daryo was cradling the apprentice. Helli picked up a blanket and wiped her hands. She was crying silently.

'My uncle,' she said, barely audible over the crashing against the door.

'I am sorry, Helli. I saw the Vanguard slain.'

'My father tried to save the Calm but the Captain-General was killed too. The Shrewd and the Ranger are still fighting; they made it into the Castle.'

'The Arrow Nymph is dead,' said the apprentice through her sobs.

'I think many are.'

Herren Downe was making his way towards the tree at the centre of the Sanctuary, apparently counting the survivors, or perhaps simply seeing if he recognised anyone. Daryo saw Yi near the top of the cave but he seemed to have lost his arm. Another man below him had an awful wound to his face. The Trident was near the tree, bleeding heavily from the side of his head. Daryo could hear still hear the slamming against the door. It became like the beat of a heart. It pounded into the night. The torches began to burn out and someone organised the burning of surplus blankets and broken weapons along with small doses of flame oil. Provisions were taken out of their boxes and the boxes burned. The pounding continued. One apprentice went mad with the constant noise and started screaming and cursing. When someone tried to calm him, he seized a sword and began slashing wildly. Calmly, Herren Downe took a bow and shot the crazed boy down. The hammering was unceasing as the Vidmarians were frustrated by the outer portcullis and door. It became part of life, the constant dull thudding sound reverberating down the tunnel. A constant throbbing, a constant beating on the door, never hesitating. Daryo reclined under the branches of the tree. Darkness had come and gone. Light was starting to filter through the hole in the rock. Someone had tried to get close enough to the rock to secure a rope and climb into it but the tree was far too low compared to its life-giving cleft. Helli Downe had helped one of the healers create an injured ward near the top of the Sanctuary, the unwounded moved down to the lower shelves. Herren was the most senior official of the Order and had organised sentries in watches for the Threefold Door, shifts of hygiene workers to bury the waste and tasked shifts with checking and examining the food for anything rotten or spoiled. Daryo had spent a few hours checking through barrels of apples and potatoes for mould or decay. He wondered if it was worth rechecking, the potatoes were damp. Someone moaned from near the door and Daryo looked up. He had not heard any noises across the Sanctuary before. The pounding on the entrance had drowned out distant noises. The pounding had stopped.

'Herren!' he shouted, scrambling for Temma's Sword and his shield. 'Herren!'
Herren Downe had been asleep and was roused by his Brethren next to him. 'Walker?'
'Listen!'
'To what?'
'That is my question too!'
Herren Downe listened for several moments before he realised. 'The battering ram stopped. They broke through.'
A Member emerged from the tunnel, a bow in his hand. 'Commander Downe! The battering ram has stopped but there are no soldiers in the tunnel!'
By this point, many were scrambling up the levels of the Sanctuary. Herren Downe picked out three of his Brethren and four Members of the Order, including Daryo. Then they unlocked the innermost of the Threefold Door and began to unset the traps. It took an hour before the traps were released and the three doors opened. Daryo and the other Members led the way up through the tunnels. The door was still shut and apparently undamaged. There was a hatch up in the top. Daryo crouched and allowed Herren Downe to stand on his back to open the hatch. The portcullis had all but given way but there were no Vidmarians in sight.

'Looks like the world is ours,' said Herren, stepping off of Daryo and helping him up. The Commander of the Brethren unlocked the door and as he opened it the ruins of the portcullis collapsed. Herren drew his sword as he stepped outside. It was snowing again and scattered like fallen trees in the snow were dead Vidmarians. And very live Batribi. Dostan spread his arms in welcome. 'My kin. Welcome back into the air. I am sorry that we took so long to arrive. The assembly took much convincing.'

Only fifty-one Members had survived and every one was injured in some way from Daryo's nicked side and the Ranger's broken arm to Yi's lost arm. Thirty-nine apprentices were alive and most were unhurt. Only thirteen of the Brethren survived. The Batribi had arrived with nearly five hundred warriors. Most of the Vidmarians had fled when a horde of screaming Batribi, most bearing twin curved swords, had charged while the remaining Order warriors had fired volley after volley of arrows into the retreating forces. Nearly three thousand, a third of the attackers, had been killed. The rest had been routed into the forests south of the road. Only ten Batribi had been killed. The senior surviving Member of the Order, Kitsun the Shrewd, rallied his forces before the Wooden Fortress.

'We have lost hundreds,' he said, his voice hard. 'We have lost comrades, kin and loved ones. But this was victory in a battle. The enemy were surprised and fell back. They are commanded by men driven by greed and misguided vengeance. They will return and we will all die as our comrades did. We must disperse. Each of us must go their separate ways. There is a cluster of ours in Sinsebil, some may go there. There are Boskinians, Gourmini, Jaboens, Adacans, a Silver Islander, a Batribi among us. We must return to our peoples, or seek out new ones. We must cast away our Order, its symbols and our sword names. But I beg of you, my friends; do not cast aside your Promise. Remember your pledge to support those in need and defend those without the means to defend themselves. Remember that you are sworn to do this. Remain good, remain just, remain righteous until you are discharged by death. I pledge to you all to the end of my days, my sword and my service.' He raised his sword in salute.

All of those around him did the same and echoed his words in a solemn oath and prayer: 'My sword and my service.'

# Book 2- Seas and Roads
# Year 359 of the Empire Age of the Yashoun

## Chapter 15

Almost all of the little caravan were wounded, some were near death, all walked with the shuffling gait of a beaten and dispirited army. Thirteen men and ten women trudged through the light snow covering the forest road towards the Tember Pass between Gourmin and Jaboen.

At the head of the column was a young Batribi man wearing a dark green cloak over an old-fashioned, rust-coloured armoured jerkin, woollen leggings and low boots. The raised hood of his jerkin covered a thin but dense layer of curly black hair that was mirrored by a short patch of beard just below his mouth. The smoothness of the skin around round eyes and a wide nose showed his youth but the look in his eyes suggested a much older man. From the wide leather belt around his waist hung a curved Batribi sword and a short knife. On his back, the handles just visible over his shoulders, were two shorter, straight swords, their pommels moulded into animal heads. On his left arm was slung a shield with a single sword-over-shield device painted on it. At the pommel of the sword was illustrated a Yashoun milepost flanked by a harlequin and a blindfolded child.

He glanced back at the small column behind him and stopped to allow them to re-join him. The first to reach him was a young woman only a few seasons older than the Batribi, dark brown but bloodshot eyes looked at him from under heavy lids and thin eyebrows. She was clutching the shattered bottom half of a shield to her chest like a child with a doll; just visible between her arms was a golden cockerel holding a sword.

'Keep walking, Lana,' said the Batribi kindly.

The girl shook her head. 'It hurts.'

'I know. My wound hurts too. But if Sevant's army comes back, we cannot be anywhere near the Five Towers.'

'Three Towers.'

He shrugged. The Temple Tower had been demolished by missiles from a catapult, the escaping defenders had set fire to the ancient Wooden Fortress Tower before withdrawing. Most had gone east towards Aslon from the all-but destroyed home of the Order of the Shield and Sword. Only a small group was heading west for the Pass. Lana, once confident and personable, had become something of a mistreated child over the time of the siege, whinging and complaining about her lot, the life in her eyes had been

replaced by disillusionment and pain. Her wound was in her hip; an arrow had struck her sword belt, penetrating less than half an inch but right against the bone.
'Daryo, it hurts.'
'I know, Lana.' The Batribi, Daryo the Walker, had been caught just below the ribs on his left side, a gash nearly five inches long that was well bandaged. 'Just keep walking. We can rest soon.'
Most of the Batribi force that had broken the siege were covering the withdrawal but three were escorting the group towards the Pass. Another score had gone on ahead with the more seriously injured. One of the escorts was Daryo's kinsman Laulra and he nodded as he passed. He was concerned about Lana's injury and her mien and was keeping a close watch on the young woman. He and Lana led the column onwards and Daryo fell back into step alongside an elegant woman carrying a double-curved bow and a large, lumbering man with wild hair, a vicious laceration across his cheek and upper lip and carrying a mighty two-headed axe.
'Sofea, how is Lobrin?'
The stately, dark-haired woman glanced at her companion, who had a somewhat vacant and untroubled look despite his wound, the cold and his undoubtable tiredness.
'Lobrin? How do you feel?'
'I am walking. With the Racing Hart.'
'Yes, Lobrin. I am the Racing Hart.'
The big man, Lobrin, stopped sharply. The man walking behind him almost collided with the behemoth but sidestepped in time. Sofea the Racing Hart and Daryo were forced to stop too. Lobrin studied Sofea for a moment.
'You are the Racing Hart. I am walking with you.'
'Yes, Lobrin. How do you feel? Are you in pain?'
'I feel well. My feet hurt. I have walked a long way.'
'Yes, you have. Come, there is further yet to walk.'
Lobrin considered this for several heartbeats before resuming his former steady pace.
'He seems fine,' said Sofea, hurrying to get back alongside her charge and Daryo kept with her. 'It is sometimes hard to say. Lobrin is not skilled with words or feelings.'
Daryo knew that the large man had received a severe blow to the head as a youth but was in control of his actions and was a formidable warrior. Lobrin struggled with details and to answer questions but was quite capable of following instructions when they were made clear to him. His last instruction had been to walk with Sofea the Racing Hart and he was doing so, carrying his axe like a knapsack.

The road sloped up sharply as it emerged from the trees. Ahead was something Daryo had feared- the checkpoint that had been destroyed several weeks before had been reinstated and reinforced by dark red-and-brown-uniformed Vidmarian troops, flying the halved banners of the Vidmarian king and his ally Sevant the Stone, a former Member of the Order who had led the attack on the Five Towers. Daryo and Sofea exchanged looks as Laulra called a halt.

'We have to follow the road,' said Daryo. 'I know this route well.'
'We have numbers,' said Sofea. 'They may be wise and simply allow us through.'
'I doubt it,' said Daryo. 'We should get a closer look at their defences and numbers.'
Sofea nodded. 'Can you move silently?'
Daryo grimaced. 'I can try.'
'I will accompany you, my kin,' said Laulra. On his back were two curved swords similar to the one on Daryo's belt.
Daryo smiled. 'My thanks, Laulra.'
The two Batribi used the undergrowth and rocks along the road to hide their approach to the checkpoint. As they got within a hundred yards, Laulra reached up and drew one of his swords. Daryo drew his own curved blade, Temma's Sword, named for its previous owner, Laulra's cousin. They got within sixty yards without being seen but there was no cover to use further up the slope. Laulra glanced at Daryo.
'Too many,' he whispered.
'How did the others get through? The ones with the seriously wounded?'
'The checkpoint may have only just been established,' suggested Laulra.
There was evidence to support this theory: horses being unloaded, a tent being erected. Some weeks prior, Daryo had assisted in the destruction of the original checkpoint.
'Then they will have found the bodies of their comrades. They will be on alert and angry.'
Laulra nodded in agreement. 'How many do you count?'
'Eight... nine.... Nine.'
'I count twelve...'
Daryo quickly recounted. 'Ten.'
'Perhaps it is eleven.'
'We cannot turn about. Sevant the Stone's army will move up to take and search the Five Towers eventually. We cannot turn about. And some of those with us must reach our people's settlement.' Daryo's low whisper was urgent. 'They need care. We must fight through.'

Laulra nodded slowly. 'I fear so. We must see who among us can fight. Our people, the Hajma woman Sofea, the big man...'

'Lobrin will fight.'

'Come, we should return and plan our actions.'

They withdrew carefully and found the rest of the group concealed back in the trees, Lobrin leaning on his axe, Sofea with an arrow notched on her bowstring. Laulra and Daryo explained the situation to the group. Of the total of three Batribi and twenty Members of the Order, the three Batribi and five of the Members were fit to fight: Sofea, Lobrin, Daryo, Calmos the Lone Creature and Telmaza the Ford. It was agreed that the best with bows- Sofea, Calmos and the two Batribi brothers, Turyo and Krai- would fire into the encampment. They hoped that it would be enough with just the bows. If not, the others- Daryo, Laulra, Lobrin and Telmaza- would attack with blades. The injured were all sworn Members of the Order and capable of self-defence and the detachment were confident they would be safe if left alone. The attackers, Laulra in the lead, hurried back towards the checkpoint, weapons ready. The archers notched arrows when in range. Sofea took Lobrin's arm. 'Lobrin, you are going into battle. The red and brown uniforms are the enemy.'

'Battle?'

'Yes, Lobrin. What uniforms are the enemy?'

'Battle with the red and brown uniforms,' repeated Lobrin, an eager look on his face. 'I can kill them.'

'Yes. Stay with the Walker.'

'Stay with the Walker. Battle.'

'Yes, Lobrin.'

The big man seized his axe just below the head and at the base of its shaft. Daryo and Laulra led the attackers out of cover. As soon as those at the checkpoint saw the attackers coming, the concealed Order archers released their arrows. The range was long and the arrows caused more confusion than pain among the Vidmarians but it caused enough of a distraction for the melee fighters to close with their targets. Daryo caught the blow of a tall, bearded swordsman on his shield, shoved him back with it and opened the man's throat with the outside of his curved blade. Laulra and Telmaza the Ford both wielded two blades; Laulra bore twin curved Batribi blades, Telmaza had a short stabbing sword and a dirk. Lobrin fought without finesse but with a brutally violent method, his axe cleaving though armour, flesh, bone and wood with a vicious abandon. His comrades stayed a respectful distance as he remorselessly hacked through everything that approached him. Whenever there was enough space and a clear target, an arrow hissed out of the trees. A black-fletched Batribi arrow struck a Vidmarian in the throat and Daryo cut him down and the flare of battle died. Lobrin held his axe by the very bottom of its shaft and swung it down, decapitating a writhing, wounded opponent and cast around for another target.

'Done, Lobrin!' called Daryo. Sofea was sprinting up the slope, calling to Lobrin that the battle was finished. The big man lowered his axe, a look of profound disappointment on his face. Laulra had lost one of his blades, the blade had sheared near the hilt. He studied the truncated handle for a moment and then cast it away. There had been eleven Vidmarians, all had been felled. Telmaza and Calmos were confirming that all were dead; one man writhed and cried and Calmos's dirk was driven into his throat.

'Bring up the rest, brother,' Laulra said to Daryo. 'The less time we tarry here, the better.'

'I concur.' Daryo hurried back to where the wounded had been left. There were some nervous looks as he approached at a run but he smiled quickly. 'Come. The road is clear but we must be moving soon. We do not know when the checkpoint may be relieved or reinforced.'

One by one, the wounded stood, except for Guva the Spider's Sword. He had taken an arrow to the shoulder and nobody had been able to remove it. While the Vidmarian guards on the road had been despatched, Guva had crossed to the Next Kingdom with them. Daryo escorted the wounded back to the checkpoint, had a brief conversation with the three other Batribi and they sent the rest of the party on ahead. Daryo, Laulra, Krai and Turyo returned to where Guva's body lay and they excavated a shallow grave with their swords. Turyo surrendered his cloak to make a shroud and they laid the Gourmini in the earth, covering him with the loose earth and snow. Daryo raised Temma's Sword, point down in the salute of the Order.

Laulra intoned: 'We commend this man to the ground. We commit his spirit to the care of the Gods and Goddesses of the Pantheon. We commit his honour to the pages of history. We commit his memory to our minds. From the First God, we ask health. From the First Goddess, we ask bounty. From the Second God, we ask resolve. From the Second Goddess, we ask loyalty. From the Third God, we ask recovery. From the Third Goddess, we ask compassion. From the Fourth God, we ask security. From the Fourth Goddess, we ask that we shall one day stand alongside our comrade in her halls.'

Daryo recited the Order's Promise: 'With my heart, my mind and my honour, I promise to do my duty as a Member of the Order of the Shield and Sword and to follow orders as given on the authority of the Captain-General and his Aides. I swear my Shield and

Sword to the defence of the just, the righteous, the innocent and the weak. By this oath, I pledge my sword and my service until I am discharged by death.'
Guva's sword had been left on the ground nearby. Krai drove the point down into the mound of earth and the four Batribi stood in silent respect for several heartbeats.
'We should go,' said Turyo softly.
Daryo nodded slowly. 'We should. We must catch up with the others.'
They turned as one and jogged towards the road.

Dauern the Constant died just before the straggling group reached the entrance to the Pass. With the rocky ground too hard, too poor and too frozen to dig a grave in, the four Batribi collected stones to build a cairn over the body of the young Hajma. Barely ten seasons older than Daryo, one of the youngest Members of the Order, had been struck by falling masonry from the collapsing Temple Tower. His left arm and shoulder had been badly crushed and he had taken a blow to the head also. Daryo had a strange thought that burying him below a pile of stones was somewhat disrespectful but there was no other option. When the poor man was interred, Laulra again prayed over the grave and the party moved into the Pass; Daryo at the head, Krai and Turyo at the rear. The Tember Pass was the most usable connection between Gourmin and Jaboen but was barely ten feet wide in most places, unpaved and dangerous. As well as the natural hazards of landslides, avalanches and the poor road, the Peak Tribes ranged through the wild landscape attacking travellers. Daryo walked with Temma's Sword in his hand and his shield ready. Sofea was close behind, an arrow notched on her bowstring but the string relaxed, and Lobrin was mere feet behind her, trundling along like a content plough horse.
'Daryo! Daryo!' called someone from behind.
The Walker stopped and looked back. Calmos made his way through the group.
'We have to stop, Daryo. The Stricken is... as her name suggests.'
Daryo nodded and glanced up at the sky. The cloud was thick and threatening snow again. 'We cannot wait for long. It is well past midday. We must be clear of the Pass by sundown.'
'I understand.' Calmos went back down the line. Sofea returned her arrow to its quiver and sat on a rock. Lobrin stood over her, a looming presence. Daryo's fingers worked on the hilt of his sword.
'I should scout ahead,' he said finally.
Sofea nodded. 'Do not go too far, Walker.'
'I will stay within hearing.'

Daryo proceeded along the Pass and rounded the next corner. He paused and thought for a moment. The last time he had traversed the Pass, several Peak Tribesmen had been concealed in the rocky slopes to each side and had ambushed him and his companion. He had not seen any signs of them but Kitsun the Shrewd, travelling alongside him, had known they were there. Desperately he scanned the slopes looking for some suggestion of a concealed person but nothing was evident. He continued on for a few more yards and found a cart, it had thrown a wheel and any cargo it may have carried was long taken. Daryo hurried back to the others.

'There is a cart up ahead,' he announced. 'One wheel is gone but we could remount it. We could put the most seriously wounded on the cart so they do not have to walk.'
Sofea nodded. 'Excellent. A large cart?'
'Could take three or four sitting in it.'
Sofea called Calmos and Telmaza up, told Lobrin to accompany them and left the three Batribi to protect the remainder of the group. Lobrin's huge size and Daryo's strength from his youth as a smith's apprentice meant they were able to easily lift the cart. Calmos and Sofea slid the wheel back into place on the axle. Calmos identified a suitable piece of wood from which to fashion a pin and cut it down with his dirk before slotting it in. Sofea had a piece of rope in her pack, she tied it between the shafts to make it easier to pull. Lobrin and Daryo then pushed the cart back along the pathway. The three most seriously-injured were loaded onto the cart, two with bad wounds to their legs, the third with several arrow wounds in the chest and abdomen, and the same pair of draught-animals took the rope and hauled the cart onwards.

After two miles, Daryo was replaced in the shafts by Calmos. The indomitable Lobrin simply marched on, hardly noticing the weight of the cart and its occupants. The snow began to fall just after Sofea and Daryo persuaded Lobrin to rest and Laulra took station pulling the cart. Darkness came and the group were not out of the Pass. Daryo was very insistent that they continue and, at the minimum, clear the Pass itself. Laulra agreed and the small column pressed onwards, led by Krai with a lit torch and drawn sword. In the dark, the pass was even more difficult. Every divot became a pit, every rock became a boulder, each hole was a turned ankle. Whenever the person in the front stopped or slowed, it caused a landslide of collisions down the line of travellers. Colliding with Lobrin from behind was akin to walking into a stone wall. Having him run into the back of one was similar to being run down by a horse. Soon the only person that would suffer to have Lobrin walk behind them was Krai, who continued to lead the group despite the hazards with a brand of determined cheer that none of the others were able to assimilate.

Finally, well after dark, they left the Pass and found a suitable clearing among the forest of evergreen trees and made a makeshift camp. Daryo drew second watch, woke Telmaza at the end of it and made himself a makeshift shelter under the low branches of a tree with a windfall branch before wrapping himself in a blanket and going to sleep.

# Chapter 16

The roar was of anger, fury and challenge. Daryo threw off his blanket and groped out of his shelter in the lee of a huge tree. He had slept with the hilt of the Horse in his hand and he seized the Bear as he emerged, reversing it ready to protect himself. Lobrin was roaring, stood over a hollow part-covered in branches. Daryo remembered that Telmaza, Sofea and Lana had been sleeping in it. He looked around the clearing and then saw the blood under the cart- the three seriously injured from the cart had been sleeping under their transport.

'Hart!' bellowed Lobrin. 'HART! HART!'

'Peak Tribesmen! No doubting!' Laulra called to Daryo over the din, examining some footprints nearby. 'Known to carry off women for breeding!'

'HART! HART!'

'Lobrin! Silence!' barked Krai, crouching beside the cart. 'Three dead!'

'HART! HART! HART!'

'Lobrin!' moaned Daryo, hurrying to check elsewhere. The other eleven had apparently been well-hidden and were unharmed and unmolested. Turyo joined Laulra.

'HART!'

Daryo hurried across to the big man and seized his arms. 'Lobrin! The Hart has gone away! She will come back! Who else did she say to follow?'

Lobrin went silent for a moment. 'Walker. And Lone Creature. And Telmaza. And tall dark man.' The tallest of the Batribi was Laulra by almost a head.

'Then stay with the Lone Creature. The tall dark man and I will go and meet the Racing Hart and bring her back. Yes?'

'Yes. Hart will come back.'

'Yes, she will. I will bring her back.'

'That is good.'

'Do as Lone Creature says.'

'Yes, Walker.'

Daryo smiled at the big warrior and then joined his kinsman. 'What do you think, my brother?'

Laulra had moved to another set of tracks. 'At least six. Maybe as many as ten. Approached from the north-west. Who was on guard?'

'It must have been last watch,' said Krai. 'I woke Telmaza for last watch.'

'They cannot be more than a few hours ahead then,' said Turyo, joining them.

'We have to get them back,' said Daryo, in a tone that brooked no argument.

Laulra nodded. The brothers deferred to him and looked for instruction. Laulra took several long, slow breaths to think. 'Krai, Turyo, take the rest of the wounded, Lobrin and Calmos. Go to our people at Stannia Lake. Do not stop until you get there. Swear on a God.'

'On the Second Goddess, we swear,' said Turyo immediately.

'Daryo and I will pursue the tribesmen,' Laulra continued. 'I can track them, Daryo is best with a blade and probably fastest on his feet.'

Daryo nodded his assent. 'We should take bows as well.'

'I agree.'

Daryo went and relayed this to Calmos and Tohmanz the Stricken, who was the least wounded of the others. Reluctantly they agreed and Calmos gave Daryo Sofea's bow and quiver, which had been left by her blanket. Lobrin was persuaded to follow Calmos. Laulra was given a Batribi bow, with bronze finials on the tips, by Krai and, wordlessly, Laulra and Daryo began tracking their lost comrades.

Fortunately, Laulra was an excellent tracker and the Peak Tribesmen were not known for subtlety. Their tracks were relatively easy to follow, especially as after about a mile, there were long, deep drag marks suggesting that they were having to tow one of their captives for periods because she could not or would not walk. Laulra paused at a small stream. He pointed silently to a shred of cloth on a spiky shrub and then saw a boot by the water. Branded onto the sole was an Order mark. The boot was a very small size, suggesting Lana. On some weeds on the far side was a smear of blood. An accompanying torn section of cloth was alongside, a small strip from a sleeve or leg of a garment. All of the tracks turned slightly north. Laulra hurried onwards. At one point, he reached for an arrow but then decided not, returned it to the quiver and hurried forwards, Daryo close behind. They wound through the trees following the tracks but Daryo noticed that Laulra was having more difficulty. The trees were progressively larger and closer together, there was no underbrush to disturb and the ground was hardened by the cold. Several times Laulra told Daryo to wait and scouted ahead for more tracks before returning and beckoning the younger man on.

The fourth time it happened, Laulra's signal was much more urgent and Daryo hurried to reach him. Laulra put a finger to his own ear to indicate Daryo should listen. Daryo did so but heard nothing. Laulra raised the finger in the air to signal patience and then Daryo did indeed hear voices; they sounded like two people arguing, to the west of their last direction. Laulra nodded, smiled grimly and notched an arrow. Preferring blades, Daryo drew Temma's Sword and followed Laulra on towards the noise. Cresting a ridge,

Laulra suddenly stopped and knelt down slowly. Daryo did the same and crawled alongside. Down a short but steep slope was a small clearing. The three Members of the Order were laid face down on the ground, their arms tied to poles stretched across their shoulders. Lana and Sofea had been gagged with cloth, Telmaza looked to have been knocked senseless. Two of the fur-clad, unkempt Peak Tribesmen were arguing, the thinner one gesturing repeatedly to the north, the other disagreeing. Five other Tribesmen were stood around, some holding rough swords, one holding a stone axe, the thinner disputant had a spear with an iron point on each end. Sofea tried to get up and the spearman hit her viciously across the back with his spear. Daryo lunged forwards but Laulra restrained him swiftly.
'Patience, my brother,' he muttered. 'Patience, consideration.' He reached for his arrows, studying the situation. 'I cannot see any behind the man with the spear. Go around to the right-' he pointed '-wait for my first arrow. Protect the captives, let me deal with the rest.'
Daryo nodded and slipped away, keeping as low to the ground as he could with sword and shield. He found a shallower slope and scrambled down, using the point of Temma's Sword to aid his balance as he descended. He turned into towards the captives and caught sight of a Tribesman, still watching his arguing companions, through the trees. He glanced back up the slope and saw Laulra draw his bow. Daryo broke into a run. The first arrow struck the spearman's companion in the side just below the ribs. The second struck the same man in the side of the neck and he fell heavily onto Lana. Daryo smashed through a small sapling and decapitated the spearman in a simple swipe and a fountain of blood. The first Tribesman to respond with a bellow and a charge was shot down by Laulra. One Tribesman had a sling and was reaching for a stone when Laulra shot him. Only one of the remaining Tribesmen charged Daryo, a huge but rough sword swinging. Daryo parried the blow with his shield, stepped around his assailant, swung Temma's Sword at the man's back but it was caught by the Tribesman's sword. Daryo pushed forwards, his blade slid down the other and he shoved the other blade away with his own. He put his shield ready to protect himself but Laulra's next arrow struck his opponent in the back of the neck, nearly passing out of his throat. The Tribesman coughed bloodily and crumpled into a heap at Daryo's feet. Daryo stepped back and quickly slit Sofea's bonds. Sofea pulled her gag out and moved to help Lana. Daryo tried to rouse Telmaza. He turned her onto her back, her bottom lip and nose were bloodied and there was a red-purple bruise above her left eye and another on her left cheekbone. The breath through her nose was ragged and the pulse of her heart through her chest was exceptionally fast. Laulra hurried down the slope to them and

helped Sofea to free Lana and clear her mouth. Lana was moaning incoherently and tears ran down her face. The bindings on her wrists had cut into the skin leaving deep, bleeding grooves.
'Are you wounded, Sofea?' Daryo asked, carefully checking Telmaza for other injuries. She had not been bound as tightly or as extensively as the other two but Daryo suspected the blows to her face and head would be more injurious. Laulra confirmed that Lana was not in immediate danger of death and then joined Daryo in checking Telmaza. He looked grim.
'The blow to the front of the head... that looks serious,' he said. 'She needs a healer. Find two long branches and one short, we can make a sled.'
Daryo eased Telmaza's shoulders back to the ground, sprang up and hurried away but Laulra swiftly called him back.
'We were not fast enough,' he said simply. 'She has passed.'
Daryo stifled a gasp. 'We must bury her.'
Laulra and Daryo scraped a shallow grave with the swords of the Peak Tribesmen and laid Telmaza in it. They then piled the corpses of the Tribesmen and burned them. Laulra took Lana's hand tenderly in his and led her like a child through the trees, Sofea and Daryo behind them.

They had to stop when the light failed. Lana stopped, sat against a tree and was asleep. Sofea was almost senseless by that time and fell asleep quickly. Laulra and Daryo stayed awake through the night, naked swords on their laps, sat either side of a small fire facing in opposite directions. As soon as there was sufficient light, they roused a drowsy Sofea and an uncooperative Lana and began to walk again, Laulra again leading Lana by the hand. After nearly eight miles, Laulra turned south, joining a narrow dirt cart track that wound through the trees. In places, forks presented themselves with no signposts but Laulra seemed to unerringly know which option to take. They passed what looked like a rocky outcrop until Daryo saw a pair of eyes studying them from within the skilful disguise. The head that the eyes were within inclined very slightly when they saw Daryo looking. A Batribi sentry.
'Laulra? We are near the lake?'
'Yes. This is the very edge of the watch line. There is a more overt line closer to the settlement as well as the ring of sentries around the settlement itself. We are very conscious of how dangerous the Vidmarians may be to us.'

The more overt line was a wood and canvas shelter with two Batribi sentries just out of the trees. From there, the track became a better roadway down to the cluster of tents and ramshackle buildings alongside the lake.
Laulra smiled. 'Home.'

The Batribi healers had several large versions of the normal Batribi conical *kaff* tent as their base with blue banners hung above each entrance. There were nearly thirty Members of the Order of the Shield and Sword in various states of injury. Lana's physical wounds were relatively minor but her mental injuries seemed severe; in contrast, Dava the Three Crystals had a severe and deep laceration to his face and neck that had nearly killed him and Tenuso the Frayed had an arrow in the chest that nobody could remove. He was in a deep sleep due to some concoction of the healers', when he awoke someone would have to tell him that his wife, Emrea the Ascent, had been killed when the Temple Tower collapsed. When Lobrin saw the Racing Hart, he gave her an almost bone-crushing embrace and it took five Batribi and Sofea's protestations for him to release her.
A healer eventually managed to seat Daryo on a stool and help him to remove his jerkin and the shirt beneath. The wound in his side was healing neatly. The healer found some clean bandage cloth, rebound the wound and suggested that Daryo take at least a full day to rest. Daryo decided that he was too tired to argue and he was found a hammock in a wooden building nearby. Despite it being just after noon and so cold as to be paralysing, Daryo slept.

'Master Daryo? Master Daryo?'
Daryo woke, feeling as if he was climbing from the bottom of a long staircase. The light pierced his eyes painfully.
'Master Daryo? I am very sorry to wake you.'
Daryo opened his eyes and saw a girl only a few seasons younger than him standing over him. 'Is there anything wrong?'
'I do not know, sir. My cousin Dostan asked that I wake you.'
'Dostan?' Dostan, the leader of Daryo's clan, had led the Batribi force that had relieved the siege of the Five Towers. He had been commanding the Batribi that had remained screening the Order's withdrawal and dispersion.
'Yes, Master Daryo. He returned early this morning.'
'What time is it?'
'Shortly before noon.'

Daryo coughed and sat up quickly. He had slept almost an entire day. 'My thanks. Where is he?'

'He was going to the Assembly site and then the temple.'

'Again, my thanks.'

The girl smiled and departed. Daryo had only removed his boots and weapons before sleeping, he quickly stamped into his boots and buckled his sword belt. The building he was sleeping in was full of Members of the Order and Batribi warriors, some sleeping on straw mattresses, others in hammocks, and he had to take great care as he left not to jostle or kick any sleepers. The day was clear and cold enough to make the muscles of his back tighten in protest. The temple was the only building in the small Batribi settlement that was any larger than the forest of *kaffa* a large log-built building with a wooden dome that was not-quite complete; two sides of nine of the dome were still under construction and a hole in the top of it would serve as a chimney. With the open sides, the whole dome was doing the task. The doors were closed but unlocked, Daryo slipped inside. A large fire was burning in a stone ring in the centre, making the temple warm and inviting. The smoke rose out of a hole in the ceiling into the dome. Around the fire were carved wooden symbols of the Pantheon: a tree, a wheatsheaf, a spear, a flame, a ten-pointed star, a crystal, an anvil and an orb representing the dead moon. Dostan had laid his sword against the pedestal of the Second God's spear and was sat on one of the log rings that served as seats. Daryo stood back by the door until Dostan had finished his prayers and looked up.

'Daryo, come, sit.'

Daryo drew Temma's Sword and laid it against the pedestal alongside Dostan's blade before sitting next to his adoptive kinsman. 'I am pleased to see you unhurt, Dostan.'

'Ramini told me you were injured.'

'A minor wound, almost healed.'

'That is good news. The Five Towers is empty. All of the Members of the Order and the Brethren have escaped successfully. All but the very last of our people are safely away as well. We are expecting the last party to return here very soon.'

'What if the Vidmarians attack the settlement?'

Dostan shrugged. 'Then our people shall walk again, as our people have always done. We shall return to the roads. It is already death to be within Vidmaria, there will simply be a larger area that is not passable to us.'

'I would hate to be the cause of the breakdown of the settlement.'

'You are not the cause, my brother. The Assembly of Clans chose to intervene. Anything that comes down upon us, we bring down on ourselves.'

Daryo smiled thinly and Dostan clapped him on the shoulder. He addressed Daryo as brother but felt an almost-paternal feeling towards the younger man.

'I know of no threat that the Batribi people cannot face down, you could stay with us and aid us in our work to build the settlement.'

Daryo looked at him. 'I do not know what I wish to do. I had just started a new and exciting adventure and it has been curtailed. I think I would like to put my name to use, walk the roads, learn what I can, help those that need it, explore the land.'

Dostan nodded. 'I have a small *kaff* near mine that is unoccupied. Only some stores are kept there. I will set up a canvas bed for you in there. No Batribi is turned away from the settlement and no kin of mine will be dismissed either. Stay for as short or long a time as you wish. If you wish tasks to do or responsibilities in the settlement, arrangements can be made.' Dostan stood up and retrieved his blade. 'Any time you need me, night or day, rain or snow, I am at your call, my brother.'

'My thanks. Thanks for everything you have done, Dostan.' Daryo stood, picked up his blade and held it by the hilt, point down, the pommel at eye level. 'My sword and my service, my brother.'

Daryo spent several days dividing his time between the Members of the Order being cared for by the Batribi healers and the settlement's guard force. Dava the Three Crystals and Jurio the Gate were the most severely hurt but the healers were convinced that neither was in danger of death. Each day that Daryo was at the settlement by the icy Stannia Lake, a few more Members of the Order left for their own destinations. On the second day, Sofea the Racing Hart and Lobrin the Harsh departed. They intended to return across the Tember Pass and sneak through to Allesbury in Gourmin. Daryo was most surprised when Lana came to bid him farewell as she was returning to her family in Boskinia. Her mind had recovered from its shocked stupor and her wound was well on the mend. The healers had given her permission to travel. She was joining a group that were travelling north into Jaboen. She was going to the port of Nalb, then she would take a ship from Nalb to Sitak in Gourmin and follow the road along the Armynyan border and cross into Boskinia from the east. It was a long, convoluted route but necessary to avoid the Vidmarian army in southern Gourmin that had attacked the Five Towers. She embraced Daryo warmly, mounted her pony and she, four other Members and an escort of three Batribi headed north from the lake settlement. Daryo resumed his patrol of the settlement's perimeter. Sundown came and he was relieved by another and he returned to his *kaff*.

The next day seemed somewhat empty. The only Members of the Order remaining were Dava, Jurio and Tessio the Red Road, too badly hurt to move. Dava had the vicious slash on his cheek and neck, Jurio had taken several arrows in the back and Tessio had been struck and burned by a flaming arrow in the arm and the burn was more serious than the puncture. Daryo had no duty on the perimeter watch and the injured Members of the Order were in sleeps brought on by the healers' potions. A hunting party, organised by Krai and Turyo, provided an afternoon's distraction as six Batribi crept through the forests on the far side of the lake. Although not confident in shooting with bow, Daryo shot a boar. Krai claimed a deer and several rabbits, Turyo a rabbit and one of the others, a woman named Vimma, shot a particularly huge boar and hit a deer, which escaped the hunters even though wounded. The party returned with a significant amount of meat on an improvised sled and delivered them to the smokehouse on the edge of the town for preservation and the use of the town.

He visited the makeshift forge and spent some time making use of his apprentice's training as a blacksmith, repairing and sharpening a few blades, a small woodsman's axe and a saw. Dostan came past and offered his own sword for attention. Daryo set to sharpening at the grindstone, watched by Dostan.

'We could surely find you a position in the forge if you wish, Daryo.'

Daryo glanced up. 'I think not.'

'No?'

'I was an apprentice for nearly ten seasons. The smith, Vehllal, thought I had talent but I would be happier doing the work that the Order did. I think it may be time for me to leave the settlement.'

Dostan nodded. 'I thought it may be. When will you go?'

'With the dawn.'

'Then tonight we shall have the clan join for a meal and give you a farewell in the old fashion of our people.'

'I would be happier simply leaving with my own company.'

Dostan smiled. 'I shall see you before you leave, my brother.'

'My thanks.'

Dostan left Daryo in the forge. Daryo finished working on the small pile of blades and then began sharpening arrow heads. A cooking cauldron had been dented and he spent a good part of the afternoon returning it to perfect shape. After the cauldron, he moved on to some damaged chain. It was almost dark when he decided to stop. The settlement's forgemaster had long left so Daryo damped down the fire before leaving. He slipped between two rows of *kaffa*, walked around the temple and stopped completely as he was

greeted by a roaring fire in front of Dostan's *kaff*. Nearly forty men and women and their children were sat around the fire, two sheep were being cooked on the blaze and there were jugs of drink being passed around. Dostan emerged from the small throng, grinning broadly.
'I am sorry, brother. I lit a small fire in front of my *kaff* and soon all of the clan was around it.'
Daryo laughed despite himself. 'I see I have no option in my leaving meal.'
'Not as the fire is right behind your bed. It may keep you awake this night. Join us.'
Daryo nodded. 'I would be honoured.'

The lamb was superbly succulent and accompanied by fire-roasted potatoes, onions fried in butter and vast amounts of the strong Batribi ale that Dostan called *cairus*. All of those present were blood kin of Dostan and Laulra in some fashion- Temma, the large, hairy man named Tuai was Dostan's cousin; Turyo and Krai were nephews by marriage; Setini, a mother of seven children, was a cousin by marriage; Vralra was her eldest son and father to four daughters of less than ten summers. The evening was convivial and even the children were present late into the night. By an hour before midnight, the clan of Dostan were sat around the fire in a loose circle, replete with food and drink and warmed by the white glow of the embers that could be felt twenty yards away. As the conversation died down, Dostan started thumping his fist against a box rhythmically. Soon all the assemblage were keeping the rhythm, some clapping their hands together, some slapping their knees or stamping their feet, one couple had his hand cupped and her fist tapping into it. Daryo recognised that this was the inevitable prelude to the Verse, an age-old Batribi custom, a spoken-word recitation with a chorus and the stanzas improvised by the speaker. Dostan began:
'*Our people walk and walk again,*
*This fate of ours is each one's bane,*
*To sleep beneath the stars each night,*
*To walk and walk again in flight.*'
'*The fire's growth stands for our clan,*
*The light is bright, heat warms our hands,*
*Fire warms the skin and clan the heart,*
*Together as one, even as we part.*'
The clan joined the chorus again:
'*Our people walk and walk again,*
*This fate of ours is each one's bane,*

*To sleep beneath the stars each night,*
*To walk and walk again in flight.'*
Vralra spoke next:
*'The path we walked was long and steep,*
*But some traditions we all must keep,*
*The Verse, the Faith, the tales we say,*
*Are surely always the Batribi way.'*
*'Our people walk and walk again,*
*This fate of ours is each one's bane,*
*To sleep beneath the stars each night,*
*To walk and walk again in flight.'*
A young boy had stood at the far side of the fire from Daryo.
*'My first words at fire said,*
*The words I thought of in my head,*
*My mother speaks when the Verse is done,*
*A way that is followed by her son.'*
The chorus was delayed by a beat as there was a murmur of approval at the boy's first words of the Verse.
*'Our people walk and walk again,*
*This fate of ours is each one's bane,*
*To sleep beneath the stars each night,*
*To walk and walk again in flight.'*
The next contributor was a woman, Temma, for whom Daryo's sword was named:
*'The walk is done, the town grows on,*
*Batribi people with buildings are strong,*
*The old ways last despite the new,*
*Carried as always by the Batribi few.'*
*'Our people walk and walk again,*
*This fate of ours is each one's bane,*
*To sleep beneath the stars each night,*
*To walk and walk again in flight.'*
The Verse finished as no new speaker contributed and gradually the pulsing beat faded. Daryo looked around at the gathered clan. Some of the young had drifted into sleep, as had an elder. A young couple were whispering together, giggling like children and exchanging kisses. Small knots of people were holding private conversations, others were drifting away towards their beds. They were not blood by birth, he knew nothing of his

true parents or clan, but he had been made kin by Dostan and treated as such by Dostan's father Stai. The kin of Dostan were the closest Daryo had to a family and he knew he would miss them greatly.

Inauspiciously for travelling, the morning's rain was persistent and cold. Daryo dressed quickly: fresh underclothes and stockings, a thick black linen shirt and leggings, next his armoured jerkin and boots. He buckled his sword belt and checked Temma's Sword from pommel to tip before sheathing it. Stai's Twin Sword's harness went on next and the Horse and the Bear were both checked thoroughly before returning to their own sleeves, their hilts just protruding above Daryo's shoulders, the rest hidden when he put on a black hooded cloak. Dostan had made sure that a full pack was ready and this went on top of the cloak. Daryo checked that he had left none of his possessions in the conical *kaff* tent and then ducked out into the rain. Standing a short distance away, he could see a figure shrouded in the murky lakeside air. Knowing it would be Dostan, Daryo drew Temma's Sword and raised it, point down, in salute. 'My sword and my service, my brother!'
Dostan raised a hand in farewell. 'Walk lightly, brother! Gods' Guidance to you.'
'And to you. Until we meet again.' Daryo sheathed his sword, shifted the weight of his pack slightly and turned north.

## Chapter 17

The rain did not abate. Daryo felt the pathway get wetter and less passable with every mile. The first town he would come to, as he joined the road from the Tember Pass and turned west, would be Lalbi; but Lalbi was known for its discomfort and sometimes hostility towards Batribi people. The area around Stannia Lake where the Batribi town had been established was perfect in almost every respect but that its nearest established neighbour was the least welcoming of Jaboen towns. The dilemma this presented was that Daryo knew that the next-nearest towns, Hef and Three Rivers, were another day's walk on the other side of Lalbi. As he continued west, downhill, Daryo was trying to think of a way of finding warm and secure shelter overnight. In the meantime, he continued to walk.

The rain was increasingly intense, shrouding the hilly forests below the Tember Pass is a grey haze of moisture. The trees dripped their loads with greater intensity in the gusting wind that seemed to be channelled down the Pass. The noise of the rain, the constant spattering, married with rush of the wind and the creak of the pine trees were an unceasing and strangely monotonous noise. The road, switching back down the hill in wide, meandering curves was gradually becoming a stream. Daryo wondered if it was wiser to return to his bed in the *kaff*, let the skies clear and then restart his journey but every step made it more difficult to turn around. Lalbi was hidden from view by the murk and Daryo simply had to continue walking until the raised town walls came into view above the trees. Thinking as he approached, Daryo remembered somewhere he thought he may be able to get sanctuary. The Beacon Inn was against the deeper cliff on the west side of the town, a thatch-roofed stone building with a small stable nearby. Daryo ducked inside the low door. The inn was deserted but for the proprietor- short and squat with a poorly-closed scar.

'You should not be here, Batribi,' he called as Daryo entered. 'Lalbi does not welcome your sort.'

'You welcome my sort,' said Daryo. He showed the device on his shield. 'My blade is sharp but my eye is sharper.'

The other studied him for a long time and suddenly had his inspiration. 'You are the boy that came? Sent by the Ranger, collected by Kitsun?'

'I am.'

The innkeeper gave a short bow. 'Welcome as ever. Come, I will open the hidden room for you.'

Below the inn, concealed behind a wine cask, was a concealed room with a bed, table and chairs, a fireplace and a small armoury lined one wall although it was less well-stocked than on Daryo's first visit. The innkeeper lit a fire and promised Daryo a meal. Daryo stripped off his wet clothes and hung them to dry in front of the fire below an olive green banner of the Order. Daryo sat himself at the table and closed his eyes. The innkeeper returned with bread, cheese and apples.
'My thanks... Adil?'
'Indeed.'
'I am Daryo the Walker, kin of Dostan.'
'You are a Member now, you spoke your Promise. Is it true, the rumours? The Order fell?'
'It did. Sevant the Stone led a Vidmarian army against the Order. Some escaped, some survived, including Kitsun and Vilya, but many died.' Adil nodded sadly but said nothing. 'I will rest a while and be on my way.'
'Where are you heading to?' asked Adil.
'I have no destination in mind. Westwards.'
'Soon?'
'I have no cause to delay.'
'You can stay as long as you wish.'
'My thanks. But I shall be gone by dawn.'
'If that is your wish. Excuse me, I have work to do.'
'Of course.'

Something was awry when Daryo woke. The fire was barely giving light, the candle on the table had been extinguished. The smell of damp and fire smoke was overwhelmed by that of men.
'He fell asleep.' A deep voice, near the door.
'He trusted the fat innkeeper,' said another voice, closer to the fire.
'Never trust a tavernier. Kill him here?'
'No, the traitor wants to see prisoners. Just make sure he does not wake for a while.'
A dark shape loomed over Daryo. Daryo had moments to think. He threw himself off of the bed into the figure beside the bed. His legs struck his assailant at about the knees, knocking the dark figure back with a yell of surprise. Daryo rolled quickly to his hands and knees and flung himself to the fireplace. Propped against the side of the hearth was Temma's Sword. He seized the sheathed blade and swung around just in time to block a swingeing slash with an axe. Daryo kicked out at the axeman's shins and threw himself forwards. By the shouts, there were at least two more assailants in the room but Daryo

had reversed the surprise and had Temma's Sword unsheathed. Without looking, he slashed outwards and downwards and screams told him that he had connected with both attackers. A shadow lunged from near the door but straight onto the point of Temma's Sword. As Daryo retracted his blade, there was a searing, penetration pain as a blade was driven into his side, just at the hip bone. In the near darkness, he slashed downwards until Temma's Sword bit into bone and the blade fell. The fourth attacker was fleeing. Daryo decided it prudent to let him go. He found the candle and relit it from the embers of the fire. The three assailants were wearing the brown uniforms of the Vidmarian army. Two were definitely dead, the third was groping for his sword. Daryo took a deep breath and slit the man's throat. Quickly, he gathered his effects and, without bothering to dress properly, burst out of the hidden room's door. The wine cellar was beginning to fill with smoke; the escaping soldier had tried to compensate for his lack of personal bravery by burning the inn with Daryo in it. Daryo hurried up the cellar steps into the inn's hall. Adil the innkeeper was dead in the centre of the floor, a single arrow in his chest. The chairs had been thrown into the fireplace and the inferno was growing. Daryo stamped into his boots quickly, swung his bag over his back and opened the front door only as far as necessary to escape. A crowd was beginning to form, buckets being carried to try and extinguish the fire that was starting to take hold on the wall behind the fireplace and the roof at the far side of the inn where a torch had been put to the straw. Nobody saw the dark-clothed, dark-skinned Batribi slip away into the night.

Daryo stopped after nearly half a mile, the wound in his hip felt like a flame held to his skin, the inside of his skull was pounding like a war drum and the taste of smoke lingered in the back of his throat. He stopped and found shelter under a pine tree that had fell against a rocky outcrop. Within a short period, he had a small fire built and used the light to inspect the wound. It was a ragged hole, almost as far across as his thumb was long. The blood was oozing from it rather than pumping and he knew that this was the better of the two possibilities. He dug into his pack, found a shirt and ripped a piece to cover the wound. He then used a bandage strip to tie it in place but the position was awkward, just above his sword belt. As he stood, the sword belt dug against the pad over the wound. It was uncomfortable at best but there was no option. Aware of the coldness of the night, he dressed properly including his twin swords, cloak and pack and began to walk.

The constant off and on pressure on the improvised dressing covering the wound soon became more than uncomfortable. With every step, Daryo felt as if the Vidmarian soldier's blade was piercing his skin again. Without any way of telling his direction, he walked blindly, using the crescent moon as a guidepost. The ground was particularly uneven but still sloping downhill overall, suggesting at least that he was not heading north or east. After three miles, he was forced to stop and rest. He felt under his shirt and found his improvised pad sodden with blood. Another one was made from the same spare shirt, the bandage retied and he continued slowly through the darkness.

Daryo estimated that he was only six miles from Lalbi when the sun came up and told him that he was walking almost exactly west. With light to see by, Daryo stopped again and examined his wound. It was being kept open by the pressure of the sword belt, on and off with each and every step and the new dressing was black with blood. He threw it away, tore the sleeve from his spare shirt, folded it into a new dressing pad and pressed it against the wound, wincing as he did so. The bandage strip was wet where it had been against the dressing pad so it was retied in a slightly different position. With no wish to further aggravate the injury, Daryo removed Temma's Sword from its sheath and fastened the sword belt around his pack tightly so that the sheath hung on the back. Holding Temma's Sword, he decided to continue west and hope to join the road to Three Rivers.

A full day and a night later and Daryo had been unable to find the road. Convinced that he was correct, he continued to walk. His wound was better, not bleeding as profusely, but its location on his hip meant that eventually it reopened with walking. The only option, Daryo knew, would be to find some kind of permanent shelter and wait for it to heal but there was nowhere suitable. He had come through the forests around Lalbi and was instead traversing the rough and rocky heathland that stood east of the Riy River. Frequent small streams had left his boots and feet somewhat damp, if not wet, and a harsh southern wind kept the air cold. A stop in the night to sleep had been disturbed, uncomfortable and brief so the Walker had pushed on. A pause to drink from a stream had been troublesome when he had almost fell when standing up. After that, Daryo had not stopped despite his thirst.
*The pain is too much. The blood is thin and spent. Stop and lay down.*
Daryo tried to ignore the pain. He knew little of blood other than its colour but knew that to stop would be dangerous.
*The cold is intense. Stop, build a fire, get some sleep.*
The cold was being kept at bay by his constantly moving legs, the weight of the pack on his shoulders, the feel of Temma's Sword in his hands.

*The pack is heavy. Leave it. The swords are heavy. Leave them. The shield is heavy. Leave it.*
The pack contained vital items to his survival. The swords were gifts and may be needed. The shield was a gift and may be needed too.
*The road is not there. Turn back. Go back and hide in the town.*
The road was west of Lalbi. To turn back would be to undo two days and nights of walking to return to a hostile and possible dangerous town for no gain.
*There is a cave ahead, sit, build a fire, rest.*
The cave was as stony ledge, barely three feet high and less deep. It ran north to south and would act as a funnel for the wind.
*There is nothing ahead. Turn back.*
There is Three Rivers ahead. Warmth, food, a healer.
*There are healers at the Batribi settlement. The clan would have plenty of food and firewood to share. You would be welcomed and nursed and be given time to heal.*
The settlement by the lake was three day's march in the opposite direction. The clan would care for him though and the *kaffa* were warm and food plentiful.
*Turn back. The argument is no argument. Turn and go back to the lake.*
Daryo stopped, shifted his grip on Temma's Sword and turned to face east. Below the pointed peak of one of the mountains was Stannia Lake. Daryo turned west again, resolutely. 'Stop talking to me, Darkest Goddess. I have no wish to join the Harlequin just yet.'

*Stop walking, Daryo. Stop walking. Stop here. This place is good. Lay down. Stop here and lay down. Your body needs rest. Your mind needs rest. Stop here and lay down. Lay down. The ground is softer than it looks, is it not? That must feel better than walking. The burning of your wound. The beating pain in your skull. The ache of your legs and feet. They all go away when you lay down.*
Daryo threw down his sword and felt himself sink to his knees.
*Lay down. The Harlequin, the Calm, the Blind, your mother, they all stand at my side. They all wait for you to join them. Lay down and rest. Close your eyes and be with them. Join the ranks of those who serve the dead moon.*
Daryo shrugged his pack off, feeling the welts in his shoulders scream in protest. He lay down to one side.
*Close your eyes, wounded warrior. Let it come as sleep.*
Closing his eyes was a relief. The world was closed away, the pain in his legs and hip reduced from shouts to whispers and the darkness of rest was as inviting as anything he had ever known.

The light was painful. The light was unnatural and unwanted. He wanted to reach out and destroy the light but he could not lift his arms. Next came the heat. The heat was worse than the light. The heat was causing him to sweat and pant for breath. The heat was suffocating and oppressive and he was glad when the darkness took both away. The darkness was kind but with darkness came cold. The cold caused him to shiver and this brought pain. The cold also brought noise. The noise was unnatural and unpleasant and would not desist. The noise faded slightly and returned. The return of the noise brought the heat. The heat brought the darkness and the darkness was kind.

## Chapter 18

'Batribi? Can you hear me?' Something was pushed into his hand by the hoarse voice. 'If you can hear me, squeeze my finger. I hope you speak the Common Tongue. Squeeze my finger if you understand me.' With exceptional effort, he squeezed his hand around the finger. It was hard and knobbly like a stick. 'Thank the Third. I thought you were as dead as a fish on a mountaintop.' The finger was withdrawn. 'Can you open your eyes?' He tried to open his eyes but the light was too much. He squeezed them shut again 'Oh! Of course! The lamp! Wait.' The noise receded with the voice and the light was extinguished. 'Better?' He tried to open his eyes again and the light was much less. He opened his eyes.

'Good evening,' said the hoarse voice of the old woman bent over him. 'I truly thought you would die. Fortunately for you I found you when I did and the Third God's guidance and my skill kept you with us.' The woman had a pinched, hollow-cheeked face, a thinning mane of silver hair and squinting eyes. 'Do you have a voice?'

'My name... Daryo... kin of Dostan.' His own voice was strained and dry.

'I am Fayi.' The old woman helped him sit up a short way and gave him a cup of broth. It tasted strongly of mushroom but was one of the most exquisite things that Daryo had ever swallowed.

'My thanks, Fayi. Is this Three Rivers?'

'Three Rivers! Huh! Not within forty miles!'

'Where am I?'

'My home. In the land by the Riy River west of Lalbi. You have been here for four days. This is no town, this is a house alone. I found you by the roadside. Nearly broke my back dragging you onto the sled. Huh!'

Daryo looked past the woman. The house was tiny, no bigger than a Batribi *kaff*, its roof patchy in places, he on the only bed, a fire in the centre and nothing else visible in the gloom. 'I do not remember.'

'Cold sick. The chill stops the body, slows the brain. And that wound in your hip was not helping. I patched it and it is closed but you need rest.'

Daryo was then aware that he was unclothed beneath a sackcloth blanket. 'You...'

'Yes, yes, I took your clothes away to get your wound. I have been dealing in hurt bodies for more winters than you could count, you have nothing that another man does not,' she said dismissively.

Daryo, embarrassed none the less, lifted the blanket and found a poultice tied with a fresh strip of cloth to his hip. 'My thanks.'

Fayi waved her hand dismissively. 'More the Third God's work than mine.'
'I heard... I thought I heard... the Fourth Goddess. She told me to stop and sleep.'
'The cold sickness. Plays tricks on the mind. Maybe the Fourth Goddess works that way, I cannot say. I follow Spellis and not the others. It had me cast out of Lalbi many, many seasons ago when I would not and did not attend the festival of the First God after the harvest.'
Daryo smiled weakly. 'Your devotion to the Third God saved my life. I am no person to judge.'
'Hm.' The woman turned to the fire. A pot was bubbling on it and she stirred it firmly. 'I heard you ask for Three Rivers? Is that where you go to?'
'I was going to Three Rivers, yes.'
'You would have died before you got there. What was it? A boar, a bear?'
'A sword.'
'A sword? Guards? Are you being sought?'
'No, an ambush.'
'Robbers?'
'Something of that nature. They were more interested in my capture.'
'And you fought them off?'
'I have skill with a blade... I had swords with me. Are they...?'
'There's a shed against the house where I leave my sled. All your possessions are in there. Your clothes are under the bed. Your boots are by the door.'
'My thanks.'
'None needed. You are not strong enough to leave. Three days and nights. Maybe more. That wound must be closed and you must be hale enough to walk.'
Daryo nodded. 'Your knowledge of these things is greater than mine.'
Fayi ladled a mug full of broth and handed it to Daryo. 'Finish that. It will help you sleep. Sleep is the best thing for you. I am sleeping in the shed. You need the bed more than I. If you call, I shall hear.'

When Daryo awoke again, it was day but the sky, visible through a gap in the ceiling on the far side of the hut, was dark grey. He felt under the bed, found his underclothes and pulled them on. He then swung his feet out and tried to stand. His right leg was stiff and uncooperative and he fell with a crash. No-one came and he forced himself upright again, doing hobbling circuits of the tiny home making his leg work. The wound site was painful but not badly so and he was able to dress with care- leggings, shirt and boots and then his cloak before venturing outside. The hut was, if possible, on a worse state outside than inside- the entire structure leaned to one side, the roof was exceptionally poor and there was a small pile of rubble to one side that suggested that what had been a chimney had collapsed long in the past. The shed was slightly more robust-looking and through its open doorway, Daryo saw his swords, shield and pack laying on the ground. The tracks of a sled led out of the home's little hollow and up onto the higher heath. There was a staff in the shed and Daryo took it to afford himself a little more stability as he walked around the hollow to make his stiff limb work as normal. The stiffness was gradually replaced by a soreness and he decided to return to his bed. As he hobbled back to the door of the hut, the old woman came down from the heath.

'You should be careful. Not fully healed yet, that wound.'

'I had to get out of the bed and try to walk. A walker who cannot stand on the road is not much of a walker.'

'But a dead walker is even less. Get back to that bed.'

'I am doing so.'

Fayi watched the Batribi limp back into her home. She had managed to snare only two rabbits and a squirrel but had gathered some firewood and a small basket of wild mushrooms. She strongly suspected that the Batribi in her bed was a fugitive but the Third God did not discriminate against those in need of aid, he simply healed them.

Daryo remained in Fayi's home for another four days before she decided that he was strong enough to leave. He had gradually spent longer walking around the hollow over those days and the pain in his leg had become no more than a dull ache above his hip. When Fayi departed for her daily foraging and to check her snares, Daryo dressed properly in fresh clothes from his pack- a russet shirt, looser brown hose and fresh underclothes. He then returned his sword belt to its normal position around his waist. There was no discomfort from his wound. He strapped Stai's swords to his back and pulled on his cloak with his pack on the top. Temma's Sword was withdrawn, checked and returned to its sheath, his shield went onto his left forearm.

'You are leaving.'

Daryo slid his shield up towards his shoulder before he turned. 'I have imposed on you long enough, Fayi.'

'No real imposition. But it is probably best that you make your way.'

'I must thank you. Without your efforts and prayers, I would not have lived.'

'The Third God guides me.'

'The Second and Fourth Goddesses me.'

Fayi seemed to find this amusing. 'Truly? Brokea may guide you, Daryo, but the Darkest Goddess commands you. Tell me the story of the Eight of the Pantheon.'

Daryo looked quizzically at her. 'The Pantheon always were. They created the world so that people may come to know them and serve them. All but the Fourth Goddess were venerated for that which they gave so the Darkest Goddess made it so that all who lived would one day die and become her servants regardless of their desires.'

'It is as you say. Some people, though, do not wait until death to become her servants. You carry three blades, three instruments of her work. You may wish to walk the roads and learn of the world but nonetheless...'

Daryo nodded and smiled faintly. He then drew Temma's Sword and held it up by the hilt, point down. 'My sword and my service, Fayi.'

'Gods' Guidance, Daryo, kin of Dostan. All of them. Go four miles west. That is the road from Lalbi to Three Rivers.'

Daryo clambered out of Fayi's hollow and walked westwards, the rising sun at his back. After an hour's steady walking, he found the road, running from the north-east to the south-west. In the latter direction, Daryo could see a bridge. He knew it would be the ancient Seareu Bridge over the Riy and he turned in that direction, towards Three Rivers. The bridge was older than anyone had knowledge of, an edifice of three stone arches supporting a wide, paved roadway. From the corners, thick wooden arms reached up to the centre of the bridge, from where they met hung an acorn the size of a man. The builders, and the reason for the extraordinary design, were utterly lost to history. A banner had been nailed to the ancient black beams at the corners of the bridge. The banner was midnight blue with a single white star in the corner, the emblem of the Seatless Squire, the junior of the lords of Jaboen, often employed to enforce the law and collect taxes and tolls on behalf of the king. A dozen men were spread along the hundred-yard bridge, a cluster of tents at the far end. As Daryo approached, a spear-wielding man stepped forwards to demand a toll. Daryo suspected the fee was increased for an armed Batribi but paid reluctantly and headed for the Midstream Inn in Three Rivers. An uncomfortable night in a damp cellar passed and with the sunrise he continued west.

As Daryo approached, the guard on the north gate of Thiel, where the three roads from the town joined, was interested only in Daryo not being Vidmarian. Daryo could appreciate why Thiel's lord would be concerned so the defences were being reinforced- a wooden palisade being replaced with a stone wall. The Vidmarian nation was known for its aggression against its neighbours and after its thrust into Gourmin against the Order, not only would they be unlikely to withdraw but it would encourage other acts of aggression as well. Thiel was the closest of Jaboen's towns to Vidmaria and therefore the most vulnerable. Daryo felt that he knew Thiel. He had never visited the town but was sure that he knew it. The town was positioned on the steep south bank of the River Soiliy, many of the houses built along steep, twisting lanes that snaked down to the temple square by the banks of the river. The temple itself almost overhung the river. Daryo slipped inside. It was a temple of Spinel, the Third Goddess, bringer of compassion and reason. Above the small circular altar was a glass crystal. In respect of the Goddess, Daryo removed his sword belt and Twin Swords and laid them alongside his shield just inside the door. A young woman by the altar looked up as he entered, her face changed from peaceful to nervous and she took a wide route around and behind Daryo before hurrying out of the door.

Daryo was accustomed to the reaction to Batribi of many Jaboen and he ignored the occurrence. He knelt by the altar and tried to control the racing thoughts in his mind. Reason and clarity were two of the qualities given by the Third Goddess.

'Syrza was right,' said a soft voice. 'A Batribi in the temple.'

Daryo opened his eyes. An elderly, dun-robed priest had knelt across the altar. 'If I am imposing or offended the lady, I can leave.'

The priest shook his head. 'Not at all. Syrza is timid, there is no harm done, Master Batribi. I can preach the Third Goddess's message of tolerance and understanding but I cannot compel my congregation to follow my teachings. I know that many, no, that is unfair, that most of your people are honest, hard-working, decent and faithful.'

'We are.'

'You pray to the Pantheon?'

'I follow the Second Goddess. I follow the way of duty and loyalty.'

'As do all followers of the Pantheon.'

'I felt a sense of loyalty to this place,' Daryo told the elderly priest. 'As if I know Thiel.'

'Perhaps your clan spent a lot of time around Thiel when you were young.'

'Perhaps.' Daryo looked up at the crystal above the altar. 'I thought perhaps Spinel would guide me as to why I thought this. I have had an... eventful season, I have recently recovered from a serious wound, I thought it may just have been a trick of the mind.'

The priest nodded. 'It may be.' He closed his eyes for several heartbeats and appeared to be praying silently. His eyes opened again. 'May I tell you a story, Master Batribi? It may explain something of your mind.'

'Of course.'

'I have been the priest here for eighteen summers. Seventeen springs past, I was the new priest, my first appointment having been a novice at the Great Temple of the Pantheon in Ossmoss. I was awoken one night, very late, very late, by a commotion. Much of the village was awake. This was shortly before the Yashoun withdrawal and a force of Yashoun soldiers were trying to move a camp of Batribi from the area by taking them to the old bridge at Sul and forcing them across into Vidmaria. As a military operation, the plan was working particularly well but one woman, a young mother, escaped the cordon and ran into the town, pursued by a soldier on a horse. She fled to the temple, carrying her child and tried to gain entry. The soldier, the captain, knocked her down with his horse. She fell down the steps. The fall killed her but the baby in her arms was only injured, a gash above its eyebrow.' The priest smiled faintly. 'A gash that would be a faint, pale scar by this time.'

Daryo unconsciously reached up and touched the slight groove that ran from his hairline down and slightly split his left eyebrow. He knew that it was a pale brown colour, much lighter than the rest of his skin. 'I was the baby?'

The priest nodded slowly. 'I think it most probable. You were too young to remember this place as you would remember it now but maybe that is why you feel that you know Thiel. You have been here before, just many seasons ago.'

Daryo took a long, slow breath. 'My mother. You said she...'

'She died. The impact of the captain's horse... the fall... I cannot say.'

Daryo bowed his head. 'May the Fourth Goddess guide her steps.'

'And the Third bring us to know the reason for our loss,' recited the priest. 'I could show you where she is buried.'

Daryo looked up quickly. 'Truly?'

'Indeed. Come with me.'

The burial ground was on the edge of the town at the foot of the wall, near the river but on a section of bank high enough not to flood. The grave markers were mostly iron or stone. One round, flat moss-covered piece of stone close to the wall was unmarked.

'I could not mark a name or anything else on the stone, as I knew nothing of the poor woman,' said the priest.

Daryo knelt by the stone and brushed as much of the debris away as he could. 'They named me Daryo, mother,' he whispered. 'They told me it meant alone but I have nobody to say otherwise. I hope you approve. I have thought about you sometimes. Who you were, what you were, how you died... I know a little more now. I am glad to have come here this time.' He stood up.

'You may stay as long as you wish,' said the priest quietly.
'My thanks but I would rather not. I would ask one thing of you.'
'Anything you wish.'
'Mark this stone: *A woman of the Batribi, a mother to a son.*'
'Certainly.'

Daryo felt uncomfortable trying to stay in Thiel. The inn was small but looked comfortable, most people had been polite if not pleasant; despite this the familiarity he had felt with the town had evaporated like frost before fire. He supposed it was the knowledge that his mother was buried there after many seasons of not knowing his mother's fate had soured the town in in his mind. Instead, Daryo returned to the road and turned west once again.

# Chapter 19

The border post between Jaboen and Yashoun was thirty feet above the Dithithindil River. A squat, square, stone tower was between the road and the precipice. A series of ten spiked wooden barricades were staggered along the road to make it difficult for traffic to pass through. There was a small queue of people waiting to be passed through the gateway formed by the last two barriers. Daryo looked up at the tower, two Yashoun archers were on the top of the fifty-foot-plus tower. Three men with the short Yashoun army sword were clearing people through the barriers after they were questioned by a portly, bald man in a black robe. Two more men stood by the tower door with shields at their sides and spears in hand. Daryo joined the short queue behind a Jaboen trading caravan, a farmer and his boy with a cart and a wealthy-looking mounted traveller with two attendants. The portly man, a guard at his shoulder, exchanged only a few words with the traveller and moved on to Daryo.
'Where are you going to, Batribi?' he demanded. Portly was perhaps a kind description, the man was positively obese, multiple chins and rolls of neck fat below a flabby face and piggy eyes. His tone of voice was that of a man completely convinced of his own importance.
'Ossmoss, sir.' Daryo had already decided on his exact story and was determined to give only the information requested.
'Why?'
'My mother's death. I wish to pray at the Great Temple.'
'Where have you come from?'
'By Stannia Lake.'
'That is a long walk.'
'A pilgrimage, sir.'
'Where is your clan?'
'By the Lake.'
'They are not with you.'
'No, sir.'
'Why not?'
'My mother had no other children. I wished to make this pilgrimage alone in her memory.'
'Why are you carrying swords?'
'The roads are dangerous, sir. Thieves, bandits, Peak tribesmen, Vidmarian raiders, for all I can tell.'

'You know what happens to those who use blades offensively in Yashoun?'

'They have their hands and then their heads removed in Gourmin, sir.'

'Indeed. Keep the blades sheathed.'

'I will, sir.'

Daryo was given a permissive nod and followed the mounted man and his valets through the barrier.

'Nice blade,' said one of the swordsmen manning the barricades, pointing to Temma's Sword.

'A gift from a kinswoman,' Daryo told him, stopping for a moment.

'The curved blade will give you an excellent slashing capability.'

'But limits the stabbing capability.'

'It requires more skill to use,' said the soldier.

'A little.'

The soldier smiled but the pleasant smile turned to a vacant surprise. He fell forwards, an arrow protruding from his back. It had the distinctive double-fletching of a Vidmarian arrow.

'Ambush!' roared one of the spearmen, seizing his large, rectangular shield.

Daryo quickly pulled his own shield down to his forearm, the outer strap in his fist. He turned to where the arrow had come from, a sharp ridge above the road, crouched and covered his vulnerable legs with his shield. He then shucked his pack rapidly.

The two swordsmen by the barricades had no shields and only leather armour and they were running for the tower. Both were struck by several arrows in the back as they ran. The noble-looking traveller and his attendants had kicked their horses on to the gallop but men with spears raced out of cover to intercept them. Daryo stayed behind his shield as more arrows flew. Two struck his shield, one broke against the road near his foot, the fat official had been struck in the ribs and stomach and was rasping for breath on the ground. The Yashoun archers on the tower were firing randomly into the undergrowth on the ridge, hoping to hit the invisible archers. The two spearman had retreated inside the tower and Daryo thought it best to do so as well.

He waited for the next score of arrows and as they struck around him, he ran for the tower door. One of the Yashoun soldiers looked as if to block him but his comrade permitted Daryo inside. A flimsy wooden screen was pulled across. The ground floor of the tower was totally empty but for the foot of the stairs.

'Are you injured?' the second spearman asked, slightly taller, broader and darker than his comrade.

'No,' said Daryo. 'I think the official is dead.'

'Stuki, Sodakimo and Aksakari are dead,' said the other spearman.
'Thunaki!' came a voice, shouted down the stairs in the far corner. 'We can see at least eight now!'
'Hold them away from the door!' was the response from the man who had asked after Daryo's health. 'You can use those blades?'
'Very well,' said Daryo simply.
'You may need them to get out of here.' Thunaki threw down his spear and drew his own sword. 'Sino, get up there, get a bow.' The other spearman nodded and hurried up the stairs. 'If I am dying beside you, I should know your name.'
'Daryo, the Walker of the Order of the Shield and Sword, kin of Dostan.'
'The Order! I am privileged. I thought your type something of a legend.'
'We may be soon,' Daryo replied darkly, discarding his shield and drawing the Horse and the Bear, inverting the Bear quickly. 'How many archers up there now?'
'Three, but not many arrows.'
'This screen will not hold long.' It appeared to be only a few thin planks nailed together with feet attached to the bottom, just wide enough to block the door. 'A single man could knock it down.'
An arrow struck the screen and most of the tip punched through the thin wood.
'It is a windbreak not a fortress gate,' admitted Thunaki. 'Are they Vidmarians?'
'I believe so. Do you have reinforcements nearby?'
'No.'
Another arrow struck the screen, near the top, and the screen swayed. Daryo moved from the same side of the doorway as Thunaki to the other side.
'When they come through, cut low,' Daryo told the Yashoun. 'Cut at the knees. It may not kill the first man but it will obstruct the others. If we are overwhelmed we retreat up the stairs if possible.'
Thunaki nodded. 'A sound plan.'
'Thunaki!' called the voice from above. 'Thirteen now. We have few arrows left.'
'Only fire if you have a clear target!' Thunaki called. 'Then come down to help us!'
'Understood!'
A man charged the screen and smashed it down. Thunaki slashed downwards as the Vidmarian fell on top of the flimsy barricade and cut into the man's back. Daryo stabbed downwards with the Bear and laterally into the doorway with the Horse, where it struck the second attacker full in the throat. Thunaki had raised his shield and turned to block the doorway for a moment. He was shoved backwards by the force of another charging Vidmarian soldier but the attacker ran straight onto the raised point of the Bear. Daryo

spun into place blocked the doorway and was nearly run through by a spear. He parried
it aside and slashed with the Horse. Thunaki was back on his feet and Daryo backed
away from the door just far enough to allow Thunaki to stand alongside him. The
Vidmarians were now pouring through the door. Both Thunaki and Daryo were forced
back towards the stairs, blades flying to protect themselves. Daryo managed to get inside
the swing of a greatsword and slash across the Vidmarian's inner arm and ribs. Suddenly,
the other Yashoun soldiers, Sino and the archers, came down the stairs like a raging
torrent. The remaining Vidmarians fled. One of the archers hurled his sword after them
and struck a fleeing opponent in the back. Daryo lowered his weapons, panting for
breath.

'Go out and check the men outside,' Thunaki instructed and the three archers trotted
outside. The Yashoun laid his shield down and mopped his brow. 'Vidmarians on
Yashoun soil...'

'Probably not the first either,' said Daryo. He saw a movement. A Vidmarian, the one
with the greatsword, stood up and lunged. '*Thunaki!*'

The Yashoun spun just in time and shunted the slash of the huge blade aside with his
own sword. Daryo saw an immediate opportunity, leaped sideways onto the third of the
stairs and jumped at the Vidmarian, leading with the Horse. The Vidmarian saw the
threat a heartbeat too late and tried to turn but the short, straight Batribi sword was
driven into his ribs with all of Daryo's weight. For insurance, Daryo spun the Bear point-
up and drove it into the Vidmarian's gut. He held both blades for a heartbeat, turned
them both slightly and withdrew his swords. The Vidmarian gurgled bloodily and
collapsed to the ground. Thunaki exhaled slowly.

'My grateful thanks, Daryo the Walker. You saved my life if not my shirt.' He indicated
his left arm; the Vidmarian's greatsword had slashed his sleeve almost off and nicked the
flesh of his arm. 'I owe you a great debt.'

'Your gratitude is payment enough,' replied Daryo politely, cleaning his weapons on a
Vidmarian's leggings.

Sino returned. 'All dead, Thunaki. Stanei, the other three, and all of the Vidmarians
that remain. Two, perhaps three, escaped.'

Thunaki nodded. 'They will likely return. We should withdraw. Gather what we can. We
make for Namixo.'

The two archers were named Tankiro and Sayi. They had collected the last of the food
and their own packs from the accommodation level in the tower. Sino and Thunaki then
did the same. Daryo recovered his own pack, returned it to his back and then returned

his shield to his arm. Feeling somewhat vulnerable on the road, he drew Temma's Sword again. The four Yashoun soldiers joined him. All four now wore beige linen cloaks and iron-reinforced helmets with a rounded top, slightly flared neck guard and fixed cheek plates. All had their standard short swords sheathed at the left hip, quivers of arrows on the right, bows over their shoulders, knives in a sash on the chest, spears and shields.
'The Yashoun Army travels light,' said Daryo with a grin.
'The Yashoun Army prides itself on every soldier being able to fight with every weapon,' replied Sino defensively.
'And I do not wish to leave any weapons for the Vidmarians,' said Thunaki. 'I am sure that they supply their forces with adequate arms. All the surplus weapons went in the Dithithindil. Are you coming with us, Daryo the Walker?'
Daryo nodded. 'I was travelling west anyway. I would be safer travelling with you so I shall be coming with you at least as far as Namixo.'
Thunaki lifted his shield. 'Move out.'

After a mile of walking, Daryo sheathed his blade and asked: 'How far is Namixo?'
'About ten more miles,' Thunaki told him.
'I do not know Yashoun. Is Namixo a town?'
'A small town but it is the great eastern fortress of Yashoun. Vidmaria cannot attack southwards across the mountains. If Vidmaria is to attack Yashoun, this is the only point of attack. Jaboen, Gourmin and Boskinia are much more vulnerable.'
'You seem to know much of these matters.'
Thunaki smiled. 'I know something of these matters. The Dithithindil Road is the weakest point of the Empire regarding the Vidmarians so Namixo and Kakuo are heavily fortified. To the north of the road, beyond that ridge...' he pointed to the high ground to their right, 'is the Northern Wastes, a waterless and desolate land. No army could cross it. So the road is defended.'
'If this is so, should you not have a way of warning Namixo from your border post?'
One of the archers, Sayi, snorted. 'Our pigeons escaped two days ago. We were waiting for a new one.'
Daryo could not help but smile. The rain began soon after, a steady fall that soaked the four Yashoun soldiers but Daryo's cloak was much more resistant to the wet. The road was well paved, befitting the main conduit from Yashoun to Jaboen and Gourmin, and the rainwater drained off the edge of the road and cascaded over the drop into the Dithithindil below. The rain got heavier over time until it was a constant barrage of cold water. Sayi opined that it would be drier walking in the Dithithindil. He was the

youngest of the quartet, of an age with Daryo, and a keen hunter. He alone seemed able to stay positive and ebullient in the face of the rain, his cheeriness only enhanced by unusually fair hair, a round face and lively eyes. He had discarded his sodden cloak and seemed to embrace the rain.

Apart from their footsteps, a gusting wind, the torrent of the Dithithindil below and the pattering of the rain were the only sounds. The road became more difficult as it became wetter. Puddles joined to become small lakes and the lakes joined to become miniature seas. Lower parts of the road became ankle-deep in rain water and even higher parts became carpeted by mud.

They passed something Daryo was well acquainted with, he had a Yashoun milepost on his shield, flanked by Kym's harlequin and Leroyfa the Blind's girl child. It was a cylindrical stone pillar four feet high with a double-kite shaped tablet on top. There were two carved arrows on the tablet: the one pointing east read *Jaboen 6 miles, Thiel 82 miles,* the westward arrow was marked *Namixo 5 miles, Sictan 144 miles.*

'Not far now,' said Sayi, with a wide smile.

'Does anything depress you, Sayi?' asked Sino bitterly.

'If I could only eat fish. That would depress me.'

The others exchanged amazed looks and wondering smiles. The young man moved forwards to take the lead of the group. The road began to slope downwards towards the raging torrent of the Dithithindil. They were slightly downstream of the confluence of the Soiliy and the Dithithindil and the river was both navigable and treacherous from the confluence all the way down to the sea at the twin cities of Ossmoss and Paloss. A dark shape loomed through the rain between the road and the river.

'Shaxsho Tower,' Thunaki announced. 'The old border between Jaboen and Yashoun. There are rumours of ghosts and phantoms now.'

The tower was identical to the one at the new border but was crumbling, the ramparts were gone, the windows were black holes, there was evidence of a fire against the wall and a makeshift gate had been made with Yashoun Army shields and logs. Daryo stopped and regarded the barricaded door for a few heartbeats. The noise of the river and the rain made it hard to tell but he was sure he could hear noises from within. The Yashoun soldiers had stopped and were watching him curiously. Daryo gave Thunaki a significant look and drew Temma's Sword. Thunaki looked curious. He laid down his spear and bow and drew his sword. He murmured instructions to the others; Sino and Tankiro quickly left their spears and bows with Sayi and drew their swords too. Sayi was apparently to stay with the spare equipment. Thunaki trotted across to Daryo.

'What is it?' he whispered.

'It may be my mind playing tricks,' Daryo replied, equally softly. 'But I am sure there is someone in there.'
'Finding shelter.'
'So why barricade the door like that. And it would be barricaded from the inside, not the outside.'
Thunaki considered this and then nodded. He waved his comrades forward. Tankiro and Sino seized the barricade, cut the ropes securing it and pulled hard. The shield-covered barricade was made of several dense logs lashed together and it fell forwards, crashing to the wet road. Daryo raised his shield and led the way inside. The lower floor of the tower was deserted. The staircase had gone but had been replaced by a ladder.
'Someone has been here very soon,' said Daryo in a bare whisper. 'Why else replace the stairs?'
'Anyone who climbs first would be very vulnerable,' Thunaki replied, moving to the foot of the ladder and looking up into the darkness. 'There is very little light up there.' He moved away, back to Daryo. 'Perhaps we just abandon subtlety.' Daryo frowned but Thunaki then shouted: 'This is the Army of the Emperor of Yashoun! This structure is Imperial property! Surrender now and you will be dealt with mercifully!'
'Oh Gods! Help! Help us!' came a muffled cry from above.
Daryo lunged for the ladder but Thunaki was faster, unencumbered by a pack. The Yashoun dropped his shield and scrambled one-handed up the ladder. Daryo quickly dropped his pack and followed, Tankiro close behind. The second floor of the tower was also empty but the remains of the staircase led upwards. The cry for help was renewed and Thunaki clattered up the stairs with Daryo at his heels but was thwarted by a trapdoor.
'It needs a key.'
Daryo came up alongside him. The trapdoor was locked on one side. 'No, we can dismount the lock. Give me your sword.'
Daryo passed Temma's Sword back to Thunaki in exchange for the short, stout Yashoun sword. He pressed the point of the straight sword in behind the lock and used his shield as a makeshift hammer. He then put the point behind the mortice and repeated the process. Sensing weakness, he pushed hard on the sword and used it as a lever. The mortice broke free of the wood ceiling and dropped to the floor. The trapdoor swung down, narrowly missing Daryo's head and he charged up the stairs. The room above had been furnished with two unpadded wooden beds close together and a jug on a stool between them as far from the trapdoor as possible. The only light was the empty window space above the trapdoor. A man was sat shackled on one of the beds, his face obscured

by a hood that moved frantically as if he were looking around. A woman was cowering behind the other bed and she screamed when she saw Daryo. Her face was badly bruised and her hair looked as if it had been very roughly cut. The hooded man was making noises as if he was unable to speak. Thunaki and Tankiro pushed past Daryo, the latter going to the woman, Thunaki pulled the man's hood off. He was unkempt and bruised as the woman was and his mouth had been gagged with cloth, which Thunaki removed.
'I am Thunaki, a lieutenant in the Imperial Army. My comrade Tankiro and our travelling companion, Daryo the Walker. We are here to help you. Is there a key?'
The man coughed, shaking his head. The woman was crying hysterically as Tankiro tried to release her. Both captives were shackled with rusted iron manacles on their wrists and ankles. The man had the two also linked by a short chain and a second around his waist.
'Let me look,' said Daryo. 'I have a lot of experience of smithing.' The woman was still wailing so he went to the man. The manacles and chains were not heavy, they were sturdy but rusted. 'I need a hammer. And a spike ideally.'
Thunaki thought for a moment. 'Sino and I are probably fastest and I have the authority to get what we need. We will run to Namixo and return with horses, tools and reinforcements. Tankiro, you and Sayi will stay with Daryo until we return.'
Tankiro nodded. Thunaki patted the captive man on the shoulder and scrambled down the stairs. Daryo followed him.
'Thunaki? Is this wise? We know nothing about these people.'
The Yashoun shrugged. 'The man's half-starved, the woman's beyond sense. They are obviously captives and I doubt legitimately so. The only legitimate authority in this land is the empire.'
Daryo nodded. 'I suppose you are correct.'
'We will leave all the weapons and equipment but our knives.' Thunaki stopped at the top of the ladder. 'Until I return, you are in command, Daryo.' He took a bronze badge from his sleeve and handed it to the Batribi. 'Protect the captives with your lives.'
Sino helped Sayi relay all of the Yashoun equipment to the first floor and then, with nothing but knives, Sino and Thunaki began to run westwards.
'Block the door again and haul up the ladder,' Daryo instructed Sayi. 'I am going to see if I can get to the roof.'

The top floor, and the roof beyond, were inaccessible from the cell. It meant that there were only two perspectives: the window on the first level looking west and one on the second looking south onto the Dithithindil.

'At the least we will be able to see Thunaki returning,' said Sayi brightly as he and Daryo hauled the ladder clear of the hole in the floor. The three of them had substantial numbers of weapons but only a total of fourteen arrows for their four bows. Tankiro had managed to work the staples holding the captives' chains to their beds loose and one bed had been lowered down and put across the ladder's hole. Sayi had managed to calm the exhausted woman with his bright attitude and she had collapsed into a deep sleep. The man had regained his voice with some water from Tankiro's flask and explained that they were a wedded couple, farmers with a smallholding nearby. They had been captured and imprisoned by uniformed men without reason or excuse. Their captors returned at irregular intervals to torment and beat their prisoners and to rape the woman in front of her husband. The man wept as he spoke and Tankiro had listened sympathetically. Free from the bed, if not his chains, the man was cradling his sleeping wife as best he could. The pain, turmoil and stress of the exploits had taken their toll on him as well; he was asleep but restlessly so. Tankiro draped his cloak over the sleeping couple carefully.
'Why?' he asked softly as he came down the stairs.
'Perhaps the Third Goddess will guide us to the answer,' said Daryo. 'Let them rest.' He went to Sayi, who was at the window, craning out of it trying to watch the road in front of the tower. 'No sign of movement?'
'Nothing, sir. Not even an animal. The rain's here to stay. May be a real storm coming. Thunaki and Sino will be near drowned.'
'As long as they return with horses and tools.'
'They will.'

It was almost dark when the sound of horses stirred Daryo from his post watching the still-sleeping captive couple. He quietly made his way down the stairs. Tankiro was at the west window but was scrambling out of the recessed window towards the ladder.
'Thunaki and several riders!' he said excitedly.
Daryo helped him to put the ladder back down to the ground and they held it steady while Sayi climbed down. Daryo then followed him down as Tankiro went up to wake their charges. Sayi and Daryo had the door unblocked as Thunaki reined in his horse. The Yashoun officer looked tired and bedraggled but pleased. He was accompanied by eight comrades and each man had a rider-less but saddled horse alongside his own. One of the men was carrying a bag over his shoulder. Thunaki took it from him and handed it to Daryo.
'Your tools.'

'I will put them to use.' Daryo quickly scaled the ladder and stairs and found Tankiro talking softly to the still-groggy couple. 'I trained as a smith,' he told them. 'I am going to break these chains off.'

He opened the bag and found the tools he wanted- a steel spike and hammer. First the woman was helped to kneel by the bare bed, her wrists resting on the edge. Daryo carefully placed the spike in the lock holding one of the manacles. A hard, precise smack with the hammer and the lock broke. A few heartbeats later, the other wrist and then her ankles were released. Shortly after, the man was free of his shackles as well. Thunaki had brought up another bag while Daryo was busy, this one with warm clothing for the couple. Tankiro and Sayi helped them dress.

'There are horses, we will escort you to Namixo,' said Thunaki. 'We will have to get some information from you, about your captors and why they took you but that can wait until we are somewhere more secure.'

The Yashoun Empire was not known for its fortresses. Temples and grand houses, beacons and halls rose in the cities but fortresses were typically simple and elementary. The Empire depended on the professionalism, skill and commitment of its army to defend itself. Nonetheless, Namixo was a special case- the most vulnerable part of the Empire to Vidmaria and one of the Emperor's Nation's easternmost outposts. On a bluff above the small riverside town of the same name, the fortress of Namixo towered over its neighbours. Accessible only by a narrow, steep and winding track, the curtain wall surrounded the edge of the plateau summit completely. Two angular bulwarks topped with catapults projected either side of the towering gatehouse and the outer portcullis. Between the portcullis and the gate were a dozen arrow-loops cut into the walls on either side. Inside the first gate was another portcullis, another gate and a third portcullis before they emerged in the castle bailey. Built against the curtain walls were stone buildings of two and three levels with high, stout towers at regular intervals. Seven towers in total ringed the wall, each with its own catapult. In the centre of the bailey, a square keep over four hundred feet high dominated. The bailey was bustling with scores of Yashoun soldiers at their tasks; some conducting weapons drills, some performing chores, one seeing to the slaughtering of several sheep. Men came forwards to help with the horses. Thunaki was the first to dismount.

'The lady and gentleman, find them comfortable quarters,' he instructed. 'Feed and clothe them, treat them as the noblest guests.'

A young man, a page or valet, came forwards and helped the lady dismount before leading the couple towards one of the towers. Thunaki beckoned to Daryo.

'We should speak with Lord Chemito,' he said. 'He commands the fortress.'
The commander's chamber was several floors up and protected by a thick, metal-barred door and a guard.
'Thunaki.'
'Serihan. Is he in?'
'Yes.'
Thunaki pushed the door open and led the way into a small but well-furnished chamber. Sealing documents at an expansive desk was a stout, balding man who scowled at the new arrivals.
'My lord commander, we were forced to abandon the tower.'
'What?'
'We were attacked.'
'And you captured an attacker? Why did you not disarm him?' demanded the lord.
'No, my lord. This man did not attack us, he aided us.'
'A Batribi?'
'Yes, my lord.'
'A spy,' said the lord angrily.
'No, my lord!'
'I doubt that very much! Take the Batribi's weapons!'
'My lord!'
The lord stood up, taking a short sword from beside the desk. 'Disarm the Batribi, Thunaki! Disarm the Batribi!' He lurched to the side and pulled on a rope. Somewhere further up in the keep, a loud bell clanged.
Thunaki looked from his commander to Daryo, indecisive and torn. He made an apologetic expression to Daryo and drew his blade. 'Daryo, please relinquish your weapons.'
Daryo's hand dropped to his sword and one hand took the hilt. He was a fraction from pulling the sword loose when the door burst open and a dozen Yashoun soldiers rushed in, weapons at the ready. Daryo's hand moved from the sword hilt to the belt buckle and his sword belt crashed to the floor.

The cell was just below ground level on the west of the keep. The only window was nearly eight feet above the dirt floor, barely a foot square, with an iron-banded wooden door opposite it. A pot, already foul, was in one corner; there was a blanket and a poor straw mattress beneath the window. Daryo seized the window bars and pulled hard, using his feet against the wall for leverage, but the bars were firmly embedded in the stone. The door was bolted at least twice on the outside and there was a jailer at the end of the corridor. He had no knowledge as to where his weapons were, his armoured jerkin had been taken too, leaving him in just a shirt. The sun rarely penetrated the cell's window and it was chilly, almost too cold. Daryo could think of only one course of action. He lay on the mattress, covered himself with the blanket and closed his eyes. Sleep was not forthcoming but it gave him the opportunity to review his thoughts and to allow his legs to rest from the walk. A dungeon was not what he had hoped for: a warm inn and a good meal would have been infinitely preferable.

Daryo had expected interrogations or torture. Instead, he was told simply that his plan had failed and was then left alone. For two days he was given no food or water. On the third evening, Thunaki slipped a waterskin through the bars of the cell. Daryo rationed it for as long as possible but was particularly thirsty. It took all his restraint not to finish it before sundown. On the fifth day, Daryo began to think of death. His mind was cast back to the Jaboen wilderness and the whispers in his ear. Since then, many nights had passed to let him think about those whispers and it had brought him to the conclusion that a voice of that sort could only have been that of the Fourth Goddess. Kitsun the Shrewd had often talked of how the Goddess of Loss and Death and Endings had whispered in his ear, trying to tempt the old warrior into doing something foolish or reckless to send him on to the Next Kingdom. Daryo now knew that this was correct. He could almost hear the deceptively soft voice in his ear.

*There are ways to die in the cell*, it told him. *Use the blanket, make a noose and hang from the window. Smash the chamber pot to fragments and use the longest as a dagger. Drown in the chamber pot.*

Leave me alone, Daryo told the voice. I am not dead yet, not dead or dying yet. Return when I am.

He sat against the wall and contemplated the damp ceiling. A shadow passed across the window, temporarily blocking the light, but it passed on. Another shadow passed and there was a thud. From the curse and the following noises, Daryo guessed that something had been dropped. A few heartbeats later, something hard fell on Daryo's head. Then a second and a third. Daryo rolled aside. They were pears, somewhat wrinkled and old but pears. Daryo seized them and stuffed them into a hole in the mattress. He peered up at the window and saw a silhouetted figure outside the window, still collecting fruit.

'You are not forgotten, Walker,' it hissed, before standing up and moving on. It was not Thunaki; Daryo thought it may be Tankiro.

Daryo smiled to himself, extracted one of the pears from the mattress and ate it. It was sour but it was such a welcome gift that he devoured it, pips and all. He said a silent prayer to the First Goddess for the food and to the Second Goddess that at least some of the Yashoun thought of him as a comrade.

Over the next three nights, odd accidents happened outside the window of Daryo's cell- another few pears, a box of cooked potatoes, a carrot, a small block of cheese; never a large amount but enough to stop him from starving. Then the bell began to ring. An alarm bell. The soldiers were running to battle positions; there were shouts for archers; an instruction for the portcullis to be lowered; the catapults were called to readiness; Namixo was being attacked.

Daryo grabbed the bars of the window and lifted himself up to look out. There were many pairs of running feet. Daryo had to drop back to the floor, he had little strength in his arms. There was noise at the door, the bolts were thrown back and Daryo came into the centre of the room. The door opened and Lord Chemito stepped inside, escorted by two guards.

'Your friends have arrived, Batribi.'

'They are not my friends,' said Daryo, the first words he had spoken in days.

'A spy working for his own profit rarely has friends.'

Daryo threw his hands up in frustration. 'I am no spy, Lord Chemito. Release me and I will aid you. Leave me here and we both die.'

'Release you and you will aid my quicker passing to the Next Kingdom. When this attack is defeated, you shall die.' Chemito turned and stepped out of the cell. One of the guards closed the door and bolted it shut again.

If you are so keen for a follower, take him, Daryo thought to himself. In response, the voice inside his mind chuckled in amusement.

The sounds of battle were unmistakeable but were somewhat detached as they were funnelled through the tiny barred window. The catapults whistled and crashed; fires blazed; thuds sounded like a ram against the gates; men shouted and screamed. By night, the catapults stopped firing but the battering ram continued. With the dawn, the Yashoun soldiers were withdrawing to the keep. The flow was steady but sure away from the curtain wall. Daryo could think only that they had a secret way out and were gradually making their way out of the fortress by the clandestine means. Which would leave him alone, defending the eastern fortress of the Empire with no weapons from a subterranean cell. He almost laughed at the prospect but was immediately sobered by the thought that his very existence as a Batribi was a crime punishable by execution according to Vidmarian prescript. Discovery would mean swift death. This prompted Daryo to make another keen exploration of his cell for an escape route but there was none. The door was solid, the bars deeply set, the walls continuous, the floor made of stone. There was no escape. But someone was at the door. The bolts were thrown back and Thunaki stood there.

'Master Batribi,' he announced formally, 'You are invited in the name of the Emperor to escape with your skin intact.'

Daryo chuckled. 'I would be delighted to do so.'

'Follow, quickly. There is little time.'

# Chapter 20

'We are betrayed,' said Thunaki as they hurried through the fortress. Daryo's jerkin, weapons and shield had been beneath the jailer's bed and Thunaki had retrieved them quickly. Daryo pulled his jerkin on, unlaced, took his weapons and shield and clutched them as they went deeper into the fortress. The Yashoun defenders had all fled.
'Why is the fortress being abandoned?' Daryo asked as they skittered down a stone spiral staircase.
'Because Chemito is a fool,' said Thunaki simply. 'He thinks it better to save the men. We have the greatest castle in Yashoun and we could hold it with ten score men. But Chemito is a fool. All of the lieutenants have tried to reason with him but he is refusing all counsel. I will have to report this stupidity; he is sacrificing our greatest fortification.'
'Who will you report to?'
'Whomever I can locate!' Thunaki reached the bottom of the stairs and Daryo found that they were in a small cellar, almost empty but for some rotting casks. Some had evidently been moved aside, exposing a section of wall to the right. Thunaki slid his hand into a crack in the wall and pulled on something concealed within. There was a dull clunk and the section of wall next to the crack seemed to shiver. Thunaki then simply pushed it open like a door, revealing a torch-lit tunnel through the rock beyond.
'The Passage,' he said, sliding through the stone door. Daryo followed through and Thunaki heaved the door closed behind them. There was a second noise as the door locked and Thunaki took an unlit torch from a bracket and lit it from a burning one.
'We follow to the end,' said Thunaki. 'This will take us nearly two miles from the fortress, towards the north. There is a small camp for the training of recruits near there.'

The tunnel took nearly an hour to negotiate. It had evidently been carved from the solid rock with chisels, Daryo could not fathom the amount of labour and time needed to excavate it. The air was cold and stale but there was a slight flow of breeze back towards the fortress from the far end. The tunnel sloped upwards after a mile, slightly down and then sharply uphill once more, the floor became a long flight of precipitously steep stone steps which required the travellers to use their hands on the steps above for balance. The ascent was difficult and left their legs burning from exertion but a narrow patch of grey-blue sky was visible above and it grew to reveal a wide cleft in the rocks and Thunaki clambered out, extending a hand back to help a grateful Daryo through. The tunnel gave out onto a narrow rock ledge and a dirt track led down a very steep slope down towards the green-brown plain beyond. In the distance was a small enclosure just visible with some wooden buildings inside.

'A training base for new soldiers,' said Thunaki. 'Lord Chemito was taking the garrison west to Kakuo.'

'How did you remain?'

'I feigned death,' said Thunaki simply. 'You saved my life; I could not leave you to forfeit yours at the hands of the Vidmarians.'

'Consider any debt repaid, my friend.'

They began the descent down the track, walking carefully and often sideways to avoid falling. A keen wind at their backs made the travel particularly difficult, threatening to blow them off of their feet. There was little vegetation to hold for support and they had to struggle downwards, sometimes almost sliding on their rears. The wind brought some persistent rain and this caused the air to become colder. The weather was thoroughly foul by the time they reached the foot of the slope. What had been a dirt track was almost a stream by that time and Thunaki and Daryo had both lost their footing several times, resulting in muddy slips and slides. They reached the flat covered in brown mud and drenched to the skin.

'Never did like that climb,' said Thunaki conversationally as they began plodding towards the camp.

'A useful addition to the fortress nevertheless.'

'Indeed. Built by the Jaboens back beyond any knowledge. The tunnel predates the current citadel, there was supposedly a wooden fortress on the cliff before the stone one replaced it.'

'You do know much of these matters.'

'I studied them. Not all soldiers of the empire are farm boys wishing for better meals and good boots. If this rain would stop, I think I would feel much happier.'

'I have got used to walking in all weather,' said Daryo. 'I hardly notice rain anymore.'

The mud was becoming sticky and their boots were sinking almost to the ankle by the time they reached the gate of the fort. A single Yashoun soldier stood on watch.

'Lieutenant Thunaki of the Eighteenth Company from Namixo,' he told the guard. 'I need to see the training commander.'

'The garrison troops are regrouping at Kakuo, sir. And the camp captain is not here.'

'I do not need the captain, I need the training commander.'

The guard looked confused. At closer inspection, Daryo could tell he was very young, younger than Daryo, probably no more than fifteen winters. He had no sword, only a stave and a pair of knives on his belt.

'I am commanding that you admit us and take us to the training commander,' said Thunaki.
'But, sir... and the Batribi...?'
'Is my companion. Admit us.'
'Yes, sir.' The young recruit turned and banged on the gate. After a short pause, the gate was opened and the guard relayed the information to the man inside the camp. The training commander was summoned as Daryo and Thunaki were ushered through the gate. The commander was approaching elderly, his hair and beard grey, with dark brown eyes and broad arms, a long sword at his hip and wearing the same uniform as Thunaki, whom he seemed overwhelmed to see.
'Thunaki!'
'Sinriro. Chemito yielded the fortress. Has my uncle been informed?'
'Kakuo would send the message.'
'I need you to do so as well. A message from the only man to know my true birthright will carry the weight required.'
'As you wish. I shall have someone find lodging for you.' Sinriro turned away.
Daryo nudged Thunaki. 'Tell me of this uncle of yours.'
Thunaki smiled ruefully. 'My uncle. The Emperor.'
Daryo chuckled. 'Truly?'
'Truly. Only a very few know this. The training commander here is an old friend of my father's. Lord Chemito knows, hence why he delights in my torment and issuing commands. And the Commander of Soldiers at the Palace holds the records. My father is Huishoda, younger brother of the Emperor. I could have spent my life somewhere in Ossmoss, safe and secure, but I always wanted to be a soldier. My father made the necessary arrangements and I joined the army. I have always simply been Thunaki from Ossmoss to my comrades.'
Daryo nodded his understanding. 'If only I could have hidden my skin so well.'
Thunaki smiled and clapped a hand on Daryo's shoulder. 'It is nothing to hide, my friend. Come, we should find some dry clothes and some hot food. I am exhausted.'

It took several days for the messages to be exchanged and conclusions drawn. Thunaki had offered Daryo the opportunity to leave but he decided to remain and possibly aid if required. With the permission of the training commander, he joined some of the more experienced recruits in their training. He had significant experience with his blades and fighting alone but the Yashoun soldiers were proficient with four weapons and at working in large units. Daryo joined the recruits as one of them: he was a fair bowman;

proficient with the knives as they were little smaller than his Twin Swords; he disliked the stave fighting and thus was reluctant to expend much effort on it; with a sword or sword and shield he was unparalleled- Vehllal, Kitsun and Kym had all taught him well and he was comfortably the finest swordsman in the camp. Twice, the training commander had joined in the training and he had weighed into the practice with his own blade. Daryo, wielding Temma's Sword, had comfortably beaten him both times. The Yashoun recruits quickly adopted Daryo as a mixture of brother and role model. They gathered around him at mealtimes, on the week's eighth day there was almost a scuffle to be able to pray alongside him and, although he could disarm and defeat every opponent, all of the recruits wanted to spar with him.

Thunaki was more withdrawn. Daryo was a curiosity, unrestrained by the Imperial Army's command and discipline, but Thunaki had technically deserted his post and defied orders and thus kept away from the recruits as much as possible, spending much of his time in the room that had been assigned to him and Daryo in the senior officers' building at the rear of the camp, forbidden to recruits.

Five nights after their arrival at the camp, Daryo was at the open-air altar of the Second God, praying in the light rain as the sun went down. The rain was an irritation but his experience in the Jaboen forest and in the cell had led him to feel a deeper connection to the Pantheon. The Second God, the bringer of conflict, was the most common deity for soldiers but Daryo struggled to feel a real bond. The Goddesses gave him a much more secure feeling when he prayed. The priests at the School of the Temple when he was a child had taught that faith was a highly personal relationship with the Pantheon and that true allegiance to a single deity was much more valued by the God or Goddess than a professed belief in the entire Pantheon. Most priests joined the vocation because of a particularly strong pull towards one of the Eight and some laity joined particular trades or professions based on their faith- soldiers of the Second God, farmers of the First Goddess, healers of the Third God, craftsman of the Fourth God and onwards in infinite diversity.

'Daryo, the kin of Dostan.'

Daryo opened his eyes, stood and turned towards the voice. A short, dignified looking man with a balding pate and a neatly-trimmed beard stood a short distance away. He wore the uniform of the Yashoun army with a gold braid on the shoulder.

'Yes, I am.'

'My name is Rimuto, I am the captain of the training camp. I have just come from talking with Lieutenant Thunaki. He speaks most highly of you.'

'I must thank him.'

'I have spoken with Lord Chemito. He told me of a very dangerous Batribi spy, working for the Vidmarians, whom he left imprisoned in the cells at Namixo. It was suggested that I execute him if I came across him again.'

Daryo inclined his head. 'Good advice.'

The captain nodded. 'If, when we retake Namixo, I find a Batribi in the cells, I shall allow you to take whatever measures you deem necessary.'

Daryo smiled. 'I may do that. There is a plan to retake Namixo?'

'There is.'

'I would be willing to assist.'

'That is not my decision. There is much that must be done. Namixo is a fortress.'

'One that was abandoned.'

'Unfortunately, Lord Chemito has many friends in Ossmoss and is unlikely to suffer anything but removal from command. Such is the way of the Empire.'

'Such is the way of the world.'

'Indeed. I wanted to meet you, Lieutenant Thunaki, as I said, was most complimentary. Are you staying in the camp any longer?'

'If there are no plans to retake Namixo soon, I may continue on my way.'

'Where were you going to?'

'I was heading towards the Twin Ports.'

'If you do so, on arrival, please find the commander of the Erita Tower. He is a friend of mine. Tell him that you may interest him.'

'Interest him?'

'Trust me.'

'Certainly.'

Daryo decided to leave the next day. He thanked Thunaki and promised the captain that he would make himself known to the captain of the tower when he arrived. Rimuto provided Daryo with a satchel of provisions and an escort of three recruits westwards for nearly two days before they reached the Dithithindil Road north of Kakuo. Daryo thanked the soldiers and continued on his way north-west.

# Chapter 21

Ossmoss and Paloss, the Twin Ports and capital of the Yashoun Empire, sat at the mouth of the Dithithindil but lesser-known Twins were a hundred and eighty miles upriver. The Yashoun town of Sictan and Tovein, its Hajma counterpart, faced each other across the river. Centuries before, the Dithithindil road had skirted the monolithic Tuukyo Mountain Range, running between the cliff and the mountains, but over time the river had claimed the land and left the river as the quickest and most practical means to round the mountain and continue to Stimoss. Daryo took the overnight ferry downriver to Stimoss and then resumed his walking north-west. He knew nothing of his route but there were the ubiquitous kite-shaped mileposts and there seemed to be no other roads of any note- only the long, wide and populous Dithithindil road which was never more than a hundred yards from the mighty, ship-bearing river. He had thought of buying passage on one of the craft down to the Twin Ports but decided it would be spending coin that he did not have and may not increase the speed of his journey by much; many of the barges on the river seemed to be moving at barely walking pace.

After two days' walk, Daryo had his first view of the Twin Ports from the top of the ridge above Ossmoss. On the north bank, the same as Daryo, was the Imperial City, Ossmoss. A tall, thick and ornately-carved wall surrounded the larger twin, centred by the largest buildings in the known world: the towers of the Imperial Palace on the north of Ancients' Square and the immense dome of the Great Temple of the Pantheon, centre of the faith. The houses were large, grand and built of a pleasant light stone. On the south bank, the smaller but much more crowded Paloss was held in by its ancient earth and wood defences. The smaller twin was the site of the commercial docks and was protected by the ancient Erita Tower where the wall joined the sea on the north and the Old Castle where the wall terminated at bank of the Dithithindil to the south. The Twin Ports were not easily threatened but the defences remained strong as they were the capital of the Empire and together were surely the largest city in existence. The road was a constant, steady flow of walkers, carriages, carts and wagons into and out of the cities. Daryo followed the traffic down to the River Gate. There was a small camp of Batribi a few hundred yards from the open gate- three *kaffa* and a tethered pack horse. Daryo left the road and crossed the short grassy stretch between the highway and the camp.

'Are you one?' asked a woman tending the horse.

'I am Daryo, kin of Dostan.'

'Salini, this is my kin. You walk alone.'

'Yes. I am meeting someone with whom I have a mutual acquaintance.'

'We walk the roads as we always do. We are leaving with the next dawn.'
Daryo nodded. 'A safe journey to you.'
'And to you. Step carefully in Ossmoss. We are not welcome.'
'And in Paloss?'
'We are safer.'
'My thanks. Gods' Guidance.'
'Gods' Guidance.'
Daryo returned to the road and proceeded through the city gates. A small group of Yashoun Imperial Guards were stood just inside and one looked curiously at Daryo.
'Gods' Watch,' said Daryo politely. 'I am looking to find the Erita Tower.'
'Why?'
'An appointment.'
'Far side of Paloss. On the river. Easiest to follow the bank of the river right around.'
'My thanks.' Daryo found his way to the Upper Bridge, the furthest upstream of the seven bridges that crossed the Dithithindil and turned right to follow the river. It was more difficult than he had anticipated. No street seemed to be longer than fifty yards before it turned or terminated. There seemed to be no plan or design to the roadways and it took Daryo a significant time to make his way through the maze of houses, roads, people and miscellaneous obstructions to find the docks. A Batribi stevedore on the docks pointed him to Erita Tower. It was less impressive than he had expected, a squat pentagonal tower, barely taller than the wall beside it with a low parapet, a small number of arrow loops and a somewhat light-looking gate. A single Imperial Guard, red tabard smart and clean, stave in hand, stood watch.
'Stay clear, Batribi!' he instructed.
Daryo spread his arms wide to show that he meant no harm. 'I have a need to see your commander. I was sent by a captain of the Army.'
'Which captain?'
'Rimuto.'
'Wait here.' The guard unlocked the tower gate, admitted himself and closed and locked it behind himself. Daryo stepped forwards a step to let the traffic past as he waited. A cart full of fruit passed, followed by another loaded with squawking chickens. The guard returned.
'Why did you wish to see the commander?'
'I may interest him.'
The guard clicked his heels in salute and inclined his head. 'Correct, my lord. Please, follow me.'

The guard led the way into the tower's entrance, a low chamber occupied by a further trio of guards and a rack of staves and swords. They passed through another locked door and up the staircase, almost to the top. A small chamber with a wide loop looking over Paloss was set up as a bedchamber and office. A particularly muscular man was sat at a table with a large book. He looked up as Daryo was ushered in.

'Ha! Very amusing.'

'I do not understand,' said Daryo.

'Rimuto, he was quite right. You would interest me, sir. Dauke, commander of the Erita Tower, captain in the Imperial Guard.'

'Daryo, kin of Dostan, the Walker of the Order of the Shield and Sword.'

The captain indicated a seat for Daryo to sit in. He had a rather square head, his dark hair cropped unusually short, his chin and jaw shaved clean and he was wearing the scarlet of the Imperial Guard as a tunic under a leather cuirass. 'Rimuto is an old comrade of mine. I am in command of some... special arrangements for the city's governor. I have a mission that requires some discretion and secrecy and Rimuto promised that should an appropriate individual present himself, he would send him to me.'

'I must be that individual.'

'Precisely. You must have proved some skill with those blades and a certain level of integrity.'

'I am flattered.'

'Please be mindful that this job may be dangerous but that the payment is considerable.'

Daryo shook his head and smiled. 'I am not interested in payment.'

'What interests you?'

'I swore a solemn oath to defend those who require defence and to aid those without means to aid themselves.'

'Then this will interest you, my friend. What do you know of the Silver Island?'

'Only a little. The home of the Silver Islanders.'

'As you say. There is a large mine, crucial to the Empire, in the hills above the town of Suxin. But those who do not live within the towns are intercepting the supplies. The miners have no reserves of food and no equipment. We have tried sending the supplies through other routes but always they are intercepted. My commander believes that there is a spy somewhere passing information to the raiders. So he has taken the task away from the normal commander of such matters and ask that I arrange a less overt shipment to the mine.'

Daryo nodded. 'And how could I be of aid?'

'I need men skilled with their swords to escort the supplies. I would pay thirty gold halves.'
'I am not interested in the payment.'
'As you said. Would you be interested in my enterprise?'
'Perhaps. I have had a lot of travel and am tired. When would your... venture be leaving?'
'Not for at least a day. The ship would take around six days and then just two days to the mines.'
'Then I will find a tavern.'
'You would be welcome to remain here.'
'My thanks but I will arrange my own affairs.'
'As you wish. Simply send word as to where you are staying but I would recommend somewhere you may wish to stay.'

Following Dauke's directions, Daryo found a tiny alleyway near the cattle market. It followed the rear wall of the market along a ramshackle line of wood and plaster houses with a small bakery and what looked like a particularly unpleasant brothel with several sailors drinking in the doorway. The next building had steps in front of it down to a cellar, separated from the lane by a low stone wall. A small pole had a wooden shield nailed to it. On the shield was a black hand and the words 'The Innocent Thief'. Daryo grinned involuntarily; theft was probably the thing that Batribi were accused of more than anything else. He descended the stairs, ducked through the low door and found himself in a small tavern, the counter less than twenty feet away, the ceiling was barely seven feet away. A few rickety-looking tables and stools were scattered around the straw-strewn floor. Light came from smoking fat lamps in recesses in the walls and a candle the size of Daryo's head on the counter. An elderly Batribi woman stood behind the counter.
'Gods' Watch.'
'Gods' Watch,' replied Daryo. 'I am told that there are safe beds for our people here.'
'There are. Are you a mercenary?'
'Of a type.'
'Do not use those blades in here.' The woman stepped aside, revealing a crossbow on the shelf behind her. 'If you keep those blades sheathed, you are welcome at The Innocent Thief. You keep a name?'
'Daryo, kin of Dostan.'
'I am Somma, of no kin any longer. This is my inn. There are two rooms up the stairs behind here. Take whichever you wish. Your belongings are safe here.'
'My thanks. Do you have a boy? Or a servant here?'

'I do.'

'Please send them to the Erita Tower with a message for the captain, simply tell him that I am here.'

'Certainly.'

The rooms were on the ground level, both had shuttered and barred windows, a straw-mattress bed, a large bowl of water and nothing else. The door could be locked from the outside with a key and the inside with a heavy steel bolt, both reassuring, in addition to tavern-keeper Somma's crossbow. Daryo took the opportunity to undress completely, wash himself and then rinse through the clothes that he had been wearing. He then opened his pack and found fresh clothing and some thin rope to improvise a drying line from the barred window to the bedpost. With fresh underclothes and hose, Daryo took some time to check and clean his swords. The Bear had been given a slight knock and was a tiny increment off of straight. It was perfectly serviceable but Daryo wanted to get it remedied. The Horse and Temma's Sword were both without fault. He replaced them and then took some time simply to lay on the bed and allow his body to rest. There was a slight twinge in the area of the almost-disappeared wound on his hip and some sore patches on the insides of his legs from the walking. Rest and dryness seemed to be the best course. He closed his eyes for a few heartbeats and then sat up.

Daryo had obviously slept. The daylight had become twilight. Daryo rose, pulled on a shirt and his sword belt then a cloak and boots. He went down to the inn's hall, which was becoming busier as the sun set. After a good meal of pork and rice and a large mug of beer, he felt much happier and rather content. The vast majority of the clientele of the Innocent Thief were Batribi, some in clan groups, some alone, some with small clusters of associates. A girl with a long, wooden flute was sat by the bar playing lilting tunes. Some of the Batribi occasionally sang to melodies that they knew. A good few hours after starting, the girl finished playing and there was a general noise of praise and approval. The girl took a mug from Somma and looked around for a seat. The nearest available was alongside Daryo and she sat down, laying her flute across her lap. She was pale-skinned for a Batribi, her complexion was applewood rather than dark oak; black coloured hair with a hazel tint in places was loose at her shoulders, wide eyes were enhanced by a red colour that matched her linen dress and a wide leather belt encircled her very narrow waist. She smiled sweetly as she caught Daryo's gaze.

'Gods' Watch,' she said after a few heartbeats.

Daryo found he had not quite understood. 'Sorry?'

'Gods' Watch,' she tried again.

'Yes, yes, of course, Gods' Watch.'

The girl grinned. 'Do you have a name?'
'Daryo. Daryo, kin of Dostan.'
'Lapini, kin of Boulra. Did you like the music?'
'Yes! Yes, of course I did!'
'My thanks. Are you new to Paloss?'
'I am. I walked from Namixo. From Jaboen before that.'
'I thought so. I play here a lot, I would have seen you before. Do you play?'
'No. No, I do not. Do you play only here?'
'Not solely. I have a few places that will allow me to play, we are welcome in some places in Paloss, but the first and second days I spend here. What has you here?'
'I have some work that I have agreed to do. I am waiting to hear from the man who engaged me as to when he requires me.'
'What sort of work?'
'An escort for some goods.'
'You are a guard?'
'A swordsman.'
'A mercenary?'
'A traveller. I was recommended speak to my employer by a mutual friend. I try to aid those in need and the mission is one of succour.' He noticed that she had finished her drink. 'Talking of succour, may I buy you another drink?'
'If you wish.'
Daryo bought another two drinks and returned. They spent a convivial evening together and when the tavern closed, Lapini kissed Daryo lightly on the cheek as they parted.

A man in normal clothes, not overtly a soldier, was sent for Daryo just after dawn the next morning and escorted him not to the Erita Tower but directly to the docks. On one of the dozens of wooden quays that extended out into the Dithithindil River, a small ship rocked slightly on its moorings. A black bird formed the figurehead with the bowsprit emerging from its mouth. The bird's wings swept back to form the bulwarks of the low forecastle. Two masts, both painted red, stood on the main deck and the sides of the poop deck were also carved as the wings of a bird but were unpainted. Just above the waterline, the oar ports were visible. A single, wide plank led aboard and sailors were loading barrels with the aid of a rope to tow them up through the gangway. Dressed in an unmarked red tunic and dark breeches, Dauke was watching the loading procedure while in conversation with a Silver Islander sailor. He saw Daryo approach and hailed him.

'Your transport, the *Black Dove*.'

'A fine-looking vessel.'

Dauke dismissed the sailor. 'The last of the supplies are being loaded. I am just waiting for my other... specialists. The captain wishes to sail with the tide, which is not far away. You should get aboard. Do you have any other baggage?'

'I carry it all.'

'Your space is in the fore cabin.'

'My thanks.'

Daryo waited for a barrel to be hauled to the top of the gangplank and then followed it up. The fore cabin was low and rather dark, lit only by small portholes under the wings of the bird figurehead. A series of five hammocks were slung from the beams above. Most of the deck was full of coils of rope and squat, knee-high barrels. Daryo picked his way to the forward hammock and dropped his pack below it. It was one of the first true spring days, the air was warm and so Daryo dispensed with his cloak. The cabin door opened and a huge figure stooped through.

'Dauke said there was another Batribi,' it said.

Daryo regarded the newcomer: nearly seven feet of very dark-skinned Batribi, his hair not shaved away but allowed to grow in a huge bush that made him look even bigger. His nose was misshapen, as was the mouth below. He wore rough leggings and boots but an incongruously good-quality tunic. In his hand, held like a toy, was a recurved bow.

'Gods' Watch,' said the giant affably, dropping a bag on the closest hammock to him.

'Gods' Watch,' replied Daryo politely. 'I am Daryo, kin of Dostan.'

'Viulra, kin of... I cannot say honestly. I have been out of speaking with my kin for several seasons. I was kin of Camma.'

'You have been away for a long time?'

'We separated. A disagreement. I chose to leave them. That was two winters ago in Nudakso. I do not know where they are.' He shrugged massively. 'And you, Daryo, kin of Dostan?'

'I walk alone. My kin is dear to me though, they are at Stannia Lake, the settlement that is growing there.'

'I had considered going there.'

'All are welcome. How did you get involved in this?'

'I got talking to a Yashoun soldier in a tavern, it was Dauke, and he invited me along, promised good payment. And you?'

'Referred by a mutual friend.'

'Swordsman?'

'I am. You appear to be an archer.'
'A man my size should wield an axe,' said Viulra with a grin. 'I have heard that so often.'
'Actually, I was about to say the range on your arrows must be exceptional.'
Viulra gave a booming laugh that seemed to shake the ship's beams. 'Enough to shoot someone in the Next Kingdom!'
Daryo took an immediate liking to his huge compatriot, it was difficult not to, and they returned to the deck so that Viulra could stand up straight. He was seven feet high without doubt and three feet broad. Daryo was not small, two yards in height and strong from his apprentice's days, but Viulra was like a tower beside him. As well as his bronze-tipped bow, he carried a short Yashoun-style sword.
The captain was apparently a Silver Islander- dark hair, sallow skin, narrow eyes and standing at the tiller giving instructions to the crew. He noticed that the two Batribi were watching him and he bustled down the ladder and across the deck. 'Dauke's men?' he asked, his voice accented but his Common Speech still clear.
'We are,' said Viulra.
The captain was nearly two feet shorter than the Batribi archer. 'I am Captain By Dee of the *Black Dove*. My ship, my command. You make trouble, over the side.'
'Yes, sir.'
The captain nodded and strode away. Dauke had boarded, flanked by two men with identically pale, mousy hair and beards hanging to their shoulders, beady eyes and weak chins. Both were in identical clothing, long blue cloaks and their faces were alike to a hair. They were carrying long bags on their backs and small crates.
'You met each other then,' said Dauke, with a satisfied smile. 'Viulra and Daryo, this is Cambitilian and Dororossi Mardno.'
'I am Dororossi,' said the slightly smaller one in a monotone.
'Yes, of course! My apologies. Dororossi and Cambitilian Mardno. Very experienced sailors as well as soldiers.'
The twin men exchanged looks and passed the others, heading for the fore cabin.
'Talkative individuals,' said Viulra with a derisive snort.
'But excellent men in a fight,' said Dauke. 'I have several witnesses and I trust them.'
Daryo nodded. 'We met your captain also.'
Dauke smiled. 'An excellent man. Follow his instruction while aboard and he is perfectly reasonable.'
'You accompany us?' asked Viulra.
'I do. I am ensuring this transport personally.'

'Commander Dauke, we have to leave,' said the captain, appearing at the Yashoun soldier's elbow.

'At your discretion, captain.'

'*Tu lan! Tu lan!*' bellowed the captain, striding back to his tiller, and his crew burst into action. The gangplank was hauled in with a crew member still stood on it. Another scrambled up stays to the deck. Two on the dockside cast off the mooring lines and were hauled aboard by their crewmates. Daryo was almost knocked aside as a tiny Silver Islander man raced up the rigging. Many of the crew were headed below through the central hatch, just aft of the mast. The noise of oars being unshipped and shouted orders filled the air. The *Black Dove* was already being pulled slowly away from the dock. The starboard oars struck water and there was the roll and then thump of a drum as the first stroke, and a hard lunge on the tiller from the captain, swung the *Black Dove* out into the Dithithindil's centre. Another roll of the drum and another thump and soon the rhythm of the drum was steady as the oars came into stroke. The ship rocked with the first real rush of water and the captain brought the tiller over to point the ship out towards the Sea of Dith.

Daryo took a step back and took a hold of the ship's rail.

'Not a sailor, Master Daryo?' asked Dauke, amused.

'Never on more than the Dithithindil ferry,' admitted Daryo.

Dauke clapped a hand on his shoulder. 'You will find that you adjust quite swiftly. The great advantage of the Twin Ports is that they are so far upstream, so the sea is a distance away and it tends to be quite calm.'

'This is calm?' asked Daryo, transferring a second hand to the rail.

'Very.'

Daryo moaned slightly. The motion of the ship was causing uncertainty in his legs as the deck moved and a distinctly sour sensation was rising quickly in his throat. He turned to face off the ship and allowed everything to flow. Dauke rested a hand on his back until the retching faded.

'Better?'

'A little.' Daryo spat. 'By the Third God...'

Viulra chuckled and wiped a splatter from his sleeve. 'Unpleasant. Some of us have control over our innards, Daryo, kin of Dostan.'

'My sincerest apologies.' Daryo spat again. 'Things are always best shared with others, are they not?'

Viulra laughed and nearly knocked Daryo overboard with a slap on the back. 'Timing is all! Timing is all!'

# Chapter 22

Dauke had not been fooling that the Dithithindil was a millpond compared to the Sea of Dith. As the wind caught the sail and almost ripped the *Black Dove* out of the mouth of the river, the bow dived into a trough, only to be thrown upwards onto the crest of the next wave. Daryo was hanging over the stern rail as the last contents of his stomach were left behind. Viulra stood alongside him for much of the time, offering fresh water and supportive comments. The sailors ignored the Walker's plight, wrapped up in their duties. Dauke seemed to go from tiller to bow and back again. The twins, who Dauke had said were Tibilian, had not emerged from the cabin. Viulra went back to the cabin to check and found them talking together. They had stopped when he entered and started again when he left.
'Very unsocial,' said Viulra.
'Very,' agreed Daryo dully, sinking down to sit with his back against the stern. 'I have never…'
'Been to sea before,' Viulra replied calmly.
Daryo gave him a weak smile. 'My thanks, Viulra.'
'I have a strong gut and kind soul,' said Viulra with mock-nobility. 'Some food?'
'Not yet.'
'I understand. I am going to walk the deck and clear the air in my head.'
'Of course. And my thanks again.'

Daryo finally struggled to his feet just after noon. The pitching and rolling of the ship was still unpleasant and he had to grope his way along the rail, twice necessitating sailors standing aside.
'Yoo bad ill?' asked one, another Silver Islander with a particularly thick accent.
'Better now,' said Daryo.
'Noo sailing is hard. Lots silva ill first sail.'
'My thanks.'
Daryo made it amidships and then lurched inwards to the mast, sitting down on a large box of complaining chickens. He could still faintly see the Yashoun coast, the twin hills that flanked Kalimoss Bay, behind the ship. The ship seemed to be carrying onwards at a much faster rate than Daryo had anticipated. Out into the Sea of Dith, which lay between the Twin Ports and the Silver Island, the *Black Dove* was keeping to its name and veritably flying through the water. Ahead of the racing ship was open sea merging into the sky on the horizon and a dark shape became more distinct.

'*Chu'ulai!*' shouted a voice from the foremast. '*Chu'ulai! Yashu!*'
Daryo looked around. Nobody seemed to have reacted. He regained his feet and staggered back to the tiller. 'What is that, captain?'
'Ship.'
'Another ship?'
'Yes. Yashoun ship. This part of sea very busy. Ships to Silver Island from Ports and Kalimoss. Ships from Jaboen, ships from Sodidor.'
Daryo nodded. 'Hostile ones?'
'Few. Too many Yashoun.' The captain pointed out to the approaching vessel. It was flying the scarlet flag of the Empire, wheel and spears in the centre, from the bowsprit and main mast. The *Black Dove* was flying the Silver Island banner: a black triangular mountain with a gold summit on a red flag. The crews hailed each other. The Silver Islanders of the *Black Dove* were shouting in their own language and Daryo guessed from the tone of their voices that they were being rather abusive. The Yashoun vessel's crew were mostly being friendly and the banter was mostly humorous. The ship was bigger than the *Black Dove* with a third mast and several of the huge naval catapults of the Yashoun Navy mounted on the flanks. The name on the stern read *Pride of Durat* and soon it was receding into the distance, leaving the *Black Dove* to sail onwards alone.

The crew assembled for their evening meal, cooked by one of only three men on the crew who were not Silver Islanders- a rotund Jaboen named Behriz. The other two, Armynyans, were talkative and curious about the Batribi in their midst, having never met a Batribi before and only seeing them from a distance. Daryo had managed some bread around mid-afternoon and was happy to eat the fish and potato stew cooked over a brazier on deck. The food made him feel much better and he was soon content and joining the conversation as much as possible between Dauke, Viulra, the two Armynyans and the cook. The Tibilian twins had come out, eaten and returned to the cabin without a word to anyone. Soon, Temma's Sword was out and being passed around the crew, none of whom had ever seen a Batribi sword closely.
'How do sword swing?' one sailor asked.
Daryo took his blade with a smile, took a few steps away and practised some of the sword drills he had learned from Kym the Harlequin. The fantastically sharp curved Batribi blade whistled through the air under the control of its master in precise and swift patterns. To make the display a little more impressive, Daryo inverted his blade, returned it to his belt and drew the Horse and the Bear, turning the show into that of a whirlwind of two swords. After several minutes of intense work, Daryo brought his swords up to

salute and gave a slight bow. The sailors chorused their approval and Viulra gave an impressive salute.

'Good, Batribi. How good?' asked a voice from behind.

The twins had emerged from the cabin again. One, Daryo thought he was the slightly taller one, Cambitilian, had a four-foot metal weapon in his hand- sharpened as a sword blade at one end, square in section and with a studded metal ball at the opposite end.

'Can you defend yourself?' asked the other twin.

Daryo glanced around. 'Yes.'

'Do so.'

Daryo reversed the Bear in his left hand. 'These swords are sharp.'

'Is the mind holding it? If it is, the sword will not touch my flesh.'

'And your mind?'

'Sharper than yours.'

Daryo brought the Horse up to a high position and the Bear in front of him. The unarmed twin stepped away from his brother, who hefted his weapon, took hold near the sword end and swung the weapon over his head, the ball swinging down but well away from Daryo. Daryo darted forwards and almost walked onto the sword point. He just shunted it aside with the Bear and swung the Horse down. The Tibilian slipped aside, using the movement to flick his weapon sideways and almost drag the Horse out of Daryo's hand. Daryo swung his elbow and kicked out sideways as he turned. His boot caught the twin's gut and knocked him back. This angered the Tibilian who again swung the ball end of his weapon like a club. Daryo dropped to the deck and rolled forwards, past the Tibilian and again kicked out. The Tibilian jumped the kick and landed hard on Daryo's foot. The Walker cursed and rolled away, just escaping the downward-stabbing sword point. He sprang up to his feet and found the side rail. Daryo pushed away from the rail, the Horse straight out in front like a lance but inches from his opponent, he rolled to the right and slashed sideways. The Tibilian barely blocked the swing and Daryo came on to guard.

'Very well done, gentlemen!' said Dauke quickly. 'An excellent display! Truly excellent!'

Daryo glared at the Tibilian for several heartbeats before straightening up and sheathing his swords. 'Well fought,' he said calmly.

The Tibilian snorted derisively, turned on his heel and followed his twin back to the cabin. Viulra came alongside Daryo. 'Keep a close watch on both of those men,' he advised.

'I will.'

'Come, sit, the sailors have some strong wine, which is rather good.'

'Gom, gom, gom,
Tan lum so lom,
Gom, gom, gom,
Tan HO!
Gom, gom, gom,
Ti san yo,
Gom, gom, gom...'

The Silver Islander crew had a seemingly endless litany of sea shanties as they worked, some repetitive and memorable, others long and complicated. The 'Gom, gom, gom' verse seemed to be the most popular with the sailors.

Daryo was sat on the chickens again listening and watching as the sailors opened up the foremast sails and the lookouts were changed; one atop each mast, two in the bow and two in the stern.

'Gom, gom, gom,
Tobi si li hanni ho,
Gom, gom, gom...'

A senior-looking seaman was splicing a rope by the rail, a group of men were scrubbing the deck near the forecastle and the captain was being spelled at the tiller by one of the Armynyans. The Jaboen cook was scrubbing pots and singing along absent-mindedly to the crew's song. Viulra had a small bag and was fletching some arrows sat on the forecastle steps. They had seen no other ships for the whole day. Daryo wondered at how alone it felt. On the roads, one knew that other travellers were somewhere on their journeys, travelling towards or away, but the sea gave Daryo a feeling of loneliness and isolation, as if the ship were alone on the seas.

'Look! Look!' the huge Batribi jumped up and leaned over the rail.

Daryo hurried across. There were several large fish, the size of a man, swimming alongside the ship. They had long noses and forked tails and seemed to swim effortlessly, occasionally breaking the surface and blowing water from a hole on their heads.

'Incredible,' said Daryo, as another of the fish jumped slightly and blew out a spout of water. He could not recall seeing anything like them before.

'What are they?' wondered Viulra.

'Fish,' said the captain, coming alongside. 'Like chasing ships. Harmless, good to eat.'

Daryo watched the fish for a long time until they dived beneath the surface.

By sunset, a heavy rain squall had blown in and it drove all but the on-watch crew inside. Daryo retreated to the forecabin. As soon as he entered, the Tibilian twins, sat in their hammocks, stopped talking.

'Good fight, Batribi,' said one of them.

'And by my opponent,' Daryo responded politely, climbing up into his hammock.

'You do not like us, Batribi.'

Daryo looked at the pair. 'You have been very unsocial. And my name is Daryo.'

'We are Tibilian,' said the closer twin. 'There are no other Tibilians here. We have no reason to be social.'

'You could simply be so. The Third Goddess's way is that of an open mind.'

'We do not believe in the Yashoun gods,' said the further twin.

'What do you believe in?'

'The strength of a man's arm, the breadth of his shield, the range of his bow.'

Daryo considered this. 'I would concur. I simply believe that there is a guiding force to those qualities.'

'Gods.'

'Exactly.'

The twins exchanged looks. 'We think you are wrong.'

Daryo shrugged. 'And if it matters to anyone, I think you are wrong.'

He pulled off his boots and laid down in his hammock. The Tibilian twins remained silent and Daryo eventually found himself asleep.

The long, shallow bay to Suxin was protected by cliffs to either side. The wind was lost and the crew had to row for nearly ten miles into the anchorage. A huge pier led from the shore, nearly half a mile into the bay. The *Black Dove* moored towards the end astern of a huge Sodidoron cargo ship, the *Broken Promise*. A small taskforce of dockers came trailing along the wide pier and the crew began preparations to unload. Dauke found Daryo and Viulra sat on the bowsprit, taking their first look at the Silver Island's largest town and best port.

'Would you gentlemen take guard on the pier?'

The two Batribi nodded and shimmied back down the bowsprit. Viulra retrieved his bow and Temma's Sword from the cabin and they took position on the landward side of the mooring while the ship was unloaded. The Silver Islander stevedores had several carts that they were loading but Dauke left the ship and returned with a wagon and pony. The cargo for the mine was then transferred to the wagon: salt beef and fish, sacks of rice and apples, lamps, oil, shovels, axes and many other crates and barrels. Dauke brought the Tibilian twins from the ship as the crew finished loading the wagon.

'We are simple travelling merchants,' he told his four men. 'The previous convoys to the mine have been military escorts. This is just a wagon with a few men. We go north from Suxin to Vinyu, then west into the mountains to mine. If all goes well, we are there in three days and back again two later. The ship will wait for us here.'

# Chapter 23

Suxin was a small town. From the harbour, its streets led steeply upwards, a difficult climb in the dry, hot air. The town square had the wood and plaster homes of the Silver Islanders on two sides, a market in the centre, a new-looking Temple of the Pantheon on the north side and a large house in its own grounds on the east with the Yashoun flag hung from all points.
'That is Half Moon House,' said Dauke as they passed. The Tibilian twins were driving the wagon, Dauke sat on the rear, the Batribi walking behind. 'The home of the Governor of the Silver Island, a personal appointment of the Emperor himself.'
'Who leads the Silver Islanders?' asked Viulra.
'The Governor.'
'Which of them?'
'There is none,' said Dauke, looking puzzled. 'The Governor is all that is needed to govern on behalf of the Emperor.'
'The Silver Islanders have no voice in their government?' asked Daryo.
'Why would they need one?'
The two Batribi exchanged looks but did not reply. There was no need to comment on such a statement, Daryo could see a look of disappointment in Viulra's eyes. A sextet of Yashoun guards were stood at the gates of Half Moon House, swords in hands, as if they expected an assault at any moment. The road led between the great house and the temple, and on up the hill through more houses. The houses became smallholdings, the smallholdings became farms and it was clear that they were out of Suxin. Another mile along was a heavy wooden palisade, surrounded by a moat, and studded with watchtowers. Each tower had at least three archers in and the gate was protected by four Yashoun soldiers, again with swords drawn.
'The garrison,' said Daryo. 'The guards are very alert.'
'Perhaps there is... unrest among the Islanders,' suggested Viulra.
'The Silver Island has been peaceful for generations,' Dauke interjected. 'There are no problems.'
'Except for whoever is stealing your supplies, intercepting your convoys and betraying you to the raiders,' suggested Daryo.
Dauke went quiet; Viulra nudged Daryo and gave him a quick grin.
Beyond the garrison, the road levelled out and followed a high plateau. There were no trees but the sides of the road were littered with rocks, prickly bushes, thick shrubs and long brown grasses. The road forked just before noon.

'Go to the right,' Dauke directed. He had taken over driving the cart, Viulra was sat beside him, the Tibilians were in the back and Daryo was walking ahead. Daryo complied, the road to the left looked recently built. 'That road leads directly to the mine,' Dauke called. 'But it is where the other shipments were stopped. We go in to Vinyu and then follow the river west.'

'Would this road not be watched too?'

'Possibly. But this is not a military shipment. And we are not headed to the mine,' said Dauke. He had on his uniform but under a plain brown cloak. 'A merchant and his aides, remember?'

'If I were a bandit, I would not discriminate,' said Viulra simply.

'Nor I,' agreed Daryo.

'Is this what the Batribi do?' asked a voice from in the wagon. 'Plan banditry and its practice?'

'As much as the Tibilians sit idly in hidings conversing in secret!' snapped Viulra.

'Silence, Batribi!'

'Silence yourself, Tibilian!'

'What would you do to make me?'

'What Daryo did on the ship!'

'Need a Yashoun to intervene?'

'Before he killed you!'

'Viulra, peace,' said Daryo, glancing back and shifting his shield on his arm. 'It serves no purpose.'

'Listen to your comrade!' came a voice from in the wagon. 'He speaks more sense than you ever have! And he has more skill with a blade!'

Viulra went to retort but thought better of it. Daryo turned his attention back to the road and the surroundings. He had the uncomfortable feeling that he was being watched from only a short distance. His left hand dropped to the hilt of Temma's Sword on his hip and his right hand flexed. The feeling had been growing since they had left Suxin and it was almost unbearable.

'Viulra, what can you see?'

The huge Batribi stood up on the wagon seat, clutching the roof for support, and searched the landscape with keen eyes. 'Heath, more heath and heathland, my friend.'

'Surely?'

'Surely as the sun rises.' Viulra hopped down from the wagon, it rocked wildly as he did so. He took a few long, quick strides and caught up the yards to Daryo. 'What do you see?'

'Nothing. That is what concerns me. The Fourth Goddess is speaking in my ear.'
'What does she say?'
'That she has agents in the heath who have designs on our lives.'
'Do the Pantheon... speak often in your mind, Daryo?' asked Viulra softly.
Daryo chuckled. 'Not often. And only the Darkest of them. An old warrior told me that she whispers in the ears of the valiant and the bloodied, to try to lure them into her halls.'
Viulra guffawed. 'If you believe it, my friend.'
'I have heard it. At times of great injury or great danger. The soft and beguiling whisper in my ear.'
His huge comrade shook his head in mock-despair. 'A terrible thing, those that hear voices are often mad. Or worse.'
'No... no... this is...' Daryo stopped and, behind, Dauke had to sharply rein in the horse.
'What is it?'
'Bow!'
As Daryo dropped his shield, Viulra threw him the bow. Daryo caught it, the arrow that followed, notched, drew, aimed and fired in a swift movement. With the single shot, he was already throwing the bow back. The arrow struck about twenty yards from the road and there was a shout of anger, pain and shock. Daryo broke into a run, drawing Temma's Sword as he did. A man lurched out of a hollow, the arrow buried in his upper arm. He looked like a Silver Islander but was of darker skin, his hair beyond his shoulders and wearing only a pelt skirt. He had a long spear and nothing else and it was jabbed viciously in the Batribi's direction. Daryo used his shield as a ram, crashed into the man and knocked the spear aside with his shield. He slashed open the man's chest and then throat. Viulra reached the scene just as the scout's body crashed to earth.
'Who is he?'
'The Fourth Goddess's voice in my ear! Do you think that I am still mad, Viulra?'
The big man chuckled. 'I do, my friend, but this is some mitigation to your condition, I think.'
Dauke joined them. The Tibilians had stayed with the wagon. 'One of the Nar Silver. The other people of the island. The wildmen of the north. They have their own lands and rarely come south, the Imperial presence and the Silver Islanders' hostility is an effective deterrent.'
'Could they be your raiders?'

'No. There is no purpose to their raiding this sort of shipment. And why, then, would there be such evidence of a traitor? A traitor working for the Nar Silver? Nobody can even speak their language.'

Daryo thought through Dauke's words. 'As you say. We should hurry. If he is alone, he will be missed soon.'

Nightfall came and Dauke insisted that they stop. Both Batribi and, surprisingly, the Tibilians thought it better to press on but were overruled. Dauke even took the horse from the wagon and tethered it a few yards away as if to forestall argument.

'Rolling three-man watches until sun-up,' said Daryo. 'We keep patrolling the heaths too. Keep any light to a minimum. Do not show any sign we do not have to.'

'Who has first watch?' asked Dauke.

'I do,' said Viulra immediately.

'And I,' said one of the twins, Cambitilian, Daryo thought.

'I will too,' said Daryo.

'Not in my lifespan,' said the second twin. 'Leaving my brother alone at night with two Batribi. You might slit our throats and steal the wagon yourselves.'

'Who do you think you are to make such a claim?' demanded Viulra, rounding on the Tibilian and towering over him. The Tibilian's hand dropped to the knife on his belt.

'A man too wise to close his eyes and leave his kin with two bandits.'

Viulra's club-like fist swung and nearly knocked Dororossi across the road. Dauke, Daryo and Cambitilian all shouted and jumped in. Daryo seized Viulra's arm. Cambitilian got between the giant and his twin, pulling out his double-ended weapon. Dauke had one hand on his own sword and the other on Cambitilian's chest.

'You see, brother!' shouted Dororossi, scrambling back to his feet. 'You see it, the treachery and violence of the dark people!'

'Kick a dog enough times and it will bite you, fool!' snapped Daryo. 'How many taunts and insults have you thrown at us on our people and our ways, how much derision? And then you complain that he strikes you! Are you really *that* foolish?'

'How dare you call my brother fool!?'

'I call him what he is, by Dule's Hammer!'

'And you waving your stupid, ignorant beliefs at us!'

'Dauke!' Daryo turned to the Yashoun. 'You are leading this mission. You engaged us. State the truth.'

Dauke spread his arms. 'I cannot say. I believe that the taunting and abuse has been on both sides. Both equally guilty in my eyes. Every jibe has been replied, every push countered with a pull.'
Daryo sighed. 'Then say what you will, Dauke.'
'If you can bear to be within proximity until dawn, Daryo and Viulra can go ahead as scouts. Cambitilian and Dororossi will stay with the wagon.'
Daryo exchanged glances with Viulra and then nodded. 'As you wish.'
Dauke looked at the Tibilians. 'Is this acceptable? If anyone dissents, return now to the *Black Dove*.' The twins looked at each other and both assented. 'Then find some rest. Or not. Take your choice. We move at sun-up.'

Daryo and Viulra took alternate watches behind the wagon through the night and the Tibilians at the front. When the sun rose, Dauke emerged from the wagon and began returning the pony to the traps. Daryo and Viulra began to walk ahead. They were nearly four hundred yards ahead before the wagon began to move.
'Make sure we can see the wagon,' said Viulra. 'If we get too far ahead and they are attacked, we might know nothing about it.'
'Agreed.' Daryo shifted the shield on his arm. 'Of course, we may be attacked and they do not aid us.'
'Perhaps the Tibilians would not but Dauke would. He stands more chance of success with four escorts than two.'
'Perhaps. But the Third Goddess tells me not to trust him either.'
They walked for several miles in companionable silence, the wagon always around four hundred yards behind them. The land grew more barren but rockier; large piles of rock and boulders littered the landscape with only thin mosses and grasses around. At intervals, Viulra would leap atop a convenient point to survey the landscape.
'They are still watching us,' he said after the fourth such climb.
'Where?'
'I cannot say. I would have picked out the scout with my bow.'
'Hunt them?'
Viulra considered this. 'Continue walking. I shall return. Keep a sharp eye.' He signalled a positive to Dauke and lumbered off of the path, sliding into the grasses to the right of the road. Daryo continued walking, his palm itching for the hilt of a sword. He expected an arrow to strike him at any moment but he walked for a hundred yards, half a mile, a mile, with nothing interrupting his stride. It was nearly three miles further on when there was a crunch from the underbrush and Viulra reappeared.

'I thought you fell down a hole,' said Daryo.
'I did,' said Viulra with a sharp intake of breath. There was a gash in his leg. 'Too big and slow.' He sat on a rock and inspected the injury.
Daryo stopped beside him. 'Is it deep?'
'A scratch. I had all but got the man at my arrow's point when he saw me. Lashed out with a spear and caught my leg. But I stuck him through. Another Nar Silver. I should have shot him from a greater distance but I was over-confident.' He took his water bottle and washed the wound quickly. Daryo had some bandage cloth in his cloak and he handed it to Viulra. He bound his leg and stood up.
'Good.'
The wagon had reached them and Dauke dismounted. 'Is there a problem? Where were you, Viulra?'
'Another Nar Silver watching us. He scratched me but he paid with his blood.'
'Can you walk?'
'Well enough.' Viulra took a few steps and nodded. 'Perfectly well.'
'Let us not risk that,' said Dauke. 'Cambitilian, Dororossi, go on ahead. Viulra will ride on the wagon, Daryo follow behind.'

Vinyu was barely a town- a cluster of wooden houses with either wood or canvas roofs, none more than a single level high, stood alongside the confluence of two little rivers. A single watchtower stood on the side of the road, a single Silver Islander with a slingshot on guard. It looked pitifully vulnerable for a village in a region known for bandits and wildmen. There was no wall, no other defences or precautions of any kind, just the lone tower and lone man at the top.
'I was expecting something more impressive,' Viulra told Daryo. He had walked the last few miles, confident in his own strength. 'A clan of our people in their *kaffa* would be a more impressive sight.'
Dauke reined the horse in. 'The original track to the mine is on the far side of the village. We will follow that up to our destination.'
'How far is that?' asked Viulra.
'About ten miles. We should be there by nightfall.'
'Tiring, Batribi?' asked one of the twins.
Viulra ignored him. Dauke glanced from one to the other and whipped the horse on. Viulra strode past the wordless Tibilians and took up position as the forwards scout, Daryo took advantage of the situation to jump up alongside Dauke.
'Need a rest?' the Yashoun asked.

'I may be the Walker but there is a limit to my endurance. I am not long recovered from a serious wound and it still does not feel at its utmost. I think the Third God has more to do.'

Dauke nodded. 'My guardian is the Third God. My father was a physician and he felt a very strong connection to Spellis.'

'Are you from the Twin Ports?'

'Yes, Paloss from birth. My father is still caring for those in need.'

'And your mother?'

'Passed to the Next Kingdom two winters ago.'

'May the Fourth Goddess guide her steps.'

'I pray that she does. Your guardian?'

'I could not say. I was brought up in the School of the Temple in Salifa. All the boys there were dedicated to Dule but I find little in common with the Fourth God. The Darkest Goddess, or the Second Goddess, would be the closest I have to a guardian.'

'There is nothing to prevent a grown man choosing a guardian for himself. I know several who have done so. Some even change their guardians.'

'I may consider that.'

'The Third God is not an obvious choice for a guardian for a solider but I have been wounded in battle. It healed well so the Third God obviously cares for his disciple.'

The wagon was already out of the village and the track turned up and away from the rivers towards the mountains. The track got narrower, it had obviously been carved through the rock. Viulra had to trot to stay in front of the pony. The wagon lurched over a rock and Daryo had to grab onto the seat to stop himself being thrown.

'The road is...'

'Not a road,' said Dauke. 'This is only a track. But it is much more inconspicuous than the new road and hopefully it means we can get through to the mine.'

The incline became steep. The pony was struggling so Daryo got down and walked alongside Viulra.

'We are being watched again,' said Viulra softly.

'You believe so.'

'I think your madness is infectious: I am hearing the Darkest Goddess in my head.'

'Trust her.' Daryo drew Temma's Sword. 'Where do you think?'

'Left. I can do this.'

'Are you sure?'

'Sure.'

'Do not injure yourself again.'

Viulra chuckled and hopped up onto the rocks to the left. Within moments he was out of sight. Daryo signalled to Dauke that all was well and continued walking. After half a mile, he became concerned. Then there was the noise of running footsteps. Daryo looked up, expecting Viulra to emerge over the rocks. Instead, a Nar Silver hurled itself over the edge at Daryo. He barely got his shield up when the figure crashed into him. He heard Dauke shout and the horse whinnied. Daryo kicked out and swung his shield out. The Nar Silver's nose disintegrated as the shield's rim struck. They staggered back and Daryo was able to recover himself. The Nar Silver wiped blood away from their face and Daryo realised he was fighting a woman. She had a rough sword and hurled it at Daryo. He deflected the missile with his shield and she threw herself bodily at him. The impact knocked Daryo to the floor. Before he could react, bony fingers were clawing at his face. Suddenly the fingers went stiff and the weight of the body stopped moving. Daryo shoved the body off. An arrow had struck the Nar Silver in the side of the neck. Viulra was on the rocks, another arrow notched. Dozens of Nar Silver were boiling over the rocks on the right and down the track. Viulra released another arrow. The Tibilians were out from behind the wagon, Cambitilian wielding his two-ended weapon, Dororossi with a pair of short swords. Dauke drew his own sword and joined the fray. Viulra fired one more arrow, drew his sword and was into battle too. Daryo ducked a blow from a rough axe, slashed the axeman's gut open with Temma's Sword and dodged another blow from a sword. Viulra stabbed the swordsman and Daryo took the head off. Cambitilian was fighting back-to-back with his twin, Dauke was wielding his sword two-handed. The Batribi protected each other as the back of the Nar Silver assault was broken and the survivors began to flee. Viulra took his bow again and started firing after the escaping Nar Silver, cutting down another half-dozen until the battle was done.

'No attacks on this route?' demanded Cambitilian bitterly, trying to staunch a wound in his arm.

'I cannot believe it,' said Dauke. He shook his head in confusion. 'I cannot believe it.'

'We should keep moving,' said Viulra, relaxing his bow.

'We should turn back,' argued Dororossi.

Daryo used the pelt leggings of a dead Nar Silver to wipe his sword clean. 'We should keep moving. We get these supplies to the mine and complete our task.'

Dauke still had his sword in hand. 'We move swiftly. I will drive the wagon, Viulra will be alongside me with his bow. Daryo, Cambitilian, Dororossi, all three of you will be ahead. Go as fast as you can for as long as you can. We make for the mine.'

It was a hard run. Weapons in hand, eyes scanning the countryside, Daryo ran at the head of the little column. Occasionally he thought he saw a part-concealed figure in the landscape but no ambush came and they continued. After two miles, Cambitilian insisted he could go no further and Viulra gave up the bow and wagon to run alongside Daryo. The incline got steeper and what Daryo had initially thought was mist ahead around the mountain soon resolved itself to be smoke. The mine was burning.

There was a ditch and a high wooden fence making a compound, protected by a gate and low watchtower. The tower and gate were peppered with arrows and surrounded by little piles of slung stones. Parts of the fence were burning, as was a pile of rubbish at the base of the tower and most of the tents and buildings in the compound. The wooden doors across the mine door were still ablaze. Yashoun bodies were strewn across the ground as if scattered by a giant child.

'I think we are too late,' said Viulra in a flat tone.

Dauke was white-faced. 'I knew almost all these men.' The Tibilians were checking the bodies for survivors. Viulra picked up a rusty iron sword, studied it and threw it aside.

'Why?' Dauke asked. 'Why would the Nar Silver do this? This is not even their land.'

'Is it close?' asked Daryo.

'A few miles.'

'Maybe it is territory. The Nar Silver want this land, or believe it to be theirs, and the establishment of the mine is an invasion in their eyes.'

'There's no reason. This is Yashoun land.'

'This is the Silver Island,' said Viulra. 'It belongs to the Silver Islanders and the Nar Silver.'

'And it was taken from them!' snapped Dauke.

'Taken! As you say! Precisely as you say! If I took your sword, you would want to take it back!'

'Or I would find another!'

'If I took your wife? Or your sister?'

'I would kill you!'

'And that is how you have made the Silver Islanders and Nar Silver feel!'

'What would you know, Batribi?' demanded Dororossi.

'I know because I am from a people that are thrown out of any land we are in for more than eight days! I know because my people have no land! I know because everything my people have is taken from us unless we fight with swords, spears and teeth!' Viulra had crossed the distance to the Tibilian and was towering over him by fourteen inches.

Daryo saw Dororossi drop his hand to his sword. He drew Temma's Sword, Cambitilian had seized his own weapon. The hurled stone struck Cambitilian on the back of the neck. The Tibilian spun to face the threat and the second hit the side of his head, knocking him to the ground like a felled tree.

Daryo raised his shield just in time to block a stone aimed at him. Dauke reacted quickly, diving behind the wagon and grabbing the shield of a dead man. Viulra notched an arrow and fired in the direction of the stones. Dororossi had been forced to abandon his twin and use a smouldering shed for cover. Cambitilian was motionless, face down on the ground next to a Yashoun corpse. Viulra joined Dauke behind the wagon.

'I cannot see them,' shouted Viulra.

'In the high ground above the mine entrance!' Dororossi called back.

Viulra notched another arrow, swung around the wagon and fired in the direction indicated. Daryo used the diversion to run to the shed alongside Dororossi.

'Is my brother dead?'

'I cannot tell. I do not think so.'

Another of Viulra's arrows flew into the high ground.

'Hold your arrows, Viulra!' Daryo called. 'Save them for targets!'

A few more slung stones cracked off of the wagon and the ground.

'We cannot hide here forever, Daryo! If they can, they will have support coming!'

Daryo glanced around the corner of the shed and got a picture of the scene. 'I can get forwards. I have the only shield. Dororossi, will you aid me, follow my instructions?' The Tibilian assented. 'When you are prepared, out towards the mine entrance. There is an overturned cart. Shelter there.'

Dororossi took a long breath and rushed out, after twenty yards, he broke right and dived behind the cart. Simultaneously, Daryo ran the other side of the shed and sprinted forwards to a wooden screen that had once been the back of a woodpile. He slammed into the screen and kept his head down below the top. Another small shower of stones came down. One bounced and fell alongside Daryo. It was a little smaller than his fist, knobbly and, from the speed, was definitely from a slingshot.

'Viulra! The black rock at the top of the mine entrance!'

'Can see it!'

'I believe there is one behind that rock! Two quick arrows!'

'Two!' Viulra's arrows flew and Daryo peered up and over the screen as the arrows struck near the rock. There was a swift movement: a Nar Silver recoiling. Daryo saw another piece of cover, a mine cart, and ran forwards. Another stone came from the right of the black rock. Dororossi emerged from cover, the slinger on the right had to stand to fire

and Viulra shot him. The second Nar Silver tried to escape. Viulra fired again, the arrow struck near the tribesman and he scrambled to safety. Daryo stood up cautiously.
'We should leave. He will go for aid.'
Dororossi went to his brother. Cambitilian was awake but seemingly beyond sense. There was a lump like a duck's egg growing above his left ear and he seemed unaware that his twin had lifted him to his feet and was enquiring how he was. Instead he stood, swaying slightly, his weapon aside, a thin trickle of blood coming from his right ear, eyes unfocused.
Dauke and Daryo had a fierce debate as to what to do with the supplies. Viulra and Dororossi eventually sided with Daryo. The pony was turned loose and the wagon burned. Dauke took a shield from the ground and the small party hurried south again.

The decision was unanimous to avoid the road. They went south-west, across country, to join the Suxin-Vinyu road. The pace was as rapid as possible given the rocky and unstable ground and Cambitilian's insensibility. Viulra climbed available sites at intervals for a better view. He could not see a single Nar Silver clearly any time but it was clear that they were being pursued: the movement of the bushes against the breeze, odd clatters and whistles that were not made by animals. The feeling of being pursued grew, a feeling of prey and predators.
Daryo leaped a ditch and an animal started. It was like a goat but larger, with longer legs and curved horns nearly as large as its body. It raced away with bounding leaps, its dun coat blending it into the landscape in moments. After three miles, Cambitilian, being dragged by Dororossi and pushed by Daryo, stumbled into a hole and there was an ominous, sickening noise. Despite his dazed condition, Cambitilian screamed.
'Viulra, watch for the Nar Silver!' Daryo called. 'Dauke, give me that staff.'
Dauke had taken a staff from the compound as a walking stick. He threw it to Daryo. The Batribi pushed Cambitilian down, pushed the staff against the snapped lower leg and bound it tightly with his last remaining bandage strip. Viulra had a spare bowstring and Daryo used it to bind the leg to the staff. Dororossi had rammed the hilt of a knife into his brother's mouth to stop him biting through his tongue and to reduce the noise of his screaming.
'Wine, anything,' Daryo appealed. He had seen healers administer wine to the injured. Dororossi had a small flask of strong wine and poured it straight into his twin's mouth. Cambitilian swallowed and sobbed in agony.
'He cannot walk,' said Daryo firmly.

'We cannot remain,' replied Viulra, readying an arrow. He had only a score left. 'I can see... three... four... five, possibly.'

'Shoot one,' said Daryo.

Viulra drew, aimed and loosed. There was a thud as the arrow struck its target. 'One struck.'

'We have to carry him,' said Dororossi.

'I am strongest,' Viulra suggested.

'I can shoot,' said Dauke. 'All Yashoun soldiers can shoot bow.'

Viulra handed over his bow and quiver of arrows. With little apparent effort, other than a grunt, he hauled Cambitilian over his shoulders, hooked his arm through Cambitilian's uninjured leg, grabbed the Tibilian's arm with the hand and stood up. 'Go.'

The party moved on, much slower, Dororossi at the front, scouting for hazards; Daryo behind Viulra carrying Cambitilian and Dauke at the rear with the bow. Cambitilian lost sense after less than a mile and vomited soon afterwards, covering Viulra's back and legs. They had to stop again. Viulra put Cambitilian down on his side but the Tibilian was soon shaking violently.

'He is passing,' Dauke muttered to Daryo.

'And not well,' said Dororossi firmly, standing up. 'Dauke, give me the bow.' Dauke glanced at Viulra, who had taken off his cloak and thrown it away. Viulra nodded and Dauke handed over the bow and arrows. 'I will hold them back as long as I am able. The faster you move, the more time I can make for you.'

Viulra looked at Dororossi for a long few heartbeats. 'You could come with us.'

'You know I will not. Cambitilian is my twin, born within heartbeats of me. We are beyond brothers. When he dies, I die beside him.'

'Whatever you believe,' said Daryo, 'I hope they receive you well.'

'Your sacrifice will never be forgotten,' added Dauke. 'I will ensure that.'

Dororossi nodded and turned away resolutely. 'Go.' He drew the bow.

Dauke, Viulra and then Daryo turned their backs and began to run again.

Dororossi's stand brought the two Batribi and the Yashoun enough time to reach the road. They turned south and were able to increase speed. By nightfall, they were within sight of Suxin's barracks. With a huge effort, they managed to reach the gate. Dauke asked the Batribi to hang back and he spoke with the sentries. After a lengthy conversation, one of the sentries went inside the compound and returned with an officer. The officer had an exchange with Dauke and then went back. He returned with a superior, who also had a long talk with Dauke. After this, three soldiers brought half a dozen horses and Dauke, Viulra and Daryo were escorted back to the *Black Dove*.

Dauke paid both Daryo and Viulra when they reached the ship. Thirty gold halves was a very good sum of money, although the risk to their lives and the loss of the brave, albeit prickly, Tibilians made the gold feel somewhat inadequate. Dauke insisted that the ship would not leave the Silver Island for another two days and that both Batribi's berths were available for them. That night, they retired to their hammocks aboard ship. At times, they tried to converse about their experiences but words failed and they fell into silence and sleep.

## Chapter 24

The next dawn, Daryo and Viulra went ashore. They found a bowyer and fletcher in a small square near the harbour, surrounded by various similar craftsmen and tradesmen. Viulra spent an entire gold half on an imported Adacan recurved bow and another three silver halves, at six silver to a gold half, on four-score steel-headed arrows. For a small amount, a smith allowed Daryo to use his grindstone to sharpen his blades. Viulra had his boots repaired and bought a new cloak, one of green and brown, to replace the one soiled and lost. The two Batribi then walked across town to the temple. It was a Temple of the whole Pantheon and there were altars in a circle, each adorned with a carving of the God or Goddess's symbol, around the central one made in the form of the Eightfold Circle. Daryo prayed at the Second Goddess's altar, Viulra at the First God's.

Afterwards, they walked across the town, exploring the place. By the mouth of the river, the older part of the town, several strange white birds with massive, long beaks, flat on the top but bulbous underneath, with long necks and webbed black feet, were perched along the edge of the water. They regarded the Batribi with indifference and seemed completely unafraid when Daryo approached them. Further up the riverbank was a squat stone building, its roof almost flat, with a wooden barricade in front of the door, which was nailed shut, and a sign had been nailed to the barricade:

*Closed by the order of the Governor of the Silver Island on instruction from the Emperor of the Yashoun.*

⸿ ×𝜤𝜀𝜤⸿⸿⸿⸿⸿⸿ 𝜑⸿ 𝜑 𝜑 𝜑⸿⸿⸿⸿ ⸺⸿𝜤⸿𝜀𝜤⸿

'I wonder what this building was,' said Viulra, studying the symbols above the door- a series of ten symbols that were made out of a mosaic of glass and pottery shards. 'It looks like a temple.'

'Perhaps it is. The Yashoun do not like religions other than that of the Pantheon. When they invaded, perhaps they had the Silver Island's temples closed.'

Viulra glanced around. They were at least fifty yards from the nearest building. 'Perhaps we could gain entry?'

Daryo chuckled. 'Were you the type of child who stole fruit from the orchards and milk from the breast of someone else's mother?'

Viulra laughed uproariously and slapped Daryo on the back. 'Oh, I was! I was! Our clan elder despaired of me! My father slapped my legs so often his hands stung endlessly!'

Daryo laughed along. 'Perhaps another time then. We have just finished being paid for honest work by the Yashoun Empire. Perhaps we should not violate the order of the Emperor just now.'

'Ha! Wise words, my friend! Wise words! Yes, perhaps we should move on and not court any more trouble.'

They returned through the old part of Suxin towards the docks. As they passed through the square, there was a large crowd of Silver Islanders outside the Half Moon House. The dozen Yashoun guard at the gates of the compound were all in armour, with bare swords in hand and shields raised. On the roof were a cluster of archers. Daryo had left Temma's Sword and his shield on the *Black Dove*, his twin swords were on his back but the growing crowd's anger seemed to be directed at the Yashoun. There were several people shouting at the Yashoun guards in both Common Speech and in the Silver Island language. The guard commander, a crested helmet under his arm, was listening to three elders who were stood at the front. One was enraged, the others trying to keep their compatriot composed. The Yashoun leader pointed back to the governor's house and raised his hand, suggesting perhaps that either the governor was powerless or that the captain was powerless to influence the governor. The Silver Island elders had a quick discussion between themselves. The angrier one was hoisted onto the shoulders of three younger men. The crowd quietened.

*'Yi an to merro ten, tai lan te tes ton lan!'*

The crowd roared and began to move up the road that led out of the town towards Vinyu. Daryo and Viulra hurried aside as the mob funnelled down the narrow road. The Yashoun leader spoke with some of his men and three-quarters of them followed the crowd out of the square.

'That looks like a protest,' said Viulra. 'The Islanders are not happy with something.'

'Dauke may know,' Daryo suggested. Their employer had just emerged from Half Moon House, wearing Yashoun uniform. The Batribi crossed the square and waited outside the compound for Dauke to reach them.

'You saw the assembly.'

'We did. What caused it?' Daryo glanced up the road at the withdrawing mob.

'The Nar Silver are becoming very active. There are many villages in the island interior and they are being attacked. The Islanders do not feel the governor is doing enough.'

'Is he?'

Dauke turned towards the port and the Batribi fell into step. 'The governor is doing all he can. There are too few Yashoun on the island to act.'

'The barracks...'

'Are almost empty. There are less than a hundred Yashoun on the island, and some of those are civilian. They left the camp and the equipment but most of the soldiers have left. Swords lay rusting in the armoury.'

Daryo and Viulra exchanged looks. 'The Imperial possession is a sham.'

'It is.' Dauke sounded defeated. 'The Islanders are either demanding action or to be armed.'

'And the governor will not do either,' Viulra suggested. 'There are insufficient resources to deploy soldiers and arming the Silver Islanders would risk Yashoun being thrown off of the island entirely.'

Dauke nodded dully. 'I have been asked to stay and assist but the governor is not my commander. I have my own duties, I am returning to the Twin Ports with the next dawn as planned. One captain cannot have an impact on this situation, not without a company of men.'

They reached the ship. Dauke and Daryo boarded but Viulra pleaded a desire to return to the temple.

'Daryo. Daryo. Come along, Daryo.'

He could not tell what time it was other than it was the very earliest time of the morning.

'Viulra? What is it?'

'Shhh, stay quiet, my friend. Come, we have somewhere to be.'

'Dule's Anvil, Viulra, what time of day is it?'

Daryo struggled to sit up in his hammock. Viulra was holding a single candle in one hand and Daryo's boots in the other.

'Not long past midnight. Come, come. I have your boots.'

Daryo took his boots, pulled them on and scrambled out of his hammock. 'What is it?'

'Somewhere we must be. Come.'

The big Batribi handed Daryo his cloak and twin swords. Daryo pulled his sword harness on and then his cloak. 'Where are we going?'

'Ashore. We must be careful. There is a curfew in the town.'

Daryo yawned. 'Why are we going?'

'There is somewhere we must be. Come.' Viulra ducked out of the cabin, Daryo close behind. They slipped out onto the deck and over the side onto the dock. Instead of moving into the town, Viulra went to the left and around towards the river. Twice they had to duck into cover as a pair of Yashoun guards passed nearby. Several of the large-beaked birds were roosting along the side of the river and the Batribi passed them carefully. They were near the closed-up old temple, Viulra hurried across to a nearby wooden hut and tapped on the door.

'*Un ta?*' came a whispered voice from inside.

'*Hensi,*' Viulra whispered back.

The door was opened and Viulra led the way in. A Silver Islander, no more than twelve summers old, smiled at them, shut the door and pulled aside a bed mat to reveal a hole and a ladder descending into it. Viulra scrambled down, followed by Daryo and the boy. At the base of the hole, nearly twelve feet down, there was a three-foot high tunnel, lit by fat lamps in recesses. Viulra carefully crawled along to the other end and then beckoned Daryo on. There was another hole and another ladder at the far end and Viulra helped Daryo over the edge. They were in the corner of a low stone building, about twenty yards square. The door and window shutters were shut and barricaded, the interior was lit only by a few lamps. About a dozen figures were visible in the dim light. The boy scrambled out of the hole and spoke quickly to one of the figures. They picked up a lamp and came closer.

'You say all Batribi on island.' It was the elder, the angry one, from the market square crowd.

'And I spoke truthfully,' said Viulra. 'There are two of us.'

'How will two Batribi help?'

'We are warriors, trained warriors,' Viulra insisted. 'And my companion, Daryo the Walker, is one of the members of the ancient Order of the Shield and Sword.'

'The Order of the Shield and Sword,' repeated a voice from the back of the room. A small figure, bent over and leaning on a stick, came forwards. Their right arm was missing, the face drawn and almost grey. 'Daryo the Walker.'

'Yi!' The only Silver Island member of the Order had been gravely wounded at the final battle of the Order. Daryo had assumed him dead. 'I thought...'

'I escaped. I went with Turgid and Blessed to Spiert. We found shelter, I healed as well as could be and then came home. Why are you here?'

'I came in the employ of a Yashoun but our mission failed because of the Nar Silver.'

'Why are you *here*?'

'For that, you must ask Viulra.'

'I listened to what you said, Daryo, about helping those in need. The Silver Islanders are in need. I did not return to the temple this past night, I found the crowd protesting at the barracks and spoke with the leader.' He indicated the Silver Islander elder. 'I offered him our services against the Nar Silver.'

Daryo was nonplussed for several heartbeats. 'Are you serious, Viulra?'

'Very. This is a chance for us to achieve something. We were unable to help the miners. We were unable to help Dororossi or Cambitilian. But we could help the Islanders.'
Daryo looked around the shadowy assembly of Silver Islanders and into the earnest face of his huge companion. He turned to Yi, drew a sword and held it up by the hilt, point down. 'My sword and my service, Islander.'
'Until discharged by death, Walker.'

The dark temple yielded a dozen wooden boxes as seats and the lamps were brought to together to light the circle. There were ten Silver Islanders, seven men and three women. The boy had clambered onto a shelf high above a window to keep watch.
'What do we have available?' asked Daryo.
'We have men,' said Yi. 'We are not cowed as the Yashoun think. We have own company of men but no weapons.'
'So we need weapons,' said Viulra. 'The barracks, there are weapons there.'
A young woman was translating for the elders, one of whom voiced an objection. Yi assented. 'There are hundreds there.'
'No,' Daryo told him. 'The Yashoun we were working for told us that there are less than a hundred.'
This provoked a wave of comment and debate. It took a considerable time before Yi was able to say: 'We were talking of taking back our island. We will take the weapons, offer the Yashoun to join us. If they refuse, they can be confined. If they accept, we can fight with them.'
Daryo nodded. 'Very wise. We need someone who knows the Yashoun barracks. We will need to know where the armoury is, who keeps the keys and the patrol routes. Then we need a method to transport the weapons. We must have a mustering point for the company, a training regime and a commander.'
'They are trained,' said Yi. 'The commander can be decided. The rest can be put in place. Be at the Yashoun Temple at noon and we can put our plans in movement.'

Daryo and Viulra crept back to the *Black Dove* undetected and were quickly asleep once in their hammocks. With the new light, they gathered their belongings and equipment and informed Dauke that they had decided to stay on the island and explore the land while they had the opportunity before paying for passage back to the mainland. Dauke was surprised but was happy for them to do so, noting that they had been paid and were not obliged to follow his lead. He assured them that they had until the *Black Dove* sailed to change their decision if they so wished but that, if they remained, they did so with his grateful thanks. Just before noon, the *Black Dove* rowed out of Suxin Bay, unfurled its sails and set a course west of southwest for the Twin Ports of Ossmoss and Paloss. The two Batribi took their packs to an inn and then hurried to the Temple of the Pantheon.

# Chapter 25

The sun was long down. The dead moon of the Fourth Goddess gave no light among the stars. In the darkness, two Batribi and two Silver Islanders crept through the broken ground alongside the road until they reached the edge of the moat of the Yashoun fort. One of the Silver Islanders, the boy lookout Sen, slid carefully down the bank and into the water. His companions heard him hiss as he entered the cold water and some gentle splashes as he swam to the other bank. Viulra notched one of his new arrows to his equally-new bow, aiming at the dark shape of an archer in the nearest watchtower, about thirty yards away and about the same high. There was a tap-tap, then another and a third. Sen signalling. The other Islander with them, a young woman named Hai, had a long rope. She threw one end across to Sen, who quickly pulled it tight so it did not splash in the moat. First Daryo and then Viulra used the rope as a guide to slip down into the moat and across to the other side. The water was breath-stealing in its chill and Daryo was glad to scramble out on the far side despite the fact his clothing was sodden. Sen gently paid the rope back into the moat and Hai pulled it in. She would stay on watch. Sen led the way along the fort's wooden wall to the base of the watchtower. Instead of upright wooden pillars, it became horizontal slats to the top of the wall. Sen climbed up first. He progressed slowly but absolutely silently. At the top of the eight-foot palisade, he gave the tapping signal again and then dropped down inside the wall. Daryo followed next. He had only his Twin Swords again, shield and Temma's Sword left at the inn, and was able to climb almost as quietly as Sen had. At the top, he also gave the tapping signal and dropped down. The ground was soft and yielding but stank. It occurred to him he had landed in the garbage pile from the kitchens. Sen was crouched nearby. The sentry on the watchtower was pacing and his footsteps masked Viulra's climb and heavy fall on the other side. The kitchen was a wooden building with a wide stone chimney. Beyond it was a pathway from the gate and then a structure with lanterns hanging outside that faintly illuminated the sign: '*Officers*'. The man that they had met in the temple, a former horseman at the fort, had said that the armoury was directly behind the officers' building. Daryo slid past Sen to the corner of the kitchen. The building alongside was a store with a narrow alley left between them. Daryo crept along it, checked the thoroughfare and sneaked across. He looked back and beckoned. Sen scuttled across, then Viulra. They passed the officers' building, a couple of voices audible inside. Behind was a stone and wood building with a tiled roof and no windows. The armoury. The door was onto another thoroughfare, facing the parade square. The keeper of the key would be the duty officer, based in the guardhouse by the gate. But at regular intervals, the duty officer checked the doors...

He was alone, without a helmet, sword at his hip, stave in hand. The keys were on a loop in his hand. It was simple enough for Viulra to allow him to pass, slip up behind him and knock him senseless with a stone cupped in his fist. The Batribi then dragged the insentient Yashoun back into the shadow. The keys had been dropped and Daryo scooped them up. There were a dozen keys but the second one tried unlocked the iron-banded armoury door. Daryo took one of the lanterns from alongside and stepped inside. The small building was a single room. Racks of swords lined three walls, barrels were full of staves, Yashoun combat knives were bound in pairs on the central tables with shields stacked underneath and the door's wall was bows, arrows and coiled strings. Daryo gave the knocking pattern on the door and soon Viulra and Sen had joined him.

'More than enough,' muttered Viulra, counting swords. 'At least ten score.'

'Four score bows... enough staves for three companies,' Daryo added. 'Perfect. We must wait for the transportation now. Hai will have signalled them.'

'What if the guards at the gate do not admit them?'

'Then we have our second plan.' Daryo hoped it was unnecessary. The second plan called for eliminating the guards at the gate, shooting the archers in the towers and taking the fort in a rapid stroke, but they had insufficient men and weapons to do so effectively and it would mean no chance of the Yashoun agreeing to aid the Islanders. He reached up and drew the Horse. Somehow he felt more secure with the sword in his hand. A cart was coming up with three Silver Islanders, ostensibly to empty the latrine. Concealed in the cart were six more to help load. The cart would then drive out and the six assistants would follow Sen and the two Batribi out over the fence. Nearby, another twenty Islanders were concealed, the attack force for the second plan. Daryo went to the door and glanced out. Sen, who could not speak a word in the Common Speech, smiled supportively.

'They should be here,' Daryo muttered.

'Patience,' was Viulra's response. 'Patience. Trust to the Third Goddess.'

'The Fourth is too vocal.'

'Talk softly but keep your sword close.'

'I try to.' He pulled the door ajar again and peered out. 'This is not right.'

The young lookout, Sen, looked fantastically unruffled. He was perched on a table full of daggers, inspecting one of the pairs of blades. The Yashoun fighting knife, a foot long and simply made, were a peculiarity of the Empire: no other army issued its soldiers with such weapons but Yashoun soldiers were all taught to fight with swords, staves, daggers, bow and fists.

Daryo heard voices, then footsteps and slowly closed the door.

'Should Masuki have said something like that?' one man asked as they approached.

'I think he should. Someone had to.'

'But all it does is get Tauo angry and that makes life harder for everyone.'

'If nobody says it, how will he ever know?'

'Does it have to be said so... bluntly?'

'Perhaps not but Masuki never was subtle.' The footsteps stopped. 'Dule on them!'

'What?'

'Some fool cannot count. Look. Supposed to be two lamps. And that *is* Tauo's job.'

'Maybe Masuki had a point!'

'That was what I was saying. Fool, a total fool.'

'Best to get another.'

'Not at this time. Daiki will be abed and as much as Tauo angry is bad, Daiki angry is even worse. We would be hearing about this until the sky falls. No, let the guard officer find it and give Tauo a smack. It might sort the twice-cursed idiot.'

'Ha! Some chance!' The footsteps resumed and the guards moved away.

Daryo released a breath he had been unaware that he had held. He glanced back at Viulra, who had an arrow drawn. The big man relaxed his bowstring and mopped at his brow. 'The Fourth Goddess is getting to me, my friend.'

'Welcome to madness,' muttered Daryo, cracking the door open again. This time he could hear hooves and the creak of wheels. 'This could be them.'

There was a donkey cart coming along the path, two Islanders leading the donkeys, an elder sat on the back of the cart. The cart stopped outside the armoury. One of the men at the front made a short pantomime of examining the cart. He removed the pin from the wheel on his side and hurled it away. He then went back towards the gate, ostensibly searching for the pin, in reality to keep watch from that side. The other donkey-tender stayed with the animals, watching the other direction. The elder slid off of the wagon and hissed an instruction. Under a sheet, covered in peat and manure, in the bottom of the wagon, six were concealed and they slid out. One doused the remaining lamp. Daryo opened the armoury door, sheathing the Horse again. Viulra already had a sword in each hand. He passed them to Sen, he to Daryo, Daryo to the first of the concealed robbers and soon a rapid chain were passing the swords into the cart, where the elder stowed them. The swords were done and Viulra began to pass the daggers out. Every heartbeat seemed to Daryo to take too long; the swords took an age to pass out, the daggers took longer, every moment was another moment that a wandering Yashoun soldier could catch them. The daggers were finally done and the bows began to be passed.

'Please! Help, wheel pin lost!' came the voice of the cart driver.

'What?'

'Wheel pin! Wheel break! Need pin!'

The six men passing the weapons froze. *'Shin no,'* whispered the elder. One by one, they slid past Daryo into the denuded armoury. With admirable calm, the elder pulled the filthy sheet back over the loot and started wandering, scuffing his feet on the ground, as his comrade continued to plead the Yashoun for help. Daryo closed the door.

'Wheel pin! Dirt cart, no pin, wheel off, no dirt cart.'

'Why can you Islanders not learn the Common Tongue properly?' growled the guard. 'I think you mean you have lost the wheel pin from your dirt cart. Yes?'

'Yes, sir!'

The Yashoun groaned. 'There is a woodpile, over there. Find a piece of wood to use.'

'Thanking you, sir.'

The guard's heavier footsteps approached as the Islander scuttled away. The guard approached the cart. 'I sent your man to find a new pin.'

*'Am niti so?'* asked the elder politely.

The guard sighed. 'Do *you* speak Common Speech?'

'Yes, sir,' said the man with the donkeys.

'I sent your friend to find a new pin from the woodpile. He should be back soon.' There was a pause. 'Did you put out those lanterns?'

'No, sir. Like that when we stopped. Light would help us find the pin.'

'Hmm.' The guard's footsteps approached the armoury door. Viulra blew out the lantern. There was a painfully long pause. 'Why can some people escape with not doing their tasks?' he muttered to himself, then addressed the Islander. 'Be quick, do your task and go. I do not like your people wandering in our camp.'

'We will be quick, sir. Very quick.'

The guard's footsteps receded. The elder came to the door and nudged it open. 'Gone,' he said with a sly grin.

Daryo nodded. 'That is most of it. Just some bows left. I think we stop now.'

'Stop now,' agreed the elder. 'Just dirt to take, then back. Good fortune.' He whistled and the other driver appeared from the shadows, taking a new wheel pin from his pocket. It was put in place, the elder sat back on the cart and the donkeys were moved on. Daryo checked every direction and slipped out of the armoury, beckoning the Silver Islanders after him. Sen led them around the armoury and back towards the watchtower.

Viulra was last to leave the armoury, some borrowed Yashoun arrows supplementing the half-dozen of his own. He closed the door of the armoury, locked it and dropped the keys next to the still-insensible officer alongside the building. The two Batribi then hurried towards their exit point. They were within yards when the alarm bell sounded. 'Quick!' said Viulra, almost throwing Daryo at the wall. Daryo scrambled up and felt and heard Viulra following. They reached the top and Daryo threw himself off into the moat, closely followed by Viulra. The pair swam to the bank and scrambled out. On the watchtower, the archer could hear the noise and started firing arrows blindly into the area. Daryo felt the rush of air as one passed his head. He found a large rock and slid in behind it. Viulra had found similar shelter a few yards away.
'They will search,' he said.
'We must get back to the temple.'
Viulra chanced a look over his rock. 'I can see nobody. We can go.'

Just after dawn, the market began to open. Farmers and their carts arrived, several stalls had fish from the harbour, a potter had a barrow of wares, a woman was selling fabric and another had woven baskets. All abandoned their posts and hurried to look as a column of their countrymen marched six-abreast through the centre of the market. They wore a mixture of old and improvised armour, archaic uniforms and civilian clothes. They were led by a group of elders, a cripple and two Batribi. The first ten ranks of men carried bows that looked suspiciously like Yashoun bows. The next score ranks had Yashoun-pattern swords. The score ranks behind had a mixture of spears, staves, knives and other weapons. The column moved smartly through the market and approached the gate to Half Moon House. The guards at the entrance to the compound stood with weapons in hand but there were only four of them. At the head of the column, a young Batribi carrying a curved blade and round shield levelled the point at the closest guard. His large companion divested the guards of their weapons.
'Fetch the governor,' he ordered gruffly, giving one of the guards a shove in the direction of the house.
The Yashoun looked up fearfully at the man and then ran for the house. The column moved into the compound, the grass-covered areas either side of the path were soon covered in armed Silver Islanders. Above the door of the great house was a balcony, the door onto it opened and a tall, heavy man in a nightshirt and robe came out with a crossbow in hand. He had apparently only half-believed the report that hundreds of Silver Islanders had taken his residence.
'This is rebellion then!' he announced.

An Islander woman of about forty springs stepped forwards. She was one of the leaders of the company and spoke the Common Tongue most clearly. 'Not rebellion, sir! This is defence! The Nar Silver are hurting our people and the Empire does nothing to prevent it! So we are taking action! The weapons have been taken from the barracks, there is another company there to ensure the soldiers do not react violently. If you order the commander to assist us, he will. If you do not, the soldiers will be confined in the barracks until we are finished with the Nar Silver.'

The governor looked around. 'You leave me little option!'

Viulra chuckled to himself. 'That was the plan.'

The governor put down his crossbow. 'You have given me no option but to surrender. But mark these words: the Yashoun Empire will not forget this act!' He turned and strode back into the House followed by some cheers, insults and laughter from the armed men outside.

'We cannot take that to be agreement to assist us, a surrender suggests he is not going to aid us,' said Viulra. 'The company has to secure the barracks.'

'Carefully,' Daryo added. 'The commander may be more reasonable.'

The Silver Islander leaders quickly conferred in their own language. One looked at Daryo a few times, who heard the words *Choi Tie*, the words for Batribi. The spokeswoman turned.

'Would *you* lead the men there?' she pointed at Daryo as she spoke.

Daryo glanced at Viulra. 'Would I? Are you sure?'

'Certainly.'

Daryo felt very strange marching at the head of a company of warriors. He had never been at the head of a company and not in such circumstances. As they approached the barracks, Daryo was aware that there would be archers observing. They were the complication, he knew. A rapid but bloodless rush to take the whole fort was likely best but the archers could cause a rapid escalation as they could fire from their towers with relative impunity. The plan had been made in advance- the same as Half Moon House. Daryo strode across the wooden bridge across the fort's moat, all of the Islander archers and swordsmen at his heels; only the ill-armed had stayed at Half Moon House but their numbers alone were more than sufficient. The guards at the gate looked completely bewildered but raised their weapons.

Daryo raised his empty swordhand. 'There need be no blood spilled!' he announced, stopping a respectful distance from the sentries. 'I must talk with the commander. I swear in the name of the Third Goddess that no violence shall be used unless we are provoked.'

One of the guards almost tripped as he scrambled through the postern gate and disappeared. Daryo noticed another three archers climb to the nearest tower and gripped his shield a little tighter. After an aching wait, the postern opened and the commander of the fort stepped out: a man almost dark enough to a Batribi, tightly curled black hair poked out from under his helmet, his naked sword in hand. He took several heartbeats to study the situation.

'What is this?' he asked calmly.

'This is an opportunity,' said Daryo. 'An offer but not one that will be given again. The Silver Islanders are taking action against the Nar Silver because the governor and you refuse to do so. You will have noticed your emptied armoury. The governor is currently arrested in his residence. This force outnumbers yours by more than two men against one. We can storm the fort and take it from you but scores will die. Alternatives are possible however: you can surrender the fort to us. Your men can disarm and you may remain in the fort until the Nar Silver have been subdued. Or you could fight with us. Your force is small but skilled, they could be an immense help. The Yashoun Empire states that the Silver Islanders are citizens of the Empire, you could make that true. Help them to defend themselves.'

The commander regarded Daryo for a long while. 'I cannot make such a decision alone. My officers and I must be permitted to speak with the governor.'

Daryo thought for a moment and then nodded. 'You will be escorted to Half Moon House.'

The market had become a throng. Daryo guessed that at least another three hundred Silver Islanders had arrived, all bearing some kind of weapon, ranging from rusty swords to pitchforks and fishing harpoons. The commander almost fell off of his horse. He had brought four men as an escort and they looked pathetically outnumbered. Daryo had the same number of Silver Islanders with him and they all laughed at the sight. The Yashoun soldier and his escort were guided into the compound of Half Moon House and up to the door. The commander and his men dismounted and were permitted inside. Daryo found Viulra sat on an elegantly-carved stone bench to the side of the house.

'The commander of the fort?' he asked Daryo.

'A rather chastened commander,' Daryo replied, sitting next to his companion.

The wait was worse than a battle. The sun moved on, the cloud came across, the cloud broke apart and disappeared. The morning became one of heat and tedium. The increasingly large Silver Islander crowd became restless and agitated. Arguments and disputes broke out and Viulra was instrumental in breaking up a swordfight. Eventually, a Yashoun soldier emerged from Half Moon House and requested the leaders of the Silver Islanders.

Daryo and Viulra were invited to join a group of six Silver Islanders- four elders and two younger leaders- that were taken inside. They were taken through the polished-wood hallway and up the stairs to the governor's chamber. He was sat behind a table, flanked by the captain and a robed civilian official. The governor stood up as the deputation entered but he turned wordlessly to the commander.

The soldier spoke. 'This decision was not simple. The governor is acting on orders from the Empire and does not feel able to defy those orders.' He glanced at the governor. 'So he had resigned his office. I am now representative and commander of the Empire here. I am not willing to send my men to fight the Nar Silver. I do not wish to defy the Emperor's orders. But I was reminded today that the Silver Island is part of the Empire and its people are therefore under the protection of the Empire. The native forces should act against the Nar Silver. The Army of the Yashoun will protect Suxin and Cansunri.'

## Chapter 26

Sonyon was a small village beside one of the rivers that ran southwards from the mountains to the sea, dependent on goats, sheep and fish, close to the Nar Silver's territory, which was marked by a series of wooden posts running along a dry riverbed less than five miles from the village. It was a small force that approached from the north, following the river. There had been less than forty suitable horses and they had been quickly commandeered. At the head of the thirty-one riders were two more figures, one in a hooded cloak with a shield on his arm, the other a huge man with a fine longbow. The column of smoke rising from the village was drifting north on the hot wind. From the distance, it seemed that every house in the village was burning. The column spurred their horses on desperately.

Daryo the Walker was the first to jump down from his horse on the edge of the village. It was not just every house burning- carts, fishing nets, even fenceposts had been thrown on the fires.

'Find the people!' Daryo shouted and the Silver Islanders scrambled down from their mounts, several drawing their captured Yashoun swords. It was impossible to enter the village, the wall of burning houses was too intense and so they were forced to spread around the outside.

A young militiaman found the first of the villagers. Three men, two women, two young girls and a boy child had been tied to stakes at their hands and feet and their faces covered with sacking or blankets. The reports of the attack on Sonyon were three days old. In the heat, all of them had died from the heat and lack of water. Another group, eight women and three older men, were found by the riverbank. Eight children and two more elders were south of the village, then a group of seven men and boys. Lacking any other action, the Silver Islanders cut the bodies free of their stakes and began to excavate a grave with their swords. They refused to allow the Batribi to assist, so Daryo and Viulra searched for signs of the Nar Silver, finding nothing but continuing to look until the Silver Islanders had buried their countrymen.

The ride back towards Suxin had been quiet and subdued until a party of men, running across the plain. The riders, their interest and tempers piqued, gave chase. It was a party of Nar Silver and, despite being on foot, they turned and fought. Daryo turned his horse sharply to avoid the thrust of a spear and it reared, dumping him hard to the ground. One of the straps on the back of his shield snapped and Temma's Sword bounced away. Daryo looked up, his back and head screeching in agony, and just rolled away from a metal spike that was almost driven through his neck. He kicked out and caught the Nar Silver in the knee as an Islander woman stabbed his attacker. Daryo had come to appreciate in just three days of training and scouting how vicious and committed the women of the Silver Island were. They were fearsome warriors.

Viulra was practising a tactic that nobody had ever seen before- fighting with a bow at close quarters, firing arrows from ranges of less than ten yards, parrying blows with the metal-reinforced bow and even stabbing with arrows when necessary. A small group of the Nar Silver managed to flee and Viulra's last arrows chased them away. Daryo found Temma's Sword under the body of one of his force. Six of the Islanders had been killed, nearly thirty Nar Silver. Two of the Islanders had been injured, Viulra had taken a slash across the back of his neck but it was barely bleeding. When they saw the smoke rising again, Viulra had to almost tie the two injured women to their horses and he escorted them eastwards towards Suxin while Daryo led the remaining twenty-three north towards the rising smoke: the burning village of Cax'xi.

Another forty Islanders, from elders to children, had been left staked to the ground. Most had been beaten beyond sense first but many had come back to waking. Several of the children were screaming as they were cut free. Only one woman had died, probably from her injuries before being bound. Daryo sent three to ride hard for Suxin for wagons, more horses, more soldiers and physicians. The remaining women in his group, four of them, tended to the victims and the others spread out as a picket line around the burning village. Daryo had been forced to leave his shield tied to the saddle of his horse as the broken strap meant it was impossible to hold. He kept Temma's Sword in his belt and drew the Horse and the Bear as he patrolled the burning village. The Nar Silver was hidden in a depression by a pig sty, surrounded by slaughtered pigs. Daryo had almost stepped on him. A short, almost crescent-shaped blade lashed out and caught Daryo across the shin. He stabbed downwards with the Bear and, as he did, another Nar Silver came running from outside the village, knocking Daryo down in a tangle of limbs and swords. He heard running feet and shouts in Common Speech, the Nar Silver tongue and the Silver Islander language as he tried to fight off his attacker. The barrage of steel, bone and flesh suddenly ceased and became a dead weight. Daryo writhed free and regained his feet, just in time to duck beneath the swing of a cudgel and drive the Bear through the Nar Silver. As he withdrew his blade, he felt rather than heard another attack come from behind. He got the Horse up behind his head just in time for it to ring against the other blade and block it. He stabbed back with the Bear, found flesh, and swung the Horse in an arc, parrying the Nar Silver's blade aside and cleaving into his neck. There seemed to be no end to the flood, dozens of Nar Silver racing forwards with spears, blades and clubs. As fast as Daryo was able to fend off an attacker, another came. A pair broke through, running for the villagers in the centre. Daryo fought his way through and managed to intercept the first just as he seized a girl by the throat. After three strikes in the face, he released the screaming child. Daryo pushed the girl away and drove both of his blades into her assailant. The other Nar Silver grabbed an elderly man and shouted a challenge at Daryo, holding a knife to the man's throat. An arrow flew past Daryo's head narrowly. It struck the Nar Silver's hand, nicked the elder's throat and caused the attacker to lurch backwards, away from his captive. The second arrow struck the Nar Silver full in the chest, killing him.

Viulra had returned with nearly a hundred, the big Batribi riding at their head without reins, firing arrows quickly and precisely as he found Nar Silver targets. Daryo raised the Horse in salute and went to check on the elder. It was only a small wound and easily staunched. Viulra's force had quickly corralled the remaining Nar Silver and disarmed them. There were nearly forty prisoners and they were roughly handled into a column to be taken back to Suxin. The villagers were to wait for wagons and Viulra almost ordered Daryo to remove himself to Suxin to have his injury tended. Daryo was too tired to make a debate and led the column of Nar Silver prisoners and Silver Islander guards back to the city. The Yashoun commander declined to guard the prisoners, so they were taken to a large warehouse store on the edge of the harbour and confined there with a dozen archers spread on rooftops around and some of the less trained and equipped Islanders on the ground.

\*   \*   \*

The Silver Islander leaders called the two Batribi to a meeting at the reopened temple to announce that they had made a final assessment of their available forces. There were a handful over three hundred men and women that had trained despite the Yashoun prohibition. Two hundred of these had either Yashoun swords or Yashoun metal-tipped spears and all had procured large oblong shields from various sources; the shields were traditional Silver Island war equipment. The other hundred of the trained were equipped and proficient with the Yashoun bows and a small group of thirty crossbowmen had been added.

'We wish our Batribi warriors to lead the Company,' said the articulate spokeswoman named Kam. It was she who had delivered the terms to the governor.

Daryo and Viulra exchanged looks. Viulra gave a short bow. 'If that is what you wish.'

'It is. You are best warriors.'
'Then we will do what we can,' said Daryo.
'There are twenty score more with weapons of some kind. Some are pitchforks, some are kitchen knives. These are not good for fighting but can protect Suxin. Some are from Cansunri and will return to protect their homes.'
'Are there other villages that are not protected?' Viulra asked.
'There is Coha, Jen Tyii, Da Tyii, Neisunri and Vinyu.'
'We should send some of the militia to protect the villages,' said Daryo. 'At the least, the most exposed.'
Kam explained this to the other Islanders in their own language, most of the elders had only a basic knowledge of the Common Tongue. One responded: '*Coha i Vinyu ju maa.*'
'Coha and Vinyu are in need,' Kam translated.
'Perhaps fifty to each,' said Daryo. This was discussed by the elders and the settled number of three score to each village was decided.
'How is the Company to be used?' Viulra was studying the rather poor map of the island that they had available.
'The Nar Silver that attack the villages must be stopped,' said Kam. 'They attack Cax'xi and Sonyon so they must be near here.' She pointed to an area west of Cax'xi. 'South there is no water. They must be here.'
'We can sweep across the ground from Cax'xi,' said Viulra. 'Move west and into Nar Silver land. If there is a large number, they cannot hide easily. We stay on the high ground and it should be simple enough, with the Second God's help.'
Daryo nodded. 'Perhaps the prisoners may yield some information too.'
Kam frowned. 'There are few Islanders that speak Nar. And fewer Nar Silver that speak your speech or ours. But it can be tried.'

Viulra took command of the first search, taking half of the Company out towards Cax'xi. Daryo accompanied Kam and the translator to the harbour. He had been expecting, as few Silver Islanders spoke the language of the tribesmen, that the translator would be aged, a survivor from an age when Nar Silver and Islanders coexisted more closely. Instead, the translator was a boy, younger than Daryo at only fourteen or fifteen summers, with the darker skin and thick, curled hair of the Nar Silver. Still he spoke the Common Speech well and the Islanders' language too. Daryo guessed that he was of mixed origins, or perhaps an orphan brought up by Islanders. The main doors of the warehouse had been barricaded with wooden bars and an overturned wagon but had four men on guard nonetheless. Around the back was a smaller door, guarded by two men and three women with a mix of old swords; one was nearly as long as the woman holding it. She went inside and extracted a prisoner, a woman with her hands bound and a small gash on her arm. She stared with undisguised hostility at Kam and Daryo and spat at the boy translator. The precedent seemed to have been set. All the Nar Silver were silent towards Daryo and Kam and outright unpleasant or even aggressive towards the young translator. The most useful information gleaned from thirty-eight prisoners was that the Nar Silver were intent on killing as many Silver Islanders as possible. One lashed out at the translator and received a vicious thump on the side of the head from Daryo before he was escorted back into the barn. The entire exercise proved somewhat fruitless. Daryo walked away from the barn, trying to contain his frustration, and sat down on a large brown rock. The rock moved.

He jumped up as a long neck and legs emerged from the rock and the animal began to move towards the water. Daryo took another few quick steps away as the animal sedately moved onwards.

'Kam!'

The young woman came across. 'Yes?'

'What is that?!' He pointed at the animal.

'A shellback,' said Kam. 'There are many around the island but are they are not often near Suxin.'

Daryo took a wary step forwards. 'Are they dangerous?'

'Not often,' said Kam calmly. 'The mouth's bite is hard but they do not bite people unless they are threatened. Some people catch and eat them.' She went closer. The shellback looked up, a slow twist of the head, round black eyes regarded her with a sedate interest, before it lowered its head and trundled forwards. It stopped and took a bite of some shrubbery, chewing thoughtfully before plodding away.

'I have never seen such a thing,' said Daryo. 'A rock with legs...'

'A shellback,' said Kam with a grin.

'Why does it look like a rock?'

'I cannot say. Only nature knows. Perhaps it is to hide. The shell is very hard and protects the animal. It cannot live outside the shell.'

Daryo followed the animal for several yards, observing the slightly scaly green skin, the odd triangular tail and ridged mouth. The animal took a bite from another plant, ignoring its observer. The young translator joined him.

'Infinite rock,' he said. 'That is what the Nar Silver call the shellback. They live for twice the life of a man and are as hard as the rock of the mountain. The Silver use this form in war, making the rock with their shields.'

Daryo nodded. 'Very clever. I shall have to see that.'
A horse and rider arrived outside the barn and the rider dismounted as soon as he saw Daryo. 'Master Batribi, the searchers have been attacked. Please, you must come back to the square.'

The Third God has much to do, Daryo thought. There were nearly two score injured soldiers, several physicians were already at work. Daryo helped bind a gashed leg and the next mat had a very large figure laying on it.
'Daryo.' Viulra's normally booming voice was a rasp. 'Daryo.'
'Dule's Hammer, Viulra! What happened?'
'Ambushed. River. Hiding in the water. Arrows.' He lifted his cloak aside. There was the broken shaft of an arrow stuck just above his hip and another just between the ribs. He sighed and laid his head back. 'Dying.'
'I can get a physician!' Daryo went to stand up.
'No!' Viulra seized his wrist. 'Dying. No physician can help. I pray to Fourth Goddess.'
'You are not going to her yet, Viulra!'
Viulra coughed and sobbed in pain. 'Very soon. Be careful. Nar Silver... very good... clever...'
'Shh, rest...' Daryo looked around wildly for a physician.
'No! Dying. No time. They are out there, Daryo... expect attack anywhere... be strong... Would have left my bow but lost it... Pray for me, my friend.'
'I will. I swear.'
'The Dark Halls await me... always worshipped by name... I am ready to meet Vashine.'
To speak the name of the Fourth Goddess was believed to bring her action upon the speaker. Viulra died within heartbeats. Daryo stayed by his friend's side for a long time, ignoring the chaos around him. It was much later before he could think of the right words.
'I commend this man to the care of the Gods and Goddesses. From the First God, I ask health. From the First Goddess, bounty. From the Second God, resolve. From the Second Goddess, loyalty. From the Third God, recovery. From the Third Goddess, compassion. From the Fourth God, security, and I beseech the Fourth Goddess to guide the steps of Viulra to her halls and to protect him in the Next Kingdom as his bow did in this life.' He covered Viulra with a sheet and went to find someone to help with a grave.

The dam was only improvised, a pile of rocks and logs, but it had been enough to divert the flow of the river over an area of low land, a pebbly beach, alongside the houses of Vinyu. With the help of a dozen Islanders, Daryo managed to pull it apart enough for the water to complete the work. The water returned to its original course and revealed the secret it had almost concealed. The irregulars defending the village had either been killed outright or staked out, the houses had all been burned but the inhabitants had been bound on the beach and the river diverted. When the first body was moved, water poured from the mouth and nose. The people had been drowned by the diverted river.
'We have to find the Nar Silver camps and destroy them,' said one of the commanders with Daryo.
Daryo shook his head. 'No. This has gone far beyond that solution. Where is the Nar Silver's largest town?'

\*   \*   \*

The entire trained company of Silver Islanders were on the march. They had massed at the deserted and devastated village of Vinyu and then headed northwards across open country. The going was poor, the heat intense, the ground rocky and broken, but it was the best direction it had been decided. The Nar Silver were attacking from south of the mountain so the Islanders were moving north of the mountain to attack the one known town in the Nar Silver lands. The entire irregular force had been deployed to defend the remaining villages, leaving Suxin in the charge of the Yashoun garrison.
As he scrambled over yet another boulder, Daryo was struck suddenly that it was eight days since Viulra had died. Eight days, a full eight days and he wished that he had the opportunity to pray to the Fourth Goddess in a temple. He had no such opportunity and so continued to scramble across the awful terrain. The heat of the sun was such that the rocks were almost too hot to touch. The Company were spread across almost a mile, struggling to stay together in such broken ground and searing heat. Every man was carrying a shield, sword and several spears or bow and arrows and spears. All had been found helmets and some armour from myriad places, all mismatched but to add as much protection as possible. Several of the Company were replacements, drafted into the group in place of those injured or killed in the same ambush as Viulra. They had been ceaselessly drilled by an elder for a full day before being permitted to join the Company and some recruits had been rejected as insufficiently able.
Daryo stopped and took the waterskin from his belt. They would need another water source by nightfall, he knew. Everyone was draining their waterskin at least three times

each day. They were north of the central mountain of the island, a conical peak that Daryo had been told was named Hen To and was considered sacred by both Islanders and Nar Silver. The east face was sheer and the ground at the foot of the mountain flat but the north side seemed to have been subjected to many rockfalls over many generations and was endless piles of rocks, dissected by narrow gorges and infinite numbers of small crevices. Some of the larger ones were negotiable by improvised crossings of various degrees of sturdiness and the narrow river that they had passed had been traversed by a relatively sturdy wooden bridge, complete with side walls and a series of symbols carved into the planks, all of which looked less than ten seasons old. This joined a rough track, little more than an oft-travelled route than had worn down a pathway along the rock. As they continued westwards, it became a more defined trail and some sections had unmistakeably been sculpted by chisel to make travel easier. This made progress much swifter and after sundown Daryo was sure that there was the glow of a town visible on the horizon.

It was certainly a town but Daryo had never seen anything of the like. The entirety had apparently been built on a wooden platform that stood astride a series of ravines. It resembled an immense landlocked raft surmounted by the wooden homes of the Nar Silver. All that separated the Islanders and their young Batribi leader from the town was a sparse, rocky two miles of ground and a rapidly-growing force of Nar Silver. The Company had made no secret of its movements at any point. The Nar Silver spies had undoubtedly been observing them and the bulk of the raiders had apparently been hurriedly recalled to confront the Islanders bold attack. Daryo quickly rallied his men, the archers in the centre, protected by four groups of the Company, one on each side. The Nar Silver were a single mass, shouting, hooting, beating drums and blowing horns, over a mile away and still audible. A few skirmishers were dissuaded by arrows from Islander bows. This was taken as a signal for the mass to begin advancing at a brisk pace. Daryo called for Kam, who was acting as his lieutenant.
'Is everyone prepared?' he asked.
She nodded sharply. 'Prepared.'
'I must trust this to you. I have no experience of this style.'
'We know. We can do this well.'
'Continue.'
'*Ye lafa!*' Kam called and the groups quickly came close in to the archers, forming a box around them. Daryo found space in the centre. '*Koi ha!*' The archers were infiltrated by their comrades. '*Tof fan!*' The outsides of the box formed a wall, overlapping their large

oblong shields. The Nar Silver were beginning to run. '*Tof hainto!*' The men in the centre all raised their shields above their heads, forming a solid roof of shields. Daryo, with difficulty in the close circumstances, checked his own smaller, round shield and drew Temma's Sword. '*Suh hyua me!*' Spears were pushed out through the gaps in the shields. The Company of Silver Islanders had transformed themselves into a spear-and-shield version of the shellback creature. The noise of the Nar Silver attack had reduced slightly; they were unnerved by the new development and unsure of how to penetrate the defences. A short burst of arrows and stones rattled off of the shield shell. As soon as it finished, Kam shouted: '*Pen!*'

The shields dropped, the men forming the walls knelt swiftly and the archers let fly into the Nar Silver, less than two hundred yards away. As soon as the arrows were loosed, the walls and roof of the shell were back in place. The reason for the harsh and repeated training was suddenly obvious- a mistimed movement would be fatal. The Nar Silver charged the shellback but the force of the collisions only pushed the formation tighter together. As spears were lost into enemy bodies, men on the walls took the spears of their comrades in the centre.

'*Fas to!*' shouted Kam. Every man in the walls with a spear in hand thrust it outwards, drew his sword, broke with his neighbour and slashed out. '*Pen!*' Again the drop, the single volley of arrows and the reform of the walls. A single Nar Silver threw himself into a gap. Daryo darted forwards and slashed him across the neck, then the chest. The shellback had closed up again and the Nar Silver's body was left inside. The formation was again battered by a Nar Silver surge. The formation held, more spears were lost in more Nar Silver bodies. Daryo was well aware that the Nar Silver heavily outnumbered his own force but the Silver Islanders were confident in their shellback technique and it was holding well. Another hit from another charge and an Islander was cut down. Seamlessly, the man behind him took the place in the wall. This began to happen more regularly and the number inside the formation began to reduce. Kam ordered another arrow volley, then the archers began sniping through the gaps between their comrades' shields. The signal seemed to take forever to come; Daryo was beginning to think that the other half of the scheme had collapsed again some unseen or unexpected obstacle. But the signal came- a repeated blast of a wooden whistle, echoed by dozens of others. The Nar Silver attack faltered as the significance dawned on the Nar Silver. Some of the Islanders in the shellback began to lower their stance, opening their shields. Slowly the formation broke apart. Daryo expected some resistance from the Nar Silver but the sight of their town beginning to burn had taken all thoughts of fight from their minds.

As the Company had demonstrably and obviously attacked from the east, the irregular militia had taken the Nar Silver town from the south, sneaking into the barely-guarded town and capturing it. Only a few buildings were fired and the population corralled. The elders had been gathered in the town square and met by their contemporaries from the Islanders and the Yashoun commander to negotiate a cessation of hostility.

The period of negotiation continued for nearly eight days. The Nar Silver were insistent on their right to land and to the restriction of the Islanders. The Islanders were certain of their own innate rights. It was the Yashoun mediation and the perseverance of the Islanders that eventually found a resolution. The villages burned by the Nar Silver, where the populations had been killed, would remain uninhabited: Vuyin, Cax'xi and Sonyon. The Silver Islanders would not reoccupy them but neither would the Nar Silver take them. It was also agreed that the two peoples would build a road through the ruins of Cax'xi to join the Nar Silver town to Suxin. A peace concluded and representatives exchanged, the Islander force began the journey back to Suxin.

'Master Daryo.'
'Gods' Watch, Kam.' Daryo had learned that Kam was a content and confident follower of the Pantheon. He had been sitting on the edge of the long jetty looking out to sea. She sat alongside him. 'We are most grateful for your assistance.'
'I was doing my duty.'
'The regular trading ship from Yashoun is due later today. Passage will be secured for you to return.'
'My thanks. I have enjoyed your island though. Some of the animals...' He pointed further along the jetty. A large black bird with a hooked orange bill, spotted neck and scarlet legs and feet stood on a barrel preening. 'Fantastic. Amazing creatures.'
Kam looked at the bird. 'There are many of those. They fish in the harbour. There are stories that the Nar Silver catch the birds and use them to catch fish.'
Daryo shook his head, smiling. 'Amazing.'
Kam smiled. 'You could remain. You are most welcome in Suxin. A house could be found for you, a position in the new militia.'
'My thanks, but I was here only to do a task. I think I should return now.'
'Of course.' Kam kicked her legs a little and stretched them. 'Please do speak to the elders before you leave, Daryo. We are most grateful.'
'You are most welcome. And I shall.'

Daryo stayed on the pier for most of the afternoon, watching the birds and animals that passed. A small Jaboen ship arrived and he had a brief talk with the captain. One of the crew was half-Batribi and it stirred the emotions that Daryo had suppressed for nearly twenty days. He had immediately felt close to Viulra when they had met; they were lone wanderers, skilled warriors without a clan to travel with, somewhat mercenary but with a real sense of reason overwhelming any want for reward. There was some voice in Daryo's mind that said that Viulra's death had been without purpose and he wondered if perhaps there was some truth to the thought. It made him wonder if his father had died with purpose somewhere in Jaboen or Yashoun. Had he fought in defence of an innocent or to protect his family, or had he been killed by an accident, or a fall, or a thief? The thoughts dredged the memory of his mother, how she had died, from his mind and Daryo was soon wandering despondently through Suxin. He found himself outside the temple and almost ran inside, searching desperately for an answer or a helper. Instead he found an almost empty building. Even the candles on the central altar had been allowed to burn out. With the Yashoun presence at its minimum and imperial control broken, the Islanders were apparently forsaking the imposed faith. Daryo's breath came in rasps, desperate pants for air, he wondered briefly if the wetness on his face was tears, sweat or both. The saltiness stung his eyes. He collided with something and lost his feet. In total and almost blinded panic, Daryo crawled and found something blocking his way. He reached up and felt a round shape on a larger obstacle. The altar of the Fourth Goddess. Weeping, sweating, mind in turmoil, Daryo whispered urgently: 'Take me as well, please, Vashine, take me as well!'

# Chapter 27

The sound of the drum was exceptionally loud and the blazing fire made it even less bearable. Daryo tried to cover his eyes but moving his arms was painful.
'Daryo? Daryo?' The voice was exceptionally loud.
'Oh... quiet... please.'
'Daryo, this is Kam. The elders sent me. You were found this past night.'
Daryo groaned. 'Quietly, please.'
'I am sorry.' Kam's voice was much softer. 'You were found late this past night, not long before sunrise. You were in a tavern, beyond sense with drink. You tried to... attack the watchmen who found you but you had too much drink. You are suffering this morning.'
'I... I do not remember. I do not remember any of it.'
'You must have drunk too much. There is a beaker by your bed, I had a physician mix a potion to help you improve.'
'My thanks.'
'When you are feeling better, please come to the True Temple. The elders wish to speak with you as soon as is possible.'
'I will.'

Daryo did indeed feel better after drinking the physician's brew. He was in a room that he did not recognise with a low bed, a small stool where the beaker had been placed, a basin of clean water and a pile of belongings- Daryo's belongings bought from the inn. He found clean clothes from his pack, stripped, washed and dressed. His weapons had been brought and were laid carefully on another stool. After his boots, trousers and a light shirt, Daryo buckled his swordbelt and left the room. It was a room in a small house, although there seemed to be nobody else at home. The house was near the harbour and he found his way to the old temple, passing a friendly Yashoun patrol on the way.
A small congregation of elders and warriors were inside, talking in small groups. One of the elders saw Daryo enter and said something to Kam.
The Islander woman smiled and approached him. 'You feel better?'
'I do, my thanks.'
'Our physicians are quite skilled in such matters. We have had a slight setback to our otherwise successful endeavours. As you know, it was our intention to send a party of representatives to the Empire to outline what has occurred on our island and to declare our intention to remain without Imperial supervision. This has been pre-empted,

however. The governor has escaped from his residence. He bribed a sailor and ordered a small group of soldiers to accompany him. His boat is at least half a day out of the harbour. What vessels we have are being sent to try to locate it but it is literally a boat in the ocean.'

'So there may be an Imperial response.'

'Undoubtedly.'

Daryo nodded slowly. 'That may be... severe.'

'It may be.'

Daryo noticed that the others in the temple had gathered around. 'I feel a touch on my shoulder.'

'We would be honoured if you would continue to assist us,' said Kam. 'Any reward that the elders and commanders of the Island have to offer is yours.'

Daryo shook his head. 'I do not do this for the reward. I took a promise, less than five seasons ago, to defend those who needed defence and to protect those needing protection. The people of this island require defence, and I can assist in that endeavour.' He drew Temma's Sword, holding it up in salute. 'My sword and my service.'

Kam translated the Common Speech for the Islanders more comfortable with their own language. One of the elders made a short speech in the staccato Islander language. Kam repeated it in the Common Speech.

'There are legends of the wind that say that a Red Wind will come to the Silver Island. A wind that will blow across the island and make it clean. The elders believe you may be the Red Wind, Daryo. You have helped us to break the Yashoun control, you have helped us against the Nar Silver. If you can assist with the Yashoun once more, the entire island is in your debt.'

Daryo nodded. 'How long would it take to reach Ossmoss from here?'

'Three nights in a small boat. Four perhaps.'

'I cannot see more less than a day to assemble a suitable force. Likely two. It is going to be eight days before the Yashoun arrive. No less than eight.'

Kam explained to the elders. One patted the wall of the temple as she replied. 'We must build defences,' Kam said.

'We must. But there are other issues to address as well. Was it only the governor and a few men that escaped?'

'It was.'

'Then I must talk to the commander.'

Ichuro Nobu had cooperated as far as he could with the Silver Islanders and their Batribi allies. He had a respect for the Islanders following nearly ten years' service in Suxin but had little knowledge or thought of the Batribi. When he was a young recruit he had been involved in removing a Batribi camp from near Shovomoss but that was the only contact he had known with them until he had met the two warriors. Now he had been requested to join the younger of the men at the governor's residence. He knew that the older man, the giant of an archer, had been mortally wounded and had died just before the resolution of the Nar Silver problem and immediately expressed his condolences. The younger man was barely into manhood; he appeared to be between eighteen and twenty years old, his head covered by thick, curled black hair with wide dark eyes, a somewhat flat nose and the start of a beard that looked to be just as dense as his hair. He thanked Ichuro for his concern politely but seemed much more interested in business than pleasantries. His voice was deep and somewhat soft.

'Kam informed me that you are aware of the governor's... flight.'

'I am. He will undoubtedly make for Ossmoss to inform the Emperor.'

'Undoubtedly.'

'And return with an army strong enough to take the island by force.'

'Exactly.'

'I can imagine why you wished to talk to me, Master Batribi. Or may I use your name?'

'My name is Daryo.'

'Daryo. You wish to talk to me about the possibility of my assisting you against the Imperial Army. I agreed to work with you to protect the Silver Islanders against the Nar Silver, I did not and do not believe that such protection was contrary to my orders. Silver Islanders are as much citizens of the Empire of the Yashoun as my own brother. But I cannot take arms against the Empire. I am a soldier of the Emperor, as are my men. We are all Yashoun. We will not make war on our own people.'

The Batribi smiled thinly. 'I would not ask you to do so, sir. Despite what many think, the Batribi people understand loyalty and honour better than most.'

'So what would you ask of me?'

'Passivity, sir. I would ask that your troops lay down their weapons and play no part in any attack. It will make an impossible task slightly easier if the Islanders are not constantly looking over their shoulders for your assault from behind. If the impossible is accomplished and the Yashoun landing is repulsed, your men will be released and free to either remain on the island or return to Yashoun. If the landing succeeds, you were forcibly disarmed and held prisoner by the savage islanders and their deceitful Batribi accomplice.' Daryo raised his eyebrows ironically.

Ichuro chuckled despite the severity of the situation. 'And if I decline either option?'
Daryo's expression froze in a blink. 'Then the Company of soldiers will take the fort by force, sir.'
Ichuro held his hands up quickly. He had expected the options to be those offered as soon as the governor's escape became known to him. 'The Second God would gain nothing by such an action, Master Daryo. I will not ask my men to push themselves to such action, it would serve only to end their lives needlessly. I will instruct my men to disarm. All weapons will be surrendered and we will place ourselves in your care.'
'Will all your men comply?'
'They will follow the orders of their commander and I intend to tell them the reason for my decision. I believe that they will accept rationality and reason.'
'My thanks.'
'The fort is a defensible position but the direction of the assault...'
'Your men should remain there. It will still protect them and it can easily be masqueraded to be a prison.'
'I can have my men work on the illusion.'
'Again, my thanks. I am sorry that the situation is such, Commander Ichuro.'
'As am I, Daryo. It suggests that the Second God has a sense of humour, does it not?'
'He and the Fourth Goddess.'
'Ah, now she is a different subject entirely...'

*'Lem hi van yan tom lii aan. So to too ly en ma?'*
Daryo raised his hands. 'I cannot understand you.'
The stout little man groaned in frustration and pointed to a stone pillar of the long pier. *'So... to... too.. ly en ma?'* he repeated.
'I cannot understand you when you speak slowly either,' said Daryo, equally slowly.
The man, the trustee of Suxin pier's structure and repairs, sighed and sat on the pillar that he had indicated. *'Nas ya.'*
'I cannot speak my own people's tongue, I cannot speak yours either.' A welcome sight came walking up the pier. 'Kam! Thank the gods!'
The man stood up and quickly explained his position to Kam. Kam nodded. 'Hui thinks that you cannot destroy the pier. The stone pillars are too strong.'
'But the deck is wood. Only the supports are stone.'
Kam translated this. 'That is true.' The harbourmaster gave another opinion, which sounded reluctant. 'He says it would mean that rebuilding the pier would be easier.'

'My thanks, Kam. Please ask him to ensure that as much flame oil as possible is soaked into the deck as soon as possible.'

'Certainly.'

From the harbour, Daryo checked preparations in the roads. Learning from the battle of the Five Towers that he had fought in, defending his Order of the Shield and Sword, he had recruited teams of Suxin townsfolk and soldiers to dig pits in the roads. These would then be lined with stakes and spears and covered to form traps. Other groups were erecting traps on other streets- rigged crossbows, spiked spring-loaded traps, tripwires and fake ambushes. Small red-painted rocks marked hazardous areas and watchmen, mostly children of about fourteen summers, ensured that the uninitiated did not wander into danger. Half Moon House was something of a fortress and was to be manned with archers but a few extra features were being hurriedly added. The barracks was now a prison. Locks had been removed from the inside, weapons removed and the ladders to the guard towers moved to the outside; all that was required was the gates to be shut when the Yashoun landing came. Similar plans were in place at Cansunri but, as a much shallower and smaller anchorage, it was considered highly unlikely that the Yashoun would land there.

The lodgings that Daryo had awoken in after his bad night was that of an unmarried soldier without family killed in the attack on the Nar Silver town. One of the elders had arranged it for Daryo and he was happy to remain there as he visited only to sleep. His time was taken up entirely by the preparations for the Yashoun landing: training with the Company and others, organising and installing traps, checking and ensuring supplies and with only brief pauses for meals and a daily visit to the temple to pray. The first day had been to the altar of the Second God but soon Daryo found himself gravitating to that of the Fourth Goddess. He decided not to request anything more than lessening the loss of life. To ask for his own after all would have been too much to ask, even of a goddess.

He had been unsure of where to take position after the landing. Some had counselled that he command from the new command post, a large house on the edge of the town; others had suggested he be in the centre of the defence at Half Moon House. Eventually, he had decided to lead the militia and then join with the Company outside the town. Work proceeded well, more and more of the town had been readied. A significant number of people had moved from their homes, either away from the harbour or spread out into the villages.

The elders had been relocated to Jen Tyii under guard, leaving just four captains in Suxin along with Kam, who had continued to act as Daryo's lieutenant. For most of each day, she tailed behind her Batribi captain, assisting his work, translating for the Islanders that struggled with the Common Tongue and fetching food and drink as required. Daryo had tried to spend a short time each day teaching her to defend herself. She was indifferent with a sword and an average shot with a bow but showed some promise with a spear or stave, even though a spear was a more difficult weapon.

Working in relays, fishermen from Suxin, in addition to their normal work, were keeping a sharp watch for approaching ships. A Jaboen trading ship was diverted to Cansunri, as was a Sodidoron vessel that arrived two days later. On the tenth day after the governor's escape, Daryo was looking over a new trap on the harbour side when a fishing boat was rowed into the bay. The fisherman splashed ashore, shouting to Daryo. 'Sail! Sail!' he shouted. 'Sail!'

'Yashoun?' called Daryo, skirting the trap and hurrying down the jetty. '*Yausa?*' He had learned a few of the Islanders' words. *Yausa* was the word for Yashoun.

'*Yausa, tel! Tel!*' *Tel* was an affirmative.

Daryo exhaled slowly. '*Sento. Thu su da.*' My thanks, tell boss.

The fisherman waded ashore and made his way into the town, heading for the command post. Daryo went back to his lodgings, taking care to avoid the traps, and dressed for battle- armoured jerkin despite the heat, Temma's Sword on his sword belt, the Horse and the Bear in their sheathes on his back, his shield on his left forearm. He hurried to the command point, meeting Kam and the commanders. The plan for the defence had been established days before but it was quickly rehearsed. Another fisherman came in, reporting that a single ship was approaching Suxin Bay, flying a flag of truce. The commanders, Kam and Daryo agreed to go to the harbour.

The Yashoun ketch launched a boat from half a mile off the jetty and it was rowed inshore. A soldier stepped ashore and tied the boat up and a man stepped ashore, dressed in a flowing scarlet cape over a bronze cuirass. He seemed slightly surprised that his welcoming party was four men, a woman and a Batribi.

'Do you speak the Yashoun tongue?' he asked slowly. One of the commanders answered affirmatively. 'Excellent. I am Consul Suto Tachi, representative of Emperor Ueda the First of the Yashoun. On the ships anchored in the bay are nearly three thousand Yashoun soldiers. If I do not send word, ten thousand more will leave Nudakso in two days and reinforce my army. The Silver Island is a part of the Empire and it is to remain so. Where is the garrison commander?'

Daryo stepped forwards. 'Sir, I am Daryo, kin of Dostan, appointed representative of the Silver Island people. The Islanders have the garrison safely confined. The Nar Silver threat has been resolved and the Islanders wish to retain much of the independence and self-government that they have gained during the conflict. The Imperial governor deserted his post and the garrison commander has acceded to the Islanders' wishes. They wish to agree a new status and recognition within the Empire.'

'This is not possible. No part of the Empire has any different status or recognition,' replied the consul smoothly. 'There is only one result that I can accept: the complete surrender of the Silver Island.' He clutched the hilt of his sword.

Daryo put his own hand on Temma's Sword's pommel. He glanced back at the Islanders and saw four negative expressions from the commanders. Kam looked rather scared. 'That is not an option to the Islanders, consul.'

'Then the Island will be taken by force,' he warned, drawing his sword.

Daryo did likewise, the Islanders behind him drew their swords. 'The Islanders will resist.'

'And they will die.'

The Silver Islanders insisted that the ketch would be allowed to leave unmolested. The Yashoun ships began to move deeper into the bay on their oars. There were seven in total, six transports and an escorting naval brig. The two smaller transport ships rowed in towards the jetty. Daryo had removed himself to a new watch point in the beacon of the warehouse which had held the Nar Silver prisoners. It had a commanding view of the whole harbour but was a safe two hundred yards from the harbour end of the jetty. Concealed in the rocks to the right, the south-west side of the bay, were two score of archers with a good range to the jetty and the ships, just over ten score yards. The furthest ship from the archers, the closer to Daryo, reached the jetty first. The main deck was covered by black and brown clad Yashoun soldiers. The gangplanks were pushed ashore and as the Yashoun soldiers began to hurry ashore, the archers began to fire. Every arrow was fire-tipped and aimed at the ships and jetty. The barrage was slow but constant, the sails on the second ship began to scorch. Some arrows struck the Yashoun troops, some hit the jetty and it began to burn. Four barrels of flame oil had been poured on the wooden pier and it soon became a half-mile-long strip of fire. Yashoun soldiers were throwing themselves into the bay, some running back onto the ships. The ship closest to Daryo was beginning to catch light; soldiers were leaping off of the ship on the opposite side to escape the flames. Sailors were desperately trying to extinguish the fire but the heat of the burning jetty and the continuing fire-arrows were beginning to ignite the rope and sails. The other ship was still a way from the pier and the oars had reversed to push the transport away from the pier. The ship was also using archers to fire

back towards the Silver Islanders. The crew and soldiers on the burning ship were all abandoning it, the ship's deck was alight. Daryo hurried down the steps from the beacon to the warehouse floor. Nearly four hundred militia were crushed in together. Daryo squeezed his way to the front and drew Temma's Sword. Kam appeared at his side.
'All ready?'
'Ready, Daryo! *Ji tun!*'
The doors of the warehouse were thrown open and the militia raced out. They were soon at a run as the Yashoun pulled themselves out of the water, some burned, some near drowning from the weight of their armour and weapons. Only a handful tried to make a battle of the situation but they were soon overwhelmed by the Silver Islanders. Weapons were taken and armour stripped before the nearly ten score of survivors were escorted to the barracks and imprisoned with the island's deposed Yashoun garrison. The second transport had escaped out of arrow range. Daryo had left the militia to escort the prisoners and had returned to his watch post. The escort ship was moving into the bay and it archers and ship-mounted ballista began to fire into the rocks where the archers were but belatedly; as soon as the pier had begun to burn, the archers had orders to withdraw. The remaining transports began to move in behind it, archers bristling from the sides and bows. Daryo decided that the Fourth Goddess would be satisfied soon enough and left the warehouse, choosing his route carefully across Suxin, out of the town and up a sharp slope. The Company were concealed among the rocks and shrubs. Daryo scrambled into a hollow alongside a young soldier, receiving a wide grin. The position gave a fairly good view of the harbour and most of the town. Two of the larger transports began to row hard for the harbour, arrows and catapults firing into the rocks where the Silver Islander archers had been and into the town as well. These ships were significantly larger than the first pair, three masts and with a strange, flat front. They were not slackening speed as they approached the still-burning pier and first ship, they used the momentum to ground themselves in the harbour, as close as possible to the shore. The flattened fronts revealed themselves as ramps, dropping into the shallow surf and allowing hundreds of Yashoun troops to surge ashore without difficulty, wading through only a couple of feet of water. Shields raised, spears levelled, the Yashoun men began to form up on the edges of the harbour. Daryo still had Temma's Sword in hand. Kam, not a warrior, was safe with the elders so an Islander with the Common Tongue had been drafted to the Company as Daryo's lieutenant.
'Now?'
Daryo shook his head. 'We wait. The town is ready for them.'

The Yashoun companies began to advance into the town and the noises of the traps being sprung began to be heard- the rumbles of stones, the clang of metal, the thud of wood and, over all, the screams of men. Daryo murmured a prayer to the Fourth Goddess. The noises continued and, before long, several Yashoun began to return to the harbour. Even from a distance, many seemed wounded, scared or both. Many weapons had been discarded.

Daryo stood up and raised his sword. The Company of the Silver Island stood up from their cover. 'Kill only if necessary!' he shouted. 'You know where to go! Forwards!'

The battle was brief, brutal and effective. The Company attacking from the west, and support from militia from the north, took nearly a hundred prisoners but many more resisted and were killed. The Company then stormed the beached transport ships. The crews were taken without a single death. An officer from one of the ships was put in a boat and told to row out to the consul's ship with the message that not only Silver Islanders would die.

## Chapter 28

### 12th *Day* of *Summer* in *Year* 360 of the *Empire* *Age* of the *Yashoun*

Just over two hundred miles south of Suxin, two hundred and sixty miles west and north of Nudakso and nearly four hundred miles west and south of the Twin Ports, the islands had no individual names and little to offer other than anchorage. Any ship blown off course while navigating Yashoun's Long Cliff Shore had a chance of being serendipitously guided to the safety of the Dule's Boon Islands, hence their naming after the Fourth God, the giver of security and safety. Over time, a small and motley collection of pirates, shipwrecked sailors, rebels and fishermen formed a community one of the islands, informally known as Dule's Joke, suggesting it was not as much of a gift as it may first appear. It was little more than a ramshackle village, rarely visited by those ships blown off-course as it was on the north-western island and difficult to access through treacherous waters. The one ship that regularly arrived at the little jetty of Dule's Joke was one from Cansunri on the Silver Island, bringing the fresh produce and goods that the island could not provide for itself, trading for the simple vegetables and fish that were found and produced on the island. The ship's crew were unloading almost as soon as they docked. As well as the crew there was a single passenger: a young Batribi man stepped ashore, carrying a large pack in one hand and a shield in the other. He reached the top of the jetty and looked around, hoping to find a harbourmaster or similar official. With nothing in evidence, he decided to rely on experience and headed for the nearby inn on the harbour. It was early in the morning and the inn was all but empty. The publican was a hook-nosed Sodidoron, easily seventy winters old, and looked askance at the new arrival.

'Not many Batribi here,' he said bluntly.

'I was told that in Suxin,' said the Batribi. 'I am looking for a ship to Yashoun.'

'Not many of them. Only ship comes into the Joke is the one you just came in on from Cansunri.'

'No others?'

'None regular.'

The Batribi dropped his pack and sighed. 'Can I get a bed?'

'Nobody turned away in the Joke, that's what they say. Bronze half a night.'

'Done.'

'The beds are through the back. Only one resident so pick any bed but the last one.'

'My thanks.'

'What brings a Batribi here from the Silver Island? Who are you?'
The Batribi picked up his bag. 'My name is Daryo the Walker, I might have angered a Yashoun consul.'

Over a morning meal, Daryo the Walker laid out his story for the innkeeper, Irither, who was much more amenable when he heard that his Batribi guest had angered a Yashoun official. The consul's message, when told that the Silver Islanders were quite happy to kill Yashoun, was that the reinforcements would be summoned from Nudakso. By Summer's First Day, another twelve troop transport ships had arrived. Using their landing ramps and boats, over ten thousand Yashoun soldiers were landed, completely overwhelming the defences of Suxin. The Company had tried to resist but been swept aside. The Silver Islander commanders had surrendered to the Empire, the elders had pleaded ignorance as prearranged and a small group including Kam had spirited their Batribi comrade out of the town and south to Cansunri, too small to be attacked from the sea, and the trading captain had been persuaded to take a passenger to Dule's Boon. Daryo was then encouraged to explain how and why he had been on the Silver Island to begin with, which soon became a life story.
'An eventful time,' said the innkeeper, somewhat impressed.
'I have had good fortune. The Fourth Goddess has claimed others instead. But if there is no path away from Dule's Boon, then the events may become less significant.'
Irither shrugged. 'There is always a path. Other ships come but infrequently. Ships blown away from the Empty Shore stop in the southern bays, making repairs and finding supplies before resuming their voyage. There is nowhere to go to though, there is no town on any other island. You would be waiting on an empty beach for something that may never arrive.'
Daryo shrugged. 'Then I must wait. I cannot swim.'
Irither laughed. 'You are welcome to stay for as long as your coin lasts. No man is turned away from the Joke.'
'My thanks.'

The long-term resident of the inn was a Silver Islander with very little Common Speech. He had a small boat and worked independently of the other fishermen out of Dule's Joke. He seemed quite content to be sharing his lodgings and kept his own business. Daryo found little to occupy his time. Dule's Joke had no temple, only the single inn, no market and no entertainments or diversions. He spent his days out in the rocky hinterland of the island, hunting the few animals that lived there or simply practising drills with his swords, switching from one blade to another in mid-action, fighting with different combinations of his three blades and his shield. After sword drills, he started to run, the steep slopes and lack of paths making the exercise more difficult but also more rewarding. Each day's sword work and running left him a little less breathless, a little more confident for the next day. After seven days, Daryo took the eighth as one of rest. He tried to teach himself to swim but almost drowned in Dule's Joke's harbour so spent the rest of the day outside the inn. With the next dawn he resumed his training, pressing harder than he had in the days before; fighting with more ferocity, hunting smaller and faster animals, running harder and longer than before up steeper slopes. After four more days, a mast appeared, approaching the harbour but it was the trading ship from Cansunri, flying the Yashoun flag and its crew augmented by a cluster of Yashoun archers. He returned to the rocks and his work. By the twentieth day, Daryo was struggling to keep motivated to go back out beyond the township and continue training. Rather than wishing to go outside, Daryo found he had to almost drag his own body outside to fight and run. The slopes of the western plateau seemed a little steeper and a little higher than on previous days. At the summit, Temma's Sword was heavier, his shield more cumbersome, the twin swords unwieldy and awkward. On his return, he almost slipped down the slope and grabbed a branch just in time to save himself. The sight of a mast in the harbour almost caused him to fall again.

\*     \*     \*

After nine days at sea on the Adacan ship *Arrettzi*, Daryo decided that the sea was not his preferred method of travel. He had no trouble with calm seas but the unpredictability of the water and weather was infinitely less desirable than the surety of walking on a road. He knew little about the port of Kalimoss other than it was south of the Twin Ports and at the mouth of the River Sentsho. From the river, the town sprawled along the south bank and looked unremarkable: a large temple dome on the east edge, several smaller ones in among the houses, a number of grand houses on the west side of the town and a small but bustling harbour. When the *Arrettzi* had moored, Daryo thanked the captain profusely and gladly went ashore. Even the landing tariff, blatantly and uncompromisingly raised for a Batribi passenger, of two silver halves was a payment Daryo hardly noticed making. He followed the harbour eastwards as far as possible and then had to go into the town to look for the gate. At the corner of the main street, searching for the right direction, he collided with a young woman, who dropped the cauldron she was carrying on his foot.

'Oh, I am so sorry!'
'My error, my apologies,' said Daryo, picking the cauldron up. It had a large crack in the bottom. He straightened up. 'Oh! Gods' Watch, Miss.'
The Batribi girl, about sixteen summers old, with her long hair wound around in a knot at the back of her head, smiled shyly. 'Gods' Watch.'
'I am sorry for colliding with you, I was looking for the gate, I do not know the city. Your pot appears to have cracked.'
'That was not your doing! I was looking for a smith but nobody in town will work for a Batribi, whatever the price.'
Daryo studied the offending pot. 'I may be able to help. I apprenticed as a smith.'
'You did? That would be wonderful! My clan are camped outside the walls. Where are yours?'
'The Batribi Lands. I walk alone.'
'Oh. My name is Carini, kin of Moulra.'
'Daryo, kin of Dostan.'
'My pleasure, Daryo, kin of Dostan. This way.' She pointed north and began to walk, Daryo alongside, still carrying the pumpkin-sized cauldron. 'Where have you come from?'
'However bizarre it may sound, from the Silver Island by way of Dule's Boon.'
'Truly?!'
'Truly.'
'Are you returning to your clan?'
'Perhaps. I had not made certain plans.'
She smiled and pushed a stray strand of hair aside. 'You are a mercenary?'
'Of a sort.'
The road turned east and passed through the town gates. A few hundred yards from the gates were a small cluster of *kaffa*, two horses tethered nearby. A single woman was standing watch.
'Carini!'
The girl smiled at Daryo. 'Daryo, kin of Dostan; this is my mother, Namma. I met this man in the town, mother. He says he worked as a smith and might be able to fix our problem.'
Namma nodded. 'Is this true, Master Daryo?'
'Yes, Madam. I will do my best.'
'We should introduce you to our clan elder before you start work.'
'Of course.'

The clan elder, Moulra, was of around sixty summers and caring for the horses when Carini introduced Daryo to him. He had Daryo explain something of his background and why he was in Kalimoss before consenting to Daryo trying to fix the cauldron. Carini was put at his disposal and they began to gather wood. There were large groves of olives and a spread of vineyards across the land around Kalimoss and there was plenty of dry, dead wood available. There was a fire in the centre of the camp and as Carini collected wood, Daryo began to build up the blaze in its shallow pit to create the necessary heat. The clan was small- Moulra; his son was Carini's father, Namma's spouse; Moulra's daughter, her husband and their four children; and a cousin of Namma's. Two of the children, boys of eight and nine summers, enthusiastically assisted in collecting the wood and building the fire. Soon the fire was intense but Daryo had kept it small, piling his belongings nearby. The two older children, another boy of fifteen summers and a girl of sixteen, were despatched with to fill a water barrel at the river. Daryo found some large metal pincers and a hammer that he thought suitable among the clan's possessions. Carini continued adding wood at Daryo's direction and he went down to the river to assist those with the barrel. The fire was mostly olive wood and burned at a high temperature. He had Carini continue to stoke the fire while he found a suitable stump of wood- a little narrower than the cauldron and about three feet long. He buried the wider end in a small hole alongside the fire and packed as much earth as possible around it to hold it upright. The fire was blistering, white-hot before Daryo removed the cauldron's handle and put it base-down in the very centre. Soon the metal was beginning to glow a dull red. He used the long pincers to lift the pot. He examined it and put it back in the fire, trying to push it down a little deeper.

'Not right?' Carini asked, perching on a large box.

'Not hot enough,' Daryo told her. 'Still waiting for the right heat.'

'Will it take much time?'

'Not much.'

'You were an apprentice?'

'I was a ward of the School of the Temple in Salifa, in Jaboen. All the boys had to work apprenticeships and the smith was the only man in the town that would take a Batribi.'

'You enjoyed the work?'

'It was pleasant enough and I learned much from Vehllal, the smith.' He checked the pot again. 'Excellent.' He picked the pot out of the fire with the pincers and lowered it quickly over the stump of wood so the inside of the damaged item was against the top of the stump. Holding the pincers tight, Daryo struck the slightly-rucked edges of the crack and began to push them together. This closed them flat but left a gap between them of about a finger's width. Daryo levered the little cauldron back off of the stump and put it back in the fire.

'Can you not fix it?' asked Carini anxiously.

'I can, it just must be pushed together,' said Daryo. 'It will not be as strong as it was. It should not be used directly in fire again.' He lifted the pot, laid it on its side, holding tight with the pincers and carefully knocked around the base of the pot, pushing the glowing lips of metal together. One pushed into the interior, one came outwards. When they overlapped by nearly an inch, Daryo put the pot back in the fire. He looked up and found Carini watching him intently. She smiled, slightly shyly, and looked away. Daryo retrieved the pot from the fire, put it back over the stump, hammered the bottom flat from the outside and plunged the pot into the barrel of water with a roar and cloud of steam.

'Done,' he announced, pulling the pot out of the water, averting his face from the billowing steam. 'Let it cool and do not put it deep in fire but it should do well for broth or milk.' He carefully placed the pot on the stump, the correct way up. 'I can put the handle back shortly.'

'Our grateful thanks, Daryo, kin of Dostan.'

'My pleasure and the Fourth God's gifts.'

'You must have been forged on his anvil.'

Daryo laughed. 'On the tip of the Second God's spear I think is more likely.'

'On a branch of the First God?'

'Perhaps.' He studied the repair from inside the pot. 'That does look satisfactory.'

'Would you like a drink? Some food?'

Daryo decided it would be impolite to refuse and he was hungry. 'A crust and a cup of milk would be gratefully received.'

Carini giggled. 'I am sure we can do better than that,' she said, and returned with cheese, an apple, bread and some strong mead.

Daryo ate sat on his makeshift wooden anvil, aware that although Carini had excused herself pleading chores, she passed him frequently and often found reasons to start a conversation. When he had finished eating, he reattached the tensioned wood handle to the cauldron and tested the quality of his repair with some water. He put it over the remnants of the fire to boil the water and he decided the repair was sufficient. Moulra was sat outside a *kaff*, carving some pegs for the canvas walls.

'Daryo, kin of Dostan.'

'I have finished my work, Moulra. The pot will do its service a little longer.'

'My thanks, Daryo. We have few possessions, we must care for those that we have. Have you been paid?'

'I have been given a meal by Carini. That is more than sufficient.'

Moulra nodded. 'As you wish.' He thought for a moment. 'Have you spoken with my daughter, Sraini, or her husband, Buryo?'

'No, I have not.'

'Buryo was injured by a wolf, some seasons ago. One arm has no strength and his back is weak. We have to leave Kalimoss. We are reaching that time at which the town becomes unhappy with our presence. The merchants no longer trade, the soldiers become hostile.'

'It is our fate.'

'Each one's bane,' quoted Moulra, nodding. 'Did you have a road in mind?'

'None specifically.'

'I think we should go southwards, perhaps towards Nudakso. If you would assist us in packing the *kaffa*, and walk with us as far as you would, I would be most grateful and would offer any recompense we can spare.'

Daryo considered this and, for a reason known only to his own mind, Carini's shy smile was at the front of his thoughts. 'I swore an oath on the Pantheon to aid those in need of it. I will help pack and walk with you, at least for a time.'

There were six *kaffa* to remove. Each had the canvas skin pegged to the ground and anchor lines running from the top to be undone. The ropes were then tied up, the bound support posts were pushed together, bound as a log and removed, the canvas then folded and bound tight and loaded on one of the two wagons. Then there were a dozen boxes of tools, equipment and clothing, the two large water barrels, the spare harnesses and other tack for the horses, a pile of blankets and a stack of stuffed canvas mattresses. The load was distributed between the pair of carts and, when the camp was completely gone, the horses were harnessed, Moulra took the seat of one wagon and Buryo the other. Buryo was of around thirty winters and strong in the legs but his left arm was almost stick-thin. The two younger children were allowed seats on one cart and Daryo was invited to place his pack there as well. With a curious patrol from the Kalimoss city guard watching, the Batribi clan and their new ally started down the road to the east.

# Chapter 29

Daryo found himself walking at the tail of the little convoy alongside Carini. The road followed the River Sentsho, a wide and sluggish, muddy river that oozed rather than flowed towards the Sea of Dith. At times the road was below the level of the river and the thick dirt and incongruously verdant plant life flanking it suggested that the road flooded when the river rose. After a few hours' eastwards, the road turned south, still following the silt-laden river. There were several thickets of thorny bushes and some stands of olive trees. At one point they passed a small stone farmhouse and received a harsh glare from the goatherd. Carini asked questions at irregular, short intervals that Daryo found often needed long and complicated answers: why he had been in the Silver Island, why he had three swords, what the images on his shield meant, why a smith needed a large barrel of water and a litany of further enquiries.

'Dule's Anvil...' someone moaned from ahead.

Daryo looked forwards and saw a small rockfall nearly blocking the road. Buryo was scrambling down from the cart, his older children coming forwards too.

'We can clear this,' said Namma's husband, Crai. 'Some feet to the rope and the wagon will roll.'

The clan moved forwards, Buryo and Moulra staying with the wagons, even the children helping to clear the landslip. It took only a short time and they were moving again, Carini spelling her father driving the cart. They walked until sundown with no incident until stopped by another rockfall.

'We should make camp,' said Moulra. 'Clear the fallen rocks in the morning and continue.'

Daryo assented. 'Carini, help me with the *kaffa*.'

Namma and Crai pulled a *kaffa* pole bundle off of the other wagon as Daryo and Carini took theirs. The poles were laid out, the canvas shells came next and the poles were slid into the centre and stood up so that the canvas hung like a lady's skirt. Daryo then went inside and pulled the poles apart until they stood up and supported the weight. Carini went back to the wagon to fetch the pegs. She went to lift the bag holding them and they all fell out as the bag's seam collapsed. Daryo chuckled and Carini threw one at him. It stuck his arm. She threw another, a third, a fourth, each one hitting Daryo, both of them laughing harder.

'Carini! Stop throwing equipment!' barked her father.

'Sorry, father.' She scooped up a bundle of pegs and hopped down from the wagon. She dropped a few pegs at Daryo's feet and went around the back of the *kaff*. Daryo drew his knife and used the hilt to hammer home the first peg. The work was soon done and the children despatched to find fuel for the fire.

'We should have scouted the area,' said Moulra as he started building the fire.

'Allow me,' Daryo said.

Moulra inclined his head. 'My thanks, Daryo.'

'I can help,' said Carini, jumping up.

Namma frowned but Crai assented. Daryo exchanged smiles with their daughter and both went back to the road.

Scouting the area and checking for dangers became something of a lovers' stroll. Carini slipped her arm around Daryo's and held his hand, clutching his elbow with her other hand. There was a small stream that led down to the river behind the camp but there seemed to be no other noticeable features. The pair found a fallen tree; Daryo sat down for a period with his back against it and Carini sat sideways on his thighs like a child on her father's lap.

'This looks safe here,' she said. 'I love walking the roads. I love finding new places, even if we stay only a short time.'

Daryo smiled. 'I love the road for the same reason. I have been walking for nearly eight seasons. I see new faces, new lands, every day. Who could tire of it?'

'Some new faces are more welcome than others.'

Carini leaned sideways, putting her hand on the tree so she was leaning right over Daryo, their faces inches apart. She kissed him gently. After a blissful moment's bewilderment, Daryo returned the kiss.

Carini showed no embarrassment in returning to the camp with her arms still wrapped around Daryo's. Namma looked unhappy but said nothing. Crai had stalked and shot a wild goat and it was roasting over a fire. Daryo was accosted by the four youngsters and persuaded to tell the story of the Order and the Five Towers' last battle. Simma, Srai, Viulra and Moulra the Young were attentive listeners and polite with their enquiries. After dinner, Moulra the Older sang some songs in the Old Batribi Language and Daryo shared some Silver Islander rhymes that he had learned. The *gom gom gom* verse was particularly popular with the younger ones. Sraini then sent them to sleep and Buryo produced a bottle of wine bought in Kalimoss. Carini, although a season short of being of age, was permitted to join them and she sat for most of the evening with her head against Daryo's shoulder.

'Who will take first watch?' asked Moulra when the bottle was finished.

'I will,' Daryo volunteered.

Moulra nodded. 'Our thanks, Daryo, kin of Dostan. Crai, Namma, Buryo and Sraini will wake me. Good sleep to you all.'

Shortly, Daryo was alone by the fire, his possessions were in a small *kaffa* that the clan normally did not erect, he had only his cloak wrapped around his shoulders and the Bear across his knees. Having spent so many times sleeping in the open, he had no fear of the darkness or the strange, unexplained noises that came in the quietness. At intervals he put another piece of wood on the fire. It was a warm summer's night and the fire was for light rather than heat. Looking up, there were barely a wisp of cloud covering the stars; in the patterns of sparkling light, he traced a ship, a cauldron, a sword, a chair, a horse. He then got up and took a short patrol around the camp. A startled animal scuttled away from his footsteps, squeaking in alarm. He returned to the fire and put another piece of wood on. Someone in one of the *kaffa* moved, causing a rustling. They settled and Daryo sat back near the fire. Over the rest of his watch, the person in the *kaff* seemed to be struggling to settle. Daryo had not noticed who was sleeping in which *kaff* but thought it may have been one of the younger ones.

'Daryo,' said a quiet voice behind him. Crai sat down.

'Gods' Watch, Crai.'

'I am next on watch.'

'I should retire then.'

'Daryo, I notice that you and Carini have formed a relationship.'

'We have, yes.'

'I do not disapprove, Carini is not many moons from being of age. A young man of around her age such as yourself must be good for her. However we both know that you may not be walking with us for long. Do not promise, or even suggest, something that cannot last.' Daryo nodded thoughtfully. 'Do you understand?'

'I believe so.'

'Sleep well, Daryo.'

'And you.'

Daryo got up and went in to the little *kaff* set aside for him; long and low rather than tall and round. The Bear was returned to its sheath alongside the Horse. He had a bed roll ready, pulled off his boots, leggings, and cloak and slid inside. The soft and slightly distant crackle of the fire and the soft noises of the others sleepers soon had Daryo lulled to sleep.

Dawn was the best way of waking, Daryo had found, and in a *kaff* there was no way of blocking out the sudden glare of light as the sun came up. He pulled himself out of the *kaff*, only in undershorts and shirt. The morning was brisk but not cold and he was able to dress more easily stood up outside the low *kaff*'s entrance flap. He pulled on trousers and boots as Carini emerged from their *kaff* with Simma. The two girls saw Daryo, Simma whispered something to her cousin and both laughed. Sraini called them over, setting them to work making the morning meal. The boys, the younger Moulra, Viulra and Srai, were sent to check and groom the horses. Daryo volunteered for work and was asked to assist Crai in starting to pack the *kaffa*. There was not a viable water source and the campsite was not particularly well suited so Moulra did not want to remain. The smaller *kaff*, Moulra's, was left up and after eating, each member of the clan took turns in there to wash and put on clean clothes before it was packed, put on the wagons and the clan re-joined the road.

By midday, the road had turned to the west very slightly and then back southwards, following the wide bend of the river. It rose away from the river bank and the road and river parted company as the cliff top along the edge of the river became too sharp. Carini taught Daryo to drive a wagon as they reached the edge of the pine forest that ran almost to Hajmachia.

'Another day of travel, maybe two, we should reach Roukdo,' Moulra told Daryo, the two of them walking for a period together. Moulra had difficulties with his hips and could not walk for long periods. 'Roukdo is the crossroads between the Hajmachia road from Kalimoss and the road from the Twin Cities to Nudakso.'

'Have you decided which direction to take?'

'There was much talk in Kalimoss, and before in Paloss, of the Vidmarian army around Namixo in the east of Yashoun. That is very close to Hajmachia, less than three days away from the borders and only five or six from Tovein. I do not wish to put my clan in the way of harm. I think we will head south towards Nudakso, although it is a somewhat linear progression from Nudakso to Veritimoss and Jundan. Perhaps we will turn north back to Paloss. I must discuss the matter with my kin. Which way will you go?'

'I do not know. I have not considered the matter particularly.'

'I would ask that you involve yourself in our discussion about our direction then.'

'Certainly.'

Moulra clapped a familiar hand on Daryo's arm and increased his pace, sitting himself on the rear of the nearest wagon with some assistance from Viulra on the wagon and Namma on the ground. The first wagon, driven by Carini, suddenly came to a halt.

Sraini quickly reined in her own horse, stopping the wagon. A thick, mature pine tree had fallen across the road. Daryo came forwards.

'We may be able to clear it,' said Buryo, studying where the felled section had parted from the stump. 'There is only a hand's breadth holding the trunk to the stump. We could remove it and roll the tree aside, using the horses if necessary. Viulra! There is an axe in the wagon.'

'Yes, father!' The boy began to search for it.

'No movement!' shouted a strange voice. 'Stay still, dogs!' A pair of men in black and green appeared from hollows, wielding a club and a mace. From behind the tree came three more with a sword and axes. 'You give any coins, metal and food you have!'

'We have nothing of value!' shouted Moulra. 'We have women and children! Let us pass!'

One of the axemen on the tree laughed. 'You have something of value. You will yield it! Do you not recognise your situation?'

'Do *you* not recognise your prey?' demanded Daryo. He allowed his cloak to drop, his shield and pack were on the second wagon but all three swords were in place. 'I am Daryo the Walker of the Order of the Shield and Sword!' He drew the Horse and the Bear together. 'These people are under my protection!' He spun the Bear point-down. 'I give you this chance to withdraw.'

'A dog with teeth!' shouted the man with the mace and a heavy black beard.

'A dog with teeth is still a dog!'

Daryo swung his blades. 'Clear the road!'

'Father!' Viulra had uncovered the axe and he managed a good throw to haul the three-foot tool to Buryo, who just managed to catch it with his good arm. Crai quickly jumped onto the first wagon and pulled a sword, shorter than Temma's Sword but of a similar design, from behind the wagon seat.

'Kill them!' commanded the axeman.

'Run!' Daryo shouted at the others and leaped to intercept the bearded man as he lunged towards the nearest wagon. He was large and powerful but clumsy and the Bear went straight through his chest. Daryo levered the body aside with his shoulder and just caught the swing of a short axe. Buryo shouted in distress, Daryo ducked the axe, hit the wielder with his clenched sword-fist and ran the ten yards to Buryo. His attacker had slashed him across the arm and Buryo dropped his axe just as Daryo knocked the attacker aside. He heard a cry, Namma or Sraini, and slashed the attacker across the throat with the Horse. He spun, drove the Bear back into the man and searched for the scream. One of the other axeman, a very tall man with a nasty scar across his face, had cut down Crai. Srai roared in anguish and anger and ran forwards, seizing his uncle's sword but running straight into the axe's blade.

'No!' cried Simma, watching her brother fall. Daryo tried to get there but was intercepted by the fifth attacker, swinging a huge, double-headed battleaxe. The man's first swing barely missed Daryo's head, the second knocked the Bear from his hand, the axe's handle came out like a charging animal and struck Daryo squarely in the chest, knocking him back against the road. The axe was raised for a finishing blow when suddenly a curved blade almost took the man's head off. A sobbing Carini almost dropped the sword in shock and distress. Daryo rolled and jumped to his feet. The last remaining attacker was near the second wagon. He was not looking at Daryo, he had Simma by the hair. Daryo ran with both swords raised and used his full speed and weight to drive both blades through the man and into the side of the wagon. Slowly, carefully, he withdrew the blades, trying to control his rasping breath and racing heart. All five attackers were dead. Crai and his oldest nephew, Srai, lay dead within feet of each other. Moulra had apparently tried to resist the big axeman too and the elder had a knife lodged deep in his stilled chest. Buryo was bleeding heavily from his wounded arm, Simma had a bloody head wound. Srai, the young Moulra, Namma and Carini were all crying copiously. Viulra and Sraini were tending to Buryo and Simma. Namma hurried to Moulra, her young sons went to their fallen brother. Carini was standing, sword still out in front of her, staring at her fallen father. The horse in the lead wagon had broken its traces and fled. Daryo ignored the emotional response and instead checked each of the attackers. All five were certainly dead. He then went on to check Moulra, Crai and Srai. The knife in Moulra's chest was long and had slipped between two high ribs and penetrated almost all the way. Srai had taken the axe almost vertically into his chest, leaving a deep cleave into his torso. Crai had been struck in the side of the abdomen on one side and in the joint of neck and shoulder on the other side. None of the three would have had a chance of survival. He went to Carini and gently removed the sword from her hand.

'Go to your mother,' he whispered gently, giving her a firm embrace. 'Please, go to your mother.' Carini whimpered but nodded and ran to Namma. Simma had stood up, the minor wound on her head staunched. She could not look at her slain brother and went to her own mother.

It was almost dark before the site was cleared. Buryo assisted Daryo in clearing the front, horse-less wagon and placing his wife's father, his wife's sister's husband and his own eldest son in the wagon. They and a still-tearful Carini hauled the wagon off of the road.
'We should hold a watch,' said Buryo dully.

'A watch?' asked Daryo.

'We stand guard... over the bodies. Until dawn. It is a Batribi custom that some clans still hold. Moulra would want it.'

'I will get a *kaff* put up for the children and the women,' said Daryo. 'Carini, I need you to gather firewood. Buryo, start your watch.'

With the *kaff* erected, Namma, Sraini, Young Moulra and Viulra had somewhere to shelter. Carini gathered sufficient wood to start a small fire, which Daryo sited between the *kaff* and the wagon. Buryo took the sword that Crai had used and stood vigil until Daryo relieved him. He doubted any of the clan slept, he heard soft weeping and quiet conversation all through the night. At dawn, Daryo was replaced by Carini and Namma. He went and collected a large pile of wood. With slow and deliberate sadness, Buryo helped to stack it around and under the cart. Sraini took a branch from the campfire.

'We commend their bodies to the Gods,' she said slowly, struggling to keep her words clear. 'Moulra, son of Moulra and Camma. Crai, son of Heryo and Limma. And... and Srai, son of Buryo and Sraini. We commend their souls to our memories. We mourn our clan leader, Moulra. We offer ourselves to the service of his memory and the continuation of his clan. We mourn our kin and commit their bodies to fire and the care of the Fourth Goddess, knowing we shall meet them again in the Next Kingdom.'

She plunged the burning branch into the woodpile and it was soon alight, the wagon taking fire quickly and soon the fire was too intense to approach. The clan retreated several yards and turned to the widow in their midst.

Sraini held her hand up. 'I am Sraini, once kin of Moulra. I ask now that his kin recognise me as leader of the clan.'

Buryo bowed. 'We accept Sraini, daughter of Loulra and Temma, as leader of this clan.'

Daryo felt it necessary; he drew Temma's Sword and held it up, pommel in front of his face, point down. 'I offer my sword and my service to you, Sraini.'

'My thanks, Daryo. My kin, please load what we can onto the one wagon. Harness the horse. Daryo, please take what tools you need to clear the road of that tree.'

'Certainly.'

'I wish to leave... this place as soon as possible.'

Daryo took the axe and quickly severed the fallen trunk from its stump. With Simma's assistance, he harnessed the horse to the stump end of the trunk and dragged it aside. Shortly the horse was harnessed to its wagon, the clan's belongings had been loaded, the surplus added to the pyre or buried, and the wagon was back on the road, heading westwards for Roukdo with Simma driving, the rest of the clan walking behind and

Daryo leading the way with his shield on his arm and Temma's Sword in hand. Looking forwards, he could see nothing but forest.

Roukdo was a small, pleasant market town built in a clearing in the forest with low, flat-roofed plastered houses. The temple of Roukdo was built in the centre of the town crossroads with a broad square around the centre. Each road was signposted clearly: Kalimoss on the west road, Ossmoss/Paloss north, Nudakso south and Hajmachia west. The tall, slim, domed temple had a wreathed spear carved on the doors. There was a gatepost nearby and the horse was tethered to it. All the members of the clan went inside to pray for their lost kinsmen and Daryo remained with the wagon. A young watchman passed, no older than Daryo himself, a local picket rather than a Yashoun army soldier, and he looked curiously at Daryo. His skin was significantly darker than the norm for a Yashoun.

'Are you Batribi?' Daryo asked him.

The watchman shook his head. 'Not really. My father's mother was. Are you?'

'I am. The clan I am with is inside the temple.'

The watchman nodded. 'Batribi are fairly welcome in Roukdo. There are no merchants that will refuse work or soldiers to force you to move on. As long as the camp is not in any way disruptive, it will be well tolerated.'

'My thanks. There are only eight of us, the camp is small.'

'There is a suitable stretch of land just south of the town. There is a windmill, long since unused, camp alongside. If you are thinking of moving on, the Vidmarians took Namixo some time ago and have been threatening Kakuo.'

'Again, thanks.'

The watchman smiled and moved on. Carini was first to emerge from the temple and held the door open for the others. At the foot of the steps, Sraini absently patted the horse's neck and stared at the sky for a considerable time. Her kin gathered around and waited for her.

'North,' she said eventually. 'North.'

'North?' asked Buryo.

'Nudakso is too far. None of us know the road or the land. Safer to go north.'

Buryo nodded. 'North it is.'

'We can go back to the Twin Cities. Maybe up through the wastes and into Jaboen if we can find a guide to take us through. I was even thinking of making for the Batribi lands in Jaboen. The Dark Lands, they call them..'

'Certain?' asked Daryo.

'Certain.'

'I am going east, into Hajmachia.'

'You are leaving us?' Carini's voice was high and her eyes wide.

'I am. The road north is short and one of the safest in Yashoun. I have made a promise and I believe I have fulfilled it to you and your kin, Sraini.'

Sraini nodded. 'You have.'

Daryo took his pack from the wagon and dug into a pouch deep inside, where he had put the recompense from his foray to the Silver Island. 'I came by this by the will of the Fourth God. It will help you buy some provisions and hire a guide across the Northern Wastes to Taam.' He put twelve gold halves in Buryo's good hand. Buryo went to interrupt, Carini tried to speak but Daryo continued. 'I am most sorry for your losses, I wish I could have done more. If you are bound for our people's land, when you arrive, seek Laulra, kin of Dostan, or Dostan himself and tell them of me. They will care for you as kin. Gods' Guidance to you all.'

'Daryo!' Carini tried to take his hand but he reached past her, took his bag and pulled it on.

Buryo clasped Daryo's hand, then Namma did the same. Sraini gave him a brief embrace, so did Simma. Carini tried to catch hold of him again but avoided her to tap hands with Young Moulra and Viulra. He pulled his shield up onto his arm, took Carini's hand and led her a short distance away. 'Carini, it is time.'

'No!' She seized a handful of his sleeve. 'No, I want you to stay!'

'The roads part here. You and your kin need to go and make yourselves a life. North of here in Yashoun, Jaboen, by the Stannia Lake.'

'With you.'

'Not with me. I am going into Hajmachia, the Vidmarians may be coming this way. I can be of use, doing what I promised, protecting those who cannot protect themselves.'

'I cannot protect myself.'

Daryo smiled. 'My thanks, Carini. You have been... wonderful. Be safe and be happy. Gods' Guidance.'

# Chapter 30

The road from Roukdo towards Hajmachia followed the Sentsho River east but climbing away from it as it had before the forest. The incline was slight but steady and even Daryo was finding it difficult after five or six miles. He had to stop frequently to allow the burning sensation in his legs to subside. By nightfall he had not travelled as far as he had hoped and moved off the road to find some shelter. He found a small tree that had fallen, leaving a hollow against the trunk. Sraini's kin had given him a piece of canvas for making shelters and he tied it to a branch to make a windbreak. He found a small amount of firewood and it was alight swiftly with some tinder from his bag. With the fire lit and shelter ready, he removed his twin swords and sword belt, laying them with his shield. He removed Temma's Sword from its sheath and stepped out of his temporary home. He waited for a considerable time, he counted nearly four hundred before he heard what he had waited for from the north.

'One chance!' he called into the darkness. 'You surely know I can use this sword! You have been following me for nearly ten miles! I give you one chance to come forwards! I will share my fire and food if you come forwards peacefully!' He turned towards the noise. 'No more opportunities! Come forwards now!'

There was another noise, a rustle, another rustle, not a rustle but a sniff. 'Daryo...'

'Carini!' She emerged from the trees. She was carrying a large bag awkwardly with both hands and even in the near darkness looked exhausted. 'What in the name of all Eight are you doing?'

'Coming with you!'

'Carini... Carini, no.'

'I want to. In two moons I am seventeen autumns, I am of age. Many girls my age have a man that they love and they move to another village to be with him. Just what I am doing.'

'This is not the same. Another village, yes. You have no idea where I may be in three months. Your kin will be hundreds of miles away.'

'We are Batribi; that is our life. And the clan are going to the Lake Town. I can find them there.'

'The road is dangerous, Carini. And your mother...'

'Knows why I left.'

'You saw what happened to Srai, Moulra and Crai.'

'Yes! And I do not care! I love you, Daryo, I love you and I want to be with you, wherever you are going!'

'You really told your mother where you were going?'
'I did. She was angry, very angry, but she said I was of an age to make my own decision and that unless she tied me to the wagon, I would have left regardless.' Daryo sighed. 'I can defend myself. I killed that man with the axe.'
'More by fortune than skill.'
'My father... my father said that half of fighting is bravery.'
'Bravery is only a small part of combat.'
'Then you can teach me the rest.'
'It is a skill, a difficult skill. It requires gift and ability as well as tutoring.'
'Teach me.' She took a step closer.
'Carini...'
'Teach me.' She was less than a foot away.
'This is a bad idea...'
'Daryo. Please.' She kissed him.
'As you wish.'
Carini kissed him again and dropped her bag. 'You will not regret this, Daryo.'
'I hope you will not.' Daryo waved an arm towards his shelter. 'There is little space under that canvas.'
'I brought bedding and clothes and other things.'
Daryo picked up the bag. It was rather weighty and had only a small handle. He dragged it to the shelter and put it under the canvas. 'We can look through what you brought soon. Did you bring any more food?'
'No, I thought you would be hunting.'
'I was more worried about who was following me. I have some salt fish, some bread, nothing more.'
'I am not hungry really.'
Daryo smiled. 'As you say. You should eat though, you would have had to be walking rather fast to keep pace with me. Thirsty?'
'I am thirsty.'
'Come, I have a flask.'
They sat by the small fire. Carini drank and when Daryo produced the food, her actions belied her words as she ate hungrily. Daryo found some apples in his bag too and Carini ate three. 'What bedding have you got with you?'
'Two blankets and a bolster.'
'Fine. Sleep on this side, closer to the fire.'
'I can sleep the other side.'

'Carini, sleep on this side. Stay warm. You are used to a *kaff* helping to contain the heat, I sleep in the open most nights, I will be fine.'
'As you wish, Daryo.'
Carini sorted her bedding and was soon asleep. Daryo lay awake beside her, wondering what strange whim of which of the Pantheon had brought him a sweet, pretty girl who could barely hold a sword to walk alongside him into battle.

'High, high, low. Good. Low, low, high. Move your feet. High, high, high, high, low. Carini, you must move your feet. Low, low, low, low, high.'
Daryo lowered the Bear. Carini looked puzzled but kept the Horse on guard.
'Why did you stop?'
'Because you do not listen! You cannot stand like a statue. If I am moving to your right, either move right as well or turn. You must learn to move all of your body together.'
'That is hard! I am trying to concentrate on the sword.'
'But the sword is only a small part of the fight. Like bravery, like thought, like movement. If you think only of the opponent's sword and he steps behind you, you may not be able to see his sword when it cuts you open.'
Carini's arm dropped to by her side. 'That is a cruel thing to say.'
'You want to live as I do, Carini, you could be cut open. You could be wounded, you could die.' He pulled up his loose shirt to show the wound just above his hip. 'I have been cut open many times.' He lowered the hem of his shirt and raised his left sleeve to show a scar there. 'That is just two. You have to be aware of that and ready for that. Raise your blade.'
Looking slightly chastened, Carini raised the Horse again. 'What this time?' she asked, her tone determined.
'Attack me. Try and break through.'
'To hurt you?'
'If you could stop before that happens, I would appreciate the effort.'
Carini chuckled despite herself, took a few breaths to ready herself and then attacked with surprising ferocity, using two hands to hack viciously. Using just one hand, Daryo's blade fended hers aside. The more laconic Daryo's defence became, the more frustrated Carini became and the more intense her assault was. He made the mistake of becoming too complacent and one slash knocked the Bear out of Daryo's hand. Seeing an opportunity, acting on instinct, she switched to a one-handed grip, lunged forwards with her free hand and seized Daryo's shirt by the front, pulling him forwards until the point of the Horse pricked his ribs.

'Dead,' she said with a malicious grin.

Daryo smiled indulgently. 'Dead and walking with the Harlequin.'

'The Harlequin?'

'The woman who first taught me to use a blade in anger. I am teaching you with some of the methods she taught me with.'

'Do you have any other weapons I can try?'

'I have my curved sword but that is more difficult to wield, and more dangerous to practice with. Slip with the Horse and I am wounded, a missed slash with Temma's old blade and you might just remove my arm. I do not normally carry a bow or any other weapon. We could find somewhere perhaps to purchase or trade for something. We have been here for three days.'

'Can we leave now?'

'If you wish; it is barely midday.'

The pair had soon packed and left the campsite where Carini had caught up with Daryo, heading east along the Hajmachia road. Daryo had packed the heaviest item in his pack and the rest had gone into Carini's bag. She had improvised a strap from a rope to sling the bag over her shoulder and had found a broken walking stick that was tall enough for her to use. The road continued uphill at a steady rate, making progress increasingly slow as the day wore on. Carini demonstrated the two characteristics that Daryo believed typified their people: exceptional stamina walking the roads and equally exceptional ability to talk or sing while walking. When her conversation was exhausted, she recited songs or verses in time with their steps.

The forest thinned as they finally crested the rise. The change from incline to flat was almost physically shocking. Progress was much easier on the flatter road and as the road turned south, a huge lake spread out to their left. On the edge of the lake was a small town.

'We might find a field to sleep in,' said Carini.

Daryo shook his head. 'If there is a town, we try to find the inn. Few innkeepers will turn away coin, even if it comes from a Batribi hand.'

The inn was named the Sharpened Pike, the image on the sign that of a fish with a knife-blade tail. Like almost all of the houses around it, the inn was built on legs above the ground, suggesting that the lake flooded regularly. A scrawny-looking girl was sweeping the terrace outside the door. She looked terrified when she saw the two Batribi and fled inside.

'Not a wonderful omen,' Daryo observed but led the way inside.

The inn's hall was small, the bar just inside the door. The girl was talking urgently to the man at the bar, saw Daryo and ducked behind the counter. The innkeeper was grizzled and white-haired, his right eye covered by a patch.

'What?' he demanded.

'Gods' Watch,' said Daryo politely. 'We need a room, just for one night.'

'Four silver halves.'

'Four! This is an inn, not the Imperial Palace. Two.'

'Four, or find another inn.'

'Two, no food, just the bed.'

'Done.' Daryo handed over the money and the innkeeper led the way across the hall to a low door. 'Bed in there.'

'Our thanks.' Daryo pushed the door open and ducked inside. The room may once have been a storeroom. There was no window, the roof was so low that Daryo could barely stand and the bed was barely wide enough for two but there was less than two feet on each side of it and only just enough space for the door to close.

'Cosy,' said Carini with a grin.

'Extortionate would be closer to the truth,' Daryo replied. 'I can sleep on the floor, you have the bed.' He took his shield off of his arm.

'Nonsense.' Carini dropped her bag. 'If you sleep on the floor so do I and this is the most expensive bed in Yashoun. We can share the bed.'

'I think... I mean...'

'Daryo, I have been walking most of the day,' she said, sitting on the edge of the bed and unlacing her boots. 'I am tired, very tired. If you are honourable and in control of your actions, so am I.'

Daryo smiled. 'Certainly.' He pulled his boots off and sat on the bed.

'Good.' Carini laid back on the bed. 'I cannot remember sleeping in a bed since I was tiny. When I was about a score of seasons old, I was moved onto a bedroll like the adults.'

'They had beds in the School of the Temple when I was a boy and I try to sleep in inns as much as possible. I think one sleeps better in a bed than on the ground. And the bolted door of the room is always a boon. I have wondered, sleeping under the open sky, what would happen if a bear or wolf took a liking to the piece of meat in my bedroll. If the fire went out, there would be no deterrent.'

Carini unwound the cloth from around her feet, glanced at Daryo and pulled her leggings off. 'Much better.' She slipped her smooth legs under the blanket quickly. 'Eyes off of my skin, Walker.'

'Eyes firmly on the wall,' said Daryo, looking at her face instead.
She smiled. 'That is not the wall.'
'It is a great deal more interesting.'
'Interesting?'
'Entrancing.'
'Much better.'
Carini turned onto her side and reached out, putting her hand on Daryo's leg. 'Do you always sleep fully clothed?'
'Not always.' He pulled his shirt over his head, snuffed the candles and laid down. Carini's hand was still on his leg and he felt a tightness in his stomach. 'Carini...'
'Daryo?'
'Move your hand away. Please.'
'Daryo... I would like to...'
'Not now, Carini. I think... this is just too soon.'
'Oh.' The hand was withdrawn. 'Sorry, Daryo. Really, very sorry.'
'Please... just... a little patience.'
'Of course.' Carini moved and her head came to rest on his chest, her hand on his middle. She was soon asleep and Daryo found that sleep came to him almost as quickly.

It was not long after dawn when the innkeeper rapped on the door and demanded that the occupants leave. When he threatened to evict them forcibly, Daryo opened the door with Temma's Sword in hand and suggested that the more prudent action would be to allow them to leave in their own time. Not wanting to remain in the inhospitable lodgings longer than necessary, Daryo and Carini quickly dressed and departed.
The baker was considerably more hospitable than the innkeeper, told them that the little town was named Vo, that they were around sixty miles from Hajmachia and charged just two bronze halves for a half dozen vegetable pastries, four cheese and two Hajma confections- shards of sweet, thin, crispy pastry. For another half, he filled a skin with milk and another with a thin beer. Daryo dropped a silver half, easily the full worth of the provisions, surreptitiously as they thanked him and left. Further along the street was a small smithy. Daryo was able to immediately ingratiate himself by talking about the smith's work. He bought a five-foot walking stick of dark wood with sharp, pointed ends that resembled spear points and a short, two-edged, rather simple sword for Carini. Four silver halves was a fair price.
The road kinked back east immediately outside the town and ran along the south edge of the lake towards Hajmachia. Out on the water a number of boats were fishing and a

young shepherd was driving his flock along the road in front of them, which took some time to negotiate. The road began to slope downwards away from the lake, rose slightly, dropped and rose again, another long and steady climb. The day was remarkably clear and increasingly warm and the spear-like point of the great mountain Mach visible against the sky- visible even though it was more than six score miles distant.

They stopped just after midday and after eating, Carini began experimenting with using her walking stick as a weapon. The smith had said that the stick had such sharp points for climbing steep hills but Daryo thought that they may have the extra purpose of defence. The high-quality iron tips were almost as sharp as an arrowhead. In only a short period of time, Daryo saw that she had a lot more natural ability with a longer weapon than with a sword. He took up his shield so that Carini could practice attacking. She found a natural rhythm spinning the shaft, using the shaft as a club and stabbing with the sharp ends. When she rested, Daryo got a small box from his bag, which contained his sharpening equipment. He sharpened both ends of the stick to an even keener point and then spent some time with the Horse teaching Carini how to use it to defend herself, simply stopping Daryo's attacks. They then returned to the road to find a campsite or inn.

Twilight approached and there was no sign of habitation. They were passing through yet another of the forests that seemed to cover the land. The trees creaked and rustled constantly in the wind.

'Stop,' said Carini softly. She was a few feet behind Daryo.

Daryo complied. 'Is there a problem?'

'I think... maybe.'

'Where?'

Carini inclined her head to her right.

'Wolves?'

'Men.'

Daryo reached down and put his hand on Temma's Sword. Carini put her second hand on her staff and took a deep, slow breath.

'You can do this,' he whispered to her. He glanced left and saw a movement. Ready to ambush travellers, they were now spooked by their own prey stopping.

'Ready?'

'I am.'

Daryo turned towards the threat, drawing Temma's Sword and allowing his shield to drop into position. 'Come out, cur!'

'Daryo! Behind!' Carini stepped behind him and raised her staff across her body. Three men had emerged from the trees on that side, two on Daryo's side.

'You call us cur, dog,' spat one of the men. 'I will take that sword from you. And put it down your woman's throat. After I put a larger weapon up between her legs!' The other men laughed. Carini cursed and turned. Daryo quickly turned too to stay back-to-back with her.

'How far up between your legs will this go before you fall silent?'

'I offered first.' The man drew a sword.

Carini spun her staff and raised it to strike. 'If you want to stick me, come and try.'

'Oh, I will, and then my friends can try too, yes?'

Carini felt a nudge in her back, Daryo's elbow, and then a slight push. She spun out of the way as Daryo came around again, at a run. The would-be bandit barely raised his blade before Temma's Sword slashed across his torso from shoulder to hip. The other man with him got his sword up as the men on the other side of the roadway ran to assist. Daryo felt a push and spun to confront them. He caught a swing of a mace on his shield, pushed out with it and cut low with Temma's Sword, using the momentum to swing around and block a sword aimed at his neck. The third ran past Daryo towards Carini. Daryo hurled Temma's Sword after him, striking the runner in the back. He blocked the mace again and got the Horse free of its sheath. He parried the sword, struck its wielder with his shield and stabbed the raider in the chest. With a heartbeat of time remaining, Daryo got his shield in place, drew the Horse out and hacked down into his remaining opponent. A howl of pain caught his attention, his head snapped around and saw Carini with one point of her staff buried just above the hip of her foe. Daryo quickly pulled his blade free and rushed to assist her. The man had dropped his weapon and stood with a stunned look, groping for the wound. Carini stepped back, tugging her staff out, looking equally surprised. Daryo used his shield as a ram to knock the man down.

'Unhurt?' he asked Carini.

She nodded. 'Not hurt.'

'Well done. You did very well.'

'Is he dead?'

'No. But he will not be following us. Come on, we should move on.'

Daryo put a hand on her back and managed to start her moving towards the Hajma border again. He sheathed the Horse, retrieved Temma's Sword and resolved to place as much distance between them and the site as possible. They walked for nearly a mile before Carini asked: 'I did well?'

'Very well.'

'Really?'
'Very, very well.'
It was almost dark but Daryo could see Carini's satisfied smile.

Using Carini's staff as a javelin, Daryo speared a boar, butchered it with his knife and roast the hind legs over the evening fire. Carini, in between gathering firewood, drilled herself with her staff. Daryo sat turning the spit, enjoying the smell of the roasting meat and watching Carini's movements. She was getting more confident and considered with almost every breath. The boar was excellent and the pair ate and drank well, drinking most of the milk from the baker in Vo. Daryo then rigged up the canvas over a low-slung branch, tied it down and sorted the bedding rolls. In the morning, they cooked the rest of the boar, salted and wrapped it as well as possible before leaving. The road became steeper as it left the lakeside and climbed towards the Hajma frontier. A trading caravan passed them just before midday- seven horse-drawn wagons, over a dozen people including a child and a very friendly dog that had a great interest in Carini's bag as she was carrying the boar meat. Daryo told the animal's master where he may find the remainder of the boar carcass and was given grudging thanks. About two miles further on, they met another small convoy- four wagons pulled by oxen and driven by Batribi. It was a large clan, led by a woman with two generations of her descendants and their spouses and children; nearly forty Batribi in total. They exchanged some pleasantries, Daryo used some more of his coin from his Silver Island exploits to buy some ox milk and cheese from the group before they parted ways with a cautionary note from the clan leader: 'There are many Vidmarians in Hajmachia. Take great care and keep your sword close.'

# Chapter 31

Daryo had been taught something of history in the School of the Temple as a boy. He knew that over twelve hundred seasons before, the Yashoun army had invaded and conquered Hajmachia in less than two moons despite desperate resistance. In much more recent times, a few score seasons, the Hajma had been given some control over their own rule under the supervision of the Yashoun Empire. Since then it had been run as part of the Empire in the same way as the Silver Island but with its own council permitted to make issue its own rulings and edicts under supervision.

The positions and relationship of the two societies was well demonstrated on the bridge into Hajmachia across the River Rith, a narrow and fast waterway that ran northwards, joining the slightly larger Schoud and thence on to the Dithithindil just upstream from Stimoss. On the western side of the bridge, a Yashoun flag hung from the arch, six feet across, the blue wheel flanked by a black and a silver spear on a crimson flag. On a post by the side of the road was a small, faded creamy brown pennant: a black mountain wreathed in green, a rearing white horse on one side, a lit torch on the other; the arms of Hajmachia. There was no watch on the bridge, the flag made it quite apparent to any traveller that they were still in a part of the world that the Empire considered part of its territory.

On the east bank of the Rith was Rithein, the first Hajma town. In contrast to the wooden buildings of Vo and Roukdo, Rithein was stone-built. The houses were mostly round with peaked roofs which made the town look as if it were made of fanciful castle turrets. Some larger buildings, including a domed temple, stood out between the points of the houses.

Carini yawned as they entered the town, hard enough that she had to stop walking until it passed. 'I need a rest, Daryo.'

'Perhaps we can find the inn.'

Carini approached a man watching from nearby. 'Gods' Watch, is there an inn nearby?'

'Not that takes your type,' said the man bluntly.

'You mean a woman?' retorted Carini in a waspish tone.

'A dark.' He spat and it hit Carini's shoulder.

Daryo went to remonstrate but Carini had raised her staff and levelled a point at the man's face.

'Do that again and I shall give you a new hole to spit from,' she said calmly. Daryo laid a hand on her shoulder and guided her away, leaving the Hajma man looking shocked. They continued walking along the major road and passed an inn. Unusually, it had a

large, clear notice alongside the door: 'HAJMA ONLY'. They increased their pace to pass through the little town and then began the search for a suitable campsite.
The rain arrived during the last hours of darkness. It was steady and unpleasantly cold. Carini and Daryo had to quickly gather their belongings under the waterproof canvas. Daryo moved their packs in against the tree under whose branches they had been sleeping. The pine tree and the canvas gave them good protection from the rain, even with Daryo sitting against the tree, and Carini soon fell asleep again, her head on his leg. He tried to stay awake and think but the rhythm of the rain lulled him into closing his eyes and he too was soon asleep.

The sun came up and its light woke Carini. She had half-remembered some snares from her childhood but they had caught nothing and she got boar and cheese from the bag. Daryo woke soon after, the movement and noise of Carini getting up and getting a meal was enough. After relieving himself a short distance away from the campsite and eating some Yashoun pastries, he went for a short walk out to stretch his legs. They were almost thirty yards from the road, obscured by trees and a slight incline gave Daryo a wide view of the highway as he emerged from the trees. The sight that greeted him was of a large column of Yashoun troops, shields on their arms, spears over their shoulders, packs on their bags, marching east in ranks of six with cloaked sergeants after every three-score and small parties of mounted officers at irregular intervals. A steady thump of feet interspersed with shouted orders and clomp of horses filled the air. The column stretched away into the distance deeper into Hajmachia. By the time the tail end of the column passed, Daryo had counted almost nine hundred soldiers and they were being followed by their baggage train. He retreated into the trees and almost collided with Carini, who had been coming to find him.
'A lot of the Yashoun army just marched past,' he told her. 'Over eight hundred of them marching east.'
'That clan elder was telling the truth: lots of Vidmarians in Hajmachia.'
'Or there will be soon.'
'You wish to continue eastwards?'
'I do. If I can, I would like to be of assistance if I can.'
'You go, I follow. I have nearly packed, just the canvas to fold.'
The canvas was folded and secured in its usual position under Daryo's pack. Carini went to the road while Daryo checked the campsite for anything lost or dropped, pulled on his pack and joined her.
'A few more soldiers,' said Carini. 'All on horseback, about thirty, went past.'

'The Yashoun Empire is taking this seriously.'
They joined the road, heading east, and after a few more miles of relatively level land, the road began to climb steadily once more. Daryo and Carini had to rest every couple of miles, the incline was painful on the upper legs and backs. In the distance, the rear of the Yashoun column was visible. Daryo insisted that they remain a respectable distance behind the soldiers. When the column stopped just before midday, Daryo and Carini also stopped, taking their day meal early alongside a milepost that told them that they were just twelve miles from Hajma, the capital city of Hajmachia, its ancient name the same as that of the nation's people. Carini was confident that despite the climb they would be able to reach the city by nightfall.

At the top of the climb was the ravine city of Hajma. Daryo had seen many towns but never one built across a gorge. All of Hajma seemed to be built on a network of bridges that spanned the Schoud River a hundred feet below. The bridges were lined by the buildings, the roadways in the centre, some were connected to others by narrower walkways, and there were even constructions on some of the larger footbridges. One of the few buildings not suspended above the Schoud was a large temple of the Second Goddess, which looked much newer than the surrounding cityscape. The city was busy but even to a newcomer, the air was tense. Passers-by did not greet friends or browse the stores, there were brown- and black-clad Yashoun soldiers and locals in long beige hooded tunics cinched by very wide leather belts. The Yashoun soldiers' habit of walking with their right arms at their sides so their spears were level made them look both menacing and awkward, as they occupied three times the space of a normal pedestrian. Daryo insisted that they visit the temple and as they had still some time before sundown, the temple doors were open, large braziers burning either side of the entrance and another in the middle of the altar at the centre of the dome. A priest was placing some more fuel on the small blaze and looked up as the Batribi entered.
'Gods' Watch,' he said politely.
'Gods' Watch,' Daryo replied, echoed a moment later by Carini. They left their packs against a pillar. Daryo, knelt drew Temma's Sword and placed it on the altar. Carini laid her staff next to it.
'What would you ask of the Guardian of the Dutiful and Loyal?' asked the priest, coming around the altar to where the Batribi had knelt and kneeling beside them.
Daryo thought for a moment. 'I made a vow several seasons ago, in the name of the Second Goddess. I would ask guidance on how best to serve the vow that I made.'

The priest nodded. Carini said: 'I would ask how to know how to show loyalty and devotion to something that I cannot see. Not the Goddess, I believe in the Goddess and her presence, but in my clan, who I left.'
'Clan is important for your people,' said the priest.
'Very.'
'Do you hold your clan in your thoughts and in your soul?'
'I do.'
'Then you show them loyalty. Sir, what vow did you make?'
'To defend the just, the righteous, the innocent and the weak until the Fourth Goddess claims me.'
'That is a great undertaking. How do you find these people? Those that need defending?'
'I seek them. I listen for those who may need help.'
'Then you take all measures that you can?'
'I try.'
'I believe you are both true and dedicated followers of Brokea.' The priest lifted his hands. 'I pray to the Second Goddess, the Great Lady Brokea, giver of passion, tutor of loyalty, teacher of duty that you guide...'
'Daryo, kin of Dostan.'
'Carini, kin of Sraini.'
'That you guide Daryo, kin of Dostan, and Carini, kin of Sraini, in their wishes to keep their vow to you and their loyalty to their clan, to each other and to the Pantheon of Gods and Goddesses.'
'Our thanks, sir,' Daryo said to the priest, after a few heartbeats' devout silence. 'Is there an inn or boarding house that would admit Batribi within the town? We had a less-than-pleasant reception in Rithein.'
'Hajmachia normally welcomes Batribi,' said the priest. 'I am sorry that you had such a reaction but the country is very wary of anything new. The Vidmarians are threatening the crossings of Sietviert and Tovein. They are holding a long stretch of the Dithithindil Road on the north bank and look set to attack Hajmachia as a bridge perhaps towards the Twin Ports.'
'That is why we came this way, to assist in the fight, if possible.'
'I fear that more than two Batribi warriors may be needed, but you must adhere to your vow. I will show you to the appropriate authority in the morning. Until then, there is a small lodging nearby run by one of the most faithful of the temple's congregation. I shall introduce you and you will be well cared for and able to rest easy.'
'We would be most grateful.'

The priest's constituent was an elderly man with a small but functional home on one of the larger bridges of the town. He listened to the priest and agreed to accommodate the two Batribi- the woman in his tiny guest bedroom, the man on the high-backed bench in the living room. Daryo insisted on paying for their lodgings and a meal when they woke in the morning and the priest collected them early and took them across to the east side of the gorge. There was a larger part of the city on the east bank than on the west, more warehouses, workshops, a small temple of the Fourth God, a large market and, on the edge of the town, a sheer-sided, five-towered keep surrounded by a high curtain wall. Most of the city was built of the same white-veined grey stone but the castle, in the new light, looked almost red.

'That is the Blood Keep,' said the priest. 'A name derived only from the colour, nothing macabre, I assure you. It is the seat of the Hajma Council, the Yashoun governor and the Yashoun military command.'

'Our thanks.'

The priest smiled. 'I hope that you can be of service. My name is Severin Guut. Please find me when you return. I would like to know what happens to you if possible.'

'Certainly. And our thanks once more.'

The gate of the Blood Keep's curtain wall was guarded by two Hajma archers and three Yashoun men. The Hajma looked curious at the approach of a male and female Batribi, both armed, the Yashoun were more suspicious and levelled their spears.

Daryo spread his arms to the sides. 'I am Daryo the Walker, of the Order of the Shield and Sword, I am here to offer my assistance against the Vidmarian army. My companion is Carini, kin of Sraini. I would like to speak with a commander.'

'I would like to speak to an Imperial Princess, but that will not happen today either,' spat one of the Yashoun.

Daryo nodded slowly. 'Most probably not. I am a comrade of Captain Thunaki of Namixo and the Eighteenth Company, and of Captain Dauke of the Erita Tower.'

'Thunaki of Namixo,' repeated one of the other sentries. 'How did you come by that name?'

'I am a former comrade of his. I saved his life on the Dithithindil Road and he saved mine at Namixo.'

The sentry held a whispered conversation with his comrades and withdrew into the castle. The Hajma looked mildly amused at the confusion, the other Yashoun looked slightly disbelieving too. There was an awkward silence and pause until the sentry returned, accompanied by a sergeant. He regarded the Batribi coldly, beckoned and stepped back inside. Daryo and Carini followed. Inside the gate, within the castle bailey, the grounds were full of Yashoun soldiery and a sprinkling of civilians. Daryo and Carini were led from the gate on the west wall around the keep to the east side, where a wooden walkway led up to the entrance on the second level. At the top of the walkway, inside the anteroom, Daryo and Carini were divested of their packs, weapons and Daryo's shield at the point of swords. They were then hustled down a staircase to the basement floor and locked into a cell.

'We just got arrested!' said Carini, her eyes full of tears.

'Something else is happening,' said Daryo. 'That sentry knew Thunaki's name.' Daryo checked the barred window and the wooden door. There was a bucket under the single wooden bed and nothing else. He sat on the bed. Carini pushed and then started kicking the door. When she got tired, she sat with her back against it and sobbed. Daryo moved to sit next to her and held her close. At midday, a meal was provided- a large bowl of pottage- and then the isolation returned. Carini began attacking the door again. Daryo was just on the brink of telling her to stop when the door was unlocked and pushed open. Carini jumped back. Daryo stood up from the bed.

'Thunaki!'

'Daryo!'

'Good Gods, how did you get here?'

'I was about to ask the same thing!'

'What is this?' demanded Carini. 'He locks us in a dungeon and now he is your brother?'

'I was out on a scouting mission,' said Thunaki. 'They did not believe your story but thought it worth testing. They detained you until I returned and could identify who you are. Who is your companion?'

'Thunaki, this is Carini, kin of Sraini. Carini, this is my comrade Thunaki.'

'Come, let us get you out of here,' said Thunaki. 'Oh, and I believe this is yours.' He handed Daryo his sword belt. 'I will introduce you to our commander. I assume you are here to lend that sword?'

'I am.'

'And after we talk to the general, I have to find out what happened in the Silver Island.'

'If you supply the wine.'

The Yashoun general was in a large chamber on the entrance level, studying a map on a canvas that was larger than many beds. He looked up as Thunaki entered with his companions.

'Commander Thunaki. This is the great warrior that you promised me?'

'Yes, sir. General Lord Ayumo, this is Daryo the Walker, kin of Dostan, and Carini, kin of Sraini, Daryo's companion.'

The Yashoun general studied them both for a considerable period. He was broad, almost bald on his skull but compensated with a greying black beard down to his mid-chest. Over his black breeches, high boots and short black tunic he wore a grey-blue robe with a badge of arms on the breast. A long, broad-bladed sword with a fine steel blade and a leather-bound silver hilt rested on the table. Daryo noticed that the general's right ear had been damaged; he was apparently a general who had seen combat at the point of his own sword, not just from the commander's hill behind the armies.

'Thunaki has said that you are a Member of the Order of the Shield and Sword,' said the general.

'I was,' said Daryo. 'The Order fell.'

'I had heard rumours, reports of this. The Vidmarian invasion of Gourmin destroyed the Order's sanctuary.'

'It did. Many died. My people, the Batribi of the Stannia Lake, saved as many as they could. The Order scattered.'

'Thunaki told me that you fought superbly against the Vidmarians alongside him and that you were instrumental in an important Imperial task on the Silver Island.'

'True. I also helped the Islanders fight the Nar Silver revolt and...' Daryo paused, unsure how to continue.

'You were the Batribi that aided the Islanders against the Fifty-Third Brigade's landing,' Thunaki finished. 'He is the Painted Man.'

'I was.'

The general stared at Thunaki, then at Daryo. 'You were? The Batribi that inspired an... exceptional defence.'

'Yes.'

'You were responsible for the death of dozens, scores, hundreds of Yashoun deaths... but it was masterful strategy, Daryo the Walker. Masterful strategy and I must admire the work of another craftsman. I welcome a man of your ability, Walker. The hour is later than even the Emperor thinks.' He looked at Carini. 'Your companion is a warrior also?'

'I am, and capable of using my own voice,' said Carini indignantly. She had been leant on her staff, she raised it, spun it through a series of circles, bringing it back to vertical with the thud of a steel tip on the stone floor.

Daryo smiled despite himself. The general gave a short bow. 'My apologies, Miss Carini. I did not mean to offend you. Commander, bring some drink and food for the Batribi while I show them the dispositions.'

'Yes, sir.' Thunaki clicked his heels and left.

The general beckoned Daryo and Carini to the map, which was spread across several tables. It was a large illustration of Hajmachia and the land bordering it: Yashoun surrounded the country on almost all sides but for the mountainous border with Vidmaria to the east. Along the banks of the Dithithindil, north and south, brown and gold flags had been placed. There were a cluster of little Yashoun flags stood in Sietviert and Tovein in the north, some in Tanviert in the south and the largest cluster at the illustration of Hajma, most just to the north of it.

'The Vidmarians are attacking on both banks of the Dithithindil,' Daryo observed. 'They took Namixo.'

'And Kakuo,' said the general. 'But the Imperial Army is holding Sictan, reinforcing it with each passing day. It is my task to repel the Vidmarians on this side of the river. I intend to attack here.' He pointed just east of Sietviert. 'That is where the vanguard is.'

Daryo nodded slowly. 'May I suggest a different strategy?'

'You may suggest one.'

'If the vanguard is in Sietviert, the baggage train and supplies must be coming along the south bank of the river.'

The general chuckled. 'I was hoping you would say such a thing. We must take some time to confer, Master Daryo. Perhaps you, Miss Carini, would like to rest and eat while this business is done.'

Carini exchanged looks with Daryo and nodded. 'I think that might be best. I can see you later, Daryo.'

'I will have a room found for you.'

The room was near the summit of the northernmost tower of the keep, adjacent to Thunaki's lodging and on the floor below the general's quarters. Both Carini and Daryo were given keys and told that the room was at their disposal for as long as they wished. Daryo only reached it late in the evening after a long conference with General Ayumo, Thunaki and other officers. He had eaten in conference, been excused only for a visit to the privy, and finally dragged himself to the room in the tower. There was a large, curtained bed, a chest, a rack for cloaks and weapons, a small shuttered window and a small door off of the bedchamber. A small bookshelf stood by the window. The light came from a well-carved wooden candelabra on the wall. Carini had put her pack on the chest, her staff stood against the wall. She was laid on the bed, reading one of the volumes. Her boots, cloak and leggings had been discarded and she was wearing only a tight pair of white linen shorts below the waist. Daryo was struck by the contrast between her legs, the colour of dark oak, and the stark white of the shorts. She had long legs, Daryo decided.

'Everything concluded?' she asked.

'I believe so. We will be leaving with the new day.'

Carini patted the bed. 'Then you should rest.'

'There is only one bed. I should have spoken with Thunaki.'

'Take what is given,' said Carini with a slight grin, shifting her legs.

'Carini...' Daryo put down his pack and used a rack's hook to hang his shield. He pulled off his twin swords, used one loop to hang it from another hook and then removed his sword belt. He drew Temma's Sword, laid it under the bed and hung the belt with the twin swords. He found his gaze drawn to Carini's bare legs. She noticed where he was looking and smiled.

'Strong legs,' she bent her knees, then straightened the one closest to Daryo. 'I am Batribi.'

Daryo followed his intuition, pulling off his boots and unwrapping his foot cloths, not looking away from Carini unless he had no other choice. As soon as his feet were uncovered, he pulled his shirt off. Carini sat up a little.

Daryo smiled. 'Strong arms. Blacksmith.'

Apparently raising the stakes, Carini unbuttoned her shirt and slipped it off. She had a dark linen wrap around her chest. 'Broad shoulders, my father's legacy.'

Daryo unlaced his leggings and dropped them. Carini's jaw almost dropped. 'Strong legs. I am Batribi.'

'Daryo? Are you awake?'

'I am.'

Carini's hand touched his back. 'Are you angry with me?'

He rolled from his left side, facing away from Carini, onto his back. Her hand moved to his chest. 'Why would I be angry?' The candles had burned out a while before and he could only feel and hear her.

'I know you were... unsure... before... about...'

'I was.'

'You changed your thought.'

'They moved on. Like water in a river, they moved on. I was unsure. I have known you longer, got to love you more and now I am sure.'

'I am glad. Did you... enjoy it?'

'I have never felt such feelings before!'

'Neither have I.' She kissed above his ear. 'Such an... exciting feeling...'
'I know.'
'I wonder if we can make the same feelings happen again so soon.'
'We can try.'

Daryo was woken by a young Yashoun officer not long after dawn. After he had dressed, he gently woke Carini, promised to return and followed the officer down to the entrance level and General Ayumo's map room. In addition to a dozen Yashoun leaders, a Hajma officer, wearing an elaborately-engraved bronze cuirass over his beige tunic, and with a tasselled halberd in hand looked suspiciously at Daryo.
'Daryo the Walker, this is Eldert Petros, Warden of the Blood Keep, the title of Warden is given to the commander of the Hajma army. Warden, Daryo the Walker, one of the Yashoun Empire's strategic experts.'
Daryo exchanged looks with Thunaki, who was trying to suppress a laugh. 'Gods' Watch, Warden Petros.'
'Walker.'
'Daryo is not subverting your command, Warden. He is an advisor and will be accompanied by his companion.'
'The plan is his?'
'In part. Commander Hahuro?'
'Yes, sir!?' An officer on the opposite side of the map came to alert.
'Your force will be accompanying the Hajma under the normal conditions. Walker, you will be advising the Warden on the battle as necessary, assisted by Commander Thunaki.'
'As you wish, general. May I ask what the normal conditions are?'
Ayumo looked at his nominated commander, Daryo thought rather uncomfortably before replying: 'Commanders Hahuro or Thunaki will explain at a later time. It is imperative that you leave as soon as possible.' The last sentence was addressed to Petros as well as Daryo.

It was difficult for Daryo to count the Hajma army as he had been given a mount and Warden Petros on his own horse kept up a brisk trot through the army as it began to form up. He was focused on organising his force, so Daryo and Carini kept a respectful distance. Thunaki joined them just before midday as the Hajma army started marching north-east, riding a truly magnificent palomino horse.

'A lovely animal,' said Carini, reaching across from her own mount to stroke the palomino's mane.

'A gift from my uncle,' said Thunaki.

Daryo quickly changed the topic of conversation. 'What were the conditions of the Yashoun army joining the Hajma?'

Thunaki looked around, ensuring that they were not being overheard. They were nearly ten yards behind the company ahead of them and had a lead of more over the trailing company. 'The Imperial Army has strict instructions to remain in the rear of the Hajma. If the Hajma attempt to flee, the Yashoun are to use their bows and shoot them down. If they are defeated, the Imperial Army withdraws. If they are winning the battle, the standing command is to take the field from them so that the Imperial Army is victorious.'

'That is appalling!' breathed Carini.

Thunaki hung his head. 'Those are the orders. The Empire sees Hajma lives as less valuable than Yashoun lives.'

Daryo looked back over his shoulder at the ranks of Hajma behind them. 'I do not feel comfortable with this, Thunaki.'

'By the Third Goddess, you think that I am?'

'No, I am sorry, my friend.'

Thunaki sighed. 'So am I, Daryo. Those are my orders, the orders for any Yashoun commander in Hajmachia.'

'Why would there be such an order?' Carini demanded.

'If I knew why the Emperor and the Court made decisions, I would be Emperor and not a newly-promoted commander out in the hinterland of Hajmachia.'

Daryo waited until he and Thunaki were significantly behind the others.

'Something you said to the general, this past day, you referred to me as the Painted Man.'

'I did.'

'This is not... a pleasant remark, my friend. Not a remark I thought that I would hear from you.'

'It was not intended to be an insult. A painted man is one who is not what he appears. A priest who hires whores... a small man with exceptional strength... a man painted a different colour to the way he is on the inside. A brown wooden door with red paint on it.'

'I understand.'

'What I was suggesting to the general is that you are not what, admittedly many, of Yashoun think Batribi to be. You are a painted man, a wandering traveller who is a warrior beneath the paint. A soldier dressed as a vagrant.' Thunaki winked and smiled to take offence from the remark.

Daryo laughed. 'So you are the reverse? A vagrant dressed as a soldier?'

'More than you know, more than you know.'

The journey to the plateau looking down on the town of Sietviert took most of the day. Camp was set up and Daryo noticed that the perimeter guard was Yashoun. Apparently the Hajma army was being penned in. Walking among them, he realised that the Army of Hajmachia was somewhat less well-equipped and well-trained than the Yashoun. Most of the soldiers wore the cream-brown tunic but some had armour, some had none. There were a wide variety of weapons, boots and shields. Some men had bows but there seemed to be few arrows. What worried Daryo more than anything was the lack of tents and shelters. The scattered tents that he came across would have been comfortable for himself and Carini but he found nine men squeezed together in one. The vast majority of the Hajma, Daryo estimated there were five thousand, slept in the open. It was dry but there was a chill in the air. By contrast, the Yashoun camp, around a hundred yards away from any Hajma, had one tent between three men, their equipment was good, all of them armed in the Yashoun custom with knives, swords, bows and spears. Provisions seemed plentiful, including meat, whereas the soldiers of Hajmachia had been eating pottage. Daryo returned to the Hajma camp and sought out Thunaki and then Warden Petros.

Two days after the first camp, the first Vidmarian force was sighted by a Hajma scout. Daryo's changes had been put into effect. Every evening that the army had stopped, he, Carini and Thunaki had organised a redistribution of weapons so that there were organised battalions of /halberdiers, swordsmen, a small cluster of archers and an equally small group of barely-equipped men as rear-guards and messengers. Daryo led a small group of swordsmen to intercept. It was only a Vidmarian patrol, assigned with keeping the road clear. Three of the eleven were killed and the rest surrendered without much resistance. With some physical persuasion, one of the younger Vidmarians admitted that there was the main Vidmarian force in Tovein, a smaller one near Sietviert and that the main supply laager was on the south bank of the Dithithindil, around twenty miles from Sietviert. Daryo's raiding force removed their prisoners to the camp and handed them to the auxiliary group of Hajma soldiers to guard with captured Vidmarian weapons.

Daryo immediately arranged a conversation with Thunaki and Warden Petros.

'The plan can still be effected,' said Daryo. 'Attack the Vidmarian rear, take their supplies- the Hajma soldiers can make good use of them- and then attack west while General Ayumo attacks northwards.'

'Do we know how many troops are defending the supplies?' Petros asked.

'No, but the two prisoners who would talk said that there were not many.'

'It is a risk.'

'A small one,' said Thunaki. 'There are unlikely to be five thousand soldiers defending a supply deposit.'

'What if the prisoners are lying?'

'Then we will find a deserted area alongside the road.'

'Or a trap.'

Daryo shook his head. 'Then we send a scouting force ahead.'

'My soldiers are not trained for such methods.'

'With respect, your soldiers are barely trained,' said Daryo flatly. 'We have a plan. We have orders and the Vidmarians are in your country, Warden.'

'Daryo? What is wrong? You look troubled.'

Daryo sat down heavily under the shelter. 'I am.'

'Tell me.'

'The Hajma are bold enough but their commander is timid: scared of the Vidmarians, scared of the Yashoun. Thunaki is doing what he can but there are five thousand Hajma and less than five hundred Yashoun, under instructions to only enforce their orders on the Hajma.'

'What is the solution?'

'The solution would be to remove Commander Hahuro and Warden Petros and have Thunaki in command. But Thunaki is only an advisor as I am. He has no official authority over either Hahuro or Petros and neither are likely to listen to either advice or to allow Thunaki to command.'

'So what is the actual solution?'

'I do not know, Carini! Stop asking!'

Carini swallowed hard and said in a small voice: 'I am sorry, Daryo.'

He sighed and reached out, pulling her into an embrace. 'So am I. I am tired, frustrated, I am going to find a quiet place to pray and then try to sleep.'

'The Second God or the Third Goddess.'
Daryo shook his head and looked up at the sky. 'This may be the eve of battle. There is only one I should appeal to.'

'Darkest Goddess, cruellest of tricksters, guide of the dead, force behind my blade and strength behind my shield. I have heard your voice whisper to my thoughts and I have felt your presence in the times of my life that I have felt danger and peril. I may face battle with the new day, or within but a few days. I beseech you to lend your wrath to my swords, your stoicism to my shield, your cunning to my mind and your subtlety to my actions. I beg you to accept those that I send into your kingdom and I ask that you allow me to continue in your service although not yet to walk at your side. I am fated to join you as all men are. I ask only that you do not claim my life now.'

# Chapter 32

The sun was a long time from its rise when two Batribi and six Hajma, armed with bows, slipped over a small, rocky rise and towards the road. The Dithithindil Road on the north bank was a major highway from Yashoun to Jaboen and Gourmin carrying travellers, traders, armies and merchants. The Dithithindil Road on the south bank was a cart track that linked a belligerent nation to small riverside towns in an Imperial province. Straddling the route was the Vidmarian supply laager with a wooden fence around. A sentry with a burning torch was patrolling along the fence. Inside the fence-line were a few campfires and torches. A dog barked.
Carini shuddered. 'I dislike dogs,' she muttered.
'If we keep our distance, the dogs will not even react to us. The wind is in our face so the smell cannot carry,' Daryo replied. 'Vonkers?'
One of the Hajma came alongside. 'Walker?'
'Take two men to the right.' Daryo pointed. 'I will take Carini the other way. The rest of you, remain here. If we need assistance, use your bows.'
'Yes, sir,' said one.
The slightly fat and rather ponderous Vonkers took two of his comrades in the direction indicated. Daryo beckoned to Carini and they went to the left. He had left Temma's Sword and his shield at the camp, sacrificing arms for movement and swiftness. She carried only her spike-tipped staff. They crept down a slight slope and had to clamber over a rocky outcropping. They had reached less than a hundred yards from the fence. A sentry passed less then forty yards away, a dog on a rope trotting at his heels. Carini held her breath still until the sentry was well past.
'We have to find a gate,' Daryo whispered. 'Move slowly and keep close to the ground.'
He crept to the left, hands on the ground, around the rocks and found a sharp depression to crouch in after nearly thirty yards of crawling. He could see three stationary men clustered around another torch but there seemed to be no gate there, just a place where the sentries were congregated. The men by the torch divided. One travelled only a few steps before turning towards the fence and disappeared from view.
'That must a gate or an entrance,' Daryo whispered to Carini. 'I would get closer but a dog's hearing and scenting is much better than a man's. If they know we are here, we may not get away. Back to the others, stay down and go slowly though. No sudden movement.'
Carini's movements were overly slow but it was better to move slowly and remain stealthy. They reached the three that Daryo had left on the ridge. Vonkers and his men

had not yet returned. The first twinges of dawn were visible in the east. Daryo strained his eyes for Vonkers and the other two. A dog barked again but from the other side of the compound.

'Daryo,' murmured Carini, 'peace. Lower your hand.'

Daryo realised that he had his right hand on the Horse's pommel above his shoulder, his fingers flexing restlessly. He lowered it quickly. Eventually Vonkers and his men returned. A sentry and his dog had stopped near them and they had been too nervous to try to move until the obstinate sentry moved on.

'Did you find a gate?' Daryo asked quietly.

'No, Walker. We saw nothing.'

'There is an entrance on the west side,' said Daryo. 'Perhaps the gate is on the north side. I am worried that we would not be able scout that side without being sensed by the dogs. But there seem to be little of note, no overwhelming numbers of guards, I think an attack would be simple enough. We should return to the camp and report.'

After some persuasion and cajoling, Daryo, Carini and Thunaki convinced Petros to proceed. He would send only three hundred men but the result was very encouraging. Daryo led the small force, which was supervised in Hahuro's euphemistic phrase, by nearly ten score Yashoun, to the rise overlooking the laager. Leaving three score archers to pour arrows into the Vidmarian compound, Daryo's group, half of the remaining force, went to the left to the entrance way he thought he had seen and Vonkers led a group to the right, around the compound, hoping to find the main gate on the north side. Daryo found three sentries at a gap in the fence, one tried to raise his sword and Daryo cut him down. The other pair threw their weapons down and Daryo hurried past them, leading from the front. The entrance was less than three feet wide and Daryo was almost immediately faced by another section of fence, there was another gap to the right, he turned, was forced back to the left and found himself in the supply compound. The archers had ceased firing. A small number of Vidmarians and several horses had been shot down. Most of the compound, nearly an acre of space, was occupied by canvas shelters supported by spiked poles, there were also some round tents similar to Batribi *kaffa* and a half-built wooden hut. A Vidmarian, an arrow buried deep in the top of his shoulder, hurled a knife. Daryo just raised his shield in time to deflect the blade. Another knife came and it stuck into the shield. Carini ran past Daryo and, using her staff like a lance, stabbed right through the Vidmarian's ribs. As she withdrew the staff, Daryo had to hurry past her to engage the next man, he caught a few slashes on his shield and finished the argument with a hacking downward swing of Temma's Sword.

The rest of the Vidmarians seemed to have little fight. They were not line infantry, not accustomed to battle, and even the raw Hajma troops were more than a match and heavily outnumbered the Vidmarians. The supply compound was captured and the Vidmarians rapidly being encircled and penned against the west fence by Vonkers, who had indeed located a proper gate in the north wall. As soon as the Vidmarians were confined, the so-called supervising Yashoun troops, led by a captain, entered in a rigid column and took control of the prisoners. Carini took a small group of Hajma to watch the roadway and Daryo sent a messenger back to the camp to tell Hahuro, Thunaki and Warden Petros that the supply compound had been captured without a single Hajma casualty.

The camp and the main force of troops was relocated to the supply compound. Those supplies that could be moved were taken out from under their shelters and the Hajma troops took them for their own. Daryo and Carini requisitioned one of the low, rounded canvas shelters as the closest thing to a *kaff*. A small caravan of three Vidmarian ox wagons appeared from the west, empty with just the drivers, and were swiftly taken in hand. The plans made at the Blood Keep were for the Hajma to then turn west and to attack Sietviert in concert with the main Yashoun force, which should have taken Tovein. Commander Hahuro sent a rider to find General Ayumo's command post and report their progress. After Daryo suggested it, Petros had watch posts established a mile from the compound on the roadway and on the pathway south to warn of any approaches. Carini established herself as something of a quartermaster, distributing supplies and weapons and even coordinating the manufacture of new arrows and the repairs of existing weapons. A small forge had been built on the edge of the compound by the Vidmarians, based around one of the shelters, and Daryo recruited some Hajma and a Yashoun with smithing experience to make arrowheads and sharpen blades. Three iron ingots of decent size were left and Daryo forged a greatsword, nearly five feet long, which Vonkers, who was quickly becoming a valuable lieutenant, gladly took receipt of it.

Late the next day, the rider returned with reports that the Yashoun Ninth Brigade under General Ayumo had taken Tovein almost without a fight but that the Vidmarians had withdrawn to Sietviert, which was significantly more defensible. The general's instructions came in a sealed document. Daryo was summoned to the half-built wooden hut, it had a secure roof and Petros had taken it over as his headquarters.

'The Yashoun are drilling their troops,' said the Warden of the Blood Keep. He lifted the folded parchment, sealed with wax. 'These orders have arrived from the Yashoun general and... I cannot read letters. Numbers, but not letters. I am told that you read a religious text for one of my men, that you have letters.'

'Indeed.'

The Warden took a deep breath, as if readying himself for an unpleasant task. 'Would you read the orders?'

Daryo took the document. 'Certainly.' He studied the seal. 'The seal I do not recognise but the words on the outside read: *From General Ayumo of the Yashoun Imperial Army Ninth Brigade of Infantry to Warden of the Blood Keep Eldert Petros.*' He broke the seal, unfolded the page and read the orders. 'The document reads: *Advance on Sietviert from your present position. The Vidmarian Army has taken Sietviert and fortified their positions. It is my intention to attack Sietviert at dawn, from the west on the Last Day of Summer. I intend that, at this given time, you will attack the Vidmarian position at Sietviert from the east. It is thus my intention to give the Vidmarian Army battle from two directions. The Second God guide our actions and signed thus General Ayumo of the Ninth Brigade.*'

The Warden took the paper and looked at it. 'I must take your oath that you speak truth, Batribi.'

'By the Third Goddess, those were the words. I can seek out one of your countrymen who may have letters. Lieutenant Vonkers perhaps.'

'No. No. I trust an oath on a goddess's name whoever speaks it.'

'Summer's Last is the day after next. It would take us a day's march to reach Sietviert so we should make ready.'

'I consent.'

'I shall give the necessary instructions.' Daryo turned on his heel and went to leave the building.

'Batribi!' Daryo turned back and the Warden looked embarrassed. 'Daryo. My thanks for your assistance with the orders. I have been somewhat... curt with you. Insulting even.'

Daryo did not reply.

'I am accustomed to being watched, controlled and commanded by Yashoun. I follow Yashoun orders, am watched by their officers and commanded to do their bidding. If I follow their direction, I am paid coin and privilege. If I fail, I am sent to the dungeons below my own Keep. Or to the gallows on its wall. To then have a stranger, a Batribi from another land, thrust upon me as an advisor... and I am no new man to the sword or to battle... I was angry. I resented the... implication that I had no ability to command my own men even under Yashoun direction. I know... I know that the appointment was not your choice. I know that you intend to do all you can to assist in the winning of this battle. This is my nation, not yours, and you have put your life, and that of your companion, in peril for my nation. And for that I am grateful.'

Daryo inclined his head. 'I swore to defend those who needed it. It occurred that I knew Commander Thunaki and he has a somewhat high opinion of my ability, hence he recommended my service to General Ayumo. I am here to work in whatever way necessary to assist in the defence of Hajmachia.'

Petros smiled thinly. 'My thanks. Do you know anything of Sietviert?'

'I have never visited Sietviert.'

'It is alongside the Dithithindil but high above it, being on the south bank. The town is the highest point for several miles and has a significant stone wall surrounding it. From the west and south, the land is flat until it climbs up to the town. From the east, you must descend a sharp slope into a dry valley before climbing back towards the town.'

'The town is easy to protect.'

'Very. Do you have any thoughts as how best to take it?'

Daryo shook his head. 'Not without a clear sight of the town.'

'Then I guess it best that we ready the men to move.' Petros smiled a little wider than before. 'Would you give the order, Walker?'

'Certainly, Warden.'

'I will find our Yashoun... comrades and inform them of our orders.'

## Chapter 33

Sietviert was everything that Petros had described. It was at the top of a cliff, the highest on the south bank of the Dithithindil for dozens of miles. From the cliff top, in a wide arc, a relatively-low but broad and strong stone wall studded with four squat towers with battlements around the top. There was no gate in the east side of the circle, instead the road dropped from the ridge to the east of the town, turned south and looped around to the southern gate. There was another, smaller gate on the east side. Ranged along the south side of the wall but concentrated mainly on the east, on the plain beyond bowshot of the walls, was the camp of General Ayumo's troops. They had some small catapults and were building a storming tower.

Daryo and Petros had the Hajma camp established behind the ridge, out of sight of the town. From there, he and Carini accompanied Petros, Hahuro and Thunaki to meet with General Ayumo. The Yashoun leader was confident that no call for aid had got out from the enclosure but had eight thousand men at his disposal, plus the five thousand Hajma, and knew that there were about sixteen thousand Vidmarians inside the walls of Sietviert. He proposed that the siege be permitted to continue.

'There is one risk, General,' said Thunaki. 'The garrison could get a message away. There are substantial Vidmarian forces on the north bank of the Dithithindil, in Kakuo and Namixo, possibly in Sictan by this time. There are of course, those still in Vidmaria, if a messenger got out through the lines then we could be attacked from the rear. Until then, they would be content sitting inside the walls. As long as their provisions are good, they can resist until they are relieved.'

'How would a messenger get out?' asked the general politely, probing the theory.

'Perhaps simple stealth, my Lord. Alternatively, a descent down the cliff to the river would not be beyond imagination or capacity.'

'Many Hajma can climb cliffs and mountains,' said Petros. 'Vidmaria is even more mountainous and it is reasonable to assume that Vidmarians can climb well also.'

'If they are reinforced, we could be surprised,' repeated Thunaki. 'I recommend if we can break the siege sooner, that would be best, sir.'

'I concur,' said Daryo.

'What do you suggest, Master Daryo?' asked Ayumo.

'I would like to wait for darkness and take the opportunity for a close examination of the walls.'

'I will ensure that no attacks are made after sunset,' Ayumo assured him.

'My thanks, General. I will make sure I am ready.'

With just his twin swords, and with thick cloth wrapped around his boots, Daryo crept to the bottom of the wall close to the cliff edge on the west of the town. Above, he could see moving glows, suggesting that sentries were patrolling the wall but General Ayumo had assured him that they did not mount patrols outside the walls. The Vidmarians were seemingly quite convinced that the Yashoun force outnumbered their own, Ayumo's deceptive tactics of extra tents and campfires along the ridge were working. It lent credence to Thunaki's warning that they would simply stay within the walls and find a way to send a message to Vidmaria for reinforcements; the besieged thought themselves outnumbered but were safe in the town until help reached them. Daryo investigated a small hole in the wall but it was clearly a latrine outlet on closer inspection. He moved on. Another hole was barely inches wide and looked to be an arrow loop. After another fifty yards there was a wreck of wood, some stone debris and a foetid, rotten corpse in Yashoun uniform, stuck with arrows. Daryo guessed that this was a position where Ayumo's men had tried to climb the walls. The wreckage suggested ladders but they had been destroyed or had collapsed. There were some more bodies further along the wall, mostly Yashoun but some Vidmarians, again most of them riddled with arrows. He reached the small west gate, aware that it was most likely to be more carefully watched than the rest of the wall. He gave the gate a wide berth, nearly forty yards, making sure to step very carefully and quietly until he was away from it. Not far from the gate was a wider perforation in the wall, lined by clay. It was too narrow for a man to pass through but there may have been possibilities for sabotage. The wall between the drain and the south gate was almost featureless, a curved stone wall with just occasional arrow loops. The main gate to the town was reinforced with an extra arch of stone, a portcullis in front of the iron-banded gate, murder holes in the top of the arch and with the remains of Yashoun soldiers littering the approach. On the east were the remnants of more Yashoun ladders and soldiers. The base of a tower bulged out from the wall and there was a drop from the stone down nearly twenty feet, which Daryo had to scramble carefully down. He startled an animal that ran in a smattering of feet and terrified squealing. Daryo froze until the animal was well away, listening intently for any hostile reaction. There was a few comments from the top of the wall, almost drowned by the ambient noises and then the peace returned. Confident he was still undetected, Daryo moved on and found a way to climb back to the foot of the wall. After a few hundred more yards of arrow loops and towers, Daryo had to scramble down another escarpment away from the walls and, a few feet from the ground, lost any hold and fell to the ground. The fall was only four feet and he managed to remain on his feet. There was a slight overhang, wet and muddy at the bottom, with a drain pipe embedded in the earth. It was much larger than anything else, nearly three feet across. Daryo probed the entrance for a few feet before the darkness became complete. Not encountering any barriers, Daryo extracted himself and continued his survey of the wall up to the end of the cliff. He then retreated from the wall to the rise on the east and followed it around to the main Yashoun camp and General Ayumo's tent.

The general stood against a supporting pole of his tent. He looked up as Daryo entered. 'Walker. No incidents?'

'No, General.'

'Anything to report?'

'There was one possibility. An overhang, east of the gate. There is some sort of drain through the ground that appears to lead into the town under the wall.'

'Large enough for a man?'

'Superficially. It was rather too dark. I need something so I can see where I am going.'

'A torch.'

'A torch or a lantern. What I would like to do, if I may, is to return with some necessary equipment and explore that drain further.'

'Certainly. Not this night?'

'Not this night, dawn is approaching. I need to be able to access the drain when it is newly dark and have time to return before sun-up. If I am seen, it may give the Vidmarians a suggestion of what we are planning. They could reinforce or trap the drain on the other side.'

'Will you go alone?'

'I think it best. Perhaps one or two as assistants and to keep watch.'

'Any of my men are at your disposal, Walker.'

'My thanks, General. I am going to rest now.'

'Of course.'


The next night, Daryo, Carini, Vonkers and two other Hajma followed the reverse route of the one that Daryo had used the night before: along the ridge and down the slope, across the lowland to the overhang. To cover any noise that they might make, a small force of Yashoun were attempting to storm the west gate.

'Ensure you stay under the edge,' whispered Daryo. 'Light that lamp.' Vonkers did so. 'Thuyt, Gruesen, stay here, stay alert. Carini, Vonkers, follow me.'

Daryo took the lead. The drain was clay, slightly less than three feet high, inclined upwards slightly with a small trickle of water along the bottom. Rather than walking

painfully bent over, Daryo crawled awkwardly holding the lamp in one hand. Progress was painfully slow and uncomfortable. After less than thirty feet, Daryo had to stop and hand the lamp to Carini and stretch his back out. After continuing for a few more yards, they passed under a connecting pipe that was only inches wide. There were several more pipes in the next few yards. The drain then sloped upwards more sharply and became harder to negotiate. Daryo was glad when they reached the end- the pipe curved upwards to vertical and, around ten feet above, finished with a barred cover. With some awkward and uncomfortable manoeuvring, Daryo managed to get into a standing position in the upward pipe with Carini stood on his shoulders and Vonkers bracing his legs. She reached up and got her hands on the grate.
'Wooden,' she whispered. 'I think it is under a water pump.' She tried to move it. 'The grate is heavy but loose.' She tried again. 'Sorry, Daryo, it is just too heavy.'
'How strong are you, Vonkers?' Daryo hissed.
'Perhaps strong enough to lift you, Walker. I can try to do so.'
There was more shuffling, squeezing and contortions before Daryo stood on Vonkers' shoulders, with his head almost touching the grate.
'Excellent.' Daryo took a grip of the bars and pushed. The grate moved. Daryo pressed harder and the grate lifted and its weight pulled it aside. 'Success. Can you get me a little higher, Vonkers?'
'I can try.'
Daryo felt the lift of Vonkers underneath, gripped the edge of the drain and pulled himself up, bringing his head to the top. The grate was indeed under a water pump, situated in a small square surrounded by stone houses. There was a fire burning in the middle of the space nearby. A number of sleeping forms on the square could have been Vidmarians and Daryo decided it was too perilous to investigate any further. His arms were burning with the strain and he carefully lowered himself down again. A slightly-rounded but firm surface under his feet was Vonkers' shoulders and Daryo was able to haul the grid back over the drain. With Carini's help, Vonkers lowered Daryo to the bottom of the pipe.
'It is under a pump,' Daryo whispered. 'There are possibilities. Carini, go first down the pipe, go carefully.'
The descent was easier, using arms and legs to propel themselves down the drain on their backs, Carini with the lantern again. They reached the bottom and were helped out of the entrance by the two sentries.
'No movement, sir,' one reported.

'Good. We may have possibilities through here. Make sure there is nothing dropped,' said Daryo. 'We go out the same way as we came. Stay silent now, silent until we are up and over the ridge.'

As he had been the previous night, General Ayumo was waiting for someone to return. Daryo explained the drain's layout but was sceptical about the possibilities.

'We could not get a large number of troops through there,' said Daryo. 'The pipe is too narrow. Getting out of the drain at the other end is problematic also. It is not practical for an invasion.'

'Infiltration?'

'Yes. We could infiltrate men into the town. The entrance is in a square but if the infiltrator was careful... yes.'

Ayumo nodded. 'Let me think through some possibilities. Commanders' meeting will be after the morning meal. I shall send someone for you.'

'As you wish, General.'

'Daryo, what happens now?'

Daryo was already in the bed in the tent, Carini was undressing.

'What do you mean?'

'What happens?'

'You were there, you heard the general. He is going to find a way to use the drain to our advantage.'

'And the battle is won.'

'Perhaps.'

'And then what?'

'I cannot say. The next day comes with the sunrise and no sooner.'

'Do you want to stay walking forever?'

'I cannot say.'

Carini pulled her leggings off and squirmed into the bed next to Daryo. 'The Yashoun Empire and the Hajma will be very grateful for our help, would you agree?'

'I would imagine so.'

'Could we perhaps ask for... a house?'

'A house?'

'Somewhere to live. The Hajma Army could give you a position and we could live in a house in Hajma or Tovein or...'

'I had not thought in that manner.'

'We could have a small house and you could command a company and we could think of children and a life together.'
Daryo smiled. 'We could.'
'Would you like that?'
'I think I would.'
Carini slid closer and laid her head on his shoulder. 'I know that I would.'
Daryo held her against him.

The commanders' meeting consisted of Ayumo, Thunaki and Hahuro, Daryo, Carini and Petros and the commanders of the troops that Ayumo was leading- who were introduced as Kachirou and Harasho.
'There is a key resource in Sietviert,' said Ayumo. 'No force can survive without water and Sietviert has a weakness in this regard.' He nodded to Harasho.
Harasho was older than the other commanders, of at least sixty-five summers, his hair and neat beard almost white. 'I was in command of Sietviert's garrison in my younger days. All water to all pumps in Sietviert, but for one well, is pumped up from the Dithithindil. That is nearly two hundred yards below. A hand pump cannot pull water that far. On the cliff top is a pumping station, there is a windmill on the top and the machinery can be turned by ox or horse. If the pumping station can be wrecked, there is no water to anything but the well near the west gate. If that could be fouled as well, there would be no water in Sietviert.'
'The drain gives us the best chance to get a small team inside,' said Ayumo. 'The pump station is easy to find, even in the dark, it is the only building within fifty yards of the edge of the cliff, correct?' Harasho nodded. 'Master Walker, you have given us much but I ask a little more.'
'To sabotage the pumps?'
'Correct.'
'I consent.'
'Our thanks.'
'I will go too,' said Carini. The tone in her voice and expression on her face gave no space for disagreement.
'As you wish,' said Ayumo. 'We have recovered some Vidmarian uniforms so we can equip a small number as Vidmarians to accompany you.'
Daryo thought for a few heartbeats. 'Two. They can protect the well, but Carini and I will fare better alone.'
'As you wish.'

'I would like Lieutenant Vonkers and Soldier Thuyt with Soldier Gruesen to watch the bottom of the drain.'
'Certainly. I think it best that this is done soon.'
'We will go as soon as the darkness is enough.'

# Chapter 34

Daryo and Carini both spent most of the daylight hours procuring what was necessary for their task- complete black clothing, more thick fabric to wrap their boots, rope and the like. Thunaki produced a small glass bottle, which he said was a potion that would poison the well, although not causing death. Harusho told both how to get from their entrance to either target and then from that position to the other target and back to the drain. The alternative exit route would be to head for the west wall and use their rope to climb down the wall.

As darkness fell, they met with the others. Vonkers and Thuyt were dressed in Vidmarian uniform, Gruesen in all black and carrying Vidmarian weapons. When the sun was well down and the darkness complete, the small group retraced their route along the ridge down to the drain outlet. Gruesen took position to watch the end of the drain. Vonkers and Thuyt proceeded along the pipe first, then Carini and Daryo last. At the top end, Thuyt clambered onto Vonkers' shoulders, pushed the drain grate aside and scrambled out. He carried a short length of rope, just enough to lower down and allow Vonkers, Carini and Daryo to climb up.

'If we do not return before dawn, leave without us,' Daryo whispered to Vonkers.
'Good fortune and the Second God go with you both.'

The square had several clusters of sleeping Vidmarian soldiers. Daryo had Temma's Sword in an improvised canvas sheath on his back. Carini's staff was impractical for the pipe, so she had borrowed a Yashoun sword, also in a makeshift carrier on her back. Slowly, silently, they passed through the square and found an alleyway with a forge at the top. Commander Harasho had made both Daryo and Carini recite and remember their pathways and the alleyway was the start of both. It was short and came onto a small side-street. There was a separate alley, just to the right and across the street. Daryo pointed towards it and then to the left. The two options: pump room or well. Carini pointed forwards. The pump house first.

Daryo checked that the street was clear and crossed slowly. Carini waited for his signal and followed. The alley was narrower than the first and winding. It led behind the small Temple of the First Goddess, became steps as it passed an apothecary and physicians and then reached one of the main streets across Sietviert, which Daryo knew could also take them to the well. A patrol passed the end of the alley, just as Daryo reached it. He melted quickly back into the shadows. The squad of six men, one carrying a lantern, passed at a slow pace. Their walk and their soft conversation betrayed anxiety but one also said 'arriving soon', to which the response was 'catch them from behind'. With the patrol past, Daryo peered out, looking for the next part of the route- a small street just away to the right. It was visible, a tall house on its nearest corner. The patrol was forty yards away, forty-five, fifty. Daryo hurried to the shelter of a doorway near the corner, followed by Carini. She paused alongside him and moved on to the corner. The street was only fifty yards long but seemed longer. She kept as close to the wall as possible, Daryo close behind. One of the houses on the road seemed to have been burned. The ruins were still smoking. A light became visible at the far end of the road. Carini slipped into the ruins of the burned house, Daryo close behind. The charred building ruins, their dark skin and black clothing kept them hidden as the patrol, three men all with lanterns, passed. As soon as they were beyond her hiding place, Carini hurried onwards. Daryo followed, his hand on the hilt of Temma's Sword. The road sloped sharply upwards, reached a crossroads and Carini ran across it. Daryo was close behind, they passed the last house on the street. Around thirty yards on was a stone wall with the windmill beyond, a dark shape alongside would be the pump house. They crouched behind the wall. Daryo could see at least two guards by the windmill.

'Guards,' Carini whispered.

'I can see two by the windmill.'

'Three.'

'Three?'

'Yes.'

Daryo reached behind and drew Temma's Sword. 'We have to be quick and precise.'

Carini released her borrowed blade. 'I will be.'

'Where is the third?'

'Two right at the end. The third is between us and them.'

'That one is yours. I can manage the other two.'

'Ready.'

'Go.' Carini scrambled over the wall, Daryo close behind. She made a crow's flight for the first sentry. Daryo rounded the site and broke into a run. With a silent prayer to the Second God and the Fourth Goddess, he slowed to a creep within fifteen yards. With ten yards remaining, he heard the thud of Carini hitting her target. Daryo's men did not hear their comrade's death and neither had any inclination that a Batribi swordsman had reached them. They died without knowing.

Carini joined Daryo and they both raced to the door of the mill. It was locked but Daryo was prepared. Using Carini's sword and a technique he had practised some times before, he dismounted the mortice of the lock and pushed the door open. They slipped inside the mill. From Commander Harasho's details, they knew that they had to reach the top of the mill. A short distance from the door, a single candle burned and a line of candles and lanterns were hung next to it. Daryo lit one candle from another, put it in a lantern and held it up. The room was nearly circular, around thirty feet across. A three-foot pipe came through the ground and went straight upwards with another branching off to the side, alongside a door that must have led to the pump house. The stairs wound around the inside of the walls with just a narrow protective rail. Daryo led the way up at a steady pace; lantern in one hand, sword in the other. The stairs were almost three hundred feet high before they came into the room at the top of the mill. The space was right in the top of the tower and full of the gearing and machinery for the sails and pump. The axle for the wheel outside came through a hole in the wall along with a biting wind. Harasho had identified the parts to be damaged- key joints between the sails and the pump itself. The parts were iron but the pins and pegs were wooden. There were appropriate tools in the room- bars, hammers and even a small axe for the care and maintenance of the pump. Daryo used them for the opposite purpose, smashing out several pins and pegs and managing to pull a gear wheel from the machinery. Where the hole for the axle was, Daryo hurled what he could into the Dithithindil, hundreds of feet below.

'Now to the pump house,' said Daryo. 'Be careful on the steps. That would be a horrible fall.'

They descended as quickly as possible and let themselves into the pump room- a low, cramped room, filled with pipes with a giant wooden wheel hung from the ceiling. The track around the outside suggested that the wheel was turned by a donkey or horse. Carini used her blade to pry the gear wheels free as Daryo shut the valves to the pumps around the town and did his best to jam them shut by removing the valve handles and dropping them in an open topped pipe. They splashed into water a considerable distance down.

'The well,' said Carini with a grin. 'Then back to the others.'

'We have twice the distance to cover to get to it.'

They returned to the door of the mill. Carini extinguished the candle and Daryo checked outside. They slipped out and froze. The first sentry, the one killed by Carini, had been found by a four-man patrol. Daryo caught hold of Carini's hand and tugged. Keeping his back against the wall, they slid around the mill tower and along the pump house, climbed over the wall at the far end and crept back into the town. They regained the street that ran across town and turned west. There was little cover, they had to move in sprints from one shadow to the next. At the end of the street, Daryo took the option to their left and then an alley to the right. There was a large pile of sacks, barrels and boxes in the alley and Daryo sat behind it, struggling to control his breathing. Carini almost tripped over him and sat beside him.

'Are you hurt?' she whispered urgently.

'No. Tired.'

'A little further and we can leave.'

She helped him up and they moved on, Carini in the lead. At the end of the alleyway was a single sentry. Carini acted swiftly, grabbing him from behind, driving her sword through his back, his heart and out of his chest and withdrew it quickly. Daryo helped her pull him back into the alley and cover the body with some sacks from the refuse pile. They crossed the street, raced down another and almost collided with a patrol. One went to scream an alarm but almost lost his head to Temma's Sword. Carini parried the swing of a surprised comrade and Daryo slashed across the Vidmarian's stomach and neck.

'Someone can find them easily!' hissed Daryo. 'Quick! Run!'

They ran at full speed down the street and they slid into a small drainage ditch on the edge of another square. At the centre was a roofed well, their target. Spread around the square were over three score slumbering Vidmarian soldiers.

'We cannot do this,' Daryo whispered. 'There are too many.' He took the vial of liquid from his belt. 'Thunaki could have kept this. Come, we should go back.'

'Wait,' Carini said, peering around. 'How do you sleep in the wind?'

'What do you mean?' Daryo hissed.

'You keep your back away from the wind.'

'Yes. The wind is at our backs so the Vidmarians will sleep towards us.'

'Perhaps.'

'So they cannot see the well.'

'Not on this side of the square.'

Suddenly Carini snatched the vial from his hand and sprinted for the well.

'Carini! Carini!'

She slowed as she reached the first Vidmarian sleepers, she crept on the balls of her feet past them. One of the sleepers moved and almost kicked Carini's ankle but she stepped over it just in time. Daryo could barely breathe as she stepped over a slumbering soldier, slipped between two more and reached the well. Daryo saw a movement on the side of the square. He crept out of the ditch and found a dark archway. A patrol had stopped and one was relieving himself against a fence. They were almost fifty yards from Carini but she was completely exposed. Regardless she moved on, avoiding a well-huddled group of sleepers, checking back over her shoulder and with a long step was alongside the well. Daryo was sure that he heard the pop of the cork and then Carini was threading her way back. Daryo started finding himself considering his exit routes- back towards the well and Vonkers or to take the shorter route to the wall. Both had merits, he decided, but the well was probably best as it would expose Thuyt and Donkers to less danger.

And the bell tolled.

It was an alarm, the dead men, somewhere, had been found. And there were thousands of Vidmarian soldiers in Sietviert. The time for stealth was passing quickly.

'Carini!' Daryo called, stepping into the open. 'Wall!'

Carini ran across the square, her feet darting into space among the rousing Vidmarians. She reached Daryo and ran straight past him, catching his arm to pull him after her. More bells and alarms were joining the commotion, along with shouting voices and drawn weapons. There had been one contingency put in place in case of a major alarm- a detachment of Yashoun would be about to launch a feinted assault on the south gate. The main impediment became groggy, agitated and anxious Vidmarians running to their positions. It took a painfully long time to reach the foot of the east wall, most of it spent crouched under an overturned cart as companies of Vidmarian soldiers rushed past. They crossed the last street and found themselves in an alley at the foot of the wall, feet from the steps. Daryo raced up, sword ready, Carini almost pushing past him in her haste. There was a single man stood at the top, surveying the town. He shouted when he saw Daryo and levelled his spear. Daryo used his momentum from running to barge into the luckless man and Carini drove her sword into his throat. She had their escape rope on her back and began to quickly unfasten it while Daryo stood guard. She fastened the end to an iron bracket and hurled the rest over the wall. The alarms had been silenced but the commotion below continued.

'Go!' said Daryo, watching for danger.

'I cannot climb a rope!' Carini replied. 'Not down the rope! I do not know how!'

'The same as up! Go!'

'Show me!'

Daryo looked over the edge. 'Right. Be close after!'

'I will be!'

Daryo seized the rope and climbed onto the parapet. He was moments away from lowering himself down when he saw the bowman emerge from the tower towards the end of the wall.

'Carini! Archer!'

She saw him a heartbeat too late. The arrow struck her just above the hip on the right side. Her Vidmarian blade fell to the wall with a clatter. Daryo had no thought to the drop or distance. He ran along the parapet as surely as a squirrel on a branch, threw himself off of it and landed on top of the Vidmarian archer, Temma's Sword driving into the man's chest like a cleaver. The other two men in the little tower room looked up in shock. Daryo sprang up, opened the closest man's throat with the cross-swing and hacked down into the joint of neck and shoulder. He pulled the blade free and spun full circle, taking the last opponent's head from his shoulders. He drew a few ragged breaths and ran back to Carini. She was sat against the parapet, breathing rapidly, her hands clenched around the arrow shaft in her midriff.

'Daryo... Daryo...' she moaned.

'Shh, I can get you out of here,' he said, kneeling beside her. He ripped the improvised sheath from his back and pushed it in around the wound. 'Hold that. I will pull the rope up and lower you down.'

'No... no...'

'I will not leave you here.'

'Caught... get caught... go.'

'I will *not* leave you here.'

He got up and quickly hauled up the rope. He made a loop in the end, placed it carefully around Carini's shoulders and helped her stand. She groaned as she did but did not protest. With a lot of help from Daryo, she stood on the parapet as he coiled the rope and took the strain. Carefully, she passed over the edge and Daryo fought to support the weight. Slowly, agonisingly, excruciatingly, Daryo lowered Carini down. His arms, back and legs screamed in burning pain until finally the weight was gone. Without pause, Daryo threw himself over the parapet, barely holding the rope, disregarding thought and consideration and all-but slid down the rope. Carini had extricated herself from the loop and was hanging on to make his descent easier. Daryo leaped free with five feet left, landed heavily but was up again, pulling Carini's arm over his shoulder and hauling her back to her feet.

'There should be a party of Yashoun only around half a mile away,' said Daryo encouragingly. 'We will get you to the camp, get a physician to you and you will be walking to our house in Hajma within the season. Remember that house, Carini? Think of it, picture it in your mind's eye and we will both see it.'

The town could have vanished, its garrison and archers fallen to the river below, Daryo had but two thoughts- Carini and where in the name of the Pantheon the Yashoun patrol was. Every step seemed to cover bare inches. Every breath came more heavily and with more exertion. Every burn of a muscle or twinge of a joint was increased tenfold. Carini's weight became greater and greater as she weakened. She could move her feet a little less distance with each step. Her breath was faint and panting. Daryo could feel her face and arm drenched in sweat.

'Password!' shouted a voice.

'It is the Walker!' Daryo called back. 'Help, I need a physician.'

'Password?'

Daryo thought. He heard the creak of a bowstring from an invisible threat. 'Paloss!' came to his mind.

Suddenly he was surrounded by Yashoun soldiers. A cloth stretcher was produced and they were soon hurrying back to the camp, Carini slung between them.

# Chapter 35

The tent was Ayumo's, being used as the general had a wooden-framed canvas bed. Carini was laid on the bed, undressed but for her undershorts and wrap around her chest. The arrow was still in her abdomen and the physician and three assistants were working. Daryo had been firmly but sympathetically ejected from the tent and he paced in a circle around the outside. The general had removed himself, coordinating a more concerted attack on the town for the morning. Thunaki sat on a stool nearby, watching Daryo. In the distance, the sounds of the Yashoun feint on the south gate was continuing.

'She put the concoction in the well,' Daryo said as he passed Thunaki on one circuit. 'I was unhappy about going into the square but she simply... went to the well, did what was needed, ran back as the alarms went off. They found the sentries that we killed. We had to kill some of the sentries by the mill and again in the town near the well.'

'She was very brave.'

'She is very brave. The most courageous woman I have ever known.'

Another few circuits.

'The damage to the wind-pump was simple enough, we threw a gear wheel out of the window.'

Another circuit.

'Where are Thuyt and Vonkers?'

'They heard the alarms, kept themselves safe in the pipe. They sent Gruesen back to inform us. I directed Gruesen to return, he will tell them that you and Carini have returned and Thuyt and Vonkers can withdraw too.'

Two more circuits.

'Have many been killed in the feint?'

'Not many. It is noise and nuisance more than an attack. The real attack is dawn on the west side.'

'I may join it.'

'I am sure General Ayumo will consent to whatever decision you make.'

Another turn around the tent.

'Why is the physician taking so long?' Loud enough that those in the tent would hear clearly.

'I cannot say. I know nothing of the physician's art.'

'Is there another available?'

'Mamukso is the best in the Yashoun army, in my opinion.'

'Two swordsmen, however talented the second, are better than one peerless bladesmen.'
'I trust Mamukso to ask for help if he needs help.'
Daryo was a third of the way around the tent once more when the physician emerged, his assistants in tow. Daryo turned so quickly that he almost came out of his boots.
'How is she?!'
The physician was a relatively young man, his hair unusually close cropped, he wore white gloves that reached to his upper arms. They were covered in blood. One of the physician's aides helped take the gloves off and then threw them aside. The young physician guided Daryo a few yards from the tent.
'I am sorry, Walker,' he said softly. 'Miss Carini is mortally wounded. The bleeding has stopped but, inside, there are many ruptures. The arrow is still in place, to remove it would kill her very swiftly. To leave it in will kill her slowly. I have given her an elixir to dull the pain. I cannot do more.'
Daryo felt the landscape swim around him. A hand gripped his shoulder. The physician said something consoling. One of the assistants walked back to the tent and returned. Thunaki put his hand on Daryo's back and guided him inside the tent. Carini was panting for breath, still sweating, her eyes were very wide open. A stool was produced and Daryo guided onto it. Carini's hand was lifted and put in his. Thunaki patted his shoulder and left them alone.
He had no idea how long he sat there with Carini's hand in his. Her breath stayed fast and wheezing. She closed her eyes for a period and then opened them.
'Daryo.' Her voice was barely audible.
'Carini!' He leaned forwards quickly.
'Still there.' Her free hand waved towards the arrow.
'The physician went to get some instruments to remove it.'
'Just pull.'
'I am no physician.'
'Will I die if it comes out?'
'... I said I am not...'
'Daryo.'
'Yes, my love. If the arrow comes out, you will die.'
'But I will die if it stays in.'
Daryo hung his head. 'Yes.'
Carini sobbed quietly. 'Will Moulra be waiting for me?'
'He will. My mother too. And my comrade Viulra, I told you of him.'
'The giant of the Silver Island.'

'Yes.'

'I do not want to meet them just yet, Daryo.'

'I do not want you to meet them. I want you to stay with me.'

'I cannot do that. The physician says I will go.'

'That house. The house and the home and the family that we could have had. Remember that?'

'I remember. You said that if I pictured it, I would see it.'

'I had to say something to keep you fighting.'

'Will you?'

'Will I?'

'Keep fighting. Keep fighting, Daryo. Use your swords, use that shield, do what you promised to do.'

'I do not know if I can.'

'I want you to. Swear.'

'I swear.'

She took a sharp inhale.

'What is it?'

'It hurts.'

'I can find the physician, get him to give you some... potion or other.'

Carini shook her head. 'If he does, it will put me into sleep. I want to see your face some more.'

'You can look at it as long as you wish.'

'I want... I want... guardian... First Goddess.'

'A prayer?'

'Prayer.'

Daryo thought frantically. 'I cannot think... Thunaki? Thunaki?'

The Yashoun slipped into the tent. 'I am here.'

'Carini wants a prayer to the First Goddess. I cannot think of one.'

Thunaki nodded and took a thoughtful breath. 'Greatest Goddess, Great Lady of the Pantheon, giver of plenty and bringer of bounty, please continue to bless your faithful with your gifts. Aid your servants in care of their crops, in stalking their prey and in fishing the rivers. Care for the stores of your servants, their provisions and larders and give us plenty in the years to come.'

'Thanks...' wheezed Carini. 'Prayer... good... Next Kingdom soon.' Her breath was getting shallower.

Thunaki reached down and put his hand on her leg. 'Walk well with the Fourth Goddess, Carini. Look for Suko, son of Suko, of Ossmoss, my keenly grieved-for uncle. I shall do you honour for the rest of my days.' He stepped out.

'This is not how I thought we would part,' said Daryo, feeling tears on his cheeks. 'In a house together, at a great age, perhaps. On a battlefield, fighting side to side, perhaps. Not like this.'

'Happen... battle...'

'We were so close to getting out!'

'Should... should have... seen... my fault.'

'No!'

'Tired... so tired...'

Daryo used his free hand to wipe his tears from his eyes. 'Sleep then, my love. Close your eyes and sleep.'

'Will be... end.'

'Yes, my love. Yes.'

'Do... not... want... not yet...'

'Then stay awake.'

'Cannot... tired...'

'Sleep then, Carini. Close your eyes and sleep.'

'Scared... Daryo... scared.'

'You will not be scared across The Bridge.'

'Not... scared... Walker with me.'

Daryo instinctively found Temma's Sword in his belt. He held it out for her to see. 'I will protect you, Carini. I swear. And I swear to continue fighting in your name.'

'Not scared... safe... so tired...'

'Sleep, my love.'

'Daryo... I love you... so tired.'

'I know. I love you, Carini. Sleep, my love.'

'Sleep... yes... sleep.'

Daryo sat on the stool beside her bedside with Temma's Sword across his knees. Dawn came and he knelt at the head of the bed for a long time, repeating silent prayers to each of the Pantheon in turn. Someone stepped into the tent at one point but left quickly on seeing the scene within. Midday came and Daryo returned to his stool, continuing his silent vigil. Sometime in the later day, he removed the protruding arrow from Carini's body and found a Yashoun army tunic in a chest which he managed to dress her in. The ownership was immaterial, he thought it better that she was dressed somehow, even if the tunic did not quite reach her knees. It was almost sunset before he left the tent.

'Commander! Commander!' A nearby soldier rushed into another tent and Thunaki emerged a moment later.

'Daryo? Has...?'

'Late in the night.'

Thunaki bowed his head. 'May the Fourth Goddess guide her steps.'

'She will.'

'You look awful, my friend. You need a rest and a meal.'

Daryo shook his head but his body betrayed him. He yawned massively. 'I think... yes...'

Thunaki indicated the tent he had been in. 'There is an unused bed in there. Sleep and I will find you some food.'

'I want a guard outside the tent.'

'You feel unsafe?'

'Not my tent. Hers.'

Thunaki nodded. 'Certainly. I know nothing of Batribi funerary rites, my friend. But sleep now and we can organise such things at a later time.'

Daryo stumbled into the tent, fell onto a bed and was asleep within heartbeats.

He did not wake until the next dawn. A sizeable loaf of bread, two legs of chicken and some apples had been left and he ate all of it without enthusiasm but his stomach was grateful. An accompanying jug of milk was drained. He stepped out of the tent. Thunaki stood outside what had been General Ayumo's tent with his sword drawn alongside Vonkers.

'Gods' Watch, Daryo,' said Thunaki, a kindly smile on his face.

'Gods' Watch... is she...'

'Safe.'

Daryo looked around. The camp was almost silent. 'Where is the army?'

'Attacking Sietviert. This is to be the last attack before we leave them to suffer from the results of you and Carini's work.'

Daryo nodded dully. 'I need a latrine.'

'Of course. I have Gruesen and Thuyt left with Vonkers and myself. We are all at your disposal.'

Daryo found the latrine, did the necessary and returned. 'I want to find somewhere to... to bury her.'

'Of course.'

'Somewhere... fitting.'
Thunaki thought. 'I know the perfect place. I will get the others and find a stretcher.'

On the road to Hajma, about two miles from Sietviert, the ground sloped up steeply to a ridge and then swept downwards to a valley. On the reverse slope was one more of the dense pine forests that seemed to cover much of central and southern Hajmachia. On the ridge itself was a single tree stood alone, eighty feet high, bushy and healthy, its companions lost to fire, woodsman's axe or time. In the shadow of the tree, the stretcher carrying Carini's shrouded body was put down. Daryo, Thunaki, Thuyt, Gruesen and Vonkers had a shovel each and took turns to dig. By sundown the grave was large and deep enough.
The four Yashoun tied ropes to the corners of the stretcher and lowered it and Carini into the grave. Daryo had brought her staff and he pushed it into the ground above Carini's head. Slowly the Yashoun filled in the grave, leaving the top two feet of the staff as a marker. A pony arrived carrying the priest from the brigade. He spoke briefly with Thunaki and placed an unlit lantern on the mount of earth.
'We commend Carini, kin of Sraini, to the care of the Pantheon. We commend her spirit to the Next Kingdom and her memory to our minds. The sound of her footsteps have faded, the candle of her spirit has gone but the faithful know that that candle has been relit on the other side of the bridge and that her footsteps walk the roads of the Next Kingdom alongside those we have lost before. We ask the benevolence and bounty of the Pantheon on those of us that remain behind. From the First God, we pray for strength of mind and body. From the First Goddess, we pray for bounty. From the Second God, we pray for victory in war. From the Second Goddess, we pray for loyalty and devotion. From the Third God, we ask recovery from sickness. From the Third Goddess, we ask peace and compassion. From the Fourth God, we pray for security and safety. And we beseech the Fourth Goddess to guide the steps of Carini across the bridge to her Kingdom and to care for her for the rest of eternity.' He looked around. 'Would anyone like to speak?'
Thunaki nodded. 'I knew little of Carini. I met her only at the Blood Keep and since. She was a thoughtful and clever young woman, a joy to be around and a fierce warrior. I know she was faithful to the Pantheon and that her thoughts were often with her clan but that her heart went with the man she loved.' He gave Daryo a short bow. 'Carini, kin of Sraini, did a great service to the people of the Yashoun Empire in her last evening. She was a woman of conscience, of duty and of passion. And we salute her.' He drew his

sword, as did the three Hajma soldiers, and all four knelt with the points of the swords in the ground. One by one they stood.

Daryo stood silently for a long time. 'I loved Carini. Like I have never loved anyone before. I have no memory of family. I have lost many of the friends that I have had. And then I met Carini. I loved her. We were going to find a home, start a family, find a life in a town. But I swore to Carini that, without her, I would go on fighting, go on walking the roads. I do not know how I can find the strength to do that. I pray that the First God gives me the strength.' He drew Temma's Sword, still stuck into his belt, raised it by the hilt, point down. 'I pledge my sword and my service to your memory, Carini. Every step on every road, every time I draw a blade will be in your name until I am discharged by death and meet you in the Next Kingdom.'

The return to the camp was slow and silent but the camp was anything but. Soldiers were rushing about in apparent confusion. Thunaki grabbed one and interrogated him as to the source of the excitement.

'A breach' was all he heard.

'The wall is breached?' asked Thuyt.

'We should go to help,' said Thunaki, drawing his sword. 'Daryo, are you... Daryo?'

'He was just beside me,' Gruesen said, confused.

The four began to separate to look for him but suddenly Daryo burst out of his tent. He was still wearing the dark clothing from his work in the town but now had his twin swords on his back and his shield on his arm. He was racing for the town, running as if every corpse in the ground were chasing him. Thunaki lead the pursuit but Daryo was well away, legs moving at a speed barely mortal. The east gate had fallen and Yashoun soldiers were fighting their way into the town but with the Hajma soldiers at the front. Daryo went through the Yashoun ranks like a galloping horse through parchment, through the bottleneck of the gate itself and into the town. He dived down an unoccupied alley and burst into a square full of half-panicked Vidmarian soldiers. Daryo fought blindly and unstoppably. Every slash of Temma's Sword cleaved into an enemy with a relentless force. Any riposte was batted aside by the shield. No hostile sword came within a foot of the near-psychotic Batribi warrior. Any threat was dispatched and any enemy foolish enough to confront him cut down. He had no idea how long he fought for but there was a gradual decline in the number of enemies. He became aware that Thunaki and Vonkers were fighting alongside him but the numbers of enemies were almost zero. Emotionally spent and physically fatigued, Daryo allowed himself to drop his guard.

'The Vidmarians have opened the south gate,' Thunaki told him. 'Most of them fled. How are you?'
Daryo lowered his sword. 'Tired,' he admitted.
'You sent over fifty to whatever the Vidmarians call gods. If you were not tired, I would be most concerned!'
Temma's Sword was returned to its sheath. 'I am going back to the camp. Please... give me some solitude for a time.'
'Certainly.'
Daryo turned and began to wander back towards the east gate. Thunaki beckoned to a pair of Yashoun soldiers nearby. 'Follow the Walker back to camp, discreetly. Ensure he reaches his bed safely.'

When Daryo awoke it was to the sound of music, singing and laughter. The Yashoun Army was celebrating the relief of Sietviert. He emerged and immediately had a bottle of wine pressed into his hand by Vonkers.
'Good evening to you, Walker! The Vidmarians are fleeing over the border and Hajmachia is safe for now! We have had news too, that the Yashoun Army has taken back Kakuo!'
'Good news,' said Daryo, managing a smile. 'The siege was not needed. The well did not need to be fouled. Carini gave her life for nothing.'
'Perhaps many have, Walker, but I think it best to believe that they gave their lives for victory. My brother is dead on the border, killed when the Vidmarians first invaded our country. He died for no purpose, for the Vidmarians to come and rape our land, or he died as the loss in the long road to throwing the Vidmarians back across the mountains.'
Daryo mused on the idea. 'That is a worthy thought.'
'Come, Carini and Veew would not wish us to be glum. Join the celebration.'
'My thanks, Vonkers. I would be glad to.'
Several boars had been roasted over open fires and there was sufficient drink for all. The Yashoun and Hajma soldiers mixed freely, teaching each other songs and bawdy rhymes. Thuyt, Gruesen, Vonkers and Thunaki had commissioned an army smith to make a pair of bracers in thanks to Daryo- leather panels with straps to go around the forearm with a series of closely-spaced steel bands engraved with trees, vines, snakes and a curved sword. They were of excellent quality and Daryo almost tried to refuse them, but he remembered a lesson that he had been taught before: that is was the height of rudeness to refuse an offered gift. With Vonkers' help, he put them on and even allowed Gruesen to strike one bracer with a sword to demonstrate their resilience.

The victory party was curtailed by a heavy, icy rain shower. Daryo retreated to his tent and slept again. A good time after sun-up, Thunaki went to wake him and found the tent empty and everything belonging to the Batribi removed- weapons, shield, pack, clothing. An inkwell, pen and parchment were left on the stool. The parchment was informally addressed *Commander Thunaki*. It was a letter:

*To Commander Thunaki, a true and honest comrade through much*
*From Daryo, kin of Dostan, the Walker of the Order of the Shield and Sword*

*My friend, we have arrived at a common destination from a common departure but by very different roads. I fear the time is right that our roads part once more. It was been my deepest honour to fight alongside you. You have been a loyal and true friend to a man who has few friends and comrades. The truest friend I thought that I would have has been taken from me and I now voluntarily part from the next.*
*My humble and deep thanks for your comradeship and faith, my friend. I return my boots to the road and my skills to the service of the weak, the needy and the defenceless but if ever I may lend it to your use, I pledge you my sword and service until I am discharged by death.*
*Gods' Guidance to you.*

# Book 3 - Swords and Stars
## Year 364 of the Empire Age of the Yashoun

## Chapter 36

To Dostan, of his own kin, of the Batribi Lands
From Daryo, kin of Dostan, Coenobium of the First God in Halmia
Written the Third Day of Autumn

My dearest brother, I believe my search for a refuge is complete. The Coenobium welcomes all who wish to make use of its facility to rest, pray, learn and work. I have now been here nearly six seasons. I am sorry that I have not written before this but I simply wished to make the most of the quietness and simplicity of my surroundings.

The experiences I underwent in the Silver Island, Dule's' Boon and in Hajmachia, as I described to you in my last letter, have served to bring my thoughts to those of prayer and reflection. I have killed many and seen many killed around me and my own mortality is a message that I think the Pantheon is sending to me that I cannot afford to ignore.

Life in the Coenobium is peaceful, prayerful and fulfilling. My blades are locked away untouched, my shield a wall-hanging. I pray for you, brother, for Laulra, Temma and the others of the clan as well as for the success and growth of the settlement.

I miss the roads, the excitement of exploration and travel but I welcome the absence of conflict and combat and the tranquillity of my home.

I remain, brother, your loyal kin and friend, Daryo.

*To Daryo, kin of the Dostan, formerly the Walker of the Order of the Shield and Sword, of the Coenobium of the First God, Halmia, Jaboen*
*From Dostan, son of Stai, of the Batribi Lands of Ru'uatan*
*Written on this the Nineteenth Day of Autumn*

*My brother, I am glad to hear that you have found a place of peace and sanctuary. I had worried following your last letter, your depressed state and the blackness of your thoughts were evident in your words. I know that the deaths of Viulra and Carini were difficult for you to bear and the pressure of almost constant combat is one that can only lead to ruin.*

*I agree with you that the simplicity and serenity of the Coenobium is likely to be the best course for you in the short term but I believe most keenly that the place you would be most welcome and best served here with your own people here in our settlement.*

*I ask that you give this true and clear thought, my brother. The town is growing and thriving. More of our people seem to arrive almost daily. The temple is complete, the market is commonplace and the crops have been plentiful with every harvest. A small fortification is now being built as the Vidmarian Army is still close in distance if not in threat. There are positions in the Guard if you would so wish, in the forge or any other role you wished to fill. You would be most welcome as a part of the community and, most important, as part of the clan.*

*Write as frequently or little as you wish, my brother. Any message from you is most welcome. Yours in the fellowship of our kin, Dostan.*

*To Dostan, son of Stai, of the Batribi Lands*
*From Daryo, kin of Dostan, at the Coenobium of the First God in Halmia*
*Written on the First Day of Winter*

*I apologise, brother, for the lateness of my response. The courier was forced to travel to Halmia via Three Rivers and Salifa instead of through Hef due to rockfalls and landslips on the road from Lalbi to Hef. It may be that the next rider that I hire is able to pass that way but the rain in the north of Jaboen has been intense.*

*I have found a way of life in the Coenobium that is ideal for my talents. The coenobites are devoted to the First God, they are bound by precepts of duty laid down from the Great Temple's Reverend Apostle. Even though I have not pledged myself to their Chapter, they ask that all guests contribute to the work of the Coenobium and I have arranged a very modest facility in a cellar to function as a metal-working workshop so that I may contribute using my smithing skills. This takes but a small time of each day and the rest of my day is spent in prayer and study. The darkness that held by mind on my arrival has all but passed. I am most grateful to the coenobites for their hospitality and the senior assured me just this last night that I may remain as long as I wish. I have been with the coenobites for approaching two cycles of the seasons and my stay has been beyond useful to my heart and my mind.*

*I would ask of you to write me news of the settlement and our kin. My companions are a group of less than fifty coenobites and I am perhaps ready for some company of other than the brothers. My thanks for your correspondence, my brother, and I remain at you service. Daryo.*

*To Daryo, kin of Dostan, Coenobium of the First God, Halmia, Jaboen*
*From Dostan, of his clan, son of Stai, of the Batribi Lands*
*Written on the Eve of Midwinter*

*My brother, I open with the news that my kinswoman Temma has given birth to a second daughter, a sister to Tella, whom they have named Impini after Stai's wife. She is a beautiful and wonderful little child who has made the clan a more wondrous place. My cousin Balini is also expecting a child and her brother Huryo is to be married on Spring's First Day to a woman recently arrived in the settlement. The clan is growing and would only be greater with your addition, my brother. I realise that every letter I write is encouraging you to join us but it is only because I feel it would be the best for everyone concerned if you were here. A coenobium is a peerless place to rest and to pray but the clan would be a place for you to move forwards, I hope that you are starting to believe this too after two winters.*

*The fort on the north perimeter of the town has been completed and Laulra is to be its first commander, although his work as our representative to the Jaboen Court will continue as well. He has been instrumental in some potentially successful trade deals with the Council of Gourmin as well as with the Jaboens. We are also hoping that a relationship can be formed with Yashoun Empire.*

*Think well on my words, I beg you, my brother. I look for your next letter by courier. Your brother, Dostan*

## Chapter 37
## 11 days from Winter's Last

The city of Halmia was the ancient capital of Jaboen centred not on the royal palace, as it had only been rebuilt after the Yashoun withdrawal from Jaboen. The palace was a modest construction on the edge of the city. Instead the centre of the city was the Council Hall. The Twelve Lords of Jaboen held the majority of the power of the land as the king was but a distant scion of the last true ruler of Jaboen before it was divided by its larger neighbours. Outside the city walls, another newer feature of the city as the Vidmarians had destroyed the city walls in the Third Year of the Yashoun Empire Age, was a small compound, surrounded by a wall of typical Halmian red-brown stone, nearly twenty feet high. The gates were wooden and as high as the walls. The only clue as to the purpose of the enclosed space was a small bronze engraving of a spreading tree on the bell hung on one door. The Batribi traveller dismounted and studied the gate for a moment before ringing the bell. He waited for a considerable period in the rain before ringing the bell again. Eventually a hatch at eye level in the other gate opened.
'Yes?'
The traveller lowered his hood. 'My name is Laulra, kin of Dostan. I am the emissary of the Batribi land to the Lords of the Council. My kinsman is a guest of yours. I hoped to speak with him.'
'Of whom do you speak?'
Laulra, kin of Dostan, almost laughed. 'How many Batribi guests do you have?'
'Of whom do you speak?'
The Batribi sighed. 'Daryo, kin of Dostan, sometime known as the Walker.'
'Wait here.' The hatch closed.
Laulra stood closer to the gate in the hope of a little shelter. He had ridden from a meeting with a trader in Salifa to Halmia and the rain had persisted the entire distance. He was wet through and cold, some of the more sheltered puddles of water were frozen. The Coenobium of the First God was on a hillside to the west of the Jaboen capital and exposed to the elements. The wind was from the south and bitter. Laulra was not a patient man in the best of circumstances and the wait in the wind and rain was not conducive to his patience. He rang the bell a third time, stamping his feet trying to generate some warmth. The hatch opened again.
'Admission to the Coenobium is only by the permission of the Coenobarch. We are waiting for his decision as to whether he is to admit you. Master Daryo has requested no guests and did not inform us that you would be arriving. I wish to ensure that the

Coenobarch and Master Daryo are content for you to be admitted. Please be patient.'
The hatch closed again.

Laulra groaned in frustration and patted his sodden horse's neck. 'Patience,' he muttered, more to himself than to the animal. He raised his hood again, protecting himself against the rain. 'Come along...' he murmured.

There was a small series of metallic thuds and the gate opened slowly, just sufficient for Laulra and his horse to pass through. Laulra took hold of his horse's long rein and led it inside the compound. A man in the light brown robe of a priest, the cast of his eyes and brow identifying him as the man behind the hatch, gave Laulra a short bow. 'I will take your horse to the stable.' He indicated a wooden building against the inside of the wall. 'Please proceed to the temple, the Coenobarch is inside and awaits you.'

'And my kinsman?'

'The Coenobarch would speak with you first.'

From the gate, a gravel-covered pathway led into the centre of the compound where a small stone temple stood. There was a much larger building, a small mansion almost, behind it, a barn to the right with some pigs snuffling around, a small, fenced planted area was to the left. Laulra walked quickly along the pathway, lined with small fruit trees, to the little temple. In the entrance porch, Laulra removed his travelling cloak and hung it from an empty candle bracket to give it the chance to dry. Under his cloak, he wore the traditional Batribi hooded tunic over a shirt, leggings and with a curved sword at his hip. The door of the temple was ajar and Laulra pushed it open.

The temple, like most, was circular in plan with a round altar, a carved wooden tree in the centre, a piece of exceptional sculpture complete with branches, fruit and leaves. On one side, a circular glazed window showed a green tree surrounded by a dark blue sky. Simple, curved wooden benches formed four rings around the altar. A man in a black robe sat in the front row, his hands clasped in prayer and his head bowed.

'Come in, Master Batribi.' The voice was slow and measured.

Laulra closed the door, laid his sword down and moved between the benches, sitting about a fifth of the way around the circle from the man. He looked to be of at least sixty winters, his hair turning white, his eyes looked milky as if his sight was faded.

'You are kin of Daryo?'

'I am. My name is Laulra, kin of Dostan.'

'I am Zayn, Coenobarch of this chapter. Daryo has been our guest for some time now.'

'Yes. He has been corresponding with my brother Dostan, our clan leader.'

'Why do you come here?'

'Simply to visit him. I have been in Salifa and am due to meet the Lords of the Council this day. The Coenobium was on my route into Halmia and I wished to take advantage of this opportunity. I have not seen my kinsman in nearly twenty seasons.'
'He has not asked for visitors. He spends his time in work and prayer.'
'I know. I was hoping he may assent to seeing me.'
'When he came to us, he was greatly troubled: haunted by death and war. He has come to peace under the care of the Mightiest of the Mighty.'
'I know, and I do not wish to disturb his peace, but I was hoping that our bond as kinsmen would mean that he would see me.'
The Coenobarch shook his head. 'I am sorry, Master Laulra. I do not want to disturb him.'
Laulra sighed. 'I would like to hear it from him.'
'I cannot allow that.'
'Surely that is Daryo's decision. I wish you to simply ask for his decision. Tell him that he has a visitor, who I am and ask if he will see me.'
'As you wish.' The Coenobarch stood slowly.
Laulra sensed duplicity. 'Swear on the God.'
The Coenobarch's eyes betrayed but a flash of anger but it confirmed Laulra's suspicion. 'I swear on the name of the First God Dravin.'
'My thanks.'
The Coenobarch shuffled out. Laulra sighed and stretched his legs. He had been on a horse for a long period and luxuriated in the warmth of the temple and the opportunity to sit on something still. Again, the wait seemed interminable. Laulra suspected that the Coenobarch was taking the opportunity to dissuade Daryo from allowing a visitor. Even through the stone roof and walls, he could hear the rain continuing to fall. The wind whined around the temple's low dome and was joined by a draught from the door.
Laulra stood, ready to argue his case further with the Coenobarch.
'Laulra!'
'Daryo!' Forgetting he was in a temple, Laulra hurdled the benches and pulled the younger man into a fierce embrace. 'Gods' Graces, Daryo, you look well!'
Daryo smiled. He had allowed his hair to grow out a little, forming a small halo around his head, his beard was neat, no wider than his mouth and reaching just from the bottom lip to the end of his chin. He was dressed in a thick black robe, woollen trousers and low boots. 'As do you, brother. Sit, sit.'
They both sat on the nearest bench.
'How do you like the Coenobium?' Laulra asked.

'The peace and reflection was exactly what I needed after my experiences of Hajmachia and the Silver Island.'

'You have been here for several seasons, have you not found it somewhat... dull?'

'Not at all. I saw so much death and so much blood that the simple life of the coenobites has been so rewarding and so healing.'

'I am glad. You have... no plans to leave?'

'No immediate plans, no.'

Laulra nodded. 'If ever you require somewhere else to stay, the clan will welcome you with open arms. I am loath to leave so soon but I must meet the Lords of the Council this day.'

'My thanks for your visit, Laulra. I hope to see you again soon.'

'The feeling is mutual, brother. Gods' Guidance to you.'

'And to you.'

After Daryo had taken Laulra back to his horse, he trod the well-worn path back to his chamber. The main building was devoted to communal areas such as workshops and the kitchen on the ground floor, accommodation for the coenobites on the first and other rooms in the attic rooms at the top. Daryo used the main staircase and followed the corridor at the top to the last room. He lived simply: a bed, a chair and desk, a chest beneath the window and another under the bed, which he rarely even touched. On the wall above the desk hung a dust-covered shield, almost obscuring the images painted on it. He closed his door and sat on the side of the bed. A book was open on the desk and Daryo picked it up. He had been reading it when the Coenobarch had come. It was a text by the previous Coenobarch of the Chapter entitled *Interpretations of Creation*, a scholarly look at the philosophical and moral lessons of the creation story and the gifts given by each of the Pantheon. Daryo was particularly interested in his current chapter, he had read it three times, as it was one that dealt with the antithesis of the creation; the Fourth Goddess's contribution of making all men mortal to ensure that she had followers after death as they did not worship her, the bringer of loss, while living. As he read, Daryo noted passages to raise in his regular meeting with the Scholar of the Chapter. The discussions between a man with an intense interest in the Fourth Goddess's work and a devoted Scholar of the First God, the Bringer of Life, were often intense but always intellectual and concluded amicably.

From the tower at the far end of the house came the hour bell, followed by the three rapid rings that signalled mealtimes. Daryo marked his passage and proceeded to the dining hall. Six long tables filled the room. The coenobites ate together at every meal,

there was a system to divide labours such as cooking that benefitted everyone. Daryo had taken his turn the previous day. He was one of two so-called guests, not sworn members of the Chapter, but long-term residents of the Coenobium. The other greeted Daryo with a short bow, he was a man of thirty-two winters, he had been a soldier who had lost an arm and eye in battle with Peak Tribesmen, now he served the First God in fulfilment of a promise in exchange for his life. He was to leave at the end of the winter, his vow completed.
'Gods' Watch, Master Daryo.'
'Gods' Watch, Master Ihabasit.' They tended to sit at the far end of the room from the majority of coenobites, who ate in silence but permitted guests to converse on the condition that it was quiet. Occasionally a Senior of the Chapter would join them.
'You had a visitor?'
'Briefly. A kinsman.'
The meal was served, a vegetable stew, a bowl for each man, and the Chapter Priest, the third member of the Seniors of the Chapter with the Coenobarch and the Scholar, stood and the rest of the attendees of the meal did the same. 'We of the Coenobium of the First God give grateful and humble thanks for this meal. We give thanks to the Mightiest of the Mighty for his gifts of health, strength and life. We offer our lives to his service. We rededicate ourselves to his great will and works. We pray especially on this day for soldiers, for warriors, guardians, protectors and watchmen. We pray especially for the people of Taam in Jaboen, Nudakso in Yashoun, Aslon in Gourmin and Hivamakia in Boskinia. We pray especially for our dear brother of this Chapter, Hayzan, who is ill and we beseech the First God's intervention with the great Spellis, Third God, in bringing our brother back to wellness. We pray especially for our guests, Daryo, kin of Dostan, and Ihabasit, son of Haarun. We pray especially for those that have donated food and wood to this Chapter in the past eight days. Hear our prayer, Dravin, Greatest God among Great Gods.' After a moment's silence, the Priest sat and the meal was commenced. Each meal was preceded by a prayer, who and what was the subject was determined on a schedule of rotation and changed day by day. The familiar rhythms and calm dignity of each ceremony was of great benefit to Daryo's spirit.

After the meal, Daryo finished reading the book and returned it to the Chapter Library below the bell tower. The Scholar was sweeping out the room by candlelight and greeted Daryo as he always did; like a friend who has not visited for many seasons.
'Master Daryo! So good to see you here! Returning Coenobarch Saadam's tome?'
'I am.'

'What opinion do you have of it?' The Scholar was very elderly, he had told Daryo that he had lived through seventy-nine summers, was small and wrinkled but sprightly, something like a keen bird.

'I disagreed with his thoughts on the Fourth Goddess and on the legacy of The Deluge but in more broad terms, I found it most instructive.'

'The Deluge, truly?'

'I think it an act of the Pantheon as a whole. A... correction, akin to keeping only the strongest pup of a litter. Not a vengeful act by one Goddess.'

The Scholar chuckled. 'I expected nothing else of your mind. Why do you think I recommended such a book and not one that gives simply the Reverend Apostle's writ on the Creation? I wanted to suggest another interpretation, particularly after our discussion of the Deluge before.'

'I think Coenobarch Saadam was too... focused on the First God's work and is rather dismissive of the Darkest Goddess. He seems to view her as an inconvenience. A bad child scaring the chickens.'

The Scholar laughed so hard it made him cough and splutter. When he recovered himself, he had to sit down to recover his breath. 'Daryo of the Batribi, you will kill an old man with such comments before summer comes! To describe the Fourth Goddess so... oh, my young friend, you make me smile!'

'I do not describe her so, but I believe that Coenobarch Saadam does so.'

'The very thought! Ha!' The Scholar wiped a tearful eye. 'You wish further reading?'

'If you can suggest suitable material.'

'Certainly, certainly.' The Scholar got up slowly and tottered among the lines of shelves, Daryo close behind. They stopped in a far corner, near the wall. 'The shelf at the top. The... darker volume.'

Daryo reached up and brought down a wooden tube, which proved to contain a scroll, much older than many others and the books around it, with no identifying marks. 'This one?'

'Yes. A less... hostile author to the Fourth Goddess, this text examines her relationship with Dravin and suggests analogies and relationships as well as conflicts. I think you will find it most entertaining, yes. *On Partnerships* it is called, a copy of a manuscript by a Reverend Apostle who was elderly when I was but a boy.'

'My thanks, Scholar Riheem.'

'It is almost time to extinguish. You should return to your chamber. We have until this coming evening before our meeting, I would ask you read as much of the volume as you can. It will raise some questions, I hope.'

'As you wish. Gods' Guidance, Scholar. Sleep well.'
'And you, Daryo. I shall see you in the temple at dawn.'
'Of course. Have ever I not attended?'
'Not to my knowledge. A good night to you.'
Daryo returned to his chamber just before the Extinguish Bell sounded. He undressed, snuffed out the candles and retired to bed.

## Chapter 38

A short time before dawn, the bell ran to wake the Coenobium and summon those within to the temple for the daily service of worship. A simple morning meal, normally bread and milk, was served afterwards before the brethren dispersed to their tasks- some for the care of the compound and buildings, the Coenobium had three horses that required care, there was a planted area of vegetables to be tended, clothing to be washed, the kitchen to be tended and a myriad other tasks. Two of the coenobites travelled daily into Halmia to give instruction in the schools and temples.

Daryo retreated to the small cellar. Alongside the stores, in one corner, was a high fireplace, a work table, a small anvil and a chest of tools. There was little metalwork needed but Daryo's experience as a smith's apprentice had lent him some skill and it allowed him to give some service to the Coenobium. Ihabasit worked with the horses as his tasks. A metal tethering ring had been pulled apart by an ill-tempered mare and Daryo was attempting to repair it. He stoked up his fire, still warm from the previous day, and was soon heating the iron ring to bend it back to shape. The work was simple and he was finishing the work as he became aware of an observer.

'Scholar Riheem.'

'My sincere apologies for interrupting you.'

'I am almost finished, Scholar. There is no cause to apologise.'

'Are you free of duty for the rest of this day?'

'I am.'

'I find myself called to Halmia. A long treatise from the Emperor has been received by the Lords of the Council. They have asked for me to examine it and to draft a response, as the Council's scribe has fallen ill. Would you accompany me?'

'Accompany you?'

'It would mean I miss our meeting and I thought that we could talk while on the road. I should not be at the Council Hall for long.'

Daryo thought for a considerable time. He had barely left the Coenobium since his arrival and said so.

'There is no compulsion. If you wish to remain, you should do so.'

Daryo nodded. 'I would prefer to do so.'

'As you wish. I could meet with you after the next dawn service?'

'My thanks, Scholar. It would give me some time to read the text that you gave to me.'

'Until then. Gods' Guidance.'

'Gods' Guidance.'

Daryo finished his work, left the fire to burn down and removed himself to his chamber to read the *On Partnerships* scroll. The thrust of the argument that it presented was that the Fourth Goddess was a partner to the First God, that death was an inevitable part of life and that all things, not simply man, died, therefore the Fourth Goddess's creation of death for man was simply an extension of that which she applied to all other things. Death ensured that there was always adequate space in the world and sufficient food, else everything would be consumed as man procreated and populations grew. Again, Daryo found himself disagreeing with the author but respecting the arguments made. The next day, he greeted the scholar after the morning worship and meal and they retired to the library, finding armed chairs by the small fire.

'I find my fire a little larger every day,' said the Scholar, sitting down heavily. 'It is as if the cold gets a little deeper into my bones with every new day.'

'If we are fortunate and virtuous, age comes to all.'

'Fortune, I think, is the key to the lock.'

'Not faith?'

The Scholar chuckled breathily. 'Fortune and faith. What did you think of the text? Allow me to pre-empt, you disagreed with the author.'

'I did.'

'May I ask why? In this case?'

'The suggestion is that the Fourth Goddess was almost a product of the First God. That because he created life, and all things die, man is fated to die by rote.'

'Indeed.'

'But were not the Pantheon always so?'

The Scholar nodded in response.

'So the Fourth Goddess was always so, as was her work.'

'If I am a tree-feller and you a carpenter, is not your work a product of mine?'

'But my work could exist without you. I could fell my own tree.'

'Equally my work would be foolish without yours. Felled trees would pile up with no purpose. So without either of us, the other's work is either without purpose or much more difficult. The producer of goods and the supplier of the materials are mutually dependent on each other. The Fourth Goddess depends on the First God for live souls. The First God relies on the Darkest Goddess to remove the living to make room for more. If the elderly, sick and wounded do not die, would there be room for the new-born babes?'

Daryo nodded slowly. 'I think I see.'

The Scholar stood up and took another scroll from a nearby shelf. It had a new leather case. 'This is another text on a similar subject. It is named *The Flowing River- Birth to Death, The First God and the Fourth Goddess.*'

'Who is the author?' Daryo had learned early in his meetings with the Scholar to always question the source of the material.

'I am,' said Scholar Riheem with a modest smile. 'It is a short essay. And I invite you to disagree heartily with my own views if you so wish.'

Daryo returned the smile. 'I shall try to moderate my disagreements.'

There was a knock on the library door and one of the younger coenobites, a man of about Daryo's age, entered.

'Brother Scholar, I humbly beg to interrupt.'

'Brother Haisel, how can we assist?'

'I apologise, Brother Scholar, but Master Daryo has another visitor.'

Daryo sighed. 'I am deeply sorry, Scholar. Who is it, Brother Haisel?'

'He gave his name as Dostan, Master Daryo.'

'Dostan!?'

'Yes, Master Daryo.'

The Scholar raised a hand. 'Bring him here to the library, Brother Haisel.'

'Yes, Brother Scholar.'

Daryo looked at the elderly coenobite as the younger man left. 'I am sorry, Scholar. I know visitors to guests are discouraged and I have had two within three days.'

'They are your kin, Daryo. You should welcome them.'

'They are not truly my kin. I was declared and accepted as part of the clan by Dostan's father, Stai. When he passed to the Next Kingdom, Dostan took leadership of the clan and has named me brother.'

'Then he is your kin. If the Coenobarch proclaims a man brother, is he a coenobite and brother?'

'He is. You think the two are the same?'

'Completely.'

Daryo massaged his head with his hands. 'I am finding all the... mental exercise difficult.'

'You manage it very well, Daryo.'

The knock on the door came again.

'Enter!' called the Scholar.

Dostan was beginning to grey, his hair turning the colour of iron, his eyes wrinkled at the corners. There was a green tunic and trousers under his heavy travelling cloak.

'Gods' Watch, my brother.'

Daryo stood up and embraced him. 'Gods' Watch, Dostan. You have travelled a long way.'

'I have. With good reason though.'

Daryo turned to his original companion. 'Brother Riheem, Scholar of this Chapter, this is my brother and the head of my clan, Dostan, son of Stai.'

The Scholar stood up slowly and clasped Dostan's hand. 'Gods' Watch, Dostan.'

'Gods' Watch, sir.'

'I should allow you to talk,' said the Scholar. 'Tell me, Master Dostan, has the rain ceased?'

'For now.'

'Then I shall take the air in the compound. Excuse me.' He let himself out.

Daryo waved Dostan to the vacated seat and retook his own.

'Were my messages insufficient?'

Dostan chuckled. 'Of course they were sufficient, my brother. One cannot have the same relationship with a message as with another person face to face. You really have taken to life in a coenobium. I never thought it possible.'

'The whims of the Pantheon are strange.'

'Indeed.'

'You come to persuade me to return to the clan?'

'In a way of speaking, I have.'

'I thought my messages were most clear.'

'They were. And I respect the decision that you made at the time you made it.'

'But now you do not?'

'The circumstances have changed, brother. A condition of the gift of our land from the King of Jaboen was that we accept a degree of fealty to him. We pay no taxes or duties to him but have... responsibilities towards our Jaboen brethren. Particularly in mutual assistance in times of need. Such as war.'

'War?'

'The Vidmarian Army is still holding Namixo in Yashoun and, to do so, hold a small corner of Jaboen. This is apparently insufficient. They have given notice to the Lord of Thiel that if the town is not abandoned by the Tenth Day of Spring, they will take it and kill all who resist. The Lords of the Council, when they met with our brother Laulra, have given a formal request for Batribi assistance, much as your Order did before.'

Daryo hung his head. 'You wish me to join you.'

'You are a fine warrior, Daryo,' said Dostan earnestly. 'If half of the stories Laulra and I have heard of the Batribi warrior in the Silver Island and Hajmachia are true then you may be greatest Batribi warrior walking. We need you, Daryo. You are a leader and a combatant and my kin.'

'I do not know if I can, Dostan. I have seen so many people that I care for die, many because of my own actions. I have peace and contemplation here. Devotion to life, not death.'

'What about your duty?'

'My duty?' Daryo's head came up.

'You swore an oath.'

'To a body long since perished.'

'Until discharged by death.'

'It did not specify whose death.'

'You lie to yourself and to Brokea if you think that, Daryo!'

'And what would you know!' Daryo stood up, nearly knocking his chair over. 'I saw Viulra killed by Nar Silver! I left the Tibilians to die to save my life! Carini died in my arms! And what of the Order? What of the Harlequin? Tell me, Dostan!'

Dostan stood up. 'Peace, my brother. Peace. I cannot say that you have not seen terrors and lost those that you loved. But you swore an oath, in the name of the Second Goddess, and to me you pledged sword and service. I am asking for those now, Daryo. I did a great service for you, the entire Batribi settlement risked itself to help your Order and we cared for the wounded and asked for nothing in payment. I ask for payment now.'

'You ask for a large payment, brother. One I am not sure I can meet.'

'I require payment nonetheless.'

Daryo shook his head, trying to clear his thoughts. 'One moment I am grappling with finer points of the Pantheon's work, now I am contemplating leaving this place where I have found real sanctuary to return to what I was trying to escape from.'

Dostan sighed. 'I am most sorry, Daryo, but I would not have travelled such a distance if I did not believe that you were needed.'

'I have to talk with one of the Senior Coenobites, Dostan. I cannot just decide to leave.'

'As you wish. Winter's Last is in eight days. The Batribi Company leaves the settlement in six. If you come, be with us by then.'

Daryo sat alone in the library for a long time. Most of it he spent simply staring at the fire. He wept at times. The Scholar returned just before the evening meal.

'You were missed at the midday meal, Daryo.'

'I was not hungry.'

Riheem sat down. 'Your brother's visit was difficult.'
'I came here for the clarity and peace that I knew only a coenobium could offer. Now someone comes to take me away from it.'
'Back to a life that you once led. A life you had some success in.'
'And a life that cost me so much.'
'What would you say is your greatest skill, Daryo? You can wield a sword, you can hammer iron, you can study text, what is the greatest of these?'
Daryo sighed. 'My sword. I have fought off scores of men unaided.'
'Is that... ability, that talent given by the Second God, being used here?'
'No.'
The elderly coenobite was silent for a while, studying Daryo's face. 'I shall miss our meetings, Daryo. Your companionship and conversation have been great boons to me. I ask you to keep my text, I can rewrite it. Read it if you should have the chance to do so.' He stood. 'Your kinsman has not yet left. I shall inform him.'

The long box under the bed was untouched in seven seasons, it had gathered a thin layer of dust on the top. Daryo pulled the box out and lifted it onto the bed. The catch was stiff but clicked open. In the top was a dull green-brown canvas pack which he removed. Beneath was an array of items including a bowl, water skin, a fire-starting kit, a coin bag and some other equipment on a small pile of clothing. All of it went into the pack. A pair of high, Hajma leather boots and a pair of steel and leather arm bracers sat alongside. Most of the clothing and a good blanket went into the pack, the boots and bracers put aside as well as a jerkin. Under the clothing was a leather harness and a sword belt with scabbard. These were removed and also laid aside. Under these was a long parcel of slightly-oiled canvas. He unwrapped the parcel carefully. First was a knife, slightly curved at the tip, a single cutting edge on a bone handle, around six inches long. Next was a thin, two feet long sword, two edges with an offset point, the pommel of its hardwood hilt carved into the image of a bear's head. Third was a sword identical to the previous one but with the pommel that of a horse's head. Lastly was a curved blade of almost three feet, a vicious point flaring out to nearly five inches wide before tapering back to the leather-wrapped hilt. Daryo ran his fingertips over the flat of the blade. It was named for Dostan's kinswoman, Temma. The Bear, the Horse and Temma's Sword. Daryo removed his coenobitic robe and the underclothes beneath, exchanging them for grey woollen undershorts, a black shirt, brown wool leggings, foot wraps and then the boots. Next was the jerkin, thick hardened leather with thin steel plates over the chest and ribs, lining the elbow-length sleeves and covering the shoulder blades. He buckled the bracers on to his forearms then the harness on his back and the sword belt around his waist. The Horse and the Bear went into the sheathes on the harness, the knife and Temma's Sword into theirs on the belt. Hung on the back of the chamber door was a waxed fabric hooded cloak and this covered everything. Lastly, Daryo took the shield from the wall and used a corner of the bed blanket to clean it. The shield was painted a dark brown with a circle, in a lighter brown, running around just inside the metal rim to represent a shield. Down the centre was a simple illustration of a sword. At the base of the sword, over the pommel and hilt, was a white Yashoun milepost flanked by a scarlet and green harlequin and a white and gold girl child, dressed in rags and wearing a blindfold. The harlequin was that of Kym the Harlequin, Daryo's first tutor in the ways of war, and the child that of Leroyfa the Blind, both of whom had given their lives to save that of Daryo and a group of children. The two were holding hands over the milepost. Together they formed the badge of Daryo the Walker of the Order of the Shield and Sword.

Daryo was surprised but not shocked to see that Laulra was waiting with Dostan outside the Coenobium stables, both wearing a broad grin and they had a spare horse with them.

## Chapter 39

After all the time spent in his self-imposed confinement, Daryo was almost overwhelmed by leaving the Coenobium's compound. The walls were high and it gave the interior a sheltered effect. The wind was strong outside the compound although the early-morning rain had abated. Daryo mounted the horse and it took a mile before he was comfortable with his seat.

'Is the mare causing a problem?' asked Laulra at one point.

'No. I have not ridden for a long time.'

'The skill stays even if the memory fades,' said Dostan kindly. 'The change from a sheltered chamber to the road again must be jarring.'

'Somewhat. Tell me of the settlement. Does it grow?'

'It does. We were but a village before, a few hundreds. We are a town of sixty score.'

'That is impressive.'

'The temple is a joy to behold and has been wonderfully decorated. There is a permanent forge now, by the lakeside, two bakeries, crops are to be planted with the spring, the fort is strong and well-sited and Laulra negotiated the purchase of an entire ten gross of sheep and goats from the Jaboen king, so many of our people are learning swiftly to be shepherds. We have cattle, although less than a score, and poultry by the score. The lake is our most important resource, the fish feed our people.'

'Has the settlement been named?'

'There have been many suggestions. The Lake Town is the most common, or Stannia, for the lake beside the town. A growing number have been calling for the land to be named Ru'uatan.'

'I do not know that name?'

'Some stories suggest it is the name of the land that our people left so many countless seasons ago. Before we became the travellers of the road.'

'I think that would be a fitting name.'

Dostan nodded. 'I agree, but our brother does not.'

'The new land should have a new name,' said Laulra firmly. 'There are enough of our people who can speak the Old Tongue that we should use it to create a new name and a new title for our lands. Mrai, kin of Fyryo, suggested that we should use the words *He'ath* and *Urr*, the words for sanctuary and gift. *He'ath'urr*, the Given Sanctuary.'

'It has merits,' Dostan conceded. 'But I am loath to give anything, including sanctuary, to Mrai, kin of Fyryo.'

'Why not?' asked Daryo.

'Mrai attends the Assembly of Clan Leaders in place of Fyryo. The Assembly is supposed to be attended only by the leaders of the clans with, perhaps, an assistant if they struggle with the Common Speech. Instead Fyryo sends Mrai, as he cannot trouble himself to stir, and Mrai is a most obstructive, vocal and unpleasant individual.'

'He is short-tempered but affable enough if one talks carefully,' Laulra suggested.

'You are the only man that I know capable of talking carefully enough, brother. All others are cursed and insulted. It is probably only because he lacks any ability with sword that someone has not offered to put it to duelling to resolve his issue.'

'I have never heard of our people duelling,' said Daryo.

'It is very rare,' Dostan told him. 'Very rare. But there are still, on occasions, especially among the older people and in the more traditionally-inclined clans, the tradition persists. It is something that the Assembly is uncomfortable in retaining and it is heartily discouraged.'

The road gave the travellers the option to pass through the gates into Halmia or to follow the road around the south of the city. The three Batribi followed that option, a bridge crossed the River Huba and the road immediately turned to follow the river eastwards for a period. They were passing through the normally lush grass and farmland that surrounded Halmia but winter made the landscape empty and dull; the fields were fallow, the trees bare but the sky was clear. The wind, coming from the mountains to the south and west, was icy and swept across the relatively flat ground around Halmia without interruption, making for a piercing gale. Daryo held his cloak tightly to try to defeat the wind.

'Could you not have called for me in the summer?'

Dostan and Laulra laughed.

'I can make my next mission one to Vidmaria and ask them to delay their advance next time,' Laulra offered.

'I would be most grateful.'

'Giryo's clan opined that it was most upsetting for them to attack in winter,' said Dostan. 'They had found work in road and wall repairs in Tonamaz but when the Vidmarian attacks came, they were told to leave.'

'I do not know Giryo.'

'They arrived not ten days ago. Only eleven, one of them an infant. A pleasant group.'

'You were able to meet them?'

'I was. I try to meet as many new arrivals in our town as I can,' Dostan explained for Daryo's benefit. 'It ensures that they have one name to call if they are in need of aid. It was also beneficial that Giryo's son, a lad also of the name of Giryo, incidentally, is

something of a carver in wood or bone. There is only one other in the town and people always desire decorations or embellishments of some kind.'
'We could do with another man skilled with his tongue, in diplomacy,' said Laulra. 'I cannot work with the Jaboens, the Gourmini and the Boskinians alone. We need an envoy to Yashoun.'
'Could you be an ambassador, brother?' Dostan asked Daryo.
'I think not. I was a warrior and something of a coenobite. Neither calling has had much need of my knowledge of diplomacy. I cannot see my place in the court of the Emperor.'
'Can you see your place in the town? As part of our clan?'
'Perhaps, brother, perhaps. That I have left from the Coenobium is maybe the next step on my road.'

The road turned southwards after a dozen miles and parted company with the river. A farmer, leading an ox that towed a wagon of potatoes, almost collided with a tree to avoid the three Batribi riders. Dostan urged his horse on to a greater speed and the three kinsman were soon engaged in a good-natured race, encouraging their horses to higher and higher speeds as they galloped south and then east. The clear sky and wind meant that they were almost frozen by the time that they reached the first halt, a complex of buildings that incorporated a farm as well. Dostan went inside to ensure that the innkeeper was not inhospitable to Batribi guests. They were welcomed for a meal and spit-cooked chicken and bread were produced and the Batribi welcomed the opportunity to sit in front of a large fire, warm themselves and allow their damp clothing to dry.
'We should reach Jonat by nightfall,' said Laulra as they remounted. 'The Lord of Jonat is a friend of mine, he broached the purchase of the sheep with the king on my behalf. We can get secure lodging there.'
'And more besides?' suggested Dostan slyly as they kicked the horses on. Laulra sighed and said nothing. Dostan winked at Daryo. 'Laulra has a... friend at the house of the Lord of Jonat. A... good friend.'
Daryo chuckled. 'I pray it is not the lord's wife, Laulra.'
Dostan laughed too. 'Almost. His daughter. Laulra may be given a bed by the lord but I swear on the Fourth God's hammer that he will not stay in it.'
Laulra swore and kicked his horse on to a canter, followed by Dostan and Daryo's laughter.
'I shall have to find him a wife,' said Dostan, still chuckling.
'You have a wife?'
'Certainly. Limma, daughter of Vimpini.'

'But no children?'

'Not that we have not tried.'

Daryo smiled. 'I am not sure that was necessary to pass on.'

'I do not complain but Limma is trying somewhat drastic measures. There is a Gourmini tradition that says that a particular bed is good for prospective parents. So a woman who wants to become with child should lay with her man in the bed of another woman who conceived. We seem to have seen every bed of every mother in the town.'

'I hope with the owner absent.'

Dostan groaned. 'One walked in on us in mid-act.' Daryo almost fell off his horse laughing. 'Not the most conducive action to romantic feelings, another woman standing there.'

'Some may find that stimulating.'

'Not I.'

Laulra had slowed his horse to allow the others to reach him. 'Enough jokes spread with my name?'

'We have moved on to making jokes with my name,' Dostan assured him.

'Very thoughtful of you, brother.'

'I have a thought on that,' said Daryo. 'Dostan. That is not a name like any other Batribi name that I have heard. There seem to be... conventions on a Batribi's name. Dostan does not seem to agree with those conventions.'

Dostan nodded. 'You are correct, brother. Dostan is a Gourmini name, not Batribi.'

'I do not know another Batribi with a name that is not of our people.'

'My father named me for a man of Spiert in Gourmin. Our clan, the kin of Stai, although led then by Stai's brother Laulra, was travelling from Sinsebil towards Riverhelm in Gourmin. There were only ten, one was a pregnant woman. Our mother, Impini.' He indicated Laulra. 'They were surprised and attacked by Peak Tribesmen. They killed another woman in the clan and a small boy before an archer began firing arrows from a concealed location drove them off. Some of the tribesmen were killed and the rest fled.'

'The archer was this man Dostan?'

'He was. A well-regarded hunter and fur trader from Spiert. One arrow struck a tribesman just as he was poised to kill our mother. In gratitude, Stai and Impini pledged that they would name their child for him: Dostan if it were a son, and Efeda if a daughter, for Dostan's sister. A moon later, I was born and named Dostan.'

'Have you ever met him?'

'I did once try to seek him. I was a young man and the clan was near Allesbury. I left the clan and walked alone to Spiert. I made some investigations and found that he had died some time before. I would have liked to thank him and perhaps to know him but I will have to wait until I reach the Next Kingdom and find him there.'

Jonat was not much more than a village with a small temple to the First Goddess, a bakery, a butcher and a small forge. A small but well-built manor house stood on the edge of the village overlooking the leafless orchards, the building forming one side of the courtyard square, the stables the second and a low stone wall the other two. The village was pleasant and well-kept. The Batribi travellers had attracted some attention as they passed through the village and they were met by a young woman in a smart, bronze-coloured tabard. She smiled broadly as they dismounted.
'Master Laulra, welcome back to Jonat.'
'My thanks, Balija. My brothers, Dostan and Daryo. Would Lord Hafal consent to our staying for the night? We have travelled from Halmia and are going back to our lands.'
'The lord and Lady Fathi are in Nalb at a celebration. Miss Sibeena would be happy to accommodate you, I am sure.'
Dostan and Daryo laughed until they cried as the mystified housekeeper led them into the courtyard.
Sibeena was of about eighteen winters, not tall but well-proportioned and with a face made even more appealing by the pink-cheeks caused by the cold air in the stables and the fur around her collar. She blushed further pink when she saw Laulra and was happy to give them the two guest rooms in the house. Dostan and Daryo immediately volunteered to share one room to allow Laulra his privacy, as they continually repeated. The young woman was a vivacious, talkative and polite host over dinner and even showed the travellers to their rooms. Both rooms had a pair of beds with good mattresses, thick blankets and large fires. Daryo offered to lock Laulra's room for him, for his own security, and narrowly missed a thrown boot as he retreated.
In a short time, both Dostan and Daryo were in bed. Daryo, recalling old habits and necessary precautions, laid the Bear naked on the floor beside the bed.
'Expecting to be attacked in the night?' Dostan asked, barely visible with the candles doused and the receding fire.
'Just being careful. I have slept in the open and in hostile environs too often to have a blade too far away.'
'Less than a day out of the coenobium and already thinking as a warrior again.'
'It kept me alive, brother.'

'That is why I came.'

'I do not understand.'

'We could have fought a battle without you, Daryo. If you had remained in that place, you would have been breathing, the blood flowing in your veins, but you would not have been alive. This is the life you know, the life you are best served in.'

'This life could kill me.'

'It could. But it would be a significantly better life until the end.'

'I have spent a long time in the company of those devoted to the First God. The principle of life is key to them.'

'And its quality?'

'Surely a factor.'

'My thoughts entirely, brother.'

Daryo smiled to himself in the near-darkness. 'I must say, I do like that word.'

'Brother?'

'Yes. Not something that I hear often and a word I could get quite accustomed to hearing.'

'Then I shall use it at every opportunity, my brother.'

# Chapter 40

The road the next day led through Salifa and Hef, where Laulra had an associate who ran the inn and they stayed there before pressing on for the Stannia Lake Township. The road from Lalbi turned west towards Gourmin and a fork, without signpost, presented itself after a few miles. Laulra led the way to the right and down towards the Lake. The Batribi's fortification was a wooden tower, built on a natural rise north of the lake, with a stone wall around the base of the hill. A border fence, built of pointed wooden logs, was being erected westwards from the fortress's wall by a group of men towards the rocky cliff at the edge of the pass. The new road led down to the growing settlement- an amalgam of some stone buildings, wooden houses and the traditional canvas Batribi *kaffa*, looking increasingly like a small town rather than a temporary village or an encampment. The temple, Assembly Hall, forge, a large barn and a long stable building stood out from a distance. At the perimeter of the town, Dostan dismounted.
'No ridden horses in the town,' he explained. 'We should take them to the stable, I shall have to at least speak to Limma and then find Temma.'
'Temma?'
'Temma is in command of the Company in my absence,' said Dostan. 'I have been... honoured with the leadership of our soldiers.'
'Which is why Dostan wanted you to be here,' Laulra told Daryo. 'So if something goes awry, he has some kin to blame it on.'
The stables on the east of the town were large and, apparently, for the use of those in the town that would need a horse. Ponies, riders, plough horses and colts stood side by side in the stalls. One of the women talking to a stable girl was who they were seeking: Temma was tall and unusually dark-skinned, wide eyes highlighted by a red colour on her upper eyelids, her dark hair was thick and plaited and then bound in a shell shape on the back of her head. She wore a dark blue tunic under a lightweight dark leather cuirass and a curved Batribi sword on her back.
'Dostan! You are back a day early. Laulra!' She hugged both brothers and then Daryo stepped out from behind his horse. 'Daryo the Walker.'
'Temma.' He smiled and accepted her embrace. 'I kept your sword safe.' He laid his hand on the hilt.
'It is your sword, my friend, not mine. How was your time in the coenobium?'
'Restful and most beneficial. I am very content with my own thoughts now.'
'I am so pleased that you decided to return.'

'I was very happy to hear of your new daughter, Dostan wrote of her. You named her Impini?'

'We did. We have to make sure you are introduced to her. She is almost two moons old.'

'And already you are in combat?'

'Not yet. I was commanding the training and drilling while Dostan was absent. I still have duties to my daughters. Tella is almost six springs old and she is being cared for by a young woman who is also wet nurse to Impini. But I can resume being their mother now.' She looked to Dostan for confirmation.

'Absolutely,' he replied. 'How many in the Company?'

'Three more joined. Ten score and thirteen.'

'Ten score and fourteen,' said Daryo.

'And I have to go back to Halmia and attend the king,' said Laulra with a mocking cheerfulness.

'Think how jealous all of us will be,' said Dostan. 'We have four days before we have to leave, I think it best to call the Company together with the new day.'

The group left the stables and Dostan pointed down the lane in front of them.

'At the end of the lane is the Temple Street,' he told Daryo. 'For now, at least now, our clan is at the far south of Temple Street. Beyond that is the area where the Company are training. Laulra and I have to speak with some others in the Clan Assembly.'

'I can take Daryo down and find him a bed,' said Temma.

Dostan nodded. 'We will have to hold a clan meal tonight. Can you try to have all invited, Temma?'

'Certainly. Tella will send the word around. She will enjoy that.'

'As you wish. We will see you later, Daryo.'

'Of course, brother.'

Temma led the way down the street, a somewhat muddy track that the Batribi had tried to pave with split logs in the mud.

'Some of the roads in the centre of the town, around the temple, have been stone-laid,' Temma told Daryo. 'We do not have enough labourers to pave this far yet. As the town grows, and when the Company returns, we should be able to do so.'

Most of the houses in that quarter of the town were wooden and seemed to be attached to *kaffa* by canvas-covered tunnels. One was a little larger than the others and had a pale green piece of sheet hung outside, on which someone had crudely painted a sword and a horse. Temma smiled.

'Tella is a keen artist. Her flags seem to change with every three days.' She pushed the door open. The house was tidy with a wooden floor, well-built beds in two corners,

flanking a hearth with a large fire. A low table was surrounded by stools. A chest and a set of shelves built of scrap wood flanked the door. On the right, a curtained doorway apparently led to the connected *kaff*.
Sat on the smaller bed was a young woman of Daryo's age, cradling a baby in her arms and with another asleep on the bed beside her. A girl with her hair done in the same way as Temma's was sat in front of the fire with a small scroll in her hand, reading aloud slowly. She stopped when Temma entered, from her face she was undoubtedly Temma's daughter.
The woman on the bed stood up carefully so as not to wake the babies. 'Impini has been asleep a while, Temma. I have just finished feeding Tlai.'
'My thanks, Jarini. I hope that she had been behaving well. This is Daryo, of our clan.'
'Gods' Watch, Jarini.'
'Gods' Watch, Daryo. Welcome home. Do you need me to return later, Temma?'
'Dostan and Laulra have returned so I think you can devote your time to your child. There is a clan meal tonight if you and Gnai wish to attend.'
'I am sure we will. I shall see you tonight. By the lake?'
'I think so. If we are not there, look for us where the old *kaffa* were.'
'Certainly.' She passed them and closed the door behind her.
'Tella,' said her mother. 'This is Daryo, a clan-uncle. He is going to be staying with us for some days.'
The girl put her scroll down and regarded Daryo with uncertainty. 'Gods' Watch,' she said quietly.
'Gods' Watch, Tella.'
'There is a bed in the *kaff*,' Temma told Daryo. 'It is a storeroom but *kaffa* are usually warm. It would give you more privacy than taking Tella's bed. Tella, would you help your clan-uncle move the boxes from the bed?'
Tella nodded, got to her feet and led Daryo through the curtained doorway, along the two yards of canvas connection and into the conical *kaff*, which was full of boxes, crates and sacks and also with a wooden floor. On one side was a simple bed, stacked with boxes of potatoes. Daryo put his pack down and helped Tella move the boxes to the other side of the *kaff*. The girl went away and soon returned with an armful of blankets.
'Mother said you would want these,' she said, barely audible.
'My thanks, Tella.'
'Mother wants me to go and tell the clan of the meal. I have to go.'
'Certainly.'

The girl hurried out. Daryo spread the blankets out on the bed and rested his pack against the bed. He removed his boots, changed his foot cloths and replaced them. After some thought, he removed his weapons, replaced his cloak and went back into the house. Temma had moved her baby to a crib at the foot of the bed.

'Is everything in order, Daryo?'

'Quite suitable. I would like to explore the town a little. It has grown so much in the time that I have been away.'

'Of course. To find your way back, find the temple and turn south. Look for the flag outside!'

'My thanks. I shall not be too long.'

The town had grown significantly in the twelve seasons that Daryo had been away. There were dozens more wooden houses, most of them with a *kaff* attached to the side or rear. The temple had been completed and Daryo went inside. The wooden walls on the inside had been plastered white and the interior of the dome was painted black. There was a stone ring altar with wooden carved symbols of the Pantheon stood on it, with hammered bronze shields behind them to protect them from the heat. Split-log benches had been added, eight forming the first circle around the order, sixteen the second row and there was space for at least two more rows. An elderly man was conducting a small service to a dozen attendees in front of the Third God's star. Having only been at services to Dravin in the coenobium, Daryo unobtrusively joined the worship. With the Company going to battle, most of the prayers were for any who were wounded to recover swiftly. The recent bright moons were praised and their help to the hunters was lauded. After the service, Daryo found the bakery and then the forge. When he had been in the town the last time, the forge was a temporary affair on the north side, it was now beside the lake with a stone-built fire ring, a large anvil, good tools and a stone building alongside, as well as its own pump. The smith, Coryo, had a similar background to Daryo's: an apprenticeship having been at a School of the Temple of the Second Goddess in Tiverta. He had taken the forge's ownership when the previous smith died. After the Gourmini invasion, he had fled Tiverta and came to the Batribi Land. The previous smith in the town had fallen ill and Coryo had taken over running the forge. He invited Daryo to return at any time and told him that he was quite welcome to do any work while there. What had been the assembly site for the clan leaders had been raised with earth so that it was almost eight feet above the waters of the lake, paved and it had become the town's market square. A little way north from the market was a longhouse, built of logs like the temple but with a thatched roof, almost a hundred yards long with long green banners outside. A member of the town watch, leaning nonchalantly on the wall with a spear in her hand, told Daryo that it was the Assembly Hall of the Clan Leaders. Alongside was a small building that proved to be the command post of the Watch.

'Pardon me,' said a voice and Daryo turned.

'Gods' Watch.'

The somewhat squat woman gave a jerky nod. 'Gods' Watch. You are that... Wanderer from the Order.'

'Daryo the Walker, kin of Dostan.'

'I am Komma, kin of Solvan, Commander of the Watch. Are you volunteering?'

'I have been drafted into the Company by my brother.'

'At the rate Dostan is conscripting, there will be no Watch remaining! I have less than thirty left and most of us are too old to wield a sword.' She marched past Daryo into the hut and a slightly stunned Daryo moved quickly on.

He found the series of *kaffa* that were used by the physicians to treat the Order's wounded, a two-storey building was being erected nearby, presumably as a replacement for the *kaffa*. This was almost the northernmost building in the town and Daryo found himself looking up the newly-paved road towards the fort. Beyond was the Stannia Pass and then the road from Lalbi through the Tember Pass to Gourmin. Daryo turned around and walked back towards the temple.

A huge cauldron of stew was set on a large fire by the side of the lake and several other fires, much smaller, were put around the area to help keep the clan warm. There were around sixty that were connected to the kin of Dostan and they had a lively and convivial evening together. The Verse was recited, Tella and two of her friends performed tunes on their flutes, a boy just about of age gave a demonstration of juggling, in turn, clay jars, burning torches and knives. Tella sat beside Daryo for the entire evening, responding to questions but not offering any. Dostan seemed to be in attendance for only brief periods but Laulra stayed throughout. A woman of around Dostan's age, a few less than forty summers, introduced herself as Liua, Dostan's lieutenant commanding the Company. She was the niece of the less amicable Komma, commander of the town watch, but was much more polite and less abrupt than her aunt. She was at the gathering by virtue of being the wife of Halvan, of Dostan's clan, and was an attentive listener after requesting some of Daryo's tales of the Silver Island. Some of the clan drifted away after sunset but many stayed late into the night.

'Physician! Somebody fetch the physician!'

Daryo parried the weapon swung at his head. 'Hold!' he said, lowering the Bear. He was assisting Liua with training for the Company, the woman he had been sparring with lowered her weapon. Daryo hurried through the crowd of practising Batribi warriors towards the shouts.

Another female warrior, a little older than Daryo, was sat on the ground clutching a bleeding wound on her upper arm, blood pulsing from between her fingers. A young boy, barely sixteen summers, stood beside her looking dumbstruck, a short sword in his hands, the edge bloodied. Dostan was nearby and had called for the physician.

Daryo slashed the sleeve of his tunic away, knelt beside the woman and pressed the wad of cloth against her wound. 'We need to hold that tight against your arm.'

Dostan had a woollen scarf around his neck, he pulled it off, added it to the dressing and then snatched the sword away from the boy. 'Get gone, Brai! You are a useless warrior and a pathetic excuse of a man! Get gone!'

The boy turned and fled, colliding with the physician and almost knocking him down. 'A slashing wound,' Daryo told him. 'Not deep.'

The physician took over the care of the woman. Daryo stood up.

'Who is that boy?' he asked Dostan.

'Brai, kin of Solini. I have never seen a worse wielder of a blade. If he is firing a bow, stand directly in front of his target and you will be safer than you were in the coenobium. Hunting with him is like hunting with a pack of barking hounds beside you. Leave him to tend a fire, the fire goes out before you know it was even burning.'

'Let me help him.'

'Brother, I need you fit to fight. Train that boy and you will be unable to hold a blade for many moons.'

'There are three days before we leave for Thiel. Three days, if you can spare me from the Company.'

Dostan shrugged. 'Good luck to you then. Do a favour for me, brother, try not to lose any limbs. A finger or an ear would be acceptable, but no limbs.'

Daryo patted his shoulder and ran after the boy, Brai. The Company were training on a flat, slightly elevated area south of the town, a slope ran down from the training ground. There was a track that had been worn into the ground and it joined the street near Temma's house leading to the temple. Brai had already reached Temma's home and was still fleeing but was tiring, his feet beginning to drag on the road as his pace reduced. Daryo was more athletic, by a large measure, than the young Brai; conditioned by many years of walking and fighting. By the time that the boy had reached halfway along the

street, he had slowed to a walk. The sound of Daryo's pounding footsteps made him turn and he shrieked.
'Please do not kill me! Is she your kin? Did I kill her? Please! Did I kill her?'
Daryo realised he was still holding the Bear. He quickly sheathed it on his back alongside its twin. 'No! No, it was just a wound. She is not my kin, just a comrade. I am Daryo, kin of Dostan, my brother's lieutenant.'
'He sent you to kill me!'
From closer range, the boy was younger than Daryo had thought, his eyes were wider while scared, a weak chin and a large nose gave him a little of a warrior's look. He was wearing the indigo tunic of the Company but appeared to have been trying to pull it off.
'He did not send me to kill you! He sent me to help you.'
'Help me? How?'
'I am going to train you.'
'Train me? To do what?'
'To fight.'
'But I am dangerous! I hurt eleven people in training! Eleven!'
'If they were enemies, that may be commendable. But a warrior with no control is, as you said yourself, dangerous. I can teach you control.'
'You might get hurt. I... I might hurt you.'
'I will take that chance.'

Beyond the training ground was a small stand of trees and Daryo led young Brai behind them, out of view of the rest of the Company. He had his twin swords on his back and had retrieved his shield from Temma's home when they passed. He drew the Horse and threw it the two feet to Brai, who dropped it.
'Watch the sword's hilt, not the point.'
'But the point is dangerous.'
'Yes, but you cannot catch the point. You can and will catch the hilt. Watch the hilt.'
Daryo picked up the fallen sword, wiped the mud off of it onto his leggings and threw it again. Brai's hand made contact with the hilt but the Horse still fell in the mud.
'The hilt will not hurt you, Brai, kin of Solini.' Again, Daryo retrieved the sword, cleaned it and threw it again. Brai almost dropped it but held it just in time. Daryo nodded.
'Better.' Daryo drew the Bear and transferred it to his right hand. 'Can you defend yourself?'
'No.'

'Attack me then.'

'Pardon?'

'The best form of defence is to attack. In some cases. Attack me.'

'You will need your shield.'

'Brai, I pledge to build you a house with my own hands and wait on you day and night until your natural death if you scratch my skin.'

The boy could not suppress a laugh. He raised the Horse, studied Daryo for a minute with a particularly nervous expression and then slashed wildly. Daryo caught the slash and shunted it aside. The boy felt the rush of blood and swung again. Daryo again caught the overhead slash, the third, the wild horizontal swing at his waist missed him by a foot, the following slash came much closer. Daryo blocked it with the Bear and pushed the Horse aside. Brai dropped the sword.

'Stop,' he said firmly. Brai froze, half-bent to retrieve the sword. He stood straight. Daryo stooped, picked up the Horse, wiped it clean again and threw it to Brai for another time. The boy somehow caught it. 'If you keep dropping my sword, the Horse on the pommel may bite you.' The boy promptly dropped it again and Daryo sighed. 'Last time.' The procedure was repeated.

'You are a small man, Brai. Seventeen summers?'

'Sixteen winters. My sixteenth born-day was at the dead moon.'

'You are not two yards tall.'

'Not by a few inches.'

'You are not built like a smith or a miner.'

'No.'

'You are trying to fight like a large man. Was your father a large man?'

'I do not know. He is dead, when I was not big enough to walk, he died.'

'I see. I never met my father either. You are trying to fight like a large man, hard swings, slashes from over your head, powerful strikes. You do not have the strength. You have a loose grip, which compounds the folly of fighting so.' The boy seemed to have tears coming to his eyes but Daryo pressed on. 'I do not know who taught you to fight, Brai, but they were particularly misguided and you have been taught badly. But I am going to correct that. Are you comfortable with the sword? Would you prefer a spear or an axe? Or a bow?'

'They are too long. And I cannot shoot well. I am better with the sword.'

'Then we shall leave you with the sword. Is your right your stronger hand?'

'I think it is.'

'Take a stronger grip. Firmer. Imagine it to be an animal that is trying to escape but a small animal that could be injured. A firm grip. Not a breaking grip.'
Brai did so. Daryo took a close look at his hand and agreed that the grip was appropriate but the blade position was not.
'Hold your arm straight in front of you, sharp edges of the blade forward and back. Good, much better. Now flex your elbow slightly, lower your hand a little, keep the point towards my face. That is a good guard position. You have to keep the grip firm but your wrist, elbow, shoulder, they must all be flexible to absorb any shocks.' Daryo used his free hand to slap the flat of the blade several times, increasingly hard, to test Brai's readiness. 'Good. You are improving already. These things are most simple, it is a matter of practise and confidence. One you must do, one I can hopefully give you.'
The boy grinned enthusiastically.

'Tired, Daryo?'
Daryo had trudged into Temma's home and yawned cavernously just before he was greeted by her husband, Tella's father, Yiryo. He was of about an age with Dostan, larger across the shoulder but shorter from head to ground with a ready, broad smile.
'A little. I have been teaching.'
Yiryo chuckled. 'I am sorry, Daryo, I tease. Temma told me that you were training Solini's nephew to be a swordsman.'
'Trying to.'
'A challenge?'
'The boy tries but combat is like... musical talent or sculpture. One either has the necessary ability or not.'
'Does he?'
'Only a little. Much enthusiasm and he is no fool but he is a challenge, yes.'
Yiryo waved towards the fire. 'There is stew in the pot, bread on the side. Eat what you need. I tapped a cask of mead, I'll get you a cup. After working with that boy, a strong drink is probably just what you need.'


'Look along your arm. Do not point the arrow, point your arm. Do not stop your breathing; it causes tension. A tense archer misses more easily.' Daryo walked around from behind Brai to in front of him, studying his stance. 'Spread your legs a little further. At about the width of your shoulders, you are at the most balanced with your feet at that distance. Draw back a little further.'
Brai complied, his drawing arm shivered with the strain. 'I cannot hold it.'

'Hold it. Breathe.'

'I cannot...' He released and the arrow thudded into the tree, around seventy yards away, nearly ten feet above the straw target that Daryo had erected. It joined three others, two were in the tree to the right and a score more in the trunk below the target and in the grass. The boy sighed and lowered the bow.

'You did not hold, you did not keep your aim and you did not continue to breathe. You let the strain be too much, your pulling arm became a weight and pulled the arrow back as you released.'

'My arm is tired! I have shot more than two dozen arrows!'

'And an archer in battle may carry five dozen arrows or more and fire all of them.'

'Then I am no archer. I was better with the sword.'

'Defend yourself.' Daryo drew Temma's Sword, the only weapon he was carrying. Two days before, he had purchased a good steel sword, similar to his twin swords, from the blacksmith. Brai had stuck it into the ground and seized it quickly. He barely got it up in time to parry Daryo's blow. In two days his archery and long-weapon work had not progressed if at all but he had improved with his sword. He was capable of protecting himself against basic attacks and of countering when prompted. With the round shield that Daryo had also purchased, Brai had also displayed an instinctive talent for using his shield as an impromptu weapon, swinging to use the edge as a blunt blade or clubbing with the metal boss. The shield was being painted so he was only wielding his sword, as Daryo was.

'Much better,' said Daryo, approvingly. 'You are improving beyond any expectation.' He looked up at the sky. 'It is approaching noon. We should ensure we are ready to leave. I shall see you at the temple at midday?'

'You will.'

# Chapter 41

With the Company due to leave the town, the priest had called them all in to the temple for a service of blessing and prayer. Most of the population seemed to be thronging the square outside. Daryo, his armoured jerkin over the indigo tunic of the Company, managed to work his way through the crowd to the temple doors. The round building was completely full of the Company, Daryo barely made it inside out of the sudden rain shower but the people of the town crowded around the building regardless. The priest, a young man of around Daryo's age, had no schooling from the Great Temple of Ossmoss but had been apprentice to a priest in Jaboen before moving to the Lake. He had been accepted by the clan leaders as the most suitable and most learned to be the town's holy man. He stood in front of the spear of the Second God, wearing the beige robe of a junior priest. Daryo could see Dostan and Liua near the front of the congregation.

'All of us have gathered here to mark a new chapter in the story of our people,' the priest announced. 'So significant is this chapter that nearly all of this town has come to mark it. Not many seasons ago, a small group were able to leave the town and scare a Vidmarian army for a short time to allow a small group to escape from their impending death. This is not the same. This time, a significant number of our people are leaving to go to war and it is likely that many will never return but go on, instead, to the Next Kingdom. Perhaps one out of six of our people are leaving to fight for the land on which we are living.

There are some of those here that believe we should not be any relationship to Jaboen. But this land is the daughter of the land of Jaboen. Without Jaboen, without the King's benevolence, without the gift of this land, we would have no settlement as we do.

'It is right, it is *right* that we help the Jaboen King to defend his land. If Thiel falls, do we aid then? If Three Rivers falls, do we aid then? If Lalbi falls, do we aid then? If the Vidmarian Army, the Vidmarians that have declared death to any who have the temerity to be one of our people, if they stand at the mouth of the Stannia Pass, if they camp by the Lake, will we then decide it is time to resist? We take this action both in thanks to the Jaboen people for the gift of this land, and to protect those people that remain.'

Daryo found himself wondering if the priest was not perhaps better suited to being a diplomat or a clan leader.

'Why do I speak of these things?' the priest continued. 'People have come to the temple not to hear political arguments but to hear prayers. But I speak of this because it is the will of the Gods and Goddesses of the Pantheon that we have come to this point. The First God, Dravin, has brought us this land. The First Goddess, Tahili, gives us the fishing, hunting and crops of this land. The Second God, Thiney, has given us the means to defend our people. The Second Goddess, Brokea, teaches us that we must care for our land and our kin. The Third God, Spellis, will heal those wounded in war and the spirits of our people. The Third Goddess, Spinel, teaches us that we must have compassion and consideration for our Jaboen neighbours. The Fourth God, Dule, gives us the security and safety of this land. The Fourth Goddess, the Darkest Goddess, will take on those who are killed protecting this place; a special place is reserved in her kingdom for those lost doing their duty. We are Batribi, we do not fear the Fourth Goddess, we accept her presence. Do we not?'

There was a murmur of assent from those assembled.

'The Fourth Goddess is the constant companion of the soldier but also of the hunter, the physician, even the miner knows her presence. The Second Goddess is the constant companion of the soldier but also of the mother, the clan leader and the watchman. The Second God is the watcher and guide of soldiers. I ask all of those present in this temple now to pledge themselves to the service of the Second God, to the Second Goddess and to the Fourth Goddess.'

The priest raised his arms in salutation and the congregation did so as well. 'Dravin, bringer of war, watch over your soldiers, lend them strength to their shields, keen edges to their weapons, resilience to their souls and sharpness to their minds. Brokea, teacher of duty, give your soldiers passion for their cause, loyalty to their leaders, devotion to the Pantheon and honour in their deeds. Darkest Goddess, guide the souls of those that fall in their service to the Next Kingdom and watch over them until their kin join them, as all men must.'

The priest lowered his arms and bowed his head. There was silence for a considerable time, broken only by isolated coughs and the soft crying of a baby. The priest eventually raised his head, caught Dostan's eye and stepped aside. Dostan stepped up to beside the altar and paused for a moment, contemplating the spear of the Second God before turning to face out again.

'Soldiers of the Batribi!' he cried. 'Soldiers of the Company! We go now! The wagons are loaded! The swords are sharp! The time is now that we go to defend our lands! I led the small force that relieved the Five Towers and we showed the Vidmarian Army that Batribi swords are to be feared! This battle will not just be one of surprise and shock of an unprepared enemy! This will be a battle between armies, in towns and costing many lives! We are not a warmongering people but we are warriors! Are we not warriors?'

'Yes!' called a few of those in the temple.

'Are we not warriors of the Batribi?'

'Yes!' was the louder response, Daryo joining it.
'Are we not the loyal warriors of the Batribi?!'
'YES!' was the thunderous reply.
'Then let us go to war!'
'YES!'
The throng outside the temple parted as the Company streamed out. On the market square were nearly three dozen horse-drawn wagons carrying the baggage of the Company. Each wagon had two people already on the seat. The Company formed rough ranks at the front of the line, stragglers joining as they said farewell to kin, spouses and children.
Limma, Dostan's small but fiery wife, gave Daryo a fierce embrace as he passed her, Temma and Tella both did likewise, Yiryo gave him a hearty slap on the back and a flask of mead. Brai was in deep conversation with his mother. Liua passed Daryo and pointed to the front of the ranks. Daryo nodded his understanding and parted from his kin.
'Daryo!' Laulra lurched out of the crowd and caught Daryo's arm. 'Good fortune go with you, my brother.'
'You are going back to Halmia?'
'No, I am staying here. I am leading our clan and Buren's clan while they are with the Company.'
'You may need more fortune than I!'
'Perhaps. Gods' Guidance to you, brother. Come back safely.'
'Gods' Guidance, Laulra. I will endeavour to bring Dostan back too.'
'Oh, that is of little concern!'
Both laughed and embraced again. Daryo made his way to the front of the assembling Company accompanied by two large men with equally large drums. Liua was already stood waiting. Dostan appeared and raised his sword. The last members of the Company joined the irregular lines.
'The Batribi Company goes to war!'

The march was a quick pace, if nothing else a Batribi Company could walk. They joined the road to Lalbi still keeping a fast pace. Dostan lead from the front and his speed was exceptional, little short of a trot for mile following mile. Some of the Company struggled to keep pace and, after nearly fifteen miles, Daryo and Liua insisted on a halt to allow the stragglers to catch the vanguard. He sat on a log alongside Liua and pulled off his boots for a few moments.
'We will have to camp around Lalbi,' he said.

Liua nodded. 'Not ideal, I know. Then Three Rivers, we should join the Jaboen Army there in another day.'

\*        \*        \*

On the road from Three Rivers to Thiel was a patchwork forest of brown, green and black canvas long-tents. Among them were visible the men of the army of Jaboen making the necessary preparations for the battle, weapons being sharpened, armour being polished, shields being repaired. At nearly three hundred yards from the camp, the Batribi were intercepted by two spear-carrying Jaboen pickets, the red winged boar of Jaboen painted above the metal boss of their shields.

'Dostan of the Batribi Lands,' said the Batribi leader. 'This is the Batribi Company, come to join the battle.'

One of the sentries nodded. 'Follow me, I will show you were you are to camp and then take you to the Seatless Squire.'

Dostan followed the man towards their camp. Daryo took some quick steps to come alongside his kinsman.

'The Seatless Squire?'

'In times of war, the Seatless Squire is often the first choice as Jaboen commander. The king is no soldier, the Seatless Squire is currently Rashad, his brother by marriage, he is a soldier and someone we have had some dialogue with, as he is a Lord of the Council I have met him several times, so has Laulra.'

'A good man?'

'A practical man. He was an officer in the Yashoun Army, then the Jaboen Army. He is well-versed in military and civil matters. Laulra has much respect for him and I respect our brother's judgement.'

As they approached the camp, a man came out on horseback, wearing an almost-black blue tabard with a single star embroidered on the breast. 'Hail, Dostan of the Batribi!'

'Gods' Watch.'

'I am Fassal, aide to the Squire. Please, there is a commander's conference about to start. The Squire requests that you and your lieutenants attend.'

'Certainly.' Dostan nodded to Daryo and Liua. He paused and studied the first ranks of the Company. 'Rymma, lead the Company to our camping area. We will join you as soon as possible.'

The largest tent, black canvas and with man-sized banners of the Jaboen winged boar at all sides, at the centre of the camp was their destination. All around, the Jaboen army was readying for battle: weapons checked and sharpened, shields painted, boots repaired, armour polished and adjusted. An axe-wielding sentry stepped aside as the aide dismounted and led the three Batribi inside the tent. There were a score of Jaboen, two women and the others men, and a man wearing a Yashoun Army uniform, clustered around a long table. At the far end, a man in almost white robes, with a heavy black beard and small eyes below dense eyebrows, stood up from leaning on the table.
'Gods' Watch, Dostan of the Batribi.'
'Gods' Watch, Lord Rashad. My lieutenants, my brother Daryo the Walker of the Order of the Shield and Sword, and Liua, kin of Solvan.'
Rashad, a man of approximately fifty springs and well over two yards tall when stood erect, inclined his head to both. 'This conference is to explain how we intend to conclude the battle of Thiel. I had just introduced Captain Meula of the Yashoun Army, a comrade of mine from my time in Yashoun and the architect of this plan.'
The Yashoun glanced at the Batribi and then back to Rashad. 'I am so glad the Batribi have arrived. My lord, your forces are currently occupying the town of Thiel. That forces numbers...'
'Four thousand, three hundred and nine swords' said a young woman near Rashad, not looking up from her parchments.
'The army in camp numbers...'
'Fifteen thousand, eight hundred and seven,' said the same young woman. 'That does not include the Batribi.' She looked up.
'Two hundred and sixteen,' said Liua.
'Sixteen thousand and twenty-three.' She returned to her papers.
'The town has sufficient defences to hold the Vidmarian army,' said Meula. 'It will need relief and the simplest direction to relieve it from is from the east. The town is confined against the river to the south. The Vidmarian army can be swept aside from the town simply.'
'Sir,' interrupted Daryo. 'Can you tell me, please, where the Vidmarian river crossing is?'
Meula looked affronted. 'That is irrelevant.'
'Would you tell me?'
'Three miles downriver, west of the town.'
'If the plan goes correctly, that is the direction that they will flee,' said Daryo.
'Likely,' conceded the Yashoun.

'If they found their way blocked, they would have much less chance of striking a counter soon. More injury could be inflicted and a larger statement made.'
'The man has a good argument,' Rashad said. 'Remind me of your name.'
'Daryo, sir.'
'Daryo, proceed.'
'The Batribi Company are not accustomed to fighting in line and charging with a large body. We have been able to train but not within the confines of an army, only as a Company. As a unit, we are a strong and dangerous one. I suggest that you make use of this, my lord, the Batribi Company will hold the river crossing.'
Rashad raised his thick eyebrows. 'Alone.'
'Alone.'
Dostan jabbed Daryo in the ribs with his elbow. 'Brother,' he muttered, 'what are you doing?'
'Saving Batribi lives,' Daryo murmured back.
The Yashoun captain studied his maps and glared at Daryo a few times before replying. 'That would be acceptable.'
'Details of Vidmarian positions can be furnished for the Batribi,' said the woman by Rashad's side.
'Our thanks,' said Dostan, still slightly confused. 'Ahem. Liua, can you remain for the remainder of the conference? It will be necessary for us to know the remainder of the plans relating to Thiel. Daryo, we should see to our people.'
He almost dragged Daryo out of the tent and around fifty yards away.
'I trust you implicitly, brother,' he hissed, 'but what compelled you to say such a thing?'
'Honesty, brother. It is the best use for our Company. And you heard the attitude of the Yashoun captain? He has no liking for our people, we would have been the vanguard, at the thick of the fighting, and taken massive losses.'
Dostan considered this. 'And how does your plan diverge?'
'We have excellent abilities as individual soldiers, in general, and our talents lay in concealment and movement, not in fighting in battalions. We can lay traps and ambushes on the approach to the crossing and limit our exposure to danger until the Vidmarians arrive, then take them unaware.'
'You should not have committed us to such a thing so readily, brother.'
'I am sorry, Dostan. I am not accustomed to this situation. I have had my opinion sought before.'
'I do not chastise, I believe you have made the right decision. Come, let us find where our people are camped. We may not be here for long.'

'Daryo, Daryo the Batribi lieutenant?'
He had been demonstrating a snare to some of the Company and stood up. The young woman that had been at Rashad's side was there with a small pile of documents.
'Yes.'
'I am Lord Rashad's clerk, Suhla.' She handed over the pile of parchment. 'I bring the maps and reports of the Vidmarian positions between Thiel and their river crossing point and then between the crossing of the Soiliy and their crossing of the Dithithindil.'
'My thanks.'
Daryo deposited the documents with Dostan and returned to his tutoring. Dostan, Daryo and Liua met just before sundown in the small *kaff* that Dostan and Daryo were sharing; the whole Company were sleeping in the smaller, dome-topped versions of the Batribi canvas homes. The parchment and scrolls were spread across the floor. Some scraps had been scrawled and drawn on- rough maps and sketches of ideas mostly of Liua's doing but Daryo also recognised Dostan's hand among the scribbles.
'We have a plan, I think,' said Liua. 'If there is one thing that Jaboens can do, it is take records and notes. The Vidmarians have built a bridge across the Dithithindil opposite Lichon and a smaller one across the Soiliy. There are around... fifteen score Vidmarians at the bridge and three score at a camp south on an improvised road from the Dithithindil crossing.'
'Fifteen score is not a huge number,' said Daryo. 'But more than we have.'
'Surprise will be crucial,' Dostan said. 'Or we need to lure a portion of that force away from the rest.'
Daryo nodded, lost in thought.
Liua smiled. 'Simple. Vidmarians see themselves as wolves, don't they? What do they like to chase?'
'Prostitutes?' asked Dostan.
'Rabbits. Prostitutes, Dostan? By Dule's forge, your mind is deep in the cesspit.'
'It is no fault of mine, it is attached to the rest of my body...'
'What if the Jaboen attack on the siege fails?' Daryo asked. 'The Jaboen attack drives the Vidmarians towards us in a state of confusion, at worst, in a rout at the best. But only if the city is relieved.'
'Captain Meula suggested that we could form another attack, come from the west,' Liua told them. 'It may depend on how many casualties we take whether we have enough swords.'

'We have to be careful with our people,' said Dostan. 'We have few to lose, every lost Batribi could be an empty *kaff* beside the lake.'

'We will be very careful, brother.'

'The Vidmarian deadline for Thiel's surrender is the next sundown. We have to be in position by then. We leave at first light, with no wagons, only a minimum of items.'

# Chapter 42

Carrying only small bags, a few bundles of poles, canvas and their weapons, the contingent of Batribi left as soon as the darkness was total. A Jaboen guide led them to a ford across the Soiliy and left them there. The Company scrambled across the river, Liua and Dostan in the lead, Daryo at the rear, turned right and began to run. The grassland was relatively even and flat and the Company were able to keep a good pace. By keeping the river to their right, it was inevitable that they would reach the Vidmarian crossing. They splashed through several streams and ditches than ran down to join the river. In the darkness, there were trips, stumbles, turned ankles and twisted knees but the pace slackened barely at all. The Company ran onwards through the night. A startled flock of roosting birds took off as more than ten score Batribi thundered across the plain. Daryo found Brai running alongside him, a look of determination on his face. After nearly three miles, Dostan called a rest and the Batribi all dropped to the ground, sitting, kneeling, prostrate on the floor. Daryo sank to his haunches, gasping for breath.
'I have... never... run... so far...' wheezed Brai.
'Not so far and so fast,' agreed Daryo, bringing his breath back into measure.
'Are you afraid?'
'Afraid?'
'Of fighting. Battle.'
Daryo considered this. 'A little perhaps. A little fear is good for the body, quickens the heart, sharpens the mind, but one gets accustomed to battle. The first time a child goes in a river, they are scared; when they can swim the river has no terror. Battle is similar, one gets accustomed and the fear is reduced.' Daryo took out his water bottle, drained half and passed it to Brai.
'My thanks. Make me a promise, Daryo, kin of Dostan.'
'Certainly.'
'Stay near me in the battle. I do not know how well I will do. If you are close, you can protect me.'
Daryo smiled and laid a hand on the boy's shoulder. 'I will do all I can and promise in the Second Goddess's name to protect you to the best of my skill.'
Around them, the Company was regaining its feet, metaphorically and literally, and Daryo quickly went to the river, just a few yards away, to refill his water. The Company were soon hurrying along the bank again, Daryo and Brai at the tail, Dostan at the head. They passed Thiel on the opposite bank, the river too treacherous and fast past the town to be bridged and too rapid to be traversed by boat. Further downstream, the bridge was

simple- long logs split in half and turned flat-side up, a single trestle underneath in the centre of the river, shallower and narrower than before the bend. In the darkness, lit only by a half moon and the stars, the Batribi crept into the rushes and grasses beside the river, less than a hundred yards from the bridge. A few sentries were visible on the bridge, some with torches. Daryo crawled up alongside Dostan, Brai close behind.
'Ready, brother?' Daryo asked softly.
'As ready as I shall be.'
Dostan nudged the man alongside him, one of the big Batribi drums lashed to the man's back. The drummer reached back and thumped the drum skin once with his fist, making a dull but carrying thud. At the prearranged signal, seventy of the Batribi melted away from the others, Liua among them. At the next thud, thirty of the remainder went with Dostan, including the drummer. Daryo gave a low whistle to call his group around him. The Company had been schooled as thoroughly as possible in Liua's plan and all were near twitching in anticipation. From the other side of the Vidmarian bridge, the noises of camp could be heard: voices, horses, fires, music.
'This seems like a sensible place!' came a loud voice, Dostan's. 'Near the river! Flat for a camp! We can cross after dawn and make for Thiel!'
'Very well, Dostan!'
Sparks lit, lamps were ignited and a blaze of light illuminated the sight of Dostan's group beginning to erect a cluster of the smaller, domed *kaffa* right on the Vidmarian's track south, about four hundred yards from the bridge. The Vidmarian sentries could not help but see the activity. There were shouts among them, in the torchlight swords were drawn. From the camp was an increased surge of activity, the volume of voices rose. A force of Vidmarians began to form by the bridge, weapons in hand, many with torches, an officer at the front bellowing instructions. Daryo flattened himself to the ground as much as possible, the key to the plan was that the Vidmarians only saw Dostan's diversion. The work of the *kaffa* party had stopped as they, apparently, noticed the Vidmarian encampment and began to argue over the best course of action. Some of Dostan and his party began to arm themselves, the rest were quickly striking their *kaffa*. The Vidmarian force now numbered around a hundred and, with their officer in the forward rank, began to cross the bridge at a trot. Dostan's party were now abandoning their *kaffa* and forming a small knot, a defensive circle, weapons ready. The Vidmarian company cleared the bridge and its officer shouted a challenge that Daryo could not hear but Dostan replied defiantly. The Vidmarian shouted again and drew his sword and led the charge. Dostan's group turned to flee, abandoning their tents and running south but, as the

Vidmarians gave chase, Liua led her group out of concealment and struck the Vidmarian company from the rear.

'Move!' shouted Daryo. The Batribi concealed with him rose and, with Daryo at their head, rushed for the bridge.

The Vidmarians had been wise enough to leave their sentries on the crossing but Daryo's group had a score of bows in their arsenal and they were shot down before they were aware of the attack. Daryo tried to ignore the noise of battle behind him and focussed on crossing the bridge- the flat centres of the split logs covered with a carpet of mud and straw. The river was less than thirty yards wide and the north end of the bridge was unguarded. Following their plan, the Batribi spread out silently. Every weapon that was found was taken, every fire extinguished, every waking man killed as swiftly and silently as possible. Temma's Sword sent nearly two dozen to whatever form the Vidmarian afterlife may have taken before the general alarm was raised but it was too late for the Vidmarians. Liua's warriors had eliminated all but a few of the company that had chased Dostan, the survivors had surrendered, and Liua had led her group across the bridge and into the camp.

There was little fight to be had. Most of the Vidmarian personnel guarding the bridge was asleep, despite the hubbub caused by the Batribi encampment group and the formation of an attack force. Over a hundred were awoken by Batribi blades at their throats. The prisoners, disarmed and bound, were corralled against the river bank.

'Well done, brother,' Dostan hailed Daryo as he approached.

'And you, a very presentable rabbit you made. You are wounded.'

'A slash to the arm, nothing more. A minor thing.' The wound had been bound with a rough bandage. 'None escaped?'

'Not that were seen. Liua is checking the tents now in case any escaped our notice.' Dostan slapped Daryo on the back and winced. He had used his injured limb. 'I was supposed to lead the attack on the Vidmarian baggage train but I think I should find Geryo and have this seen to properly. Would you...?'

'Certainly.'

The base camp was a small assemblage of canvas tents, wagons, a few wooden huts and a trio of log-built defensive positions that were unoccupied. A single sentry was shot by a Batribi archer and the rest of the Vidmarians were overwhelmed by the surprise Batribi attack. They were quickly penned in near the centre, not outnumbered but almost totally shocked at being taken so easily. Bound to a series of heavy felled trees were three score Jaboen prisoners. Daryo had them immediately set loose and rearmed and they agreed to guard the Vidmarians, quickly bound to the same trees. A runner was sent to the bridge to report and Dostan decided that it was safer to have the Vidmarians confined further from the front. The bulk of the Batribi troops escorted their prisoners back and, once bound as effectively as possible, left the released Jaboens to guard the Vidmarians with their own weapons.

None of the Batribi slept that night. Daryo, with Brai never more than ten yards away, supervised the construction of as many traps as possible- shallow pits were being hastily dug, heavy objects hung from trees, a series of crossbows were rigged covering the approach to the bridge but kept unloaded until necessary. The holes were excavated by teams of four and took most of the night before they were around five feet deep and three to four feet across. There were nearly thirty, dug at random within a two hundred yard arc from the bridge. They would be covered and disguised when finished. While this was done, the Vidmarian camp was being disassembled and removed across the river by another squad under Dostan's leadership. Liua had taken half a dozen to form a lookout post on the most likely approach for the retreating Vidmarian army. It was after dawn before Daryo collapsed back against the new palisade that he had helped construct just before the bridge to give some shelter to archers.

'You are tired, Daryo,' said Brai, sitting down alongside him. 'You have worked harder than any other.'

'Except perhaps Brai, kin of Solini.'

The boy grinned. 'I want to be useful. I may not be able to fight well but I can dig a hole.'

'You did very well.'

'When will the Vidmarians arrive?'

'That depends on how long the siege takes to break. If the plan goes as proscribed, the Jaboen attack will take place at any moment. Perhaps by midday, if the Vidmarians are overwhelmed quickly.'

'Is that possible?'

'Possible, yes. The Jaboen army is near twice the size of the Vidmarian one.'

'Will that defeat the Vidmarians for all?'

'I doubt it. Vidmaria has a force in Yashoun, still holding the fortress of Namixo, and a presence in Gourmin.'

'Their army is large.'

'Yes it is.'

'So will we not be overrun?'

'Sometimes war is not about a decisive victory. Sometimes it is about causing sufficient injury to put an army beyond action, sometimes it is causing confusion, sometimes about dissuading an enemy from trying again. This is the former, causing injury and leaving the Vidmarian army in no state to attack again. And also sending a statement to the Vidmarian king that Jaboen, and the Batribi, will not simply lay back and allow him to send his armies wherever he chooses.'
'We could march on Namixo. Help the Empire take it back.'
'I doubt that, Brai. There are too few of us and we are not equipped to break a siege.' Daryo yawned expansively. 'I will check on the progress of the bridge.' On seeing Brai's quizzical look he explained: 'The bridge is being set so that it can be burned when we withdraw.'
'Trapping the Vidmarians on the north side with the Jaboen army.'
'Precisely.'
'That was a cunning idea, Daryo.'
'It was not mine. It was Liua's plan.'
'Liua is kin of mine. Her father is the uncle of my cousin's wife.'
'You should be proud of her.'
'We are. Solini is very happy to know her. As am I.'
'I am also. Come, let us see to the bridge.'

By the time that the sun was up, most of the Batribi were asleep and only a small number stood watch. Daryo had made a canvas shelter with a piece of the *kaffa* from Dostan's diversion. He, Dostan, Brai and a physician, Geryo, who had joined the Company's mission slept beneath it. The scout's horn blew just after midday. Within a short time, the drum was beating rapidly, summoning the Company.
'This is the time,' said Dostan, stretching the stiffness from his muscles.
'Good fortune, my brother,' said Daryo, embracing him tightly. 'The Second God guide you.'
'And you. Brother, if I should walk home with the Fourth Goddess, not with you, would you speak to Limma for me?'
'If I am not walking alongside you.'
Dostan smiled encouragingly and hurried away, calling 'To arms!'
Daryo pulled on his harness, sword belt and shield. Brai drew his sword and had appropriated a diamond-shaped, gold-painted Vidmarian shield. The Batribi Company was assembling on the Vidmarian bridge, a rank of seven warriors filled the bridge from side to side. On the south side, two people were giving each passing Batribi a captured

Vidmarian spear or pike. Behind the forward ranks, the two score Batribi archers were mustering. Daryo, despite Brai's concerns, made his way through the growing throng to the front rank, drawing Temma's Sword. A running figure came into view, a Batribi carrying a bow. He slowed to negotiate the traps safely and jogged up to Daryo.
'The Vidmarians, sir. Around a mile away. Retreating in near-chaos.'
'The Jaboen army?'
'I could not see. There were many Vidmarians in my line of view.'
Daryo could not help but smile. 'You know your post.' The man held up his bow. 'Go. Gods' Guidance.'
'Gods' Guidance.'
Daryo strained his eyes but could see no sign of approaching Vidmarians. The sun at his back lit up the plain. The noises of the waiting Company beside and behind him drowned out the noises of birds overhead and the water of the river. Beside him, Daryo could feel Brai trembling.
'Take some slow breaths,' Daryo advised. 'Relax your grip on your sword a little. Try to stay calm. Think of what you learned with me.' There was a growing sound, a low rumble, the sounds of distant shouts. 'This is the time.' He stepped out of the line and turned to face the others. 'Warriors of the Batribi! Gather your courage! You know the plans, you know what must be done! We fight for our kin, for our lands and for our people! Honour and courage!'
'Honour and courage!'
Daryo stepped back into the rank and drew Temma's Sword. He had forsworn a spear or pike, preferring the sword in his hand. Brai had also decided not to or forgotten to take a long weapon but dozens bristled around them. Daryo tried to keep his eyes forwards, he knew that Dostan was with the archers and that Liua was somewhere in the rear ranks. Brai had been beside Daryo but suddenly moved behind him. Daryo did glance back and took a long step forwards as Brai was heartily sick on the floor. Those around him made way and the woman behind him patted him on the back sympathetically.
'Happens in many a first battle,' the man alongside Daryo observed.
Brai recovered his composure and stood upright. The Batribi ranks closed again. The first Vidmarian soldiers were visible. They were trotting quickly, apparently being pursued and they seemed to not even notice the absence of the encampment that had stood before the bridge. A group of those at the very front ran at full speed into the first pit trap. The men behind stopped almost instantly, shocked by the trap. This seemed to be the first they noticed of the missing encampment, the absence of their comrades and then the Batribi force occupying the bridge. With the obstacles present, they quickly

formed a group and were joined within a very short period by dozens, then scores, then hundreds of their comrades.

*Darkest of Goddesses*, thought Daryo, *cruellest of tricksters, guide of the dead, force behind my blade and strength behind my shield, I stand here once more about to do your service. I ask that you spare as many of my people as you will, I pray that you think on those that would be left and that you choose to take these lives at another time. All men are fated to join you, I pray you show mercy and patience and accept those that I send you in exchange for sparing my kin and my comrades.*

A few Vidmarian archers began firing towards the Batribi blockade but their arrows fell considerably short. Along the front of the Vidmarian ranks in their red and brown uniforms, several officers in fur-edged cloaks, two of them on horseback, were organising their forces. One of the mounted men galloped to the Vidmarian left, the most organised-looking section, shouted orders and waved forwards. The left wing of the Vidmarians began to move forwards in disciplined ranks. They travelled less than forty yards before a dozen hit the first pit trap and disappeared from view, screaming as they were impaled on the spears and spikes below. This slowed the advance as the Vidmarian soldiers began probing the ground for more traps. Despite their caution, more fell into the pits and one unfortunate soldier triggered the concealed, tripwire-activated crossbows. Four crossbows fired from their concealed position in a natural dip and all four struck the soldier that had triggered them. This caused a small amount of panic in the rear of the advancing Vidmarian section. The forward ranks were urged on by their mounted officer and they pushed on, into range of the Batribi archers on the bridge and the south bank of the river. The Batribi archers' volleys were enough for the already-scared and demoralised Vidmarian troops and they were soon retreating in disorder despite their officer's bellowing and chased by Batribi arrows and jeers.

'Why do they not attack?' asked Brai nervously.

'They are trying to find the best way to do so,' replied Daryo, watching carefully the activity opposite.

The Vidmarian right was organising into files, moving much slower and each file led by a man with pikes, jabbing the ground hard to trigger the trap pits. Three files crept forwards. Daryo felt a tug on his arm, looked around and found Liua there.

'We should hold here,' she said. 'They are reluctant to-' She cut off as there was the familiar clunk of the crossbows went off, followed by noises of surprise and pain. A few Vidmarians with bows fired in the direction of the crossbows, as if trying to hit concealed archers. 'They are reluctant to attack us directly.'

'They are already scared and demoralised,' Daryo replied. 'They have been chased here by the Jaboen army and then confronted by pits and hidden crossbows as well as their comrades' absence and our force blocking their retreat.'

The Vidmarian right was still inching forwards in columns but the momentum was lost as the pits became larger and closer together. When they were within two hundred yards of the bridge, the Batribi archers started firing again. The Vidmarian columns again broke in confusion, many as they tried to flee fell into pits. The Vidmarian officers were trying drastically to rally their men but the troops were obviously, even from nearly four hundred yards away, were in the throes of disintegration but seemed unable to retreat. The sound of horns came from beyond the Vidmarian army.

'The Jaboens!' said Liua with relief.

'Maybe not such a good thing,' Daryo replied. 'They have no other options now. Be ready!'

'I should go back to my place.' Liua suddenly sounded nervous and hurried back into the Batribi ranks.

The Vidmarians were definitely aware of their predicament and, in increasing numbers, began to run in the only direction that they had: towards the Batribi.

Daryo flexed his sword-arm and brought his shield in front of his torso. The Vidmarians still had pits to negotiate and rigged crossbows between them and the bridge but the phalanx was beyond such concerns. It was a cross between a charge and a flight.

'Hold!' shouted Daryo. 'Hold! Hold!' The leading Vidmarians triggered the last rigged crossbows, less than ten yards from the bridge. 'Forwards!'

The Batribi ranks took a large step forwards and roared a challenge. Some of the Vidmarians tripped in surprise and some stopped in total shock, there was trampling, vicious shoves and chaos in the bottleneck at the bridge and the Batribi were into the battle. Daryo found he could not push forwards as he wanted to as he tried to keep Brai within a sword's length at all times. He found himself fending blows with his shield and only being able counter direct assaults against his own person as he was not able to step away from Brai. The boy was surrounded by competent and capable warriors and was not called to step into the front rank. From well beyond the Vidmarian army was the blowing of the horns of the Jaboen army and several of the Vidmarians looked over their shoulders in fear. From behind the Batribi, a steady drumbeat started. Daryo shoved the Vidmarian in front of him back and Temma's Sword cleaved into the man's neck. The drumbeats suddenly stopped. The Batribi all had been told the signals and, in a disciplined unit, began to move backwards across the bridge. The move was carefully timed so that the Vidmarians were distracted by the Jaboen move on their rear, but had to be equally carefully executed so the Vidmarians did not rush the bridge and turn the pullback into a rout. The Batribi archers covered with ceaseless volleys of arrows and the Vidmarians, wary of more traps, the Jaboens and the Batribi manoeuvre made them reluctant to follow. With some separation between the Batribi and the Vidmarians, the Batribi archers changed to flaming arrows and began to put a burning barrier between the two groups. Daryo, as he backed away from the enemy, noticed at least ten Batribi left dead on the bridge as it began to burn. The Batribi Company made it off of the bridge under cover of their archers and the other distractions and reformed to the right of the bridge as the bridge began to burn more fiercely; the Batribi had put small barrels of flame oil along the edges of the bridge. The Batribi archers reverted to conventional arrows and to firing at the Vidmarians, who were entering a state of chaos: some were throwing down their weapons and spreading their arms in surrender, others tried to swim the river but were dragged under by their weapons and armour. Some of the Batribi moved to the bank of the river in case some of the Vidmarians made the crossing but the vast majority of the Vidmarians surrendered on the north bank to the Jaboens.

The final count of prisoners, given by Suhla at the commanders' meeting, was seven thousand, nine hundred and eleven. They had all been counted and removed from the battlefield to be taken to arrangements at Tonamaz, Lalbi and Salifa escorted by Jaboen militiamen. The estimated dead and injured of Vidmaria were around half that number. The Jaboen army had lost a total of a thousand and the Batribi had nine killed and a score wounded. There were prisoners taken and held by the Vidmarians, the few that had been captured had been held had released by their countrymen.
'We have them well-beaten here,' said Lord Rashad proudly. 'All did a very fine job, including our Batribi allies. My grateful thanks to you all.'

'We could do more, brother.'
Dostan was laid back in his blanket in the small *kaff* he and Daryo shared. The Batribi Company had set up a camp on the side of the Jaboen army's in the shadow of Thiel. It was well past sunset and the pair had finally been able to retire, exhausted but exhilarated by the day's events.
'More?'
Daryo turned onto his side to face towards Dostan a foot or two away, feeling a surge of energy and enthusiasm. 'It is logic. I thought as you do?'
'Truly?'
'If you divest a man of his breeches, how do you embarrass him further?'

Dostan chuckled in the darkness. 'Take his smallclothes too.'
'Exactly. The Vidmarian King just had his breeches taken, let us take his underclothes too.'
Dostan shifted in his bed. 'What do you mean, brother?'
'We have beaten a field army, one that was expected to take a Jaboen town but did not. It has now been thoroughly beaten and most of it captured. The Vidmarians expected to be able to take Thiel and to hold it. Fortunately they did not. Now we have to strike back, show the Vidmarians that they are vulnerable to attack as well.'
There was silence as this was suggested. 'How?'
'A small strike force. The Company, maybe an equal number of Jaboens too.'
'Where?'
'A Vidmarian fort or camp inside their border. One should be locatable.'
'When?'
'As soon as possible. To keep them unbalanced.'
'You think it possible?'
'If we pick our target carefully, and plan the attack in detail, absolutely, brother.'
Dostan was silent again as he thought. 'I will speak with Suhla with the new dawn and see if she can identify a target.'

Daryo was barely able to eat as he waited for Daryo to return from his consultation with Suhla. As expected, Dostan returned from with a small stack of papers and he, Daryo and Liua retired to the *kaff*, sitting on their folded blankets.
'Three options according to the Jaboen reports,' said Dostan. 'Loidee to the east, Nivel in the centre and Lichon to the west.' He passed one bound pile of documents to Daryo. 'Loidee is a fortified camp. The Vidmarian soldiers are in huts and canvas homes, the wall is wooden but high, the moat is water-filled and deep, the towers are well-armed. Nivel is a citadel, a high-walled city with a strong gate and high towers. No moat and a small garrison but thick, high walls. Lichon is a fort, a stone keep and wall on the banks of the Dithithindil. It is strong, a large number of men and supplies are kept there, it is the staging post for the attacks on Yashoun and Jaboen. The walls are actually being rebuilt, reinforced, as we speak.'
'The small garrison could be a vote in Nivel's favour,' said Liua. 'Fewer sentries, less danger, less risk.'
Dostan frowned. 'But it may be difficult to infiltrate. And we do not want to injure innocent people, a risk if there is combat in a city. I would say Loidee is not an option. Even from these reports, it is too strong.'

'All of which leaves Lichon,' said Daryo. 'A fort, so very few people other than soldiers. Near the river is easy to reach. A large amount of supplies that can be destroyed, which will help the efforts of our soldiers and the Yashoun war efforts as well. The walls are being rebuilt so there is a vulnerability in the defences.'

'Lichon,' agreed Liua. 'I think that is the best target.'

Dostan nodded and studied the papers carefully. 'There could be eight or ten thousand men in the fort.'

'A smaller force is better then, surely?' said Liua. 'Less chance of detection.'

'Agreed.'

'We need small boats,' said Daryo. He took up a map. 'We take them... here.' He indicated a bend in the Dithithindil. 'We follow downstream to the fort. We use the construction work to gain access to the fort. We destroy as many supplies as we can; if there is flame oil or something equally flammable, that can be ignited; barricade the gate from the outside, if that is practical; then withdraw the same way as we entered.'

Dostan nodded slowly. 'I can see some potential issues but nothing fatal to the life of the plan. There is to be another commanders' conference at sundown. I will talk with the other commanders.' He looked at Daryo and grinned. 'Lord Rashad has barred lieutenants from attending following an outburst from a young Batribi.'

Daryo felt his face get hot with embarrassment. 'I am sorry, Dostan.'

'No apology needed. I simply try to think and act as you do, brother, and the results are much the same.'

Daryo spent the next morning working with the Company, focusing on personal fitness and movements as a unit rather than weapon training. When Dostan returned from the commanders' conference, he immediately called Daryo and Liua together.

'Lord Rashad is unwilling to risk Jaboen troops on what he considers to be a fool's pursuit,' Dostan told them flatly. 'However, he believes we are at liberty to act against Lichon if we wish to do so.'

Liua and Daryo exchanged looks and nodded.

'We go ahead, brother.'

'I agree,' said Dostan. 'I will find Suhla and see if there is either a guide or a good map to take us to the bend in the river. And we need boats.'

The boats were commandeered from Thiel and Three Rivers, further upstream. They were mainly the narrow but long canoes of those who fished the Soiliy, which could take three or four passengers, mixed with some larger boats that could take up to ten. In total, it was decided that the boats could only safely carry ninety-five of the Company and Liua made most of the decisions as to who was to be taken. Brai was not among those chosen and, although he commiserated the youngster, Daryo was inwardly glad. He decided it best that the inexperienced boy be kept as far from further combat. The three leaders took lots to join the mission; Dostan drew the brown egg to remain with those of the Company not going to Lichon. Equipment was to be minimal again and Daryo decided that, as stealth and speed would be crucial, he would leave Temma's Sword and his shield with Dostan at the camp and to take only his Twin Swords. By sunset that day, carrying the boats in pairs, the Batribi Company made for the Dithithindil.

# Chapter 43

'Absolute silence,' said Daryo to the rest of the Company, clustered closely around him. 'Paddle the boats only when necessary. Remember: when the trees stop, move to the left bank and wait until we are all assembled. First God go with you all.'
The Batribi boats were slipped into the water. Daryo was with three women in a fishing canoe and the first to push away from the bank. The Dithithindil was swift and several feet deep. The current, as it rounded the southwards curve, picked up and swept the boats downstream. Daryo, at the prow of the boat, was using a small paddle to steer and keep the boat clear of obstacles. The sun was down and it was all but dark. The Batribi had timed their movement carefully- they had crossed the ground from Thiel to the Dithithindil in two days and moved onto the river just after dark to arrive at Lichon in total darkness. The river was rough, the rushing water eddied, crossed and collided, tossing the lightweight boat about. Daryo clung to the side with one hand and used the paddle to try to guide the canoe with the other. Behind him, his comrade reluctant sailors were also both clinging to the craft and paddling to try to avoid collisions. With every dip of the bow, water cascaded up and sprayed Daryo; with every shudder he expected to have holed the boat and to be sinking. He wondered why the Pantheon kept guiding him into the water to get where he needed to go. The banks were lined with large, spreading, cascading trees that glimmered in the half-moon above. The river turned right, slightly north of westwards, and the trees stopped abruptly as the bank was too rocky.
'To the left!' called Daryo and all four in his canoe began to paddle furiously on the right of the canoe. Within a hundred yards, the canoe hit the bank and Daryo scrambled ashore. There was a rope loop at the front of the boat and Daryo seized it to haul the canoe onto dry land as his comrades came ashore too. Within minutes, the other Batribi boats began to reach them; those in Daryo's boat helping to bring them ashore.
The Company were soon assembled; all but one boat had arrived safely. One of the larger boats, with eleven Batribi on board, had not arrived and had not been seen. It was assumed that they had missed the landing ground and hoped that they would return safely somehow. With the Batribi warriors mustered, Daryo and Liua left twenty to guard the boats and sixty-two joined their commanders on the short march west towards Lichon.

After just three miles, the walls of the fortress loomed over the Batribi. The walls were white plastered and seemed to glow. The wall closest to the bank of the river was lower than the rest, covered in wooden scaffold and there was stone and wooden debris spread around: obvious signs of the work being conducted to reinforce Lichon. Daryo pointed to a small group of Batribi who had detached themselves from the main one. He made a fist and the dozen of fighters nodded as one; they were to remain and protect the exit. A second group detached itself and began moving to the right, back towards the river. On the far side of the fort, they would barricade the gate from the outside. The remainder began to search for routes upwards using the ropes, pulleys, ladders and other building paraphernalia. Liua was one of the first to the top, drawing her sword as she climbed over the parapet. Within short minutes, Daryo reached the summit too, one of the last to do so. A Vidmarian soldier, to the right of the building work, may have seen some movement as the Batribi soldiers found hiding places on the walkway at the top of the wall. He came across to investigate, showing no particular alarm, and was unaware as a Batribi slipped over the edge of the construction and drove a dagger into his neck. The lifeless body was quickly divested of his weapons and lowered down to the first level of scaffolding, out of view of any other sentries.

Daryo took a score to the left and the rest followed Liua in the opposite direction. Within the wall was a towering keep and the compound was surrounded by the shelters, canvas tents and other evidence of an army sheltering within the walls. The camp fires were burning down although some lights showed from the keep's lower levels. Another sentry was several yards in front, leaning on the parapet looking out into the darkness. He never heard Daryo approach, may have been aware of a sharp pain across his neck and then found oblivion. The man behind Daryo tossed the Vidmarian over the top and there was a dull crunch as he hit the ground nearly seventy feet below. They found a wooden staircase leading down to the compound below. Daryo, the Horse ready in his hand, led the way down. Liua's group would split as soon as possible, one part making for the gate to make a diversion, the others were to fire the stables. At the base of the stairs, Daryo beckoned his troops into shelter behind lines of stacked barrels. They were marked WATER on the sides. Daryo found a specific man and whispered: 'Stay here. When the time comes, use your axe and hole as many as you can, as swiftly as you can.'

'Yes, sir,' was the hissed response. 'Misini has an axe also.'

'Both of you then. Have her remain with you.'

He crept forwards again, leaving the two with the barrels. To the left they moved, silently and hidden in the darkness of the night against the grey stone of the fort's walls. A small construction with a smoking chimney presented itself; Daryo left two more with the instruction to block the chimney when possible. The Batribi team continued onwards. Another small building was a meat store. With some nearby pieces of wood and empty

crates piled nearby, Daryo had a trio began to build a fire alongside the meat store. A snoozing sentry had his throat cut by the Horse and the body was put back in the meat store. They moved another forty yards around the inside of the wall before finding a dozen carts loaded with supplies ready to move. Daryo divided his remaining warriors between them, almost all of the Batribi were carrying phials of flame oil and they poured it liberally on the carts before using them as shelter, waiting for a signal from the others. Daryo slid under a cart alongside a small-framed comrade with a short, straight sword.
'Done?'
'Ready, sir,' he murmured back. 'Cart soaked in oil.'
'Just waiting for Liua.' Daryo tried to peer around the wheel of the cart towards the gate but could see nothing through the darkness. Every noise was a threat, a signal, a catastrophe, a warning. He gripped the Horse's hilt a little tighter.

The bang echoed back from the walls and keep like deep thunder. A shaft of flame nearly as high as the keep shot into the night air, blinding those look at it with its brightness.
'Now!' shouted Daryo over the sudden din, pulling himself out from under the cart. Flints were struck, sparks flew and smaller blazes flared. The Batribi knew to immediately start their escape, Daryo counted his force back past him and then began to run. A Vidmarian responding to the fire by the meat store was speared by the Horse's point and Daryo veered around the luckless one, drew the Horse out of the body and completed his circle to slash across the gut of another foe. He shouldered the Vidmarian aside and found his running pace again. The shouts and cries of the Vidmarians mingled with the roar of fire and clatter of weapons. The axeman was just chopping into the last barrel, two dead Vidmarians alongside him.
'Go!' Daryo shouted.
The axeman turned and received a crossbow bolt through the neck. Without thinking, Daryo charged the crossbowman, who barely had time to see the Batribi appear out of the darkness. Daryo drew the Bear and used a vicious double-outwards cut to decapitate the Vidmarian before racing up the stairs to the top of the wall. Only two Batribi had bows and they were firing ceaselessly, adding to the confusion in the fort's courtyard. Batribi warriors were already scrambling down the section of wall being repaired. Daryo paused at the top. A man ran past him.
'Who's group?'
'Goulra,' was the response. The group that had gone to the stables.
He caught another. 'Who's group?'

'Goulra.'

Another. 'Who's group?'

'Yours.'

Another. 'Who's group?'

'Yours.'

Finally, a man older than many of the other warriors staggered along the wall. Daryo rushed to help him. 'Who's group?'

'Liua's! All dead!'

There was a loud noise, suggesting something collapsing. 'What?!'

'All dead. Liua, all others, too close to guardhouse, crossbows.'

Daryo, for the first time, saw the crossbow bolt in the man's hip. 'All of them?'

'All.'

'Liua?'

'First shot.'

Daryo moaned in anguish and frustration. 'Come, let us get you down to the ground. Pull back! Everyone down! Pull back!'

Daryo the Walker was the last Batribi to climb back down the walls of Lichon.

Of forty-two that had climbed the walls, twenty had been lost. One of the party that had barricaded the gate had been killed by a sentry. With the confusion inside the fort and the gate barred from without, the Batribi were able to retreat back to the Dithithindil and their boats. With the current against them, the Batribi simply crossed the mighty river and then began the long hike back to Thiel.

The return hike took four days and was conducted in a remarkably silent manner; a single line of Batribi stretching across the landscape marching at a brisk pace and stopping only briefly. The cavalcade, exhausted and dispirited, trudged into the encampment near Thiel with Daryo at its tail. Without pause, they had their comrades assembled, the priest from Thiel was summoned and he gave a service in memory of the lost. Afterwards the Batribi dispersed to their *kaffa* to sleep but Daryo could find no sleep with Liua's empty space in the *kaff*. He walked around the camp, too tired to sleep, and found himself wandering through the silent streets of Thiel; most of the inhabitants had fled. The temple loomed up and Daryo found the door unlocked. He went inside and sat for a long period beyond thought.

'This is the second time I have found a Batribi warrior sat in the temple,' said the priest, sitting down alongside a startled Daryo, who had not heard the man enter. 'The same

Batribi warrior. The last time, twelve or thirteen seasons ago, you were overwhelmed with strange familiar feelings towards our town and I was able to show you where your mother lies. What brings a disciple of the Fourth Goddess into the house of Spinel for a second time?'

'A search for reason. I have lost two women close to me: one some six seasons ago, one just a handful of days ago. The first woman that my life knew was buried very close to here. I see no reason in any of their deaths and my continued life.'

The priest nodded. 'Such feelings are common on a bereavement. You are a warrior. Losses are a part of the path.'

'I tried to leave the path. I was for a time at the Coenobium of the First God in Halmia.'

'I have spent a season there myself. The path of the Coenobium is not an easy one and one must have the character and the disposition for the life. For someone of your youth and activity, I am not surprised that you did not find the Coenobium to be a home.' The priest thought for a while. 'You truly believe, do you not?'

'Truly.'

'Your guardian?'

'I have none. I have chosen the Fourth Goddess, I would imagine. I continue to fight, I continue to wield a blade and send men to her.'

'Then have you not answered your own questions? You serve the Fourth Goddess. All men are fated to join her. It is simply a matter of when, where and how. Some fear death by the sword. Others fear drowning or falling from a cliff or the bite of a dog. Other men fear death in their bed. A man on your path will lose people: kin, comrades, allies, more than a man on the path of a potter or a baker. It is a truth that you must come to see. Do not pity the dead but do not forget them either. The reason behind their deaths is the ultimate truth, Master Batribi: all men are born, all men live, all men die. We shall see all of them on the other side of the Bridge to the Next Kingdom when our own time comes.'

# Chapter 44

Their duties discharged, the Company had returned to Stannia Lake and their people, to be given a rapturous welcome. The entire township seemed to be in the market square. Tired but elated, the Company formed up to be given a grateful and congratulatory address from the clan leaders. A great feast was prepared and huge amounts were eaten and drank. Daryo was offered his berth in Temma's home and gratefully accepted, stumbling back to it not long before dawn feeling almost ready to burst, beyond satiety and sobriety and he slept for nearly an entire day and night in total contentment.

\*     \*     \*

It was unaware of his presence; he had been careful to stay downwind. It was facing away, its head against an oddly-arching tree root as it reached for something. The head came up, perhaps sensing danger, dark eyes with long lashes blinked slowly. He moved slightly, trying to bring the bow clear of the branch in front of him, trying to keep his movements slow, controlled and silent. The head turned, the deer looked right at its predator and fled, its tail flashed white in the sun and then was gone. Daryo swore aloud and fired his arrow into the trees in frustration. He had been hunting for most of the morning but there had been no success. Every time he was ready to strike, something had occurred and the target had fled- rabbits, a boar, two deer, Daryo had suspicions that his luck would allow even a dead animal to escape him. He decided that a poor day's hunting was a poor day's hunting and decided to abandon the pursuit and return to the town.
Ten days after the Company's return, spring was becoming a warm and benevolent season. Trees were starting to bud, the grass was becoming lush and green. Daryo had been hunting in the forests to the north of the lake towards the Tember Pass. He walked south, using the sun, until he cleared the trees and had a view down into the valley below: the narrow river running from the mountains down to the lake, the town mostly on the other side of the river following the bank of the lake but starting to spread north of the river. A pair of horses and riders were following the road down towards the town. Even from the distance, Daryo could see activity across the river where a new bridge was being constructed around twenty yards upstream from the old one. He crossed the grassland to the road and began to walk back towards the town, bow over his shoulder. He had taken only the bow, two dozen arrows and his knife and dressed as lightly as possible but something had not been with him. The sun was warm but the clouds to the south suggested that rain may be on its way. To the sides of the road, the Batribi were

beginning to plant. An ox was towing a plough led by a young girl. A dozen people on the other side of the road were planting saplings with a small dog running about. Further along a fence was being completed, enclosing an area of about an acre. The First Goddess had not blessed Daryo's hunting but he hoped that she would be kind towards the farmers that supported the Batribi community. To the east of the town, Daryo could see herds of goats and sheep that were perhaps the most vital resource that the Batribi had but for the lake.

'Gods' Watch, Daryo, kin of Dostan!' called one of the fence-builders.

Daryo had to think for a moment. 'Saryo, Gods' Watch!' The priest apparently doubled as a labourer.

'Tahili does not guide your arrows?'

'Not this day.'

'Your brother just rode in.'

'My brother?'

'Laulra.'

'I did not know he was expected. My thanks, Saryo.'

'Eighth Day is the next, will I see you in the Temple?'

'Certainly. Gods' Guidance.'

'Gods' Guidance.'

Daryo continued into the town, past the House of Healing that was nearly completed and crossed the old bridge. A passing woman had seen the riders arrive and pointed south. Daryo assumed that they were going to the headquarters of the Company at the far side of the town as there was no sign of them near the Assembly Hall. The building was nothing impressive, a small wooden hut behind the town stables with a shield hung outside. Two horses were tethered outside and Daryo recognised the larger one as Laulra's bay gelding. He knocked on the door and it was opened.

'We were just about to send someone to find you, brother,' said Dostan with a smile. 'Enter, please.'

Daryo stepped inside, he had spent a lot of time in the building as Dostan's lieutenant since returning from Thiel. Laulra was sat on the rough bench by the window, its curtain pulled aside for light. He smiled and nodded to Daryo. Sat on the only proper chair in the room, instead of a bench, was a man in rich black and green robes; not a Batribi, his skin was pale, his hair a pale brown, wide and milky eyes gave him a somewhat unfocused look.

'Ingit, Marshal of Aslon, this is our brother, Daryo the Walker, of my clan.'

Daryo inclined his head. 'Marshal.'

'Sir.'

'Marshal Ingit is here from the Lord of Aslon to see you personally, Daryo,' said Laulra. 'He came to Court at Halmia to try to contact you.'

'To see me?' Daryo stepped further in and Laulra made room on the bench.

'Yes,' said the Marshal. 'The Lord of Aslon has sent me personally to find you. Lord Meyidaro died around three seasons ago and his son, Lord Hess has asked that I find the great Batribi warrior that was once a member of the Order of the Shield and Sword. You were the only Batribi in the Order, correct?'

'Correct.'

'Then it is you I seek. The Order fell but before it did the Lords of Aslon were always supportive of the Order and the Order had a close relationship with the Lords of Aslon.'

'Indeed.'

'It is because of that relationship that I come. The Vidmarian army that attacked the Five Towers withdrew from the forests around to Tiverta. Tiverta has been held by the Vidmarian army ever since and it was believed, and now evidenced, that their attention was elsewhere: Yashoun and Jaboen. Our spies now report Vidmarian armies moving east again and it is believed that they are moving to Tiverta to launch an assault on Gourmin. If they do, Aslon is the first city on the road to Allesbury. The Lord of Aslon, Lord Hess, formally requests that you aid us.' He handed a small, sealed document to Daryo.

Daryo nodded. 'I understand. I am sure you appreciate that I cannot decide such a matter instantly.'

'Certainly I do. I must leave for Aslon with the new dawn. I must take your answer back then.'

Dostan turned to his other brother. 'Laulra, could you find the Marshal some accommodation? The inn is perhaps best.'

'Of course, brother. Marshal?'

Laulra and the Gourmini left and Dostan sat opposite Daryo as Daryo opened the document.

*To the Batribi of the Order of the Shield and Sword, known as the Walker.*
*From Hess, son of Meyidaro, Lord of Aslon and the Forests, Officer of the Mountains, Steward of the West Road.*

*Sir, I request that in return for the friendship and aid given to your Order in the past, you consent to lending your talents for combat and warfare to the defence of Aslon. The Gourmini Army is*

*small but professional and is committed to the defence of its land but you have personal experience of engaging and defeating Vidmarian armies, something that is lacking in the Gourmini army and in Aslon.*
*I appreciate greatly that this task will be difficult and dangerous but as incentive, as well as your sense of integrity and honour, I offer the friendship of Aslon and Gourmin to the Batribi Community at Stannia Lake and to the Batribi people in general. I am aware that your compatriot, Laulra, kin of Dostan, is negotiating trade deals with Gourmin at this time and your assistance would greatly benefit his efforts. I am also willing to ensure that the Gourmini Council permits Batribi people the same freedoms within Gourmin as a native of these lands.*
*I hope that your response is positive. Your services are greatly needed and your efforts would be of great benefit to both our peoples.*
*I remain, Master Batribi, your friend under the guidance of the Gods and powers of the world.*

'There is no option to my mind,' said Daryo, after allowing Dostan to read the letter.
'There is always an option, brother.'
'I cannot refuse a request for aid. Particularly not from an ally of the Order.'
'Brother, the Order has gone. There is no obligation on you.'
'I disagree, Dostan. The Order has not gone, we are spread apart and alone but we still have an oath to keep, one that is perhaps more important now that we do not stand together. What is the trade that Laulra is trying to organise?'
'There are several, mostly for cloth and grain.'
'And that work could be advanced.'
'The Gourmini have no king, the country is run by their lords and they are all more interested in their own designs than the greater good. One lord will not have the influence to deliver what he has promised.'
'But he will try. I may not deliver what he wishes. Aslon may fall. Then neither of us will deliver the goods that were promised. He does not ask for the Company, he asks for one man. And our town is as close to Allesbury as it is to Halmia. If Vidmaria took southern Gourmin, they could attack through the Tember Pass, cut us off from Jaboen entirely.'
Dostan smiled thinly. 'You speak truth, brother. I do not think that you should go alone. At least take a small group.' He thought for a moment. 'Laulra may be a useful companion, he knows Gourmin. I would have recommended Liua but obviously... I will see who would join you from the Company.'
'Dostan, I think it better that the Company remain here. If you will accompany me that will be sufficient.'

'As you wish, brother. I still do not believe that you have to go but if you think it is best, Gods' Guidance.'

For the fifth time in his life, but only the second on horseback, Daryo entered the Tember Pass. He had been given a young but pleasant black mare from the stables and was riding a few yards ahead of Dostan. By midday they had passed through the narrow ravine and into the forests of Gourmin. The road sloped down out of the mountains and suddenly Daryo reined in his horse.
'Dostan, there is something I have to find.'
'Here?'
'Here. Keep watch on the left of the road for one tree that seems to be two.'
'As you wish.'
They continued for nearly three miles before Daryo saw what he had sought. 'Here, this one.'
The tree indeed seemed to separate into two trunks but was simply badly damaged in distant history. Daryo dismounted and led his horse to the side, Dostan close behind.
'What is this, Daryo?'
'An old home. Somewhere I have not returned to since I left. And I have to see.'
Dostan nodded. 'I think I know what you mean, but continue.'
They tethered their horses to a tree several yards off of the road. Daryo drew Temma's Sword. Dostan studied his brother for a moment and then drew his own blade.
'Trouble?'
'Potentially.' Daryo checked their surroundings. 'Stay close to me. It is possible some of the Order's traps are still in place and operational.'
'Traps?'
'Such as the ones that we had at the Soiliy bridge. Step carefully and do not touch anything that appears unusual.'
The two Batribi proceeded carefully through the evergreen trees. At intervals, fallen trees and odd debris suggested that the forest had been the site of a significant presence of people. A large chunk of rock was embedded in one tree, obviously not by natural occurrence.
'We are near to the Five Towers, are we not?' said Dostan, stepping carefully over a pile of rotting canvas and wood.
Daryo nodded and continued walking. They began to pass more evidence of a past battle- abandoned weapons, damaged trees, further stones littering the larger clearings, then a band of trees that had been badly scorched by fire. Daryo ducked some low foliage and

had a full view. The ancient, ruined village that stood before the wall was much as Daryo had remembered- low ruined walls and stones part-covered by vegetation. The main gatehouse had been smashed in places by flung stones and the gates and portcullis ripped aside. To the left, the round Twin Towers had an air of dereliction, a tattered Vidmarian banner flew from the Secondborn Tower on the right of the two. To the right of the gate, the Temple Tower had been felled by a catapult and demolished the wall. Behind the breach was the Castle Tower. The tallest tower, the Wooden Fortress, was black and had partially collapsed. Daryo advanced slowly, Temma's Sword in hand at his side. The gatehouse looked unstable, leaning forwards slightly and Daryo eyed it nervously as he passed through the gate. The Compound was a mess, every building in it had been burned and destroyed- the forge, the bakery, the stables. The Wooden Fortress had obviously been subjected to an intense and repeated attempt to burn it, the shell was blackened and the front wall had taken the most damage, large charred holes had been burned through the three layers of wood to the interior. The heat of the fire to be able to burn through nearly four feet of ancient timber would have had to have been exceptional, the Vidmarians would have needed to put a large amount of time and fuel into such a blaze. Dostan crouched and picked up a discarded dagger that was covered in rust. Beneath it, covered in dirt and some vegetation was a shield. He dropped the dagger and picked up the shield instead. On its face was faded and damaged paint, a pale circle and a simple sword were described and, at the base of the sword image, was that of a broken pot.

'One of the Order's?' Dostan asked, showing Daryo.

Daryo studied the badge. 'I do not recognise whose badge that is but it is an Order shield. Someone killed in the battle perhaps.'

Dostan leaned the shield against some nearby stone from the gatehouse. 'I am sorry, Daryo. You lost many comrades and friends here.'

Daryo nodded and turned left toward the Twin Towers. The remnants of the bakery and dairy were against the Secondborn Tower. The smithy, a short distance away, had also been burned, only a stone trough remained above ankle-high. Daryo pushed the door to the Firstborn Tower and stepped inside. The interior had been looted and he was inside for mere heartbeats.

'Time to go?' asked Dostan.

'There is one more place I want to go,' Daryo told him. 'Do we have a light?'

Dostan shook his head.

'We will need to be careful.' Daryo headed towards the back of the Compound, to the left of the wrecked Wooden Fortress Tower. A cave in the rock that had once been

protected by a door and portcullis had been returned to its original state- a simple hole into the cliff.
'Keep to the right side,' Daryo told Dostan as they entered. 'Keep your head low as well.'
After less than forty yards, they were in total darkness as the tunnel through the rock turned away from the entrance. Progress was slow, each footstep was taken with care, right hand on the tunnel wall, left groping in front for hazards.
'What is this, Daryo?' asked Dostan through the dark.
'The last refuge of the Order,' Daryo told him. 'I want to see the Sanctuary.'
'It is dark, brother.'
'There will be light in the Sanctuary.'
They stumbled onwards and passed through what felt like a small chamber.
'I think that was the Threefold Door,' Daryo said. 'We are nearly there.'

The Sanctuary was just as Daryo remembered- a stepped auditorium in a massive natural cave with a seemingly impossible tree growing at the bottom, a cleft in the rock above allowing light into the space. A tattered banner had been nailed to a branch of the tree. The detritus of the Order's retreat to and confinement in the Sanctuary littered the tiers- storage containers, weapons, blankets, clothes, personal possessions. Daryo found a shield with a shell at the base.
'This is the shield of Yi the Islander,' Daryo told Dostan. 'I met him on the Silver Island when I was there. It is a shame that I cannot return it to him. We hid down here, barricaded ourselves in when the Compound fell. When Dostan brought our people, we were able to leave. I think that I was one of the last to leave this place before we dispersed.'
Daryo began to climb down the levels of the steps to the bottom, up on to the dais around the tree and pulled the banner out to see it properly. It was a Vidmarian banner, two rearing wolves, halved with the image of a sword-wielding statue; the symbol of the traitorous former senior Member of the Order Sevant the Stone. Daryo tore the banner down, scrunched it into a ball and threw it aside in anger.
'I am sorry, brother,' said Dostan. 'I know this is not an easy place to be, giving how you knew it, to see it like this...'
Daryo nodded sadly. 'So many people died here. Not just Members of the Order. Hundreds, maybe thousands of Vidmarians. And... they deserved it, Dostan.' Daryo turned to look at his brother. 'They deserved to die. The Order was no threat to Vidmaria, had nothing of real value, no lands, no treasures, but one treacherous dog sold us to them! And they came expecting glory and victory and we killed them in their

droves!' Daryo found he was brandishing his sword and, in a moment of self-consciousness, lowered it.

Dostan smiled supportively. 'Then let us go and send some more to join their comrades.'

## Chapter 45

Standing alone above the grass and fields, its back to the river, Aslon was visible for miles around, walls nearly a hundred feet high with half-moon towers at regular intervals around them. The city was clearly being readied for war- ballista were being erected on the towers and the sluices by the river were open, filling the moat. A few people were working around the outside of the walls in the fields and a small group of boats were visible out in the middle of the river.

'I see a problem already,' said Daryo, reining in his horse.

'Oh?' Dostan stopped his own mount too.

'What time is it? The season?'

'Spring, Spring's Ninth Day.'

'There will be little food to harvest.'

'Agreed.'

'So, tell me, brother: how does Aslon survive a siege with no supplies?'

Dostan thought for a few moments. 'I do not know.'

'Neither do I.'

They rode onwards towards the town. Around half a mile from the gate, a flimsy barricade had been erected and was manned by three men in chainmail carrying spears and a fourth with a crossbow.

'Halt,' commanded the archer, hefting his weapon. 'This area is not safe. Aslon normally does not refuse Batribi, but the Vidmarians are advancing and this area will not be safe for you or your people. You should return to Jaboen.'

'Our thanks for your warning,' said Daryo. 'But we are here at your lord's request.'

'Oh. You are the great Batribi commander.'

'Your words.'

The crossbowman studied them for a moment. 'And your companion?'

'I am his kinsman,' said Dostan. 'His... lieutenant.'

'Proceed into the city,' said the crossbowman. 'The defence of the city is being led from the temple, it is the most suited building to the task.'

'Gods' Guidance.'

'And to you.'

The Batribi kicked their horses on and guided them around the barricade. The city gate had only a single, very young woman sentry with only a staff. She looked at the Batribi and seemed to lose any words or actions to prevent them entering Aslon. The thatched, stone houses were as Daryo remembered but the riverside market was deserted. The

temple's dome rose above the surrounding buildings, a bronze spear, twice life-size, stood before the doors. Above them, the banner of Aslon, the moon emerging from the river, was hung from the roof of the entrance porch. Daryo and Dostan dismounted and tied their horses nearby. There was no guard and they were able to walk straight inside.
'Master Daryo!' Marshal Ingit left a planning table, which Daryo realised was really the altar. 'Master Dostan! Our grateful thanks for your coming.' He ushered them further in. There were only half a dozen others in the temple. The seats had been moved aside and stacked haphazardly, the altar was covered in parchments, a nearby table had weapons and shields on it. One of the men, wearing a tight leather jerkin over a brown shirt, left the altar. He had shoulder-length black hair, thick eyebrows that almost concealed the eyes beneath and a prominent nose.
'Daryo the Walker.'
'Lord Hess.' Daryo drew Temma's Sword, holding it point down in salute. 'My sword and service. This is my brother, Dostan.'
'I believe you may have known my younger brother. Toxiz, known as the Coalfire. He had some severely disfiguring growths on his neck, it made him quite distinctive.'
Daryo was surprised but nodded keenly as he lowered his sword. 'Toxiz. Yes. I fought alongside him at the fall of the Five Towers. He was an heroic fighter, a most honourable man. I do not know if he survived the battle.'
'He did but barely. He was mortally wounded and survived long enough to return to his home before he passed to the Next Kingdom.'
'I mourn him, sir.'
'As do I. We shall meet again, I am sure. How do you intend to save my city, Walker?'
Daryo smiled. 'You are direct, Lord Hess. I have had little time to study the defences or forces.'
'Here,' said Marshal Ingit, indicating the altar. Daryo went to the altar and was handed a piece of parchment. We have a city guard of four hundred, a militia of seven hundred and a Gourmini army detachment of two thousand less than a day away. Another seven thousand mustering at Allesbury.'
'That is barely three thousand,' said Dostan.
'There is another two thousand at Riverhelm,' Ingit told them.
'How many Vidmarians are at Tiverta?'
'We do not know,' said Ingit, glancing at Hess.
'Why not?'
'We did not have the men to send fruitless scouting parties to their deaths,' said the lord imperiously.

'So you do not know the disposition of the forces facing you,' Daryo replied flatly. 'You may be outnumbered ten against one and be exposing your town not just to attack but to destruction. Marshal, I need a scouting party formed immediately.'

'How—'

'Sir, you requested my assistance. If you want me to help you defend Aslon, I must have all the information necessary. I must be able to give instructions and commands to direct the defence.'

Hess glared at Daryo for a few heartbeats and then glanced at Ingit. 'Have the scouting party readied to go to Tiverta.'

'Yes, my lord.'

Daryo smiled tightly. 'My thanks, sir. What supplies does the city have? How long would provisions last?'

'Infinitely,' said Hess proudly. 'We have the river.'

'But a Vidmarian army encircling the town could contaminate the river, foul it,' said Dostan. 'The fish would be inedible, the water poisonous.'

'They may not.'

'They may,' said Daryo, trying hard to keep composed. 'How long if the river was polluted?"

The Marshal consulted a woman nearby. 'About ten days, Walker. It is too early in the season, our winter stores are exhausted and we have not been able to replenish them. We are trying to collect as much as possible before the Vidmarians arrive.'

Daryo nodded slowly. 'I would like to inspect the defences.'

'You are worried, brother.'

Daryo sniffed derisively. 'My thanks, Dostan, but I already know.'

The two Batribi were stood on the town's eastern gatehouse next to a small catapult, its counterweight being filled with rocks by a team of townsmen.

Daryo continued: 'The Vidmarians will surround the town, contaminate the river, try to force entry and if that fails, they will starve the city into submission. If they have the numerical advantage that we think they may, they can besiege the city and still defend themselves against a Gourmini counter-attack.'

'Not a good position,' Dostan agreed. 'I know little about fortified towns. What is your opinion of the defences?'

Daryo considered this. 'The walls are strong enough, unless the Vidmarians have some major siege equipment. If they have travelled a long distance, hopefully it has been

delayed. The gates are old but fairly strong. The ballista and the catapults are small and the arrows for the ballista will soon run down. There are not enough men to defend the town effectively with just the city guard and the militia. The Gourmini army... I do not know what their experience and ability is like. They may be the superior of the Vidmarian army but I cannot say.'
'We should have brought the Company with us.'
'What good would ten score Batribi swords do against ten times that of Vidmarian?' Dostan shrugged.
'We need an alternative to standing and fighting,' said Daryo. 'I have to think.'

'I will not empty the city.' Lord Hess folded his arms defiantly.
'It is a sound strategy,' Daryo replied. 'If the Vidmarian army attacks and finds nothing, they will take time to occupy and defend the city. In that time, the troops marching this way and those at Allesbury will have time to rally together and form a coherent force.'
'And my people will be left in the wilderness.'
'For a short period.'
'No.'
'Lord Hess, if you try to hold the city, the Vidmarians will pin you down and you will helplessly trapped inside. If you leave the city, join the main army, find a defensible position then there is a chance.'
'I will not empty the city, find another way.'
'There is no other way.'
Dostan intervened. 'There is somewhere that the people could go and find shelter. The Five Towers, they are in disrepair, looted, empty, but three of the towers and the caves beneath the cliff are still usable. If you wish, I can send a messenger to Stannia Lake and have the Batribi Company protect them there.'
'No.'
'Lord Hess, if you try to do what you are proposing... how many people in the city?'
'Eleven thousand,' said the marshal.
'They could all die.'
'I will not.'
Daryo stepped away from the altar. 'Then there is no reason for me to remain.'
'Say that again.'
'There is no reason to remain. You ask me here to assist in the defence of your town, I formulate a plan and you reject it. There is no reason for me to remain here.' He turned to Dostan and nodded. 'Come, brother, if we ride hard we could reach home by

sundown.' He turned on his heel and, with Dostan close behind, strode out of Aslon's temple. Slightly into the town from the temple was the stables where their horses had been housed.

There was not sufficient light for them to reach and cross the Tember Pass before the sun went down and they were forced to improvise a campsite.

'Laulra was hoping for a few days without me. I believe he only consented to be our representative to escape his older brother's supervision,' said Dostan. They were practically the first words that they had exchanged since leaving Aslon. He struck his flint, the third strike caught the tinder and the fire was soon blazing.

Daryo nodded dully. 'How much older are you?'

'Six seasons. He was born on Winter's First, thirty-five winters ago. This will be my thirty-seventh summer. How old are you, Daryo?'

'I am not exactly sure. I think, and think only, that this is my twenty-fourth spring.' Daryo leaned back against the trunk of a tree. 'I am sorry to have brought you this distance for no reason, brother.'

'I enjoy a ride,' said Dostan with a grin. 'Think no more of it.'

'I feel that I am disappointing, perhaps even... perhaps even dooming Aslon. Not the lord but the people.'

'Perhaps. But you cannot aid one who will not be aided.'

'I know. It does not salve my feeling though.'

'When we return to the lake, we should mobilise the Company and contact the Court at Halmia. It may be that the Tember Pass needs to be blocked.'

Daryo nodded. 'I think that wise. It may be more... diplomatic if the Jaboens can do the task but we can assist them as much as possible.'

'You could lead our efforts, if you wish.'

'I will consider it... can you hear horses?'

'I can. It is late for people to be travelling.'

'Gourmini?'

'Perhaps.'

Daryo drew Temma's Sword. Dostan reached for his own blade. They were nearly thirty yards from the road, nearly obscured by the pine trees. Dostan doused the fire with earth and they made their way carefully to a place where the road was clearly observable. In the near darkness, two horses were approaching from the direction of Aslon. One rider was carrying a lantern, the horses were panting as if they had been galloping.

'They are Aslon men,' murmured Daryo. The city's arms were on the shield carried by one rider, illuminated by the lantern of the other.

'... too far,' one of the riders was saying.

'Just two horses and riders, we got this far,' said the man with the lamp. 'We should turn back.'

'Marshal said to find those Batribi. Keep going.'

Dostan got Daryo's attention. 'They are seeking us.'

Daryo nodded. 'Stay here,' he whispered before stepping out onto the road. 'Gods' Watch, gentlemen!'

The riders halted their horses. The lantern was raised. 'Are you the Walker?'

'I am.'

'Marshal Ingit sent us to find you, sir,' said the man with the lantern. 'Lord Hess is...' The man coughed nervously. 'Marshal Ingit begs your pardon, sir, and asks that you return to Aslon. The scouts have returned, the Vidmarians are closer than we thought. Please, sir, Aslon needs you. You will be given all authority necessary to command the city's defence using whatever you feel necessary to do so.'

'Your lord was not keen on my authority earlier in this day.'

'Sir... that is not a problem. Marshal Ingit sends his assurance.'

Daryo beckoned to Dostan, who emerged from concealment. 'What do you think, brother?' he asked in a low voice.

'I think it a chance for us to assuage your bad feelings.'

## Chapter 46

The Marshal was talking with a young man with a crossbow on his back. When the Batribi entered, Ingit dismissed the soldier. There were no others inside the temple, it was near midnight, the only illumination was an oil lamp on the altar. Ingit looked pale and beaten in the lamplight. A long, two-handed sword was laid beside the lamp.
'Walker. Dostan. My thanks for your return. You are most welcome.'
'You have persuaded Lord Hess to permit us to command the defence?' asked Daryo.
The Marshal bowed his head, leaning on the altar. 'Lord Hess is no longer in command.'
'No longer in command?' asked Daryo, curious. 'He is the lord of the city. There is no resignation procedure, is there?'
Dostan rounded the altar, looking at something. 'Brother.' He lifted the sword slightly. There was a red-brown stain on one edge of the blade. Blood, nearly dry.
Daryo looked at Ingit, shocked. 'You killed him.'
Ingit took a deep breath. 'I killed him. He was endangering everyone in this city. He would not allow anyone to leave, not even children. He was determined to see his great city burn around him, a great hero of Gourmin resisting the invader. I could not allow it. I killed Lord Hess.'
'Who is his heir?' asked Dostan.
'He has none. His wife is barren. The next lord would have been Master Toxiz. In the absence of an immediate heir, according to the Conventions of Gourmin, the town's Marshal is vested with responsibility until the Convened Council of Lords can decide on the rightful new lord.'
'What will you tell the people?'
'They have been told that the strain of the impending attack was too much for the Lord and he died of stress-induced collapse.'
'I am not sure you have taken the right road, Marshal.' Daryo glanced at the bloodied sword again.
'It is done,' was the reply. 'Will you help me, now, to confront the Vidmarians?'
Daryo nodded. 'I will.'
The Marshal handed over a small piece of fabric with a wax seal. 'Your authority from my office, Walker. The scouting party returned not long after sundown. The Vidmarians are coming from the south, across country. They counted nearly twelve thousand.'
Daryo frowned. 'That is many. How close?'
'Here the day after next.'
Dostan took a sharp breath. 'Very close.'

'Then we must act fast,' said Daryo. 'Their scouts will be observing the city. We must be careful but swift. Tonight, the people must be evacuated across the river, guided by the most capable navigators west to the ruins of the Five Towers. That must continue as long as darkness is enough to hide them. The militia will cross last and go to the Five Towers. The City Guard can then withdraw. Send a messenger to the army group on its way and tell them to find a defensive position. Send another to Allesbury to have the main force join us there in two days.'

Ingit made quick notes with chalk on a writing slate. 'It will be done.'

'It is critical, *critical*, that the Vidmarians do not see the population of the town. They must use the forests north of the river to conceal themselves.'

'I understand.'

'You should go to work, Marshal. There is much to do.'

The Gourmini studied the Batribi warrior's face for a few moments and then hurried out. Daryo looked at Dostan, finding his kinsman staring back at him.

'You are worried, brother.'

Dostan pointed to the sword before him. 'The man leading this operation killed his lord.'

Daryo rocked his head from side to side indecisively. 'He did but for a good reason. There is no denying that he had given the people of Aslon a greater chance of survival.'

'An evil act, even if done for good, remains evil,' quoted Dostan. It was a well-known passage from the Writs of the Third Goddess.

'Sacrifice the cow to save two calves and your milk will double,' replied Daryo, a more obscure passage from the Writs of the First God. 'I do not believe he should have killed his lord, Dostan, but I do believe he did so with honest intentions and I do believe that he may have saved many hundreds of lives by taking one.'

'We will not agree on this.'

'I doubt that we will. If you wish to return to the lake, brother, I will see you when I return.'

Dostan shook his head. 'I swore to accompany and assist you, brother. I will do so and I have the same respect and love for you as I ever have had. But do not ask me to trust Ingit again.'

'I understand and I am grateful.'

Whatever reservations Daryo had about Ingit, he was capable of acting quickly and organising effort capably. The militia were swiftly going from house to house passing on

simple instructions: *Take only what you can carry. Food and clothing, nothing else. Do not leave your house until told to by the militia or City Guard.*
With every house visited, the militiaman left a chalk mark on the door so that no house was visited twice. Some people were obstreperous, some were abusive but most saw sense when the threat was outlined or they spoke to a militiaman that they knew. When the militia had been through the city, a group of civilian officials went out to seek the owners and operators of boats on the river, having them ready their craft to cross the river. Shortly behind them, City Guardsmen began to move people out of their houses and down to the river. Dostan was one of the first to cross the river to organise the operation on that side, along with the city's priest and minor landowner from near the town. Daryo walked through the town, carrying bundles for some families and directing traffic towards the river. Near one wall, he found a small group of militiamen grouped around a tower door muttering to each other.
'Is there a problem?' he asked.
The men looked at him, some with hostility, but one recognised the Batribi commander that had been asked to help defend the town. 'We know not what to do,' he said, glancing at the door. 'This is the House of the White Lady.'
Daryo vaguely remembered the Harlequin mentioning it on his previous visit to Aslon. And a young woman walking naked through the market. 'What is the issue?'
'The women are... naked.'
'They come outside, I have seen them.'
The militiamen exchanged nervous looks and shuffled their feet. 'It is not encouraged to be knocking on the door,' said another. 'People from out of the city think this is a brothel.'
Daryo sighed. 'When will they need to leave?'
'Not until next night.'
Daryo slipped past the militia, dismissed them and knocked on the door. 'City Guard!' he called. 'City Guard! This is important!' He knocked a little harder.
From a window above the door, he heard a quiet voice, then another. There was the sound of a lock opening and the door swung inwards. Daryo peered inside and stepped through the door. The little room was only eight feet square, lit by only two candles in a stand. The only other feature of the room was another door; the exterior door of the room closed and, when it had, Daryo saw an elaborate system of levers on the back that apparently let someone in the room above control the door without having to go into the little atrium.
'Hello!' Daryo called. 'City Guard!'

The other door opened a short distance and a woman of about forty springs stepped through, wearing a white gown of such a fine gossamer that it barely hid the fact that she was unclothed beneath it. The woman had a proud, haughty demeanour and carried a candlestick.

'You are not City Guard,' she said angrily.

'My name is Daryo the Walker, of the Order of the Shield and Sword. Marshal Ingit of the city has asked me to assist in the town's defence against the Vidmarians.' He showed the Marshal's seal.

The woman inspected it by the light of her candle. 'What matter is this to us?'

'The city is being evacuated, Madam. It cannot be held. The population are being removed across the river.'

'We cannot leave,' said the woman bluntly.

'If you remain, you will die,' said Daryo, equally firmly.

'Then we die in the care of the White Lady and will join the righteous at her side.'

Daryo sighed. 'A noble end but unnecessary. It is hoped that the people will be able to return within days. You can return to your seclusion.'

The woman shook her head. 'Impossible. Only two of us can step outside the doors and only as we gladly risk our bodies for our sisters.'

'You will be well-protected,' said Daryo. 'The City Guard-'

'Will take advantage of us as soon as they can do so! They are men, they are soldiers, I know what soldiers can do!' The woman sniffed and waved her hand dismissively. 'I was used as a sheath for a soldier's *mighty* weapon before I came to the White Lady.'

Daryo thought for a moment. 'Then you need a guard that is neither man nor soldier. I know that there is a score of women in the militia. They will be your personal guards. I will ensure that they keep you separated and secluded from the rest of the population and protect you from any that would impinge on you.'

The woman considered this. 'We have no clothing, it would be impractical. We give up all that we have. This gown is only for use in this room to meet with a stranger. We can take no possessions.'

'If a possession was loaned to you, with the strict proviso that it was to be returned?'

The woman smiled thinly. 'You are most astute, Master Daryo. I must consult our texts but it may be... sufferable.'

'My thanks, Madam. Madam...?'

'We give up all that we have. Including names.'

'I understand.' Daryo gave a short bow. 'Your escorts will need to take you to cross the river with the next night. They will be here at sundown.'

'As you wish. I will have the door opened.' She turned on her heel and stepped out of the atrium. The inside door closed, there was a clunk of mechanisms and the outside door opened, allowed Daryo to leave. Outside, the militiamen were still standing in a group, whispering among themselves but they stopped when they saw Daryo.
'Tell the Marshal to have every woman in the militia meet at the temple as soon as possible,' Daryo ordered one. 'The rest of you, should you not be doing your duties?' The militia scattered like beetles before a flame. Daryo took a deep breath, pushed the image of the near-naked woman from his mind and resumed his duties.

As soon as dawn came, Daryo ordered the evacuation halted. He did not want any chance of the Vidmarians noticing the civilians being removed from the town. He sent a unit of a hundred City Guard across the river as the last transit, with orders to head east along the river, out of sight, re-cross and march brazenly into the town as if reinforcing it. A messenger arrived from the Gourmini army, they had halted around ten miles north and east of Aslon. Daryo personally briefed the twenty-two women from the militia on their specific assignment. To add to the security of the Devotees of the White Lady they would be the last to be evacuated from the town and, after some discussion and a message sent to the tower, Dostan would be personally responsible for their safety and would accompany them to the Five Towers, where they would be found separate accommodation in the ruined Castle Tower, while most of the people went in the Sanctuary and the Twin Towers. Until their removal, the women of the militia stood guard outside the White Lady's tower.

By midday, the fake reinforcements had arrived with much cheering and celebration from the other City Guards, playing their part well. Daryo had the entire Guard line the walls, preparing ballista, catapults, bows and other weapons, demonstrably preparing to defend the city. Meanwhile the militia were preparing the rest of the town's population for evacuation, for which a large timber barge was unloaded for use.

Shortly before sunset, the first Vidmarian banners were sighted to the south but they did not advance and by dark there were fires visible as the Vidmarian army set up camp within sight of the walls of Aslon. As soon as it was dark, Daryo ordered the evacuation concluded. The pace was quicker but also calmer than the previous night; the militia knew their role and were more confident with the marshalling of the people to the river and onto the boats. Not long after midnight, the last boats were loading for the crossing. A middle-sized barge was towed a short distance along the bank away from the others and, from the almost-silent town, a small procession of women emerged, sixteen shrouded in a motley of black and grey robes of various origins, twenty-two in the belted tunics and carrying the various weapons of the militia, led by a single male Batribi with his curved sword drawn. Waiting by the barge, Daryo and Ingit watched as the ethereal cavalcade approached, the robed figures all barefoot and with the hoods of their cloaks drawn up over inclined heads. The odd group boarded the barge, Dostan last. He reached ashore and clasped Daryo's hand.

'Gods' Guidance, brother. If all is well, I shall see you within the eight days.'

Daryo nodded. 'If the Second God favours us. Thiney is known for capriciousness, without the Fourth Goddess's tricks as well.'

'With both willing, we will see each other soon. I will protect the devotees of the White Lady with my life. I swear on our kin's honour.'

'Good fortune and Gods' Guidance, Dostan.' Daryo nodded to the boat's owner at the tiller and cast off the lines. The boat was rowed out by half a dozen of the women of the militia and was soon out of sight in the darkness.

After a few moments' silence, Daryo turned to Ingit. 'Have the Guard light the sentry fires and withdraw to the temple square. The militia to meet inside the east gate. We withdraw as soon as we can. We must be gone by dawn.'

The Vidmarian attack after dawn was the swing of a fist against empty air. The militia had escaped along the road with barely a sound, Marshal Ingit at its head. Shortly behind, led by Daryo, the City Guard withdrew from the town after destroyed the ballistas, catapults and the locks and bars of the gates. They withdrew east in silence, only the noise of marching feet with strict instructions not to speak a word. The road was rough, no lights were permitted, but Daryo insisted on a rapid pace despite the treacherous road and the darkness. After two miles, they caught up with the militia. Daryo pushed through to the front and increased pace. Just before dawn, the watch-fires of the Gourmini Army became visible. Tired, dirty, thirsty and famished, the militia and Guard of Aslon, their Marshal and their Batribi commander traipsed into the camp.

## Chapter 47

The Gourmini Army was camped on the reverse of a ridge just over ten miles from Aslon towards Riverhelm and, beyond, Allesbury. The vast majority of the army seemed to be sleeping in the open with only a blanket between them and the air. By the light of the watch-fires, the City Guard and militia of Aslon joined their comrades. A sentry guided Ingit and Daryo through the rousing camp as dawn approached. The men of the Gourmini army wore green and most had leather cuirasses over their tunics not too dissimilar in design from Daryo's jerkin. Around the camp like trees growing in an orchard were gold-edged green banners with the brown hawk of Gourmin in the centre. The Gourmini soldiers were mostly armed with metal-tipped spears and broad daggers as well as long, narrow shields. Two were stood outside a bell-shaped black canvas tent with a man-sized hawk on every canvas panel. Inside it was a broad, circular wooden table had been erected and surrounded by elaborately-carved but foldable chairs, six large each flanked by a pair of smaller, an elaborate throne stood apart from the table. The tent was deserted.

'Please wait,' said the sentry. 'The others will be here soon.'

'The others?' Daryo asked Ingit as the sentry left.

'The Lords of Gourmin,' said Ingit. 'Mergret of Allesbury, Aedan of Spiert, Theach of Sinsebil, Drest of Sitak.' He paused. 'There is no Lord of Aslon so his Marshal deputises. And Lord Sechlann of Tiverta is a Vidmarian captive. I do not know who would deputise if his Marshal is captured also.' Ingit moved forwards to study the chairs and found one with a moon and river carved on the back. He sat down and indicated the chair to his right for Daryo. Within a short period, the other noblemen of Gourmin arrived, all accompanied by a small retinue. Mergret was only a little older than Daryo, heavily built and shaggy; Theach, elderly and barely able to walk with a stick; Drest was of about forty summers, dark-skinned enough to suggest at least one Batribi ancestor and dressed for battle in armour; Aedan was bald-headed, scarred and missing his right eye and leaned heavily on a staff. Last to arrive, alone, was a young man, not even of Daryo's age, wearing black but with a scarlet doublet on top. He looked around and mumbled apologies as he took his seat.

'Master Cadern,' Ingit mumbled to Daryo. 'Lord Sechlann's son.'

'Gentlemen,' said Aedan, standing up painfully. 'The King.'

The Gourmini all stood, turned towards the empty throne and bowed before resuming their seats.

Aedan continued: 'The Convened Lords of Gourmin recognised as lawful representatives Cadern, son of Sechlann, of Tiverta. And Ingit, Marshal of Aslon.' He looked around the other lords and received a slow, deep nod from each. 'Marshal Ingit, this Council does not approve of your abandoning of Aslon. The army should immediately reoccupy the town.'

'With respect, sir,' said Daryo. 'The town was not defensible with the resources that we had.'

'And who are you?' demanded Lord Drest.

'Daryo the Walker,' was the reply. 'I was a Member of the Order of the Shield and Sword, Lord Hess asked me to come to help against the Vidmarians, as I have significant experience against them.'

'And your method of... helping was to abandon a city full of innocents?' croaked Lord Theach.'

'The city is empty, my lord,' said Ingit. 'They were taken out in the darkness and are hidden at the Five Towers. The Vidmarians will find an empty wall stripped of many of its defences.'

'We have bought Gourmin some more time,' Daryo told them. 'The Gourmini Army can join together and fight a battle of its choosing, instead of having to break a siege.'

There were some hostile looks around the table. Several lieutenants whispered into their lord's ear. Only Cadern looked interested.

'Debating the point is fruitless,' said Mergret of Allesbury. 'The course must be decided.'

'Attack. Quickly,' said Drest.

'No, the Batribi is correct,' retorted Aedan. 'Find a battle site.'

'Forwards of here,' said Mergret.

'Closer to Allesbury,' said Theach with a croak.

'Closer to Aslon,' Mergret replied.

'Hold Riverhelm,' Drest suggested.

'I do not want Riverhelm destroyed,' said Mergret.

'You are concerned only with your own lands!' scoffed Aedan.

'And you care nothing for our capital!'

'Closer to Allesbury buys more time!'

'Closer to Aslon is safer for our people!'

'That is sacrificing our army!'

'Instead of sacrificing our nation!'

The cacophony grew as assistants and lieutenants joined the argument. Daryo was agog at the chaos; only young Cadern remained silent, looking rather bemused amid the

tumult. Daryo noticed that the boy lord-ling had particularly long hair, very delicate features and his scarlet doublet was elaborately embroidered with horses and deer.
'My lords!' bellowed Ingit. 'My lords, this solves nothing. We must make a decision.'
'We will defend Riverhelm,' said Drest.
'No! Withdraw closer to Allesbury!' said Aedan.
'Attack,' insisted Mergret.
'Withdraw,' said Theach.
'Then we must choose a commander,' said Cadern, so softly that the tent full of people had to go silent to hear him. There was a muted chuckle around the table and some sarcastic remarks. Ingit sighed.
'What is wrong?' Daryo whispered.
'That requires a vote,' Ingit whispered. 'And each Gourmini would only ever vote for himself. However...' He raised a hand. 'I nominate, on behalf of my lord, Daryo the Walker, as commander of the Gourmini.'
Daryo went to object but Drest cut him off. 'I nominate Drest, Lord of Sitak.'
'I nominate Mergret of Allesbury.'
'Theach of Sinsebil.'
'Aedan of Spiert.'
'Daryo the Walker,' said the soft voice of Cadern.
There was silence for a heartbeat and then uproar as each lord and his retinue demanded that Cadern change his vote. Daryo could not help but laugh at the quiet confidence and assurance of the boy.
'Gentlemen! Gentlemen!' barked Aedan over the din. 'Gentlemen! The vote is taken! According to the Convention, the vote *is* binding... Master Daryo, you are now commander of Gourmin's armies.'
There was silence again as every pair of eyes around the table turned towards the only Batribi in the tent. Daryo looked around, suddenly rather intimidated.
'How many troops are mustered here?' Daryo asked quietly.
'Twenty-two hundred,' said Mergret grudgingly.
'And assembling at Allesbury?'
'Seven thousand, two hundred,' replied Aedan, his voice betraying a little amusement. 'They are assembled already and were due to march towards us as soon as dawn came.'
'You intend to hold this place?' demanded Drest.
'I do. The ridge is difficult to crest from the direction of Aslon. The river protects our right flank. The only way to attack is to attack the ridge.'
Aedan nodded. 'A sound plan.'

'I propose that the ridge be used to help deceive the enemy. The force from Allesbury can be hidden behind it. The current force masquerades as our only army. They then withdraw, drawing the Vidmarians into the main army.'
'You are commander,' said Aedan.
'We should also put scouting parties in place, with fast horses, so that we have a full picture of the Vidmarian army's actions and intentions. We also need to know if they are mainly mounted, mainly infantry and so forth.'

The conference lasted until almost midday before business was pronounced finished. The other lords and their retinues departed one by one. Daryo and Ingit were left alone with just Lord Aedan and his aides, who were dismissed by their master, who hobbled back to the table.
'Would you excuse us, Marshal?'
Ingit gave a short bow. 'Certainly, my lord.' He stood, nodded to Daryo and followed the others out of the tent. Daryo remained seated.
Aedan's dark-blue left eye regarded Daryo, the skin of his right eye had been sealed shut and a scar ran from the eye to under his right ear, his head was shaved clean, the skull marked by the white scar of a burn. Daryo assumed that the badge on his dark blue sleeveless robe was that of Spiert: a white ship against a black shield. When Aedan moved, Daryo could see a sword at his side as well as the long staff in his hand.
'Tell me, Daryo the Walker, who the most dangerous man at that convention was?'
'I do not understand. In what way?'
'The one most likely to cost lives.'
Daryo thought for a moment. 'It is difficult to say.'
'Speak freely, I will take no retribution.'
'Either yourself, sir, or Lord Mergret.'
'Why so?'
'You, sir, strike me as the closest to a leader as the Convened Lords have. Lord Mergret is Lord of Allesbury and seems the most vocal of the others.'
'Astute but incorrect. Young Tiverta.'
'Lord Cadern?'
'He is not a lord. He is the youngest of four children, two sons, and only representing his father, who is captive in Vidmaria. And he has chosen you as commander. I do not believe that you are an incorrect choice, sir, in fact you are likely to be as capable as any other, but Young Tiverta is easily led and a known... nonconformist. He is reputed to lie with other men, even with young boys. He is no soldier, nor a diplomat or a merchant.

He chose you because he felt it would be the most disruptive act, the biggest statement of defiance possible. May I tell you a tale? I assure you it will be relevant.'

'As you wish.'

'I am the third child of my parents. The oldest, my sister is the wife of the Lord of Salifa in Jaboen. I am the younger of the two sons by less than a cycle of seasons. My older brother was... dim. The faculties given to other men, such as reason, thoughtfulness, consideration, control of temper, even speech, were denied to my brother. In Yashoun, such a man in a noble family would be hidden from view, if not killed as an infant. My mother and father, as I do, follow the tenets of the White Lady and their priestess counselled them to care for Brennun in the hope that one day the mind would grow to join the body in maturity. My father was known for being... nonconformist, for wanting to appear different and combative, and so he accepted this advice.'

'A compassionate act towards a kinsman.'

'By the time that I came of age, it was not a wise decision. Brennun was a boy of eight or ten seasons encased in the frame of a man larger than his father. The stress of his care aged our mother particularly and she died that summer, young. Brennun was more... volatile than before, prone to fits of anger and violence. One Midwinter Day, about a season after I came of age, he somehow came by a small flask of flame oil, I know not how. He could not have known what it was but some small part of his mind knew that he should not have it. He ran out of the keep and I saw him run and pursued. He ran into a building in the courtyard. It was the stables with the grain store alongside, although well separated. He ran into the room used by the grooms and threw the flask into the brazier in an attempt to dispose of it.'

'And it exploded.'

'Indeed. The winter was dry and cold, the timbers of the stables dry and the burst of fire into the hay of the stables caused an inferno. There were two dozen horses in the stables and there was the grain. I raced in to release the horses.' He raised a hand to his scarred scalp. 'I went to the horses closest to the fire first.' He moved to his eye and a finger traced the scar. 'One horse, wearing winter-spiked shoes, kicked out.' He pulled up his left sleeve, revealing a blackened skin. 'I freed all the horses and stood outside listening to Brennun screaming as the flames took him.'

'You could not reach him in time.'

Aedan looked Daryo straight in the face. 'I could have. I could have saved Brennun first and then the horses. I let him burn.' He came around the table and Daryo stood up swiftly. Aedan stopped inches from Daryo. 'My father put Brennun in that situation, by being so permissive and by trying to make a statement in caring for an idiot son. So beware of young Tiverta, Daryo the Walker, his decisions could put all of us in danger. My father made the wrong decision but with good cause. Cadern has that same facet to his character. And beware of Aedan of Spiert. I am the man who let his brother burn. I will not hesitate to treat you the same if you fail Gourmin.'

'A useful conversation?' asked Ingit, as Daryo emerged from the tent.
'Instructive,' Daryo replied after a few moments' thought.
'The militia have been separated from the Guard. The City Guard can be easily absorbed into the rest of the army. I was going to suggest, sir, that the militia could be used for the scouting missions that you described. They are all from around Aslon and know the land and its quirks better than any soldier.'
'As you say. I need to know the numbers of the Vidmarian army, the balance between footmen, cavalry, archers and others, their organisation and how they are disposed: are they ready to attack or are they defending themselves? Have they occupied the city?'
'I understand.'
'I also want someone who is particularly knowledgeable about the north bank of the river. Preferably a fast rider.'
'Yes, sir. I will find you accommodation.'
Daryo looked around at the army. 'Does the rest of the army, the Aslon City Guard, have tents and canvas beds?'
'No.'
'Then neither do we.'
'But, Walker...'
'Marshal, if the men sleep under the stars, so do we.'

A single Gourmini scout crept through the darkness with a Batribi close behind. They scurried across the Aslon to Allesbury road and into a depression a few yards to the north side. From the lip, the city of Aslon was visible. Around it were several watch fires but not a huge number. The majority of the Vidmarian army seemed to be inside the walls.
'That is... foolish,' Daryo whispered to himself.
'Walker?'
Daryo adjusted his position. 'The whole Vidmarian army... cooped up in Aslon. Exactly what we wanted to avoid for our own men. We have to get back to the camp. We have an opportunity.'

By dawn, the Gourmini army was marching on Aslon. The Lords had all been very unhappy at being shaken awake and told to report for a conference. Aedan had been coldly disapproving, Drest and Theach surly but Ingit, Mergret and Cadern all agreed that Daryo's plan was the best course of action. The Aslon City Guard, Daryo at its head, formed the vanguard, the force from the ridge behind, with the army from Allesbury under orders to follow.

In the daylight it was clear that the Vidmarian commander had indeed occupied the town with no thought to being attacked. The gates were being repaired but the workers fled as the Gourmini army approached. Those Vidmarians outside the walls stampeded inside.

'Aslon City Guard! West Gate!' Daryo ordered, stood to the side of the road on a rock outcropping. 'Sinsebil Company, East Gate! Spiert and Tiverta Companies to the West Gate! Sitak to the East Gate! Allesbury Company to cover the south walls!'

The Gourmini Army streamed past, the lords and standard bearers stepping aside where Daryo stood. A fading and surging plume of smoke was rising from the north.

Vidmarian archers began to fire from the walls, a few Gourmini arrows responded.

'We need screens to protect our men,' Daryo told Ingit. Take a score of men from each company, they need not be complex.'

'Understood, Walker.'

'What about the river?' demanded Lord Drest, dismounting his immense black horse. 'The Vidmarians can send their men across the river and attack us from behind!'

Daryo grinned. 'Not this time, my lord. Did you notice the smoke? In the time it has taken us to advance the eight miles on foot, a section of the Batribi Company has travelled almost fifty by horse. The Batribi are now encamped on the north bank of the river and making a show of being a much larger force than it is. The Vidmarians will believe that they are encircled.'

Drest nodded in satisfaction.

'We should establish an encampment,' said Daryo. 'As many of the men should be sheltered as possible. Food and water need to brought up.'

'I will arrange that to be done,' said Cadern, with a sudden brightness. 'There are few of my men in the army, we will not be missed.'

'My thanks,' said Daryo politely.

'If the siege is established, there is no danger,' said Lord Drest with satisfaction.

'Not yet, my lord. I must go forwards and ensure that the Vidmarians are indeed secured inside Aslon. I need to see if there are natural or other features that we can make use of. The men need to be made aware of vulnerabilities on both sides, the areas of risk of

Vidmarian sallies, any weaknesses in the defences that we could exploit.' Daryo identified Marshal Ingit among the small throng. 'Marshal, can you please have the Aslon militia deployed on watch for any Vidmarian reinforcements? Concentrate on the south and west.'

'Certainly.'

On the north side of the road, the small number of Gourmini cavalry, all bearing the unmistakeable image of the Archive at Allesbury on their shields.

'Lord Mergret, your mounted men will be rather useless in a siege but they could also be a very useful patrolling force, especially towards Tiverta.'

Mergret sighed, as if Daryo's suggestion was a great imposition. 'You are the commander.'

'My thanks, Lord Mergret.' Daryo commandeered a spare horse and rode down to the siege lines.

The Gourmini soldiers had effectively surrounded Aslon. The lines of Gourmini were sheltering behind anything that they could find from the thin rain of arrows from the Vidmarians on the walls. The Vidmarians had managed to somehow erect the east gate back in place, the west gateway was barricaded with wagons, carts and furniture from houses in the city.

'My Lord Batribi!' called one soldier, the ship of Spiert on his shield. Daryo reined his horse back. 'It came to me, my lord, that if the Vidmarian army decide to leave Aslon, we are outnumbered.'

'By Dule, Scour!' swore one of his comrades. 'Say that a little louder and they might attack before midday!'

Daryo smiled. 'You are correct in a way, soldier. But they have only two narrow exits. It is easy for us to contain them in Aslon as it takes only a few men to block the gateways. The defences that they think are protecting them are also a prison.'

'Who is the force on the north bank, sir?' asked another soldier.

'My people, the Batribi.'

'Hurrah for the Batribi!'

'Hurrah!' was taken up by several around.

'Are they here to help us storm the city?' someone asked.

'They are not in enough numbers but they will prevent the Vidmarians escaping across the river.'

'When *do* we storm Aslon?'

'Not for a while. A siege serves a purpose.'

'Will the river be poisoned?'
'We are looking at options.'
'Have we catapults?'
'I am sure Lord Mergret is going to organise such things. Look to your front, watch for the enemy. Good fortune be with you.'
Daryo rode around the south of the city for a second time, sun and river of Aslon and the ship of Spiert replaced by the plain scarlet of Allesbury, then the crossed spear and spade of Sitak and the halved brown and white, split by a black bar, of the Sinsebil men. Moving like rats through a maze, men wearing the distinctive orange flame on violet of Tiverta went about their given work of provisioning and supplying. On the east side of Aslon again, Daryo took a while to study the river, at a safe distance from the city walls. It was over seventy yards wide, slightly less west of the town, and was navigable so he assumed that it was at least six feet deep. On the far bank, through the trees, was visible a group of Batribi were rapidly erecting *kaffa* and lighting fires. A few yards away, some men of the Sinsebil Company were butchering wagons to provide screens; the floor had been split in two, given legs made of the sides and then the simple defences were being carried towards the walls of Aslon. A small group were also trying to construct something of a catapult.

By sunset that day, the siege was well established. Most of the Gourmini positions had been provided with wooden screens to protect them from archers, trenches and traps were built in front of Aslon's gates and even some ramshackle shelters were materialising. The lords of Gourmin had engineered a private enclosure of their own on the ridge, nearly half a mile from the city, their well-made and luxurious tents in a small, guarded group around the black tent used for their meetings. Only Cadern lacked such comfortable quarters but he had appropriated something like a large *kaff* and a small amount of furnishings. The orange and purple standard of Tiverta was the largest of any. Daryo found some canvas to make a shelter spread between two rocky outcroppings, secured with loose stones and rocks, one end closed by his pack, the other by a damaged barrel. Daryo had filled his waterskin at the river, retrieved some bread and salt pork from his pack, and then sat on the ground on the ridge, surveying the town and the siege as the night's fires came to life around the Gourmini camp. Someone sat beside him.
'Walker.'
'Master Cadern.'
'Are you happy with the disposition of the men?'
'It is acceptable.'

'My men will camp on the west of the city, it will create a good camaraderie with the other Companies, I hope.'

'I hope so.'

Young Cadern gave an amused-sounding sigh. 'You dislike me, Walker. I can hear it in your tone.'

'I am simply tired, sir, I mean no disrespect. I have had little time to form an opinion of you or the other nobles.'

Cadern laughed. 'You say so but I know of your conversation with Lord Aedan after our first meeting. Do not be concerned, that is the way that all in the Convention of Lords operate. One must be aware of what one's rivals are doing.'

'Are you not colleagues in the leading of Gourmin?'

'I am no colleague. My father is the Lord of Tiverta.' Cadern took a long, slow breath. 'The Lords of Gourmin are all interested in their own lands and their own interests. The only common bond is that their lands are within Gourmin, that they are bound to be members of the Convened Lords and that they are each as self-interested and self-serving as the others. The reason they do not let Tiverta and Aslon fall is that they know that it will then be Allesbury, Sitak, Sinsebil and Spiert falling like young girls before a handsome squire.'

'There is no reason to think that future will be so. The Vidmarians are well contained.'

'For this day.'

'And many more. Do you doubt your men?'

'No. I doubt those of Mergret and Theach. They will not hesitate to take each of their men back to their own city if they feel the battle is lost. They will look to their own ends. Why else was Tiverta allowed to fall? When Vidmaria showed no further interest, when no other lands were threatened, Tiverta was left to its fate: fire and pillage. Even now, three thousand of my father's men and my father and brother are captives of the Vidmarians and the town of Tiverta is theirs. All our sawmills, all of our potteries, are in the town. They will all be lost.'

'I am sorry, sir. Perhaps when this business is done, the other lords will consent to the relief of Tiverta.'

'And perhaps tonight Lord Mergret will become a ravishing beauty of a girl and offer her body to me. But I have little faith in that occurrence.' He stood up. 'I will see you with the morning, Walker.'

'You shall.'

Daryo watched the young lordling disappear into the twilight and sat alone, regarding the siege, until well into the night.

The first signs of something awry came with next day. Large numbers of the Allesbury and Sinsebil Companies fell ill with severe stomach pains, a chronic flux of waste and considerable vomiting. Later in the day, the Aslon City Guard and the Spiert men were similarly affected and by the end of the day, the Sitak Company was affected as well. Only the lords and the Aslon militia seemed to be unaffected. A physician accompanied Lord Theach reluctantly visited with some of the afflicted from the Sinsebil and Aslon men. He administered a concoction to three men of the Aslon Company and not to another three but by midday, two of the men in the first group and one of the second were near death and another had driven his own dagger through his heart. The Lords of Gourmin held a quick meeting while Daryo had gone forward to take a stock of how many men were remaining. The first notice that Daryo had was a minion of Lord Drest's informing him that the lords were withdrawing immediately to Riverhelm in case the problem was contagious. Daryo had only a short tour of the siege lines to discover that the vast majority of the Gourmini were sick- perhaps eight of every ten men. There were perhaps only four or five hundred, including almost the entirety of the seven score Tiverta men, who were unaffected. Daryo had a man from each Company report to where the lords had been encamped; there was no man of the Spiert Company well enough to reach the meeting. A message had been send out and the men of the Allesbury cavalry and the Aslon militia had been recalled. With great reluctance and a sense of real embarrassment, Daryo gave the orders that the remnants of the army, all those that could move, should retreat east towards Riverhelm.

# Chapter 48

'There is something very clear to me, gentlemen,' announced Daryo, patrolling the Lords' meeting tent like a caged beast. Only two hundred and eleven men of the army, plus ninety-one Aslon militia and one hundred and twenty-two cavalry, had left Aslon and united with the main Gourmini army force just west of the village of Riverhelm. The Lords of Gourmin were encamped just south of the village.

'What is clear is that this was not accidental. The Aslon Guard had its own supplies and most ate only bread. The Allesbury Company had its own supplies and ate pork. The Sinsebil Company had its own supplies and ate pottage. The Spiert and Sitak men fished. The Tiverta men ate cheese and apples. However nearly a hundred score Gourmini are dead or near passing outside Aslon. One in seven of the Gourmini army is lost without the Vidmarians swinging a sword. We held a decisive advantage over the invader and it had been sacrificed in a mess of vomit and shit.' Daryo paused to allow his words to settle on his audience. The lords, with Marshal Ingit and Cadern and around two dozen attendants in total, sat in silence. Elderly Lord Theach shook his head sadly. 'I have been talking to as many of the men as possible, to yourselves and to as many of those we were forced to abandon as I could manage.'

'And did this lead you to any conclusion, Walker?' asked Aedan.

'It did, sir. Every man drank water from the river at some point last evening. Could this have been the source?'

'The Vidmarians could have contaminated the water,' suggested Drest.

'Indeed. But at risk of fouling their own supply. And the men of the Aslon and Spiert Companies were upstream of the city and would not have been affected. Incidentally, after talking with the physician, I believe that any contamination would have taken three or four dawns to affect men in such large numbers and, of course, the Aslon and Spiert men should have been unaffected.'

'A disease then,' said Marshal Ingit. 'Plague.'

'A plaque affecting so many so quickly? And not infecting men who slept back-to-back with those killed by it?' Daryo shook his head. 'I did entertain the theory, a plague was a possibility. But again, the speed of the action, the totality of the effect, according to the two physicians that I have found, is not consistent with any illness known to them and is too complete in its impact. Even under the most vengeful attack of a plague, some remain unaffected and there is always a small number of sick that begin the wave. The first stone of an avalanche.'

'What else could this be then?' demanded Aedan. 'Holy wrath?'

'Do not speak so lightly of such things!' warned Theach. 'The Third God may not spare you!'

'If the Pantheon is so mighty, they would not have allowed this,' retorted Aedan. 'The White Lady teaches us that disease is a thing of the world, not the will of a god.'

'You speak of what you do not understand, Aedan,' scoffed Mergret.

'And you would know of it?'

'I worship the Pantheon. I know more of what I worship than of what I do not.'

'Then you are closed and small, Mergret! A man should learn of everything around him, other faiths, other places, other peoples, not just what he finds within his own walls!'

'Closed and small? The Patron of the Archive? Find a mind and lose your mouth, Aedan!'

'A patron of knowledge but not a practitioner!'

'This gets us nowhere!' barked Daryo suddenly. The bickering silenced. 'There is only one possible cause of this... illness. Poison.'

There was uproar. Daryo sighed and waited for the noise to subside as anger, fear and scorn flowed like water around a bowl. Only Cadern remained silent amid the din. When quiet returned Daryo spoke:

'Both physicians, one of Allesbury and one from Sitak, agree that the men were poisoned. Most likely by mushroom or something akin to it.'

'An infiltrator,' said Theach wisely.

'I do not believe so,' Daryo replied. 'Think on it. The army was camped on the ridge when the men of Aslon joined it. There were no Vidmarians within a mile of Aslon when the last of the City Guard left it and a stranger in such a small group would have excited comment and questions immediately, would it not? The men of Aslon would have recognised a new face among them. The army then moved and surrounded Aslon, the Vidmarians barricading themselves in. The Companies had different supplies, different camps and were spread in an arc almost three miles across. If a Vidmarian escaped notice in the Sitak Company, would not someone in the Spiert or Allesbury Companies seen him? The food was all under guard, a spy would have been seen eventually. No guard was found dead, so the spy did not kill any guards to do his work. The spy would, of course, had to have exit the town undetected and breach a very alert siege line without being noticed.

'I spoke to nearly twenty score men outside Aslon, searching and searching for a reason for the illness and eventually it came. A man in the Allesbury Company mentioned it first and every Company, *every* Company's men corroborated what he said. Just after dark, a series of men brought broth to each and every encampment and offered it to the men retiring to sleep. Those unaffected were those at the front of the lines watching the town.'

'Broth!' exclaimed Drest. 'Poisoned!'

'Exactly, my lord.'

'Not one spy, many!' breathed Theach.

'No, sir,' said Daryo sternly. 'No spies. Traitors.'

'Traitors!?' was the universal exclamation.

Daryo nodded as he came around the table and drew the Horse from over his right shoulder. He brought the flat of the blade down on Cadern's shoulder. 'The broth was supplied by the men of the Tiverta Company.' Cadern stayed silent and Daryo continued. 'The broth was vegetable, I found some. With some large chunks of mushroom in it. Every single man who is not affected did not eat the broth. Every man who became ill took the broth. And it was made and passed out by men wearing the flame and purple badge of Tiverta, who were taking responsibility for the provisioning of the men because, how did you put it, Master Cadern? *There are few* and *will not be missed*? Not missed, well found. And found out.'

The tent was silent: shocked, stunned, beyond belief of the case put before them. Eventually Aedan stood. 'Cadern, son of Sechlann of Tiverta, do you deny the charges put to you?'

The young man's face had gone parchment white and the hand resting on the table trembled slightly. His head fell forwards and rocked from side to side in what could have been a negative response.

'Why?' asked Mergret. 'What could you possibly...' He sighed. 'Your father. The Vidmarians have him. If you hand them Gourmin, they hand back your family.'

A slight nod from Cadern.

'They would have slain your family as soon as they achieved their goal,' said Drest, almost kindly. 'You would have found yourself with naught but ash, Cadern. Naught but ash.'

Daryo caught the eye of Ingit. 'Marshal, I think it best that the Aslon Militia immediately disarm and confine the Tiverta men.'

Ingit nodded but Mergret interjected: 'I have wiser counsel. Meachm, have the First Company of the army disarm and execute the Tiverta men.'

'NO!' screamed Cadern suddenly. His cheeks were now streaked with tears. 'I gave the orders! They did only as told! I told them what to do! They only followed my orders!'

Mergret held up a hand to stop his lieutenant. 'Do you accept lord's culpability, Cadern?'

The boy sniffed and nodded sharply.

Mergret looked around the table. 'I see no alternative if the boy has taken lord's culpability for such a crime.'

'No alternative,' agreed Aedan, still standing. He drew his sword. 'Cadern, son of Sechlann, it is the verdict of the Convened Lords of Gourmin that you are guilty of the heinous crimes of treason against the Gourmini people, conspiring with the enemies of Gourmin and you have accepted lord's culpability for the actions of your men in poisoning the soldiers of Allesbury, Aslon, Sinsebil, Sitak and Spiert. For these... unforgiveable crimes, in the name of the King, you are sentenced to die at the break of the next dawn. All those that condemn bear witness to my words.'

Theach stood shakily, was handed a blade and drove it into the ground beside him. Drest drew his sword and did the same. Mergret took a deep breath, accepted a sword from his lieutenant and spiked it down. Ingit stood, took his sword and, with an air of reluctance, drove the point into the ground. Aedan raised his blade but looked at Daryo.

'Daryo the Walker, as bringer of these charges, you must also choose to condemn or to spare.'

Daryo looked around. 'I am not a lord, I am not even Gourmini.'

'Our laws are clear.'

Daryo sighed and looked down at the boy in the seat beside him. 'I pray guidance for your soul, Cadern. I truly do.' He removed the Horse from the boy's shoulder and drove the point into the ground.

Finally Aedan drove his own blade down. 'Condemned. Shurno, take him to his tent and confine him there until the time comes.'

One of Aedan's lieutenants drew his sword and went around the table to Cadern. With Daryo's help, the lord's son was pulled to his feet and the lieutenant escorted the boy from the tent. One by one, the lords resumed their seats, Cadern's now conspicuously vacant. Daryo returned to his place alongside Ingit.

'We must find one to speak for Tiverta,' said Drest, after a painfully long silence.

'No,' was Theach's immediate reply. 'We cannot trust any man of Tiverta now.'

'I agree,' said Aedan immediately.

'Capitation by Proximity,' suggested Drest.

'Aye,' said Theach. 'Capitation by Proximity. That is Mergret.'

'Not Allesbury,' said Aedan. 'Aslon.'

'Aslon is the closer,' said Mergret. 'Marshal Ingit, as representative of Aslon, by the principle of Capitation by Proximity, you now speak also for Tiverta. This is not the Council gifting you the land, this simply permits you to speak for Tiverta and command its men until a suitable man of Tiverta, or other man chosen by this Convention, is named.'

'I understand, my lord.'

'Then we should resume conduct of the war,' said Aedan. 'The Vidmarians still hold Aslon, we now have a much larger force than we have before. We could resume the siege.'

'The area around Aslon is now full of festering corpses,' said Mergret. 'We cannot occupy the same space.'

'We have a watch post still,' said Daryo. 'In case the Vidmarians leave Aslon, we have a warning.'

'Is that what they are likely to do?' Drest asked.

'I do not know,' admitted Daryo. 'I cannot know the thoughts of the Vidmarian commanders. They may choose to remain, safe, and wait for reinforcements. They may think that we are beaten and come forwards to complete their victory.'

'What would you do?'

Daryo thought. 'I would consolidate my position, strengthen Aslon and send for aid from Vidmaria so that the rest of Gourmin could be taken with overwhelming force.'

'We have near to eight thousand men here,' said Mergret. 'We could take Aslon.'

'We still are outnumbered by the Vidmarians,' said Daryo. 'Storming Aslon may not be successful.'

'What is our commander's decision?' asked Drest, not entirely sarcastically.

'Renew the siege, but at a greater distance,' replied Daryo. 'The dead around the walls may even work in our favour, they may cause disease among the Vidmarians. If reinforcements arrive from Vidmaria, we would be in a position to strike. If they do not, the siege will be effective. The only complication is that provision will have to be made for the people of Aslon at the Five Towers.'

'That can be arranged.' Aedan looked around. 'Equal shares from each. Any other matters that must be addressed? Then we adjourn until just before dawn. A man of each city?'

'Two,' said Theach.

'Two from each. Crossbows.'

One of Aedan's men woke Daryo well before sunrise and Daryo dressed quickly, before being led out to a small copse just to the east of Riverhelm. Nearly three hundred men were in ranks making three sides of a square, the copse forming the fourth side and the lords in the centre. Daryo noticed that on one side were the Tiverta men, all bound by the wrists and guarded by Allesbury men. On the opposite side a cluster of ten men, each with a crossbow, were waiting. Shortly, a group of Spiert men arrived with young Cadern at the centre, dressed only in a long black shirt. He was half-led, half-dragged to the closest tree of the copse and tied with his back against it. Aedan drew his sword.

'Cadern, son of Sechlann, you have been found guilty of treason and conspiring with the enemies of Gourmin. You have also accepted lord's culpability for the actions of your men in poisoning the army of Gourmin.' Aedan turned to the captive Tiverta men and addressed them. 'You are all guilty of this crime. Your lord has admitted culpability for your actions and thus your lives will be spared. But you will be branded as guilty and you will be exiled from Gourmin. Any man of you found within Gourmin within eight days will be liable to execution.'

He looked across at the crossbowmen. 'Take position.'

The crossbowmen came out into a line in front of the trees and turned to face the bound Cadern about thirty yards away. A young woman, wearing a white dress, followed the crossbowmen, a priestess of the White Lady. She went to Cadern's side and whispered some words in his ear. The boy shook his head and struggled but the woman continued with her words of conciliation. When she was finished, she moved quickly aside.

'Cadern, son of Sechlann!' declaimed Aedan. 'Your crimes have only one just and reasonable punishment. In the name of the King, I declare that your life is forfeit. Do you have anything to say?'

The lord's son simply sobbed and struggled against his bonds.

'May whatever faith or belief you hold be of comfort to you now,' Aedan continued. 'If it pleases, let them forgive your crimes. Ready.'

The crossbowmen checked their weapons and placed bolts in the slots.

'Aim.'

The crossbows were lifted, ten steel bolts aimed at the still-struggling figure against the tree.

'Loose.'

There was a quiet click as the bolts were released and a wet thud as the bolts all found the young man's torso. The body stiffened and then slumped in its bonds. One of Mergret's lieutenants went forwards and drew a knife across the throat to confirm that the young man was dead. The lieutenant looked back at the lords, inclined his head and began to cut the body free.

'Let it be known by all of Gourmin!' barked Aedan. 'Those who betray their countrymen and allies will die in the name of the King!'

The Gourmini ranks shouted in unison. 'The King!'

Daryo had returned to the camp to order preparations for the renewed siege of Aslon. He had packed his bedroll and shelter and was heading towards the lords' encampment when a rider arrived in the uniform of the Aslon militia.
'Walker! Walker! The army is advancing!'
'It should not be yet,' said Daryo, confused. 'I have not given any orders.'
'No, sir! The Vidmarian army! They are leaving Aslon! Advancing towards us!'
The realisation hit Daryo. 'Sound the alarm.'

In the time it took the Vidmarian army to leave Aslon and organise, the Gourmini army was able to reach the ford across the Docus River. It was fast and fairly narrow, the road crossed at a well-established ford that was only inches below the surface but the water either side of the ford was several feet deep. Daryo had the Gourmini infantry divided into three units, placing one blocking the road on the east of the ford, flanked by the other two, with the archers behind and the cavalry in reserve. The lords of Gourmin established their position on the high ground further to the east overlooking the ford. By midday, the outnumbering Vidmarians on the west bank also had three battalions assembling although Daryo could see no sign of cavalry or archers.
'I do not understand,' he said to Ingit. 'Why do this?'
'Perhaps they are too confident,' said Ingit. 'Or it may be a trap. Did you get the messenger to the Batribi?'
'I did. The Batribi company will be sending scouts into Aslon already. I think there is something at work here that we have not seen.' Daryo looked southwards. 'Are the militia out?'
'Yes, Walker. They will sound the alarm if we are being outflanked.'
'You have the instructions that I gave you?'
Ingit brought out a scroll from under his robe. 'I do. Ensure that the Vidmarians attack and I can follow your instructions from there.'
'I will be in the main battalion.'
'Lord Aedan has insisted on leading the cavalry.'
'Acceptable. Ensure the remaining lords stay back on the high ground. A captured Gourmini lord could create more... trouble.'
'I understand. Good fortune, Walker.'
'And to you, Marshal.'

Daryo left Ingit on the high ground behind the Gourmini positions and hurried down the road to where the Gourmini army had formed up. He hurried through the ranks of archers just as the Vidmarian advance began and the hurry became a run. The Gourmin were all equipped with oval shields, nearly five feet long but only two feet wide in the centre, and spears with conical points almost eight inches long with broad daggers on their belts. Daryo raced through to the forward ranks, shield on his arm, and drew Temma's Sword. A Gourmini trumpeter came alongside him.

'Ready, sir.'

Daryo nodded. 'Hold fast.'

The trumpeter blew three long blasts as the lead Vidmarians splashed into the ford. The Gourmini ranks shifted slightly, nervously, spears were levelled.

'Again!' Daryo ordered.

Three more long blasts to signal the Gourmini ranks to hold. Daryo raised his shield and the first lines collided, Vidmarian leaf-bladed spears and long swords, Gourmini narrow shields and narrow-tipped spears, wood, leather, iron, flesh and bone. The shouts and roars of men added to the crash of weapons and bodies. Daryo was five rows from the front of the Gourmini defenders. A Vidmarian crashed through the front ranks right before Daryo. He staggered and was unable to defend himself against Temma's Sword. The Vidmarian assault was dangerously fierce. A second battalion of Vidmarians joined the fray, pushing against the Gourmini defenders.

'Archers!' bellowed Daryo.

The trumpeter blew a single long note. The Gourmini archers, behind the main battalion, began firing over their comrades' heads into the Vidmarian attackers. Another unit of Vidmarians were joining the attack, an almost overwhelming force. Daryo found himself suddenly in the midst of the fighting. The Vidmarians were mostly wielding spears but they all had swords as well. There was a real sense of anxiety and desperation in the vicious attacks of the Vidmarians, each man seemed to be fighting as if there was no other path, battle or death. Many were impaled on Gourmini spears, cut down by Gourmini daggers and several were slashed open by the curved sword of the Batribi at the centre. The second Gourmini battalion was coming to the aid of the first. The third, Daryo saw briefly, was engaged on the right as yet another Vidmarian force tried to wade the river further downstream from the ford, where a cluster of small islets had been formed in midstream.

Daryo caught another thrusting spear with his shield, stepped forwards hard to push the spear down and away before spinning left, using the sharpened inside of Temma's Sword to hack into the Vidmarian's neck. Daryo pulled his blade free and parried a sword thrust, knocking the assailant sideways into the Gourmini soldier next to him. The young trumpeter's dagger slashed the Vidmarian's throat and in the next breath the boy was blowing the 'hold fast' signal.

The third trumpet seemed to panic the waiting cavalry. In a rush of hooves and shouts, the Gourmini mounted soldiers were suddenly galloping south, behind their infantry and away from the battle, followed by abuse from some of the Gourmini at the rear of the formation. The Vidmarian assault continued across the ford. The soldiers that had crossed downstream were being held by the third Gourmini battalion but even with two units, they were struggling to hold back the waves of Vidmarian attacks. Daryo had been fighting on the very edge of the river but found himself almost twenty feet back from the ford. Fighting just feet from him was the young trumpeter, struggling to defend himself with dagger and trumpet. Daryo tried to keep him close but the force of the Vidmarian attacks continued and he found himself driven back by the numbers. The trumpeter was run through by a spear. Daryo allowed his focus to wander for but a heartbeat and received a vicious hit in the back. A Vidmarian spear had struck one of the steel plates in his jerkin. Daryo spun and Temma's Sword lodged in the spear's shaft. He shouldered the wielder aside, freed his blade, cut down a Vidmarian to his right and then the one that had struck him.

'Retreat!' came a cry. 'Surrounded! Retreat!'

The shout raised from the Vidmarian ranks with increasing urgency. Daryo shoved the nearest Vidmarian in the side, cut across the man's knees and then his neck as he fell. The Vidmarians were in retreat and Daryo found he had a few yards of space. On the far side of the river, the Gourmini cavalry, guided by some of the Aslon militia from the area, had crossed a second, unmarked ford a mile upstream and attacked the Vidmarian commanders behind the main force before falling on the group trying to cross upstream of the main ford. The Vidmarians were now fleeing in disarray, harassed by the Gourmini cavalry. Daryo sent a soldier back to the archers to stop the Gourmini firing on their own men and found a man that could use the trumpet to sound an advance. The Gourmini began to advance across the ford, stepping over the dead and wounded of both sides, the larger Vidmarian force already scattered and beyond resistance as the Gourmini mounted men caused further chaos and death. A group had already broken off, with orders to retake Aslon. A few Vidmarian stragglers were resisting but they were soon overwhelmed by the exultant Gourmini. A much larger force was running before them and the Gourmini pursuit was tireless and bloodthirsty.

Within three days, the people of Aslon were back in their town. Houses had been ransacked, anything moveable either taken or destroyed, the temple desecrated by apparently having been used as a latrine. The Tower of the White Lady had been used as a dormitory by Vidmarian soldiers. The Batribi detachment, only thirty of the Company, had crossed the river as soon as possible with instructions from Dostan to start making the temple and tower serviceable quickly. The Aslon militia had immediately posted a watch on the wall and the city's banners had been hung in as many places as possible. With the town in such disarray, including a still-smouldering bonfire of furniture in the market area, the Gourmini lords held council in their tent outside the walls.

'The cavalry have followed their quarry back to Tiverta,' said Aedan. 'There is a small garrison of the town but the main force is that of the army routed from the ford. Lord Drest, you were talking with the Vidmarian commander that was captured?'

Drest nodded. 'A man who gave his name as Thery Merthelon. He is a fairly junior officer but was an aide of the commander, who was killed. He says that they left Aslon because the commander, not an experienced man, a lord in the position by patronage, believed that our army was smaller and could be easily defeated. When the cavalry struck their rear, the commander panicked and ordered a retreat.'

'The commander of Tiverta?'

'He professed not to know; that the previous commander, a former Member of the Order of the Shield and Sword-' Drest's eyes flicked to Daryo '-was removed from the post and a new man sent from Vidmaria.'

'And where is the old commander?' asked Daryo.

'I did not ask but can try to ascertain that.'

'My thanks.'

'Then it remains that we must decide what is to be done next,' Theach croaked, thumping the table.

'We should push on,' Drest suggested.

'Push forwards and take the rest of our lands back,' Ingit agreed.

'Next we must attack Tiverta,' said Aedan.

Theach nodded. 'I concur.'

'Aye,' said Ingit.

'Aye.' Drest.

'Aye.' Mergret. 'Daryo the Walker, we appreciate that the purpose for which you were called is fulfilled. However, Gourmin is still in danger as long as the Vidmarians hold Tiverta.'

'What price would you ask to assist us in retaking Tiverta?' asked Theach.

'I would ask nothing for myself, sir,' Daryo replied. 'However, my people are still a young country and seeking trade and allies. Your cooperation and understanding with our people, a representative to our settlement, would be gratefully received.'

Aedan nodded. 'I think that is acceptable. A permanent Batribi envoy would also be welcomed.'

'I am to meet my brother later, he can have that arranged by our Assembly of Clan Leaders. Does the council wish me to remain as commander?'

Aedan looked around and received affirmative signals. 'It does.'

'Are reinforcements available? A larger number of men may be needed to mount a proper siege, as well as machines: catapults, rams, the like.'

'Such things are being brought from Allesbury,' confirmed Mergret. 'There is not much more manpower to draw on but that is also coming. Perhaps six thousand. A significant force is needed in the east on the Armynyan frontier.'

'I understand. I think that the men available should be moved forwards quickly. I do not know Tiverta well. Is it easily defended?'

There were a few chuckles from the assistants and lieutenants around the table.

'You do not know Tiverta at all?' confirmed Ingit.

'Not at all.'

'Perhaps you should ride forwards soon, Walker,' said Drest. 'You have much to learn. The best way for you to learn of Tiverta is to see it with your own eyes and to make your own decisions.'

'I will do so. I may be able to go this day, my brother will ride with me.'

## Chapter 49

As well as Dostan, Daryo was joined by a dozen members of the Batribi Company's detachment, who chose to remain and assist while the rest returned to Stannia Lake. The road southwards towards Tiverta was little more than a track, rough and rocky and the horses were forced down to a walk after less than five miles.

'This road is... eventful,' said Dostan as his Gourmini horse negotiated a sharp slope to join Daryo at the bottom.

'Appalling,' replied Daryo, encouraging his horse onwards.

'I was being charitable. How far is Tiverta?'

'Almost fifty miles.'

'At this speed, it will be dark before we arrive.'

'By then, we should reach the Gourmini cavalry encampment. They are in sight of Tiverta from some high ground to the north and west.'

'Did the Convened Lords say how close behind us the army would be?'

'The army is leaving Aslon this day. The rest should reach Aslon by next day but may require some organisation before they follow.'

'And if the Vidmarians attack again?'

'Then they will find the Gourmini army coming to meet them. Would you wish to be attacking over this ground?'

'I can think of better.'

'The lords' opinion also.'

'And yours?'

'And mine.'

'What do you know of Tiverta?'

'I am concerned; all that anyone would tell me is that the town is easily defended. A militiaman from Aslon also told me that there is no road out of Tiverta except this one. The road ends in Tiverta.'

'So the Vidmarians came across country?'

'Or built their own road. There must be a passage through from Tiverta southwards towards the Dithithindil.'

Dostan nodded. 'If the Jaboens would agree, we could perhaps send a small force to investigate, it might be a passageway that could be blocked.'

'Perhaps.'

The path crossed a stream via a rocky ford and started to slope downwards steadily towards a cleft in the increasingly high peaks to either side. To one side of the path on a small piece of flat ground was a small campsite, four of the Aslon militia around a small campfire, a horse ready to speed a messenger back to the town if the Vidmarians advanced. By the middle of the day, the sun was starting to be uncomfortably warm. The Batribi stopped and many removed one or two layers of clothing before they continued. The road continued to descend into the valley with the hills on either side becoming mountains, grey-topped and sheer-sided.

The Gourmini cavalry detachment of ten score men and their horses were encamped in front of a sharp rise in the ground. At the top, a watchpost was looking towards Tiverta. The Batribi had brought a pair of *kaffa* and got to erecting them before the darkness became total while Daryo sought out the cavalry commander, a nephew of Lord Theach's. When Daryo questioned him about the defences, he simply said that the defences were strong and were easier examined than explained. The Batribi *kaffa* were soon set up on the edge of the cavalry camp and, with some quick foraging, the dozen Batribi soldiers had a substantial fire burning between the doors of the two canvas shelters and the horses tethered nearby. They found various items to sit on, some simply folded their blankets. A few rabbits had been shot on the route and Dostan rigged a spit to roast them over the fire.

'In a straight line, we not far from the lake,' said one of the women. 'If we could cross the mountains, over the top.'

'Throw a stone, try and hit my brother,' suggested another and the other Batribi chuckled.

'And I thought that the kin of Camma were the most united clan of all, Jayini' said Dostan.

'If we were the only clan left, we would be!' This raised a louder laugh.

'Is it not the kin of Dostan?' one of the soldiers asked.

'I cannot stand even the sight of my clan leader,' said Daryo, his tone flat.

'Or his brother,' added Dostan.

The Batribi all laughed.

'Kin of Camma? Is a kinsman of yours the smith?' asked Daryo.

The woman, Jayini, of about Dostan's age, nodded. 'Camma is my father's sister. Her husband is the smith. Your brother works with the Jaboen court.'

'Laulra, yes he does.'

'He negotiated the purchase of the sheep, which most of my clan care for.' She indicated her rather-rigid padded jacket. 'Stuffed with our sheep's wool.'

'It looks good work,' said Dostan, leaning over for a closer inspection.

'It is a good design. The wool is very densely packed inside making it almost as armour.'
'Very good.'
The rabbits cooked, Dostan removed them from the spit, chopped them into sections and handed the pieces around. Most of the Batribi had bread and other items brought from Aslon and the elements all combined made a good meal shared between the fourteen Batribi. A large jar of ale was passed around. Some of the more high-spirited Gourmini soldiers were singing the bawdy and ribald songs typical of soldiers.
'Such poor songs,' said one of the Batribi. He began slapping one fist into the open palm of his other hand. Soon the other Batribi were keeping the same rhythm.

*'Our people walk and walk again,*
*This fate of ours is each one's bane,*
*To sleep beneath the stars each night,*
*To walk and walk again in flight.'*

Dostan spoke: *'We ride to war as kinsmen bound,*
*Our swords and spears in Gourmin found,*
*Our blades are sharp, our minds are keen,*
*We wait for battle under the white moon's sheen.'*

*'Our people walk and walk again,*
*This fate of ours is each one's bane,*
*To sleep beneath the stars each night,*
*To walk and walk again in flight.'*

'No wolves of hair seek this place,' said a woman.
*'But wolves of Vidmar' will show their face,*
*Do we fear the fight, the task ahead?*
*We do not fear, wolves can be bled!'*

There was a chuckle as the next chorus began.

*'Our people walk and walk again,*
*This fate of ours is each one's bane,*
*To sleep beneath the stars each night,*
*To walk and walk again in flight.'*

Daryo contributed: *'The Darkest One is near us now,*
*To her laws even kings must bow,*
*Pain and death are always at war,*
*We take them to Tiverta just one time more.'*

*'Our people walk and walk again,*
*This fate of ours is each one's bane,*

*To sleep beneath the stars each night,*
*To walk and walk again in flight.'*
One of the older men of the group:
*'Our kaffa decay, the houses grow,*
*The ways we had are the ones we know,*
*Our paths must change as sand and sea,*
*The Batribi path is long and free.'*
*'Our people walk and walk again,*
*This fate of ours is each one's bane,*
*To sleep beneath the stars each night,*
*To walk and walk again in flight.'*
The Verse faded as the Batribi began to retire to sleep. In a short time, only Daryo was sat in front of the fire.

'Darkest Goddess, bringer of death, cruellest of tricksters, strength behind my sword and fortitude in my heart, I sit among my kin and comrades before another battle. I have faced this foe before and seen allies killed by them, taken injury at their hands, killed these enemies with my own weapons. In battle, you have always spared my life at the expense of others. I know that in my future I must pay for this account but I beseech you, Darkest Goddess, to add this to my debt to you. I ask that you spare my life and those of my brother and my people and accept those of the enemy that we send to you. I know that I am fated to join you as all men are. I ask only that you do not claim my life in this battle.'

'Daryo. Daryo!'
Daryo yawned hugely as he awoke. 'Dos...Dostan?'
'Yes, come, the sun is up. There is something that you should see.'
Daryo struggled out of his bedroll and groped for his boots. The morning was painfully cold and Daryo wrapped himself in his cloak before ducking out of the little *kaff*. The Gourmini were beginning to rouse themselves, going to tend to their horses. The Batribi were almost all up and at work. Dostan led the way up the sharp incline towards the watchpost at the top. The sun had risen fully but was giving little warmth. At the rise, the Tiverta valley was spread out illuminated by the fresh sun.
Daryo moaned slightly. 'The Fourth Goddess did *not* listen last night.'
Tiverta was built alongside a small, clear lake, surrounded by a wall that looked to be at least seventy feet high, studded with round towers with a huge gatehouse and immense

tower in the south-west. A moat surrounded the east of the town, the lake ran the length of the southern wall and a dry but deep ditch protected the northern and western half. The towers were topped with large catapults, the walls were bristling with men and the gatehouse had a large, ominous fire burning on the roof. Halfway between the ridge and the town, an angular tower stood guard beside the road, with dozens of arrow loops at every level.

'Not the simplest task,' said Dostan quietly.

'We have to take the tower first and, while doing that, we will be in range of the gatehouse.'

Dostan nodded. 'Without doubt.'

A sigh in response. 'Do you ever feel as if you are being tested, brother?'

'Sometimes, yes I do.'

A short, strongly-built man strode up the ridge. Over brown leggings and a green shirt he had on a chainmail vest and bracers on his arms similar to Daryo's. They had met the previous evening, he was Cahn, the cavalry commander.

'I think my men will not be of much use,' he said ruefully. 'Tiverta is a citadel. The Great Tower has never been breached, not in fifteen generations. The gatehouse is a fortress in its own right. The Triangle Tower covers the whole road from the bottom of the slope to the gatehouse. There could be thirteen or even fifteen thousand Gourmini in the town. And a population of maybe ten thousand, mostly women and children.'

'This will be difficult,' said Daryo. 'If we try to starve the garrison, we starve the people of Tiverta as well. Any assault could cause death to the people. And if we do break through, there are hundreds of hostages that could be slaughtered.'

'If only we had a battle in open field,' said Cahn, slightly sadly. 'A wide plain, some high ground to defend or attack, maybe a watercourse...'

'Much more suited to a cavalry commander,' agreed Dostan.

'And my men.'

'Surely there will be tasks that you can perform?'

'Picket duty, carrying messages, perhaps bringing up water for the men on the ram.'

'There must be another path,' said Daryo. 'How else did the Vidmarians bring up so many troops? They must have a passage to the south and west, a road, a pass, there must be something.'

'Perhaps the cavalry could investigate when the siege is established,' suggested Dostan.

'I was thinking the same, brother.'

Cahn nodded. 'That sounds a... productive operation. It would stave off the boredom of messenger duty.'

Daryo shook his head. 'We will have to wait for darkness again before making a closer inspection of the defences.'
'I have a farrier from the town, I will send him to you as soon as possible. There may be a detail that he knows that an investigation in the dark from outside the walls will not reveal.'

The farrier, Fealean, was not of much use. He seemed to be unhappy with being interrogated, in his words, by two Batribi and insisted that he knew little of the town's defences: entrances other than the gate, he knew not; openings on to the lake, he knew none; the location of barracks or similar, he could not recall; the lowest point of the walls, not something he had ever examined; the likely places for a defensive stand, he claimed to be no soldier. He then immediately excused himself and returned to his work.

Just over ten thousand Gourmini soldiers congregated against the ridge at the head of the Tiverta basin like water behind a dam within a day. The major obstacle to their progress was the triangular-shaped tower. A Gourmini force that tried to storm down to the gatehouse of the town were so badly assaulted by arrows, bolts and rocks from the tower that they withdrew in chaos. The Vidmarians were apparently trying to construct a catapult on the roof of the tower but progress appeared slow, hampered by the location and, it was assumed, a lack of materials. Tiverta's gatehouse had a pair of catapults that occasionally fired in the direction of the Gourmini on and behind the ridge but the range, about five hundred yards, was a little long. Only a few missiles even got close to the ridge and one even came within a foot of striking the tower. The tower itself was more of a problem for the Gourmini, at least the few that manned the ridge, as the crossbows and longbows of the tower were within a long range and a harassing fire came at irregular intervals, necessitating the construction of screens with some urgency. With the rear-guard and the siege engines, three days after Daryo's arrival, came a message from the Convened Lords of Gourmin, entrusting the action at Tiverta to their nominated and elected commander: Daryo the Walker.

# Chapter 50

'Walker, this is Kandecov, the Armynyan miner I told you of.'

'My thanks, Jayini.'

Daryo had been observing Tiverta from behind one of the screens on the ridge. He stepped down and sat on a log, positioned there for specifically that purpose. 'Kandecov, sit down.'

The big man did so, he was tall but stooped, almost hunchbacked, with a balding head and a thicket of a beard. 'Batribi, you are leader?'

'I am. Jayini said that you have a way of breaking into the town.'

'Yes. I work in mine. We have big rocks. Break with fire.'

'Fire?'

'Put fire with big rock. Hit with hammer. Rock cracks.'

'And you think this would work against Tiverta's walls?'

'Work on rock in mine, will work on rock in wall. All rock from same place.'

'My thanks, Kandecov. If this works, I will ensure that the Lords of Gourmin reward you.'

Daryo called together his key lieutenants on the ridge: Dostan, Cahn of the cavalry, Ruprect and Menrad of the infantry, Luitiger of the siege battery. He outlined the principle of Kandecov's methods.

Menrad nodded. 'I know of the principle, my lord. It is practical.'

Daryo smiled. 'I am no lord, Menrad.'

'I am sorry. Walker. My family is from Sinsebil, there are many mines and quarries. A fire, if stoked to sufficient heat, will either crack rock or leave the rock vulnerable to breaking.'

'Then we must get to the foot of the town wall,' said Dostan. 'To do that, the tower must be taken, brother.'

'Not necessarily,' Daryo replied. 'Commander Cahn?'

The cavalry commander nodded. 'In the past two days I have had mounted scouts get to the other side of Tiverta. We have found the Vidmarian's road on the other side of the town, there is a narrow, forested path that the Vidmarians have begun to lay with stone but the road is deserted. The soldiers must all have been brought up to defend Tiverta. If the scouts have got through, we believe that foot-soldiers could also sneak past Tiverta. They could then establish a mine on the west of the town while we lay siege on this side. When the tower is taken, a second mine, and a third, and however many others we desire can be dug.'

Daryo nodded. 'I think this a sound plan.' He looked around the others and received affirmatives. 'Menrad, you will lead four hundred. Ensure that at least a third have some knowledge of quarrying or mining and give Kandecov, the Armynyan, a position of leadership. The rest will be there to defend them. Cahn, send the majority of your men too, they will ensure the road from Vidmaria is blocked. I want them ready to leave at sunset, as soon as it is dark, you have my authorisation to depart.'

'Yes, Walker.'

'Luitiger, bring up all your weapons. Ignore Tiverta, focus on the tower. I want to breach those walls as soon as possible.'

'At once, Walker.'

'Dostan, half of our people should go with Menrad, would you lead them? I will keep the rest here.'

'Certainly, brother.'

'If the Vidmarians try to flee Tiverta, make a show of resisting, then allow them past. If reinforcements from Vidmaria come, send a message and hold them as long as possible. Gods' Guidance to you all.'

By midday, the six Gourmini catapults had been dragged to the ridge and were gradually finding the range of the tower, their stones beginning to strike their target as those in command of the great machines calculated the range and angles. The thrown rocks were the chip of the sculptor's chisel on the triangular tower's walls. The majority struck the near-flat wall facing the ridge, the larger boulders causing the whole structure to quake. For nearly eight days the rhythm was established: as soon as there was light to aim by, the catapults were loaded and then the clunk and crash of the firing trebuchets. Just after sundown, the firing stopped, followed by a messenger from the west of the city and the mining party. The Vidmarian defences continued to fire back at the Gourmini on the ridge but the range was extreme from the walls to the ridge and only a few missiles came close, causing only a few injuries to Gourmini soldiers and slightly damaging one of the Gourmini catapults. The half-built Vidmarian catapult on the top of the tower was smashed when the damaged catapult released its shot as it was hit for a second time.

Just before sunset on the ninth day, the evening's ritual was performed: the commanders assembled on the ridge as the Gourmini catapults, reduced to five with one damaged, were loaded and then fired in unison. Two shots clipped the ramparts, sending Vidmarian soldiers running for cover, one struck about ten feet from the top, the other two hit about ten feet from the ground. The tower shook and a massive crack appeared, splitting the wall.

Daryo and the commanders looked at each other in eagerness. Unbidden, Commander Ruprect hurried down to ready the infantry.

'Reload!' ordered Luitiger. 'Reload! Quickly! Same shot!'

The men around each catapult, around seven to each, were quickly in action. One man at each weapon was entrusted with choosing the missiles, a difficult skill to learn and a difficult technique. Each one had a simple balance and a master stone and each shot was weighed against the master stone. Shortly all five catapults were loaded. A scarlet banner was held aloft and then lowered quickly. On that signal, the five trebuchets fired. A shot again struck the top of the tower, one sailed over the tower and missed entirely, one hit near the base but the remaining two struck near the large crack in the wall. Several chunks and flakes of the tower wall rained down.

'One more!' Luitiger bellowed. 'Quickly! Quickly!'

The men were a step ahead and all but one loader were already weighing shot as the catapults were reset. As soon as they were ready, the shot were loaded, the red flag raised and lowered and the missiles let loose. Two shots missed, one hit the base of the crack, one to the side and one hit almost in the centre. The crack became a canyon and the side of the tower began to collapse, the canyon becoming a cave.

'Ladders!' roared Luitiger. 'Ladders! Gourmin to arms!'

Daryo peered excitedly into the gathering darkness at the tower. The tower had a gap in the walls, ten feet above the ground and nearly twenty feet wide over at least three floor levels. The Gourmini infantry were hurrying up and forming lines, siege ladders being passed forwards. With a deafening roar, the remainder of the side wall of the tower collapsed. Daryo kept himself prepared for battle every day, he had his twin swords on his back even if nothing else. He drew them quickly and inverted the Bear by habit. Over a thousand Gourmini soldiers were already massing on and behind the ridge. A pair of trumpeters appeared.

'Advance.'

The advance was sounded but it was no advance, it swiftly became a charge. Daryo started at the front but bloodthirsty and angry Gourmini soldiers, attacking the invaders of their land, were soon pounding past him down the three hundred yard slope to the critically-damaged tower. The Vidmarian defenders were overwhelmed, outnumbered and shocked at their sudden reversal of fortune; from being safe behind stone walls to being exposed and attacked from the ridge. The defence of the tower was its walls and one was gone. The Vidmarians barely resisted, a dozen were killed and the remaining surrendered. The Vidmarian black and gold wolf banner was cut down and a Gourmini hawk replaced it as the light faded to night.

'Have the rest of the infantry moved up!' Daryo bellowed as suitable messengers appeared. 'Ensure the town is surrounded! Catapults up to fire on the gatehouse! Send a message to Commander Cahn! Siege tower forwards to the ridge! Ram up with the catapults! Archers to congregate behind this tower!'

Lit by torches and lanterns, the Gourmini army swarmed into predesigned places around the town, the five smaller towers each had a watching force, a larger one for the gatehouse, the archers behind the ruined Triangular Tower, the catapults were pushed forwards alongside by teams of up to three score men and a dozen oxen. Behind them, two almost-built siege towers were trundled forwards, then the simplest of the battering rams, a single trunk of a pine with ropes around it to facilitate carrying. A second, with a cover and wheels, was being constructed behind the ridge. More mining teams were being formed and they would be put to work as soon as possible. A few barrages of fire arrows were sent over by the Gourmini archers and soon a counter-fire from Vidmarian archers were directed at the encircling Gourmini. Many of the Batribi were good bowmen and found weapons to join in the archery, the rest leant their shoulders to moving the catapults and siege towers. Daryo sent instructions for Dostan and Cahn to join him at daybreak at the Triangular Tower and for a full report from the cavalry pickets on the Vidmarian road on any activity or any signs of reinforcements for the Vidmarians. He then hurried forwards towards the gatehouse to inspect the Gourmini positions.

Dostan and Cahn did not appear at dawn the next day, Summer's First. Ruprect sent a messenger, who did not return, Daryo was fearing the worst when finally all three appeared, filthy and wet.

'The mine flooded,' panted Dostan. 'The walls crumbled and water rushed in. We were trying to get the men out. Three got out but six were drowned before we could get to them. There are two missing but they must have died by this time.'

'Fourth Goddess guide them. Kandecov?'

'Was sleeping at the time.'

'The mine was too close to the lake, Walker,' said Cahn. 'We will need to dig on the north of the town.'

Daryo nodded sadly. 'I will give the order. You both should rest, you look exhausted.'

For the rest of the day, the catapults exchanged shots. All of the catapults on the towers of Tiverta were now in range of the Gourmini ones, and likewise the Gourmini catapults could hit most of the town. The Gourmini archers had spread around the town and were concentrating on the defenders on the ramparts. Mines began to be dug, one by the northernmost tower, one to the west of it and one by the gatehouse behind the cover of the largest arrow screen. A shield had been improvised for the ram, two wagons tied together upside-down and then the wheels mounted on the bottom. It allowed five men on each side to shelter underneath and work the ram and it was put to work on the gates under a hail of arrows from above. In the middle of the afternoon one of the Vidmarian trebuchets hit the ruined Triangular Tower and showered masonry on the Gourmini catapults, damaging one and necessitating it being withdrawn to behind the ridge for repairs.

With sunset, the first siege tower was wheeled forwards, first by oxen and then pushed forwards by over three hundred men to the left edge of the gatehouse. The tower was nearly a hundred feet high, protected on three sides by nets and screens with ladders inside up to the top. From the summit platform, a hinged bridge was dropped down to the gatehouse and the Gourmini army, led by Captain Menrad and four Batribi, surged onto the roof of the gatehouse. The response by the Vidmarians was barely credible- all the catapults began firing flaming pots at the tower, even at the expense of killing their comrades on the gatehouse. The Gourmini were valiant and more men climbed the ladders even as the structure began to burn. By midnight, the siege tower was ablaze and Daryo gave strict orders that nobody be allowed to try to climb it again. By dawn, the inferno had collapsed into a pile of smoking, ruined, charred timber. Over twelve score Gourmini had been killed in the attack. The mines continued, although the catapults of the gatehouse had changed their aim, apparently trying to hit the westernmost of the excavations and the most exposed of the three. Daryo climbed the second siege tower around midday for a better view of the town. With a clear day and a bright sun, the whole town was visible from the incomplete tower on the ridge. A small river running through the town looked like a ribbon of silver in the sunlight. Just beyond the shadow of the Great Tower was a well-appointed, fortified grand house that was undoubtedly the former home of the lord of Tiverta. Two domed buildings were Temples of the Pantheon, Daryo thought that he could see a large anvil outside the larger one. Three other buildings, one close to the manor house, could have been chapels of the White Lady. Groups of soldiers moved in the streets, there was not a townsperson in sight.

The following day, Daryo ordered a halt to all offensive operations but for the excavations. The two damaged catapults were given more attention, the larger second covered ram was finished. He received a messenger from the Convened Lords but all he was told was that an official dispatch was due as soon as the Lords had agreed a text and it took another two days to arrive.

*From the Convened Lords of Gourmin met at Aslon*
*To Daryo the Walker, nominated Commander of the Armies of Gourmin*
*Written the Fourth Day of Summer*

*Sir, it is requested and required of you in the name of the King to bring the siege of Tiverta to a conclusion with all haste. The Convened Lords accede that Tiverta is a well-defended and highly difficult to assault however the city must be taken as soon as possible. The resources and numbers of men that we can send to reinforce your army are limited and this may hamper your efforts. If this is so, delay is appreciable and acceptable to this Council. Should you require more forage, provisions, men or weaponry, any request will be given due consideration and all measures that can be taken to assist you will be implemented with all despatch.*
*Signed, for and on behalf of the King of Gourmin,*
*Mergret, Lord of Allesbury,*
*Drest, Lord of Sitak*
*Theach, Lord of Sinsebil*
*Aedan, Lord of Spiert*
*Ingit, Marshal of Aslon and Capitate of Tiverta by Order*

Dostan found the text humorous. 'They say that no reinforcements are available but they will send anything you need, and that the siege should be ended soon but any delay is acceptable!'
'I thought that also. Everything and anything that the Lords of Gourmin do seems to be confused and conflicted. They are more interested in their own means than in the common victory and so squabble over petty issues. Sometimes I believe that they do so simply for the sake of the argument. It is almost a point of pride to disagree with your neighbour. I cannot see how any place could possibly be run successfully in such a way, and yet they do so.'
'At least most of the Clan Assembly can appreciate when a suggestion is in the interests of the town as a whole. There may be squabbles and disagreements but the good of all is what the Assembly puts first.'
'Oh, I believe the lords do so, but that does not stop them from arguing the point anyway.'
'What a way to rule a country!'

'Precisely. But even that is a façade of sorts. Everything done in the name of the non-existent King! They act in the name of a man who does not exist and that is because they cannot agree on who it should be.'

'It does not suit them to choose a king. They would lose their power. Few men would ever choose to relinquish power, especially the amount of control the Lords of Gourmin have.'

'Perhaps. But is not Jaboen an example of a king holding little power and the nation being run by its lords?'

Dostan nodded thoughtfully. 'Gourmin has always been a strange nation. Where else could an Armynyan miner, a Batribi wanderer and the Fourth God's guess of what else serve under the same banner?'

## Chapter 51

Daryo ran from an arrow screen behind a rocky ledge of the ground. Behind it was a simple hole in the ground, nearly three yards wide. Daryo dropped into it and crouched down. Ahead, a wooden-framed tunnel of about three feet square stretched downwards and outwards towards Tiverta. He crawled down the tunnel carefully. The floor had been covered with bundles of rushes and straw, wooden shoring at regular intervals. Occasionally was evidence of the diggers- parts of tools, a headscarf, an axe handle. After twenty yards, Daryo found a small depression, six feet wide and a Gourmini miner was sat on a small box inside it. Daryo stopped to stretch.

'About forty yards further, Walker,' said the miner. 'We have reached just under the ditch.'

'My thanks.' Daryo resumed crawling. Forty yards in such cramped conditions was difficult work and took a significant time, slowed by miners passing canvas buckets of earth and stones back towards the entrance. He eventually reached the digging face. The big Armynyan, Kandecov, had two blades in his hands like large spearheads and was digging with both hands, pushing the waste between his legs and a man behind him was scraping it aside for others to push into buckets. He glanced back at the disruption caused by Daryo's arrival.

'Batribi.' He returned to his digging.

'I was told that you have reached the dry moat,' said Daryo.

Kandecov indicated upwards with one hand. 'It is above us. Only two feet, three feet. Wood is needed soon so no fall.'

'There was a small collapse near the gatehouse but has been repaired. This mine is the closest to the wall.'

'Ten feet,' said Kandecov with surety. 'By dawn, we are at the wall.'

'We will be staging a feint towards the gatehouse at midday. While that is happening, the fire must be set in the mine.'

'Yes.'

'You will be ready.'

'Yes.'

Daryo began to extract himself. 'Good fortune.'

'Yes.'

The attack was led by the newly-finished, covered ram and nearly half a thousand Gourmini soldiers attacked the gatehouse. Meanwhile a large amount of broken and waste wood was piled into the central mine of the three dug, supervised by Dostan. Daryo commanded the attack, coordinating a catapult bombardment and support from archers as the attack proceeded. He found Temma's Sword in his hand twice as he fought his own natural instincts to join the battle and help his allies. The Gourmini attackers were determined but the defences were strong and the attackers suffered heavy casualties.

A runner reached Daryo as a large vat of boiling water was emptied from the gatehouse. Some splashed on the accompanying troops, the cover on the ram shielding the wielders. The screams of the scalded men were piercing.

'Sir, the fire is set in the mine,' said the messenger.

Daryo sighed. 'Thank the Pantheon.' He signalled a trumpeter. 'Sound the withdrawal.' The Gourmini army fell back from the town, out of range of the gatehouse defenders. As soon as Daryo was content that the main danger was passed, he hurried around to the mine. The Gourmini miners were emerging at irregular intervals, running for the cover of archery screens and rocks. The entrance to the mine had a small stack of barrels visible in it.

Dostan and Kandecov were sat with their backs against the closest screen to the mine. Daryo hurried behind the cover as a Gourmini archer tried to shoot him down.

'We lost many men,' said Daryo. 'I hope this is successful.'

'We are confident,' said Kandecov.

'Proceed,' Daryo invited him.

The Armynyan signalled to an archer a short distance away behind another screen. The archer turned away and returned with arrow notched and the pitch-tipped arrow alight. He exposed himself and calmly fired the arrow into the top of the stack of barrels, ducked away, returned with a second arrow and it joined the first in the barrels. The barrels were all coated inside and out with pitch and were soon burning fiercely, the fire spreading down to the props and an oil-soaked cable of ropes that took the fire down the shaft to beneath the walls of Tiverta. Soon the only evidence of the fire below the ground was a column of smoke from the entrance. Daryo watched for a long time but only the smoke continued.

'What now?' he asked, puzzled. 'When does the wall come down?'

Kandecov smiled and chuckled. 'Fire burns. Heats stones to crack. Then the hammer is used to crack stones. Then wall comes down.'

'So we must put the ram against the wall.'

'We must.'

'We must fill in the ditch,' said Dostan. 'We can use the waste from the mine when darkness comes. We will need another diversion.'

Daryo grimaced. 'I will find a suitable force. We will attack south of the gatehouse, perhaps even use the second tower.'

'Do not be too keen, brother. The ram will work but we will need the night to keep the Vidmarians' attention away.'

'I will do my best. I will try and find some rest until then.'

Dostan nodded. 'I will have you called if we need you, Daryo.'

Sleep was little rest; images of death and defeat swirled through Daryo's mind when he slept and fear haunted him when he awoke, exacerbated by the daylight. By sunset, Daryo felt as if had been walking for the whole day instead of resting.

'Daryo?'

He sat up, yawning. 'Yes, yes.'

Dostan squatted down next to Daryo's bedroll. 'You look awful, Daryo. Did you not sleep?'

'I did but I had no rest.'

'Mind too busy?'

'Far too busy.'

'You have a difficult task. You are responsible for the lives of thousands of warriors and all those in Tiverta. It is not a light burden.'

'And I feel I am betraying my pledge.'

'To whom?'

'To the Fourth Goddess.'

'What do you mean, brother?' Dostan sat down on his own bedding.

'Before a battle, I pray to the Fourth Goddess. I always have. I have always offered her a... bargain: that I will send the souls to her in return for her sparing my life.'

Dostan nodded slowly. 'I imagine many people make such a bargain, silently and with their lives threatened.'

'I am not keeping my part of the trade. I am not using my blades and sending those souls to the Next Kingdom. Instead I send others to die, or to kill, without doing the deeds myself. This is not the trade I promised.'

'Say, for the argument, that you did the deeds yourself, that you had led the attack on the gatehouse while the fire was being built in the mine. A Vidmarian shot down the prominent Batribi commander of the assault. You passed to the Next Kingdom. Tiverta was held by the Vidmarians as the leaderless Gourmini were thrown back. You failed in your obligations much more than you did before: to the Fourth Goddess, to the Gourmini lords, to the Gourmini people, to the people of Tiverta and to your people. A commander must act through others, if he is simply killed then there is no leadership. You are fulfilling your obligations, brother. And if you truly wish to lead the army through the breach in the walls, then I know that no man here will stop you from doing so.'

The second siege tower was brought forwards, its walls and roof covered in water-soaked hides to protect against fire. It was wider and stronger than the first tower with more loops for the Gourmini archers and a larger capacity of troops. While the tower, with an accompanying barrage of catapult stones and arrows, was pushed forwards towards the tower to the south of the gatehouse, the covered battering ram was moved away and hurried towards the burning mine. A fortunate misfire of a Tiverta catapult had smashed a hole into the mine just before the walls and it allowed some brave or foolhardy of Kandecov's miners to pack more wood into the mine and increase the heat. As the sunlight faded, cracks were becoming visible in the walls of the town. In the darkness, more and more of the Gourmini army left their positions around the town and made their way to the north side ready for the attack. At the screen closest to the wall, Daryo and Dostan stood waiting along with Commanders Reprect and Luitiger. Kandecov returned with his arms burned and hair singed.

'Ready,' said the Armynyan proudly. 'The fire can be felt on the stones.'

Reprect hurried away to have the men readied. The battering ram was pulled forwards. In a symbolic gesture, the commanders drew their swords. The ram was directed by Kandecov across the section of filled ditch just to the side of where the mine reached the wall. The regular smack of the hardened wood ram, capped by solid iron, against the stones was soon shaking the walls of Tiverta. The progress was slow but sure. More cracks began to appear, the stones began to chip and shear. The Vidmarian defenders were soon responding, arrows, spears and rocks began to rain down but the ram was well-protected and the attack from the siege tower on the other side of the town was not insignificant, diverting their attention. The hammering of the ram continued all through the night, just before daybreak it paused and then resumed with a re-stoked fire in the mine beneath. And in the middle of the morning, there was a mighty cracking noise, bringing Gourmini soldiers running from all directions. The men wielding the ram were suddenly fleeing for their lives as masonry rained down. The wall was tumbling forwards, the cracks at the base splitting stone from stone. With an abrupt roar, the wall collapsed into the defensive ditch, burying the ram but filling in more of the ditch and opening a pathway nearly twenty feet wide.

Commander Reprect was the first through the breach at the head of the Gourmini army. Daryo immediately sent Dostan south to order a push from the siege tower and then led the second force of Gourmini soldiers up the ramp of fallen stone and into the city. Reprect would be heading to the gatehouse to break the gates open. The Walker's force began to fight its way towards the lord's house and the Great Tower beyond. The streets of Tiverta were wide and relatively clear, given that the town had been under siege and it was a great disadvantage to the Vidmarians as the Gourmini forces poured through the breach and they were able to quickly spread through the town, killing almost every Vidmarian that appeared. Within a short period, the people of Tiverta were emerging: peasants, women, young boys, with axes, knives, scythes and hammers and the Gourmini army suddenly acquired hundreds of vengeful, angry and murderous auxiliaries who were desperate to liberate their homes. The tide of Tivertans with the Gourmini army swept the Vidmarians aside and soon the Vidmarians were surrendering in huge numbers. A huge cheer went up as Daryo took a dozen Vidmarians in hand and, looking up, he could see a Gourmini banner being waved above the gatehouse. It would allow the rest of the Gourmini army easy access to the town, led by the cavalry. Daryo pushed through a crowd of defeated Vidmarians, passed the large Chapel of the White Lady and found himself below the walls of the lord's residence. The gates were being assaulted by a posse of townsfolk with hammers and axes. There were shouts that the Vidmarian commander was inside and that there were still a thousand Vidmarians within the grounds. Daryo ignored the house, circumnavigated the perimeter and led a small company of soldiers through the main marketplace, which had evidently been used as sleeping place for townspeople from the detritus. A broad street to the large open space around the base of the Great Tower of Tiverta, with its smaller tower before it. There were Vidmarian soldiers on the top of both towers, at every window and the doors were firmly closed. There were still dozens of Vidmarian soldiers in the plaza and they were still fighting. Daryo raised his shield and rushed to help a Tivertan battling against a sword-wielding foe with just a metal stake. Daryo despatched the first Vidmarian only to be confronted by a mountainous man wielding an axe. The Vidmarian roared a torrent of vile abuse and swung his huge weapon at Daryo, who nimbly leaped aside and slashed at the big man's head. He ducked out of the blow, staggered and fell with a Gourmini arrow in the side of his neck. Daryo slashed the falling man's throat open, kicked the body down and just deflected a sword blow with his shield in time. He parried the second blow and the third gave him an opening to cut across the Vidmarian's thighs, step past and slash through the back of the Vidmarian's neck. The clattering of horse's hooves joined the noises of battle and the Gourmini cavalry, Commander Cahn at the head of the column. The remaining Vidmarians outside the tower surrendered themselves.

'The city is ours, Walker!' cried Cahn, brandishing his spear in triumph.

'All except the tower,' replied Daryo, looking up at it.

'Perhaps not for much longer!' Cahn pointed and the Walker turned to see the doors of the tower opening. A Vidmarian in a plate armour cuirass over a mail shirt, crested helmet under one arm, emerged. Cahn quickly made a path, using his horse and Daryo followed.

The Vidmarian was dark haired with a horseshoe of a moustache and thick eyebrows. He glared at Daryo and then at Cahn as the latter dismounted.

'I am Merchon of Nivel, Royal Viceroy of the Vidmarian Throne, lord of Tiverta.'

Cahn suppressed a laugh as Daryo reached them, followed by a wave of Gourmini.

'I am Daryo the Walker, commander of the Army of Gourmin. This is Commander Cahn of Allesbury.'

'Commander,' said the Vidmarian. 'I am here to negotiate the withdrawal of my men.'

Cahn glanced at Daryo.

'You can negotiate with me,' said Daryo. 'I am in command of this army.'

The Vidmarian frowned, looking at Daryo. 'I do not negotiate with dogs.'

Daryo still had Temma's Sword in hand, the outer edge streaked with Vidmarian blood. He raised the blade across his chest. 'I have killed several of your men this day, Viceroy. If I cut you down now, the Gourmini army and the very angry people of this town will storm the towers and kill many of your men. If you wish to have your men walk out of this town alive, you *will* negotiate with me!'

The Vidmarian paled. 'State your terms.'

'Your men will surrender every weapon. They will be escorted by Gourmini soldiers to the border of Vidmaria and the escort will leave them there. Any Vidmarian prisoners elsewhere in Gourmin are not part of this arrangement. Any Gourmini prisoners, army or otherwise, are to be released to my charge. In return, no man of the Vidmarian army will be harmed and you will be permitted to keep any provisions or supplies other than weapons.'

'All Vidmarian prisoners will be released.'

'I cannot speak for the lords of Gourmin on their prisoners,' replied Daryo bluntly. 'Only those in my custody will be released.'

'The catapults and such will have to be dismantled. My men will require time to do that.'

Cahn scoffed. Daryo shook his head. 'Catapults, ballistas and the like are weapons. They will remain here.'
The Vidmarian sighed. 'Your terms are acceptable, Batribi.'
'I am glad, Vidmarian.'

The people of Tiverta, with a cordon of the army holding them back, lined the main street as the Vidmarians emerged from the towers, threw down their weapons and marched out of Tiverta. The prisoners already taken had been formed into a column outside the town and, closely watched by Gourmini cavalry and archers, they began their trek around the town to join their own road back to Vidmaria, nearly a hundred miles to the south and west.

The Lords of Gourmin had arrived the following day and the Batribi contingent left immediately after their ceremonial entrance to Tiverta. Daryo had handed over the Vidmarian leader's sword, pulled the cord to free the Gourmini banner from the side of the Great Tower, excused himself and met the other Batribi by the gatehouse. Three had been killed and so nineteen Batribi rode from Tiverta for Aslon and then their own lands beyond the Tember Pass.

\*     \*     \*

The Walker found himself at rest in the *kaff* adjoining Temma's home within three days. He had spent a day completely at rest, barely leaving the dwelling, enjoying the rare opportunity of having no place to visit or task to perform. The next, Daryo devoted to his equipment: every item of clothing was washed, his boots and belt cleaned and polished, his shield required some repairs that he was able to do to the rim and to the straps, all three swords and his knife were sharpened and polished to absolute perfection. Three days after returning to Stannia Lake, Daryo allowed himself some further relaxation before midday and spent the afternoon in the temple as it was the week's Eighth Day. He met the smith at the evening worship and thus was engaged to help build a small furnace for the forge, which took most of a day- a small clay construction was erected and strengthened with a second layer of clay. It gave the facility for the forge's scrap metal to be melted down and reused, reducing the wastage. With the work done, Daryo sought out Dostan, who had been at his usual work of the construction of the new bridge and was trudging home.
'A good day's work, brother?'

Dostan sighed tiredly. 'A long day. We have the downstream parapet in place now. When the ramp on the north bank is built, we can finish the pathway to the bridge and it can be used.'

'How long do you think?'

'Three days. Four perhaps.'

'Excellent. I do not think I will see it though.'

Dostan chuckled. 'I am not surprised, Daryo. You are never comfortable with the sedentary life, are you? There is something of the town or city that does not sit well with you. It is why I knew the coenobium was not right for you. And it is how I know that you would not stay here for long.'

'I am sorry. I know that deep in your soul you would like all Batribi to come and live here, Dostan, and your own brother leaves at every opportunity. It is not the example you wish to show.'

They reached Dostan's home, a few yards from Temma's and went inside. It was of identical design but with no children, there was no need for a second bed and Dostan had instead a large chest that doubled as a seat, covered by a thick cushion. Daryo sat on it and Dostan pulled up a stool. There was a large jug of milk by the empty fireplace; Dostan took a swig and passed it Daryo, who did the same.

'Where will you go?'

'I have been thinking. I might head back and try to see more of the Twin Ports, then Jaboen, perhaps explore Gourmin: Sinsebil, Spiert and Sitak. From there, perhaps even Armynya. Or I could go south, that would be Boskinia. I do not know the roads of that region.'

Dostan nodded. 'We have some contact with Boskinia. The king is aged but sympathetic to us and the people are generally accepting of a Batribi face. The land is pleasant and productive. You will return?'

Daryo was silent for a significant time. 'I do not know, Dostan. Every time I am here, I feel this... wrench. I want to walk the roads, my mind and body and soul need it, really need that freedom. But when I am here, I have this burning feeling that I should stay and help the town grow but I am not a townsman, I am not of a clan by upbringing, I am not a man of family, I am a lone soul, a Batribi orphans among Jaboens, a walker among settlers. I swore an oath to the Second Goddess, as you have reminded me. And I have a great debt to the Fourth Goddess that I cannot ignore.'

The two men stood and embraced.

'If ever you tire of wandering, know that your home is here, Daryo.'

'My thanks, Dostan. You and Laulra have been blessings to me. Gods' Guidance, my brother. We will see each other again.'

## Chapter 52
## Two years after the relief of Tiverta
## Summer's Third Day

The port of Nalb was Jaboen's only workable commercial port but was still restricted by towering cliffs on either side as the River Huba reached the sea. The town was crowded into the gorge and climbed the steep slopes on either side of the river. Although small in size, Nalb was known for its busyness; all sea trade from Jaboen to Gourmin, Yashoun and beyond was forced to go through Nalb as the only suitable anchorage. The road from Halmia reached Nalb through a man-made cutting near the top of the canyon and followed a series of steep, torturous switch-backs down into the town with houses and businesses perched precariously on the ledges between the roads. Some harsh looks and muttered comments came towards the Batribi traveller but he ignored them. The steep roads needed careful negotiation and he was glad when he reached the bottom of the hill where the few native businesses and industries of Nalb were clustered alongside the inner harbour. The houses and other buildings were tightly-packed on the little flat ground available, thatched roofs touched when walls did not.

The Walker identified the sign of an inn on the far side of the harbour and found a small, low bridge over the river a few dozen yards upstream near the neck of the gorge. The inn was little larger than some of the houses and shops around it with the sign of a bottle with a ship painted in the centre. The door was open and Daryo stooped inside. The hall was tiny, a bar and three tables with a long ladder at the far end of the room to access above and below. A small group of sailors were clustered in one corner.

'No Batribi,' said the innkeeper immediately. 'Get back to your shelter.'

'I have no shelter,' Daryo replied crossly. 'I am not with a clan. I require a bed for the night and can pay for it.'

'I do not give beds to Batribi.'

'What is the rate for a room, for a Jaboen?'

'A silver half.'

Daryo suspected that was double the normal cost but still carried a significant amount of money from his work in the Silver Island for the Yashoun. 'Two silvers. I am tired and have walked from Halmia.'

'Two and two bronze.'

'Sold.' Daryo got out the money.

'Go down to the cellar. The left side room.'

Daryo nodded and clambered down the narrow ladder into a low-ceilinged cellar with only a small space between two doors. Daryo pushed open the one to the left and nearly walked into the bed. There was a bed and nothing else. Light came through a very small window, the walls were running with damp. Daryo removed his shield, pack and the Twin Swords on his back, pushing them under the bed. He then let himself out of the cell-like room, locked the door and ascended the ladder, leaving the inn without a glance at the proprietor. A baker nearby sold him a small fish pie and Daryo sat by the harbour watching a large Yashoun ship in the outer part of the bay, furling its sails and dropping its anchor. A small fleet of tenders began to row out to bring the cargo ashore. The pie was spicy, hot and enjoyable and Daryo returned and bought a second. As the tenders began to come ashore and the cargoes unloaded, he noticed a commotion around the shore line. A woman screamed and someone swore loudly. Daryo hurried forwards to where a small crowd had gathered around one of the tenders. A shaggy-haired man dressed in little more than rags had hold of some type of harpoon and he was lashing out randomly at the people gathered around.
'Grab his arms!' someone shouted.
'Fetch the guards!'
'Cut him down!'
A stevedore lunged at the delinquent but was slashed across the arm by the harpoon. Daryo pushed through the small crowd and drew Temma's Sword. The man lunged with the harpoon, Daryo used the curved back of Temma's Sword to catch behind the barb of the harpoon, he twisted aside and grabbed the harpoon's shaft, pulling it out of his opponent's grasp. A band of Jaboen stevedores jumped on the little man, knocking him to the ground and pinning him to the quayside.
'*Cisa lobirogo mon! O Istos tomogote!*' babbled the man. He looked gaunt to the point of skeletal, his hair was matted and his beard straggled to his neck, what had once been a long garment like a brown cape that covered all over his body was ripped and stained, the light leggings beneath were filthy and his feet were bare. His skin was burned a dark brown by long exposure to the sun. A couple of guards belatedly arrived and the harbour workers moved aside as two crossbows were aimed at the prone man.
'Stay your bows!' said Daryo earnestly. 'Do not shoot!'
'The man's a lunatic!' protested the injured stevedore, showing his wounded arm. 'Shoot him!'
'No!' Daryo objected. 'He is terrified, look at him.'
One of the guards looked at Daryo. 'Do you know this person, Batribi?'
'No but I know a terrified stranger when I see one!'

'He attacked me!' barked the stevedore.

'Defending himself.' Daryo tossed a silver half to the stevedore. 'That should have you healed by a physician with a jug of wine to dull the pain.' He turned to the guards. 'My name is Daryo the Walker. I am staying at the inn yonder. Release this man to my charge, by the Third Goddess he needs care not chastising.'

The guards looked at each other and shrugged. 'Any further trouble, it will be your head, Batribi.'

'My thanks.' Daryo sheathed Temma's Sword, crouched down next to the man and said kindly: 'Come, we should get you looked after.'

'*Olo murtogus mon!*'

'Shh, I am no threat to you, I swear.'

'He doesn't speak Common Speech!' exclaimed a woman. 'A barbarian!'

'Peak Tribes,' suggested one of the guards.

'No, I know something of their language,' Daryo replied. 'He is not of the Peaks. *Choi tie, tel?*' The only words in the Silver Islander tongue that he recalled. 'Nor the Silver Island.'

'*Rubac!*' barked one of the guards. When the crowds looked at him, he said, somewhat self-consciously: 'Learned a few words of Armynya.'

The little man on the floor shook his head in bewilderment. '*Koun vo dores? Koun vo dores? No murtogus mon!*'

Daryo reached into his belt pouch and found a single gold half. 'Please, someone find him some clothing, shoes, food.'

'I will,' said a robed woman nearby. 'Keep your money, Batribi, I can show charity, I follow Spinel. Bring him to my home.'

'On your feet, boy,' said one of the guards, not unkindly.

Daryo and the guard helped stand the dishevelled man up.

'Come along,' said Daryo. He spread his arms in a gesture of welcome. 'Nobody will hurt you. Come.' He pointed to the woman and put a guiding hand on the man's arm.

The little man looked at the woman. '*Vo hilpus mon?*'

'I am a friend,' she said calmly.

'As am I,' said Daryo.

'*Vo hilpus mon?*'

'A friend,' Daryo repeated.

The man suffered himself to be led along the harbour, while the guards dispersed the crowd. The lady walked past the bridge towards the neck of the gorge and then turned to climb a set of steps to perhaps the largest building in the port, its roof tiled and the windows glazed. A rose-coloured banner, emblazoned with a black anchor, hung from the small balcony above the main door.

'This is your home?' asked Daryo.

The woman smiled back at him. 'I am Kalila, my husband is Jussef, Lord of Nalb.'

The room was probably for a guest to reside in- a large fireplace facing a well-padded framed bed with chests, hanging rails, a rack for weapons and a carved statuette of a seabird in front of the glazed window. The strange man was encouraged to sit on the bed, a servant brought warm water, a tunic and leggings and several pairs of boots for the man to try. Daryo and the Lady of Nalb withdrew for a few moments to allow the man to wash and change and then food was brought: bread, cheese, oat porridge and a jug of mead. He ate as if afraid that the food would be snatched from him, sat on the bed, devouring everything, muttering '*denkun*' as he did so. His skin had been tanned so dark he looked almost Batribi, his matted hair framed a heavy brow, a beaked nose and small, very dark eyes.

'He has not eaten in a long time,' said Daryo. 'His body... every bone shows.'

'Do you know this man, Batribi?'

'No, Madam, I simply intervened for him on the harbour.'

'Why?'

'I know what it is to be adrift in a strange land and to feel threatened by those around you.'

'What is your name? Where is your clan?'

'My name is Daryo the Walker, my clan resides beside Stannia Lake. I walk alone.'

'Our... hungry guest must have a name.'

Daryo got the man's attention as he devoured an apple, core and all. He put his hand against his own chest. 'Daryo.' He pointed to the lady. 'Kalila.' He pointed at the little man.

'Phorun,' was the reply, hand against his chest. He pointed to Daryo. 'Dar-yo.' Then the lady. 'Kar-lee-la.'

The Batribi and the Jaboen smiled. 'Yes,' said Kalila. She looked at Daryo. 'Let me try something.' She held out her left hand and ran the fingers of her right hand over it. 'Jaboen.' She took Daryo's hand and stroked it the same way. 'Batribi.' She pointed at the little man.

'Ondogino.' He pointed. 'Ka-li-la... Jaa-bo-wen. Dar-yo... Bat-rib-ee.'

'Phorun, Ondogino,' replied Kalila with a smile.

'I do not know a land of Ondogino,' Daryo said. 'I do not have a great education in such things.'

Kalila shook her head. 'I do not know it either.' She went to the door and called a servant. 'Find Master Naioki.' She returned. 'Master Naioki is the town's tutor, a most learned man from the famed College of Jundan, and a scholar of the Archive in Allesbury, he teaches my children and speaks many languages, he may know.'

Phorun had finished his meal and looked around hopefully. 'Kalila. *Ostes toi plo bunvuli?*'

'I think he is still hungry,' said Daryo.

There was a bowl of fruit by the window and Kalila offered the peaches, grapes and apples to Phorun, who gratefully took the bowl and began eating with a few '*denkun*'s between bites.

The door opened and Daryo's immediate reaction was of a kindly, grandfatherly figure, slightly stooped and walking with the aid of a stick. He smiled widely. 'Madam Kalila.'

'Master Naioki, do you know of our guest?'

'I had heard, yes.' The elderly man tottered into the room.

'Phorun,' said Kalila clearly and pointed at the tutor. 'Naioki.'

'*Ca tou ostes voe menjegu?*' asked Phorun, suddenly looking concerned.

Naioki smiled. 'Would you say a little more, young man?'

Phorun looked at Kalila and Daryo in consternation. '*Mo ni cumprines. Koun mo bozunes firo?*'

Naioki made a placating gesture and took Daryo and Kalila a little aside.

'Do you understand him, Master Naioki?' asked Kalila.

'A little, Madam. He is speaking a dialect of the old language of these parts. Many generations ago, perhaps as many as fifteen generations, the state of Crimir occupied much of what is now Boskinia, Gourmin, southern Jaboen and some of Vidmaria. To the north, along the coast, was Sindipinda. Nalb was known as Kenjunu Keju and was one of the ports of the land, along with Spiert. Allesbury, Sinsebil and Jonat were also settlements in that age, Halmia was a tiny village. The language has been preserved in the Archive of Allesbury, some of the oldest Jaboen texts known are in the tongue known as Ondogine.'

'Phorun said that he was Ondogino,' said Daryo.

'Truly?'

'So he is from some... lost enclave?' asked Kalila, glancing back at Phorun, who was negotiating the eating of a peach.

'I think not, my lady, I think that the most likely possibility is that is from the Kyi Sun islands.'

Kalila frowned. 'Master Naioki...'
'I know that nobody from the Kyi Sun have been seen for many, many seasons, my lady, but the evidence fits: the language, the physical appearance, he arrived by sea... I would like a chance to talk with him. I speak something of the Ondogine tongue and may be able to converse with him.'
'Certainly,' said Kalila. 'Master Daryo, would you consent to remain with Master Naioki? I am afraid I have some business to attend to in my husband's absence.'
'As you wish.'

The conversation between Naioki and Phorun started as a tentative exchange of words, the Yashoun tutor sometimes pronouncing a word in several different ways before Phorun understood it. By dark, they had been talking for over an hour in what Daryo took to be a relatively fluent conversation. With the fading light, the conversation stopped and Naioki stood up from the stool he had asked for earlier in the day.
'Phorun wishes to sleep,' Naioki told Daryo. 'He is exhausted. We should find Lady Kalila and I can tell you both the story of our guest.'
Kalila invited Daryo to remain for dinner and she, Daryo and Naioki sat down to eat in the house's main dining room, with the lady's three children, all aged between six and twelve summers, around the circular table with them.
'He was a... dissident,' said Naioki. 'The reign of the Kyi Sun king is harsh and exact and Phorun and his comrades wished change. They attempted a revolt, to overthrow the king. Many joined the revolt but the army of the king was too strong. Hundreds were killed and Phorun escaped on a boat, with no means of navigation, little food and with no oars. The wind carried him away, he believes north and then west. He was caught in a storm and fortunately rescued by the Yashoun ship that brought him here.'
'How long was he adrift?' Daryo asked.
'Twenty-three days.'
'I am surprised that he did not starve,' said Kalila.
'He had some food and rationed himself.'
'It is truly the gift of the First God that he is still alive.'
'Mother, can we meet the Kyi Sun man?' asked Kalila's daughter, a girl of about nine summers.
'Perhaps, Niha, he needs rest and food for now.'
'Is he a nice man?'
'Very pleasant, Miss Niha,' Naioki said.
'What did he do? Was he a soldier?'

'No, he was a clerk.'

'What job do you do, Master?' young Niha asked Daryo.

Daryo smiled. 'I am a soldier. I travel from place to place fighting for those that need it. Such as Phorun.'

'Will you keep travelling?'

'I will. I was only planning on staying in Nalb this one night and then following the coast road into Gourmin.'

'You are welcome to remain in Nalb for as long as you wish, Master Daryo,' Kalila told him.

'My thanks, Madam, but I will be moving on with the new day if Phorun is happy in your care.'

'I am sure he will be, he is equally welcome to stay here for as long as necessary. I doubt he will want to return to his native islands. It may be that he wishes to remain in Nalb indefinitely, in which case I will ensure that some task can be found for him.'

# Chapter 53

The road out of Nalb was as steep as the road in. Daryo was gasping for breath by the time he reached the top of the cliff. He had made sure to say goodbye to Kalila before departing and, through the tutor, had also been able to accept Phorun's profuse and grandiose thanks and ardent embrace. In thanks, Kalila had given Daryo some provisions and some guidance as to what to expect on the road into Gourmin.

The road followed the top of the cliff to the north and east and after a few miles Daryo passed the statue of a hawk marking the border with Gourmin. The road curved away from the cliffs slightly, joining a slight valley that skirted the mountains of the Jaboen-Gourmin border. The road was wide and well-paved with flat stones and seemed to follow the little depression, around three feet below the surrounding ground, as the path of least resistance; the ground to either side was broken, rocky and dotted with small pools and springs. Daryo assumed that after heavy rain the road would become something of a river. As the road grew further from the sea and closer to the peaks, larger trees began to appear along with bracken and shrubs that made the landscape most picturesque in the summer sunshine. Just after noon Daryo stopped to eat and take some rest before continuing. The road became less even and climbed steadily into the hills at the base of the Peaks. He wondered vaguely if Peak Tribesmen, known to be brutally violent and aggressive, strayed so far down the mountains and took a moment to lower his shield from its normal travelling position high on his left arm into a battle posture: the outer strap in his left hand and the inner just below the elbow. It was not as convenient when walking but the defensive benefits in hostile ground were obvious. By mid-afternoon the road was high in the foothills of the mountains and passing through a lush woodland. A large type of deer started and fled at the Walker's approach. Birds maintained a continual chorus. A small rockfall required some careful negotiation and on the far side a chance look downwards for an obstacle caused Daryo to stop.

A thin cord, barely more than twine, ran across the road and disappeared into the underbrush. Daryo had fought enough battles and hunted enough animals to know a trap when he encountered it. The position suggested it was not set by a hunter of game. With painstaking care, he stepped over the line, drew the Horse from over his right shoulder and, at the limit of his arm's length, cut the line, leaping backwards as he did. There was a rushing sound of something falling, a clang of stone on metal and a weighted net descended from the trees above. It fell on the area where the trip line had been, Daryo's evasion meant he was well outside its reach.

'Stop where you stand!' cried a voice from the trees. 'You may have missed the net but there are four blades and a bow around you! This road is subject to a toll!'
'On who's authority?' Daryo called back.
'The authority of the four blades and the bow!' was the reply. Another voice, a little distance from the first laughed. 'The people of Sinsebil and the villages are starving! We will take one in five of what money or valuables you carry!'
'I will not be robbed!' returned Daryo crossly. 'However, perhaps there is a way that I can be of use.'
'You can be of use by handing over one in five of what you have!'
'I will not surrender anything to a disembodied voice! Come forth and claim what you want if you have a scrap of courage!' Daryo kept his sword and shield by his sides.
Someone whistled and three figures, one carrying a bow and the others swords, appeared on the higher ground to his right. Another swordsman appeared on the road in front of him and the fourth clambered down a tree before drawing their blade. All of them were dressed in a motley of brown, green and black with raised hoods. One of those on the high ground slithered down the slope nimbly. They carried an outdated style of sword- a single piece of steel about a yard long, the handle round and wrapped with leather and no guard between the round grip and the flat, rather unpolished blade. The figure was slight and quite small in frame, when they lowered their hood, it became clear that the small frame was that of a young woman, her golden hair cut short, sharp blue eyes above a slightly-pointed nose and a scarred right cheek. She levelled her sword at Daryo.
'One in five of what you carry,' she demanded.
'I said you must claim it,' Daryo replied, thinking on the weight of his pack on his back and how it would affect his combat. 'I will not surrender it. You could take what I give you and use it for your own ends.'
'We are using it to help feed the starving!' the young woman snapped. Daryo heard the creak of the bowstring.
'How could I trust those words from a group of ruffians that fix traps and ambush innocent travellers?'
'We swore an oath to defend those that require aid and that cannot aid themselves! In the name of the Second Goddess Brokea, we will use your coin to feed those who are hungry!'
Daryo frowned, the words ringing in his ears. He slowly raised his shield, showing the badge. 'The second word.'

'My,' was the immediate response. The woman studied the shield for a moment, looking confused, she looked around at her comrades. She turned her sword around and raised it, point down, in salute. 'My sword and my service, Daryo the Walker.'
Daryo returned the salute. 'Until discharged by death. How do you know my name?'
The woman seemed to blush as she pushed her sword into its sheath. 'I could not forget the man who first saw me bare.'
He frowned and then realisation came. 'Jenni!'
'It has been some seasons, Walker.'
Daryo almost dropped the Horse as he ran forwards to embrace her. 'I did not recognise you! The Gods have been kind to you.'
Jenni smiled and hugged him tightly. 'Come down!' she called to the others. 'I have been fortunate. Come, we will take you to our camp.' They started through the trees, off of the road, going downhill. 'We are all of the Nest, all but I went to Sinsebil as the Vidmarians approached. Noth…' A tall and somewhat gawky adolescent, 'Calleso…' Smaller and more solid with a severe countenance, 'Jamil…' A little older than the other two but younger than Jenni and exceptionally muscular, '…and Solpa.' Another young woman, probably the youngest of the group, of only about sixteen summers, dark haired and small-featured, the archer. 'We were all part of the community in Sinsebil and life was always difficult but we lived. Then old lord Theach died two summers ago, not long after Tiverta was taken back. His son is a madman, he trebled rents and food prices and controls all food stocks and everything else that he can. He cares only for money and it means that people in Sinsebil, but especially in the villages around, are starving because they cannot afford to buy food and pay their fees and taxes. We all thought that we could use our skills to get some money from those rich enough to pay it: merchants and the like travelling between Gourmin and Jaboen.'
'I can see the reasoning. Have you been successful?'
'Seventeen families still in their homes and still fed because of us,' said Calleso firmly. 'And we feed dozens of homes. We steal from Lord Oram when we must.'
'Jenni, I lost you in the battle at the Five Towers,' said Daryo. 'What happened?'
Jenni sighed. 'I was hurt, when the Secondborn Tower was hit by a rock, I was struck on the head. One of the Brethren thought I was dead and I was removed to the burial cavern but I was saved, maybe the Third God, maybe the Fourth Goddess was too occupied, and I came awake. I was one of the last to leave the Five Towers when the Batribi left. I went to Allesbury with Dibat the Trident's group first, then went to Sinsebil because the others from the Nest were there. Where were you?'

'In the Sanctuary with Herren Downe. I left with Sofea the Racing Hart and Lobrin the Harsh and went to my people's town by Stannia Lake.'

'Where then?'

'It is a long story.'

They reached the crest of a low cliff. Jenni laughed and leaped off. Daryo almost shouted and looked over the edge. Twelve feet below was a piece of canvas stretched out and Jenni had landed squarely in the centre. One by one, the rest of the small group jumped and landed on the canvas. Less than ten yards away was a small camp- half a dozen tents around a smouldering campfire. Noth threw some small pieces of wood on the fire and crouched to blow on the embers to encourage flame. Jenni took her swordbelt off and dropped it outside one of the little canvas shelters.

'Is that Leroyfa the Blind's sword?' asked Daryo.

Jenni shook her head sadly. 'No, I lost that at the Five Towers. I dropped it when I was knocked down and it was lost. This is... a copy. I shovelled out nearly thirty stables for an entire autumn and winter to earn enough money to have that made by the smith in Boarteth.'

Jamil helped Daryo remove his pack.

'How long have you been here?' Daryo asked.

'Since late winter,' Jamil told him. He had a design inked on the skin on the back of his hand: two figures holding pikes that extended up the back of his forearm.

'Nura the Guarded's badge?' asked Daryo.

Jamil nodded. 'Indeed. My mother. Noth is Moded the Archer's son. Calleso is the son of Jurio the Gate and Semmania the Tile. Solpa is the daughter of Corun and Sexul Downe of the Brethren.' Daryo noticed that Solpa was wearing a dark yellow hood, she was unstringing her bow and she gave Daryo a shy smile.

'Some of you do not know,' announced Jenni. 'Daryo the Walker was a battle-born Member of the Order, he was the tail of Kym the Harlequin. His kin led the Batribi warriors that gave the survivors time to withdraw.'

'You saved us from the Nest,' said Calleso.

'I escorted you, along with the Brethren,' Daryo replied, a little embarrassed. 'I did not save you; Kym the Harlequin and Leroyfa the Blind gave their lives for you and for me. That is why their symbols are on my shield.'

'We would not have survived without you, Walker,' said Solpa firmly and the others chorused agreement.

Calleso and Noth departed to reset their trap, Jamil to keep a watch on the road south, Solpa to hunt for some dinner. Jenni remained with Daryo and he told her of his exploits since they had last met. She listened incredulously.

'We heard that there was a Batribi leading the army at Tiverta but did not believe it,' she said when he had finished. 'You have had such a wonderful opportunity.'

'I have been fortunate.'

There was a long whistle. Jenni looked up and grabbed her sword. 'Travellers on the road. Come along!' With that she was hurrying away through the trees.

Daryo had his twin swords still on his back and raced after her. She was ascending the cliff apparently without aid and it was only when Daryo was right next to the rock that he saw a fantastically-camouflaged rope ladder. He followed Jenni up the cliff as fast as he could. At the top, she was already disappearing into the trees; her clothing made her one with the trunks and foliage. Daryo darted through the underbrush and nearly tripped over her. She had ducked down into a hollow within yards of the road, which was around five feet above them. He guessed it was where they had been concealed when he had come past. There was a quick flash of metal from the top of the slope above the road and Jenni's hand rose in the air briefly in response as Daryo crouched beside her.

'Noth and Calleso,' she whispered.

'Jenni, I do not feel this is right.'

'This is my choice, not yours,' she hissed back, looking angry. 'Stay here. Do not interfere.'

Three horses, one towing a wagon, the others with riders, came around the rockfall.

'Traders,' Jenni muttered to herself, drawing her sword.

The first horse passed the trap somehow without springing it but the second, pulling the wagon, broke the cord. The net fell, ensnaring the horse and wagon driver.

'Stop where you stand!' shouted Jenni. 'This road is subject to a toll!' With a rustle, Solpa appeared alongside Daryo, notching an arrow. 'There are five swords and a bow around you!'

'What do you want?' shouted the man at the front of the procession. 'Who are you? Show yourself!'

'I am the person exacting the toll!' Jenni replied. 'The people of Sinsebil and its lands are starving. We will take one in five of the coin or valuables you carry to help feed the people!'

'This is robbery!'

'This is justice! Taking from those who can afford it for those who cannot!'

The trader looked at his fellows, one struggling beneath the net, and sighed. 'You swear on whatever gods you keep to do no harm?'
'If you give us what we ask, I swear on the First Goddess Tahili to do no injury!'
'Be quick!'
Jenni whistled. She and the others broke concealment and hurried forwards, Solpa staying back with her arrow ready. Noth helped the horse and wagon free of the net. Coin was produced, counted by Calleso and one in five was taken. The traders were then permitted on their way. The little band withdrew to the hollow where Daryo had remained to check their takings.
'Nineteen silver halves and fifty-seven bronze,' Calleso announced. 'They were Gourmini, returning to Allesbury. They had made money selling vegetables in Nalb.'
'We could go straight to Boarteth,' said Noth.
'We should,' Jenni agreed. 'Split the money in two, Calleso. You take Noth and Jamil through the high ground. Daryo and Solpa will come with me through the valley.' She looked at Daryo. 'See all of what we do before you dismiss it, Walker. Please.'

The walk to Boarteth took until past noon. Jenni had led Daryo and Solpa through a shallow gorge just down from the roadway. They re-joined Calleso, Noth and Jamil on a rocky ridge overlooking a small village almost surrounded by a narrow river, a small chapel of the White Lady at the centre and an even-smaller temple of the Pantheon on the riverbank.
'That is Boarteth,' Jenni told Daryo. 'Sinsebil has one of the largest estates of Gourmin and Boarteth is the largest of the villages. It is also known for... resistance to the new Lord of Sinsebil and so it suffers: low rations, high taxes, frequent extra rent demands. It needs our help the most.'
Noth scrambled forwards on the rocks a little, peering down at the village around three hundred yards away. 'I cannot see any guards... not more than the constable.'
'The constable is in our pay,' Jenni explained for Daryo's benefit. 'He is the man of the Lord but lives in the village and suffers the same rents and privations as everyone else.'
'A silver for each house?' asked Jamil and Jenni nodded.
'Noth stay up here, watch for trouble,' she said. 'Come, we should move quickly.'
Leaving the lean young man on the ridge, Daryo accompanied the others down to the village of wood and render, tile-roofed homes. Around the perimeter of the village were several large earth kilns.
'Boarteth makes tiles for much of Gourmin,' said Jenni. 'But the lord takes the money.'

A young woman of about Daryo's age was grinding flour at the front of her house. She looked up and smiled shyly. Leaving her work, she came forwards a few feet and Calleso went across to her, taking out some coin. She took the money and said a few soft words of thanks. A boy of about five summers came running out of another home.
'Hunting lady!'
Solpa grinned and Calleso passed her some coin. She knelt down next to the boy. 'Good day, Shurn. Is your father working?'
'Yes, works on tiles.'
'Can you keep the money for him?'
'Yes, I can. I will put it safe for him to get later.'
'Good. Go quick then, put it safe.' The boy hurried off, leaving Solpa beaming widely.
'We keep these people fed,' Jenni said, passing a stipend to another woman. 'If we did not give them this, they cannot buy food. The rents will be due soon, so the need for coin is greater.'
'I understand what you do, Jenni. I am not sure about the way you secure the money.'
'We take it from those who can afford it for those who cannot.'
'From innocent people.'
'Defending the weak.'
'But not defending the innocent.'
Jenni frowned and walked away from him to a home smaller than the others. She went inside and emerged a little later. 'Tell Thera that. Her husband is dead, her leg is injured, she cannot work and she has four children. We can take coin from traders and merchants or we can let those children die hungry.'
Most of the villagers were in a few unwalled shelters around the temple at the business of making clay tiles. It allowed Jenni's group to distribute the rest of the money quickly and Daryo could not argue with the fact that the money was needed and received with genuine, deep gratitude by the people. One woman, apparently the priestess, gave Calleso a blessing and requested that her portion be given to another. Their work done, the group reunited by the Chapel of the White Lady, returned to the overlook and then departed for their camp in the greenwood.

'We could use the bronze,' suggested Noth as the group sat around the fire that night. 'There is a lot, we could go to Great Gap and distribute the bronze there.'
'Bronze is good, it creates less attention when the people spend it,' agreed Jamil.
Jenni nodded slowly. The others all seemed to defer to her leadership. 'You are right, Jamil. Could we do Little Gap in the same day?'

Calleso thought for a moment. 'Yes. Neither would get as much and it would nearly empty our reserves.'

'Nevertheless.'

'As you wish, Jenni.'

'What of you, Walker?' Jenni asked.

Daryo had been thinking of what he wanted to do for a while. 'I do not condone your methods,' he repeated, looking around the small gathering. 'But I cannot deny that your work, the things you do for the people of these lands, it is all quite astounding and so necessary. I have been thinking quite keenly and I would like to do something to aid you. I have some coin that I earned working in the Silver Island that I will gladly give, more than one in five. However I believe that there is another way that you could help these people.'

'Kill the lord,' suggested Noth keenly.

'No. Humiliate him. He must have great reserves of money from all the taxation and income.'

'In Sinsebil Castle,' said Jamil. 'I used to be a servant there. There is a vault in the cellars beneath the great hall.'

'Is there a way in?'

'The main gate?'

Jenni and Noth chuckled. Daryo smiled. 'Something less obtrusive?'

Jamil nodded. 'I think so. But someone has to get inside.'

'I can do that,' said Solpa.

Everyone looked around in surprise. 'Are you sure, Solpa?' Jenni asked.

'I think so. I know one of the maids in the castle. I think I can get inside with her.'

'You could not have a weapon, or anything else that might get you in trouble,' said Daryo.

'I know.'

'Are you sure?'

'Yes.'

'Then my plan may be workable.'

## Chapter 54

Jamil fetched some horses at dawn and they rode southwards. The road forked to pass either side of a steep-sided hill and the pre-determined action was for Jamil, Solpa and Noth to go right to Great Gap, in the larger pass, and the rest went left to Little Gap, in the narrower western pass. The charitable work went apace and then Daryo, Jenni and Calleso rode hard for Sinsebil. Half a mile from the town, in view of the walls but within the trees, they tethered the horses in a hidden depression on long reins. They were soon joined by the others, all of whom looked pale and their horses exhausted.

'What happened?' Jenni asked, helping Solpa dismount.

'Provincial Watch,' said Noth. 'Lots of them in Great Gap. We were chased but lost them in the woods.'

'Sure?'

'Completely.'

'If you are sure.'

The mounts were tethered with the others and Noth set a handful of traps to dissuade thieves.

'Is that sufficient?' Daryo asked warily.

Noth nodded. 'There is a toll gate within fifty yards. The man who keeps it is in our pay and he will care for the horses.'

The group straggled into the town so as not to attract attention. There were heavy patrols of soldiers in the distinctive brown, white and red colours of Sinsebil. Daryo kept the hood of his jerkin raised and his cloak's cowl as well. He attracted a few curious glances but nothing more. The town was unnaturally quiet and tidy. The houses were three floors high, of wood and render with tiled roofs and shuttered windows, the upper floors slightly overhanging the streets. The market near the polygonal castle was only a few stalls, none selling food. In the marketplace, Solpa left them to go and meet her friend that worked in the castle. Jenni led the way down an alley, past a Chapel of the White Lady, darted across a main street and knocked on the door of the house. There was a few moment's pause and an elderly man answered. He recognised Jenni and opened the door wide. She beckoned to the others and they were swiftly inside. The house was very sparsely-furnished: a bench in front of the fire, a rough table and rushes on the floor, stairs leading up in one corner.

'Daryo the Walker,' said the man. 'You were the Harlequin's tail.'

Daryo thought frantically for the man's name, he was of about Daryo's height, dark haired and with a thick beard. 'I am sorry, I cannot recall your name.'

'I am Roedan, once the Wolfhound. You spoke at Muster after I proposed moving the young ones here.'

'Yes! Yes, I recall!'

'This was the house that they were brought to. I escorted them here and have remained here ever since, keeping a safe place for those who were in the Order. And those who continue our works,' he said, smiling fondly at Jenni. 'What brings you here?'

'The Walker has a plan to strike against the lord,' Jenni told him. 'We are getting into the castle with dark.'

'That is dangerous,' said Roedan. 'The curfew comes at sundown.'

'I know. Curfew means that the guards are either asleep in their beds or out enforcing the lockdown. It should make entry easier.'

Roedan sighed. 'I trust your judgement, Jenni. You need somewhere to wait until dark?'

'Please.'

'You know where to go.'

Jenni nodded and beckoned to the others. Behind the stairs, a portion of the floor came up and away, revealing a small, hidden cellar accessed by a knotted rope. When all five were inside, Roedan passed down a lit candle and closed the hatch behind them. Jamil used it to light several lamps in the cellar, illuminated a bare, earth-walled space around ten feet square. Jenni sat down on a barrel with her back against the cold wall with her sword across her knees. Jamil sat on a box; Daryo, Noth and Calleso on the floor.

'The castle keeps two shifts of servants,' Jenni told Daryo. 'So the lord can justify not paying a wage to anyone. Solpa will deputise for her friend in the castle and let the rope out of the garbage chute from the kitchens. We have two guards at the gate to the outer yard to remove, then we climb up the rope into the kitchen.'

'Is the chute large enough?'

'I can fit,' said Jamil. 'I left employment at the castle after I was accused of stealing food. They tried to get me to the dungeon but I broke free, found myself in the kitchen and threw myself down the waste chute.' The others laughed. 'If I can get down the chute, everyone here can get up it.' More laughter.

After some silence, Daryo nudged Jenni. 'May I ask a question of a personal subject?'

'Of course, Walker.'

'You have never mentioned your parents. Who were they? What role in the Order? What were their names?'

Jenni smiled sadly. 'They were not in the Order. My mother, I have no memory of. My father was a mason, an excellent mason, in Tiverta. He helped in the building of the Great Tower of Tiverta and was well-respected. He was travelling to Aslon to help with

some repairs. I was in the cart, he walked alongside. A known killer of women was fleeing on horseback from a Member of the Order, a Jaboen woman named Shara the Caged Bird. The fugitive rounded a corner and his horse collided with my father, knocking him to the ground. Shara's horse could not stop, her horse trampled my father. He died on the road. She stopped, she abandoned her pursuit, to tend him and then she saw me. She took me back to Tiverta but when she learned I had no kin there, she took me with her to the Five Towers. I was then passed on to the Nest. I was there for something of twenty-one, twenty-two seasons before I met you for the first time.'
'A tragic story, Jenni. I am most sorry.'
'It is my past. I was a young child. I remember very little of it. I have visited my father's burial in Tiverta once. And I honour Shara the Caged Bird's memory. It would have been my sword name had ever I taken my Promise.'
'She did not survive?'
'She took ill, not long after I reached the Nest. She did not survive that winter.'
'So much loss.'
'Indeed. But you are not lost. And this motley band of fools that I have found. They are my family now.'

The opportunity to rest was taken until late, when Roedan reopened the cellar cover and they clambered out. He had a single lamp lit on the table. Jenni was the last to scramble out of the cellar, just as there was a hard knock on the door. Everyone looked around startled, the knock was repeated with a more urgent tone.
'City Watch!' came the shout outside. 'Open the door!'
'They must have caught Solpa!' hissed Noth, reaching for his sword.
'Or just a random raid, it is quite common,' said Roedan. He went to the unused fireplace, reached up inside the chimney and brought down a short-handled battle axe with a spike opposite the blade. A fragmenting tapestry on the wall was pulled away and he took down his shield.
Another harsh crash at the door: an axe breaking down the door. All the occupants of the Order's once-safe house reach for their own weapons. Daryo squared his shield and drew Temma's Sword.
'They know we are here!' said Noth, taking position beside the door. Jamil went behind the door. Daryo and Roedan stood right before the door, Jenni behind them, Calleso to the right in the most space as the only one with a buckler. The axe blows continued accompanied by cries of 'City Watch!' and increasingly angry and bloodthirsty responses from Noth.

'Make for the castle as soon as possible!' Jenni instructed. 'Meet in the alley by the Outer Yard gate! Second God be with you all!'

There was a clang of the City Watch's axe striking the lock of the door and then another and the door gave way, swinging inwards. Jamil timed a vicious kick to knock the door closed and it hit the lead City Watchman in the face. When the door opened again, Noth's blade swung out at throat height, taking down the next Watchman. Daryo and Roedan charged the attackers and Jenni was quickly involved. There were a dozen of the Watch but they had not anticipated quite what they were facing. All six of their targets were excellent wielders of a sword and fighting in defence of their lives. Daryo smashed one in the face with his shield, ducked and slashed across the Watchman's exposed thighs, stood and opened the luckless man's throat as Noth ran him through from behind. He was the last Watchman to fall dead. One remained outside and he began to run but Jenni was in pursuit. She was fast, remarkably so and unencumbered by armour, and within yards leaped forwards and her weight and speed drove her blade through the back of the Watchman's neck, sending them both to the floor into a pile of limbs and blood. Daryo reached the scene with the rest of the group behind him. Calleso and Noth helped Jenni up.

'Roedan and Noth are going to clear up the... mess,' said Jamil. 'Then create a diversion if we need it.'

'Quick, drag him in here.' Daryo checked the alley and returned to the dead Watchman, helping Calleso drag the body into cover. There was nothing to be done about the blood on the stony street but hope that the gathering darkness hid it.

'Curfew cannot be far away,' said Jenni. 'Come, quickly. I pray Solpa is not caught.'

They jogged down the narrow alley, it widened at the far end and Jenni stopped alongside a house with a barricaded door and with the shutters nailed closed.

'Evicted for not paying rent, most likely,' Jamil hissed to Daryo. A few short yards away was the castle's tallest tower, its conical wooden roof silhouetted against the nearly-dark sky. Below it and outside the main wall of the tower was a thin outer wall, barely six feet high, with an archway into the area beyond.

'The Outer Yard,' Jenni whispered. 'Two guards, normally just inside the arch. The waste comes out at the far end. The wood store and dung heap are in there too.'

'Kill the guards quietly,' suggested Calleso.

Daryo shook his head. 'No. Incapacitate them. There is no need to kill them.'

'They work for the lord and enforce his laws,' Jamil growled.

'And have wives, children, sisters and parents as you do,' Daryo replied. 'Jenni?'

She sighed ruefully. 'I suppose I could.' She swiftly removed the sheathed sword from her belt and put the belt on again, but just under the bulge of her breast. She opened her shirt's laces a little to show a little more of her chest, pushed her leggings a little lower on her hips to show some of her flesh around her waist. 'Can you manage with me?'
Daryo nodded. 'I will be as close as a shadow.'
'Stay here,' Jenni told Calleso and Jamil. 'Wait for my signal.'
Jenni strutted confidently out of the shadows and across the open street towards the archway. When she was halfway across, Daryo ran the distance to the Outer Yard's wall and took refuge in the castle's shadow. Jenni reached the archway and leaned in.
'Good evening,' she said huskily to the guards, out of Daryo's view. 'A little chill tonight. It could be a long time out here for you. I could help you keep warm.'
'We are on duty, slut,' said one man.
'And we do not pay, we take,' said the other.
Jenni stepped through the archway. 'I could not hope to hold off one of you big, strong soldiers, not to say both of you. I say, just look at the size of those spears you both have in hand. You could pin me down and... do anything. Pin me here against the castle wall and I would be helpless.'
Daryo could only admire Jenni's work: he now knew there was two soldiers, with spears in their hands and that Jenni was against the castle wall.
'What if we did?' growled the second soldier, apparently interested.
'I could scream,' Jenni suggested.
'And who would help?'
Daryo chanced a look around the corner of the arch. Jenni was facing him, her back against the main castle wall, one soldier about six feet from her with spear in the crook of his arm, the other with spear in hand between Daryo and the first man.
'Ooh, maybe your comrade would run to my aid.'
'Or mine.'
The soldier closest to Daryo snorted. 'I would run her through well.'
Jenni gave a coquettish giggle. 'I wager you would. Why not show me?'
The man stepped forwards but his comrade was quicker, seizing Jenni's arm, pulling her away from the wall and into his grasp. 'Me first.'
Daryo stepped through the archway, raised Temma's Sword and brought it down hard on the back of the closest man's neck. The thud attracted the attention of the other guard, who's head turned and it met Jenni's fist travelling in the opposite direction. The force of the blow turned him around half-circle, Jenni drove her foot into the back of his

knees and, as he crumpled, Daryo's shield smashed him across the side of the head, sending him to oblivion with his comrade.

Jenni shook her hand and flexed the fingers. 'Perfect, Walker.'

'Well done to you. A masterful performance.'

'Not my first,' she admitted. She hurried to the archway and gave three short, low whistles as Daryo found some rope and bound the first guard, stuffing some cloth from the garbage heap into the mouth. Jamil and Calleso arrived. Jenni checked the garbage chute and sighed.

'Solpa got the rope in place.' From a square portal about eight feet up in the castle tower, just over three feet square, dangled a knotted rope. 'We need a guard down here. Calleso.'

He nodded. 'As you wish.' He pulled the jerkin off of the second guard, put it over his own clothes and took up a spear. 'I can watch our two prisoners as well.'

Daryo handed over his shield. 'Take this too. I cannot take it up the chute.' He removed his swordbelt as well, Temma's Sword would also likely be too bulky. He laid it next to the garbage pile and pulled some fat-soaked cheese-cloth over it.

Calleso accepted it and took up position with spear and shield blocking the archway. Jenni went to take the rope but Daryo got to it first.

'Strong before sweet,' he said flatly and began to scramble upwards, boosted a little by Jamil. The passage was tight, slimy and rancid but less than ten feet long. He found the top, gripped the metal-lined edges and pulled himself out, landing in an inelegant heap on the floor of the castle kitchen. He looked around quickly, drawing the Horse from over his right shoulder. The walls of the tower room were lined with large working tables, a barrel of potatoes was nearby, the fireplace warmed only by embers, the metal spit smoking slightly in the heat, a large grain ark next to the milling stones. Tallow candles on several candelabras lit the room. The rope was anchored to a beam from where meat and vegetables hung. There was a scrabbling noise and Jenni's head appeared.

'Any signs of Solpa?'

'None.'

'Safe?'

'Safe.'

Daryo helped her up through the rubbish shaft and called down. 'Come up, Jamil.'

He turned away as the grain ark opened and Solpa emerged. Jenni gave a cry of surprise and rushed forwards to help her clamber out of the huge chest full of grain.

'I heard my name,' said Solpa brightly.

'We thought you have been caught!' said Jenni. 'The Watch raided Roedan's house!'
Solpa shook her head. 'No, nothing, I hid in here. Is everyone safe?'
'Yes, no harm done.'
Jamil appeared from the chute. 'How unpleasant,' he remarked dryly, drawing his sword.
'Do you know how to get to the vaults beneath the hall, Jamil?' Jenni asked.
'Yes. We are in the square tower. Down the stairs, follow the passage along the back of the hall and down the stairs at the far end.'
'Likely guards?'
'Possible. Possible. Someone will be closing down this night: locking doors, putting out candles and such.'
'Then we need to be quick.'
Daryo drew the Bear and gave it to Solpa. 'I will want that back.'
She grinned. 'I prefer a bow.'
Jenni took some empty sacks from a nearby counter and nodded. 'Go, Jamil.'
The big Jaboen opened the kitchen door, glanced out and led the way down the curved stairs. At the bottom, ground-level, a narrow passageway led away from the tower. A decorative slit in the wall gave an obstructed view of the castle's great hall. The passage was deserted and unlit, the foursome had to grope their way along the stone wall to the far end, nearly a hundred yards, to where the stairs downwards were lit by a burning torch. Jamil took the torch from its bracket and was first down the stairs. At the bottom was a locked door. Jamil dealt with the issue by simply knocking. The guard inside unlocked it, opened to see who was trying to gain entry and was struck precisely between the eyes by the butt of Jamil's sword. He fell back, smacked his helmeted head on the stone floor and sank to oblivion. Jamil stepped delicately over the prone man and dragged him clear of the door to allow the others ingress. Jenni relieved the guard of his weapon and keys. The guard had been sat on a stool by the door in a small entryway that then led around and the main cellar stood directly under the great hall. Metal cages were set into the wall for the first twenty yards: cells, each loaded with prisoners. There was an immediate clamour for release but Jamil silenced them quickly promising aid in return for silence and patience.
Jenni locked the door and left Solpa on watch there. Beyond the cells, the cellar was a regular storeroom for vegetables and hardware. One corner was a stone box about seven feet high and five square out from the basement corner with a heavy wooden door, reinforced by iron bars.
'What do you think, Jamil?' Jenni asked anxiously.

He handed the torch to Daryo and took a closer look at the lock. 'May as well try the keys first.' Jenni handed them over. There were five and none fitted. Jamil produced a small back of lock-breaking tools and got to work.

'Hurry up,' hissed Solpa from by the door. 'What if there is a guard change?'

'I cannot go any faster than I am!' snapped Jamil, not looking up.

Daryo handed the torch on to Jenni and went to Solpa. 'Undoing locks is tricky. Best to let Jamil concentrate.'

Solpa sighed and waved the Bear, Daryo's blade, around a little aimlessly. 'We could be caught.'

'Batribi!' someone hissed from the cells.

Daryo looked around and saw a dark face behind the nearest bars. 'Are you one?'

'Trai, of my own kin.'

'Daryo, kin of Dostan. How were you caught here?'

'My clan set up camp on the edge of the town. The guards appeared and demanded a fee. We could not pay. I was given the choice to surrender myself or the clan's horses in payment. We had only three, we needed them to carry the *kaffa*, so I gave myself over.'

'Where are your kin?'

'They headed to Stannia Lake.'

'My kin are there. How long have you been here?'

'Twelve days, I believe, by the changes of guard. You should not be disturbed, that guard had only just taken post.'

'My thanks. We shall have you out in a short while. All of you,' Daryo said to the prisoners at large, roughly counting more than thirty.

Jamil cursed, stood up from the lock and then crouched back to his work.

'The lord has the key,' said one of the female prisoners on the opposite side to the Batribi captive. 'We have seen him some times; evil, money-thirsty whore-son.'

'I have heard some very unpleasant tales,' said Daryo.

'My children are having to fend for themselves,' said the woman crossly. 'Vaun is only twelve summers, Kera and Grita are only seven summers, alone in Whiteburn.'

'Not for much longer, I swear on the Second Goddess,' said Daryo.

'Dule's sweating stones...' swore Jamil, adjusting himself and reaching for another tool.

'Jamil...!' whined Solpa.

'Solpa, quiet!' barked Jenni, glaring at her.

'Shh!' insisted Daryo. 'Let him work.'

'Listen to the Walker!' growled Jamil. 'I have to focus.'

Solpa moaned to herself. Daryo put a comforting hand on her shoulder. The moments were measured in rapid heartbeats and quick breaths, only the sound of small movements of bodies, the burning torch and the clicking of Jamil's tools broke the silence.

'Jenni!' said Jamil suddenly. 'Quick, quick!' She dropped the torch and leaped to Jamil's side. 'The long... no, the other one. Yes, straight through... little more... twist right.' There was a click and Jamil gave an almighty howl of triumph, pulling the door open. The stone box was stacked with small boxes and bags of coin, mostly bronze and silver but some gold.

'Take the gold and silver first,' said Jenni, as Solpa and Daryo hurried to her side, taking the sacks from tucked in her belt. 'Quickly.'

The sacks were quickly filled and Jamil improvised a yoke with some rope. Solpa found a handled box that she could carry and Daryo took a large bag of coin, Jenni another. The vault was about three-fourths empty and Jenni pronounced herself happy.

Daryo picked up the keys, removed the one for the cellar door and tossed the remaining on their cord loop to the nearest prisoners. 'I assume that you can effect your own exit?' One of the prisoners chuckled. 'Can you?'

'They can,' said Daryo, jerking a thumb at his companions. 'Personally I might struggle.' He unlocked the cellar door and glanced up the stairs. 'Stairs are clear.'

'Go,' Jenni urged. Daryo hurried up, Solpa close behind.

At the top of the stairs, Daryo checked the passageway and, despite a sword in one hand and bag in the other, ran down the passage. He could hear voices in the great hall through the decorative window slits but continued running regardless.

'Go on, go on,' said Daryo, pausing at the far end. Solpa, Jamil and then Jenni ran past him. As Jenni set foot on the stairs, Daryo saw movement at the far end. He dived out of sight but heard a shouted challenge. 'Run!' he bellowed after the others and almost tripped as he tried to keep pace with the others. Solpa reached the kitchen, bashed the door open and squealed in shock: a castle guard was in the process of extinguishing the candles. He froze, startled for a moment. Jamil shouldered the diminutive Solpa aside and lashed out at the guard, his sword cleavering in the guard's neck before the unfortunate man could reach his own weapon.

'Out!' Jenni shouted. Jamil turned, grabbed Solpa and almost threw her down the garbage chute. Daryo dived into the kitchen and kicked the door shut, Jamil threw his shoulder against it.

'No lock!'

'Jenni, go!'

'Not without the both of you!' she argued.

'Jenni, go!'

'No!'

'Go!'

There was a thud on the far side of the door and Daryo leaned his weight in as well.

'Jenni! Solpa needs you! Go!'

'Go!' agreed Jamil.

'Be close behind me!' she insisted. She clambered onto a table, put her feet into the garbage chute and pushed herself down.

There was another bash and the clamour of several voices outside.

'I think we woke the garrison!' said Jamil.

'Just the armed ones!'

'We cannot hold this door all night.'

'I can hold it until the Fourth Goddess claims me!'

'I can hold it at least a heartbeat longer!'

'One of us can hold them.'

'Is there not a table that can be put across it?'

Daryo turned to put his back to the door and surveyed the kitchen. There was nothing that could be moved, everything large enough was anchored to the floor. Another impact from the other side of the door and an alarm bell began. 'Nothing.'

Jamil spat. 'Do me a boon, Walker.'

'Now?'

'Tell Noth and Calleso that they are simpletons, thank Jenni and hug Solpa.' He took a leather cord with a bead on it from around his neck and pressed it into Daryo's hand.

'Jamil, we can work a device...'

'No, Walker. Go, please. My mother is calling my name from across the bridge.' Another hit on the door.

'Jamil...'

'Go, Walker. Jenni would never forgive me if I came out and you died here. Just one moment.' He stepped away from the door and hurled the bags of coin down the waste passage, grabbed a meat cleaver and took station bracing the door again.

Daryo gripped his hand. 'Does it mean much to you? Your heritage?'

'Everything.'

'Say the Promise.'

'With my heart, my mind and my honour, I promise to do my duty as a Member of the Order of the Shield and Sword and to follow orders as given on the authority of the

Captain-General and his Aides. I swear my Shield and Sword to the defence of the just, the righteous, the innocent and the weak. By this oath, I pledge my sword and my service until I am discharged by death.' Jamil said the Promise of the Order at high speed and wiped away a tear. 'Jamil the Doorbolt.'
Daryo almost laughed. 'Jamil the Doorbolt. Die well.'
'But not before I take down a dozen men with me to line my route over the bridge to the Next Kingdom. Go now, Walker.'
Daryo waited for the next smash against the door, crossed the kitchen quickly and threw himself head-first down the garbage chute, pursued by Jamil's roar of defiance. Within a heartbeat, Daryo landed on his belly on the pile of waste in the castle's Outer Yard.
'Walker!' squealed Jenni. 'Where is Jamil?'
Daryo swallowed hard and picked himself up. 'Fighting the Fourth Goddess's efforts. We have to go.'
'We cannot leave him!' insisted Solpa.
'He gave his life for us to escape,' said Daryo. Calleso passed over his shield and Temma's Sword. 'We must go.' He buckled his belt quickly. Roedan and Noth had arrived and emerged from concealment.
Jenni stifled a sob. 'Solpa, Noth, Walker, north gate. Calleso, Wolfhound, with me through the flood drain. Meet at the northern milepost.'
Calleso shucked his guard's disguise and checked that the street was clear. 'Quickly, we can go now.'

\*       \*       \*


The small group gathered around the campfire and Jenni put Jamil's necklace in the flames.
'Walk with your mother, Jamil. She would be proud of you.'
'You gave so greatly and took so little, you will be rewarded in the Next Kingdom with the greatest of rewards and every one of them earned by your valour.'
'Your memory will last forever.'
'I miss you, Jamil, I miss your hand on my shoulder and voice in my ear and I will never forget either.'
'You were the embodiment of sword and service, Jamil. A truly worthy Member of the Order. Res well.'

'May the Fourth Goddess guide you to our fallen brothers and sisters, Jamil. Look for Hoyuz the Calm, Leroyfa the Blind, Kym the Harlequin, Toxiz the Coalfire and they will honour you as we do, Jamil the Doorbolt.'

'Jamil the Doorbolt,' echoed the others.

After a few moments' silence, Jenni shook her in wonder. 'The Doorbolt!'

The shared laugh dissolved the tension.

'Where you will go now, Roedan?' Noth asked the elder.

The Wolfhound thought for a moment. 'Gourmin is my home. I tried to make a home in Sinsebil but that has been taken from me. I think I should return to the home I knew as a child: Allesbury. I will go south to Whiteburn and I can get a boat from there to Allesbury.'

Jenni retrieved one of the small boxes of money. 'This should buy you what you need, Roedan. It is because of us that you have lost your home, it is only right that our efforts help you find a new home.'

Roedan gave a short bow. 'My grateful thanks.'

'I will come with you,' Daryo told him. 'I still have more of Gourmin to see. I will come as far as Allesbury with you.'

'You are most welcome, Walker.'

Jenni looked appalled. 'Are you not staying, Walker?'

'I am not. This is the life you chose, Jenni, and a worthy one it is. But I am the Walker, it is what I must do.'

'You could be so helpful to us,' Noth said.

'I know... but nonetheless.' Daryo went to his pack and brought out the money he had left. 'One in five, I believe was the toll.'

'But we took so much from the lord!' protested Solpa.

'A little more wine is never too much,' said Daryo with a smile. He counted out the coin. A good proportion had gone since he left the Silver Island but he was still able to hand over twenty gold halves and seven bronze to amazement from Solpa and protests from both Noth and Calleso. 'I give only one restriction. If you find the Batribi that was in the dungeons, Trai, then give him four of the gold halves. If not, then it is yours to distribute as you wish.'

Jenni seized his arm and pulled him a few yards away from the others. 'I want you to stay, Daryo.'

'Jenni, no.'

'Why not?'

'Because I cannot. I would come to care for you again, Jenni, and I have lost too many people that I care for. You are a fine woman, Jenni, a wonderful woman, a true leader and a formidable fighter. And I thank all of the Pantheon for bringing us together again once more.' He kissed her on the forehead. 'Gods' Guidance. I pray we may meet again one day.'

Noth escorted Roedan and Daryo on horseback along the forest tracks through Little Gap and then around the eastern side of Sinsebil. They crossed a river and followed another network of paths until emerging from the woods on a paved road leading from Sinsebil to the south and east.
'We are nearly twenty miles from Sinsebil. Follow the road and it will lead into Whiteburn and Riverhelm beyond. Whiteburn is well less than a day's walk.'
'My thanks, Noth,' said Daryo as he dismounted. 'You have been a great boon. Good fortune to you.'
'And to you, Walker, Wolfhound. Gods' Guidance.'
Daryo and Roedan began to walk south as Noth and the horses returned to the trees.

## Chapter 55

A timber barge had, for a significant sum, had agreed to take Roedan and his "servant" downriver from Whiteburn to Allesbury. On the dock at Allesbury, they parted as friends. Daryo spent some time wondering at the fantastic, extravagant step-shaped building containing the renowned Archive, soaring for over half a mile in length and scores of feet high. Then he crossed the near-empty square to the Temple of the First God and spent a significant time praying there.

'What are you doing?' asked a voice.

Daryo looked around. A priest, very fat and of about forty summers was waddling across.

'Praying, sir. Are Batribi not welcome in the Temple?'

'Of course they are. Do you not know of the trouble?'

'Trouble? I know of no trouble. I arrived in the city only in the forenoon.'

'The tax rises this season have caused much upset. Many people, particularly from the city Without the Wall, are marching on the lord's house in protest.'

Daryo nodded and stood. 'I came in through the southern gate. What other exits from the city are there?'

'The Archive Gate,' the priest replied. 'Beneath the top level of the Archive, a smaller gate into the Town Without.'

'The road to Spiert?'

'Through the Town Without and you will find the road.'

'My thanks.'

There were noises and shouts, voices chanting and Daryo walked quickly through the portion of Allesbury that stood outside the walls. The road to Spiert was easily found and he left the city behind.

Gourmin could easily mean 'the land of perpetual forest' or 'endless tree country', Daryo decided. Both sides of the road were lined with trees, all full of summer foliage, the ground between them strewn with bracken and other shrubbery. The land was almost flat and the road well-paved. After a few miles, Daryo stopped for a brief rest, sat against a round, flat Gourmini milestone. The clear day and bright sun were conducive to walking but the hot weather was difficult. He stripped off his armoured jerkin and tied it on to the top of his pack before continuing. The trees went on and on. A deer on the path ahead saw Daryo's approach and skittered away into the forests.

'Oh... oh no.' A figure emerged from the trees; dark skinned, only about fourteen summers old, he was dressed in only a vest-like sleeveless linen top, leggings and boots, carrying a bow and with a quiver on their back. 'I was hunting that all morning.'
Daryo smiled apologetically. 'I am very sorry. I did not even see the deer until it ran. Are you one?'
'I am Exalra, kin of Reryo.'
'I am Daryo, kin of Dostan. I am travelling to Spiert.'
'My clan is camped nearby. Our ox is injured, we are having to wait for it to heal before we move on. You would be welcome.'
Daryo nodded. 'My thanks.'
There were only three *kaffa*, a single ox and a cart in a small clearing not far from the road. The ox had an ugly-looking poultice on its neck where the yoke would have sat as it stood, tied by its nose ring, a short distance from the *kaffa*. There was no fire, no watch, just three elders sat by a *kaff*, two youngsters of less than ten summers and a woman that appeared to be their mother. The adolescent who had met Daryo passed a few cursory words with the woman and ducked into a *kaff*.
'Daryo, kin of Dostan.'
'Siua, kin of Reryo.' She was small and looked somewhat haggard, her hair dusty and in disarray.
'The boy Exalra was kind enough to invite me to your camp.'
'My eldest son.'
'He was hunting deer but unfortunately I startled his quarry.'
'He is not a good hunter.'
Daryo was concerned by the woman's monotone voice and barely-awake look. 'If I may, can I meet Reryo?'
The woman shook her head. 'Reryo is dead.'
'Are you not kin of Reryo?'
'We are. He was my husband.'
'I am sorry. When did he pass?'
'In the winter.'
'You have been two seasons calling yourselves kin of a dead man.'
Siua nodded dully. 'Burel, Bulvan and Brai too old. Exalra, Toulra and Nurini are too young.'
'And yourself?'
She shrugged as the young girl, Nurini, came up. 'Mother, I am thirsty.'
'There is no water,' her mother said flatly. 'You must wait.'

The girl, no more than twenty-four seasons old, looked confused. 'But I am thirsty.'
'And there is no water.'
Daryo dropped his pack, overwhelmed by sudden anger, the three elders barely looked up. He took the waterskin from the side and gave it to the girl. 'Here, drink what you wish and pass the rest to your brothers.'
The girl looked as if she had been blessed by a god and took the skin, opening and drinking greedily.
'Exalra?'
The boy came out of the *kaff*. 'Yes?'
'There is water in the skin that your sister has. While you were hunting, did you find a water source? A stream or river?' The boy thought and nodded. 'You have a water barrel?'
'On the cart.'
'I will fill it. When you, your brother and your sister have drunk, collect some firewood.'
'It is too hot for a fire,' protested Siua.
'Do it,' Daryo instructed. 'Firewood.'
'Yes, sir.'
'Where was the water?'
'A stream, just on the other side of the road, sir.'
'Good. Get to it, Exalra.'
'Yes, sir.'
'This is my clan,' said Siua plaintively.
'No, it is Reryo's clan,' retorted Daryo, going to the cart and finding the small water barrel. It was totally empty and barely a foot long or wide. Returning to the road, crossing it, he found the stream, barely ankle-deep and filled the barrel as well as he could. Returning to the campsite, he noticed that the three *kaffa* were badly erected, their anchoring lines slack and badly pegged. After pouring water for the three elders, he had Siua build and light a fire while Daryo showed Exalra how to erect and secure the *kaffa* properly.
'How long have you been here?' Daryo asked the boy.
Exalra thought. 'Four mornings.'
'Do you know why the ox is wounded?'
'No.'
'The yoke is not secured properly. It has been rubbing on the animal's back and causing the sore. Where were you travelling to?'
Exalra shrugged. 'We were in Allesbury.'
'So towards Spiert.'

'If you say, I do not know.'
'Away from the rising sun.'
'Yes.'
Daryo nodded. 'That is towards Spiert. Who is deciding where you travel?'
'My mother.'
The *kaffa* secure, Daryo took Exalra out, with only a bow and a dozen arrows to hunt. 'You must mind the wind's direction,' Daryo told the boy in a whisper. 'If it is in your face, your prey cannot smell you. If it is at your back, it will know you approach. So when you hunt, move with or across the wind.'
They crept from tree to tree, Daryo having Exalra choose when and where to move and referring to the wind. Eventually a small deer came into sight.
'Move very slowly and make no noise,' Daryo hissed. 'If the animal looks, stay as still as stone.' Very carefully, Daryo nocked an arrow and very slowly raised the bow. The deer froze but looked in the wrong direction. Daryo levelled his aim, breathed out slowly and as he reached the end of his breath he released the arrow. The deer was alerted a heartbeat too late and the arrow lodged deep in its neck, knocked it down. Daryo quickly stood up, nocked another arrow and fired again as the deer kicked in its death-throes. The second arrow struck just under the doe's jaw and the deer went still.
'A Gods-given shot!' said Exalra, impressed.
Daryo led the way through the trees to the lifeless deer; it was small but sufficient and Exalra helped lift the animal onto Daryo's shoulders and he carried it back to the campsite. Siua had retired to sleep; the elders were sat around the fire, tended by Exalra's younger brother Toulra; Nurini and Exalra watched Daryo butcher the deer and put some of the meat over the fire to cook.
'What part of the deer is that?' Nurini asked.
'The shoulder,' Daryo told her. He put his hand on her shoulder. 'That part.'
'How do you cut it up?'
'You watched me.'
'Could you show me?'
'Perhaps not with a deer, Nurini. It is bigger than you are. If I can catch a rabbit, perhaps I could show you with a rabbit.'
'I do not know if mother would want Nurini cutting up a rabbit,' said Exalra, glancing at the *kaffa* where their mother was sleeping.
'How old are you, Nurini?' Daryo asked.
'Nine summers.'

'Easily old enough to be learning to cut up rabbits.' Daryo turned the meat over with his makeshift wooden spit, winking at Nurini, who giggled. 'And you, Toulra?'
'Eight winters.'
'I could show you as well if you wish.'
'Yes!'
Daryo smiled and turned the meat again, glancing at the three elders, sat nearby, wordlessly staring at the sky in a concerning, vacant manner. Siua was still in the *kaff* and the sound of regular snores was audible. Daryo gave Nurini instructions on how to turn the meat and then went to examine the ox. The sores on its back were almost healed. Daryo decided that with the new dawn it could travel a little further as long as the yoke was properly secured; if in the correct place the yoke may not even touch the wounds.
'Exalra, I think it best to move on with the new day.'
'Mother wanted to stay here until the ox was fit.'
'I think it is. If the yoke is properly secured and padded then it should do well.'
'Where would we go?'
'You were walking towards Spiert, so was I. I can escort you that far. If there is another clan of Batribi there, or on the road, it may be good for you to join them, at least for a short period.'
'You could stay with us,' said Nurini.
Daryo smiled. 'I have to keep on beyond Spiert to Sitak but my gracious thanks for your offer, Nurini.'

'No.' Siua folded her arms across her chest defiantly.
'Mother...'
'Siua, the ox is fit to work, this is not an ideal site to camp and, speaking frankly, I think it would be best that you had some... assistance.'
'What do you mean?'
'When I arrived there was no fire, no water, the *kaffa* would have blown down in a decent wind.'
Siua frowned. 'Everything was adequate.'
'It was not,' Daryo replied bluntly. 'Your children were thirsty and you were telling them to go without water.'
'They are *my* children.'
'They are your children and you were not caring for them. What would you eat tonight?'
'We would find something.'
'Windfall fruit and roots?'

'Perhaps.'

Daryo shook his head. 'Exalra, excuse us for a moment.' The boy nodded and hurried away towards the ox. Daryo looked straight into Siua's eyes. 'Siua, your clan has no leader, no direction. How long would you have camped here? Truly? How much longer would you have gone on calling yourself the kin of a dead man?'

'That man was my husband!'

'And he is gone, Siua. I am sorry, I am deeply sorry, but he is gone. The Fourth Goddess does not allow those we love to return any more than she allows those we hate to return. I have lost comrades, kinsmen, the woman I loved and one must learn to accept that. The man who first named me kin died but it is important, especially for our people, to have a strong clan and a leader that can take their kin forwards. With no bellwether, the flock is lost.'

Siua's face was streaked with tears. 'I loved him.'

'As I loved Carini. But we must move on. Along the road and in our hearts. With the new dawn, we will leave for Spiert. It is my hope that we can find another Batribi clan that you could join with, they would be able to support you and to help you with your needs. There is no shame in being unable to lay a fire, someone can teach you or assist you in doing it.'

Siua nodded. 'At dawn?'

'After dawn, I will have Exalra help me take down the *kaffa* and prepare to leave. I will take you as far as Spiert.'

## Chapter 56

With the yoke padded with a blanket and properly secured, the ox's sores were untouched and it gave no protest as Daryo harnessed it to the cart. Siua and Exalra cajoled and persuaded the elders in while Daryo started to strike the camp, helped by the youngsters. In a short space of time the cart was loaded and Siua in the driving seat, the children walked alongside with Daryo as they headed east on the road to Spiert.

After a few miles, Toulra jumped up to ride alongside his mother, Nurini the same soon afterwards, leaving just Exalra trotting next to Daryo. The day was warm and windy, the breeze at their backs as the road tilted downhill towards the coast. The forest thinned out and became a bare moor by the end of the morning. In the long distance was the dark smudge of a town against the coast.

'Is that Spiert?' Exalra asked.

Daryo strained his eyes towards the blot. 'I think it may be.'

'Have you been to Spiert before?'

'I have not. Although I have known some people from the town.'

'Who were they?'

'Just some soldiers.'

'You were a soldier?'

'Not... not precisely that.' Daryo briefly explained something of the Order and the battles he had fought with them, alone and with the Batribi of Stannia Lake; Exalra listened in total enthralment.

After a brief rest at midday, one of the elders began getting agitated, crying for aid and rejecting any attempt at reason. Siua guided the ox cart into the shade, Daryo and Exalra helped her to get the elderly man down. Nurini fetched water and it took some time to calm him, the late Reryo's uncle, and then return him to the cart. Siua tried to urge the ox on to greater speed but by mid-afternoon Daulra, son of Reryo the older, had passed to the Next Kingdom. The little procession stopped and a tearful group of youngsters helped Daryo gather wood for a small pyre. By sunset, Noryo, also son of Reryo, had passed along with his brother. Only Liua, Siua's aged aunt, sat by the small campfire that night.

Exalra, tears running unheeded, set the light to the pyre bearing the two pitifully small shrouded figures.

'Daulra and Noryo, walk well across the bridge to the Next Kingdom,' said Siua quietly. 'Look for your father's son, my husband, the father of my children, Reryo, son of Reryo the older. May the Fourth Goddess guide him and you.'

She walked away, leading Nurini and Toulra by the hand, leaving Exalra and Daryo watching the fire burn.

'My father did not get a fire,' Exalra said calmly. 'He was very sick and he died in the winter. The wood was too wet and cold to be burned and mother and I used an axe to make a hole in the ground.'

'I am very sorry for your losses, Exalra. I have no knowledge of my father. I never knew him and I do not know when or where, or even if, he died. He could be alive somewhere unknown.'

'What of your mother?'

'Died in an accident when I was an infant.'

Exalra stared into the fire. 'Do you think that the Fourth Goddess guards the bridge or does she walk the dead across it?'

Daryo shook his head sadly. 'I do not know. I think that perhaps she escorts the dead to the bridge and then they can walk across at their leisure to meet their friends or their kin.'

'So my father will be waiting for his brothers on the far side?'

'I hope so, Exalra. I truly hope so. When my time comes, I hope that my mother and father wait for me, alongside... some significant people to me.'

'Who?'

Daryo smiled sadly to himself. 'Kym... Leroyfa... Carini... Viulra... some others.'

'Should we put up the shelters?'

'I think so, yes. Just two: one for your mother, her aunt and your sister; one for us and Toulra.'

'Can I do the work and you can watch and assist if needed?'

'As you wish. Confident as to what to do?'

'I think I am. You watch and assist.'

Exalra, with a little help with the heavier support poles, erected two *kaffa* very competently. Nurini, with Daryo's guidance, rebuilt and lit the campfire before starting to roast some more of the deer from the previous day. After eating, Daryo felt distinctly content. The evening was warm and still, the fire dying, Nurini had drifted off to sleep, Toulra was whittling, Liua and Siua were asleep in the *kaff*, Exalra was carefully wiping the ox's harness with a piece of cloth.

'What is this?' asked an unfamiliar, gruff voice.

Daryo started and went to rise. Two Gourmini men, both with bows, had appeared from the twilight and the cover of some rocks.

'Stay still, Batribi!' ordered one, his hand dropping to the knife at his belt. Both men were wearing black tabards with a white ship badge.

Daryo stayed on the floor but raised his hands to shoulder height. Outwardly a gesture of submission but taking his hands close to the hilts of his twin swords over his shoulders.

'We mean to do no harm. We are simply staying for this night and we will leave with dawn.'

'Who shot the deer?' asked the second man, taller than the first, slightly older and with a sword as well as bow.

'Who asks?'

'I am Jaben Blyk, Warden for the Lord of Spiert.'

'I am Daryo the Walker, and I shot it,' said Daryo. 'Three days ago near Allesbury.'

Exalra's eyes widened but he said nothing.

'The deer of Gourmin belong to the lord.'

'I did not know this,' replied Daryo. 'I have a little coin, I can pay the value of the animal.'

'That is not acceptable. You pay with a hand.' The man drew his sword. 'You will all come to Spiert and be given to the command of the sheriff.'

Daryo ignored the previous caution and stood, keeping his hands raised. 'You will not touch these people. They are not my kin, they have simply allowed me to travel a short distance with them. I will accompany you. They remain.'

'All will come and all will answer for the crime.'

'Two children who cannot draw bow?'

'I said all.'

Daryo shook his head. 'Unacceptable.'

'This crime is unacceptable, Batribi. And by the laws of the Lord of Spiert, the whole of the group will answer for it.'

Daryo's hands went to the hilts of his twin swords. 'I will defend these people with my life.'

'Then you forfeit that.'

Daryo drew his weapons and without thinking spun the Bear point downwards. Toulra shrieked and dived into the *kaff* in which his mother was asleep. Exalra leaped to his feet, reaching for a spare pole for the *kaffa*. The shorter man was closest and got to the wooden pole first, seizing it and clouting Exalra on the side of the head, knocking the boy aside.

Daryo acted without thinking: he hurled the Horse at the miscreant, tossed the Bear to his right hand and right it just in time to block the incoming sword blow. The Spiert

man was big but surprised by the sudden aggressive resistance. He tried to attack again and walked on to Daryo's flying left fist. As he staggered, Daryo struck his assailant in the face with the butt of the Bear and planted his boot in the Gourmini's gut. The swordsman fell and Daryo trod on him as he went for the other. The smaller Gourmini thought of resisting and decided that the sword-wielding Batribi was too much of a challenge and threw the pole down.
'Take your comrade and get out!' instructed Daryo as Exalra staggered to his feet.
'You will die for this, Batribi!' The man picked up his winded and stunned colleague and they withdrew quickly. Daryo retrieved the Horse ruefully, noticing Nurini was awake.
'How is your head, Exalra?'
'Hurts.'
'It will pass.' Daryo inspected it. 'There is no mark or blood.'
Toulra and Siua came out of the *kaff*. 'What happened?' she asked, her son clutching her tightly.
'Some of Spiert's men. Apparently unhappy that I killed their deer. They struck Exalra but he will be quite fine. I must leave you though.'
'No, we need you!' said Exalra immediately.
Daryo smiled fondly. 'I am sorry. They will return to Spiert, fetch reinforcements and come looking for me. I wounded their pride more than their bodies and for a man like that, that will sting more than arrow or sword. I recommend you turn about, go back west, as the searchers may not distinguish between one Batribi and another.'
Siua looked up and down Daryo for a long moment. 'You have been a great help, Daryo, kin of Dostan.'
'My thanks, Siua, kin of Reryo.'
'No.' She looked at Exalra and Nurini. 'Would you name us kin?'
Daryo was surprised. 'I am not the leader of my clan. But my brother is.' He thought for a moment. 'If you are going to go west, and can make it such a distance, go to the Batribi settlement by Stannia Lake. Find a man named Dostan and tell him that you have met me. If he questions it, tell him I suggested that Nurini would make a good wife for our brother when she is a little older, that will prove your credentials.'
Siua nodded her understanding. 'My thanks, Daryo. For all you have done. Gods' Guidance to you.'
'And to you, all of you.'

Daryo had expected the hunting party. There were nine, all armed with swords, shields and with some bows in evidence, wearing the black and white of Spiert. The warden,

Jaben Blyk, was at the head alongside a man with a gold and green leaves in an arc around the ship on his tabard and a jewel-pommeled sword in hand.

'That is him!' exclaimed Blyk, with Daryo around a hundred yards away.

Swords were drawn and arrows nocked. Daryo spread his arms apart.

'I am not going to resist,' Daryo replied, stopping still.

The man alongside Blyk stepped forwards. 'I am the Under-Sherriff of Spiert. You are hereby arrested for the crime of poaching. You will be taken to the guardhouse and put before the sheriff with the new dawn.'

'I plead the right of referral,' Daryo replied simply.

'The...?'

'I have the right to appeal directly to the Lord of Spiert, not to the sheriff.'

Blyk glanced at the Under-Sherriff. 'Is that true?'

The Under-Sherriff thought for a long moment. 'I will have to confirm that with the Sherriff. Disarm him.'

Daryo drew his weapons one by one and handed them over to one of the soldiers. Another relieved him of his pack, his wrists were manacled and he was escorted towards Spiert.

Unlike Sinsebil's castle, Spiert's was built into the city walls, the gate of the city was also the western gate of the castle, all traffic therefore had to pass through the castle gates and courtyard to reach the town itself. In the long courtyard, Daryo was taken to a guardroom, directed into a small basement cell and locked in. It was almost sundown before he was extracted, led through a succession of back corridors and staircases to the main hall. The day's business was apparently concluding, several well-dressed traders and important-looking personages were leaving the hall. At the far end, sat behind a large tables, flanked by a clerk and a robed official, was a bald-skulled man with a missing eye and badly scarred visage wearing a black tunic with a small silver brooch of the ship of Spiert on his breast. His single blue-tinged bloodshot eye regarded the new arrival.

'I know you, Batribi,' he said.

'Yes, sir. You do, Aedan, Lord of Spiert. You were most perturbed when young Cadern and Marshal Ingit nominated me as commander of the army.'

The lord seized a staff and pushed himself upright from his chair. He rounded the table quickly and stared into Daryo's face. 'The Walker.'

Daryo gave a short bow. 'Indeed, sir.'

'What is this man doing in chains?' demanded Aedan, looking around.

Blyk stepped forwards. 'My lord, he shot a deer on these lands.'

'Not on these lands, sir,' Daryo responded calmly. 'Much closer to Allesbury, well within Lord Mergret's jurisdiction. I was unaware that to do so was unlawful or I would have hunted another animal.'

'Ignorance is no defence,' snapped Blyk.

'I had encountered a family who were starving. And I repeat that if I had known shooting a deer was a crime, I would have hunted a pig.'

'The crime is still a crime, my lord!' Blyk protested. 'A woman is still a housewife, a man is still a man, the sun still rises in the east!'

Aedan glared at his warden. 'This man did untold service to Gourmin, Blyk. A wrongdoing through error is nothing compared to victory at Aslon and Tiverta, is it not?'

The warden inclined his head in submission. 'Release the chains.'

Reluctantly Warden Jaben Blyk unlocked the cuffs on Daryo's wrists. 'My lord.'

'Bring any baggage, weapons and other items he carried.'

'Yes, my lord.' The warden withdrew reluctantly.

'My grateful thanks, Lord Aedan,' said Daryo when the warden was gone.

'I apologise for Jaben. He is rather inflexible and sees no further than the rules he enforces.'

'Nonetheless you must be aware of the nature of the deed I have just done on your behalf.'

'And I am most grateful, Lord Aedan.'

'You will dine here tonight as my guest and be welcome. However, to uphold the laws of this nation, I must command you to leave Spiert with the dawn.'

'As you wish.'

## Chapter 57

The room that Daryo had been given was a basement chamber with a bed and nothing else. He was glad to leave. The guard at the city-side gate refused to let Daryo enter the town and directed him through the opposite exit. With a weary sigh, Daryo turned on his heel when a commotion by the doors of the main hall attracted his attention. There was a rush of people out of the hall, one of them was Aedan leaning on a sturdy staff. He sighted Daryo.

'Walker! Batribi!' he beckoned Daryo over. 'Do you still travel?'

'I do, sir.'

'Then you may have seen this before. Come.'

Daryo decided not to argue. Aedan was helped into the saddle of a waiting horse and a small retinue of around a dozen men, including Daryo, headed into the town. The streets were narrow, the houses timber and the town remarkably flat. It was also a small town, within less than a mile they were on a stone breakwater that curved out to protect the harbour, a beacon on the end. It took Daryo a few heartbeats to realise the incongruity: the harbour had no water. The boats were sat on muddy sand, a large warship was laying on its side, masts parallel to the ground.

'Where is the water?' asked one of Aedan's aides.

Aedan hissed in frustration. 'You dolt, the water is gone, that is why Manser fetched us!' He looked around. 'Walker, anything like you have seen?'

'No, sir,' admitted Daryo. 'Never. If this were a river, I would blame a drought but how can the ocean suffer drought? Is it known how far the water has receded?'

'It cannot be seen from the beacon,' replied a grizzled man of at least fifty-five summers bearing a staff similar to Lord Aedan's.

'Where is higher than the beacon?' Daryo asked immediately.

'Only the tower,' replied the man, pointing back at the castle. Alongside the city gate of the castle was the tallest of the three towers.

'Can I get a look from there?' Daryo requested.

'You can,' said Aedan. 'Manser, go with him.'

The staff-bearer nodded. 'Certainly, my lord.'

The return to the castle and climbing to the summit of the tower was painfully slow. Manser, accompanying Daryo, had a distinctly slow gait and leaned heavily on his staff. At the top, Daryo craned over the edge to get the best view towards the sea. He struggled to see through the hazy morning light. There was nothing to see and nothing to hear but the rush of wind. Manser realised the fact as Daryo did.

'There is no wind,' the older man said.

'What is the noise?' asked Daryo, looking around from the tower. 'There is no cliff for a landslide.'

'It is not coming from the land side,' said Manser. 'It seems almost to be coming from the sea.'

Daryo crossed back to the seaward side of the tower where Manser was stood. The tower's watchman joined him, curious. 'It is getting louder... a wave!' He pointed out to the centre of the bay.

Manser peered out. 'I cannot see it.'

'A wave heading towards the harbour. Maybe a freak of the tides?'

'I can see the wave now.'

The rushing noise was increasing. Daryo was increasingly aware that the wave was immense.

'That wave is large, far too large.'

It was approaching, speeding up the bay, the rush becoming a roar, the wave was towering over the harbour wall, now the beacon, a wall of water that looked over sixty feet tall. It was a brown-blue battering ram as wide as the bay.

'My honoured Lady...' breathed Manser.

'First God, giver of life, preserve us,' Daryo whispered in the same instant.

The wave hit the harbour wall and demolished the beacon like a pile of sand before a kicking boot. The wall then followed, the boats were demolished by the relentless force of water and with a indefinably terrible crash, the wave broke on the first buildings of the town. A black tide of water smashed the houses, the chapel of the White Lady crumbled, warehouses, shops, the temple, every other structure in Spiert was crushed and swept along with the irresistible torrent of water, sand, mud and debris. The water hit the castle and Daryo heard a piercing scream over the roaring of water and crashing of debris. The tower rocked like a tree in a storm but remained standing. Only the very tops of the gatehouses remained but the city side gate's outer parapet was demolished by a rush of debris. The other two towers of the castle also rocked but their summits remained untouched.

'My wife! My daughter!' screamed the watchman, sinking to his knees.

Daryo stood transfixed, horrified, beyond any real thought as the dark surge battered onwards inland, his ears full of the growl of waterborne debris and rushing water. In what felt like half a day but perhaps it could have been an hour, the water became a turbulent lake, covering almost all of the town. Daryo tried to move, to do anything that he could find to help with the situation but the harbour wall had crumpled like parchment before the wave and he could think of nothing to do. Gradually, black and strewn with debris and floating bodies, the waters began to recede towards the sea.

'My honoured Lady...' muttered Manser again, walking around the tower wall. On the other two towers, clusters of figures could be seen. He stepped carefully around the watchman, sat sobbing against the parapet. Daryo went to him.

'They would have known nothing- swift and painless, without suffering,' he said kindly. 'I cannot say any words to assuage your pain but the few of us that survive are going to be needed. What is your name?'

'Failber.'

'Failber, I need you to think and focus your mind on the necessary.'

The man wiped his eyes and allowed Daryo to help him to stand. 'Yes, sir.'

The waters by that time were visibly retreating back towards the harbour, an ebbing tide of filth and destruction.

'What could cause such a thing?' Manser wondered aloud. 'What notion of a god could consider such a tragedy? All those children, all those women and their children...'

'Not just women and their children,' said Daryo. 'Men, horses, cows. By Dule, even the Lord of Spiert. Lord Aedan must be killed.'

'The lord dead?' asked the watchman.

'He was by the harbour. Undoubtedly.'

'His son survives,' said Manser. 'He is in Tiverta, leading our city's company of the army. He is of age.'

'Does the lord have a wife, other children?'

'Lady Geta and the lord's daughters are summering in Jaboen.'

'I pray they are not in Nalb,' said Daryo.

'No, they are in Halmia.'

'Could this be everywhere?' asked Failber.

Manser considered. 'I think not. Imagine throwing a stone into a river. The ripples lap the banks on either side but upstream and downstream they are swallowed by the current. If such a... wave is from a great impact, a rockfall into the sea from a cliff perhaps, the wave will dissipate out in the bay. I pray it does.'

'What of Sitak?' Daryo wondered. 'That is also on the bay.'

'But guarded by the Rocks of the Gulls,' said Manser. 'The Catch Bay is kinder to Gourmin than the Sea of Dith to Yashoun.'

The waters were draining faster, the tops of houses and the shattered dome of the Temple of the Pantheon became visible; the seaward side of the dome was entirely missing. Daryo remembered passing it earlier on the route to the harbour and recalled it being a Temple to the Third Goddess. The Fourth would be most concerned with Spiert henceforth. A body, halfway between draped and impaled on the roof of the temple, became visible and Manser shuddered.

'What was your role, Manser?' Daryo enquired, searching drastically for something to fill the void in his thoughts.

'I am... was... the lord's steward.'

'Someone will still need to maintain control.'

'There will be few to control.'

'Do not believe that. A horse must be found, soldiers must be brought in or those who prey on destruction will soon arrive to plunder Spiert.'

'Spiert is a dead city now.'

'It does not have to be. You can rebuild. Bring in those from the villages, welcome Batribi clans, the soldiers will be returning, labourers and craftsmen can come and rebuild and be welcomed as the new citizens.'

'You are most... hopeful, Batribi.'

'I simply believe that nothing is beyond hope or help.'

Shortly before midday, the waters had all but faded. Daryo led the way down from the tower, leaving everything but his twin swords on the top. Halfway down, the stairs were covered in thick, slippery filth and debris, requiring a lot of care to avoid a nasty fall. The castle courtyard looked like a ploughed field after a rain storm- thick mud and sand with deep puddles- but scattered with pieces of stone, wood and bodies. From another tower, a small number of men emerged, looking bewildered and scared. A single woman came from the gatehouse, holding her shoulder and sobbing. Another woman came from the great hall. The third tower disgorged the greatest number- six. Daryo went to the woman near the gatehouse. She was covered in muck and bleeding from an injury to her head. Her left arm hung from its joint, useless.

'I was... water... against the wall,' she panted. 'Arm broken.'

Daryo examined it carefully. 'I believe so. Try not to move it. I have some wine in my pack, I think so at least, I will get some as soon as I can. What is your name?'

'Corin.'

'Corin, come over with me.'

Manser had gathered the others by the city side gate. There were five guardsmen including Failber, a stableboy, a page, one of Manser's stewarding staff, the castle's apothecary and two masons, a baker, Corin was a maid and the other two women were of the castle's dairy.

'Feid, Athfeail, I want you to walk out of the city,' the steward instructed the page and his aide, trying not to glance at a broken body only yards away. Feid go south towards Tapspiert. If the village was also hit by the wave, go inland to Vierdale. Find a horse and ride for Sitak for aid. Athfeail, there is the farm to the north, Master Kindre.'

'I know it, Steward.'

'Take a horse and ride for Allesbury. Whatever needs, if the horse dies as you reach the Archive, so be it.'

'Aye, Steward.'

'Go now.'

The two men began to wade through the mud towards the outer gate.

'Ducich, was your chamber affected?' The apothecary shook his head. 'Prepare a potion for Corin to dull the pain. Can anyone here signal?'

'Aye, Steward,' said the page.

'Up to the summit of the north tower, Ingit. Watch for any signs of aid. Or of danger. If any ships approach, signal them away.'

'Aye, Steward.'

'All of the rest of you... we must start assembling the bodies, naming any that we can. Groups of three, bring them to the courtyard here, it is the best that we can do. Beware of spoil and of damaged walls and the like. Be careful, there has been enough death here this day.'

Daryo found himself working with one of the women, a motherly lady named Carra, and the older of the masons, a bluff-faced, distinctly swarthy man named Santejoso. With Manser's group in the great hall and the other groups in the towers, Daryo led his companions out of the city gate and they were immediately confronted by a low barrier of debris against the arch of the gateway and a wall of bodies thrown into the wreckage. They began to extract the sodden, lifeless figures from the mess: a girl of around twelve summers, an elderly man, a man in the uniform of the city, a man of Daryo's age stripped bare by the current but for the shreds of a shirt, a dog, another girl with her chest grotesquely crushed by an impact. Each one was carried into the courtyard, arranged with some semblance of dignity and covered with whatever fabric, cloth or box that could be found. The apothecary, a man of letters, had chalk and wrote the gender and an approximate age for each on their covering.

\*     \*     \*

Aid took three days. Sitak had been unaffected and a score of men arrived, four of them physicians but they soon became simply grave-tenders as pits began to be dug west of the castle. A priest of the Good Shepherd came from one of the villages and was willing to join the filthy, stinking work. The sun was hot and the muddy sand dried to a hard, salty crust that cracked underfoot and turned to powder when broken. The number of bodies was in the hundreds but Manser guessed that many more had been washed out to sea by the water as the total should have been many more. The city itself was a brown-coated wasteland. Not a single building was intact, the castle the only structure to escape fatal injury. The chapel of the White Lady was erased entirely, also anything within fifty yards of the harbour. The immense basket from the top of the beacon pole was found twenty yards inland of the castle. With the fifth day, a significant convoy of men and supplies arrived from Allesbury, with a promise that more would follow swiftly. Exhausted, stinking and filthy, Daryo and the other survivors retired to the camp established by the Allesbury men to rest.

After eleven days of helping clear the dead and detritus of Spiert, Daryo left the town, emotionally drained and physically tired, his progress southwards towards Sitak was a slow plod. Over two hundred men from Allesbury and thirty from Sitak had arrived and a further hundred had been promised by messenger from Aslon. The new young lord, Themar, son of Aedan, had been summoned from Tiverta and Daryo felt that his contribution had been more than sufficient, a sentiment echoed by Manser when the Walker excused himself for the final time.
With just half a day's travelling done, Daryo decided to give up the day as a poor one's effort and set up camp. The day was fantastically hot and, within just a few miles of the shore, there was little cover on the road. Daryo left it by a few yards to find a cluster of trees to shelter under. He slung his canvas as shelter, stripped to just his underclothes and laid on a blanket on the thin, pale grass in the shade to rest. He fell asleep in the heat and was woken by the cool of the evening, shortly after sundown. He was just about to reach for some clothing when he heard a voice.
'He could be dead.'
'No. Sleeping.' The voices were Gourmini and close, less than twenty yards.

Daryo remained absolutely still, laying on his back, head to his left side, trying to recall where he had laid his weapons. Half opening one eyes, he could see the rim of his shield just shining in the last light of day. His swords were under his shield, he thought.

'Definitely Batribi. Where there's one, there's normally a whole herd.'

'No, he is alone.'

'Why kill him? Take the bag and the shield and leave him asleep.'

'No, he might wake. And we want only what we can carry easily. There will be a lot more to take in Spiert. Cannot be weighed down by rubbish.'

'Fair.' The sound of a sword being drawn. 'Neck?'

'Simplest.'

A few footsteps, moving to Daryo's right hand. He waited as long as he dared, heard the attacker inhale sharply as he raised his weapon. Daryo rolled to his right quickly, into the swordsman's legs. The man yelped in surprise and lurched backwards, the surprise become pain as Daryo's bare foot struck him square in the groin with some force. The man's comrade exclaimed something and Daryo heard another sword draw. He rolled back to the left quickly, over his blanket, over his shield and seized it as a sword swung down. Daryo came to rest on his back, his shield with the inner side facing up, as the sword drove into the ground pinioning his sword belt. With as much force as he could Daryo hurled his shield at the attacker and then tugged his blanket, causing the first swordsman to stagger again. It was the heartbeats he needed to draw Temma's Sword, using the pinning sword against the belt as resistance. The Gourmini that had gone to kill Daryo saw the curved blade and moaned in fear, tripping and stumbling as he tried to flee. His comrade, braver, freed his blade from Daryo's belt and stabbed downwards with both hands. Daryo rolled aside again and used the momentum to stand, bringing Temma's Sword up ready. The remaining thief stared wide-eyed at the near-naked Batribi swordsman before him.

'You chose the wrong Batribi,' growled Daryo, allowing his anger to burn like a fire. 'You filthy, cowardly parasite!'

Daryo paced forwards slowly, menacing, raising Temma's Sword in his right arm, his left out for balance and extra malice. The Gourmini decided to strike first and found his two-handed blow effortlessly deflected by a much superior opponent. Another wild slash knocked aside, a third, a fourth and then the Batribi warrior slashed in response, the Gourmini's sword was batted aside and the Walker's fist struck him on the jaw. As he reeled, Temma's Sword opened his chest, neck and gut in quick succession. Daryo shouldered the man aside as he collapsed and in blind rage chased the other attacker, who had reached the road. He turned at the sound of Daryo's pursuit and raised his small, rather stunted sword.

'No, please!' was all the protest he could make before Temma's Sword cleaved into his neck. Daryo struck five times before the body fell to the ground in a pool of blood. He stepped away, recovering his breath. The anger was subsiding and he became aware that he was sweating and wearing only a pair of linen shorts that only covered him from waist to knee. He trudged back to his campsite and dragged the other body away before dressing, collecting his equipment and starting out on the road again to find another, more secluded campsite.

# Chapter 58

Daryo was very surprised to find a good score of Batribi working in the orchards as he approached Sitak. They were pruning fruit trees along the sides of the road in sufficient numbers for Daryo to stop alongside the fence.

'Gods' Watch!' he called to the nearest man.

The man stopped his work and inclined his head. 'Good day to you.'

'I did not realise that there were so many of our people in Sitak.'

'There are a few of us. Do you seek lodging?'

'I would be grateful.'

'Continue into the town and ask after the Dark House.'

'My thanks.'

Sitak was a small port on the west side of the silt-laden, sluggish Semaht River estuary. The air, even from a mile away from the town, stank of foetid mud and rotting seaweed. The town had a dank and slimy feeling, the walls were moss-covered and crumbling in place, as Daryo passed through the gates the wood was wet to the touch. The day was not as hot as some of the preceding ones but the town gave the impression that it was permanently dank. A wandering soldier, wearing the city's colours of white and blue, pointed Daryo towards a longhouse near the river bank. It was timbered, thatched and in better condition than much of the rest of the town. Several Gourmini nearby were glaring at the house and held a whispered conversation as Daryo passed them and pushed the door open.

The longhouse was a single room, only around twenty feet wide but nearly two hundred feet long, lined by beds and with a narrow table and stools along the centre. A section at the far end was curtained off. Small windows near the roof gave light.

'Welcome to Sitak,' said an elderly Batribi man, tottering across, supported by a stick. 'This is the Dark House, I am Dorvan, this is mine.'

'I am Daryo the Walker, kin of Dostan.'

'Labourer?'

'Traveller.'

'Your first time in Sitak I take it. I offer lodging to any of our people. The town's landowners use us as cheap labour, our people are willing to work for less than Gourmini are and it is a welcome source of employment, so many people live here long-term. Do you require such accommodation?'

'My thanks but no. Just a night or two, perhaps.'

'I charge a bronze half a night.'

'Most reasonable,' said Daryo, removing his pack to get some coin.
'It is a fair price for the workers. I do not discriminate against travellers.'
'My thanks. So Sitak welcomes Batribi?'
'The landowners do, the farmers. The townsfolk are less welcoming. Especially after dark, confine yourself to the Dark House.'
'I welcome your advice, Dorvan. Can I eat here?'
'I provide one meal for your coin. If you require extra, one bronze half a meal, just do not expect to be served beef at every meal.'
Daryo smiled and paid two halves. 'I shall restrain my expectation, that coin for an extra meal and a single night. Any bed?'
Dorvan pointed down. 'There is one to your right hand with a red blanket. Take that. The blanket and such like is part of the price of your residence. If you require the privy, there is a shack behind the house. Beware of the rats and I give no joke to you. Do not pass the curtain at the end, that is the women's section.'
'My thanks.'
Daryo walked down. The fifteenth bed on the right side had a red blanket and he put his pack on the top before removing his sword belt and harness. 'Is there a smith in town?' he called but the elder did not hear. He went down to the proprietor. 'Master Dorvan, is there a smith in the town?'
'There is but he would not do business for a Batribi.'
Daryo sighed. 'A shame, my blades require some attention. Could you direct me? I could ask in person, I may be able to persuade him to allow me to use his forge.'
Dorvan chuckled drily. 'You may ask. The smith is named Vahn, the forge is near the lord's residence.'
'Is Drest still lord?'
'He is but he is at Spiert, directing the work following the flood. Lender is his chancellor and is lord until Drest returns.'
'My thanks.'
Daryo returned to the bed, removed his jerkin and changed the shirt beneath, returned his sword belt to his waist and went to find the forge.

A short exploration of the town only gave Daryo a more negative impression of the town. The population were silently belligerent; hostile glances and muttered comments followed the Walker's progress through the unpleasant streets. He saw no signs of any temple or chapel of any faith nor a market. The butcher's shop that he passed smelt of decaying meat and flies buzzed thickly from chop to joint. A fish stall was so offensive that Daryo took a wide diversion around it.

The forge was small and as disagreeable as the rest of Sitak- untidy and rundown. The particularly large smith was sat on his anvil with a bowl of cold broth.

'Out, dog,' he snorted.

'I require a smith's services,' Daryo replied politely.

'I work for those who I wish to not simply those with coin.'

'Could I not persuade you?'

'Batribi come in and put honest and dependable Gourmini out of work, because you work for less coin. So no Gourmini in town has coin because of you.'

'I am not from this town.'

'None of you are! Wandering parasites!'

'I am simply passing through.' Daryo was trying to stay calm. 'I am not seeking work in Sitak, I simply require work on my blades.'

The smith suddenly seized a hammer and lurched up, sending his bowl and the contents flying. Daryo dropped his hand to the hilt of Temma's Sword. 'Out, cur! Out! Out!'

Daryo began to back away from the forge. 'I am leaving.'

'Parasitic filth!' The smith swung the hammer, he was only ten feet away and Daryo drew his sword. 'Stinking black scum!'

'Put the hammer down,' Daryo warned, keeping the point of his sword at the big, bearded man's face.

'Cur! Shit! Leech!' The smith swung again and Daryo hopped backwards out of range. The commotion was attracting attention, passers and shopkeepers began to gather at a cautious distance. Daryo fended off another blow of the hammer, which enraged the smith even further as a pair of guards waded through the crowd, drawing their swords. Relieved, Daryo lowered his blade. One guard forcibly relieved the smith of the hammer. There was an instant clamour of accusation and claim:

'The Batribi tried to kill Vahn!'

'Vahn attacked the Batribi!'

'The dog should be hung!'

'Vahn should be hung!'

'They are both drunk!'

'What happened, Vahn?' asked the guard with the hammer.

'Batribi tried to kill me!' roared the smith. 'Will not have dogs in my forge!' He lunged forwards again and almost walked onto the guard's sword.

'Drinking your own brew today, Vahn?' asked the other guard. 'Three or four bowls?'

'Will not have dogs in my forge!'
'Maybe five,' one guard suggested to the other. He turned to Daryo. 'Vahn does not want your people in the forge. He is in drink and is not out of it very often. Go back to the Dark House, Batribi.'
Daryo took another long glare at the smith and sheathed his sword. 'Just ensure he cannot hurt anyone.'
'We will. Get along.'

Dorvan's Dark House was filling up with Batribi returning from their work in the fields as sundown approached. The elderly proprietor had been sympathetic but unsurprised at the Walker's experience with the smith, saying that it was known for Vahn to be well in drink and particularly hostile to anyone not obviously a native of Sitak. The atmosphere in the Dark House was one of casual acceptance, the new arrival was greeted politely, invited to eat the evening's fish soup with a group of men and women of a similar age and was quizzed about the great wave at Spiert. The group of nine had left a stool empty at the table next to Daryo and late in the evening, just after the curfew bell, a young woman burst through the door and bolted it quickly behind her.
'Good evening, Ramma,' said Dorvan as she accepted a bowl of soup from him. She sighed and went directly to the empty stool beside Daryo.
'Hard evening, Ramma?' one of the young men asked.
Ramma shook her head. She was particularly attractive, her hair braided close to her head with red cord plaited into it and a matching red colour on her eyes and on her beaded necklace. She was wearing a gold-coloured vest top and a black skirt that reached just past her knees. 'Not a pleasant evening, feeling is very bad.'
The man, Koryo, told Daryo: 'Ramma works in the Hallowed Hake tavern.'
Ramma looked at Daryo. 'New?'
'Just passing through the town,' said Daryo. 'I am Daryo the Walker, kin of Dostan.'
'You should have found somewhere else to sleep. The town is bubbling like a stew pot. Was it you who got in a fight with Vahn?'
'He attacked me.'
Ramma frowned. 'I cannot say I am surprised. But that is not all. Has anyone seen Lulvan?' She addressed the question loudly to the room. There was no affirmative response. 'Rumour has it that a Batribi with no hair argued with a guard and the guard killed him.' This provoked a rumble of anger. 'And a girl was knocked down and molested by the quay during the past night. The girl said that the man sounded *dark*. Her

father was denouncing us this evening, as was Vahn. I have never had so many insults thrown at me while working. The town hates us more than usual this night.'

Daryo found that the bed was not unpleasant and the blanket and pillow perfectly adequate for a good night's sleep. As the Batribi all worked, none stayed up late as they were due back at their employments with the new day.

Waking seemed to come too early. There was no light, a few stubby candles on the table but most of the Batribi seemed to be awake. Daryo saw a young woman, Ramma perhaps, going from bed to bed shaking people awake. From outside the Dark House was a noise that sounded like many people shouting. As Daryo listened, he could hear the shout was 'Kill the darks!'.

'Up! Up!' Ramma starting shouting. 'Up!'

Daryo grabbed his clothes and pulled them on roughly. In a very short period, he was dressed, armed and with his pack on his back. 'We need to get out of Sitak!' he shouted over the clamour of the rousing Dark House.

'We have to fight!' someone shouted.

'We have to fight!' agreed another.

'No! If we draw swords, it will be a slaughter!' shouted Daryo, pulling his shield on to his arm. 'We need an escape.'

'We are near the river, a boat!' someone called.

'No!' said Ramma. 'Over the roof!'

'The roof?' asked Dorvan, hobbling forwards.

'We can break the thatch, climb out of the roof and on to the roof of the storeroom behind the longhouse. Then we can get to the wall.'

'That is fantasy!' someone retorted.

'No!'

The 'kill the darks!' chant was getting louder, joined by shouts and the banging of weapons and drums.

'Take the chance or go and face Sitak!' snapped Ramma, ripping the cloths and paillasse from the nearest bed. Beneath it was a frame with a line of boards. Someone helped Ramma lift one end of the bed and another man helped Daryo shoved a table under it to hold it up. A fearful Dorvan found a wood-axe and Ramma scrambled up her makeshift ladder to the roof and began to hack at the thatch.

Koryo whistled from the door. 'Daryo! Help me block the door!'

They seized a table and pulled it across the door and lifted a bed on top. A second bed went alongside Ramma's and a second person started work on cutting a hole in the roof.

Soon a section had been removed and Ramma was first up. She leaped the few feet to the next roof, that of a warehouse.

'Come! Quickly!' she called. Dorvan was assisted up next and just managed to cross the gap. A smash came against the door. Daryo drew Temma's Sword, the next two people began to scale the ladders.

'Open the door, you scum fleas!' shouted a voice outside, the sentiment echoed by a roar of support.

'We are all of us armed!' Koryo shouted back. 'We will take scores with us!'

'Burn them out!' someone shouted and this received a much louder backing and the cry of 'Burn! Burn!' arose.

'Move!' Daryo told the nearest man, shoving him towards the exit. 'Go!'

Koryo had his own blade, a broad dirk, in hand. He looked around, a queue had formed for the temporary ladders. 'It looks like we will be last.'

The cries of 'Burn! Burn!' and crackle of flaming torches was audible near to the door.

'We may be somewhat... crisp on the edges,' said Daryo wryly. There were still two dozen to climb out.

A curl of smoke came around the door frame accompanied by cheers from the mob.

'Seared or spit-roasted?' Koryo offered as they both took a step away from the door.

'Raw, if possible.'

The amount of smoke was growing from the near end of the building as well as from around the door. The crowd were cheering and whooping loudly. Seventeen left to climb, Ramma encouraging them from above and calling for speed. Fifteen left to climb and Daryo saw the flames in the thatch above the door.

'Do you owe the Fourth Goddess much?' asked Koryo, retreating another step.

'More than I can count. Soldiers, vagabonds, robbers, savages... She is reminding me of their names at this moment.'

'I killed a man many seasons ago, defending my own life. I have regretted it often.'

'Your debt will be paid much sooner than mine.'

The flames were spreading across the thatch from both door and end. Ten left to climb. A series of thumps came against the door, Daryo guessed the mob were throwing stones. The fires flared above the door, showering the interior with burning thatch and the rear-guards scrambled back out of the raining fire. Koryo used his weapon to scrape a burning clump of straw the size of his head from a bed but the blanket was already beginning to burn. Six to climb, with Daryo and Koryo almost on top of them. The thatch was blazing fiercely and, as the last two mounted the bed-ladders, Daryo and Koryo joined them, crawling through the ten-foot ring of burning thatch onto the slightly-sloped warehouse roof, Daryo slightly hampered by his pack and shield.

'Raw indeed,' said Koryo with a grin.

They scrambled across the roof and someone had used a plank of wood from the warehouse roof to the crumbling parapet of the town wall. One by one the Batribi were crawling across, lit by their burning former lodgings behind. The mob were hidden by the dark streets below and the brightness of the blazing building. Ramma and Daryo were the last two to cross to the wall. A rope was produced that reached almost to the ground, Dorvan was lowered down and then the remainder slid down to the ground outside the town walls. There were twenty-six in total and they moved quickly away from the wall into a field of ripening corn. Progress was slow and clumsy in the dark, Koryo leading, Daryo at the rear. He knew that eventually the townsfolk would realise that their prey had escaped and it would likely make them angrier and more bloodthirsty so he kept Temma's Sword in hand. Any of the fleeing Batribi with weapons had them drawn and ready. Nobody spoke of stopping or slowing until the first light of dawn when, in the cover of some woodland west of Sitak, Dorvan sank onto a stump and protested that he could go no further without rest. The party halted and most sat or lay on the ground. Daryo squatted down and took off his pack for a few moments.

'The Gods do not make life simple at times, do they?' Ramma observed, flopping to the ground.

'Only very rarely,' Daryo nodded. 'Very rarely indeed.'

'Few people saved much. You were fortunate.'

'I travel, I walk the roads a lot, I am used to seizing what I have and moving on quickly. Where will you go now?'

'I do not know. We should decide where to go next!' she called.

'Nowhere near Sitak will be safe,' a woman said. 'And Armynya is not hospitable.'

'I may make for Stannia Lake,' another said. 'I have kin there.'

'And I,' said a man, a little older than the others. 'The lake would be a safe haven. We could be there in eight or nine days.'

'I have kin there,' Daryo told them. 'The town greets any new arrivals willing to work for others and to contribute to the well-being of all. Anyone with any skills will be found work.'

'Stannia Lake sounds best,' said Koryo. 'And we will do best if we travel together.'

'Agreed,' echoed around.

'We should rest until daylight and then start out,' Ramma suggested. 'Put as many miles between Sitak and ourselves as we can, join the Spiert road.'

'Good fortune to you,' said Daryo.

'Are you not coming?' Ramma asked.

'No. I have been by the lake. I was only passing through Sitak. I will rest with you all here until day and then start out again alone.'

'Where do you go?' Koryo enquired.

'From Sitak I was planning on going south.'

'The road goes through Armynya but it is a deserted, desolate area,' Koryo told him. 'It follows the Semaht River and then turns west into Boskinia.'

'Then that is where I shall go: Boskinia.'

## Book 4- The Warrior
### Eight years later
### Eve of Midspring Day

## Chapter 59

'Mother of all, on this night before I begin my path to motherhood, I pray that you watch over me and my children that I shall bear in your name... Mistress of men and women, on this night before I become the woman of a man, I pray that you guide me to love him as I should and that you guide him to care and protect me through our lives together... Mighty Huntress, on this night before I join a new family as a wolf joins a pack, I pray that you keep my eyes and ears sharp so that I may learn my new place and see and hear your blessings around me...'

The quiet of the Chapel of the White Lady in Serios was interrupted only by the young woman's devotions. The sanctuary used for the ritual of prayers the night before the wedding was in essence a wooden box within the chapel itself. Traditionally a female believer in the White Lady had to bare herself to the Lady in body, mind and soul so to preserve the woman's modesty the sanctuary had a door locked only from inside and no windows. A fire burned in the corner to keep her warm. A pair of candles burned by the door, the woman sat on a cushion in the centre before a painted icon of the White Lady, flanked by more candles. The White Lady was often represented as a mother with her children, a huntress with dogs, a warrior with an army, an obedient daughter, a diligent farmer but, as the sanctuary was for those about to be married, the icon was of a young woman, sat in a sanctuary praying. Before the woman, both the real and the painted, was a scroll with the Litany of the Bride's Devotion printed on it. It was said that for every time the bride spoke the entire Litany, the White Lady would reward her with a full year of blissful union with her husband. The young woman saying her Litany on the eve of Midspring Day was on her nineteenth recitation and was hoping to make thirty before sleeping.

'Blessed Daughter, on this night before I pledge myself to motherhood, I pray that you guide my children to your will and guide my hand to raise them as you.'

There was a noise outside the sanctuary. The young woman paused in her prayers but dismissed the noise. It was most likely the priestess leaving the chapel for the night. But the noise came again, it sounded like someone rattling a door, testing if it was locked. It was not the sanctuary door, it must be the chapel door, she decided, perhaps a late-night worshipper who had missed the chapel's closing. Then there was a loud bang followed by the sound of splintering wood. The door had been knocked in! The young woman stood up quickly, suddenly feeling vulnerable in her nudity. There was the sound of voices and footsteps. She hurriedly blew out the candles in case their light showed through any gaps in the wood of the sanctuary. The fire was glowing but she had no way of extinguishing it. There was another surge of the voices and a bang on the door of the sanctuary. The young bride stifled a cry and searched for a place to hide. The box was bare; the icon was nailed to the wall with no space behind it. The bang was repeated, and again and the lock gave way. Two soldiers burst in, both carrying swords, one with a blazing torch. The woman seized the cushion to cover herself.

'I told you their women were sluts!' said the soldier with the torch.

'No!' screamed the woman. 'Please! I get married in the morning! Please! Just go!'

The soldier threw his sword down. 'Then we can break you in! Your husband's probably dead already. Hold her!'

When they were done, they left the young woman sobbing and bleeding in the sanctuary. The torch was thrown down by a tapestry, which started to burn as the two soldiers left. The rest of the village was already burning, more soldiers charging around, the surviving villagers fleeing into the fields, most dead where they had stood. As the flames died, the soldiers began to move out, led by two men on horseback.

\*     \*     \*

Daryo the Walker was walking. The road south had followed the river but then turned west and uphill. The hill became a mountain and the road became little less than a climb. At the summit the road levelled out and became a narrow pass. The Walker knew that such passes, even a long distance from habitation, were often haunted by bandits. He adjusted the heavy pack slung over his shoulders to make sure that the twin swords on his back, the hilts by his shoulders, were accessible. He was not helpless should the swords be obscured, a slightly curved sword was sheathed at his left hip, a long dagger on his right hip and a shield was strapped to his left arm. The shield was painted black so that the device, a blindfolded girl child in rags and a masked blue and yellow harlequin holding hands above a white Yashoun milestone, stood out vividly. He loosened the straps to allow the shield to come down his arm into ready position on his forearm. The snows were gone even high in the pass and the road was flanked by growing banks of grasses. Ahead Daryo could see down into the valley and a small town nestled alongside a narrow river. The sun broke out through a gap in the clouds and he welcomed the warmth. He paused to remove his heavy woollen cloak. Daryo was just over six feet tall, his dark head shaved clean on top but with a short, curling beard around his chin. Under his cloak he had on a hooded red tunic, brown leggings and knee-high soft boots. He stopped, laid down his shield, removed and folded his cloak and strapped it to the top of his bag.

'Stay down, dog,' said a voice.

Daryo stayed with his head near his bag. 'I have no items of value and you can see that I am bearing swords. If you permit me to walk away, there need be no bloodshed.'

'Only your blood will be shed, dog. Do you know how many swords are around you?'

'No more than four: one with you behind me, one on the road in front of me and someone further away behind him.'

Daryo noted the hesitation before the bandit spoke again. He had not expected Daryo to know exactly how many men were around him. 'Four swords going through your gut if you don't do what I say.'

Four then, Daryo noted. He reached the point that there was no further conversation to be had. His hands were still on his bag, level with his shoulders, and it took a blink for him to reach up, draw the swords on his back and straighten up. The hilts of the swords were carved in the image of a horse and a bear; the Bear in his left hand he spun so the blade pointed down. The two behind him were closest so Daryo turned to face them. He blocked the first bandit's swinging metal-tipped club with his blades crossed, his left hand up across his face, pushed up to knock it away and slashed the man's stomach open with the Horse in his right hand. He turned a half circle, ducked down and kicked the attacking man on the other side full in the face. The bandit fell back and Daryo leaped over his pack to drive the point of the Horse into the man's chest. The man who had been further back behind him was already fleeing down the road. Daryo spun to confront his last attacker. This, he guessed, was the one who had spoken, probably the leader and definitely the oldest of the four, broad and rugged with a two-handed axe held across his body. Any confidence his voice had carried was not in his face; it was pale and the hands grasping his axe were turning white with his grip.

Daryo carefully stepped around his pack and shield on the ground, swinging the Horse in an exploratory circle from his wrist. 'I think you should have heeded my words.'

The bandit leader raised his axe slightly. 'I don't take orders from dogs.' His voice had lost its sneer.

'Lay your axe down and walk away and I will permit you to leave unharmed.'

'I said I don't take orders from dogs.'

'That was not an order, it was a suggestion. The Fourth Goddess would be happy with two souls. No need to add a third.'

'Dogs have no gods.'

Daryo allowed his patience to drain. 'I am not a dog! I am a Batribi, the people of the road! And you will learn my name from my blade!' He lunged forwards and the bandit raised his axe reflexively. Daryo ducked at the last moment, cut upwards with the Horse to push the axe further upwards and, as he turned his back on his foe, the Bear slashed sideways through the bandits leather doublet and into his midriff. Daryo completed the circle with the Horse at throat height and opened the bandit's neck. The would-be robber fell dead with his axe falling on top of him. Daryo allowed himself a few long and slow breaths to restore his calm before using a bandit's sleeve to clean his blades. Soon the swords were sheathed, his pack on, shield picked up and the Walker was pacing along the road again into the valley.

## Chapter 60

Sataos was a small but well-defended town by the side of the river. Like many towns it used the water itself as a wall and a tall line of wooden stakes with sharpened tops and a ditch encircled the town. The single gate was midway around the wall, an earth bridge connected it to the road, meaning a traveller did not have to pass through the town if he chose not to. Above the gate was a covered section of a watch tower to make a rudimentary gatehouse. Daryo had not laid in a bed since the mouldy Gourmini port of Sitak and decided that a small outlay for a bed in an inn was worth doing. A single guard stood sentry, a large rectangular shield four feet long was leaning against the open wooden town gate, three black chevrons on the sky-colour blue, and the same badge was on his simple tunic. The guard had a spear in his hand and a short sword on his belt.
'Gods' watch,' said Daryo politely.
The young sentry grunted in acknowledgement. 'Where do you go, Batribi?'
'I seek a bed. The sun is going down and I have travelled far. Is there an inn here?'
'Two: the Wallside and the Leaping Trout. The Trout is by the riverbank but may not welcome a Batribi. Follow inside the wall around that way-'he pointed to the right '-the Wallside is as it says and built against the wall. Keep those blades in their sheaths, the Seigneur does not take kindly to those who draw weapons in his town.'
Daryo inclined his head in a short bow. 'Certainly. My thanks.' He walked under the gate tower and into the town. The houses were small and square for the majority, thatched roofs with clay chimneys protruding from one end. Daryo did as advised and followed the wall around to where a long, curved building was stood using the town wall as one of its own. From above the door hung a sign- a frothing mug with the town badge on it. Inside the hall was lit by a series of high windows in both long walls, one of them being the town wall so the windows were small and rather deep. The bar protruded from the town wall side and a door behind it led beyond the hall. The inn was quiet, only one group of men drinking by the entrance door and they barely looked up as Daryo crossed the room. The rather dark-skinned young woman behind the bar smiled broadly.
'Good day to you, sir.'
'Good day,' said Daryo. 'I require a meal and a room for the night.'
'As you wish, sir. Are you travelling alone, sir?'
'I am.'
The girl smiled. 'Your room is through the door behind me, sir. The room closest to the wall, sir. I can offer you a fish pie, sir, or some boar if you prefer?'
'The boar sounds good. I shall just put my equipment in my room.'

The girl smiled and nodded. Daryo went past the bar as the girl went down a staircase that was just behind it. The room had a bed and a chest with a lock on it and the key in the lock. Daryo put his pack and the swords from his back in the chest and locked it, laid his shield on the bed and took the key with him back into the hall. The girl had returned and Daryo took his purse from his belt and paid for a night's stay, the meal and a tankard of mead. He sat at one of the long tables near the bar and the girl soon bought a steak of boar, a fresh roll of bread and a bowl of butter.

'Are you Batribi, sir?' she asked.

'I am.'

'My father was Batribi, my mother always told me.'

'You do have something of our people in your skin.'

'Do you walk the road with the clans?'

'I walk alone now. My kin have led the settlement at the Stannia Lake.'

'They are calling it the Dark Land.'

Daryo shook his head. 'It is sad that our skin is all that is seen by so many.'

'It is. For the most, Boskinian people are tolerant. There are many people of many lands here. The priest of the Temple of Tahili is half-race as I am. There is a woodcutter that is Batribi too.'

'I may have to seek them out. My thanks for the meal.'

The girl smiled and moved away. Daryo ate at a leisurely pace, enjoying the calm hospitable air of the inn. A tall and rather intimidating-looking man strode in and glared around the room. He stalked across the room and leaned on the table opposite Daryo, who slowly drained his mead before looking up. The man was well over six feet tall with heavy brows, a thick beard and an ugly, poorly healed scar across his upper lip and cheek.

'You just came to this town,' said the man. Daryo gave no response as he decided one was not needed. The man continued. 'You are a Batribi.' Again this was obvious so Daryo remained silent. 'Batribi travellers can cause trouble.' Daryo still felt no reason to answer. 'It might be better if you stayed in the inn tonight. Step outside and you might never leave town.' The man leered showing broken teeth. 'Ask the girl. She doesn't step outside in the dark. Someone might knock her down and never know.' He chuckled sinisterly. 'Stay in the inn, Batribi.' He wagged his finger in Daryo's face.

Daryo's left hand, clenched to a fist, lashed out and struck the man in the face. He leaped up, grabbed the man's collar and hurled him backwards. The man went down like a felled tree, Daryo landed on top, his knees in the man's gut and the point of his dagger at the man's gullet.

'Threaten me again and I will open your throat,' Daryo whispered. 'I shall walk where I please at the time of day that pleases me. And if you should ever touch the bar girl, or any other of my people, this knife will find you.'

The man gaped blankly, trying not to move for fear of pricking himself on Daryo's dagger. There was a noise at the inn door and two of the town guards hauled Daryo off of the man. One slapped the knife from Daryo's hand and then punched him in ribs.

'Hold! He acted in self-defence!' shouted one of the drinkers by the door, rushing forwards.

The guards looked up, suddenly unsure.

'He did!' added the girl at the bar.

'Paroy threatened him,' said the intervening man. 'The traveller was quite right to defend himself.' The guards released their hold on Daryo, who rubbed where he had been struck to ease the pain. The man looked from one guard to the other. 'You should take Paroy out of here.'

'Yes, sir,' said one of the guards. 'Come, big man, on your feet.' They hauled Paroy to his feet and marched him out of the inn.

'My thanks, my friend,' said Daryo. 'Either our large friend or those guards may have done me some harm.'

'No harm done, a good act.' The man held out his hand, fist clenched and thumb underneath.

Daryo recognised it as an act of greeting and friendship and tapped his hand against the other man's. 'I am Daryo, kin of Dostan.'

'Rayos Great-Helm. I own the town brewers and the apiary.'

'Allow me to buy you a drink, to show my gratitude.'

'Certainly.'

Daryo hailed the girl at the bar and had her bring four meads so that Rayos' friends could also drink with them. They gratefully took the tankards and invited Daryo to join them.

Berrio was the youngest of the three and supplied barley to the brewery. Niholo was a carpenter who, according to his companions, had a reputation much further than the town. They were quite happy to sit with Daryo and talk. When they finished their drinks, Berrio bought another four.

'What is your trade?' Niholo asked Daryo.

Daryo shrugged. 'I trained as a smith.'

'A smith makes daggers, he does not wield them as you do,' said Rayos. 'That sword at your side is no mere town blade. That is a warrior's tool.'

'I have some skill with a sword.'

'An army?'

'Not precisely. I learned to use my blade from a warrior. I have... travelled using my skills.'

'Gourmin?'

'Gourmin, Jaboen, Yashoun, the Silver Island, Armynya...'

'For hire?'

'Never for hire. Only to defend the defenceless and aid the helpless. In return I have sought only shelter and knowledge.'

Berrio chuckled. 'I heard that there was a group of warriors who did that in Aslon; an order of warriors who did not ask for coin. You could join them.' Daryo smiled and took another drink.

'Are you spending much time in Sataos?' asked Rayos.

'I have no definite plans. I came from Sitak and was thinking of heading further south.'

'South would be across plains towards Adaca. Have you travelled far in Boskinia?'

'I have never been to Boskinia before.'

'You should spend some time here,' said Rayos. 'Boskinia is a fine country. The towns of the east are small and hospitable. The towns of the plains are large and productive and Hamlakia is a fine city. The western villages are small but pleasant places although close to Vidmaria.'

'Maybe I could spend some weeks in Boskinia.'

'If you wish to keep on the road, head west to Iannakia and then Hamlakia.'

'My thanks. Do you have a smith? My blades need some attention.'

'Alongside the river,' said Berrio. 'My wife's brother Houyo.'

Daryo nodded. 'I will go and see him in the morning.'

The inn was getting busier as the evening got later. Several of the patrons apparently knew Berrio, Niholo and Rayos and greeted them as they entered. One came across and tapped fists with all three. He was wearing a sleeveless surcoat over his mail and had one of the longest greatswords that Daryo had come across on his back.

'Daryo, kin of Dostan, this is Samas, commander of the Sataos Guard and first lieutenant of the Seigneur.'

Daryo shook the stocky man's hand. 'Greetings.'

'Gods' Watch, Batribi. I hear that you threw Paroy to the ground and nearly opened his gullet.'

'Having been provoked,' said Daryo defensively.

'No malice intended, Daryo, kin of Dostan. I have oft wanted to throw Paroy to the ground.'
Daryo laughed along with the others. 'An unpopular fellow.'
'Quite so. But he runs the iron mine and so is very important to the town. He is also a relative to the Seigneur by marriage and that has some status.'
'Your act today may have brightened many lives,' said Niholo with a chuckle.
'I am glad to be able to help so many.'
Daryo passed an exceptionally good evening with his new companions. They taught him some Boskinian drinking songs and he taught them a song from the Silver Island that he had learned some summers before. When the bar closed, they bid him a good night and Daryo made his way to his room.

When Daryo woke there was fresh bread and honey on a platter in his room. He ate, found some fresh clothing from his bag and decided to find the smithy as his curved sword was getting somewhat dull in polish and sharpness. He ran his finger across the blade to be sure, sheathed it and left the inn, hoping that the giver of the sword, his kinswoman, was well. Temma's Sword had served him very well. The morning was warm and bright. The town was busy and the flow of goods and people suggested that it was a market day. The market square was full of stalls and customers. On one side of the square was a stone-built longhouse with a wooden roof and the door flanked by two of the town guards. Daryo assumed that it was the Seigneur's house. A temple of the First Goddess was alongside it and faced a chapel of the White Lady across the square. The houses around the square seemed to be the largest and grandest in the town with an elaborately built well in the centre of the square, today surrounded by the busy market. Daryo caught the attention of a passing guard and asked for the forge. He was pointed along the lane between the temple and the Seigneur's house and after a few hundred yards found the forge, literally on the bank of the river. The smith was gruff but polite and took very little time and coin to sharpen and polish Temma's Sword. Daryo then spent some time in the temple and the market before returning to the inn for his belongings.

'Where are you going to?' asked the girl, who he had learned lived in a room in the cellar alongside the kitchen.
'My companions last evening suggested I go westwards to Hamlakia.'
'I wish you Gods' Guidance, sir.'
'My thanks. Gods' Guidance to you.'

# Chapter 61

The prince's tent was obvious: white and green with the dark green and acorn banners hung outside, a quartet of royal guards outside and a young terrified-looking squire was tending a magnificent chestnut horse that towered over him. A portly man, the prince's acorn in a white diamond around it on his tabard, strode out of the tent and glared at the man.
'The prince was sleeping.'
'The prince will want to see me.'
'Fortunately you are correct.' The portly man turned and strode back into the tent, followed by the new arrival.
The prince was still young, not quite twenty years, tall but not overly so, pale brown hair curling around his eyes and ears, still in his sleeping garb with a dark brown cloak over his shoulders, his jewelled silver collar just visible underneath. 'My Lord Carbreo. I assume that your early arrival is bad news.' The prince's voice did not betray that he had been abed but not asleep and that it was moments after dawn.
'Yes, sire. All four villages have been burned.'
The prince had not expected that. 'All four?'
'Yes, sire. Terta, Serios, Patos and Dalmakia. The inhabitants were slain, the buildings burned. We found nobody alive and not a single building standing. I do not exaggerate, sire.'
'I do not suggest that you do.' The young prince sighed. 'All four. Hundreds of our people.'
'They were small villages, sire,' said the portly man. 'Insignificant. Your Lord Father recognised this.'
'And failed to defend them!' snapped the prince. 'Keep your counsel to yourself, Novas, I do not need to hear you try to defend my father when he has failed!' Novas glowered but bowed low and took a half-step backwards. 'Lord Carbreo, have the camp raised. We move west. There is still a town undefended, we will garrison Vhamsia. Have the fortresses at Outros and Hivamakia warned by rider. And have another message sent to my Lord Father for reinforcements.'
'Aye, sire.'
The prince turned on Novas. 'Summon my council.'

'It strikes me, my lord, that if Hivamakia and Vhamsia were taken, the Vidmarians would have all the land they demanded,' said Lord Albul.

'The same suggested itself to me,' admitted the prince. 'But if the towns are treated like the western villages were treated, that could be thirty thousands of our people slaughtered like spring lambs.'

'And an army enjoying that success would want to destroy Outros, Hamlakia and maybe Thetri as well,' said old Lord Sett. 'Nothing would restrain them.'

'Will not they be satisfied now?' asked the much younger Venni. 'They have made a statement to us and can now push forwards in Gourmin.'

Sett shook his head sadly. 'The Gourmini are resisting, rushing armies southwards to hold the Vidmarians in Tiverta. The Vidmarian King and his commanders knows that our Lord King has refused to reinforce the western defences to protect the lake cities. So he presses on eastwards.'

'The King is correct to do so,' said Novas. 'The western villages can be lost. Hamlakia and Thetri cannot.'

'At the expense of tens of thousands of our people and thousands of miles of our most fertile lands,' suggested Carbreo.

The prince nodded. 'You are both correct, my Lords. The lake country is critical to our nation but the farmlands of the west are equally important to our people. Every man here knows my feelings on my Lord Father's decision. We cannot defend our keep by abandoning the outer wall. This is why I am ordering the army forwards to Vhamsia. Hivamakia and Outros are being alerted to the danger. We must defend the western towns and Outros is the most important road to Hamlakia.'

'There is another problem, sire,' said Sett. 'The Vidmarian army is well trained, very experienced fighting in Yashoun, Adaca and Gourmin. Our army is not. Even the Oaken Companies are not battle-hardened.'

'We cannot train them and put them through battle at the same time,' said the prince. 'I think it quite clear that we must hold Vhamsia for now and then we can look beyond the now and look for the future.'

By midday, the prince of Boskinia's army was on the march. The army was small, all that the king had permitted his son to lead westwards. Only the members of the prince's council had been allowed to raise men to march-Novas, Sett, Albul, Carbreo and Venni. Although they were lords of vast estates, all but Venni had northern lands and thus few people in their villages. The prince's army had only eleven companies, barely more than two thousand five hundred men-at-arms were marching. Fewer than two score were mounted on horses. Oxen drew the baggage carts under the supervision of old men and boys. The main Boskinian army, over twelve thousand, were in camps between Hamlakia and Thetri. The prince's army had found little armament available- some swords, spears and their large rectangular shields, very little chainmail or plate. The army of peasants was inexperienced but, mostly, loyal and determined, proud to march behind their prince, who always rode at the head of the column.

Vhamsia was a small town surrounded by a deep moat diverted from the nearby river and an outward-facing barrier of spiked branches and stakes. The river was narrow but fast and deep, flowing north from the Vham lake to the Dithithindil. The prince ordered his army to make camp astride the road that ran south-west towards the destroyed towns. The Vidmarian army carried the banners of the Vidmarian king- black wolves rearing against each other on a gold field. They carried pikes and swords along with round shields. The Boskinian prince positioned his army on the slope from the town towards the lakeside, outnumbered by seven to one. The initial charge was held by the wall of the Boskinian shields, the second buckled the line, the third wave broke the Boskinian line. Then the Vidmarian cavalry, led by two elaborately-robed men, charged and routed the Boskinian force. Only the prince's council and bodyguards escaped on their horses, the prince most reluctantly, abandoning the remnants of the prince's army and the town of Vhamsia. The two robed figures led the victorious Vidmarian army into the town, slew the men that tried to defend it, raped the women, tortured the children and burned the town.

It took two days of hard riding for the prince's party to reach Hamlakia. The City by the Lake had only been the capital for a generation. The king's father had been an ill-tempered, sickly man and despised the cold and windy air of Topakia and so had ordered his entire court to the largest of the cities in the lake country. Stone had been bought from the quarries of Dalmakia and Thetri to build new city walls, buttressed by six round towers on each side of the river, a new stone bridge and as a foundation for a new wooden palace at the side of the river. The old king had the palace built to what he had believed to be an old plan- the river diverted to make the moat, four stone towers at the corners, wooden walls and gate forming three sides of the square and the stone-built palace forming the fourth. The prince's party were waved across the lowered drawbridge and in through the gates. The prince and Novas dismounted quickly. A tall, bearded man was waiting at the door of the palace and he quickly ushered the prince and his aide inside. The Royal Council had been called and was assembled in the great hall, they stood from their seats around the Ancients' Table as the prince rushed in.

'The Crown Prince Gorero!' announced the herald at the door.

'My Lord King,' said the prince, kneeling quickly. 'My Lord Councillors.'

'Take your seat, my son,' said the king slowly. In the weeks that the prince had been away, the king had aged visibly. His face had grown more lined, his grey hair longer and more awry, his beard was unkempt. The prince wondered if his father had eaten.

The table was not quite full. The prince sat at the foot of the table, opposite his father. Nine lords had seats on each side of the long table painted with the arms of all the great families of Boskinia. Only seven lords sat on the king's left, eight on the right. The four missing were out on their western lands to try to defend them. Two were known to be dead, the other two had not been heard from for many weeks.

'Vhamsia has fallen, my lords,' said the prince bluntly. 'We had two thousand men; they had fifteen thousand and a large corps of horse. We were unable to hold.'

'Hivamakia will fall next, if it has not fallen,' said Lord Salabre, whose lands of Oanis were the only habitation between Hivamakia in the far north and Thetri in the lakes.

'Then they will march east. Outros,' said the prince.

'They may go to Thetri,' said another lord, whose name escaped the prince. 'They could march south from Hivamakia through Oanis.'

The prince shook his head. 'No. They will want to take Hamlakia quickly. The north road is too slow and through too difficult terrain. The west road is faster. Hivamakia can hold out as long as Outros. They will focus their forces there. We should move our forces to Outros and hold them there.'

'I agree with Lord Jadara,' said the king. 'They will come from the north.'

'My lord, the bulk of their forces is in the west,' said the prince. 'To march on the lake country with any numbers, thousands of men would have to march back into Vidmaria and along the Dithithindil to Hivamakia. They will not march from the north, my lord.'

'Lord Jadara thinks so.'

'I believe Lord Jadara is incorrect.'

The lord in question smiled smugly and folded his arms. 'Our prince is obviously the more experienced battle leader, a man of many summers and many foes, who has led his men for many years.'

'I have been at the front, Lord Jadara!' snapped the prince. 'I have fought the Vidmarian army in these past days and seen thousands of the people of our nation slain while you have fed yourself well and bedded the whores of the capital! The best chance we have to prevent this from happening again is to reinforce Outros!'

'My lord,' said Salabre. 'Your son is obviously tired from the skirmish and from his ride.'

'My lord, I am tired of courtiers telling me how to run a battle after I am the one that fought it!'

'And lost!'

'Because the best of our army and all the numbers of it are hiding in the lake country!'
'Because that is where they are needed!'
'Five days' ride from the enemy?!'
'To protect our heartland!'
'To protect your treasures!'
'How dare you, boy!'
'Boy! I am your prince!'
'You are a child!'
'I am a soldier! You, my lord, are a coward!'
There was a sudden silence.
'This is not a tavern hall, my lords,' said the king quietly. 'My son, this is not a helpful conversation. I believe it necessary to act and to move the army.' The prince sighed in relief. 'How many men do we have, my Lord Vassua?'
'The army in the lakes is thirteen thousand, sire. The army in Iannakia is eight thousand. The army in Thetri is five thousand.'
The king nodded. 'The army in Thetri should remain. The army in Iannakia will be moved to Outros. The army in the lakes will march to Oanis.' There was a shout of objection from all sides. 'This is my decision!' the old king screamed. 'Mine! I am king! I am king and I say where my armies go!' The room went silent and the king calmed himself. 'Such a commotion for lords obeying their liege's wishes. This is my decision. Inform me when this has been fulfilled. The Council is adjourned.'
The king stood and the lords did so too. The prince was the last to rise. As the king left the hall, the prince turned to Novas. 'Summon my council to my chambers.'

The prince's council arrived in his tower chamber together. The prince had been able to remove the clothes he had been wearing for the past few days, douse himself with some water and pull on a clean grey tunic before they arrived.
'My lords, I require your aid,' he said without preamble.
The lords looked at each other. 'We are at your service, sire,' said Sett finally.
'The king will be sending out riders. He is moving the armies but not where they are needed. The largest army is in the lakes. It is being sent to Oanis. I want it to go to Outros instead of the Iannakia army. The Iannakia army should move to the lakes to be deployed as it is needed.'
'How is this to be done, sire?' asked Carbreo.
'By changing the orders,' said the prince flatly. 'The king will send riders, royal couriers. My Lord Carbreo, ride after the messenger to Iannakia. When the orders have been

delivered, you then arrive and say that the original order was incorrectly scribed, whatever excuse is your chosen one, and deliver my order. My Lord Albul, you will ride to the army at the lakes and follow the same procedure.'

The two nobles exchanged looks but both gave short bows. 'We will obey, sire,' said Albul.

'My thanks. I am sorry that you will not have time to rest but when the Vidmarian army marches forwards, I need our armies in the correct places. The rest of you are to help me with the deception- the king must believe that his orders are being carried out.'

'My prince, is this not treason?' asked Novas.

The prince grimaced. 'Protecting your country and you king is not treason. Disobeying my father is wrong but it is for the right reasons. If we are discovered, if damnation is called down upon us, then you acted on the orders of your prince on pain of death. I will take responsibility for these acts. To your business, my Lords, my thanks and the Second God guide you.'

# Chapter 62

Daryo had expected Iannakia to be a busy town, it was alongside a lake and from the hill above the town he had seen the fishing boats busy on the water. A wide stretch of land to the west of the town was tilled and farmed. The town itself was full of soldiers. Daryo guessed that there were several thousands of them, carrying large rectangular green shields with small bronze oak trees in the centre. They were forming up in the streets and squares of the city, marching outside the walls to the west and making columns there to march away. Daryo decided to stay out of the city itself and walked around the outside of the city walls. By the road on the west side was a small inn and he went in to get some food and a drink. The owner was very apologetic but explained that the commanders of the army had cleared his cellar and store-room.
'What is the purpose of the army?' asked Daryo.
'Our nation has been invaded,' said the barman. 'Vidmarians from the west.'
Daryo nodded sadly. 'I have... experience of the Vidmarian war machine.'
The barman eyed Daryo's weaponry. 'That blade at your hip looks very fine. You might be of some use on a battlefield with that.'
'I was thinking the same thing,' murmured Daryo. 'Where could I find a meal in the town?'
'I doubt you will. There is an inn on the north road. If you get there before the army do, you might get something.'
'My thanks.'
Daryo left the inn and was almost ridden down by a horse. He jumped back and cursed. The rider reined in, a two man escort shortly behind.
'My apologies, Master Batribi!' said the rider, dismounting. 'I was somewhat angry and was not watching the road.'
Daryo composed himself before replying. 'Mistakes happen. I am unhurt.'
'There are few men walking the roads in this part of the land,' said the rider. He was obviously well-bred and educated, his beard short and pointed in the Boskinian style. He had a good sword and his robes and shields were coordinated in a manner that suggested that the arms on the shield were his own.
'I was heading for Hamlakia but I hear that there is an army going in the same direction as I.'
'And one opposing it marching the opposite point,' said the man bitterly. 'You should head south, traveller. Hamlakia is likely to burn. Your best hope is to go south faster than the Vidmarian wolves do.'

'Perhaps I could lend my sword.'

'One sword is unlikely to help us much. Unless you are keen to depart this life, I suggest you go south. Or back east.'

'Surely it depends on my skill with the sword and my knowledge of men.'

The man looked intrigued. 'Who are you, traveller?'

'My name is Daryo, the Walker of the Order of the Shield and Sword. The Lone Batribi, the Red Wind to the Silver Island, the Painted Man. My sword is sworn to defend the defenceless and aid the helpless.'

The man nodded thoughtfully. 'I have heard stories of a Batribi warrior who fought in Hajmachia.' Daryo inclined his head modestly. 'Would you come with me, sir?'

'You know who I am. Whom do I address?'

'My apologies again. I am Carbreo, Lord of Outros, councillor to Crown Prince Gorero, Master of the Roadway.'

Daryo bowed shortly. 'My honour to meet you, my lord.'

'My man will find you a horse. Do you ride, Sir Walker?'

'Indeed.'

At the crossroads in the centre of the lake country they changed horses and rode even harder in to Hamlakia. Carbreo had kept up a steady flow of questions up until they changed mounts but thereafter was quiet. Daryo had little time to appreciate the city or anything else as Carbreo led the way, urging his horse on to great speed even through the streets. The sun was down by the time the small group rode into the courtyard of the palace.

'This is the Halfwood Palace,' Carbreo told Daryo as he strode across the courtyard towards the palace building itself. 'The seat of King Olyaro the Third.' They were not heading for the main doors of the palace but to the right, a smaller door into one of the towers. A guard at the door tried to confiscate Daryo's weapons but Carbreo waved him off. Carbreo took the stone staircase several steps at a time and they reached a door near the top of the tower. Daryo was ushered into a large chamber, a large bed with brown and green hangings, a washstand, a saddle, a large table surrounded by elaborately-carved chairs, two large chests and a rack with weapons and armour. A well-made rug on the floor was the same dark green as the hangings with an acorn woven in the centre. A young man, younger than Daryo, was sat at the table studying a large parchment map.

'My Lord Carbreo.'

'Sire.' Carbreo knelt.

'Rise, my Lord. What news from Iannakia?'

'I delivered your orders as you commanded, sire. The army is moving to the lake country. When I rode through, it seems to me that the lakes army is moving west.'
'Good. I see you bring back a... guest?' The young man stood up.
'My lord, his name is Daryo.'
'Daryo, welcome to Hamlakia. I am Prince Gorero, heir to my Lord Father the King.'
Daryo gave a short bow. 'My thanks for receiving me.'
'My Lord Carbreo, without being indelicate, this man is one Batribi traveller among many. I would guess that you were travelling to Stannia Lake to join your people, sir.'
'No, my lord. I left the lake many seasons ago and have not returned.'
'Sire, I wonder if you remember in the summer of your coming of age, there were stories of a Batribi warrior who trained and fought the Vidmarian army in Hajmachia?'
'I do.' The prince thought for a few heartbeats. 'Was that you, sir?'
Daryo inclined his head. 'It was.'
'Sit,' said the prince, returning to his seat. 'Motto, wine and bread for my Lord Carbreo and our guest.'
A half-concealed servant emerged, bowed and left the chamber. Carbreo ushered Daryo to the seat at the prince's right hand and then sat beside him.
'Tell me what else you have done,' said the prince. 'I want no modesty or reticence.'
Daryo took a deep breath. 'My first battle was against the Vidmarians in the Last Stand of the Order of the Shield and Sword. We were vastly outnumbered and trapped in a fortress. I had managed to persuade the assembled Batribi clans to come to our aid and their intervention scattered the Vidmarians and allowed a few of us to disperse in safety. I travelled west and acted alone for several seasons, ranging across Jaboen and into Yashoun defending the defenceless, protecting those with no means to protect themselves. I met a Yashoun army officer and he was kind enough to show me how the Yashoun army is trained and how it fights.

'I then went to the Silver Island to learn their ways. I led a company of men against the tribes of the north of the island and, when the Yashoun army launched a wave of repression, I led the Islanders in their defence. After that I went to Yashoun and then Hajmachia. The blessing of being a Batribi is that we are normally ignored and free to travel. When Vidmaria attacked Hajmachia, I offered my blade to the king and helped to lead the Hajma army in repelling the Vidmarians. In Jaboen, I assisted in the defence of Thiel and the raid on Lichon.

'I was asked to Gourmin by the Lord of Aslon and led the defence of Aslon and led the Second Legion in pushing the Vidmarian army back to Tiverta. Since that time, this past spring, I had journeyed across Gourmin, into Armynya, doing as I sworn to do as a

Member of the Order. I moved into Boskinia this spring as the tribal conflicts are becoming bloody and vengeful in Armynya. There is no justice or rightness of purpose, it is just bloodshed.'

The prince and his councillor had listened in silence. Wine and bread had been brought but lay on the table untouched. Daryo helped himself to some wine to wet his throat.

'That is quite some adventure,' said the prince eventually. 'You have fought with three armies.'

'Four, sir: Silver Island, Hajmachia, Jaboen and Gourmin, as well as learning from the Yashoun army.'

'Fighting the Vidmarians mostly.'

'Mostly, sir, yes. Also Peak Tribes, Nar Silver, the Yashoun at times.'

The prince nodded. 'I think you may be of great use to us, Master Daryo. I hereby formally ask you to join my council.'

Daryo raised his hand. 'My thanks, sir. However, why would you ask me to join your council? Surely the king leads your war and you have many lords and commanders that are better suited?'

The prince exchanged looks with Carbreo. 'My Lord Father has very... unhelpful priorities. His lords support him in defending worthless heartland at the expense of our towns, our farmlands and our people. My council is working to move our armies to where they are needed and to fight to defend our lands properly. We would greatly benefit from the aid you could give us. You may name your price.'

Daryo took another deep steadying breath. 'I ask no price. I fight for what is just. It is right that your people are permitted to live their lives under their rightful king in their own homes. I will aid in any way I can.' He stood up and drew Temma's Sword from its sheath holding it point-down by the pommel. 'My sword and my service are yours, Prince Gorero.'

'They are most welcome,' said the prince as Daryo replaced his sword and sat. 'Motto will find you quarters and bring you anything you need.' The prince fetched something from a drawer by his bed. It was a silver acorn, about the size of a small apple. 'This is my badge of patronage. This marks you as a member of my council with all the privileges that this entails. Serve well, Daryo.'

The chamber was in the tower, a few floors down from the prince's room. A white acorn and oak leaves were painted on the door. Inside, the room was almost round, the bed was of oak and well carved, surrounded by good woollen hangings in dark green and white with a small three-legged washstand beside it. A small table, with four chairs around it, stood under the glass window. At the foot of the bed was a large chest and there was a large wardrobe on the stone wall. A young boy, about fifteen summers and still lacing the front of his halved dark green and white tabard, looked up in shock as Daryo walked in. He had a rather chubby face, unruly pale brown hair and a squashed-looking nose.

'My lord! My lord? Are you the prince's new councillor?'

'I am, so I believe,' said Daryo, not entirely sure that he had truly been snatched from the roadside by a Boskinian lord and brought into the service of the Boskinian crown prince.

'I did not know you were.... Dark, sir.'

'I did not know I was to have a squire.'

'I am not a squire, I am your page, sir, my lord. I will tend your horse, polish your armour, serve your wine, whatever you require of me, sir, my lord. My name is Sal, if it pleases you, my lord, my name is truthfully Salgatro but I am known as Sal, if it pleases, but my lord may call me whatever he wishes.'

Daryo smiled. 'If your name is Sal, I shall call you by your name.' He put his pack and shield down by the table and removed his cloak. 'I think I could use some rest. I have been riding since just after dawn.' He took off his sword belt and the swords on his back.

'I could polish your armour, sir, my lord.'

'I have none. There are some steel bands in my jerkin but they are covered by leather and not easy to polish.' He started to unlace his jerkin and the boy hurried across to help. Daryo picked up the sword belt and handed it to the boy. 'Can you check the blades on there? The sword and knife?'

'Yes, sir, my lord.'

Daryo handed over the belt and removed his jerkin. It was something he had found many years ago in the store of the Order- rust brown with armour plates in the front, back and around the upper arms. It was a little weighty but had saved his life many times. He put it over one of the chairs. On his forearms he had steel-banded gauntlets that he been given in Hajmachia, engraved with intertwined snakes and curved sword blades. These unbuckled and slipped off. Sal had managed to awkwardly draw Temma's Sword and was examining it. Daryo pulled one of the chairs away and sat down to remove his boots. Sal appeared at his feet and started unlacing them.

'I can remove my own boots,' said Daryo kindly.

Sal continued his work. 'I am your page, sir, my lord. I am here to serve you. You need do nothing for yourself that I can do.'

Daryo slid his feet under the chair out of Sal's reach. 'Stand up, Sal.' The boy did so, looking nervous. 'Sit on that chair.' Sal slid into the narrow gap between chair and table uncomfortably. Daryo decided it was good enough. 'I am not a lord, Sal. I am a travelling warrior. I am not a mercenary working for gold, I have not asked for a chamber or a bed with silk hangings or a page or any other comfort from the prince. He has given them to me without my bidding. I am unaccustomed to having a manservant and being waited on. I unlace my own boots and polish my own sword because there is normally no one to do it for me. Do you understand?'

'I believe so, my lord. Sir.'

'Walker will be more than acceptable.'

'Walker?'

'Yes. I was a Member of the Order of the Shield and Sword and each Member took a name to identify himself, his experience and his person. I did much walking and my people are known for their travelling way. The Walker was the name I chose.'

'I understand.'

'Check my blades please.'

'Yes, sir. Walker. Yes, Walker.'

Sal went back to the swords and Daryo finished removing his own boots. 'Tell me of the king and the prince and the court.'

'The court, Walker?'

'Yes.'

'I am only a page.'

'Pages, squires and serving girls know more than lords and captains. You hear things that would not be said in sight of anyone else.'

Sal made a noise that suggested he stifled a giggle. 'Sometimes.'

'So...'

'King Olyaro is very old. Lord Jadara says that he is as strong as he ever was and just ageing but Lord Albul says he is ill and dying.'

'Would that make Prince Gorero the new king?'

'Yes, Walker. The king has four children but the prince is the oldest, of age and his three sisters are younger than he, none of them are quite of age. The prince has already assembled a small council. It is done that the old king's council are replaced by the prince's.'

'Lord Carbreo is a member of the prince's council?'

'Lord Carbreo, Lord Novas, Lord Albul, Lord Sett and Lord Venni. Lord Novas is the prince's chamberlain, Lord Carbreo his aide, Lord Venni is the youngest and the prince's squire. And yourself, Walker, now are a member of the council.'

'Does the council's advice guide the prince or does he lead the council?'

Sal thought for a moment. 'Something of both, Walker. The prince heeds advice but will act alone if he believes it right.'

'You knew more than you may have thought.'

Daryo pulled off the undercoat he wore beneath his armour and closed his eyes for a moment. A rather timid knock came on the door and before Daryo could move, Sal was up and had opened the door. A young girl, younger than Sal, only thirteen summers at the most, with long yellow-brown hair almost down below her waist, stepped in. She wore a blue-green bodice over a blue dress that reached her ankles. She looked at Sal and smiled in the manner of acquaintances, smiled politely to Daryo and curtsied smartly.

'My Lord, Princess Lacia requests that you attend her.'

Daryo looked at Sal, who seemed to cringe. 'Indeed. Please tell the princess that I am... not decently dressed now but I will attend immediately that I am dressed.'

'Yes, my Lord.'

'My thanks... what was your name?'

The girl seemed shocked to be asked. 'Eranya, my Lord.'

'My thanks, Eranya. Please tell the princess I will be there directly.'

'Yes, my Lord.' She stood there awkwardly.

'You may go.'

'Yes, my Lord.' She scuttled out and Sal closed the door.

'Is there a problem with my attending the princess?' Daryo asked his new page.

'Princess Lacia believes that all in the castle are here to serve her, even the king,' said Sal carefully. 'She will demand flattery and submission. She loathes her servants and any servants and anyone who does not show her the deference she believes correct.'

Daryo nodded. 'I shall be the image of courtliness.' He reached for his jerkin.

'Sir? You may want to dress for the occasion,' said Sal. 'The princess would be displeased if you were not appropriately dressed for her presence.'

Daryo chuckled. 'I think I am going to find this very difficult. What clothes would you suggest?'

The wardrobe contained a few clothes obviously considered essential for a new occupant of the chamber. Chief among them was a robe in the dark green of the prince with white trim and a fur-lined collar. It had a loop on the breast where Sal hooked the silver acorn that the prince had presented. The trousers supplied were far too small for Daryo so he went back to his old breeches and boots. Sal led the way down the tower and through the door that led to the main palace. The princess's room was near the front of the main palace and a single guard stood outside. He saw Daryo's acorn badge, knocked on the door and admitted Daryo. Sal remained outside. The room was smaller than the prince's, about the size of Daryo's, but it was obviously a receiving room and living room not a bedroom. The princess had a well-cushioned chair against one wall, several small stools were drawn up around it, most occupied by women of Daryo's age and younger. Three girls, Eranya included, were stood behind the princess's chair. The glass windows were coloured blue and green in places, the walls were all hung with tapestries mostly depicting hunts or noble scenes. A young man who looked to be of Silver Island heritage was holding a lute but not playing. The princess herself was undeniably Gorero's sister- the same curling dark hair and smooth dark skin, almond-shaped dark eyes but she had a prouder chin, an imperious arch to her brow and a slightly smug expression. She was younger than the prince as well, fourteen summers perhaps, wearing a lightweight crimson gown.

'You are my brother's new councillor,' she said flatly.

Daryo knelt. 'My Lady.'

'Tell me your name.'

'Daryo the Walker, My Lady.'

'Tell me why my brother has chosen a Batribi stray for a councillor.'

'That, My Lady, you would have to ask the prince himself. I cannot answer.'

'My maidens-in-waiting tell me that you are a warrior. Show me your sword.'

'Alas, My Lady, I left it in my chamber. I thought it would be unwise to come before a princess armed.'

The princess giggled. 'Quite true. Quite true. You know that my brother's councillors must all serve his sisters as they do him.'

'Indeed, My Lady. My sword and service are yours.'

'Of course they are!' the princess snapped angrily. 'Your life is mine. If I scream, my guard will cut your head off.'

'Quite so, My Lady.'

'I have no wish to see you anymore. Go.'

'Yes, My Lady. And may I express my thanks for granting me an audience. I have travelled widely and never before had the chance to kneel before such a beautiful example of womanhood.'

The princess giggled again and her ladies cooed sycophantically. 'You are quite correct. You may go.'

Daryo rose and walked backwards to the door, letting himself through. The guard closed it. Sal smiled nervously and Daryo grinned. 'I have never before had the chance to abase myself to such a child before. Lead on.'

Sal turned and led the way back towards the tower. 'The princess is most demanding and the servants all say that she has always been so, Walker, even before she knew her birth and station. Princess Lacia is so but Princess Galiera and Princess Vali are both much kinder, more like the Crown Prince. They are both younger of course, Walker, Princess Lacia is fourteen years, Princess Galiera twelve and Princess Vali nine.'

Daryo heard the boy's voice change. 'You like Princess Galiera?'

'She is very kind.'

'And pretty?'

Sal stuttered with his answer. 'Many girls are so.'

'The second daughter of a king; a fine match for a young esquire one day.'

'The guards say that Princess Lacia and Princess Galiera will be offered to the Vidmarian king to persuade him to end the war. It is known that Vidmarian kings take many wives. Princess Lacia could be wed now, Princess Galiera in three years.'

Daryo nodded, thinking. 'I think I should have some food and then rest.'

'Yes, Walker. I will arrange some food.'

# Chapter 63

The prince's council was convened after the morning meal in a chamber off of the main hall, lit by a huge wooden chandelier supporting dozens of candles. A table was present but no chairs. Sal murmured the names of each of the councillors as they arrived. Lord Novas was the rotund man with the downcast features and balding head. Carbreo he already knew. Lord Sett was much older than the others, a man over sixty summers with a square jaw and a look of authority. Lord Albul was quite young, maybe of thirty summers, and had a relaxed air, a man of high birth comfortable with his position. Lord Venni was of an age with Daryo, very fair and built like warhorse, a young man in his prime and, as Sal had said, the prince's squire with the prince's badge on his robes. All but Venni were attended by a page or squire, Novas had four younger men with him. None seemed surprised by Daryo's presence, Carbreo greeted him warmly. The prince was last to arrive.

'My thanks for your convenience,' he said. 'My Lords, as by now you are doubtless aware I have added a new member to our number. Daryo the Walker is a battle leader of renown with the armies of many nations and with his own blade. My Lord Carbreo and I believe a man like this is most necessary at this time.' All heads except Novas' head nodded agreement. 'The enemy is doubtless moving on Outros. Our deception and diversion of the armies seems to have worked. Additionally, I have managed to persuade my Lord Father that a company of the Oaken Guard can be spared from the capital.'

'This is of great benefit if we can give battle before Outros, sire,' said Venni. 'But if we must hold a siege, surely the Guard is better served as a reserve.'

'Indeed,' said the prince. 'It is my intention to give battle to the Vidmarian army before Outros, even if this is only a delaying tactic, one that slows their advance and show that Boskinian hearts still burn.'

'Sire, we have less than a thousand men from the army of the west,' said Sett. 'How many in Outros?'

'Eight hundred of reserve echelon, Sire,' Sett replied. 'Some ten score on horse and the men of the militia and the city watch, maybe thirty score.'

'A company of the Oaken Guard will give four hundreds,' said Venni.

'We assemble the western army into two companies with one from the reserve,' said the prince. 'And the Oaken Guard and the horsemen. Where is best?' Daryo went to speak and then stopped. The prince noticed. 'Speak, Daryo. You are a councillor here.'

'If we are opposing a large force we need to restrict their advantage. Is there somewhere with a narrow approach? A ravine, a gorge?'

'The Westward bridge,' said Carbreo without hesitation. 'It can take only one cart at a time in one direction, it is not wide enough for two, so maybe three or four men shoulders touching.'

Daryo nodded. 'Their numbers do not count for anything if they can attack only four abreast. Where do we withdraw to from there?'

'Outros,' said Carbreo. 'We would be only three miles from my city's western gate.'

Daryo nodded. 'That sounds ideal.'

The prince nodded. 'I concur. Lord Carbreo, I place you in command of the reformed army of the west. Take Councillor Daryo with you. I will remain here and try to work with my Lord Father.'

'Yes, sire.'

'Of course, sir.'

'Hold them as long as you can, then withdraw to Outros.'

'Yes, sire.'

'My thanks, gentlemen.'

'Do pages accompany their patron?' asked Daryo as they reached the tower chamber.

'That would be my master's decision, Walker.'

Daryo nodded. 'Before you even think of packing my belongings, go and find a bag for yourself. Clothing for several days, any other items you need, a weapon as well.'

'Yes, Walker.'

'Go. Be quick.'

'Yes, Walker.'

'Go.'

Sal rushed out of the chamber. Daryo leisurely packed the few items he required, removed the robe that Sal had produced earlier in the morning and changed it for fresh woollen trousers and undershirt and his armoured jacket. He cinched on his Hajma gauntlets. Sal retuned at a run and looked positively disappointed that Daryo had managed to pack his own bag and dress himself.

'Allow me to help you with your swords, Walker.' Daryo allowed Sal to help him put on his twin blades and then his sword belt. 'There are horses being readied in the courtyard. I told the groom that your page would be riding too.'

'Good. My bag is packed. How far is Outros?' Daryo took his shield and gave it a quick inspection.

'About half a day's ride west.'

Sal went to pick up Daryo's bag but Daryo was too swift and hoisted it. 'Come. Lord Carbreo will doubtless want to leave soon.'

Sal had left his small leather satchel at the door and he trotted after Daryo out to the courtyard. Two young serving women were holding the reins on seven horses, a man was loading the pack horse, an older man was brushing down the neck of one of the horses. He bowed to Daryo.

'My Lord Daryo.'

Daryo glanced at Sal. 'What is your name, sir?'

'I am Toketteria White-wheat, my Lord. I am the groom in charge of the royal stables.' He indicated the horse closest to them. 'Your mount, my Lord.'

Daryo went to strap his bag to the back of the saddle but Sal took his bag and made it fast. Lord Carbreo strode out of the prince's tower with a small retinue in tow- a boy of about eighteen who was presumably his squire, a page and a young woman with short-shorn dark hair in light armour. He nodded to Daryo, exchanged a few words with the groom and gave the order to mount. Moments later, the small procession was trotting out of the palace courtyard and joined the west road.

The road was busy with people, all heading east. Some had horses, donkeys or oxen pulling carts, some had beasts of burden, many were pulling their own carts but most carried the few possessions that had chosen to take. Children were crying and complaining and it mingled with the mutter of saddened people, the creak of wooden wheels and the noise of animals. Carbreo's squire led the line and the horses had been reduced to a slow trot against the river of life flowing against them. Daryo took the chance to learn more of his page. Sal's father was a small landowner near the town of Psephana who had sent his son to be a page first in Psephana itself where Jadara of the king's council was lord. Sal had been taken to Hamlakia as part of Lord Jadara's household and been taken on in the prince's service. He had served a young squire before but he had been called to the western army and Sal had spent several weeks in the stables before being assigned to Daryo. He had three brothers at home, his eldest brother would take on his father's land, the second was training to be a soldier and the youngest was still a child. His mother was known for her skill in breaking, training and healing horses.

Whenever the flow of people thinned, Carbreo's squire whooped and kicked his horse on to a canter. This surge led down a steep descent. In the distance was a walled town and, beyond that, a river. Carbreo slowed his horse until Daryo was alongside.

'Outros!' he announced. 'My city! The river beyond is the Hais, which leads into the Dithithindil!'

'Is the town fortified?'

'The best-defended city in Boskinia! When the army from the lakes arrives, it will be nearly impregnable!'

'How long before they arrive?'

'This coming day. The Oaken Guard will be here by sundown.'

Just before midday, Carbreo took the lead and led the way off of the main road about a mile from the city walls. Daryo imagined it had once been an ancient hill fort as was common in Vidmaria, Hajmachia and Yashoun. Stone steps had been inlaid into the slope up to a newer house on the crest, apparently built to the same plan as the Halfwood Palace but on a smaller scale. All around the man-built hill was an encamped army- most in evidence was Carbreo's yellow and burgundy but also Albul's black, blue and green arms and Sett's purple and red. There were several wounded men, many older men and boys.

'This is my home,' said Carbreo. 'Outros House. My family are safely in Hamlakia for now. These are the reserve companies. My companies and those of Lords Sett and Albul.'

'They look like they have recently seen battle.'

'Over ten days ago. This used to be the main army. It was too badly bloodied to fight on so a new army was formed from the militia and sent forwards. This then became the reserve.'

'Where is the army?'

'Sexiki, just across the river.'

'It should be pulled back across the bridge as soon as possible. Just leave scouts on the west bank.'

Carbreo pulled up his horse, hailed a man near a tent and repeated Daryo's words. The man bowed and hurried off to relay the message.

'I would like to be able to scout the battlefield,' said Daryo.

'Of course. Let us dismount, eat, and then...'

'Lord Carbreo, I would rather go now. The sooner I can decide where to position the army, the better. How far to the bridge?'

Carbreo looked slightly affronted. 'About four miles.'

'I should leave then. I require only my page.'

Carbreo shook his head. 'You will take Camali with you.' He indicated the young woman that had rode with them. 'She knows the land and is one of my captains.'

'As you wish.'
'We should at least find you fresh horses.'

The horses were produced and the threesome rode off, not long behind the messenger heading for the western army. Camali wordlessly led the way on a roadway that led around the hill-fort and then around the city walls in a wide arc to join the main highway on the other side of the city. From there, the road sloped down steadily towards the river, rose sharply, and then dipped steeply to the riverbank and the Westward Bridge. It was as narrow as Carbreo had suggested, about ten feet wide and a hundred long, with high stone walls engraved with the Boskinian king's spreading oak. The bridge and banks were nearly ten feet above the fast-flowing water below. On the opposite side of the bridge the ascent away from the bank was flatter but longer. The east bank was studded with several stands of trees and hedgerows but the west was all but bare.
'Perfect,' Daryo announced. 'I believe this is perfect.' He smiled at Sal. 'Tell me why.'
Sal looked around and thought for several moments. 'The bridge means that the enemy cannot use his numbers to overwhelm us.'
'Correct.'
'The slope will make it hard for him to reach the bridge and on this side it will make a defence easier.'
'Correct.'
'The trees on this side give our men cover but the west bank has no cover.'
'Correct. This is the best site we could have to defend with the army we have, I think.' He turned to Camali. 'We need to establish a defensive line at the bridge and about halfway up the hill as soon as possible. Then I need a full appreciation of our forces, arms and supplies.'
She nodded and turned her horse back towards Outros.

Daryo outlined his plan to Carbreo that evening in the somewhat neglected hall of Outros House. The fireplace was covered by a wooden fence; the main table was against the wall with the benches and chairs on top of it. A pair of braziers had been set up either side of an improvised table- a door laid on two more unlit braziers. A dozen candles burned on the table. Daryo sketched the map of his proposed battle area on a parchment using unlit candles, knives and a pewter mug to illustrate his plan. Carbreo nodded slowly.
'There is one flaw in your plan, sir.'

Daryo nodded. 'I need to work with the best half of the Oaken Guard Company to train them in the Silver Islander technique.'
'The Oaken Guard arrived and setting their camp on the north of the town. Their commander is somewhat elderly, he was appointed by the king. He is very wedded to his ideas. I could ask him to command the army in my place.'
Daryo nodded. 'That may be well chosen.'
'I am no infantryman. I could command the cavalry, Camali the other half of the Oaken Guard, the reserve has its own captain and he could continue in that role.'
'That would be acceptable.'
The door to the hall opened and a young messenger came in. 'My lord Carbreo, the western army has crossed the bridge and is making camp west of the town.'
'My thanks.' The messenger turned and left. Carbreo returned his attention to Daryo. 'I gave orders for scouts to be left across the river.'
'I should get some rest,' said Daryo. 'Tomorrow will need a long time in the field training.'
'Good rest to you.'
'And to you.'

The morning was bright but windy. Carbreo had suggested a large space under the walls of the town, a large empty pasture. Daryo had requested two hundred of the Oaken Guard in full battle order. Two hundred and eight, exactly half the company, were waiting when Daryo joined them, drawn up in eight ranks. Each man was dressed the same- green hose and doublet, a mail shirt, arm guards, a rather flat-topped helmet with an open face and a brown surcoat over all with the king's oak emblazoned on it. Each man had the large rectangular shield that, when on the ground, reached to a man's ribs, a short stabbing sword on his hip, a short spear the same length as the shield and an unusual weapon the size of a dagger but with a blade that curved around to cover the knuckles of the wielder.
'I am Daryo the Walker! I am a member of the prince's council and he has tasked me with commanding you in the upcoming battle!' He waited for a second, noticing the reaction. 'Some of you will be unhappy serving under a Batribi! Some of you will be unhappy fighting for a man you have never seen fight before! But let me tell you that the army marching against us outnumbers us by ten to one! If you choose not to fight under me, then step away now! But be assured that the Vidmarian army will slaughter you, take your wife and murder your children whether you fight under me or no!' This produced a

murmur of concern and comment. 'Any man who wishes to step away, step away now!' Not a single man moved. 'My thanks to you all.'

Daryo cast off the long, full cloak he had been wearing, exposing his armoured jerkin and weapons beneath. Sal hurried forwards with his shield and a Boskinian spear. 'If we are to defeat the Boskinian army, we will require discipline and bravery! The technique that we will use to block the bridge is not what you have trained to do before! The Vidmarians will not have seen it! The Yashoun army fears it! The Nar Silver tribes of the northern Silver Island call it the Infinite Rock. The Silver Islanders call it after one of the many unimaginable animals that inhabit their land. It is the shellback.' He drew his sword. 'Close ranks!'

The Oaken Guard shuffled together obediently until their shoulders were almost touching and the rear ranks were closed up against those in front.

'Front rank *except* the men on the extreme ends, form a wall of shields to your front.'

The men complied, lifting their shields and holding them together, creating a line of twenty four shields.

'Other ranks *except* the men on the extreme end, raise your shields above your heads. Rest the base on the helmet of the man in front and the top on your own helmet.'

This was done with some difficulty, some jostling and much comment. Silence and stillness eventually returned.

'Men on the ends, turn outwards from your comrades and form your own walls. Ensure you are under the shield roof.'

This was done quickly.

'This is the shellback!' Daryo picked up a convenient rock and hurled it onto the roof of shields. It clanged off. 'No arrow or stone will penetrate that roof if it holds together!' He threw another against the front wall. 'No sword will pass through that wall if it holds together! Front ranks can use their spears or swords through the gaps at the corners of the shields! Stand easy!'

There was a surge of noise as shields were lowered and comment made.

'This technique requires practise and discipline,' Daryo told the men. 'This technique is difficult but it will enable us to hold an army many times our size. You must learn to replace fallen comrades, keep the wall intact, deal with breaks in the wall, all this will you will learn if you are willing. Who is willing?' The cheer was sufficient to make Daryo smile. 'Then I am willing to teach you. Put down your shields and come closer, we must talk.'

Carbreo reached the roof of the tower and went to the parapet. Camali pointed out to the meadow. The Oaken Guard were apparently crouched in a tight group, most with their arms over their heads. They all stood up and then crouched again. The Batribi was walking along one side of the group, gesturing with a drawn sword. The Guard stood up and turned towards him before crouching again.

'I do not pretend to understand him or his ways, Camali. He said he would need to train the Guard in this new tactic and I presume that he is doing this.'

She shook her head and snorted derisively.

'You may remember a long time ago a young woman in my wife's service. She was disobedient, insolent, even violent. She tried to flee and was caught by some of Lord Jadara's men. They whipped her, cut out her tongue, shaved her head and left her for dead. She chased them, covered in her own blood, without a stitch of cloth to cover herself and slaughtered them with their own weapons before returning to Outros House in their armour. I took her back in and she is now my most trusted bodyguard and confidant.'

Camali bowed her head, the stump of her tongue feeling awkward behind her teeth.

'I trusted that renegade, that violent young woman. That man is warrior of whom stories have been composed. He has fought in many countries over many years. He has sworn himself to our prince. So I trust him. And the Vidmarians may well have a price on him so he has reason to fight well for us.'

Camali sighed and nodded reluctantly.

'Thank you, my friend.' Carbreo squeezed her shoulder. 'You were right to tell me of your concerns. I trust him to command the first group of the Guard as I trust you to command the second, my Camali.' He squeezed a little tighter before releasing.

## Chapter 64

'My Lord! My Lord! Walker!'

Daryo felt himself being shaken awake. 'Sal?'

'Yes, Walker! The enemy's coming! The scouts have crossed the bridge! Lord Carbreo has given the order to move!'

Daryo yawned. Three days of drilling the Guard had left him very tired. Two days had seen his half-company become reasonably proficient at the shellback. At Carbreo's request, he had then spent half a day with the mute Camali's half-company, briefly teaching them the shellback and then a protective circle. He had gone to sleep in the mid-afternoon that day and was now being woken. The air was cool, outside the sky was lightening. It was apparently just before dawn. Sal was emptying Daryo's bag to find clothes. The page was in rough woollen tights and nothing else.

'Sal, go and dress then find me some bread and milk,' said Daryo. 'If I have left the tent, find me by the Westward Bridge.'

Sal nodded, looking terrified, and raced from the tent. Daryo dressed hurriedly, taking his weapons and shield, and as he buckled his sword belt he heard Carbreo's cavalry gallop away. It was crucial that they were in position in the trees early or the enemy might see them head into concealment. An hour later, Daryo was marching at the head of his half-company around Outros. They passed the army that had retreated three days before. They would be forming the seven-hundred man reserve for the battle. The old army of the west that had been encamped at Outros House, eight hundred men, would be fighting as two large companies with a force of archers, Carbreo's cavalry, Camali's Oaken Guard half-company and Daryo's half-company as independent units. On the far side of Outros, the two main companies took position on the first crest up from the river, Camali's force in front and the archers to the right. The thicket of trees off on their left flank already concealed the ten score on horseback. The reserve would be concealed by the fold in the ground. Daryo marched his force straight down the road, over the rise and down the slope to within a hundred yards of the bridge. He held up his hand for the halt and turned to face his men.

'This is where we stand! This is where the Boskinian oak blunts the claws of the Vidmarian wolf! This is where we stand!'

'THIS IS WHERE WE STAND!' echoed his men.

'Stand down, rest, but be ready,' said Daryo. He turned and looked westwards. Along the line of the hills on the far bank he could see a few figures silhouetted against the now-blue sky. They were the final warning of the Vidmarian attack. Nine men with horses spaced about a hundred yards apart and with horns to sound the alarm.

He looked east. The two large companies were forming on the ridge, Camali's force in front of it astride the road, the small force of archers was forming to their right, the cavalry was completely obscured by the trees on the left. He was happy with the deployment, now just lacked an enemy.

Sal scuttled up, carrying a bag, spear, a helmet like the Oaken Guards' and two large Boskinian shields that were almost as big as he was. A few of the men laughed.

'Your shield, spear and helmet, Walker,' he said, handing one of them to Daryo.

'My thanks. And the other?'

'Is mine, Walker.'

Daryo sighed. 'Sal, no. The shield is too big, you lack the strength to hold it above your head and the height to hold it level with the others.'

'But I am your page. I am supposed to support you in battle, Walker.'

'Not like this, Sal. Please, go back to reserve.'

'I could help someone, Walker.'

Daryo thought for a moment. 'Go back to the reserve; the Town Watch is forming a support company- bringing forwards arrows, taking the wounded back.' Daryo loosened the guard on his left arm and handed it to Sal. 'Go back as my representative. You know the battle plan. You know where we will need help.'

'Yes, Walker.'

'And, in case the fighting gets too close...' Daryo handed over his dagger.

'My thanks, Walker.'

'Go.'

Sal grinned and took a few steps away. 'Second God watch over you, Walker.'

'And over you, Sal.'

A scout came in at midday but on foot. His horse had collapsed and had returned for a replacement. Daryo sent him back towards the reserves. The alarm was sounded not long after. The sentry on the far right of the line blew four long blasts on his horn, mounted and galloped down towards the bridge. The next along the line did the same a few moments later. The rest of the sentries had been warned to retreat after two warnings. Daryo's force was quickly on its feet and arming itself. They parted to allow the scouts to ride through. And then the Vidmarian advance guard, a small mounted unit appeared on the ridge. Another joined it. Then a large infantry force crested the ridge and began to deploy in a wide line.

Daryo checked his equipment- the Horse, the Bear, Temma's Sword, his Order shield on his back, his new Boskinian shield and short spear. He raised the spear. 'Oaken Guard! Rally!' The Guard began to form up. 'Form ranks!' The Guard began to form into ranks of eight as they had practised on the meadow. Daryo moved into the throng and took position in the second row. 'Do not form the shellback until told. Hold the ranks. Hold your courage. This is where we stand!'

'THIS IS WHERE WE STAND!'

The Vidmarian army grew in size. Eventually the whole ridge was full of Vidmarian soldiers. In the centre, a pair of mounted men rode up flanked by the banners and standards of the army. A cornet blew and the main line of infantry began to move forwards, supported by two smaller companies.

'Move forwards!' ordered Daryo. 'Hold the bridge!'

The Boskinian ranks marched forwards in their ranks. The Vidmarians were starting to narrow their front as they approached the bridge. About three hundred yards away they stopped and a captain moved to the front to organise his troops. The Vidmarians began to narrow to a line of five and moved forwards to the bridge. The narrowness of the bridge forced them into a line four abreast. The Boskinians reached the neck of the bridge, four shields across the roadway between the bridge wall and two either side as overlapping replacements. Daryo put on his Boskinian helmet.

'Lock shields!' ordered Daryo. The front rank, except for the man on each end, locked shields. The men on the ends waited for the order. The first Vidmarians began to run as they approached. 'Form walls!' The men on the edges of the block of Oaken Guard turned outwards and raised their shields to form the sides. 'Raise roof!' Daryo lifted his own borrowed shield above his head, putting the base on the helmet in front with the top on his own helmet; a shield came down a little hard on his helmet from behind. The Vidmarian narrow front, three brave or foolish men, slowed in confusion but were pushed on by the screaming mass behind them. 'Out spears!'

The front ranks' spears were pushed out through the holes formed by the rounded corners of the shields. The Vidmarians were on them. The front men stabbed forwards with their spears, the force of the runners shoved the shellback away. 'Step forwards!' ordered Daryo over the roars of the Vidmarians. The Boskinians closed their ranks again. 'HOLD! HOLD!'

The mass of Vidmarians suddenly found that they were confronted by an unmoving wall of shields and spikes. Spears lost in enemy bodies were replaced by ones passed forwards from comrades behind as rehearsed. They shoved forwards.

'HOLD! HOLD!' The Vidmarians pushed again and again, roaring. Projectiles, thrown knives, stones and arrows clattered on the roof. 'HOLD!' The Vidmarians, leaving a dozen dead, stopped pushing and pulled back slightly. 'DOWN!' The front three ranks dropped their shields and knelt quickly. 'FIRE!'

The next two rows had been given bows- the first knelt, the second stood and they fired two volleys into the Vidmarian vanguard. 'Reform! Reform!' Within heartbeats the shellback was reformed but the Vidmarians were trying to flee. Further back than a dozen rows, they could not see what was happening and were still pushing as the front ranks tried to withdraw. 'Archer signal!' shouted Daryo and the command was repeated. A pennant was raised at the back of the shellback and the company of Boskinian archers, about a hundred yards away, began to fire into the Vidmarians at the neck of the bridge. This caused panic in the Vidmarian lines as more of the vanguard tried to withdraw against a bigger, closer mass behind them. Daryo leaned forwards to peer through the hole between two shield corners. Behind the chaotic Vidmarian vanguard, the Vidmarian archers were drawing.

'Hold the shell!' Daryo shouted. 'Down!' In unison, the shellback moved their right feet back a foot and dropped their right knee to the ground so that the wall of shields was resting on the ground with the roof against it. The arrows striking sounded like rain, a persistent pattering of metal on metal and wood. Daryo flexed his left hand that was holding the strap of his shield and took several steadying breaths before calling out. 'This is how well Boskinian men can fight!'

The half-company cheered. 'Fight for the king and the Walker!' someone shouted. 'The king and the Walker!' echoed the others.

Daryo continued to breathe to keep his feelings in check. The rain of arrows was petering out. 'Recover!'

The Oaken Guard pushed themselves upright again. Daryo tried to peer through the gap again. The Vidmarians were reforming at the far end of the bridge but with archers in the front. On an order they drew and fired. The hail of arrows mostly struck shield. One lucky found a gap in the shields and struck a helmet. One struck a man on the corner in the exposed leg. He moaned and stumbled.

'Cover the breach!'

The injured man was hauled back by the arms of his comrades inside the shellback and the side wall moved up to fill the gap.

'Well done!'

The next charge came. This was smarter, a smaller force of men, at a higher pace. One leaped onto the roof of the shell right above Daryo. His weight made a hole in the roof and he fell into the middle of the shellback. The man behind Daryo and to his right stabbed the interloper through the throat with his spear. A spear thrust from outside the shellback caught one of the men in the front row in the side. He fell back and the Vidmarians surged forwards.

'Hold! HOLD!' roared Daryo. 'Push!' The shellback shoved forwards. 'Recover!'

The man to the left of the breach moved sideways to repair the shield wall and the man in the rank behind where he had been, outside the bridge wall, stepped up to fill the gap. The shellback was complete again. Another surge of Vidmarian pressure came and was held back. Another man fell and the shellback replaced it. The force of the next Vidmarian charge pushed them back nearly three yards.

'Hold! Hold!' ordered Daryo. 'Rear ranks, on the backs! PUSH!'

The rear ranks, many of whom had passed their spears forwards put their hands on the back of the man before them and pushed them forwards. The tightly packed ranks of men and shields pushed forwards and sealed the bridge exit again. The Boskinian archers were still shooting into the Vidmarian mass on and near the bridge. The Vidmarian archers were still firing at the shellback but their arrows were being caught on the shields of the Oaken Guard. A small breach was made right in front of Daryo as the man in front of him was caught by a slash across his shins. As he fell, Daryo grabbed his collar, hauled him backwards and stepped forwards into the front row, just preventing a tall Vidmarian from breaking through. The wounded man was causing a gap in the shellback and a couple of arrows pierced the man in the third row. He fell and there was chaos for a moment. Several men were lost as the hole grew.

'Recover! Reform!' screamed Daryo, stabbing his spear out of the hole by his right eye at the Vidmarian front rank. 'Reform!'

The ranks behind finally moved forwards and plugged the hole. Another Vidmarian push crashed into the shellback and broke on it like waves on rocks. Daryo plunged his spear into an exposed side and reached back for another spear, which was thrust into his hand. Suddenly there was no target for the spears. The Vidmarians were withdrawing.

'Hold!' ordered Daryo. 'Hold...' He lowered his shield slightly for more space to see. The Vidmarians were withdrawing quickly off of the bridge. The arrows began to come again and Daryo raised his shield again. The clatter of arrows was fierce but quickly diminished to be replaced by the clatter of horses' hooves. There were several cries and animal screams as the Boskinian archers fired into the Vidmarian cavalry. Daryo knew his men had trained for this. He had trained them.

'Hold! Cavalry! Hold! Wait... SPLIT!'

The shellback split down the centre and parted quickly, clearing the road of Oaken Guard. The score of Vidmarian cavalry had no time to rein in. They surged through the shellback. The vanguard was already several yards up the hill. The rearguard was immediately speared by the men of the shellback. The other half-company of the Oaken Guard poured arrows down onto the Vidmarian cavalry. Even as the last were killed, the front ranks of the shellback were reforming across the bridge.

'Lock shields! Form walls! Raise roof! Out spears!' Daryo found as he called the order, the Guards around him were calling out together. 'This is where we stand!' They finished in unison. Daryo found himself back in the fourth row, the Oaken Guard men were keen to fight.

'Discipline!' he called. 'Courage and discipline! Hold the lines! Hold the shell!'

At least fifty men were still loose at the back, putting the last couple of Vidmarians to the sword. Daryo had seen several Boskinians killed, maybe a score, but at least three score Vidmarians were dead on the bridge in front of the shellback and maybe as many again further back. Another rain of arrows began to come down. Daryo tried to ignore the shafts striking his shield above his head. He did not want to hold too long, eventually his men would tire and their dead and their thirst would weigh heavily.

'For the king and the Walker!' someone shouted again.

'THE KING AND THE WALKER! THIS IS WHERE WE STAND!'

'This is heroic!' he called out. 'Boskinian men are heroic! The Oaken Guard is heroic!'

'For the king and the Walker!' was the answering battle cry of his men.

The Vidmarian footsoldiers came forwards again, this time wielding spears, probing the holes at the shield corners and at the semi-exposed legs of the Oaken Guard shellback. Daryo had his men kneel again for a while and when a charge came properly they rose and pushed. A horn came from the rear: one long, high note. The first withdrawal.

'Hold the wall!' ordered Daryo. He had seen even experienced armies crumble when trying to withdraw. 'Rear ranks, turn about!'

With care, the rear ranks could turn without breaking the roof open. They did so but it took an agonising length of time as the Vidmarian push continued. 'Front row hold! All others, turn about!'

The rest of the shellback, except the front row, turned and reached back to seize the belt clasp of the man behind. 'Stay together. Hold! Hold! And on!'

The shellback began to move away from the bridge, the front rows literally dragged by the rear ranks. The Vidmarians, seeing the withdrawal, pressed forwards more urgently. The Boskinian archers started a constant barrage into the Vidmarians to give the shellback time and space to pull back. The Vidmarians began to form a line on the east bank of the bridge, crouching behind their shields to shelter from the Boskinian arrows while their force built up. After eighty yards or so, the Vidmarian pressure on the shellback stopped. Their archers were split between the shellback and the Boskinian archers.

'Hold!' called Daryo and the shellback halted gradually. 'All about!'

Slowly, all the shellback turned back to face the Vidmarians.

'Lower roof, break walls! Walk, do not run, walk back!'

The half-company of the Oaken Guard began to withdraw up the hill, walking backwards towards the crest line.

'Slow! Slow!' called Daryo.

Slowly the Oaken Guard half-company reached the crest.

'Form ranks!' called Daryo, relieved at the orderly progress. 'Three ranks.'

His half-company was now on the left of the Boskinian line, the two double-sized companies of the army on their right, the other half-company of the Oaken Guard between and in front of them. The little group of Boskinian archers were streaming back over the crest on the extreme right. Daryo, now confident that they were out of the range of the Vidmarian archers, came through his men to the front.

'You fought valiantly!' he called. 'You showed that Boskinian men have steel in their hearts! We have not won yet though! Muster your courage!'

'THIS IS WHERE WE STAND!' the men roared.

Daryo threw his spear away and drew Temma's Sword. He turned towards the other half-company of Oaken Guard and raised his sword as high as he could. An answering sword rose from the front of Camali's force and the other half-company began to fall back to form a complete line along the crest. The small party of drummers and horn-blowers crossed from the nearest company of army to Daryo's half-company. The archers were in position on the reverse slope and were starting to fire up over their army in front of them at the Vidmarians. The Vidmarians tried to spread out as the archers found their range, scrambling for cover under their shields.

Slowly the Vidmarians were starting to mass. More were coming across the bridge but Daryo could see many more clustered on the far bank waiting to cross the bridge. At a rough estimate he guessed that there was about an equal number of Vidmarians to the Boskinian force. He slipped through his men's ranks to the man with the battle horn.

'Give the signal for the advance,' Daryo ordered.

'At once, my Lord.' He raised the large curved horn to his lips and blew three long blasts three times.

Daryo took his place in the centre of his force's middle rank. 'Stay together. Lock shields!'
The front rank lifted their shields and locked them together. In the large company to the right, the captain raised his sword and his men began to move forwards.
'Walk forwards!' ordered Daryo.
The half-company of Oaken Guard started forwards down the slope towards the Vidmarians, in a line with the rest of the army. Daryo held his sword up again and the horn sounded four blows four times. The reserve company would be moving up onto the crest. The gap to the Vidmarian force began to narrow. The Boskinian archers stopped firing so as not to hit their own comrades. The Vidmarian line began to form up, weapons ready and shields raised to repel the expected Boskinian charge. The horn blew five blasts five times. The Boskinian army continued to advance at walking pace. From the trees to the left, the Boskinian cavalry charged, Carbreo leading from the front wielding a long spear, his squire galloping at his side and two hundred men behind them.

The remaining battle was short. After the cavalry joined, the Boskinian footsoldiers charged, routing the Vidmarian force. The Vidmarians crushed to get onto the bridge, several leaped into the water, many were crushed against their comrades or the bridge parapets. As the remnants were captured or killed and the final Vidmarians fled across the bridge, Camali's half-company formed a shellback against the end of the bridge to demonstrate their determination to hold their position. Over the course of the afternoon, the Vidmarian army withdrew up the slope and over the crest.
Daryo caught the sword slash easily on his shield and opened his foe's throat with Temma's Sword. He pushed the Vidmarian away with his shield and surveyed the battlefield. Many were dead, mostly Vidmarians but many Boskinians lay among them. Carbreo had been knocked from his saddle, his helmet was gone, his left arm was hanging almost useless and he carried a Vidmarian sword.
'My Lord Daryo! It looks as if we have won the day!'
'The day, yes. Not the battle, not the war. We shall need scouts stationed on the ridge again and some defence across the bridge. And you need a physician, Lord Carbreo.'
Carbreo nodded. 'I think so. I will have Camali organise what must be done and then find a physician.'

'Walker! Walker!'
Daryo turned and raised his hand in greeting to Sal. 'How goes the battle, Sal?'

'Is not the battle over, Walker?'

'It is. We have the field.'

'Is the Vidmarian army routed?'

'Withdrawn for this day.' Daryo could feel the tiredness building in his mind and body. 'I need a meal.'

'I will find you one, Walker.'

'I will go back to my tent.'

'Yes, Walker. I will bring it to you.'

Daryo started to walk back towards Outros. Carbreo had given commands for the city gates to be opened and the main road to be kept clear to allow the army to come back through the city rather than have to march around. By the gates the Oaken Guard were gathering to march through in units. Someone saw Daryo.

'Hail, Walker!' he called.

Daryo smiled and raised a weary hand.

'The Walker! The Walker!' came the cry. 'The Walker!'

'Hail Walker! Hail Walker!' Daryo found the road suddenly lined by Oaken Guard, presenting arms and crying 'Hail Walker!' in unison as he walked.

On the crest, Carbreo could hear the chanting of Daryo's name.

'He seems popular,' said the physician, a rather wizened woman from Outros.

'We are only living here and not with the Fourth Goddess because he led us,' Carbreo told her. 'Saviour of Outros, possibly of Boskinia.'

'The shoulder is out of its joint, my Lord. I can replace it.'

'Do so.'

'Aye, my Lord. He led the Oaken Guard?'

'The whole battle plan was his. He led from the front and was at the centre of the melee afterwards.'

'A brave man. This will be painful.'

'Proceed. Indeed a brave man. I must ensure the prince hears so.'

## Chapter 65

The Walker was not in his tent. Sal searched the surrounding tents and then the latrine pits. A member of the Oaken Guard said that the Walker had been seen heading into Outros on foot. Sal hurried up the road and almost ran to the city gates, nearly a mile. He questioned the sentry at the gates, who had seen the Batribi Lord walking in to town. Sal ran through the gate and found a junction. The roads were lined with plastered houses but were quiet even as the town awoke. Many had fled with the approach of the Vidmarian army. A young woman was selling apples on the corner and he questioned her. She thought she had seen a dark-skinned man go into the temple opposite. Sal jogged across the road, narrowly avoiding an ox cart and stumbled up the steps of the temple of the Fourth Goddess.

Temples of the Fourth Goddess were not common. The Goddess's patronage of the dead meant that they were considered unlucky and undesirable neighbours. The insides were always the same- bare and stark. Dark blue circles were painted on black walls symbolising the dead moon with stone slabs underneath them representing the graves of the Fourth Goddess's company. The doors were thick and heavy. The altar at the far end was circular, again representing the dead moon with a single candle in the centre. The Walker was sat on one of the plain stone stools that surrounded the altar. His curved sword was laid on the altar itself. Sal felt uncomfortable. The temple was intimidating and morbid, the air felt heavy and smelt of tallow and herbs.

'What brings you into the presence of the Fourth?' asked a crackling voice. A cloaked elderly man stepped out of the shadows, brandishing a candle, his face obscured in shadow.

Sal gulped. 'My Lord Walker. I brought his breakfast and he was not there. I am his page.'

The man pointed a wrinkled hand at Daryo, who was still sat motionless. 'The Walker is praying for those slain this day gone on the battlefield.'

'I will wait for him.' Sal could smell something worse than the rest of the temple, perhaps the old man.

'The Walker has much to speak with the Fourth Goddess about. You should return to the camp. He will return when he is done.'

Sal looked at the figure, worried that his fear would show, back at the Walker and then fled, allowing the door to slam behind him. The old man sniffed in scorn and paced across to the altar, sitting down in the next seat to Daryo.

'He is afraid.'

'He is young,' said Daryo, his eyes closed.

'You are still young, Daryo the Walker.'

'You were young once, Dava the Three Crystals.'

'A long time ago now. And the Three Crystals have become the dead moon. I am so old now my heart-beats ache. My wound has never healed.'

'It festers.'

'Slowly. I will join our comrades one day very soon.'

'They will be honoured to have you at their side again. My people cared for you well?'

'They treated me as a loved uncle. I could not have stayed there though. I owed my life to the Pantheon of Gods. The Fourth Goddess more than all of them. So I came here to Outros and her temple to live out my days. I have already seen more sunrises than the Batribi healers said I would see.'

'I am glad to have met you once more, Dava. I remember you guiding me through the caves of the Order.'

'I remember guiding you. A mere boy of an apprentice. Not the heroic warrior that now sits beside me.'

'I was well taught. The Shrewd. The Harlequin. The Vanguard. The Ranger.'

Dava nodded slowly, his face obscured by the hood of his cloak and the shadows. 'The Shrewd and the Ranger live on in Lalbi. The Vanguard was slain.'

'As was the Harlequin.'

'Many were slain. Those that linger can only mourn them.'

'And do honour to their memories.' Daryo sighed. 'Is there anything I can do, Dava?'

'No, Daryo. My thanks but I am beyond the aid of men and the intervention of Spellis. I await the Fourth Goddess's pleasure.'

Daryo bowed his head. 'As do we all.' He stood up and picked up his sword. 'It means little with the rest of our comrades in their graves but I made a Promise.' He raised Temma's Sword, point down. 'My sword and my service.'

Dava sighed. 'Until discharged by death. My thanks, Walker.'

Daryo sheathed his sword. 'I am glad to have seen you once more.'

'We shall meet again, Walker. I shall be at the altar of the Third Goddess in the next kingdom.'

'I shall find you there.' Daryo clasped the old man's hand. 'Gods' Watch, Dava.'

'Gods' Watch, Daryo the Walker. Fight well.'

'And you.'

Daryo resolutely turned away from the crippled figure and walked to the door. As soon as he stepped outside he almost fell over Sal, who was sat on the steps.

'I thought you were told to return to camp, Sal.'
'By the priest, Walker. Not by you.'
'That man was not a priest. An old acolyte near death,' Daryo told him. 'I want you to find the priest. Wherever I am, I wish to be told when the man I spoke to passes to the next kingdom. He will have left instructions as to where to be buried. I will pay for the arrangements.'
'Yes, Walker.'
'Find the priest, make the arrangements for me and return to the camp. I must find Lord Carbreo, look for me with him.'
'Yes, Walker.'
'Go.'
Sal scurried away around the back of the temple. Daryo look a long moment to think. He was tempted to pull Dava out of the temple and into the light again but the slash across his face had been evil, a dirty blade had caused a disfiguring wound that was rotting the old man's face away. Dava the Three Crystals was content to wait for the Fourth Goddess to take him on and Daryo knew to respect the old man's wish and the Fourth Goddess's patience. He turned on his heel and made his way to the city gate.

Carbreo had his left arm bound across his chest to help protect his damaged shoulder and a strip of cloth wrapped around a wound on his right forearm. His squire had been thrown by his horse and was limping badly. Camali was unscathed but the sergeant who relayed her orders had been killed. A man of over fifty summers was stood with them in the uniform of the Oaken Guard. Carbreo was in his hall at the improvised table.
'Lord Daryo,' he greeted him.
'Lord Carbreo. How is your arm?'
'Attached. The physician returned it to its place. It is sore but will heal. I have scout reports.' He beckoned Daryo to a newly-drawn map of the land between Outros and the river and the far bank. 'We hold, of course, the eastern bank.' There were three circles of parchment painted green on the eastern bank, one with Carbreo's arms in the centre. 'I have put our scouts along the line of the hill on the west, the hill the cityfolk call the Brown Ridge.' He pointed to a line of ten needles on the ridge with green thread tied to them. 'The Vidmarian army has withdrawn and set camp before Sexiki.'
'They may try the bridge again,' said the other man. Daryo now recognised him as the former captain of the Oaken Guard, promoted to command the army itself.

'They may,' said Daryo. 'But not without reconsidering their approach. An infantry advance can be repelled the same way as before. They may attack in depth with cavalry across the bridge, shatter the shellback and charge our lines with more horsemen.'
'Is that what you would do, Lord Daryo?' asked Carbreo and Daryo inclined his head affirmatively. 'We should assemble pikes and traps for horsemen. Then we can defend better against them. A messenger from the prince has confirmed that the army of the lakes has reached Hamlakia. He awaits our pleasure as to their deployment.'
Camali spread her arms wide.
'All of them?' confirmed Carbreo and she nodded emphatically. 'That leaves only the Halfwood Company to defend Hamlakia.' Camali shrugged.
'Is it my Lord's intention to hold Outros in siege against them?' asked the old commander.
'I would rather take the offensive to them,' said Carbreo bluntly.
Daryo frowned in thought. 'We could maybe not attack but raid. Lord Carbreo, I require thirty Oaken Guard, young and fast, lightly armed and armoured and they should put themselves forwards for the duty. And we must wait for the darkness.'
'You shall have them.'

Daryo met his team by the east gate of Outros just before sundown. There were twenty-six who had volunteered to follow the Walker as well as Carbreo's Camali. Daryo checked each of them, looking to make sure that their boots fitted well, they were wearing only leather armour and carrying no weapon heavier than a sword and no shields bigger than an arm shield. One man refused to remove his mail and Daryo dismissed him, another had boots that were far too large and he was also rejected. Daryo's force was now twenty-five including Camali. They had twenty-four swords, nine arm shields, a score of daggers and Camali had a Vidmarian sword- longer and thinner than a Boskinian one with a longer point and no hand-guard. Daryo had his twin swords and no other weapons. He had just three small glass bottles with him.
'We are going to inflict some damage on the Vidmarian army,' he told his small group calmly. 'We must be silent and swift, bats on the wing.' He gave one of his bottles to Camali and another to a man he recognised. 'Flame oil. Be careful with it. Stow it carefully. We are going to cause as much damage as we can using that oil, fire and our weapons.'
There was a murmur of approval from the company and Daryo motioned them forwards.

The crest on the east bank was still lined by Boskinian scouts so Daryo was able to lead his small company across the bridge and follow the road up to the ridge line. Below, the land swept away into a deep dale dotted with tents and watchfires in the twilight. Daryo surveyed the scene. Away to his left, to the south, there was a broad sweep of trees. The sprawling Vidmarian camp was all to the north of it.

'We can find shelter in there,' said Daryo. 'Wait for total darkness. Use the ground. Do not attack unless I say.'

Daryo led his group back down the slope and in a wide arc to the south, away from the camp, back over the crest and then down into the woods. The ground was relatively clear, the trees low and starting to bud. Daryo found a hollow surrounded by tall grasses, waved downwards with both hands and sat down. Camali sat next to him. He heard the rustles as his platoon hid themselves. Camali tapped Daryo on the shoulder and pointed up to the sky, then covered her eyes briefly.

'The light?' Daryo asked. Camali nodded. 'Not yet. It must be full darkness.'

Camali nodded and rested her head on the tree beside her. Daryo listened to the noises of the woods return- singing birds as the sun descended, the scurry of rodents, a louder rustle could have been a fox. Through gaps in the trees, more fires were visible, small individual fires outside tents.

'When the fires die down,' Daryo said softly to Camali. 'When the men go to sleep, the fires will die out. Then we can attack.'

Camali made an affirmative noise and flexed her fingers. She made some more noises with her maimed mouth but could not make herself understood. She tapped Daryo's shoulder again and produced a knife. She pointed to Daryo, then the Vidmarian camp and stabbed with the knife.

'Have I fought Vidmarians before?' Daryo got an affirmative nod. 'I have. With my Order and then with the Hajma. They are good warriors but very reliant on their commanders. A Vidmarian company with no commander will not fight on using their own initiatives. They withdraw and seek shelter or a new leader. They also follow their training, they are trained to fight according to their training and have difficulty adapting, especially while in battle.' Camali smiled and thrust her knife. 'As you say. Your mouth hurts? Your tongue was it?'

Camali nodded sadly, hesitated for a moment and then opened her mouth. Daryo had just enough light to see that there was an uneven stump right at the back of her mouth and gaps for several teeth at the back.

'I am sorry, Camali. Not Lord Carbreo's doing?'

Camali shook her head quickly and made a waving gesture suggesting someone far distant. She showed Carbreo's badge on her chest and gripped it with her hand. 'He protected you after?' She smiled and gripped the badge again. 'Lord Carbreo seems a most worthy man.' Camali nodded distantly. 'A great man.'
Camali smiled wistfully and leaned her head back against the tree.

Finally the darkness came and the fires in the Vidmarian camp began to die away. Silhouettes were visible against some tents and gradually they became sleeping forms. Daryo and Camali mustered their force along the tree line. At irregular intervals sentries passed around the perimeter of the camp but they were growing less common as the night grew older. Daryo drew the Horse and produced the bottle of flame oil from his belt. He led the way forwards and started splashing the oil on the tents as he sneaked past. Camali and the Guard with the third bottle followed his example. Daryo emptied the last of his bottle and crept up behind a sentry and slit his throat with the Horse, drawing the Bear as the man dropped and reversing it so that the point was downwards. He tapped his swords together twice, the arranged signal to start. Swords flashed, daggers thrust, blood sprayed like water. Some Boskinians went for the sleepers, some for the sentries. Camali led four into a cluster of tents filled with food and supplies. When they emerged, the tents began to burn. Daryo stabbed another sentry, slid the Horse back into its sheath and grabbed a smouldering branch, raked it across the nearest tent and began to run back towards the woods, sweeping his branch across the flame-oil-spattered tents as he raced. A Vidmarian rose up, clutching a sword. Daryo smacked him across the head with his branch and opened his chest with the Bear. He reached the tree line again. One by one his men joined him. Camali was the last. She had a gash in her arm and another on her forehead but looked ecstatic in the flames.
Daryo counted twenty-five and gave the signal to draw back into the trees. A good section of the Vidmarian camp was burning and every blade in the group was bloodied. 'Back over the ridge,' said Daryo. 'Meet at the bridge.'

All of the force assembled intact at the bridge in high spirits. Most of the men were laughing and singing. Camali looked around the force, lit by torches tied to the bridge parapets, and punched Daryo playfully on the arm, grinning widely. Daryo beckoned to Sal, who had been waiting with a dozen other pages, who brought forwards jug after jug of wine and pewter cups. Daryo went around the group, men offering their hands, and accepted a cup of wine from Sal.

The Vidmarian attack came after midday, a wave of cavalry struck at the shellback hastily formed and led by Camali. As the lead pair of horsemen approached, the shellback split down the centre, leaving a forest of long stakes in the ground, and reformed thirty yards back. Two dozen Vidmarian horses were impaled on the stakes; another two dozen were cut down by Boskinian archers from the ridge. The next line of Vidmarian horses struggled through the stakes and their dead comrades just as the shellback broke and charged. The Vidmarian archers on the far bank loosed their arrows but the soldiers of the Oaken Guard took cover under their shields and remade their shellback at the end of the bridge. The remnants of the Vidmarian cavalry withdrew and their archers were almost run down by the fleeing cavalry. The Boskinian archers rushed to the riverbank and fired thousands of arrows into the retreating army and jeered them over the ridge. Daryo had been among the archers and allowed himself to join the ecstasy of victory and roared defiance at the routed Vidmarians.

'How fares the enemy, my Lord?'
Daryo was laid in a depression just on the ridge line, a long way from any of the sentries, observing the Vidmarian camp. He had seen over ten score bodies loaded into wagons and counted three dozen burned tents.
'Lay down, I do not wish to be observed,' Daryo said shortly.
'As you wish. Few men command their prince.'
Daryo's head came up a few inches. 'Prince Gorero.'
The prince slid into the dip alongside the Batribi. 'Worry not, my Lord Walker. I ask no apology. You have proved yourself to be a fine general and a saviour of our lands in just a few short days. Any misdemeanour, any crime you commit will be absolved in these lands until the end of days.'
'I ask no privilege, sir' said Daryo, turning his attention back to the Vidmarians. 'I have counted one hundred and nine bodies from our raid and the wounded from the battle. The army is withdrawing.'
'Finding another way forwards.'
'Undoubtedly. They are withdrawing directly to the west.'
'Towards Sexiki. From there they can join the road north to Vhamsia and towards Hivamakia.'
'Is there any other way into Boskinia south of here?'
The prince thought. 'Only if you travel a long distance for many weeks.'
'Where?'
'Ishter. The Mountain Keep.'

'A city.'
'A nation of its own. A tiny enclave high in the Black Mountains.'
'How far?'
'I know no distances by miles. Three weeks for a man on a horse. Maybe five for an army.'
'Is Ishter friend to Boskinia?'
'Ishter is no enemy. But Ishter will not bother the Vidmarian king. But he must march his army through Adaca.'
'Adaca is to the south?'
'It is. And Adaca may resist. The road through our river counties and into Adaca leads through the citadel of Darsux and the lakeside town of Oia as well as many villages. The Adacan king is Kyomani; he is a proud man and will not be pleased to have a Vidmarian army in his lands.' The prince slapped Daryo on the shoulder. 'Come, my Lord. We have scouts here to warn us if this is a ruse. Come back to town, there is a ceremony I must attend.'

The prince and his retinue assembled on the steps of the Mercantile Hall with Daryo, Carbreo, the Oaken Guard, men of the army and the people of the city gathered below. 'My Lords and Ladies, people of Outros, men of the army of Boskinia!' announced Gorero. 'We have repelled the Vidmarian army!'
The crowd cheered.
'This victory was a victory in battle! We have repelled them but not defeated them. But this was a victory. Our first victory of this war!'
This was greeted by a louder cheer.
'By the warrant of my father the king, I grant these honours. To the army of the west, I award the king's oak banner!'
A man stepped forwards with a light green banner mounted on a pike. The men of the army cheered loudly.
'To the commander of the army, Lord Carbreo, I award the title of Defender of the West and Commander of the Armies of Boskinia!'
He beckoned Carbreo up the steps. Carbreo mounted the steps and knelt on the top one. An attendant handed a black cape lined with green and fringed with gold. Embroidered on the back were Carbreo's arms. Prince Gorero tied the cape around Carbreo's shoulders and offered his hand, pulling Carbreo to his feet.
'To the commander of the Oaken Guard, Camali Green-haven, I award a lordship, the estate of Cilano and arms as a member of my private council!'

Camali mounted the steps and was presented with a plainer black cloak with her own arms on the back- green at the top, yellow at the bottom divided by a narrow blue band. When she rose, she was also presented with a large, elaborate scroll.

'And finally to the man who ensured our victory, Daryo the Walker, Member of the Order of Shield and Sword, by warrant of my father, I grant the title of Saviour of the Nation, lordship, the estate of Scara and arms.'

Daryo sighed slightly and handed his shield to Sal before mounting the steps. The arms were half red and half black divided by a white silhouette of a sword. The cloak was the same as Carbreo's- green lined black with gold trim. Prince Gorero's hand was extended down to him and Daryo grasped it. The prince pulled Daryo to his feet. A scroll nearly a yard wide with elaborately gilt finials was handed to him. The prince handed over a Boskinian spear with a black metal tip and highly-polished handle.

'I did not ask for this,' said Daryo.

'And that is why it is given, my friend. Scara is a small village south of here and will make you a wealthy and settled man. Your page will stay with you and any other wish you have, I will grant.'

'You have already given more than enough, Prince Gorero.'

'My Lord Daryo, nothing is enough for your deeds. I would like you to take some time to rest, relax, go to your new estate. But Boskinia will need you.'

'I will answer. My most grateful thanks, Prince Gorero.'

'And mine to you. Lord of Scara.'

Carbreo provided horses. Daryo and Sal were given an escort of four Oaken Guard to ride with them and a rider went on ahead to warn the village that their new lord was coming. They stopped for the night in the village of Cilano, Camali's new estate, in the inn and then rode on to the village of Scara. They approached over a low hill and the road led down through several acres of planted fields and some grazing pastures. The village itself was a cluster of wooden houses, the spire of a small temple visible among them with a watermill and sawmill alongside the river. Several people working in the fields looked up and several waved in greeting as the small group rode past. Daryo found that he was quite embarrassed by the attention. As they reached the village, people came out of their houses, the dairy, the forge, the mill, to see their new lord.

At the centre of the village was a well with several stalls around it. The temple was on one side of the space, a gilded wheatsheaf above the door signifying a temple of the First Goddess Tahili. A little way around the space was a modest house with a cluster of people outside. Sal was smiling broadly.

'I think that is your home, Walker.'
'It may be.'
Daryo reined in his horse and dismounted. A man bowed and four women curtsied smartly. Daryo waved them up.
'Lord Daryo, welcome to Scara House,' said the older man, bowing again. 'I am Casillo, houseman. Terras, your groom.' He indicated a tall, dark woman of about Daryo's age. 'Rau, the cook.' The oldest of the four women curtsied again. 'Sergia, your maidservant.' The youngest woman, not much older than Sal, smiled and curtsied. 'Rianala, your estate's yeoman.' A dark-haired young woman, slightly younger than Daryo, in a mail shirt over a leather jerkin and with arm guards, drew her long sword and raised it in salute.
Daryo drew his sword and returned the salute. 'My thanks for your welcome. I am glad to be here. To all of you I offer my sword and service as lord of these lands.'
Everyone in his view knelt or bowed.
Casillo was first to rise. 'Come inside your home, my Lord. You must be tired and thirsty.'
'See to my escort first and to my page.'
'As you wish, my Lord.'

The house was small but well done. The hall had a large fire-pit in the centre below the chimney, flanked by two well-made tables and chairs. A wooden stair led to a gallery along the back of the hall. Two bedrooms, one much larger than the other, and a contained privy were accessed from the gallery. Downstairs were storerooms, a kitchen and the door into the servants' quarters at the rear. Daryo insisted on seeing every room and was unhappy to find that only Casillo had a window to his room and instructed that someone be found to rectify it. He quickly divested himself of his equipment and grubby travelling clothes for a fresh linen shirt, black canvas trousers and, at Sal's insistence, his lord's cloak before going for a stroll around the village with Rianala and Casillo. The watermill and sawmill was run by Ravin, Rau's husband; the dairy by Sergia's mother Ferna; the farm foreman was Terras' husband. There were just over three hundred people in the village according to the elderly priestess Vara. The village had been the prince's responsibility and Casillo had been acting as steward but seemed pleased to have been relieved of the responsibility. Scara had no inn as the road went no further south than the village but a house near the forge had been converted to a small tavern known as the Evening's Rest. Rianala had a small structure behind the Evening's Rest that she explained was the village militia's command centre. It was a large shed with an iron-barred cell at the far end and a dozen swords and shields hung on the wall. Daryo requested that all of the shields were repainted with the village arms in place of the bare wood.

'Who is in charge of the money in the village?' asked Daryo.

'There is no treasurer,' said Casillo. 'I have the records.'

'Is there sufficient to raise the income of all the workers in the village by... five in every hundred?'

Casillo frowned. 'My Lord?'

'Can it be done?'

'I believe so, my Lord.'

'Do so. I would also like someone to find a treasurer. There must be someone with numbers in the village.'

'Indeed, my Lord.'

Daryo dismissed Rianala and Casillo and took a long, leisurely walk back to the house. By the time he arrived, Sergia had set a meal of cold chicken, cheese, bread and fruit. Daryo had Sal join him and, on impulse, Rianala.

'How did you become yeoman?' Daryo asked.

'My father, my Lord. He was yeoman under Lord Nali. Lord Nali died three autumns gone and the prince became lord. My father died that winter and the prince gave commands that the title be passed down, assuming that my father had a son.'

'He did not.'

'Only daughters. Three of us. I as the eldest was given the task.'

'And you do the task keenly?'

'Indeed, my Lord.'

'Rianala, I have never sought lordship. I am known as the Walker.'

'As you wish, Walker.'

'My thanks.' Daryo stood up, Rianala jumped to her feet. 'That is not necessary,' he told her.

The young groom ran into the hall and bowed, almost somersaulting forwards. 'My Lord.'

'Slow down, Terras,' said Daryo kindly.

'My Lord, a visitor,' she said. 'A Lady.'

'My thanks.' Daryo went outside just as Camali dismounted her horse. 'Camali!'

She smiled and curtsied with a rather mocking attitude. She spread her arms and pulled a quizzical face.

'I will learn to be a lord, I hope. The village is very pleasant.'

She smiled wider and pointed back over the rise towards her new village, nodding happily.

'I am glad that you are happy. This is much more peaceful than a battlefield.'

Camali made a laughing noise in her throat and swept her cloak aside to show that she carried no weapons. She mimed drawing a sword and hurling it away.

'You may need that returned,' Daryo told her.

She waved it away dismissively. She mimed walking with two fingers, pointed at herself and then Daryo. Daryo offered his arm.

## Chapter 66

Daryo grew comfortable in his estate over the next score days. He enjoyed the rhythms of the day and the work of the farm. Despite Casillo's unvoiced disapproval, he assisted with the building of a new sheep pen and the repairs to the dairy roof. He gave Rianala some guidance on training the eleven men that made the village militia. The day before Summer's First he led the young people of the village up the south hill where there were archery targets set up and he led the day of archery practise. When he was not busy with Scara's needs, he found he was often in Cilano keeping company with Camali- walking, occasionally practising their weapon drills, he learned that she played the Yashoun three-fold tambourine and he recited and composed stanzas of his people's Verse. It seemed quite natural after a dinner in Carbreo's honour at Scara House that Daryo escorted Camali home and kissed her gently when they parted.

The rider was dressed in white. He reined in, brought a bell from his saddlebag and rang it slowly.
'Hear all! Hear all!' he called. 'Know all who hear my words that the king is dead! King Olyaro the Third has gone to the embrace of the Fourth Goddess! His son has been proclaimed king by the old council as King Gorero the Ninth!' The bell was rung again and the rider dismounted. 'Where is your lord?' he asked the nearest person and was pointed to the dairy.
Daryo was learning how Ferna made ewe's milk cheese and had not heard the rider's pronouncement.
'My Lord?' asked the rider.
Daryo nodded. 'I am.'
'My Lord, I bring the gravest news. The king has died.'
Daryo sighed. 'Grave indeed.'
'Prince Gorero has been named King Gorero the Ninth as the last act of the old council. He summons his lords immediately to Hamlakia.'
'I shall be swift.'
'My Lord.' The rider bowed low and hurried back to his mount.
Daryo immediately summoned Sal and Terras; the former to pack, the latter to ready horses. Out of habit, Daryo changed into black leggings and shirt, his well-loved armoured jerkin and his Hajma bracers with his sword belt. Sal was waiting by the time Daryo was dressed with his lord's cloak but Daryo told him to put it in a bag. By noon, Daryo, Sal and two of Rianala's militia were riding north.

Daryo halted his group in Cilano and went to the house for Camali. She, her young page and her captain of militia joined them.

It was after dark when they arrived at the Halfwood Palace. The building was hung with large white pennants each bearing the Fourth Goddess's dead moon in silver surrounding the Boskinian spreading oak. Daryo was directed to his old room in the prince's tower. Camali was given one in the main room near Princess Lacia's chambers. The next morning at the morning meal, the king's seat was left empty with a white pennant across it. Gorero did not attend the meal, Daryo had been told that the new king would fast and eat and drink only milk until he was installed as king. Daryo was eating oatmeal porridge with little enthusiasm when a squire appeared.

'My Lord Walker. I am Hussan, squire to the king. He asks that you attend him immediately in his chamber.'

Daryo found the prince discussing a matter of funeral procedure with a priest and Lord Novas. He acknowledged Daryo's waiting and concluded his discussion with the other two before dismissing them. Daryo bowed.

'My Lord King.'

'My Lord Walker. Thank you for coming. I apologise for interrupting your morning meal but I find events happen all too quickly.'

'No inconvenience, sir. My sympathies for the loss of your father.'

'My thanks. My Lord Father was elderly and ailing. It was a release and a mercy that he joined the Fourth Goddess before his wits failed and his body began to decay. My Lord, our scouts in the south-west have revealed the Vidmarian army is marching. They have been content to occupy our lands up to the Hais River thus far. But the Gourmini army has expelled them from Tiverta and it seems that all of Vidmaria's wrath will now be turned on us. They are marching south. There are enough men left in Sexiki and by the Dithithindil to make one think that they are not moving but we know differently. The army is now solely under my charge. We will leave as many as we dare to guard Outros and Hivamakia and send the rest south to Psephana. But this army is much larger than we have faced and our force on its own will not be enough.'

Daryo nodded. 'What do you require of me?'

'I require you to go to our neighbours- Ishter and Adaca. The Vidmarian army must march through both nations to reach ours. Their people, their crops, their land will also suffer with ours. Show them that they are best to join us and that we are best to fight together. I will send with you an emissary for the actual negotiations, a messenger with our trained pigeons and a small force of Oaken Guard as escort. When you have the aid we require, I can then send the army to you where it is needed.'

Daryo nodded and thought for a moment. 'I would ask, sir, that you allow Camali of Cilano to accompany me as well.'

Gorero shrugged. 'As you wish. I know that most involved would prefer to be here for my Lord Father's funeral and my installation but this is more important.'

'Indeed, sir. When should we leave?'

'By noon.'

'It shall be done.'

Amid the frantic preparations for the king's funeral at sunset, a small group met at a nondescript stables just inside the city walls. Neither Camali or Daryo wore anything showing their status and, as they were planning to journey to Ishter down the Outros-Cilano-Scara road, there was little need for them to carry much baggage. Sal and Camali's page Herro were alongside their patrons. The prince's emissary was an elderly man with a fatherly demeanour, neat beard and tired eyes, a small landowner but an experienced diplomat named Micel Grey-Sky. The messenger, Butriguno, was an apparently failed squire, rather fat and timorous who almost flinched whenever addressed directly. A guide had been added by Gorero, a woman from Ishter named Eraphi. Six of the Oaken Guard, all of whom had been part of Daryo's half-company in the battle on the bridge before Outros, led by a captain Serri Stone-Fire.

It was agreed that Daryo and Camali would ride ahead with their pages, assemble what they needed in their villages and make arrangements for their absence and the whole team would reassemble in Scara for the journey south.

The next dawn, the Boskinian deputation left Scara. Eleven men, two women, fifteen horses and four caged pigeons, two trained for Psephana and two for Hamlakia, slung on a pony. Just south of Scara was a tributary of the Hais River and it was narrow and shallow enough for the horses to ford easily. The guide, her lustrous brown hair just starting to grey, led the way on a confident grey mare with Daryo alongside.

'Tell me of Ishter, Eraphi,' he said as their horses walked through untouched natural grasslands.

Eraphi glanced across. She had very shiny brown hair left loose around her shoulders, a prominent, slightly hooked nose and although the weather was not particularly warm, she wore a sleeveless tunic with no cloak or shawl. 'Ishter is a small nation, my Lord. A tiny stretch of land stuck between the mountains. The city is alongside a lake that is the main source of water in the land. Beyond the city, there is little civilised. The small tracts of land are fought over by small tribes who pay only minimal notice to the city. They are too busy warring with each other over a few square yards of rocks.'

'Who leads the city?'

'The city is led by a governor. There is no king and, often, no governor. The city chooses senators, by lot and then by vote. All men and women over thirty name-days may be chosen as one of the thirty to stand and the people then choose twenty of them to be senators for ten seasons. They must choose one of their number as governor. If no single one can be chosen, they must rule as a senate until the next vote.'

Daryo nodded. 'It sounds complicated.'

'Somewhat. But it has served our little city for nearly ten generations.'

'Is there a governor currently?'

'No, my Lord. The Senate rules until this coming winter.'

'How many people live in Ishter?'

'In the city? Perhaps thirty thousands. In the tribal lands, no man could count. Perhaps twenty tribes, perhaps a hundred in each. Maybe less or perhaps more, there is no way to count.'

'Would these tribes trouble travellers?'

'Undoubtedly.'

Daryo silently gave thanks to the Second God that he had collected his twin swords and his old shield while in Scara. At his request, a talented painter in the village had added his lord's arms to his shield, skilfully placing them on the milestone in the centre. 'Tell me of the people of Ishter. Do they have faith, do they go quickly to war?'

'They do have faith. The Good Shepherd is the faith of the senate but there is a small temple to the Eight Gods and one of the Unconquered Sun.'

'The Unconquered Sun is a common faith in Armynya. Is there a war-like feeling in Ishter?'

'The city is sometimes attacked by the tribes but they are not large enough to bother the city. Sometimes the Senate will send out the militia to challenge the tribes but this is not needed or done often. The militia only numbers in the hundreds. The Senate's Yeomen are the only maintained soldiers in the city and normally number about one hundred but they are trained on foot, horseback and in defending the city.'

'May I ask why you left?'

Eraphi laughed. 'You may ask, my Lord of Scara, but I may not tell you.'

'Why did you leave?'

'I left because I disobeyed my father. He tried to make me marry and I chose not to. I came to Boskinia because women are freer here. I found work in the kitchen at the Halfwood Palace and then in the chamber of sweet Princess Vali.' She showed her bracelet, a leather cuff with the image of a flying blackbird clutching an acorn in its foot.
'I have not had the pleasure of meeting the younger princesses. Although I believe my page has Princess Galiera at his heart.'
Eraphi laughed again. 'Many boys his age around the court do. Princess Vali is a very lovely child, a true royal-born young lady, all grace and charm and sweetness. She loves her music and her pony who she named Spinel after the Third Goddess. She believes that the Third Goddess is the most important of the Pantheon and tries to do everything in her name.'
'Commendable. Do you have a faith?'
'I believe in the Gods. I believe that there is something beyond us that shapes the land and the skies and what happens in both. I trust in the Second Goddess to guide me in serving Princess Vali and her brother the new king. I believe the First God has blessed me with good health in my forty-second spring. I hope that my mother is safe in the care of the Fourth Goddess and that she spurned my father when he came before her. And you, my Lord?'
'I have seen too much to believe that the world is only what is seen, as you do. The Fourth Goddess has taken many followers on from my blade, she cares for many of my fallen comrades and for my parents perhaps, wherever they fell. An old friend of mine in her temple in Outros nears death and I hope he finds peace at her side. I believe the Second Goddess also guides me in the actions that I take. I swore a solemn oath several years ago to do my duty and to give my sword and service to those who need it.'
The grasses were getting thinner and there were clusters of rocks cropping up as the mountains loomed closer. The ground was sloping ever upwards as Eraphi turned her horse south-east rather than south and they soon came alongside a narrow, fast mountain river heading back towards Scara.
'We follow this river now,' said Eraphi. 'It will lead us into the pass through the mountains into Ishter. There is no road but a rough track through the pass. Ishter cannot trade with Boskinia due to the poor travel. It trades only through the Southern Gateway with Adaca. This pass is known as the Northern Gateway.'
The pass was visible ahead, a green-brown passage between black and grey mountains, topped with white snow and ice, that formed a barrier against the almost-clear blue sky. A few white clouds were drifting northwards on the breeze. A bird of prey hovered above the pass and suddenly swooped after a target. The river by their left hands was narrow

with steep, stony banks and littered with small waterfalls, rocky rapids and numerous shallow sections. A large heron took off as the travellers approached and flapped away northwards. Daryo stopped his horse to allow someone else to ride alongside Eraphi and started his horse forwards again when he was alongside Camali. He had found in their time together that conversation on his part was quite superfluous as she was unable to reply with words. Instead he had come to learn the simple body language, signs and gestures that she used and he found that he preferred communicating that way instead of speaking.

He swept his arm around to take in the landscape and then held that hand to his heart, describing *beautiful country* with his hands.

Camali nodded. She pointed at the heron and then up at the bird of prey that was hovering again and made a rolling motion with her hand. *Lots of birds, I want to see more.* Daryo made the rolling gesture and pointed forwards. *More to come.*

She smiled, pointed forwards and made a gesture like a shrug with her whole arm that Daryo knew meant that she did not know. *I do not know what is ahead.*

Daryo pointed at the bird then mimed drawing his sword. *Birds and war.*

A point to the bird, a smile, then a mimed sword and her croaking laughing noise. *Birds are good, war is better.* She pointed forwards and raised her eyebrows.

'Eraphi?' A confirming nod. He smiled and held his arm out with his fist clenched. *Strong, dependable.*

Camali smiled again, winked and kicked her horse on.

The incline got steeper and the horses slowed. The ground was getting progressively rockier and the air chiller. Eraphi stopped and donned a woollen cloak from her saddle bag. The pigeon keeper, Butriguno, was muttering a continuous stream of complaints and self-pity as they continued; that he was not a rider, that the air was too cold, the wind too strong, his horse uncomfortable, their rests too infrequent and a continuing litany of nefarious woes. He had got to the back of the line and only Micel, a silent and tolerant companion, would ride alongside him.

The pass itself was much wider than some others that Daryo had passed through, nearly a hundred yards wide at its mouth and it looked little narrower further on. As it was approaching sunset, Daryo and Camali took the decision to camp and to continue at first light. The huge baggage horse was unloaded, it carried three tents and the Oaken Guard quickly had them erected while the two lords and Eraphi gathered wood and made the fire. The fire was soon substantial and hot and Camali took two of the Guard with bows and went off to hunt for something to supplement the food that they had brought from Scara.

One of the Oaken Guard took first watch on the pass and climbed a short distance on to the top of a nearby rock pile for a clear vantage with a bow and a horn. The other three gratefully accepted Daryo's invitation to sit by the fire alongside him.

'My Lord, may I ask something?' asked the captain.

'Of course.'

'Would you tell us of your work in the Silver Island?'

'The Silver Island?'

'You fought the Nar Silver.'

'I did.'

'Would you tell us of it?'

'It was a brutal war, captain. The Nar Silver had lived with the Islanders for many generations having divided the island by a treaty. The Nar Silver broke the treaty and began attacking villages along the rivers. Every attack they burned the houses and staked the villagers out in the sun to die. Dozens of hundreds died. When the Islanders moved to defend them, the Nar Silver started staking the people next to the rivers and diverting the flow to drown them. I was asked to assist the Islanders in their fight.'

'What did you do?'

'I learned the shellback technique from the Islanders. I combined it with the use of archers, slingshots and cavalry and we successfully lured the tribes into open battle.'

'How many died?'

'I did not count.'

'Is the Silver Island at peace again?' asked one of the other Guards.

'For now. That was six springs gone.'

'You have travelled far,' said Micel. It was almost the first sentence he had said since they had left Scara.

'Very far, sir,' said Daryo. 'Jaboen to Gourmin, Gourmin to Yashoun and the Silver Island then Hajma and back through Jaboen, Gourmin and Armynya to Boskinia and now on towards Ishter. Much of it on foot, hence I am known as the Walker.'

'A lord of Boskinia with a horse now, my Lord,' said the Guard captain.

'A long way from a ward of the School of the Temple in Salifa,' said Daryo. 'That is what I was once. An apprentice to the smith and a ward of the School.'

'The Fourth God Dule must guide you, my Lord.'

'I was a ward of his temple.'

'He has brought you from there to wealth and security.'

'If not safety.'

The captain snorted. 'The Fourth Goddess is always whispering in the ears of the others.'

'Fortunately for me, they often ignore her,' said Daryo, laughing.

'Quite so,' said one of the other Guards. 'If I were a god, I would listen only to my own counsel.'

The captain laughed. 'If you were a god, Raiyo, the rivers would run with beer, the apple trees would blossom with whores and there would be good roast venison under every rock!'

The Guards and Daryo roared with laughter. The embarrassed Guard buried his face in his knees. Daryo stood up to stretch his legs and back and slapped the young man on the shoulder companionably as he walked away from the fire. The sun was down behind the Vidmarian mountains. Silhouetted against the pink sky was the spiked point of Mach, the tallest of mountains, sited between Vidmaria and Hajmachia, visible even from such a distance. Below the position at the mouth of the pass, the entirety of Boskinia was laid out- the lakes silver islands in a darkening sea, a dull glow to the north-east of the pass was Psephana, a bright point of light almost due north may have been Scara. A flight of birds swooped overhead flying down the pass into Boskinia.

Camali and her companions returned with a wild pig that was quickly butchered and put over the fire. Micel sang some traditional Boskinian songs of safety, good food and home. With much apology to Eraphi and Camali, the Guard captain and another sang some barrack-room songs of war, women, beer and debauchery. Daryo had learned several songs in the Silver Island and taught some simple repetitive verses of a marching song.

Lots were then drawn by the Oaken Guards for the night watches with Daryo insisting on taking the first as the others retired to sleep.

Daryo was awake at first light, a sudden wake as if at a sharp noise. He slid out from his blankets carefully so as not to wake the pages, Micel and Butriguno with whom he was sharing the tent. He picked up his sword belt and woollen cloak as he went. The fire was still glowing, kept alive by the watchmen overnight. He took a few branches from the damp woodpile and added them to the fire. The Oaken Guard on last watch was sat on a rock by the entrance to the pass. The fire was between him and the tents, the horses were tethered about a hundred yards away alongside the little river. One whinnied when it saw Daryo. The guardsman looked up and inclined his head to Daryo. Daryo used his finger to take in the area and around them and opened his hands as if requesting something. The guard shook his head: nothing. Daryo frowned. He pointed to the tent with the rest of the Guard in and pointed upwards, then put his fingers to his lips to request quiet. The guardsman hurried across to the tent to wake his comrades. Daryo drew Temma's Sword and strode a few yards up the pass, studying the walls of the pass, before returning to the fire. Singly, the guardsmen were emerging from the tents. Daryo got Serri, the captain's, eye and pointed to the other two tents, repeating his sign to wake the sleepers but silently. Serri nodded and hurried across to the smallest tent where Camali and Eraphi slept. The last watchman went to the tent that Daryo had slept in with Micel and Butriguno. Daryo went to the river and patted a few of the horses. He moved upstream from the tethered animals and scooped a handful of water, drinking and then splashing another handful over his face.

The attack came from the direction that Daryo had not expected, along the line of the mountains to the west and east. Butriguno and Micel were still struggling out of the tent. A dozen screaming figures charged towards the little camp.

'To arms! To arms!' shouted Daryo. 'Everyone around the fire! Around the fire!'

The Oaken Guards were scrambling into positions, most had no time to find anything more than what was to hand. The first attacker was struck down by Serri with a spare tent pole. The man was clad in skins, patterns of red and white on his bare arms and face and a rough metal axe went flying. Serri seized it. Daryo found himself alone on the east side of the camp but Temma's Sword was already bare and the first three attackers fell to it. Eraphi screamed as Camali half-pushed half-threw her towards the fire. The last watchman seized Butriguno and gave him a similarly enthusiastic shove, Micel scurried across as a short arrow whistled past him. The pages both had short swords in their hands and stood over Eraphi. The Oaken Guard had formed a defensive half-circle by the tents. Camali ran past Daryo, her Vidmarian sword swinging and she took out the next attacker. Daryo and Camali fought back to back as the tide of attackers broke around them. Daryo kicked one in the chest and ducked as Camali's blade swung across above his head to take off the attacker's head. Daryo stood straight, parried a slash at Camali three times and then countered with a double-handed stab. The next attacker was stopped by Camali, she used her blade skilfully to disarm her opponent and both of them stabbed him through the chest. They backed away towards the fire as the attackers regrouped.

Daryo, Camali and the Oaken Guard formed a circle around the fire, facing outwards. For some reason known only to his own mind, Butriguno was clutching a sword like child's comforter. Daryo relieved him of it quickly and held it point down in his left hand to defend himself with. But the attackers were fleeing back into the broken ground at the base of the mountains. Daryo lowered his weapons.

'Is anyone hurt?'

There was a short chorus of negatives although one of the Oaken Guards had a nasty slash across his forearm. Camali bound it while the rest of the Guards struck camp. Daryo extinguished the fire and saw to the horses. Fortunately none of the mounts had been attacked. Shortly the tents were packed, all evidence of the camp erased as much as possible and everyone mounted. Butriguno had been useless in the packing of camp and was still constantly complaining despite a firm word from Serri. When Camali and Eraphi led the column off, Butriguno ended up last in line with Daryo alongside.

The pass was rocky and uneven. The floor dipped and rose and was scattered with fallen rocks. The horses had to move slowly, picking a path through the stony debris, Camali was the most confident rider and on her own steed so she led the procession, finding the best path for the others. In some places they had to dismount and lead the horses on. Traversing the pass took the entire day and camp was made within striking distance of the far end. Two took each watch and Daryo drew the last with Serri. As soon as there was light to see by, they woke the others, struck camp and got underway before the sun was fully up. The pass began to slope downwards steeply and the rocks underfoot became more regular, eventually revealed as an ancient road. The old road emerged from the pass, turned sharply west and back south again and the Mountain Keep was revealed.

Many centuries before, the only city of Ishter had been constructed inside the massive mountain walls behind the lake. A natural tunnel through the rock, once perhaps a waterway had been transformed into the entrance to the citadel. The rockface above had been carved over generations into scenes of beasts, monsters and heroes. To either side, the rock wall, three hundred feet high or more, stretched to rejoin the mountains. Before the walls were two deep, still mountain lakes like blue gems in a grey sea. The causeway between them led to the tunnel to the city. From the very top of the walls, a somewhat superfluous parapet had been made and from there flew immense black banners crossed by an ice-white spear. At Sal's insistence they stopped for Daryo and Camali to don their lords' cloaks, Serri attached a Boskinian banner to his spear and then the Boskinian group turned off of the old road and onto the narrow causeway. Flanking the outer gate were two sentries bearing shields as long as the Boskinian ones but half the width, painted black with the white spear of ice upright on them, and bearing pike-like weapons with a spear point and then four half-moon blades below, points up. Both were dressed in thick bearskin jackets over their mail and fur-trimmed domed helmets. The pair of pikes was crossed in front of them. Another man stepped out of the tunnel, bearing only a sheathed sword and no helmet.

'This is the Gate of the Mountain!' he pronounced. 'Who passes?'

Daryo raised his hand. 'I, Daryo the Walker, Lord of Scara of Boskinia. I come as ambassador of the new King of Boskinia, Gorero, to the Senate of Ishter.'

The sergeant regarded Daryo for several heartbeats, taking in his cloak, Camali's cloak, the Oaken Guard and the banner. 'You will wait here.' He turned and headed into the tunnel.

Daryo looked at Eraphi. 'Is this normal?'

Eraphi rocked her head from side to side. 'It can be. These guards and the sergeant are Senate Yeomen. The long shields are Yeomen, militia have round shields.'

The sergeant returned. 'Horses may not be ridden in the city. Leave your mounts and they shall be cared for.' Daryo nodded and was the first to dismount. 'I shall take you to the Senate.'

'Sal, Herro, Butriguno, stay with the horses,' Daryo instructed.

The pikes were uncrossed and a couple more guards emerged to take the horses. The sergeant led the way into the tunnel, lit by burning fat lamps in recesses in the walls. The tunnel was nearly fifty yards long and barely eight feet high. Daryo was glad that he could see the light of day at the far end. Camali tapped his arm, pointed at the rock and held her arm out with the fist clenched. *The wall is strong.*

Daryo held both arms out, fists clenched. *Very strong.*

She pointed upwards and made a hopping motion with her hand. *Very high.*

Daryo crossed his arms in front of his chest and then mimed firing a bow downwards and clutched his throat. *A good defence, archers on the top, deadly to the attackers.*

Camali nodded her agreement.

They emerged from the tunnel inside the walls. The buildings were squat and built of the grey-black stone but their stone roof tiles were painted in bright colours, like a field of rainbow-hued mushrooms. Instead of market stalls, goods were being sold from metal-framed carts, mostly meat, butter and cheese. A Guard was intrigued by some orange-white mushrooms but Daryo ushered him onwards. The streets were wide and straight and seemed to have been built to a plan- ten houses between streets. Many people stared openly at the small procession. Eraphi explained that few Boskinians and even fewer Batribi ever walked the streets of Ishter. They passed a domed chapel of the Good Shepherd and behind it was a square building taller than all the others around it with a round section on the top.

'The Senate,' Eraphi announced.

Two of the Ishter militiamen were at the doors, bearskins over white tunics and black leggings, no helmets, small round bucklers on their backs and spears with white-painted shafts in their hands. They raised their spears in salute to the sergeant of the Yeomen and opened the doors. Inside the atrium were another two militiamen.

'Here your guards must wait and your weapons must be left,' said the sergeant.

Daryo exchanged looks with Camali. She mimed a close distance, shook her mail shirt with her hand and pointed to the sergeant then all around them. *Our men are close, we are armoured, we are in their Senate.*

Daryo nodded and undid his sword belt. Once disarmed, Micel, Daryo and Camali were led through the doors, up several levels of stairs into another atrium furnished with benches and with tapestries between wide windows. A Yeoman guarded the next door and a black-robed clerk spoke with the sergeant and slipped through the doors. The sergeant left and the remaining Yeoman suggested that the Boskinian deputation be seated.

Daryo and Micel both did so, Camali went to the window to look out over the city. *Beautiful view*, she mimed to Daryo.

Daryo checked that nobody was watching, pointed at Camali and touched his chest over his heart. *Beautiful Camali.*

She grinned and turned back to the window. Daryo glanced at Micel, who looked exceptionally calm and assured. The doors opened and two Ishteri men with the mien of merchants emerged. They nodded courteously to the waiting trio as they passed. The doors closed again. Camali watched the two men go and got Daryo's attention. She flapped her fingers against her palm in a Boskinian gesture meaning money or gold then a rolling motion followed by drawing her imagined sword. *Money before war.*

Daryo shrugged, pointed after the Ishteri then slowly at himself and Micel. He pointed after the Ishteri again, at the Yeoman, then at Micel and then Camali. *They came before us. They are Ishteri, you are Boskinian.*

Camali mimed her sword again and made a confused face. *Is war not more important?*

Daryo pointed at her nodded, then after the Ishteri and shrugged his shoulders. He crossed his arms and held his fists out. *To you, it is. To them, perhaps not. Their defence is very strong.*

The doors opened again and a black-robed clerk emerged. 'My Lords, our sincere apologies for having kept you waiting. Please enter.'

The Yeoman held the door open as they followed the clerk through, along a short hallway and then up a staircase, emerging in the centre of a half-circle of tiered stone levels. At the top of the eight steps was a full circle of glass windows. The stone levels were being used as benches by twenty black-robed men and women. At the centre of the half-circle of benches was a stone chair but it was empty and had a spiked metal bar across the seat. Daryo counted eleven women and nine men. One of the men stood. 'Ambassadors of Boskinia. You are welcome to the Senate of Ishter. Please speak.' He sat down again and Micel spoke.

He started with the news that the King of Boskinia Olyaro the Third had died and that his son had been proclaimed and installed as King Gorero the Ninth. He then went back to describe the initial attacks on Gourmin by the Vidmarians, the Gourmini resistance and the Vidmarian change of angle to attack Boskinia. He illuminated the devastation wrecked on western Vidmaria and the coming of Daryo the Walker. He told the Senate of the defence of the bridge at Outros and the repelling of the Vidmarian assault there, and later by the Gourmini at Tiverta. He then explained that the army was seen heading south towards Adaca, assuming that the Vidmarian army was either going to attack Adaca next or to march through Adaca and Ishter to attack Boskinia from the south. Micel then requested permission for the Boskinian army to be permitted to pass through Ishter if necessary to go to Adaca's aid and as counter strike against the Vidmarian army. The Ishteri senators listened in silence, voted immediately and gave their blessing.

## Chapter 67

The inn was called the Hole in the Mountain. It was a hundred yards from the cluster of houses that formed the village of Bruszo, which was another hundred yards from the smelter and other necessaries outside the entrance of the iron mine. Only half of the party staying at the small inn had completely filled its guest rooms so the rest had needed to pitch a tent outside. Even though the inn was in a quiet part of a peaceful country, a member of the Boskinian Oaken Guard stood sentry outside the tent. Daryo the Walker emerged from the inn and headed straight to the stables behind the inn, followed quickly by his page. A few moments later, an armour-clad woman and another page followed. An older man and a particularly fat young man followed later. By this time, the six members of the Oaken Guard had collapsed and packed their tent away and started loading it onto the pack horse. Daryo went back inside to pay the innkeeper for their one-night stay, then re-joined his travelling companions and they departed.

The road was built up from the surrounding ground, paved with stone and easily wide enough for four horses to ride abreast. Trees spread in a sparse evergreen forest to both sides. The sun was high and warm, the sky clear of cloud, the horses were happy and the group made good progress south-westwards. Micel, the emissary, had bought a map in Ishter that suggested that the next settlement would be a town named Olanyi, reached after a day's ride. They passed several small farms and a wayside temple to the Good Shepherd. Just before noon was a bridge over a small river, little more than a stream, with a short, wood-built tower with three-striped pennant, blue-red-blue flying from the parapet. From the side of the tower, a gate extended across the bridge. A man in mail with a blue cape strode out of the tower, drawing his sword.

'Who goes there?' he demanded.

Daryo glanced up and saw a cluster of archers come to the parapet. 'I am Daryo the Walker, Lord of Scara, on a mission to Adaca from the King of Boskinia.'

The gatekeeper looked at Daryo and Camali's cloaks, the Oaken Guards' uniforms and the pennant carried by the Guard captain. 'Where are you going to?'

Micel brought his horse alongside Daryo's. 'The capital, Darsux.'

The gatekeeper studied them a while longer. 'I will have to send word ahead. Ride on to Olanyi. Report to the captain of the guard in Olanyi. Do not ride out of Olanyi without his permission.'

Daryo frowned but nodded. 'As you say.'

The guard opened the gate on the bridge and waved them through. As the last of the party crossed the bridge, a raven took off from the tower and headed west. The road emerged from the forest and out into the heathland. After a short ride, the road dipped into a hollow and Daryo called a halt to give the horses a rest. After a quick meal, they remounted and continued south-west.

Olanyi was a sprawling market town surrounded by a fence of ten-foot wooden stakes but with farms, houses and even a temple outside the wall. Another short guard tower was built at the limit of the town, somewhat akin to a boundary marker. A soldier, in blue cape and mail, was stood with a group of comrades checking people entering and leaving the town. He approached the Boskinian party and raised his hand.
'Who are you?'
'Daryo the Walker, Lord of Scala, ambassador from the Boskinians. We are going to Darsux. They have been told to expect us but we were also told to come first to Olanyi and to report to the captain of the guard.'
The soldier nodded. 'Proceed, sir. The captain will be at the barracks on the far side of the town. Ride through town and out the other side. The barracks are next to the road.'
'Our thanks.'
The guard stepped back and waved the party through. Daryo led the way through at a slow pace, the town was busy; the streets busy with traders, children playing games, some on horseback, carts laden with goods, a group of priests were given a respectful berth by all, a thatcher was repairing one of the many thatched roofs in the town. They passed a few much larger half-timber buildings and a stone-built chapel of the Good Shepherd, a market square and a large tavern. The west gate had no litter of buildings outside but a few hundred yards from the gate was a lower fence than the town's and guard towers at each corner, surrounded by a ditch. At the open entrance, a single man was on duty.
'I am an ambassador of Boskinia,' said Daryo. 'We have been told to report to the captain of the guard.'
The sentry bowed slightly. 'He is expecting you, sir. Please come within.' He rang a hand bell and a small group of soldiers emerged to help take the horses and the baggage. The camp had a small stables near the gate and a forge opposite. Further in was a line of five long buildings with thatched roofs, all identical, with several smaller buildings beyond them. One soldier with a white stripe across his cloak escorted Daryo, Camali and Micel to the captain's building, a much smaller square construction beyond the five buildings.

The captain was small but very strongly built, his skin dark, clean-shaven unlike many of his men, with short-shorn black hair. He had no armour on but a crested bronze helmet was resting on a table alongside a broad, short sword. He smiled warmly.

'My Lady, My Lord, Master Ambassador, sir. Welcome to Olanyi and to Adaca if you have not been welcomed before. I am Kirimi, captain of the guard and commander of the province.'

Daryo nodded. 'Thank you, Captain Kirimi. I am Daryo the Walker, Lord of Scara; Camali, Lord of Cilano; Micel, Ambassador of King Gorero.'

'You are all most welcome. A representative of the king is on his way to meet you. I am told that you are here regarding the Vidmarian army bearing down on us. Frankly, I am glad that you are here. Three hundred of my five hundred men have been removed to Darsux. You bring troops behind you?'

Daryo smiled. 'Perhaps, Captain, perhaps. We must speak with the king firs'The king is unlikely to help. He is very aged, as King Olyaro of Boskinia was. His son rules as regent. The Regent is aware that you are here and who you are, the tower at the Usi sent a raven ahead, his representative left Darsux as soon as they could be sent. The Regent asks that you wait here until the rider arrives. One of the barracks is empty and at your disposal. I have ordered that a cook to be at your pleasure day and night and the building will have fresh water, candles, anything you require.'

'Our grateful thanks.'

Kirimi escorted them to the central building of the five long barracks. It was a basic dormitory that was easily large enough for a hundred. Two Adacan soldiers were erecting a hazelwood screen at one end to create makeshift quarters for the women.

'It is very simple but I hope it will serve,' said Kirimi. 'If you require anything, please talk to one of my men.'

'Is there a temple of the Pantheon that is accessible?' asked Daryo.

Kirimi frowned. 'I am sorry, sir, there is no temple to the Pantheon in Olyani.'

Daryo nodded. 'My thanks.'

'If you require anything, please talk to one of my men.'

A meal of hot chicken, fresh bread, butter and fruit was provided and Daryo then took the opportunity to sleep. It was dark when he awoke and went for a walk around the inside of the camp wall. The duty sentry, stood next to a burning brazier, gave Daryo a formal nod. On his second circuit, Daryo was joined by Camali.

She used their common language of gestures and mimes. *Everyone asleep.*

Daryo nodded. *A long ride. Sleep is best.*

*You slept already.*
*I can sleep anywhere.*
Camali took his arm and rested her cheek on his shoulder as they walked. Daryo reached across with his other hand and stroked her hair briefly. She kissed his cheek, released his arm and went back to their sleeping quarters. Daryo followed after another circuit around the walls and went back to sleep.
The next morning, Daryo asked if he could visit the Good Shepherd's chapel in the town and Kirimi provided an unarmed soldier as a guide. The chapel was of white stone, round with a domed roof and a small square entrance. The guide opened the door for Daryo and said that he would wait. Daryo opened the smaller inner door and entered the chapel proper. Inside, the walls were painted with pastoral scenes and the cushions for the congregation positioned in circles around the central altar with a small wooden shepherd's crook in the centre. An elderly woman was knelt alone on the far side of the altar. Daryo looked around for a moment before sitting on the closest cushion, feeling rather out of place.
'Your first visit, my son?' asked a friendly voice. A man in a loose black shirt with a white belt around the middle sat down. He looked to be a little older than Daryo, his pale hair loose around his shoulders.
'It is.'
'I was not aware that there were any Batribi in the town.'
'I am just a traveller passing through. My name is Daryo.'
'And your kin?'
Daryo had not expected the priest to know about Batribi naming customs. 'Daryo, kin of Dostan.'
'I am Father Huro Sani. I believe you are not a follower of the Shepherd.'
'No. I am a believer in the Pantheon but I was told by a Jaboen priest once that faith is faith.'
'I believe so too. What brings you into the chapel?'
'I needed a quiet place to think. And perhaps ask some questions. A temple of the Goddess Spinel would have been ideal but there is no temple in Olyani.'
'I will answer your questions if you wish to ask, my son.'
Daryo considered this for a moment. 'I know little of your faith.'
'That is of no importance.'
'I have a large, important task. One that will affect the lives of countless people. But I have a personal... issue that I worry will distract me from the task.'

The priest nodded slowly. 'I see. Tasks given by others are important, especially if they affect others but concentrating on a task is difficult when a personal consideration is there. A debt? A family member?'

'A woman.'

'I see. A friend?'

'Yes. She is very special to me. I have not known her long but we have spent much time together. We have even fought in battle together. But she was done a great wrong and her body grievously hurt many years ago.'

'But you wish to make your feelings plain?'

'I think that I have but I fear that she will not welcome me. I do not wish to harm her further.'

The priest looked thoughtful. 'I understand. Tell me, my son, who created the world.' This surprised Daryo. 'The Pantheon.' He noticed the priest's smile. 'You disagree.' 'Please continue. Why?'

'The Gods decided that their knowledge and wisdom could be taught so they created the world and all the people within it to teach their wisdom to. At first the people lived forever but the Fourth Goddess thus had no followers, she argued with the others and made people mortal so that she would have disciples after they died.'

'I believe that your Pantheon are just facets of the Good Shepherd,' the priest told him. 'I believe that the Good Shepherd created the world and came to the world as a lamb. He was treated well by some people, cast out by others, fed by some, slaughtered by others. The lesson that he teaches is that we must do what is right by the most innocent, as your Goddess Spinel does. What is right by your friend? Is it right that you withhold your feelings and your love for her? Or that you tell her and let her decide how she feels towards you?'

Daryo did not answer but smiled. 'My thanks. Your words have been a great help.' The priest smiled back. 'Would you consent to pray with me, my son?'

'I would.'

The priest moved to kneel on the cushion and Daryo did the same on his. 'Good Shepherd, please guide Daryo kin of Dostan. Guide his words and his heart and show him the true path.' He made the sign of the crook across his chest and nodded to Daryo.

'My thanks, sir.'

'And to you, Daryo kin of Dostan. Peace go with you.'

Daryo knew at least the response given. 'And stay with you.'

The guide that Captain Kirimi had provided was still stood outside. When Daryo asked to walk around the market, he was quite agreeable to showing Daryo the town before they returned to the barracks. The Oaken Guard were training with wooden weapons and their shields. They had practised the shellback technique that Daryo had taught as much as they could with just six men and Camali and were now doing sword drills. Daryo found a wooden blade thrust at him by Camali and seized a shield to defend himself. Camali's onslaught was vicious and Daryo was hard-pressed to ward her off. Eventually he saw an opening, grabbed the edges of his shield with both hands and pushed hard, shoving Camali's wooden weapon away and swept his leg out to knock her off her feet. He leaped forwards, seized her wrists and pinned her down, blade against the side of her neck.

'Yield.'

She nodded and Daryo eased his grip but did not get up immediately. Camali blushed slightly and squirmed. Daryo recovered his thoughts, got up and helped Camali stand.

'My apologies, Camali.'

She smiled and waved her hand in front of her face. *I do not mind.*

Daryo pointed at her, made his hand into a claw, pointed again and held his hand over his heart. *Fearsome Camali. Beautiful Camali.*

Camali smiled, blushed again and waved her hand in front of her face before hurrying back inside the barrack building.

The blown horn just after dark caused a huge commotion in the compound. The entire company raced to the gate, forming a guard of honour with weapons presented. Daryo emerged from the barracks as a pair of mounted soldiers rode through the guard of honour, followed by a cloaked rider and another two soldiers. They rode straight to the captain's home, dismounted and went inside as the guard dispersed. Daryo saw Camali watching. She shrugged and went back to sharpening her dagger. He had not been back inside for long before an Adacan soldier asked Daryo and Micel to the captain's building. They collected Camali on the way and were shown into the captain's room. Just as they entered, the cloaked rider lowered their cowl, revealing a very beautiful round, pale face, crystalline blue eyes, very full lips, a slightly curved nose and a veritable mane of pale yellow hair topped by a silver circlet. She looked to be of an age with Daryo.

'Lord Daryo, Lady Camali, Master Micel, I am honoured to introduce Princess Tari, second child of the king, representative of the Regent, commander of the Adacan armies.'

The princess smiled charmingly. 'It is my honour. To meet the heroes of the battle at Outros is truly humbling. I apologise that I am not everyone's image of an army commander.'

Daryo swallowed hard and tried to find appropriate words. Micel instead said: 'The best army commander is the most competent; there is no requirement that they are the largest or strongest.'

'Thank you, sir. I will take that you are Micel, Ambassador from King Gorero?'

'I am, ma'am.' He grasped her extended hand.

'Lady Camali of Cilano, I know you to be a celebrated warrior in your own right. You are most welcome.'

Camali gave a short curtsey and also grasped the princess's hand.

'And Lord Daryo the Walker of Scara. I have heard many stories of the wandering Batribi warrior. I am honoured to make your acquaintance, sir.'

Daryo had to think before he could manage the words: 'And I yours, Princess.'

'We must ride immediately. Through the night. My brother the Regent is going to be in Oia this coming day. We must meet him there. We have little time.'

'Ma'am, we come to ask simply if Adaca will join with Boskinia against the Vidmarians,' said Micel.

The princess smiled. 'I surmised as much but my brother must make that decision. Please, we must go.'

Daryo roused the others as Camali saw to the horses. He assembled his own items and took them to the stables and loaded his horse, leading the animal to the gate where the princess's party was preparing to depart. Daryo realised he was watching the Adacan princess when Camali elbowed him in the ribs, pointed at the princess and held her hand over her heart.

*Beautiful Princess.*

Daryo shook his head quickly. *I did not see. Beautiful Camali.*

Camali raised both eyebrows in disbelief and mounted her horse. Not long later, the eleven Boskinians, one Ishteri, one Batribi and five Adacans were riding west.

There was little time to talk. Despite the darkness, the Adacan soldiers at the front of the procession kept up a good pace. The princess rode with her leading escorts, cowl raised against the chill night, Daryo found himself at the rear chivvying their messenger Butriguno to greater speed. The dumpy man's complaints got more plaintive as the night wore on. He was not a strong rider and was obviously used to warm blankets and soft down-filled pillars. Riding a horse through the deep night in a foreign land was not an

enjoyable activity for him. When the party stopped so that the horses could rest, drink and graze, he refused to remount afterwards.
*Leave him here* was Camali's suggestion.
'I can remain,' said Micel. 'I am not a skilled rider, I am old and I could use the rest.'
Daryo shook his head. 'The Regent will want to speak with the ambassador of the King of Boskinia.'
Micel waved his hand dismissively. 'He will rather speak to the hero of the Battle of Outros, the Lord of Scara. I will stay with Butriguno and we will ride on with the morning.'
Daryo felt sceptical. 'I think it unwise.'
'The only way that our young friend here will move is at the point of a sword and that will not aid anyone's cause,' said Micel. 'I shall stay with him and join you in Oia.'
Daryo acquiesced. 'Two of the Guard will stay with you.'
'And one of my men,' said the princess.
Daryo stood up from the rock he had been sat on. 'Our thanks, princess. That is most generous.'
'Not at all. If the arrangements are made, we should remount. My brother will be waiting.'

The city of Oia was lit up by the dawn, a sprawling lake-side town with a rather crumbling stone wall, a barely serviceable moat and no gates. The princess shook her head as they passed the unwatched gate. The slightly reduced group passed through the gate and rode through the still-asleep town to the stone fort at the side of the lake. Four round turrets that looked rather weathered were joined by ten-foot walls. Where Daryo would have expected a lord's banner hung from the parapets, there was a burned piece of cloth.
'The old duke spent his money on food and women,' said the princess as they approached the gates. 'He let his home crumble around him, the town fall into disrepair and the people work themselves to death. When my brother became Regent he had the duke removed and has come to rebuild the town.'
The gates were closed and a line of four guards with two-handed swords on their backs, round shields painted blue with a golden sun and a white bull in the centre and long spears. The princess rode her horse to the front and commanded the gates opened and the guards complied. The compound of the fort was full of tents. In the very centre there was a burned skeleton of a house.

'The duke disliked my brother's intervention. He burned the house with himself inside it,' she told Daryo.

The party dismounted and several grooms hurried forwards to take the horses. The princess was met by a robed official and she asked Daryo and Camali to accompany her. The Regent's tent was large and of white canvas. Inside a man of about forty summers was sat on a folding stool at a makeshift table reading a document. The princess knelt elegantly, Daryo and Camali bowed respectfully.

The Regent smiled. He was undoubtedly the princess's brother- the same colour hair and shape to his eyes, even the same shape of his brows. 'Sister, sister, stand.'

The princess stood up and smiled at her elder brother. 'My brother, may I present the ambassadors of Boskinia, Lord Daryo the Walker of Scara, and the Lady Camali of Cilano. Lady Camali, Lord Daryo, I am honoured to introduce you to the Regent of Adaca, my brother, Prince Lallano.'

Daryo and Camali both bowed again.

'You are most welcome,' said the Regent, his tone firm but frank. 'I wish we met under better circumstances.' A servant appeared with a bundle that revealed to be a trio of the same stools on which the prince sat. 'Please be seated.' Daryo and Camali sat across the table from the prince. The princess took hers around to sit alongside her brother. The Regent then continued: 'I believe I know why you have come but I would hear it from you.'

Daryo nodded. 'Of course, my Lord. The Vidmarian army that has recently been in Gourmin and in western Boskinia is moving. The Gourmini repelled the invader at Tiverta, the Boskinians at Outros. There is still a small force against the bridge at Outros but too few. Boskinian scouts have seen the Vidmarian army moving south. They are following the river to the pass into Adaca. A monstrous Vidmarian army is about to invade your lands, my Lord.'

'Why should they do that? The nation of Adaca has no quarrel with Vidmaria. We have only a small border with them that passes through inaccessible mountains.'

'You may have no quarrel, my Lord, but the army is coming this way. If they do not intend to invade Adaca and conquer your lands they will march through Adaca, into Ishter and into southern Boskinia. If they march through Adaca, they will surely go as they did so in Gourmin and Boskinia- burning, plundering, raping and thieving.'

'So why does King Gorero send two of his army commanders to me?'

'To offer you aid, my Lord. The Boskinian army marches even now for Ishter. The Ishteri have consented to aid Boskinia against the Vidmarians.'

'And if I refuse?'

'Then the Boskinian army will stop on the border of Ishter, my Lord. And watch the Vidmarians destroy your nation before they reach the Boskinian one.'
The Regent frowned. 'They will not invade and share the spoils.'
'No, my Lord. King Gorero has enough of his own nation subjugated; he has no men or mettle to threaten another.'
'And why are you here, Lord Daryo? You are not Boskinian.'
'No, my Lord. I am Batribi, I was a member of the Order of Shield and Sword that was destroyed by a former member that worked with the Vidmarians. Since then I have travelled the land fulfilling the oath that I made to defend the defenceless and to aid those in need. The Boskinian nation needed my aid and I swore myself to do so.'
'And Lady Camali? You are Boskinian, what say you?'
'My Lord, Camali is unable to talk.'
'Unable?'
'An... accident, my Lord. However, Camali, speak your mind.'
Camali used her gestures and mimes to put her point and Daryo gave words to her movements: 'Many have died. Many will die. If you help us, we can stop this. We can take our land back, you will have peace, we will have peace.'
'A very clever way to communicate,' said the princess in soft admiration.
The Regent nodded. 'Very. Thank you, Lady Camali. Lord Daryo, as I am sure you know, I was warned as to who you are and why you come. May I see your shield?'
'My shield?'
'Yes.'
Daryo had to go back to his horse to retrieve his shield. The Regent stood and took the shield from Daryo as he re-entered the tent.
'Can you explain this to me?' The Regent's tone had hardened.
Daryo glanced at Camali. 'It is the shield that I was given by an old friend, based on my sign as a member of the Order. The Harlequin was my tutor, the blind girl was the badge of a member who gave her life to save me and a number of children, they are walking as I do past a milepost, which has my arms as Lord of Scala.'
'Did you know a Member of the Order known as Hettimiro the Furious?'
Daryo thought for a long moment. 'I do not believe I knew him but the name is familiar, my Lord.'
'Hettimiro the Furious was killed by a party of Vidmarian soldiers acting on the orders of a man named Sevant.'
'Sevant the Stone.'

'Hettimiro was my uncle. I know the pledge that the Order took and the work they tried to do.' The Regent handed the shield back to Daryo and his sister stood up alongside him. 'Adaca is proud to stand alongside Boskinia and Ishter. The Sun shall shine on the Ice Spear and the Oak.'

Butriguno, Micel and escort arrived later in the day. Camali had already arranged a message for the carrier pigeons to the army and Hamlakia. The pigeons struggled a little as Butriguno attached the messages but took off without issue and flew north.

## Chapter 68

The next morning the princess asked to see Daryo in the regent's tent. She had a long parchment list in front of her.
'My Lord Daryo, how many men does King Gorero plan to send?'
'Twenty thousand, my Lady. Of those there will be a thousand of the Oaken Guard, the finest warriors in Boskinia.'
'And the Ishteri?'
'But three hundred. They're a small nation.'
'I understand. Do you have letters, my Lord?'
'I do.'
The princess handed the list to Daryo. 'This is a list of the armies of Adaca.'

> *The Army of Darsux- 7800*
> *The Army of Baros- 4000*
> *The Army of the Mountain- 2000*
> *The Army of the South- 4400*
> *The Army of the Cali Bay- 3100*
> *The Army of Tanaab- 3800*
> *The Army of the East River- 9600*

'That gives just more than thirty thousand,' said Daryo. 'Thirty-four thousands and seven hundreds.'
'Some cannot be used,' said the princess. 'The Army of the East River and of Tanaab must remain to defend the eastern border. The Regent must withdraw the king to safety. To Cali Bay. The Army of Cali Bay must remain.'
'Eighteen thousands can march to us.'
'They do so. We may have forty thousand men if we are fortunate.'
'Very fortunate, my Lord. We would need to be very fortunate.'
'Does the Adacan nation have a force of the most highly-trained soldiers?'
'It does. The army of Darsux has the White Bulls.'
'I must work with them, if that is possible. I have travelled far- the Silver Island, Yashoun, Hajmachia, Jaboen. I could teach them some new methods of fighting. Better.'
The princess nodded. 'Of course. The Adacan soldier is used to fighting from horses, not on foot. You could teach us much.'
'Horses?'

'Horses. And archers. There are no finer archers than Adacan women in any land.'
Daryo thought and nodded. 'That could be used. The Ishteri are also trained to fight with bows from horseback. The Boskinians fight on foot. That is their strength.'
'We could put the best of Adaca, Ishter and Boskinia to use. I spoke to my brother; he cannot decide who should command the army. Will you command the Boskinian army?'
'I will. Camali will lead the Oaken Guard.'
'I will lead the Adacan army and my cousin is captain of the White Bulls. The Ishteri will send their force under Captain Umanides. He is an old friend.'
'Where will we fight from?'
'Our border guard is at Dottia. They have no reports of the Vidmarians yet.'
'They may not for another week. The Boskinian army is marching south already. The Ishteri should be at Olanyi by tomorrow.'
'We cannot hold Darsux.'
'Truly?'
'Darsux is not a fortress; it has no fort, no moat, no wall. The court, my brother and the king are withdrawing to Cali Bay on the seashore. The people will go south. Aden is a stronghold. We must confront the Vidmarians at a position of strength.'
'I agree, my Lady.'
'My Lord, if we must be so formal, this war may be over. My name is Tari.'
'As you wish. Tari. We are confronting a large army; we must try to narrow their advantage.'
Tari thought. 'I can think of nowhere. Dottia would be the only place but we would never have sufficient numbers there soon enough.'
'Further back. Let Darsux fall.'
'Darsux falls... Sibiri.'
'Sibiri?'
'Sibiri is an ancient fortification on a crest, about twenty miles from Darsux. We could hold that place between the rivers.'
'You are an experienced commander. I believe you. I will have our messenger send that to the Boskinian army.'
'We should move to Sibiri. I will have the Adacan forces meet us there.'
'And Boskinia and Ishter will come.'
Tari gave him a striking smile. 'We come together as an excellent pair, Daryo.'
'My apologies, Tari. I must go and have the message sent immediately.'
'Of course.'

Daryo left the prince's tent and hurried away to find Butriguno and his pigeons but almost collided with Camali after a few yards.

*You are running*, she said with her gestures.

*Important work*, Daryo replied. *War is near.*

*She is near. Beautiful.*

*A comrade.*

*A beautiful comrade.*

*I do not want her.*

*So sure. Beautiful princess. Beautiful.*

*I do not want her. I do not want her.*

*What do you want?*

'I want you, Camali!' *Beautiful Camali. Beautiful Camali.*

Camali blushed red. *Me?*

*Beautiful Camali.*

Daryo took her arm and led her back to the small domed tent that the Regent had assigned him. He closed the flap behind them. 'I must use voice, my Camali, I cannot put my hands to the right words so I must use my voice. I have never seen a woman as I have seen you. A fighter, a warrior but... beautiful, the beautiful Lady of Cilano as well as the fearsome Commander of the Oaken Guard. I need my Camali as the grass needs the sun.'

Camali exhaled slowly, pointed at Daryo and held her hand over her heart. *Beautiful Daryo.*

'I know that it is possible in these coming days that we both may die. If we do not, I would live at your side.' *Beautiful Camali.*

Camali nodded and they kissed.

That evening the Regent had a feast; Tari said that it was a tradition in Adaca, known as the Fortifying Banquet for those going into battle. Tables were laid through the fort and out of the gate. The people of the town were invited to come to the table and bring food to share, the Regent's cooks produced dishes and the Regent sat among his subjects. Daryo and Camali found spaces just by the gate of the fort to sit and eat. A rather sallow, pinched-faced woman offered them vegetable pie. An elderly man opposite had the signs of a veteran of wars, just one eye and a badly scarred face and neck, and he offered baked fish. Camali had gone hunting that afternoon and had stalked and shot a deer. With Micel and Eraphi's aid she had roasted it over an open fire outside the fort and then carved it with a borrowed battle-axe. She proffered the roast hunks of meat on the back of a shield. Ale and wine were being liberally shared but Daryo left it alone, drinking from a jug of sheep's milk along with the young boy alongside him.

'Why are you a colour?' the boy asked. His mother smacked his hand.

Daryo smiled. 'The boy means no offence. I am so because I was made so.'

'By the Shepherd?'

'Perhaps. There are white and black sheep, red and brown deer; it is the way all things are made. There is a whole town of coloured people as I am in Jaboen and many more travel through Jaboen, Yashoun and Gourmin.'

'Like birds.'

'Like birds.' Daryo passed the jug of milk back to the boy.

'You are a Batribi, my Lord?' asked the elderly soldier.

'I am.'

'Do you know of your people's new nation?'

'I have visited the lake, my kin are there.'

'The Lord of Lalbi has given the lake to the Batribi people in perpetuity.'

'Truly? Where did you hear of this?'

'A Jaboen going to Cali to join the ships, my Lord.'

'My thanks,' said Daryo. 'You were a soldier?'

'I was, my Lord. I fought in the east against the Armynya Tribes.'

'You must have fought valiantly.'

'I fought to live. I fought for my king and my comrades against the savages.'

'And that is valiant.' Daryo raised his cup. 'And I salute you.'

'And I you, my Lord.' The old man raised his wine bowl.

'And I!' The young boy raised his cup.

The boy's mother, the old soldier and Daryo laughed. Camali ruffled the boy's hair. A young woman in the livery of the princess, blue with a yellow prancing horse across her chest, came along the table. She reached Camali first, said something softly into Camali's ear and moved on.

Camali tugged Daryo's sleeve to get his attention and used her gesture language. *Leave at dawn.*

Daryo nodded. *Sleep later.*

Camali smiled and handed a platter of cheese to him. *Later.*

'My Lady! I am sorry to wake you but I had to come and OH!'

The serving girl stopped still, barely inside the flap of Camali's tent. Camali was still in the cot but Daryo had been up for a short time and had just pulled on his breeches. The girl tried to apologise but stuttered: 'You were missing, my Lord. Your page went to your tent.'

Daryo shook his head sadly. 'Sal must have panicked,' he told Camali and then turned back to the girl. 'Tell Sal that I will be back at my tent shortly.'

'Yes, my Lord. Sorry, my Lord. My Lady.' She fled.

Camali sat up. *My fault.*

*And mine. I was here. I should go.*

*See you soon. Beautiful Daryo.*

*Beautiful Camali. My Camali.*


'Walker! You were not in your tent all night!' Sal came running across the fort compound.

'I was safe, Sal. I am not known for being helpless.'

'No, my Lord. I am sorry, my Lord. Walker, the girl from the princess's household said that you were…'

'That I was?'

'Eating your morning meal with Lady Camali.'

Daryo stifled a laugh. 'And I am sure she would not have deceived you, Sal. Come, we need to be ready to leave. See to the horse.'

'Yes, Walker.' Sal hurried off but stopped after about twenty yards and called: 'Walker!'

'Yes, Sal?'

'I hope that Lady Camali makes you happy.' He scampered off.


The Army of the Mountain had been camped near Oia and followed the princess's personal guard of a score of mounted men, Daryo and the Boskinian party and Princess Tari at the very front, leading the army in person. The road westwards ran along the shore of the lake. Flocks of birds took off at the approach of over two thousand men on foot and two score mounted as well as two score baggage carts. A messenger bird had arrived just before the army moved off announcing the arrival of three hundred and eighty-seven Ishteri Yeomen in Olanyi. A rider was despatched by Tari to guide the Ishteri to the proposed battlefield of Sibiri. Another bird found the column late in the day relaying a message from Ishter to Darsux that the vanguard of the Boskinian army had reached Ishter and would camp in front of the city before moving into Adaca. A full day's march for the column took them only a third of the way to Sibiri. Camp was made by sundown, the Boskinians using their own tents in a small enclave alongside the princess's tent. Daryo thought it prudent to sleep in the shared tent with Butriguno,

Micel and Sal but found he was awake well before dawn. He slipped outside to dress and then began to walk the camp. Despite being in their own country and a good distance from any homes, the Adacan camp was well patrolled. Each soldier was aware of the Batribi lord of Boskinia among them and tapped the hilt of their drawn sword on the back of their shield in salute as he passed.

The next day was another day of a long march. Daryo felt somewhat saddle-sore, handed his horse's reins to Sal and joined those on foot. He was able to stretch his legs and exercise some different parts of his body than he used riding. He slept soundly but still found himself walking the camp before dawn. The marching force was camped within sight of a small lake and Daryo strolled away from the tents, sleeping soldiers and dwindling fires to its shores. Disturbed only by the twittering of birds, Daryo stripped off his shirt, knelt down and washed his face, arms and chest with the fresh cold water. There was just enough light to see by as he dressed again. The sudden pain in the back of his head was exceptional.

# Chapter 69

The tent was grey-green canvas, conical, somewhat like a Batribi *kaff* but smaller with a single central pole in the centre. Daryo moved, sat up and found his hands bound behind his back and tied to a peg that was hammered deep into the ground. His ankles were also bound and attached to another peg. His weapons and shields were gone, his jerkin and arm guards too. The light outside the tent was coming through the canvas, suggesting the middle of the day with the sun high. Daryo found himself looking at his own shadow, suggesting the sun was high and that he was facing north. He tested the strength of his bonds on his limbs and found them good. The back of his skull, where he presumed he had been struck, ached badly.

'Come forth and be known!' he called out. 'I am awake, come forth, coward!'

There were some movements outside the tent and some muffled voices before the tent flap was opened and a man stepped inside. His hair was too white to be called fair, his eyes too pale to be called blue. He looked prematurely old. He wore black robes over a black doublet but he had the appearance of a soldier although he carried no visible weapon.

'I had no idea that the Adacans had trained dogs to fight,' he said slowly. 'And the venerable Order as well. Of course, you were a puppy then, weren't you, dog?'

Daryo took a leap of judgement. 'Sevant the Stone.'

'I have not been the Stone for many years!' snapped he. 'I knew the Order was failing but to start recruiting darks!' He spat on the ground. 'So when my army crushed the Order, you fled far away. Then you have been in Boskinia helping prop up that foolish old dolt of a king. And now here working with the pompous young upstart and his simpering would-be-soldier sister.'

'Let us speak of you then,' said Daryo. 'After marching out of the Order like a child who got sent to bed, you prostitute your blade to the highest bidder.' Sevant spat again. 'You went to Vidmaria and doubtless gave them well-imagined stories of your heroism and why you left the Order.' Sevant kicked Daryo's feet. 'You agreed to be the Vidmarian king's whore as long as he let you take out your petty revenge on your former brothers.' The next kick was into Daryo's stomach. 'You fled before the Batribi and then were thrown out of Tiverta by the Gourmini! You were unable to beat the Boskinians so you march into an innocent country, no doubt murdering the innocent on the way, to try and get more petty vengeance on those that have done you no wrong!' Daryo ended shouting his words as Sevant's boot was driven repeatedly into his stomach. Unable to protect himself, Daryo gasped for air to finish and the next boot was to the side of his head. There was a searing pain and Daryo saw only blackness.

The night was cold. Daryo woke, allowed the pain in the side and back of his head to recede, tried to ignore the pain in his stomach and began to work his hands loose, rocking from side to side to loosen the peg holding them down. The sound of approaching feet made him stop and lay still. The tent flap opened and Sevant entered, a Vidmarian soldier behind him carrying a lantern. Sevant jabbed his boot into Daryo's ribs.
'Wake up, dog!' he snapped. 'Wake!' When he saw Daryo's eyes open he crouched down and produced a knife. 'Where is the Adacan army heading?' When he received no answer, he put the knife to the exposed skin of Daryo's neck. 'Where is the Adacan army heading? You are alone, they are alone, they will die as you will unless you speak!' He suddenly thrust the knife into Daryo's thigh. Daryo tried not to make a sound.
'WHERE?' Sevant thundered, putting more pressure on the knife.
Daryo groaned and tried to keep from screaming. 'Verdeeleon,' he moaned, naming the Vidmarian capital.
Sevant chuckled mirthlessly. 'Keep me laughing and I might just keep you in a cage as a jester, dog.' He twisted the knife in the wound. Daryo screamed. 'Where is the Adacan army going?'
'Verdeeleon!' roared Daryo. 'Verdeeleon! Verdeeleon!'
Sevant's free hand struck Daryo in the face. 'Tell me, Batribi, or I'll push this knife through and out the other side!' He struck Daryo again, a third time, a fourth. 'Where is the Adacan army heading?' He leaned on the knife again.
'I told you, coward!' Daryo spoke through clenched teeth. 'Verdeeleon!'
'Coward? I'll show you coward.' Sevant slapped the knife, Daryo screamed and Sevant's boot began stamping on Daryo's exposed stomach, the stamper screaming 'Coward!' with each blow. Daryo felt the blackness come again.

It was much later in the night when Daryo woke again. His head was now afire, his stomach felt under a great weight but the real agony was the open, bleeding wound in his thigh. Daryo could do nothing for a long while but rest. Without the adrenalin of combat, the wound ached viciously and a new trickle of blood came with each movement of Daryo's leg. He had to lay still and rest, the wound eventually stopped bleeding; Sevant's knife had been long and thin rather than broad. He then started to get his hands free again. He had obviously been moving when Sevant tortured him and perhaps while beyond sense and it had helped work the peg loose. With the horseshoe peg out of the earth, it was a simple matter to twist and flex his hands until the poorly made rope came loose. Daryo slid his hands out and clasped them in front of his body, allowing the spikes of agony in his back and shoulders to subside. When they were mobile, he untied the rope around his feet and flexed his legs. The left was fine but the right began to bleed again as he stood. The leg felt hard and stiff, like bad leather. A hanging strip of tent canvas came away with a tug and made a workable bandage. Daryo hobbled around his canvas prison for a good while, forcing both legs to work, stretching the ache from his arms and back. He eased the canvas aside less than an inch. A campfire was burning a few yards away. A single Vidmarian soldier sat beside it. Two tents, one large and one small, were the other side of the fire and half a dozen horses were tethered a short distance away. The soldier at the fire looked tired, his head was down, his sword stuck carelessly into the ground at his feet. Daryo wondered where his weapons and shield had been put. He put his body's weight on his wounded leg and allowed the pain to surge and recede. Then he moved. He slipped out the tent that had been his prison and crept across the grass towards the sentry, ever heartbeat brought him closer. Daryo reached an arm's length but the Vidmarian sensed movement or heard a noise and turned. He saw Daryo instantly and shrieked an alarm. Daryo punched the man hard in the jaw, grabbed the sword before the soldier and used it reversed to slice across his foe's throat. The spray of his blood splattered across Daryo but he was already concerned with the soldiers coming out of the largest tent. Most were unarmoured, none had shields and as they straggled out of the tent at stumbling runs, Daryo dealt with them precisely and without mercy. Sevant had come to the front of his tent and watched the Batribi execute his men.

'Mad dogs are always the most dangerous,' he said dispassionately, raising a familiar blade. 'I am going to kill you with your own sword, dog. Then send your head to that mute prostitute you like. Or maybe your manhood, at least she could use that for something.'

Daryo swung the sword he had taken to be sure of its weight. It was long and thin with no hand-guard and poorly made. Sevant was wielding Temma's Sword, a broad, curved Batribi blade, excellently made and well cared-for. He changed to a two-handed grip.

'Your overconfidence is your weakness, Sevant. It was at the Five Towers, again at Outros, again at Tiverta and it will send you to the Fourth Goddess today.'

Sevant stepped forwards, stooped to the ground for a moment, stood up and continued forwards, swinging Temma's Sword in wide arcs. Daryo stepped forwards to meet him and, just before he struck, Sevant's free hand flashed out. The stone that he had picked up flew precisely through the morning air and struck Daryo's leg just above his wound. Daryo winced in pain and Sevant's two-handed lateral slice came at his head. Daryo got his borrowed blade up in time to block and, as it was off of the ground, he kicked out with his injured leg. It struck Sevant in the knee and Daryo darted backwards as Sevant lashed out when his knee gave way.

'A foul blow, dog!' roared Sevant.

'And stones into a tortured and starved opponent's wound are not, coward?'

'Coward!' Sevant launched himself forwards.

Daryo parried the horizontal blow, the overhead that followed, another and the scything blow that came at his knees afterwards. Sevant leaped back a yard and thrust straight in at Daryo's chest. Daryo stepped around the blow and, his sword still down low, punched Sevant hard in the jaw. Sevant fell back, Temma's sword flying away. Sevant kicked hard and caught Daryo's wound. Daryo had to close his eyes against the pain and he found someone rip his taken blade from his hand. He opened his eyes just in time to duck Sevant's decapitating blow, dived forwards under the next and rolled heels over head to where Temma's Sword lay. The leather of the handle felt familiar and friendly in his hand as he turned.

'If you want to slay with my own blade, you will have to take it from me,' he taunted.

Sevant spat. 'I don't mind how vermin die, just that they die.'

He charged again, another two-handed overhead swing. Daryo parried; the familiar ring of Temma's Sword in his hand. Sevant kicked for Daryo's injured leg again but the target was out of reach. Daryo swung Temma's Sword and went on the offensive, two-handed high duelling strikes. Sevant parried each one and then went back to the horizontal slash to force Daryo into a leap backwards out of range of the strike. Daryo released one hand of his grip and allowed himself to relax as Sevant recovered his guard and came again. Daryo slid out of range again, ducked the next blow and used the extra reach of his one-hand grip to stab at Sevant's body. Sevant had to step back out of the way and almost lost his footing. Daryo swung Temma's Sword over his head and Sevant barely blocked; his sword horizontal, free hand on the blade for extra strength. Daryo pushed down, his weight bearing down on the edge of his sword. Sevant kicked and caught Daryo right in his leg wound. Daryo cried out from the pain and felt his knees hit the floor, which hurt more. He heard Sevant laugh and the whir of a sword through the air. He did all he could, fall face down on the earth. The approaching blade flew through empty air. Daryo opened his eyes quickly, rolled on to his back and stabbed upwards almost blind. The point of Temma's sword drove itself into Sevant's groin. Sevant wailed; an unbearable scream that increased as Daryo withdrew his blade. Daryo rolled and pushed with his uninjured leg to stand upright. Sevant fell to his knees, sword forgotten, his hands clutching the wound between his legs. Daryo struck him with flat of Temma's Sword across the face, knocking him sideways, and lashed out with his uninjured leg, striking the wound hard. Sevant's wail subsided to a rasping gasp for breath. Daryo levelled his sword-point at Sevant's face.

'Mercy,' gasped the stricken man, blood welling from between his fingers at his groin and from his nose where Daryo had struck him. 'Mercy.'

'You showed none to Kym the Harlequin. Or to Leroyfa the Blind, to Fayd the Vanguard, Liane the Ash, Huw the Glade, you showed none to the thousands killed fighting at Tiverta or Outros and your men will show none to the Adacans.'

'No... no...' Sevant's voice was a pain-wracked groan.

'You would have shown me no mercy.'

'You... you... better man. Only... revenge for my... my exile... wanted... revenge... you... sworn to protect... better man than me...'

'I will kill you, Sevant. That is the greatest mercy I can give this nation. The Adacans will have a greater chance if the Vidmarian commander is dead.'

'No... not... my army...'

'What do you mean?' Daryo added his other hand to his grip.

'Only in Gourmin... lost command... failed... came to finish...'

'Me.'

Sevant nodded and whimpered at the pain. 'Failed.'

'Yes. Yes you did.'

'Deserve... death.'

'I am not going to kill you for that, Sevant!' spat Daryo, suddenly angry again. 'I am going to kill you because you are a traitor! A betrayer! A kin-slayer and an oath-breaker! A murderer of the innocent and good! Remember the Promise you made!' Daryo reversed Temma's Sword and thrust straight down into Sevant's chest. 'With my heart, my mind and my honour, I promise to do my duty as a Member of the Order of the Shield and Sword. I swear my Shield and Sword to the defence of the just, the righteous, the innocent and the weak. By this oath, I pledge my sword and my service until I am discharged by death.' Daryo stood with his sword pommel raised, point down, covered with Sevant's blood. He wiped the blade on the grass, laid it on the ground and knelt beside it to pray to the Fourth Goddess. As he knelt he began to feel the effects of the previous two days, the constant pressure-like feeling on the base of his skull, the burning sensation in his ribs and abdomen and the searing pain in his right thigh. He got up slowly, the wound in his thigh was undoubtedly the most serious pain and likely the most damaging wound. Sevant's tent yielded no more of his effects. He thought for a moment and then realised that when he had gone to the lake, he had only been wearing Temma's Sword. Stai's twin blades, his knife, his shield, even his forearm guards would have been left in the tent in the Adacan camp. The Adacan camp. Somewhere.

Daryo went to the other tent to look for supplies and found several loaves of bread, a skin of milk and a thick black woollen cloak. He took them all, untied the two strongest looking horses and mounted the smaller. The Vidmarian camp was on a low hill above the west bank of a lake. The lake was not particularly broad but very long. At the south end of the lake, it flowed over a small waterfall and into a wide river. To the north of the lake were the foothills of the large grey mountains beyond. Daryo recognised the larger peaks as the ones at the western edge of Ishter. To him, this suggested that he was in the north of Adaca, north of Oia, so the best route was south. He made the reins of his spare horse fast to the straps of the saddle on the one he rode and kicked the horse on.

The horse was not a fast one and was slowed by its fellow tied to it. The river went south-west and then almost due west, staying wide and slow. The dawn came, blindingly, over the eastern horizon and the horses plodded onwards. The river turned south-west again and got wider and slower. As sundown came, Daryo reached the road as it crossed the river at a ford. The road ran east to west with a narrower road south that crossed a smaller river across a stone bridge. Between the roads and the smaller river was a steep bank with the ruins of a stone building part way along it. Daryo wondered it was Sibiri, the ruined fort that Tari had described. A young woman driving a cart approached from the south and Daryo hailed her.

'Do you know of the Adacan army camped near here, my lady?'

The woman looked at him in confusion. 'You are looking for an army?'

Daryo nodded tiredly. 'I am.'

'Follow the road east.'

'My thanks.'

Daryo changed mounts and kicked it on. He went to the left, north of the rise and urged the horse on. It was almost dark when Daryo was challenged by an Adacan sentry.

'Who approaches?' came the demand.

'Daryo the Walker, Lord of Scara, commander of the Boskinian army.'

'Lord Daryo?'

'Indeed.'

The sentry hurried forwards. 'My Lord! Nobody knew where you were!'

'I was abducted. I... I am injured, badly. Fetch a physician.'

'Yes, my Lord. Diviro! Salta!' Two men appeared from the closest tent. One took the reins of Daryo's horse and the other took the sentry's spear. The sentry ran into the camp. Daryo allowed himself to relax as his horse was led into the Adacan encampment. Several fires were being lit and most of the soldiers were out of their tents preparing food or talking across their fires. Many saw Daryo and some cheered. The sentry led Daryo's horses to the little enclave of Boskinian tents among the Adacans. Camali almost dragged Daryo off of his horse and embraced him hard. Daryo eased her arms away. 'Not now. I need the physician.'

She led him into her tent and helped him to lie down.

*Why go?* she asked.

*Hit. Taken.* He laid back and closed his eyes, aware of the increasing pains around his body, exacerbated by the rigours of a day's hard riding on unfamiliar horses. Several candles were lit around the tent and the physician was rushed in. He was young, angular in appearance and direct in manner. Daryo described how he had been abused. The physician used fresh bandages to dress the Batribi's thigh but said that he was more concerned that something inside the body may have been damaged. He removed Daryo's clothes with a knife and spent a long time pressing and prodding Daryo between his neck and waist, noting where the pain was felt and where there was swelling.

'Rest and faith is all I can suggest,' he concluded. 'Keep the wounds clean and bound and do no more than necessary. Exertion could be dangerous.'

Daryo could only nod weakly. 'My thanks.'

The physician gave Camali a small flask. 'This will help you sleep. You must drink all of it.'

Daryo did so with Camali's aid and within heartbeats felt sleep come.

## Chapter 70

Daryo spent several days without knowing if it was light or dark in the sky. He moved between sleep and waking without thought or effort. When he woke, Camali was beside him, sometimes Eraphi, sometimes Micel or Sal, he would spend some time trying to ignore the pain that covered him like a burning blanket and then would be plied with another flask of the physician's sleeping concoction sending him back to the blackness. In one period awake, Eraphi told him that he been gone for three days and had passed five more back in the camp. She said that the Boskinian army had arrived at Oia and was due to march to meet them. The next time he awoke, the physician returned and said his sleep draught was no longer needed and that it would be better if Daryo recovered further without created potions to aid him. As soon as he heard that, Daryo insisted on being allowed to leave the bed. Camali was summoned and she and the physician helped him to his feet. His head felt better, as well the aches within were subsiding and although there was an initial jab of pain, his stiffened legs began to respond. After Daryo had disappeared, Camali had ordered Daryo's effects be moved to her tent and he gladly inspected Stai's twin blades and his shield. The physician took his leave and Camali assisted Daryo out of the long shirt that he had been in and into a woollen jerkin and loose trousers with much kissing of his skin and repeating of her signs for *beautiful Daryo*. He kissed her lips gently.

'I should see Princess Tari. I need to know what we must of the battle.'

Camali nodded, took his hand and led him out. There had obviously been much rain, the ground was sodden and the grass trampled into mud in most places. The most commonly-used pathways had been laid with cut grass or wooden planks to form a better surface underfoot. The princess's tent had been moved out of the main thoroughfares and an unfamiliar canvas erected beside it. Camali looked inside, smiled and guided Daryo in. Tari was sat at table with a disturbingly bear-like Ishteri Yeoman alongside her.

'Lord Daryo!' Tari leaped up and came as if to embrace him but then seemed to change her mind. 'It is so pleasing to see you on your feet.'

'It is good to be on my feet,' said Daryo, trying to keep the discomfort from his voice. 'You must tell me what happened.'

'I shall, but not now. Who is your guest?'

'Of course!' Tari turned as the Ishteri stood up. The Ishteri was without doubt seven feet tall, thick brown hair and a thick beard and moustache over his uniform. 'This is Mephintes, captain of the Ishteri Yeomen.'

The huge man clapped his hand against his breast in salute. 'Lord Daryo.'

'Captain Mephintes.'
'I come with the salute of the Senate of Ishter to you, Lord Daryo: three hundred and eighty-six men in fine health, four hundred horses, and their commander, at your command.'
'My thanks to you and to the Senate,' said Daryo. 'The Boskinian army, Princess Tari?'
'Due to set camp with us tomorrow. Just more than nineteen thousands, just more than one thousand are Oaken Guard, some three thousand cavalry.'
Daryo nodded. 'As we hoped. Has there been word from the Regent?'
'He is in Cali with our Lord King. They are beyond harm.'
'And the Vidmarians?'
'Not yet in Darsux but their scouts have been seen within range of the city.'
'We should prepare at least the White Bulls and some companies for battle at Sibiri.'
'As you wish.'
Daryo took several deep, slow breaths and Camali's hands came out to support him.
'You should rest, Lord Daryo,' growled Mephintes.
Tari nodded. 'Yes, my Lord. Rest. Regain your strength.'
Daryo sighed. 'I think that wise. I plead though that I am roused when the Boskinian army arrives.'
'Of course.'
Daryo turned to Camali and smiled weakly. She took his arm and led him back to her tent. He vaguely noticed two of the Oaken Guard detachment that had escorted them on guard at the tent door. He lay down on the bed and was asleep again within heartbeats.

He woke the next morning, he had slept for significantly more than half a day. Camali was not in her cot in the tent and Daryo managed to get himself out of his own cot with only a minimum of pain and discomfort. He thought for some long moments before deciding to dress in his familiar breeches, boots, a black shirt and his armoured jerkin. The day before, he had made a slow and painful journey from his sickbed the short distance to Princess Tari. This day, he walked out of his lover's tent with his twin blades on his back, the hood of his combat clothing raised, his curved Batribi sword and his knife on his hip, his bracers on his arms and his shield over his shoulder. Several of the Adacan soldiers hailed him as he passed. Instead of going towards the heart of the camp, he spent a while touring the area, greeting soldiers and learning some names, inspecting weapons and equipment, patting some of the horses, before turning to the centre.
Behind Tari's sleeping tent had been erected a lower, longer one. Daryo was pointed to it by one of the princess's household. A long table had been erected, surrounded by the

Adacan's favoured folding stools. Maps, lists, charts and other parchments littered the table. The towering Ishteri captain slapped his chest in salute when he saw Daryo. Three Adacan commanders were present and they all bowed formally. One had been talking to Tari, who looked up and smiled warmly. Camali had been writing something watched by a man in Boskinian robes. She caught Daryo's eye and made her signs for *Good day, beautiful Daryo*, the Boskinian turned.

'Lord Daryo.'

'Lord Venni. Welcome to Adaca.' Venni extended his hand and Daryo tapped his against it in the Boskinian fashion and then clasped it in the Jaboen one. 'You are well?'

'I am. Better than I hear that you have been.'

'I am on my feet. The Third God watches me. You brought an army with you, I pray?'

'Indeed I have. Over eighteen thousands of the army of the armies of the lakes and the north as well as two-thirds of the Oaken Guard: nearly sixty score, who have all been trained by your company in the shellback.'

'Excellent.'

Tari came around Venni. 'The White Bulls are on the march to the fort, Daryo. The Ishteri have moved up as well, to block the east road.'

'We should block the southern road too, Lady,' said Mephintes.

Camali raised her hand to Daryo to get his attention and she pointed to Venni.

'Perhaps the Oaken Guard,' Daryo suggested and Camali nodded her assent.

Everyone looked at Venni, who shrugged. 'I do not command the Boskinian army, Lord Daryo and Lady Camali do. It is their choice.'

'But we value your counsel, Lord Venni,' said Daryo and Camali assented again.

'The Oaken Guard would be proud to do so,' said Venni.

'They should move as soon as possible,' Daryo advised. 'We need the base of a battle plan in place in case the Vidmarian army advances quickly.' He sat down on a folding stool, feeling a little weak. 'Have we plans for deployment?'

Camali passed over a roughly drawn map. Sal appeared from behind a canvas wall in the tent with a plate of cold meat and bread.

'Gods' Watch, Walker.'

'Gods' Watch, Sal. My thanks.'

'I will be nearby if you require me, Walker.' He retired.

'Walker?' asked Tari.

'Daryo the Walker of the Order of the Shield and Sword,' Venni told her. 'The wandering lord, the homeless warrior.'

Daryo ignored this and studied the map, checking the written report of the princess's official in charge of surveying the land. He talked with Venni about the Boskinian army, Tari about the Adacan and detailed his plan first to Camali and Venni and then to an assembly of over a score of captain, commanders and leaders. With some additions and amendments the battle plan was agreed over the afternoon meal. Daryo then retired to bed, succumbing a little to his still-healing body. Camali joined him after the evening meal as darkness fell, undressed him, cleaned and bound his wounds and gently made love to him until the candles burned out.

Darsux was taken that night. The city had followed the orders of the Regent and surrendered. Many of the civilians had fled, some to the south and Aden, most to the west past the army's encampment towards Oia. Many of the men and boys passing had been conscripted into a rough militia, several women too, and many other refugees agreed to help with the supplies, the horses or the wounded. The militia were a rough formation, numbering nearly a thousand. Some had been armed with their own weapons, some had farm implements, others were equipped with spares from the Adacan and Boskinian forces. A retired Adacan commander was among them and accepted the command from Tari. The militia assembled and straggled forwards to Sibiri, crossing paths with the advance scouts reporting the Vidmarian advance from Darsux towards the river crossing at Sibiri. Tari ordered the advance.

## Chapter 71

The Oaken Guard deployed south of the bridge along with the Boskinian archers and the small group of their cavalry. The main Adacan force deployed along the ridge, the White Bulls occupying the ruined fort, the Ishteri holding the road on the right of the line, the rest of the Boskinian army and the small Adacan cavalry hidden behind the ridge. The militia, a single battalion of infantry and half of the Adacan archers took position immediately opposite the ford. Across the shallows, the Vidmarian army massed. Tari insisted on leading from the front and joined the White Bulls. Daryo took command of the Oaken Guard. Camali remained with the Boskinian forces on the reverse slope. A line of Vidmarian skirmishers began to cross the ford as the Adacan archers, including most of the women who had joined the militia began to fire. The Vidmarian skirmishers scattered, hurling spears at the militia before retreating back across the waters. The commanders had all been taught the Adacan method of battlefield control by horn and flag. The first Vidmarian battalion marched across in ordered lines, guided by drums, the militia scattered as ordered and fled up the hill towards the ruined fort. The single battalion of Adacan forces gave battle as the archers withdrew first along the road towards the Ishteri and then up over the hill to the reverse slope. The first Vidmarian cavalry followed the infantry as the Adacan's withdrew to their prepared position on the ridge line. Instead of chasing the Adacans, they turned south and charged the wide bridge across the smaller river backed by a rain of arrows from beyond the wide river.

Daryo stepped into his position in the third line and raised his rectangular Oaken Guard shield. 'Locks shields! Form walls! Raise roof! Out spears!'

The Oaken Guards formed the shellback. At Outros it had been only a few men wide. To block the bridge at Sibiri, the shellback was thirty-three men wide. The Vidmarian cavalry reached a gallop. The shellback's centre raced forwards, forming a spearhead, spears outwards. Each thrust of spear from the shellback was aimed at a horse as the Boskinian archers alongside fired into the attack. As men in the shellback fell, those behind dragged them under the shields and a man moved around to take his place. Daryo found himself in the front line near the centre and drove his spear into a dismounted Vidmarian soldier. The Vidmarian cavalry was beginning to withdraw.

'Lower roof! On guard!' called Daryo. The Oaken Guard brought their shields down to their normal positions. 'Draw swords!' The swords were drawn. 'Charge!'

'For the king and the Walker!'

'The king and the Walker!'

The Oaken Guard charged across the bridge.

Camali had watched the cavalry assault towards the bridge from the highest point of the ruined fort of Sibiri, the remnants of the eastern tower. Alongside her were Herro, Sal, a single Oaken Guard and an Adacan bearing the huge curved horn and the flags for sounding and showing the battle instructions. The Vidmarian infantry formed up immediately in the centre with a single battalion separate on its left. This streamed up the road to confront the Ishteri as the main infantry began a slow, measured advance. Camali saw them turn diagonal to the ridge and charge the half of the Adacan army to the right of the fort. A small detachment came forwards to occupy the White Bulls holding the perimeter wall of the outer fort. The militia streamed forwards to their aid and the roar of their engagement mingled with that from below as the main Vidmarian army engaged the Adacan right. Behind their footsoldiers, the Adacan archers started their fire on the rear ranks of Vidmarians. Beyond them, the Ishteri had charged the battalion facing them, huge swords swinging from their horses. The Ishteri broke the Vidmarian line and were soon causing chaos and murder among their victims. Camali grabbed Herro and signed what she wanted.
'First Boskinians into the main battle,' Herro relayed.
The Boskinian green oaken banner was raised, waved right to left and then held to the right. An entire third, nearly six thousand men, of the Boskinian army started forwards.
'Adacan cavalry to charge in support of the Ishteri.'
An Adacan banner with a black fringe and a black horse emblazoned on it was raised, held to the right alongside the Ishteri flag, accompanied by the charge blown on the horn. The small amount of Adacan cavalry, right at the rear, began to trot along the reverse slope, along the back of the Adacan and now Boskinian line and then charged into the flank of the Vidmarian battalion. Camali looked over the parapet of her tower. The combination of White Bulls and militia were easily holding the ruined fort. The two Adacan groups on the left were still unused. The Vidmarian army seemed to be concentrating on the right, trying to push between the Adacan lines but now the Boskinians were covering the gap.
Camali had another order given.
'Boskinian force ready to advance.'

The Vidmarian cavalry had been driven back almost to the ford but the Vidmarian archers were starting to get a better range on the side and rear of the Oaken Guard. Daryo sent back a runner to order the Boskinian archers to focus on their Vidmarian counterparts but then was caught in the melee. He had discarded his Boskinian shield for his Order one, which was smaller and easier to use. He smashed a Vidmarian in the face, drove Temma's Sword through him and caught another across the back of the neck as he withdrew the blade. He became aware that there were others in the battle, infantry instead of the mount-less cavalry. The Vidmarian reserves were moving up.

The Vidmarian reserve had moved up and joined the shattered cavalry to halt the Oaken Guard's advance. Camali fancied that she saw a curved sword arcing through the air as if thrown. She had the order given for the still-concealed Boskinian reserve to wait. Venni was commanding the remaining two Boskinian battalions and could be trusted to lead them carefully. The battalion on the Vidmarian left was crumbling under the combined assault of the Ishteri and the Adacan cavalry. The combined Adacan and Boskinian line was holding the main Vidmarian force, which had tried to regroup for a second charge but seemed to be losing cohesion. The Vidmarian reserve would be better here, Camali thought to herself. The Boskinian cavalry was trotting across the bridge, readying their first charge. Camali had the Boskinian reserve ordered forwards.

Daryo felt the warhammer hit and lodge in his shield. Without thinking he pushed hard from behind the shield, allowed it to come off of his arm, slashed with Temma's Sword and drew the Bear. The warhammer's wielder, seeing his opponent now bearing two swords, ran. Daryo quickly reversed the Bear, took his opportunity to push Temma's Sword in behind the twin blades' holder and drew the Horse instead before setting to work with Stai's twin blades, a swirling blend of sharpened Batribi steel, a keen fighter's mind and a steady devotion to finishing his task. Daryo ducked another warhammer, ducked and pushed it away with the Bear, swinging full-circle to give himself the momentum to cleave through the wielder's guts. He stood, chopped down a Vidmarian confronting one of the Guard, blocked the next attack from the next man, who received a vicious Batribi boot in his groin and then a razor of a Batribi blade across his face. Daryo kicked the man down, leaped the body swinging the Bear point up and driving both blades into the next target, again using his boot to free his swords again. He heard the pound of hoofbeats and looked up. It was the Boskinian cavalry, charging the Vidmarian reserve's flank. Beyond he could see Boskinian standards crest the hill south of the fort as Venni's reserves advanced. From the tower of the old fort, the horn sounded 'right flank forwards'. Camali was pushing back the Vidmarian force and the Boskinian reserves impacted on the Vidmarian right flank, the Ishteri and the Adacan cavalry on the right. The Vidmarian drums went silent and the soldiers began to run.

Daryo suddenly found he had no opponents as the Vidmarian right crumbled and fled for the ford. He saw the signals and heard the horn blow from the tower, directing the Boskinian cavalry to the ford. This cut off the Vidmarian retreat. The reserve were mostly fled or caught, most of the cavalry was dead, the remnants of the infantry from the centre were pushed north against the river. Daryo called out and had the Oaken Guard reform. He noticed that a significant number were lost but focused on having his men rallied and marching forwards. The Vidmarian soldiery left were throwing away their weapons, holding their arms out wide to their sides to indicate being unarmed. The Adacan troops on the left of the line moved forwards, unblooded, to help sweep the remnants of the enemy north.

Tari, Camali and Venni met at the foot of the ridge below the fort and set off in search of Daryo. They found him by the bridge, limping rather badly but making his way through the wreckage of the battle with a determined air, calling help for the slightly hurt and, where necessary, despatching the seriously wounded with the Horse and a brief prayer to the Fourth Goddess. Elsewhere, other soldiers did the same duty, looted the dead and searched for lost comrades.
'My Lord, we have taken the day,' said Tari. She had fought with her men around the ruins and still bore her short poleaxe.
'We have,' said Daryo with a tired smile. 'Few escaped although we have not come across many captains slain or caught.'
'An army cannot be raised with captains,' Tari suggested.
'But it can be led by them in the future,' Daryo replied. 'One day, Vidmaria may return.'
'But not now, Lord Daryo,' said Venni. 'Rest your blade and your body. My force have have seen little battle and my sword is unsullied by blood. Allow me to do this act.'
Daryo went to decline the offer but felt the rebellion of his still-infirm body, tired from the exertions of the battle. 'My thanks, Lord Venni.'

Daryo also declined the feast that night and slept fitfully in Camali's tent. The morning after the battle, a pigeon was received by Butriguno requesting that Lords Daryo, Camali and Venni return to Hamlakia as soon as possible by command of the king.

## Book 5 - A Wandering Lord
## Chapter 72

Lord Venni was happy to be left in command of the Boskinian army as it reconstituted itself and marched forwards with the Adacan army to ensure that the Vidmarians returned to their own lands through the Verdeeleon Pass and not through Boskinia any further than necessary. Micel agreed to stay with Venni as a diplomatic envoy, Butriguno refused to leave the safety of the army. Daryo, Camali, Sal and Herro were plied with supplies and horses by Tari and they departed on excellent mounts with two pack horses in tow. The simplest and fastest route was retracing their route through Oia, Olanyi, Bruszo, Ishter and back into Boskinia. They stayed in inns in each location, passing news of the victory, and then rode hard north from Ishter at daybreak reaching Scara by dark. The whole village had been alerted by some means and flags and sheet were waved as the lord of the estate arrived home. The travelling party slept overnight at Daryo's house and then headed north with the new day.

Hamlakia was dressed for a festival. Banners, wreaths and bunting lined and crossed the streets, few people seemed to working, the markets were open but selling ale and cakes and pastries. Everywhere Daryo and Camali were recognised they were cheered. People stretched out to touch them and raised children on their shoulders to get a better look at the Lord of Scara and the Lady of Cilano. Halfway to the Halfwood Palace, an escort of Oaken Guards arrived led by an elated Carbreo, who dismounted his horse and almost dragged Camali from hers for a fierce embrace and then hugged Daryo almost as ardently.

'Heroes of Boskinia!' he pronounced in a loud voice and many of the throng that was gathering cheered.

Camali looked particularly embarrassed. Daryo laughed. 'You seem in good heart, my friend!'

'Indeed I should be! And tonight the king will reward you both beyond your imaginings! Come! Come! The feast is being set as we speak!'

The small procession led through the masses to the Halfwood Palace where an honour guard of armed men and other lords were waiting. The king stood before the front door and embraced Daryo and Camali almost as enthusiastically as Carbreo had.

'Welcome home, commanders and saviours of Boskinia and Adaca!' he announced. 'It is my privilege to have you return! Your victory will ensure that our country can rest and recover its pride and its security. Rest yourselves but briefly, come down to our halls and you shall be rewarded!'

Daryo was shown to his room in the prince's tower. Sal accompanied him, ecstatic with the attention that he was receiving as the page of Boskinia's hero. Rich clothes and vestments had been laid out, a fire burned bright in the hearth and an awe-struck serving girl hurried out as Daryo entered trying to come to terms with the rapturous reception he was receiving. He sat down heavily on the bed.
'My Lord has been given a fine choice of clothes,' said Sal, investigating the robes and other items. 'What do you wish to wear, Walker?'
'I do not know, Sal. I do not know if this is needed or appropriate. I do not do what I do for the rewards and the fine clothing. I have done what was needed because it was right.'
'But that is good, Walker!' Sal left the robe he had been holding and came across to Daryo. He hesitated and then sat on the bed beside the Batribi. 'My family live in Boskinia. If you had not aided us, I may be dead and they may be too. Lots of people would be dead and many would be slaves. I would see you rewarded, Lady Camali, Lord Carbreo and every man who fought beside you would see you rewarded. You should be honoured.'
'It is the height of rudeness to refuse that which is given.'
'Indeed, Walker. Let me fetch some warm water and you may wash and prepare yourself.'

Sal returned with the tub of water and Daryo washed while Sal sorted through the clothing left. Sal was keen that Daryo wear the most elaborate of the clothes but Daryo vetoed this immediately. He permitted Sal to select a halved black and red quilted doublet as well as a more elaborate version of his original lord's cape and some padded breeches. Sal suggested Daryo may wish to wear Temma's Sword as well and set to polishing it as a knock came on the door. It was one of the king's pages, requesting the Lord Daryo to attend in the great hall. Daryo was still only in his smallclothes and sent Sal with the page to reassure the king that he was coming. He quickly grabbed a shirt to wear under the doublet and was fastening the front when another knock came. Daryo cast about helplessly for a moment and answered it himself. Despite the Lord of Scara being almost bare, the man-at-arms bowed formally and handed over a folded and sealed document.
'Who brought this?' Daryo asked.
'A messenger from Outros, my Lord.'

'Outros?'

'Yes, my Lord. It says who it is from on the outside but I do not know letters.'

'My thanks.' Daryo withdrew into his chamber. The document was sealed with plain white wax and actually had the addressee on the outside, not the sender's name and it was simply addressed to *Daryo, Lord of Scara*. He broke the wax, conscious that he was overdue at his own celebration, and read.

*From Sanytana Grey-shod, Priest of the Fourth and Darkest Goddess of the Pantheon in Lord Carbreo's city of Outros in Boskinia,*

*To Daryo, Lord of Scara, Walker of the Order of Shield and Sword, saviour of Lord Carbreo's city of Outros in Boskinia.*

*My Lord,*

*As you requested, I scribe this letter to you with the knowledge that Dava, known as the Three Crystals of the Order of the Shield and Sword and as the acolyte of the Fourth and Darkest Goddess of the Pantheon, has passed into the embrace and eternal sleep of his death and the company of the Fourth and Darkest Goddess of the Pantheon. Master Dava was a truly faithful disciple of the Pantheon and met his final rest with dignity and welcome in the sanctuary of the temple in Lord Carbreo's city of Outros in Boskinia.*

*According to the wishes of Master Dava, his body shall be consigned to fire as is custom in Yashoun and he has requested that the remains that are left by the fire be buried in the city of his birth known as Ossmoss in Yashoun along with the shield of membership of his former Order of the Shield and Sword.*

*The information that I believe to be correct is that you left instructions to be informed upon this happenstance, the arrangements that Master Dava left for the treatment of his body after death and that you wished to finance the said arrangements. If this is so, I offer my humble thanks and shall await your response. Master Dava's body is likely to have been fired by the receipt of this missive by yourself but the remains shall be held at the temple until your wishes regarding the transport and interring become known to me.*

*I remain, in the witness of the Fourth and Darkest Goddess of the Pantheon, your true and faithful servant, my Lord of Scara.*

Daryo felt tears come to his eyes. The trappings of lordship and victory around him became hollow and meaningless. Bravely, an old man had met his destiny and the Fourth Goddess after many seasons of pain and suffering from his wound. Although he had commanded thousands in battle and seen many thousands killed in battle, the news of the death of a single old man cut him more deeply than the wound in his thigh. He sat on the bed for a long time, simply holding the memory of Dava the Three Crystals in his mind. The Three Crystals, the crystals of Spinel, the Third Goddess, teacher of compassion and understanding, three times over for her place in the Pantheon and that each compassionate act counted thrice in her eyes, emblazoned on the shield of a warrior sworn to temper his blade with her understanding and to use reason and thought before resorting to battle. Daryo reread the letter before burning it in the hearth. Then he stood and began to dress again.

'Daryo, Lord of Scara!' announced the herald. It was only as the Batribi passed him that the herald noticed. 'My lord, I think-'
But Daryo was already striding up the hall, his old brown boots on his feet, thick woollen leggings and armoured jerkin in place, his Hajma bracers on his arms, Temma's Sword and his knife slung from his sword belt, his pack on his back on top of Stai's twin blades, his shield over his shoulder on a strap and his lord's cape folded carefully and in his arms. The room was full of the rich and noble of the land, many had stood when he was announced but all now stood to stare in amazement. Daryo looked neither left nor right as he approached the high table. Everyone there was also stood and the king looked amazed. 'My Lord Daryo, the war is over!' he joked.
Daryo knelt. 'Indeed, sire. But my war is not yours any longer. I must leave.'
'Leave?'
'To fulfil a pledge to an old comrade and the Fourth Goddess.'
'This feast and these people are gathered for you, my Lord.'
'They are gathered for victory. Victory has been won and Lady Camali deserves as much the acclaim for it as I do. As for me, sire, I must decline. I fight for what is good, honourable, just and right, not for rewards. I thank you humbly for your generosity and leave your service so, sire.' He laid the cloak on the floor before the king and stood up. 'I take my leave, sire.' He turned away.
'Stop!' thundered Gorero, slamming his hand on the table. 'Stay there, sir. You are my servant, you are Lord of Scara and by every god known, sir, you shall act as such! Guards!'

Daryo turned sharply back as three men-at-arms rushed forwards. 'You are wrong. I am not Lord of Scara. That title should never have been mine. I am Daryo the Walker. And I am leaving.' He drew Temma's Sword, causing many around him to gasp, some cried out. 'My Lord, I have thanked you and done all that you ask to save your lands. I wish now to leave amicably. I will fight my way out if that is demanded but there is no reason. Make Camali your hero, Carbreo, Venni. Allow me to leave.'

'Sire...' said Carbreo softly, shaking his head.

Gorero glared at Carbreo and then back at Daryo. 'Leave. Come not within my sight again.'

The men-at-arms retreated and Daryo sheathed his blade. 'My thanks, my Lord. Gods' Guidance on your rule.' He turned and strode out of the doors.

## Chapter 73

Daryo the Walker was walking. The ground was uneven and boggy but he marched on regardless, mindful not to fall lest he break the earthenware urn in the top of his pack that held the fired remains of Dava the Three Crystals- a couple of pounds of grey-white ash and bone in a stone jar covered with a tied white cloth. To the back of his load was strapped an iron-braced wooden buckler, bearing the white outline of a sword on a shield. At the pommel of the sword were three green crystals. As well as the load on his back, his own three blades, and his shield, Daryo carried an ash staff almost as tall as he stood to help him traverse the marshy ground beside the River Hais. From Outros he had followed the river bank north, improvised a bridge with branches to cross the Hamlakia river and then continued on his route. He followed the river's bend to the east and, as it turned north and then west to join the Dithithindil, the road came into sight. Gratefully, he diverted to his right and after a few hundred yards more mud, dips and ponds, he found his feet on the raised stone of the Hivamakia-Thetri road. He took some time to wipe the sticky black mud from his boots before turning left on the roadway towards the now-visible town of Hivamakia.

The ancient capital of the fallen land of Crimir, a land which ages past had covered much of Boskinia, northern Armynya and south-east Gourmin, Hivamakia was built on the confluence of the Dithithindil from the east, the Hais from the south and a number of smaller streams that flowed into them from the north. It spanned the banks of each river and the series of islands that sat in the flow. Many of the buildings of the city were built on the wide stone bridges that linked the islands with the shore. The city's history showed on its arms, above the nine black diamonds representing the city's islands and bridges were the silver crown and white horse of Crimir. The wall was old, a little grown with weeds and moss, but thick and tall, the gate was solid banded wood and a raised portcullis hung in front of it. Four men stood on guard, all bearing the long Boskinian shields and the short spears. They were elderly for men-at-arms, the younger men were with the king's armies, the shields looked old and the spears rusted. One of the shields was laid flat on the ground as the man saw to his boot.

'A shield should not be laid so,' said Daryo as he approached. 'It may flatten and warp, then it will not stop an arrow of grass.'

The old soldier looked up. 'And what know you of shields, traveller?'

'I was a blacksmith. I made many shields and cared for many more.'

The soldier finished with his boot, picked up his shield and eyed Daryo. 'You are a Batribi. Where is your clan?'

'I walk alone. I have a grave oath to fulfil and a long road ahead. Do boats go west to Bhal?'

'Some.'

'Would you tell me where to meet such a boat?'

'I would.'

Daryo smiled. 'Where would I meet such a boat?'

'Go to Hepsos, the westernmost of the nine, the docks there.'

'My thanks. Gods' Guidance.'

'And to you, Batribi.'

Daryo stepped inside the gates. The town was much like the walls, a little worn and a little aged but still strong. There was no market but the streets were still well populated. The familiar sounds and smells of a forge made him smile. A young boy of about fourteen summers was making horseshoes. A pigpen nearby was being shovelled out and Daryo had to step around the growing pile of muck. The street became a bridge without a noticeable change, still lined on both sides by buildings, only told by a slight rise in the stone paving and then a sight of the river between a bakery and the house alongside. Daryo reached a crossroads and asked for direction to the island of Hepsos. He was pointed towards it and the next bridge was narrower and more identifiable as such. The third bridge led onto Hepsos, little more than a square rod across, its edges lined with boardwalks and boats, mostly small oar fishing boats, some larger with sails. He saw a young man checking a sail canvas before raising it and moved alongside the boat.

'Whence do you sail?' he called.

'East to Hypsios.'

'Is any boat that you know going to Bhal?'

The man cast around for a moment and then pointed at a larger boat across the island. Daryo thanked him and crossed to the other boat, hailing a broad, dark man aboard.

'I seek passage to Bhal!'

The man nodded. 'I can oblige. This is my vessel. Nine silver halves.'

'Six.'

'Eight.'

'Done.' Daryo stepped across to the moored boat. It was wide and of shallow draught, about forty feet long, a small cabin behind the prow, a single mast and a small poop-deck. He took his pouch from under his clock and handed over the fee. 'When do you sail, ship-master?'

'The wind is rising. Soon, Master Batribi. Do you have a name?'

'Daryo the Walker.'

'Daryo... Daryo... the name sounds as if it is one that I know.'
'It is a common name among my people.' Even as he spoke, Daryo wondered if he spoke truth; he had never thought to ask any of his people who may have known.
'Maybe so. There is a cabin in the forecastle. Take what rest you may in there.'
'My thanks.'
The cabin was small, as wide as the boat and only ten feet long, its deck set slightly lower than the main deck to give room to stand. A series of hammocks were slung from fore to aft, an unlit lantern hung among them, a series of round portholes along each side provided sunlight. Daryo carefully divested himself of his load and propped it in a corner, using his shield to cover the bag as protection. After some consideration, he removed his twin blades and left them there, keeping Temma's Sword and his knife on him. He went back on the main deck. The captain had a crew of three: a boy of about fifteen summers with pale-enough skin and narrow eyes to suggest a Silver Island ancestor, a woman of Daryo's age and an older man with a thin grey beard. The woman hauled a deer carcass into the poop cabin as the boy hopped ashore, cast off the lines and shoved the boat away from the dock, scrambling back aboard just in time. The captain and the woman raised the sail and the elder took the tiller as the boat moved out into the flow. The sail caught the wind and the boat began its voyage west. The captain noticed Daryo, who had perched on the low gunwale.
'What business takes you to Bhal?'
'A short step on a long journey. I go to Yashoun to fulfil a pledge to a fallen comrade.'
The captain nodded. 'A long journey indeed but with a worthy purpose. You know the river cannot take boats beyond Bhal.'
'The Vidmarians control the river.'
'As you say. Do you take the road to Tiverta?'
'I would go across country to Three Rivers, then through Thiel and follow the river. Otherwise, I must go north. Salifa... then Taam and across the Northern Wastes.'
'Better to stay close to the river; that is my counsel.'
'Wise counsel, ship-master.'
'My name is Silendro. You will have a day to learn it, Lord of Scara.'
Daryo shook his head. 'That is not my name or title, sir.'
'Ce says otherwise.' The captain indicated the young lad who was coiling rope.
'Ce is mistaken.'
'Daryo the hero of Outros?'

'No. I am a traveller, a Batribi without a clan journeying to Yashoun. A comrade of mine died and, after his body was burned in the manner of the Yashoun, I am returning the remains to his homeland.'

Silendro nodded. 'It is a worthy purpose, sir. If you are indeed the Lord of Scara that threw his cloak down at the king's feet, or the hero of the battle of Outros and Adaca, or a traveller bearing his friend home, you are equally welcome on my vessel. And should you be the former, I thank you, sir.'

'And I!' called the young woman.

'And I!' added the boy, Ce.

'I am a traveller bearing his friend home.'

'And I thank you, sir.'

Silendro was happy for Daryo to do what little roaming was possible on the boat and Daryo found the forward cabin full of deer carcasses and smoked fish. Daryo decided to retire to his hammock and rest after that as the boat sailed steadily west.

Not many years before, Bhal had been an insignificant cluster of fishermen's huts alongside the Dithithindil. With the discovery of a vein of silver, it had grown much more significant. A road was being built south from Three Rivers but had been interrupted by the Vidmarian attack northwards across Jaboen's southern woodlands towards Tiverta. Bhal was too small and too inaccessible for the Vidmarian attack to focus on and the village had been spared. The stone-built quay from the nearby foothills of the Peaks jutted out into the river and Silendro bought his craft alongside with practised skill. A cluster of low wooden buildings and a few stone ones further from the bank of the river with the short spire of a temple showing above them. The journey had taken two days and the night between and the sun was setting further along the Dithithindil. Daryo agreed with Silendro a price for a hammock from the cabin, thanked the captain and his crew and made his way ashore with the hammock rolled up and tied to the back of his pack. The temple was of the First Goddess, doubtless to guide the fishermen and miners in their works. Daryo went inside the empty little place, knelt for a few moments in prayer and then headed north-west.

The forest had no road but a well-used pathway had been trodden through the trees which Daryo followed, his pace even and steady. The evergreen trees around and above him blotted out what was left of the sun. The forest was clear below the trees, the dense needles and branches kept the undergrowth from rising, only a few small trees and some dense, prickly bushes stood between the trunks. A wild pig hurried across the path causing an agitated twittering and a flock of birds rose from their roosts in protest. The birds settled again and only a single individual could be heard singing from high in the trees. As the light failed, Daryo's eyes adjusted. The path was relatively clear and firm and did not present much of a challenge to a walker. Daryo continued walking for another few hours, beyond sunset, before deciding to stop and rest. He found a convenient hollow, built a small fire, slung his hammock and was soon asleep.

Dawn woke him better than any bell and after a breakfast of cheese and bread from his bag, he packed his hammock and started north-west again. The day was dull and threatened rain. The birds were quiet and little stirred in the woods around the path. Daryo found himself struggling to keep his pace steady, sometimes slowing to an amble before realising and then almost jogging to make up for the lost time and distance. Midday passed and Daryo paused by a stream to refill his flask and eat a brief meal before resuming his march. He knew the town of Three Rivers but knew only of the existence of Bhal; he was unsure exactly how much distance lay between them. By sundown he was feeling somewhat discouraged. The rain finally began as night fell and he spent an uncomfortable night sleeping beside a fallen tree for shelter. The rain persisted through the night into the morning and Daryo tramped onwards trying to ignore the constant rain and increasingly sticky mud of the path. The rain stopped mid-morning but resumed in the afternoon. He reached the edge of the forest and almost tripped over at the sight that greeted him: a series of conical tents, *kaffa*. He whispered a quick prayer to the Fourth God and hurried onwards. The Batribi tents were built next to the end of the road and a series of wagons all loaded with stone. Daryo guessed that the Batribi were building the road. True to their nature, the tents were built around a large fire in the centre and a sentry walked the perimeter, sword in hand.
'Halt!' he called. 'Who approaches?'
Daryo lowered his hood and held his hands out to his sides. 'I am no threat. I am one of our people. I am Daryo, kin of Dostan.'
The man studied him for a moment. 'Arvol, kin of Daril. You are walking?'
'It is the way of our people.'
'Not all of them. No clan?'
'I walk alone.'
Arvol nodded. 'Then you are welcome with us, Daryo, kin of Dostan.'
'Do you have an elder?'
'No. I am the leader of the clan. Come, you should come out of the rain.'

The clan comprised of twenty-four, ten men and their wives, two young girls not quite of age and two babes in arms. They were working for the Lord of Three Rivers to build the road between Three Rivers and Bhal. They had been working through most of the spring and a relative of one of the women was bringing his clan to assist. They had been aided by another group initially but they had left for the growing settlement around the lake.
'There are many there now,' said Arvol's brother. The clan had gathered in the largest *kaff* as the rain was heavier and the wind picking up.
'They are putting up houses of wood,' said his wife. 'A temple to the Pantheon.'
'You do not approve?' asked Daryo.
'We are a people of the road, not of the marketplace,' said Arvol. 'We are not meant to stay in one place, we are best travelling.' There was a general murmur of agreement.
Arvol slapped his knees with his hands in a regular beat. Daryo recognised this immediately and joined him. Soon the whole clan did so and Arvol spoke again.

*'Our people walk and walk again,*
*This fate of ours is each one's bane,*
*To sleep beneath the stars each night,*
*To walk and walk again in flight.*
*The road is dark, the road is long,*
*Our hearts are loud, our hearts are strong,*
*The light is our clan and the day ahead,*
*All we ask is* kaff *and bread.'*

The whole clan joined the Verse:

*'Our people walk and walk again,*
*This fate of ours is each one's bane,*
*To sleep beneath the stars each night,*
*To walk and walk again in flight.*

One of the young girls, a distant cousin of Arvol's wife spoke up.

*'Thank you gods for giving my mother,*
*For giving my father to me and no other.*
*I love them both and love my clan,*
*Watch over us and our guest, that man.'* She pointed at Daryo as she said the last words and many of the clan laughed as they continued.

*'Our people walk and walk again,*
*This fate of ours is each one's bane,*
*To sleep beneath the stars each night,*
*To walk and walk again in flight.'*

Daryo spoke.
*'Although the Towers have long since gone,*
*But brotherhood lasts as roads are long,*
*The roads stretch on, our legs walk forth,*
*We walk different ways, my road leads north.'*
*'Our people walk and walk again,*
*This fate of ours is each one's bane,*
*To sleep beneath the stars each night,*
*To walk and walk again in flight.'*
'Peace, my kin,' said Arvol. 'Who is next on watch?'
'I am, Arvol,' said one of the older women.
'Watch the fire in here until all are asleep then douse it,' Arvol told her. 'We should rest; there is still a lot of distance to cover to Bhal. Daryo, there is space in my *kaff* that you are welcome to.'
'I am very grateful,' said Daryo. He was shown the *kaff* and wrapped himself in his hammock and blanket. Arvol, his wife, two other couples and the two young girls also shared the space and the combined heat kept the *kaff* warm through the night. Daryo woke just before dawn and slid out of the *kaff* carefully, taking his things and packing them outside. One of the women was on guard and saw Daryo.
'Daryo, kin of Dostan, you are leaving?' she asked softly.
'I have a long way to travel,' he told her. 'If I remain, Arvol will want to offer me food and further shelter. I cannot impose on your clan.'
'You walk to a destination? The lake?'
'No, west. To Yashoun.'
'Walk safely.' She helped him put his pack on. 'Follow our road, it will lead you into Three Rivers.'
'My thanks. Gods' Guidance.'
'Gods' Guidance, Daryo, kin of Dostan.'
As the sun rose, Daryo started along the stone-paved road, a welcome change from the muddy path. The rain had cleared away and the sun was beginning to peek through the clouds. A flight of birds soared overhead following the road too. When he was well away and out of sight of Arvol's clan's camp he stopped to eat before continuing.

Three Rivers was named for the streams, the Haimze and the Ohlaz, coming together to form the Soiliy, which then flowed to the Dithithindil. Daryo had visited several times as an apprentice and on his travels and found that the Vidmarian invasion to the south-east had caused the old wooden walls to be replaced with higher and stronger ones, taller watchtowers, reinforced gates and a water-filled moat diverted from the rivers. The guards at the gates were armed, armoured and alert. Daryo saw at least seven bows aimed in his direction as he approached the south gate. He was questioned sharply, his effects searched and firmly told to spend no longer than three days in town. Daryo promised to leave the next day and made his way for the Midstream Inn. He had learned in Yashoun that the place to learn any news of war, politics, scandal or famine was not the house of the landowner or the temple square, it was the inn. Sat in the darkest booth he listened to the tumult around him as the inn filled that evening. The talk was mostly of the ageing lord of Lalbi who, it was rumoured, had forsaken his wife for a stable-boy but he also heard that there had been Vidmarian raiding parties crossing the Dithithindil from the fortress at Lichon and attacking travellers on the river road. Several travelling caravans had been wiped out and troops sent from Thiel to secure the road had been destroyed as well. *The only safe road is north*, he overheard a Gourmini courier saying. Daryo made the decision that safer was best and that he would head north.

The road north joined the Riy and Daryo reached the crossroads town of Tonamaz by dusk. The inn refused a Batribi guest and, when threatened by the town pickets, Daryo was forced to sleep in the open and slept badly. He was on the road before dawn, cold and unhappy. He was soon passing the Riy ford and came to the foot of the Crumbled Temple's cliff. Salifa was visible in the distance and he considered whether or not to stop in the town. Officially he may still be wanted by the town pickets. Unofficially he had lived there for most of his life and had learned much there from the School of the Temple and the smith. However the experience in Tonamaz had surprised him. He had become used to the welcoming nature of the Boskinian and Adacan peoples and the suspicion of Batribi held by many Jaboen had faded in his memory. He wondered vaguely if the column of smoke was the forge. There was another way in.

North of the town, alongside the river was a culvert, used to help prevent the town flooding. Daryo waited for dusk and then stashed all except his knife in the culvert, checking that the urn of ashes in the top was safe and intact, before crawling through the tunnel. It was just passable and at the far end was the drain beside the river. He clambered out as soon as there was peace and then he hurried along the street, ducking into recesses and alleys- a Batribi in town would stand out. He reached the house that he wanted and knocked quickly. The door opened and the aged smith looked out.
'Can I help you?' he asked. Then he squinted and his jaw dropped open. 'Daryo!'

'Vehllal.'

'Come in! Come in!' The old man almost dragged Daryo in and closed the door. The house had changed very little in almost nine summers. Vehllal had gone completely grey, he had grown a thick beard, his eyes were rheumy, more so than Daryo remembered. 'By the Gods! I never thought I would see you again, boy! Sit! Sit!' Daryo did as he had been told. 'Have a drink, tell me, how are you?'

Daryo accepted a cup of wine and took a swallow. 'I am well, Master. How are you?'

'Master? You have not been my apprentice for many seasons! I am Vehllal. So, tell me, what have you done since you left? Do you still have my shield?'

'I do. I have had it repainted but it is yours.' Daryo then detailed what he had done in the time since he had left: the Order, Yashoun, the Silver Island, his fighting in southern Jaboen, his experience in Boskinia and his journeys and battles in Ishter and Adaca before explaining how he had finally returned to Salifa.

Vehllal chuckled. 'Dule's Anvil, Daryo, you must be weary! You have done more since you left than you ever would have done staying here as a smith. A warrior, a general and a hero, not even the Gods could have foreseen it all! How much different to the youth who sharpened blades at my grindstone!'

Daryo laughed. 'I have learned much since leaving but I have learned much here as well. It did not feel right to pass Salifa and not to speak with you.'

Vehllal smiled. 'And I thank you. You should sleep here tonight. You cannot sleep at the Olives and Ferret and I will not have my old apprentice sleeping in a drain.'

'My thanks, Vehllal. You have always been most kind to me.'

'I am guided by the Pantheon of Gods, Daryo. You know this. I would not turn away anyone to have to sleep under the open sky and least of all the man who was the boy who was my apprentice.'

'Have you not had another apprentice?'

'I have had several but they have been poor; none that warrant my time or patience. They boy that I have currently is the best that I have had but he is doing his apprenticeship because he was told to do so, he has no passion or talent.'

The pair sat up long into the night, drinking wine and discussing the past seasons. As midnight passed, Vehllal fashioned a mattress from straw and found blankets. Daryo slept soundly and safely in his old friend's home.

# Chapter 74

At some point long in history, a Yashoun official had decided that there should be a permanent guard post at the Jaboen border at Taam. The border was an earthern wall, topped by a fence, with a gap in it that allowed the road to pass through. Over time the Yashoun town had grown, the Jaboen town's very name had been lost and the sizeable twin settlements had merged together but for the wall down the centre. And the guard post, which had morphed into an inspection post. It seemed that an official later in the ages had decided to count everyone and everything that passed into Yashoun through the gap in the dyke at Taam. Daryo had everything in his bag removed, studied and handed back to him to replace. His swords were examined and even the colour of his cloak noted. The young woman scribe thanked him politely, the guard over his shoulder pointed out of the door and Daryo gratefully stepped past the young woman, out of the wooden corridor that was one of dozens and into Yashoun.

Northern Yashoun was covered by a vast tract of bare rock, sand and earth. There were no water courses and nothing grew. For this reason, they were known generally as the Northern Wastes. Daryo had crossed them once and had wanted to cross into Yashoun via the river road in the south of Jaboen. The Vidmarians had put this beyond attainment, bringing him to Taam. Daryo had crossed the Wastes once before with the Yashoun army. He knew that most travellers crossed in caravans, which assembled in the Courtyard.

The Courtyard had once been the contained side area of the Yashoun squire's home. When it had been demolished and a replacement built elsewhere in the town, the newly three-sided courtyard had become the favoured assembly point for caravans due to its openness and its adjacency to the town gate. Daryo identified a single caravan-master in the Courtyard, his status shown by the bright yellow cloth wrapped around his head against the dust. He saw Daryo approach and held up his hands.

'Stop there, Batribi. I am not hiring.'

Daryo smiled ingratiatingly. 'That is convenient; I am not looking for work. I am a traveller.'

'Where do you go?'

'Ossmoss.'

'Do not Batribi travel in clans?'

'I travel on a personal mission.'

The caravan-master nodded. 'Two gold halves.'

'What does two gold halves get me?'
'A horse, safety and supplies to cross the Wastes to Rotir.'
'Reasonable.' Daryo handed over the money and the caravan-master pointed to a large black horse.
'He is yours. Gelding, only five years old, good strong mount.'
'My thanks.'
'And you may be interested in my servant too.'
'I may?'
The master pointed to the other side of the courtyard. A very large Batribi was loading an equally large horse. Daryo strapped his bag, both his and Dava's shields and, after some thought, his sword belt to his mount and then went across.
'Gods' Watch,' he said. 'I am Daryo, kin of Dostan.'
'Yoare, kin of nobody and no-one.' The huge man, nearly a foot taller than Daryo and almost the same wide, glared down at him. 'You are travelling?'
'Yes.'
'You should see to your horse.'
The Batribi stalked away. Daryo shrugged and went back to his horse. A slim young woman with a thick plait of red hair and dark eyes was struggling to lift her saddle bags onto a particularly fine grey mare. Daryo went to help. She looked a little startled that Daryo was Batribi but then looked grateful. 'I am very grateful.'
Daryo inclined his head. 'I am glad to have helped. Are you going to Ossmoss?'
'Paloss. My father lives there.'
'He has a fine eye for horses.'
The woman giggled nervously. 'Not him, me. I chose her.'
'A beautiful animal.' Daryo stroked the horse's neck. 'You live in Paloss?'
'I did. I now live in Taam, I am doing business for my father. And you?'
'I am going to Ossmoss. An old friend died, I am taking his remains home.'
'That is very considerate of you. Most selfless.'
'I have promised to serve those who need it.'
The girl thought for a moment. 'The caravan goes only to Rotir. Perhaps we could ride to the Twin Ports together.'
'Perhaps we could,' said Daryo with a smile.
The caravan-master had mounted his horse and whistled loudly. 'Assemble outside the gate!' He kicked his horse on.
Eight people and nine horses assembled outside the gate beside the road: the caravan-master and Yoare the Batribi, Daryo and the girl, whose name was Jeda, a woman of

about Daryo's age with two men who were undoubtedly guards and a Yashoun merchantman who wore a black cloth around his head like the caravan-master and was obviously used to crossing the Wastes.

'I am Tadacto, I am caravan-master. I have spent my entire life crossing the Northern Wastes of Yashoun. The Wastes are full of freak winds, dust storms, heat and sudden cold. There is no road. There are few springs. If you do not stay with the caravan, you will die. You will obey any instruction I give. Yoare was born in these wastes. You will obey any instruction Yoare gives. Stay together, obey instructions and your gold will not have been wasted. Put the others in danger and we will leave you in the Wastes at the mercy of the Fourth Goddess and believe my words that she loves this land. Many come to her from them. Questions?'

'How long will the journey take?' asked one of the guards with the older woman.

'Five nights. Anyone else? Good.' Tadacto pulled his horse around and kicked it on. Daryo allowed the merchant and Jeda to pass him and then kicked his horse to join the line. He found himself alongside the other woman in the group. Yoare, riding his massive horse, took the rear-guard place.

Daryo took a quick look at the woman riding next to him. She was slightly older than he was, her blond hair bound by a scarf and she was wearing a richly-embroidered purple tunic and highly-polished boots. She glanced nervously at Daryo and he smiled politely before averting his eyes.

'Sorry, I am not being polite,' she said. 'My name is Zalahana.'

'Daryo the Walker, kin of Dostan. Are you going to the Twin Ports?'

The woman glanced over her shoulder. 'I am. To Ossmoss. To be married.'

'Congratulations,' said Daryo. The woman glanced over her shoulder again and cast her eyes down. 'You do not seem happy.'

She looked up. 'I have never met my husband. My uncle has arranged the marriage. My father is dead and I have not found myself a husband so my uncle arranged it. I am told the man is good and rich, handsome...'

'But you have never met him.'

'No.'

One of the guards rode up next to them. She cast her eyes down again. Daryo met the guards eye and got only a hard glare in return. He looked forwards and saw only the other members of the caravan and the flat brown dusty plain in front stretching to the horizon.

Camp was made against the foot of a low cliff. From the caravan's pack horse were a series of tents, simple pairs of poles that were tied at the top that came apart to form the props for the spine pole. Daryo assisted Yoare with erecting the tents but got only a glare in response. Tadacto built a fire and cooked pieces of pork on a spit. His work on the tents disregarded by the other Batribi, Daryo sat down next to the fire. Jeda sat down next to him.

'I have travelled on caravans a few times,' she said. 'Travellers do not normally help put up the tents.'

'I like to keep myself busy,' Daryo told her. 'What business do you do for your father?'

'He works salting and packing fish. He sells it in much of Yashoun and in Jaboen. I sell it for him in Taam and Salifa.'

'Why are you returning?'

'I am returning the receipts and order details to him. I do the same journey every two months.'

'Do you enjoy business?'

'I do in its way. I like the satisfaction of making a good deal and I meet many different people. I may try and get to Hef by autumn and try and get some new business from there. You seem to be something other than a person doing a favour for a deceased friend.'

'What makes you say so?'

'You have two shields and a fantastic curved sword on your baggage and you are still wearing two swords on your back.'

Daryo smiled. 'You never know what you might meet on the road.'

'There were stories that I heard that a mighty Batribi warrior threw the Vidmarian army out of Boskinia.'

'Do I look like a mighty warrior?'

Jeda laughed. 'You could do in the fire-light. Yes, I think so. Very fearsome.' Daryo laughed with her. 'Have you looked much at her?' Jeda pointed discreetly to Zalahana.

'Why?'

'She is not going willingly on this journey. Those guards are not here to protect her; they are here to make sure that she arrives where she is supposed to arrive.'

Daryo was intrigued. 'How do you know this?'

'My father employs men to protect our warehouses and wagons. They stay close to their targets and watch everything around them. These two stand at a distance and watch her.'

Daryo had made the same assessment earlier in the day but was impressed that the young girl had reached the same conclusion. 'An enforced marriage then.'

'I think so. It is quite common in Yashoun. If the person forcing her to marry is in Yashoun, he may have even been paid by the new husband for her. But she is Jaboen, she is not used to this sort of marriage and obviously does not want to marry a stranger.'
'Would you?'
Jeda smiled. 'My father would never force me to marry.'
'But you would not comply if he did?'
'I doubt that I would.'
Tadacto brought around the chunks of pork and pieces of bread. Zalahana was eating alone, her escorts several yards away. The merchant had learned that he had a mutual acquaintance of the caravan-master and they were conversing in low voices.
The sun dropped and the temperature followed. Most of the travellers got closer to the fire but for Yoare, who disappeared with a lit torch, and Zalahana, who had retired to her tent. Jeda was talkative and inquisitive and Daryo's stories of smithing in Salifa and travelling to the Silver Island were not enough. Eventually he confided in her with the story of his time in the Order, which was met with even more excited questions. They were the last to retire to their respective tents.

The caravan was moving not long after dawn. Tadacto led them north-west before turning south-west. The caravan headed into a low ravine, Tadacto at the front, Yoare keeping Zalahana and her escorts close to the rest, the ground was dry with rock walls that rose to almost twenty feet on either side. Daryo was riding just behind Tadacto and called forwards.
'Are you sure this route is safe, sir?'
Tadacto glanced back. 'Should it not be?'
'If I wanted to ambush a caravan, I would do it here.'
'Master Daryo, are you a caravan-master with over two hundred journeys' experience?'
'No, sir, I am not.'
'My thanks for your advice, Master Daryo.'
Tadacto urged his horse on to a canter. Daryo frowned and did likewise.
'Is there a problem?' he called.
Tadacto had rounded a bend in the ravine and looked back. 'I thought it wise to investigate around the corner. As you said, this is a good spot for an ambush.'
Daryo smiled. 'I have some experience in these matters.'
'A soldier?'
'I have been.'

Tadacto nodded as they rode. 'I have been my whole life on caravans. A servant like Yoare and now master.'
'It must be an interesting task though. Many different people and purposes.'
Tadacto shrugged. 'Perhaps.'

They were almost out of the ravine, Tadacto said, when they stopped for the night. Cloud obscured the stars and the only light came from the fire. Yoare again lit his torch and disappeared into the darkness. Daryo retired early, feeling drained by the riding. Jeda had spent another day asking him about his past and then the evening telling him about her own life. She was talkative but interesting, younger than Daryo, only just in her twentieth summer, but confident despite her youth. He enjoyed her company. The Yashoun merchant, Hukad, was a trader in stone wares and was returning to Paloss for goods. Zalahana had refused any conversation from anyone and had ridden in silence. Daryo tried to put his companions from his mind and sleep.

The scream was barely human. Daryo was sharing his tent with Hukad and they were both woken by it.
'An animal?' asked Hukad sleepily.
Daryo groped for his bags. 'I think not.'
There was a small thump and the scream cut off. Daryo drew the Horse from its scabbard and gave it to Hukad as they scrambled out of the tent, then drew the Bear and grabbed his shield. A figure loomed out of the dark and Daryo raised his shield but it was Zalahana.
'Dead, they're dead!' she breathed.
'Look after her!' Daryo told Hudak and ran down to where Jeda, Zalahana and her guards' tents were. The guards were indeed both dead, stuck with arrows, Jeda still cowering in her tent.
'Stay there,' Daryo instructed quietly. He stayed away from the fire and crept along the opposite wall of the ravine. He almost tripped over a huddled figure and started to raise his sword before realising that it was Tadacto. There was a thick arrow sticking out of his back.
'Right...' he breathed. 'You were right...'
'Not now,' said Daryo. 'How many? Do you know?'
'Three... four... ten...'
Daryo left him and decided that, given where the guards were, the attackers had started at that end of the camp, then moved down to where Tadacto was and would now be

moving towards the end of the ravine to attack on the level. He hurried back to where he had left Hudak and Zalahana.

'Can you use a sword?' he asked Hudak in a whisper.

'After a fashion,' was the response.

Daryo quickly dove into the tent and emerged with Temma's Sword, which he gave to Hudak in exchange for the Horse. 'Stay here. Jeda's still in her tent but safe. Tadacto's hurt by the fire. Look after Zalahana.'

Daryo reversed the Bear in his left hand and started up the ravine following his intuition. He paused after a dozen yards to let his eyes get accustomed to the darkness. Careful not to put himself between anyone incoming and the fire, he crept forwards again. His feeling had been correct. He identified five shapes coming towards him out of the dark. He crouched behind a large boulder and allowed all five to pass him before sliding out of cover and slitting the throat of the backmarker. The other four heard the man's cut-short scream and turned but Daryo was too quick. Two had bows but no arrows ready; the other two had rough, blunt swords. A flurry of steel and all four lay dead alongside their comrade. Daryo returned to the other travellers.

'Anyone hurt?' he asked.

Hudak shook his head. Zalahana whimpered. Daryo went and retrieved Jeda from her tent. She was shaking but unhurt. He escorted her to Hudak and then found Tadacto. The caravan-master was dead so Daryo returned to the others.

'The guards and Tadacto are dead,' he told them. 'I have not found Yoare.'

'He left the camp when he had set up the tents,' said Zalahana in a small voice. 'Perhaps he is somewhere safe.'

Daryo nodded. 'If the Fourth Goddess is satisfied, perhaps he is.'

'Should we remain here?' asked Hudak.

'It would be unwise to leave now. We have no light to see by.'

'We are lost,' moaned Zalahana. 'Tadacto was navigating. We are lost.'

'True but I have crossed the wastes before. The easiest, although longer route for us, is to simply head west.'

Hudak nodded in understanding. 'We would come to the Salt River. Which we can then follow south to Rotir.'

'As you say.'

'How far is the Salt River?'

'I cannot say. I do not know exactly where we are but it cannot be more than about three days' ride. Perhaps four.'

'Four days?'

'Four days.'

Dawn came and Daryo mounted first and scouted ahead. There was no sign of life. He returned and helped Hudak and the women strike camp. They decided to keep only the horses that they needed, four riders and the pack horse, and Jeda let the rest go free. They kept just two tents and the other necessary essentials, loaded the baggage and Daryo took two bows from the slain bandits and Tadacto's short sword, which he gave to Hudak. They then started west.

## Chapter 75

The day was exceptionally hot and Daryo realised it was just a few days from Midsummer's Day. He hoped he would be in the Twin Ports by then. Zalahana looked just as reluctant to be riding west as she had been when they left Taam. Hudak told her that she was free to return to Taam or continue to whatever destination she chose but she stayed with the others. Jeda rode alongside Daryo, refusing to let him get more than a few yards away. Once clear of the rocks, the land became featureless and bare. The dust swirled across the rocky ground in the breeze and at the pace of the horses' hooves. The sun burned down unobscured. A single bird wheeled above and the horses plodded onwards.

'Do other caravans travel this way?' Daryo asked Hudak, who was riding just behind him.

'They would be coming east,' said the Yashoun merchant. 'Tadacto was the only caravan in Taam. But all the caravans go by different routes. Part of learning to be a caravan-master is that they must learn a route across the Wastes by memory alone. It is bad for business if your travellers die of thirst or heat or you get lost in the Wastes.'

'Very bad for business,' agreed Daryo. 'I thought if we came across one, they may be willing to turn about and guide us a faster route to Rotir.'

'They may be. We may be going too far north to get to the river. You sound as if you have passed this way before.'

'I have. I was with the Yashoun army many summers ago. Nine summers.'

'You were a Yashoun soldier?'

'Not so exactly.'

Hudak chuckled. 'You are a mysterious man, Daryo. A traveller armed like a warrior and a pilgrim that fights like a soldier.'

'I am as you say. I am a warrior. A warrior taking the remains of an old comrade home.'

'What kind of a warrior?' asked Jeda.

'One that swore his sword to those who needed someone to fight for them.' Daryo patted the top of his pack with his hand. 'My comrade's name was Dava. He gave his entire life serving others and serving the Pantheon. This is all I can do for him: to take him home.'

'A worthy task,' said Hudak. 'In some future day, I hope someone will do as good to me.'

'I plan to die in bed surrounded by my children,' said Jeda. 'In many, many years' time, as I have no children. Or husband.'

'The former does not necessarily require the latter,' said Daryo with a grin and Hudak chuckled again.

'It is what is correct though,' Jeda said quickly.
'Indeed,' Daryo agreed. 'You have no plans for a husband?'
'No. I am young and my father is happy that I work hard for his business. You?'
'I am a wandering man of war; I have had little time for a wife. Hudak?'
Hudak shook his head. 'My wife died of a bad wound two summers ago.'
'I am very sorry, Hudak.'
'My thanks. I miss her but am content that she walks with the Fourth Goddess. She will care for Mati until I join her.'
'As it should be.'

Daryo called a halt shortly before sundown to pitch the tents in a depression. There was little fuel but Hudak and Jeda managed to improvise a small fire. Daryo left everything but Temma's Sword and scouted the area. Finding no threat, he returned to their little camp. Jeda had the Bear in her hands and was swinging it wildly. She stopped when she saw Daryo.
'My apologies, Daryo. I thought I should learn to protect myself.'
'Not like that,' he said with a smile. He went to his baggage and exchanged Temma's Sword for the Horse. 'You are likely to injure yourself swinging a blade that way. Take a grip with both hands.' Jeda did so. 'You are not going to beat most opponents for strength so you must use speed and guile.' He swung gently from the right and Jeda blocked it. Daryo withdrew his blade. 'Keep the point at my face, or at my throat, the blade should be in front of you. Keep your arms flexed, stay relaxed. You are small so many attacks will come high. Thus.' He swung down the right, Jeda parried, he swung from the left, the right again, the left, the right and left. Jeda parried each gentle swing. 'Good. Again.' He repeated the pattern and she parried each. 'Again.' This time he moved quicker and Jeda barely stopped his swings. 'An enemy will not attack the same way twice if he is smart. You must be alert to stop whatever he does.'
Jeda nodded earnestly and parried the next pattern. At the end of the sixth swing, Daryo stabbed forwards, the point of the Horse just touching Jeda's chest before he stopped. She sighed. 'You killed me.'
'I did.'
'I did not stay alert.'
'You did not. But you are learning. That is the most important thing. Stop for now, we have ridden a long way. Practise with Hudak later.'
Jeda handed the Bear back. 'My thanks, Daryo.'
'You are most welcome.'

She went back to the fire. Hudak brought a piece of salt pork and bread to Daryo.
'My thanks.'
'Jeda is keen.'
'Young,' said Daryo and Hudak laughed.
'You are...twenty-five, twenty-seven summers?'
Daryo shrugged. 'I have no way of knowing. I remember... eighteen but I know by my growth and experience that I am likely of twenty-five or twenty-six.'
'Jeda has seen about twenty-one. She is not that much younger than you, my friend.'
This was met with a sigh. 'I was raised as a Ward of the School of the Temple in Salifa, did my apprenticeship as a blacksmith and then learned to be a warrior. I have travelled from Adaca to the Silver Island and most places in between. I have killed countless enemies and been gravely wounded many times. She is so much younger than I am.'
Hudak nodded. 'Perhaps so.'

They started early and continued west. Jeda's horse was not bred for endurance. It was a fine-looking and lean animal but highly energetic and it struggled without regular water and good food. The other animals were happy grazing the sparse vegetation that they found and drinking poor water but Jeda's mare soon got weak and slow. The result was that it had to follow on a long rein with Jeda riding with Daryo on his mount. He tried to ignore her arms holding around his waist. The day was as hot as the one preceding it. No clouds obscured the sun and Daryo ensured that he wore only what was necessary but that all his skin was covered. Jeda and Hudak were both accustomed to the Wastes and did likewise but Zalahana complained about being told to cover her skin, citing the heat. Daryo cajoled, Hudak dismissed her and Jeda took a long time trying to persuade her to listen. Eventually it was only when her skin was looking pink and dry that she relented. She then spent the afternoon hours complaining that her skin was dry and sore. Daryo used some of their water to dampen a scarf that he cut in half and wrapped around her arms, the worst affected parts. This, he knew, would produce a stinging sensation and so Zalahana refused to ride any further. The other three decided that there was little point in continuing with her so unhappy and they found a low rock pile to set camp in the lee of. As soon as the tents were pitched and the horses tethered, Jeda requested another lesson on the sword. Daryo handed over Temma's Sword and took with him his shield and secreted his knife behind it.
'Attack is the best defence,' he told her, moving a short distance from the tents. 'All I ask is that you get past the shield.'

Jeda swung Temma's Sword a few times in preparation and then slashed at Daryo. He easily blocked with his shield, she tried a few more times and he blocked each time.
'How?' Jeda asked eventually.
Daryo smiled. 'Try to put me off balance, make me open my guard, then use your speed to get inside.'
Jeda tried again, using wide attacks and then stabbing forwards. Gradually she improved. Despite the heat she persisted with her practise, driving her attacks forwards with increasing skill until Daryo decided that they were both ready for a rest. On the next thrust, he countered with a charge, shoving her blade aside and pulled out his knife. Jeda tried to retreat but tripped and landed on her backside. Daryo landed on top of her, throwing Temma's Sword aside and finishing with his knife to her breast. He found himself stopping. She was sweating, her face was red and her hair wet.
'Be ready for anything,' he told her quietly.
'I am.'


'Trouble?' asked Hudak, clambering up the rocks to where Daryo was sat.
'I have not seen any.' It was approaching dawn and there was just enough life to see by.
'You seemed to leave the fire and climb up here rather swiftly.'
'Just a feeling. The Fourth Goddess whispering in my ear perhaps.'
'Or the Third God dropping his stars.'
'Dropping stars?'
Hudak smiled. 'A child's tale, very common in Yashoun. The stars in the sky are the Third God's and in the morning he drops them into the sea to make the water sparkle. Sometimes he misses and that makes all the little noises that one hears in the night.'
Daryo chuckled. 'A lovely story. Perhaps the Third God is dropping stars.'
'The Fourth Goddess whispers to you?'
'I have been in many battles. I have sent many men to her. She will want me alongside her. She whispers in the ears of most warriors, trying to persuade them to do foolish or dangerous things in combat so that she can get her hands to them.'
'You have managed to ignore her thus far.'
'I have. And I know many men and women who have been in many more situations that I and for many more seasons and never fallen prey.'
'Your friend.'
'Indeed. Other former comrades are scattered to the winds too.'
'Why do you call yourself the Walker?'

'Each of the Order of the Shield and Sword took a sword name to identify themselves, their character and their experience. I spent much of my time there walking and come from a people who are known for walking from place to place. It seemed a good name.'
'Most fitting.'
The pair were nearly thirty feet from the ground, the camp at the bottom, and some movement around the camp distracted them. Jeda emerged from her tent, her pale skin and red hair unmistakeable, dressed in just a shirt. She looked around and stumbled behind a rock for privacy. The men averted their eyes.
'She has a real fire for you.'
Daryo glanced back towards her. 'Just a young girl's fancy... she is a very nice young woman.'
'Very confident and keen. Zalahana is ten summers older and yet behaves as if she is ten summers younger.'
'Foolish.'
'Privileged. She has never had to do things herself or obey instructions.'
'I would find that dull beyond reason.'
Hudak chuckled. 'I think I would too.' He looked east. 'Sunrise.'
'We should wake Zalahana and start moving. I hope that we are within a day of the Salt River.'
'If we stay here, with this vantage, we may be able to see it in the light.'
Daryo shook his head. 'Better that we move before it gets too hot. When we find the river, we will be able to ride easier without having to check our course. As long as we go upriver we will reach Rotir.'
Hudak nodded. 'As you wish.'

They reached the river late in the afternoon. It was narrow and fast and known for the brackish nature of its water, too salty to drink, hence its moniker of Salt River. After a brief rest, they turned south and followed the river upstream. Several wading birds skittered around in the shallow pools alongside the river and occasionally a small fish jumped from the water. The sight of Rotir's light came just after sundown and it was the last night that they spent in the open.

Rotir was a small and rather dilapidated waypoint- a temple of the First God, the town's name was even an old version of the modern name of the god, Dravin, a small longhouse in the centre of the town that lacked several coats of paint and an inn that could barely accommodate a dozen people. The innkeeper was a morose individual and grudgingly gave them two rooms, complaining that the caravans were fewer and fewer than they used to be and that the barges on the Dithithindil and the longer but safer oversea route from Nalb in Jaboen to the Twin Ports, were between them destroying Rotir. Zalahana announced that she was staying in Rotir while she decided what to do next. Hudak had business in the town. Only Daryo and Jeda rode west the next day.

The Twin Ports of Ossmoss and Paloss lined the banks of the Dithithindil just ten miles from where the river's tides became one with the seas. Although forever known as twins, the two cities were equally known for their distinct personalities; Ossmoss, the northern twin, was the city of the Emperor, the imperial palace dominated the city's skyline, three huge square towers looming over the smart stone-built houses, artistically paved plazas, libraries, temples and baths, pleasure barges lining the river; Paloss was the grittier side of the city, the docks were those that served the tradesmen, an immense canopied market, wooden houses and shacks linked by dirty roads and the Old Fort, a wood and earth military post built on a hill beside the Dithithindil east of the city.
'Where exactly do you need to go to?' Jeda asked Daryo as they passed through Ossmoss' Rotir Gate.
'The burial ground on this side of the river.'
Jeda nodded. 'My father lives on the north side, although the warehouse is in Paloss. I am sure that he would let you stay for as long as you wish.'
'My thanks but I am sure I can find an inn.'
'I insist.'
Daryo smiled. 'As you wish. Tell me where to find your father's house and I will join you there.'
'I would like to stay with you.'
'As you wish,' he repeated. 'The temple seems like the logical place to ask after the burial ground.'
'I know the quicker way, across the town.'
'I follow your lead.'

The Great Temple of the Pantheon was the foundation of the faith. The Reverend Apostle, the chosen leader of the faith, had his seat in the centre of the grand dome. The Great Temple itself was a single, colossal dome at the centre, entered by the North Door, with eight smaller domes around it like petals around a flower, the largest and grandest close to the door for the First God Dravin, to the right, and the First Goddess Tahili, to the left. They then progressed around the centre, to the Fourth God Dule and the

Fourth and Darkest Goddess behind the Reverend Apostle's throne. The benches for worshippers were of dark wood with ornately carved legs and progressed from the central altar and the Reverend Apostle's chair across the lime floor to the North Door. Each sept was fronted by a carved stone symbol of the God or Goddess that was worshipped within and the Eightfold Circle hung laterally above the altar.

'Do you have the faith?' Daryo murmured to Jeda, and she nodded. 'I would like to offer some prayers for my friend before anything.'

'Of course.'

Daryo put down his pack and removed the urn of Dava's remains and led the way to the left, passing Tahili's six-foot wheatsheaf sculpture, Brokea's flame, Spinel's crystal and finally leaving his pack by the dead moon of the Fourth Goddess. The plastered walls of the sept were painted black. The small altar was a single piece of black stone with a dead moon carved into the front and with a single candle burning on the top. Daryo drew Temma's sword and placed it alongside the urn on the altar.

He knelt before the altar and closed his eyes. He sensed Jeda kneel next to him. He took several long, slow breaths and allowed his mind to clear before speaking in a whisper. 'Darkest of Goddesses, cruellest of tricksters, guide of the dead, power in my sword-arm and strength behind my shield, I bring before you the ashes of a dear friend and a servant of yours that walks with you. Guard him in death as you did in life. Here at the end of my pilgrimage, I offer once more my blade to your service. Continue to guide me through battle and through conflict. Accept my gift of my skill with sword and spear to continue to yield up men for your realm. Strengthen my shield and armour against my foes that I may continue to work for your ends. My life has always been yours and I know that I am destined to join you as all men are. I ask only that you allow me to keep living my life in your service and that you allow me to serve you in this world before you call me to the next kingdom to serve you in that world.' He fell silent.

After a long moment, Jeda's voice said softly. 'Darkest Goddess, guide Daryo through this world. I ask that you allow him to stay in this world for as long as you are able. I ask that you guide him away from any battle he does not need to fight and that you calm the hearts of those around him that they do not wish to send him to you. Allow him to come to you in your own time.'

Daryo smiled to himself, stood up and retrieved his sword and Dava's urn. 'Come, we should find a priest and ask about the burial. And thank you.'

Jeda grinned. 'I thought a little extra might help.'

'Indeed. I hope it does. I have no wish to join Dava any sooner than necessary.'

## Book 6- The Smith
## Chapter 76
## The Second Day of Spring in the Nineteenth Year of the Reign of King Lallano the Second of Adaca

The Adacan cliffs ran from just west of the port of Baros for over two hundred miles before falling away beside the mouth of the Bhaar River. In the lee of the clifftop before the slope to the river became steep was nestled a small village: just over two score houses, a bakery, dairy, smith, potter, a large inn and a small temple of the First Goddess. At the top of the cliffs was a winch, operated by mules that allowed miners to descend to a ledge midway down the cliff that was the opening of an ancient iron mine. Ritaro was a well-known source of ore and regular loads made their way east to Baros and south-west into Sodidor and the port of Zonathor. The houses were spread along the Baros-Zonathor road, a small square centred by a covered well and the unpaved track that led up to the mine's winch.

Daryo the blacksmith was walking back from the smelter with a dozen newly-made iron ingots in a sack. He hailed Dulithon the baker's apprentice on the square on his way back home. The forge was under a wooden canopy extending from the side of the house, the fire in a stone ring in the centre alongside the anvil, a workbench stood against the house wall, a grindstone and a young boy.

'Father, I cannot get it straight.' The boy held up a rough, half-made dirk.

Daryo smiled indulgently, putting the sack down beside the workbench. 'How long have you been helping in the forge, Stai?'

'Since winter, father.'

'I started my apprenticeship at a forge when I was twelve winters too. I was in my fifteenth winter before I made a dagger that my master was happy with. Swordsmithing is particularly difficult and needs practise.'

Stai put the dirk down on the anvil. 'Can I practise today, father?'

'Not today. I have the new wheels for the mine trucks to finish.'

'The next dawn?'

'The next dawn.'

Stai nodded, took his dirk and went inside. He was growing quickly, his skin was much lighter than his father's and his hair was a coppery brown rather than black and grew in tight curls. He was developing a strong build from helping Daryo in the forge and he had also recently started helping at the cattle farm. The priest was teaching him and the other youths of the village their letters. Daryo had noticed that recently his son had started to wear a hooded short-sleeved jerkin.

The smith got to work on the wheel rims for the trucks in the mine. The old wooden ones wore away very quickly on the floors of the tunnels through the cliff so the foreman had commissioned Daryo to make iron rims to reinforce the wheels and provide better wearing. The principle was simple: two strips of iron thirteen inches long, bent into a half-circle and then the edges folded in to form a slot for the wooden wheel to fit in. Then it was an even simpler task to make a series of perforations to allow the rim to be nailed to the wheel. The mine had seven carts, four wheels on each and each wheel required two half-circles to form the rim. With one made, fifty-five would take the rest of the day and most of the next. Daryo considered calling Stai back to assist but then saw another potential assistant.

'Kym, I could use some aid.'

Kym frowned. 'Aid?'

'I need someone to help me in forge.'

'Stai enjoys it. I can find him.'

Daryo sighed. 'He went inside the house.'

Kym went around the house towards the front door. She was almost as tall as Daryo but much more her mother's daughter than his- paler skin, browner hair than Stai, eyes the colour of chestnut, lean limbs and, at almost sixteen summers, becoming a feisty young woman. She was learning to weave but showed more interest in hunting. Instead of Stai's return, Vehllal came running around the corner, waving his wooden sword that Daryo had once carved for Kym.

'Father, I have been fighting bears!' he announced.

'For sure?' said Daryo, feigning concern. 'How many?'

'Dozens and dozens! And I killed every one!'

'Thanks to the Gods for our saviour!' The young boy, not long into his sixth winter, brandished his sword again. 'Would you like to assist me with some smithing?'

The boy lowered his sword. 'I have bears to fight.' He looked disappointed.

Daryo smiled. 'Go and fight them then.'

Vehllal's face came alive again; he roared his own little battle-cry and ran back around the house the way that he had come. He was much chubbier than either of his siblings had been and was much darker-skinned. In his face, most acquaintances likened him to his father while noting a distinct streak of recklessness and a lack of fear. His favourite clothing was his so-called armour than Daryo had fashioned with some help from a woodsman out of hazel branches and some lightweight chain as shoulder straps and cinched to his body by one of his mother's belts. This day he had rejected his armour for a leather tabard that had a thong that he could stow his sword in.

Stai almost collided with his charging brother as he returned. Daryo demonstrated how to make the nail holes in the wheel rims and after a few under supervision, he was happy to leave Stai to the task alone as he continued making the rims. The regular hammering of the smith was soon punctuated by the irregular thump of his son and apprentice.

'Stai, father, mother wants you both in to eat,' said Kym.

Midday had passed and Daryo gratefully laid down his hammer. Stai put his hammer and steel needle down. 'We have to stop?'

'Do not defy your mother,' warned Daryo. 'Go.'

Stai complied and Daryo quickly tidied his tools before going inside. The interior of the house was simple- the fire pit in the centre, a table and stools on the left, Daryo's bed and the chests and cupboards on the right, a ladder against the wall led into the second level in the roof where the children had their beds. The house was stone, increasingly common for the area, with a good wood and thatched roof. Jeda was already at table. She had recently cut her hair shorter, now if fell just to her shoulders and she had taken to wearing a Sodidoron headscarf over the winter. Dressed in her daily wear of a creamy linen dress and with a black apron tied around her waist, she looked particularly pretty and Daryo, as he often did, thought a quick prayer to the Third Goddess for bringing them together.

'Working hard?' she asked as Daryo sat down on the spare stool beside Stai.

'I want to get the wheel rims finished,' he told her. 'If I do not, I know what will happen.'

'The squire's horses will come for shoeing and you will still be making wheels.'

'Indeed.'

'I will help you finish, father,' said Stai.

'My thanks, Stai.'

'Then you two will have to help with the horses,' Jeda told the other children. 'The stables need clearing and all four need brushing.'

Kym nodded and continued eating. Vehllal looked upset. 'I have no horse.'

Daryo reached across and ruffled his hair. 'You can brush my horse' and that placated him.

After their meal, the smith and his son returned to their work. The pounding of hammers and the vicious hiss of hot metal in water filled the air again. Daryo had

acquired the habit of singing while he worked and to the sounds of the forge was added a Silver Island folk song that Stai listened to and he was soon joining in with the refrain.
'A free performance,' said a voice at the entrance.
Daryo put down his hammer. 'Hail Halidir. An early finish today?'
'The pleasure of being the farmer is that I have workers to do my labour for me.'
'The pleasure of being the smith is that I have a son to take over my labour for me.'
Halidir had only daughters.
'And he seems to be labouring well.'
Stai looked up from his perforations and smiled broadly. 'My thanks, Master Farmer.'
'What brings you to the forge, Halidir?'
'My nephew. He lives with my sister in Baros and has been made an officer of the militia. He will need a suitable sword and Tursi tells me that you have some skill making blades.'
'Tursi rarely lies,' said Daryo modestly. 'I have a couple of blades that could be finished or I could make one from new.'
'There is no great speed required. From new would be most satisfactory.'
Daryo nodded. 'I can do whatever you require but I think a soldier's sword, perhaps with some extra detailing on the blade?'
'Excellent.'
'Three gold halves?'
'Also excellent. When could you do it by?'
'If the squire's horses do not come... I could start in two days and it would take me another two. If I am shoeing the horses... maybe five days before I can start. And two days to do.'
'I am not going to Baros until the end of the season, so that is very good for me.'
Daryo inclined his head. 'I have a small amount of silver left; I will even give him a silver-coated pommel.'
'You are most kind, Master Daryo.' Halidir bought out his pounch and handed over a gold half. 'To see you through the production. The rest on delivery?'
'As you wish.'
Halidir clasped Daryo's hand, then Stai's. 'My thanks to both of you. I should go. It is my youngest, Hassisa's, born-day and I promised her a gift.'
'I can offer a horseshoe.'
Halidir laughed. 'I think not. Madam Alitini makes jewellery from shells and polished stones. Something pretty will be much more gratefully received, I think.'
Daryo chuckled. 'I think so. Gods' Guidance to you.'
'And to you.' Halidir winked at Stai and departed, walking back across the square.

The smith took a piece of chalk and wrote *steel sword, silver plate stone set pommel, detailing on blade* on a long, narrow piece of slate above his workbench; his list of jobs to be done. The sword joined *mine cart wheels* and *squire's horses* as well as *Jeda's ladle*, as his wife had decided that her old wooden ladle was not good enough for her needs. The different jobs had different priorities: the squire first and foremost as the work for him meant that the forge was kept free of rent, the mine carts were a paid job as Halidir's sword was, which meant that Jeda's ladle was a low priority, something perhaps for Stai to attempt in the evenings. Daryo turned back to his work; his son was already at work making the nail holes again. He checked a couple of examples of Stai's work, approved, and resumed his own work on making the wheel rims.

'I need a rest, father,' Stai announced about a few hours before sundown.

Daryo nodded and counted up their total. 'Thirty-one. We have done more than half. I think we can stop. Damp the fire for me.'

'Yes, father.'

Stai used a rake to spread the fire out from the centre of the circle and then covered it in saturated sacking from a bucket of water. A great hiss accompanied the fog of steam that rose and Stai scampered away.

'Stai!' barked Daryo and his son grabbed the corner of the house to stop himself. 'You have finished work. Where do you go?'

'Sorry, father.' Stai turned around and started towards the temple but then stopped. 'I would like to pray with you, father.'

'Your mother may not approve.'

'I want to.'

Daryo nodded. 'If that is what you want. Come along.'

Behind the forge was the small stable block where the family kept their horses: Daryo's black gelding, Jeda's chestnut mare, a smaller chestnut gelding that was Kym's and a bay mare that Stai could ride. On the bare grassland beyond, nearly a hundred yards from the stable, was a knee-high white stone block with a hammered bronze disk on the top. Daryo took his knife from his belt and laid it on the makeshift shrine before kneeling. After some hesitation, Stai pulled out the little knife that he kept, laid it on the altar and knelt beside his father, who nodded approvingly and closed his eyes. Stai closed his eyes too.

'Darkest of Goddesses, cruellest of tricksters, guide of the dead, power in my sword-arm and strength behind my shield,' intoned Daryo. 'I thank you once more for this chance to wield a smith's hammer in place of a blade. I thank you for rewarding my service to you with my wife, Jeda, my daughter, Kym, and my sons, Stai and Vehllal. I pray that you guide the souls of their namesakes through your kingdom. On this day I pray for the memory of Fayd the Vanguard and all others who fell at the Five Towers. Use them well in your service. My life has always been yours and I know that I am destined to join you as all men are. I ask only that you allow me to keep living my life in your service and that you allow me to serve you and my family in this world before you call me to the next kingdom to serve you in that world.' He knelt in silence for a few heartbeats before standing. Stai scrambled to his feet.

'I have never heard anyone pray to the Fourth Goddess before, Father.'

'Few people do unless they are remembering a special person that has died. I have known many very good friends who have died, so I pray to the Fourth and Darkest Goddess to guide those people now that they have died.'

'Were you a soldier, father?'

'How many times have you and your brother asked me that?'

'Many times, father.'

'And what have I always said?'

'That you have never been a soldier.'

'So why should the answer this day be anything different?'

'You spoke to the Goddess about your sword-arm and your shield.'

'Many people have shields and swords, Stai. Your mother has a sword. I am making a sword for Halidir's nephew.'

'You have three swords.'

'I do. Gifts.'

Stai looked unconvinced. 'You never use them.'

'No.'

Stai still wore the same expression but nodded. 'Would you like me to finish in the forge, Father?'

'I can do it. You can go home.'

'Can I see if Satilo is busy? We were going to go down to the river.'

'Of course. Be back by sundown.'

'Yes, Father.' Stai headed across the fields back towards the forge. Satilo was a boy who lived in the house next to the bakery. His parents worked for the squire's farm. He was the youngest of ten children and the same age as Stai. The two were firm friends. There were few children in the village of that age, less than ten, and only two that were within a season of Vehllal. There were few of Kym's age; many once old enough had left for Baros or a city in Sodidor. Daryo prayed silently alone for a while longer before returning to the forge and closing up for the night. There were still an hour or two before sundown and Daryo went into his home. Kym had gone to the squire's farm and Stai would be at the temple school learning his letters. Jeda was sat by the open window shutter beside the bed, her back to the door, using the best light to sew a rip in one of Vehllal's tunic. He crept up behind her and covered her eyes with his hands.

'The prince has come to whisk you away, Madam.'

Jeda laughed and put down her sewing. 'At your command, my prince.'

He kept one hand across her eyes and stroked down her neck, and chest to her belly with the other. Jeda hummed in contentment. Daryo stroked his hand down the side of his wife's face, rested his hand on her chest and kissed her neck.

'Work done for the day?'

'For this day. Stai has been a great help.'

'His father's industry.'

'His mother's generosity of time and attention.'

Jeda turned her head to allow Daryo to kiss her lips. He tightened his embrace as he did and they were interrupted by the door opening. Jeda looked under Daryo's arm.

'Kym, how was your day?'

'Interesting. I was speaking to Lady Asa.' Asa was the squire's wife. 'The Heart Festival is in eight days.' The Heart Festival was an Adacan tradition celebrating the love between wives and husbands, parents and children and the hope of those wishing to be parents.

'It is.' Daryo moved around behind his wife so that he could see Kym as well.

'Lady Asa asked if Dorso and I would be the Guardians.' Dorso was Asa's eldest son, slightly older than Kym. Part of the traditional celebrations were that the children of the village were taken away from home by a courting young man and woman known as the Guardians to allow the children's parents some time alone.

Jeda nudged Daryo and smiled. 'Are the Guardians not normally a young courting couple? Does that mean that Dorso and you are...?' Kym bit her lip and ducked her head in embarrassment. Jeda and Daryo exchanged smiles. Jeda got up and embraced her daughter. 'He is a wonderful young man.'

'We are not marrying, mother. Just... spending time together. He is teaching me use a bow and I showed him how to shoe a horse.'

Jeda chuckled. 'Spending time together is very important.' She released her hold on her daughter. 'Just do not forget your ageing parents.'

Kym laughed. 'You are not ageing.'

'All of us are ageing on this world, Kym,' Daryo told her. 'The day we do not age is the day we walk among the dead. You will be sixteen springs on the Summer's Eve. It may be time to consider courting, husbands, children...'

Kym laughed again. 'Not yet, father.'

'Then consider mothers, fathers and brothers,' Jeda said. 'Help me find some food to feed the starving menfolk of the family.'

'Yes, mother.'


'Father?'

Daryo looked up. Kym was standing by the entrance to the forge, twisting the corner of her tunic anxiously. It was dark, Daryo had been sharpening his curved sword by the light of a lantern. 'Kym. Is something wrong?'

'No. Not wrong. I have been thinking. I have always been your daughter more than mother's.'

Daryo smiled. Kym had always been the closest to Daryo by choice. 'What is it, Kym?'

'Can we walk?'

'Of course.' Daryo laid his sword down.

'Can... can you bring that?'

Daryo frowned. 'If you wish.' He slid the sword into his belt and took Kym's hand. They walked out behind the forge and across the grass beyond the stables. 'What were you thinking about?'

'What you and mother said: about husbands and children.'

'Oh?' They were alone in the darkness.

'You were not always a smith.'

'I did my apprenticeship with a smith named Vehllal in the town of Salifa, in Jaboen. It was he that we named your brother for.'

'Father, you always say that. You were an apprentice as a boy and you met mother just a few seasons before I was born. What about the years between? You can distract Stai and Vehllal but not me. I am too old to be distracted by words. You have a sword in your belt better than the squire's and then two more hung above your bed. You have a shield underneath the bed. You have arms painted on the anvil of the forge. What do they represent? The child, the jester and the milepost?'

'Kym... I do not wish to dwell on those years.'

'Father, I need to know what kind of man my father is before I could ever think of leaving home for a husband.' Kym stopped walking abruptly and seized Daryo's arm with both hands. 'I swear not to repeat a word.'

Daryo turned to her, her features obscured in the dark. 'With your heart, your mind and your honour?'

'Yes, Father.'

'I was an apprentice to a smith but was forced to leave Salifa. I was brought to an Order of men and women of war, the Order of the Shield and Sword. Members swore to defend the defenceless, to protect justice and righteousness and the oppressed. We took names to identify our characters. The image on the forge's arms, and on my shield, is representative of Kym the Harlequin, my tutor from the Order. You were named for her. The child is a blindfolded waif, the symbol of Leroyfa the Blind, who gave her life along with the Harlequin, to save my life and those of several children. The milepost is the symbol of my name: the Walker. The Order was betrayed by a former member and fell. Many died. I spent the rest of those years fulfilling my promise as a Member of the Order, fighting for needy and for what is right.'

'What was the promise?'

'With my heart, my mind and my honour, I promise to do my duty as a Member of the Order of the Shield and Sword. I swear my Shield and Sword to the defence of the just, the righteous, the innocent and the weak. By this oath, I pledge my sword and my service until I am discharged by death.'

'You were a warrior.'

'I was.'

'You killed.'

'Many people.'

'Why did you become a smith again?'

'When I met your mother, I promised her that I would give up walking the roads and care for what is important: her. I spoke with some people that I knew in Darsux and I found about the forge, we moved here and then we were blessed by the Second Goddess with you, Stai and Vehllal.'

'Would you have more children?'

'We would never decline a gift from the Gods.'

'Do you miss being a wanderer, father? It must have been a great adventure. New places and new people?'

'It was an adventure. But also very dangerous. I have many wounds and scars.'

'Do you miss it?'

'Sometimes. Yes, I do, sometimes. But if I was still the Walker, I would not be the smith of Ritaro, or the father of Kym, Stai and Vehllal kin of Daryo and Jeda.' He squeezed his daughter's shoulders. 'I am very, very happy with my life here, Kym, and I am very, very proud of you. You are a truly worthy namesake of Kym the Harlequin.' He leaned forwards and kissed his daughter's forehead. 'Come. We should get back home. Your mother does worry.'

The last noises from the upper level went silent. Jeda was back sewing by the light of a fat lamp. Daryo undressed, changed into the light linen trousers he wore to bed and slipped under the blanket. He lay for a while with his eyes closed, listening to the rustling of Stai or Vehllal moving in their beds right above him and the noises of Jeda's stitching. Then the lamp was blown out and Jeda was moving around the room. There were a few rustles and a clunk as she closed the chest at the foot of the bed. There was pressure on the mattress, the blanket lifted slightly, the pressure increased and then Daryo felt the touch of his wife's naked body against him.

'Awake?' she whispered in his ear. Her hand slid across his chest. He grunted affirmatively. Her hand slid down to his stomach. 'Thinking?'

'Trying,' he murmured.

'What about?' Her hand moved a few inches lower.

'Kym asked me about my life on the road. I thought that she was old enough to know so I told her and I told her how proud I am of her.'

'She is becoming a young woman. Courting a boy.'

Daryo chuckled silently. 'Not courting, my Jeda, spending time together.'

'Ah, of course. Spending time together. Spending time with a boy, shoeing horses, she will be able to stop going to lessons with the priest by summer. He can teach her no more.'

'She is starting to look and act like a woman.'

'She is like you.'

'With her mother's figure.'

Jeda moved and her breasts pressed against him. 'Is that a positive thing?'

Daryo reached across and put his hand on Jeda's hip. Even after three children and nearly two decades, a life working to keep the house and children had kept her relatively slim. 'If her future husband has as much fun as I do, very positive.' He reached around to the small of Jeda's back and guided her to lie tightly against him. 'Maybe another daughter?'

'That is up to the Gods. But not all of it. You have some work to do too.'

## Chapter 77

Stai had his day learning at the temple the next day but after mid-morning, Jeda was able to help Daryo complete the wheel rims for the mine carts. With the job complete by midday he was able to take the finished product up to the mine. At the edge of the cliff were two beams on frames reaching out over the precipice. Hanging from each beam was a basket large enough to carry four large men. At the opposite end of the cable the rope was attached to a wheel that was turned by a pair of donkeys. The man in charge of the winches was a former miner, too old to work in the tunnels, and spent most of his days sat on a stool looking out over the sea waiting for the bell to be rung on the ledge below that signalled the request to lift the basket.

'Gods' Watch, Sitiro.'

'Ah! Gods' Watch, Gods' Watch, Master Blacksmith! Our wheels?'

'The rims for them at least.' Daryo put down the sack that he was carrying. 'I assume that Ferethor is in the mine.'

'He is.'

'Then I should ride down.'

'Of course, of course.'

Sitiro got up from his stool and went to the donkeys tethered nearby. They were joined by a yoke, from the top this ran to the wheel. Sitiro smacked the outer animal on the rump and the pair started. As they walked, the bar on their yoke turned the spool and the rope that ran from the wheel to the beam, through the pulleys and then down to the baskets began to be wound around the wheel, lifting the baskets together. Daryo had made several trips down to mine; he was the only person in the village that used the iron ore in any quantities. However the visits were nerve-stretching, the journey down was not always pleasant. Daryo was glad that although the sky was cloudy, the air was still. The rumbling of the wheel and the creak of the pulley and rope was a familiar sound around the village. The baskets reached the top of the cliff so that their rims were level with the ground. The baskets themselves were essentially huge wooden half-barrels. Sitiro locked the wheel in place, released a pin on the yoke to turn the donkeys around and then reattached the yoke. He then seized one basket with a hook to hold it steady as Daryo hurled his sack of wheel rims and carefully clambered in, aware as he always was that he was a hundred and forty feet above the sea suspended in a large wooden bucket by a rope held by a pair of donkeys. Sitiro waved to Daryo and Daryo waved back. He gave the donkeys a nudge, the rope began to unwind and the baskets began to descend. Daryo tried to focus his eyes on the bottom of the basket as it began to sway. The ride down seemed to take a long time. Eventually there was a bump as the baskets came to rest on the rocky ledge nearly eighty feet from the top of the cliffs. Daryo looked out to make sure that the wooden steps were in position and then scrambled out with the sack. The ledge was twenty feet wide and over a hundred long, the baskets rested in the centre opposite the tunnel entrance, an eight foot-high entrance, wide enough for two or three people side by side. Just inside the entrance was kept a lit candle in a recess alongside a row of lanterns on hooks. Daryo took one of the lanterns, lit it and started down the tunnel.

After about forty yards, the tunnel forked. Daryo went right. This tunnel was narrower but finished after just a few feet in a cave that had once been the main mining area. It had been exhausted and become the mine's office and rest area.

'Master Daryo!'

'Master Ferethor.'

Ferethor was the mine's foreman, a Sodidoron with a shaggy, greying chestnut beard and wide eyes, his daughter Mizosa was the only other girl in the village close to Kym's age.

'Are those our wheel rims?'

'They are.' Daryo put the sack down on the foreman's desk. 'They can be nailed directly to the wheels, I made them an inch wide so they should fit the wheels as you directed.'

'Excellent. And the wheels that are too wide can easily be cut down. My thanks, Daryo. Are you going to Zonathor with the iron later?'

Daryo sighed. 'I had forgotten. I probably should do so. You?'

'No, I am a few workers short. There was some foul air in a new cave we found and it made several of my men rather unwell. The physician says that they will recover with rest.'

'May the Third God protect them.'

'He will.'

'I should go then. I will have a horse to saddle.'

'Of course. My thanks again, Daryo. You were paid?'

'Before the job.'

'Good. Gods' Guidance.'

'Gods' Guidance, Felethor.'


'Father? Father, mother said you are going to Zonathor.' Kym came running up to the stable. Daryo was saddling his horse.

'I am. The iron is going to the docks.'

'Can I come? I have never been to Zonathor.'

'Truly? Then you may come.'
'My thanks, father! I shall get my riding gear!'
'Hurry.'
Kym raced back to the house. Daryo finished preparing his horse, tethered it and crossed paths with his daughter going to attend to her own mount. As it was a full day's ride to Zonathor, Daryo dressed for the road: relatively tight black trousers, a linen shirt, his old armoured jerkin and then took down his twin swords. Sometimes thieves operated on the road and it was worth his being prepared.
'Not going to fight the Vidmarian army single-handed again, are you?' asked Jeda, coming inside and helping Daryo put the straps over his shoulders.
'Not this time, my love.'
'Ferethor said you were going into Zonathor with the iron wagons.'
'I am and I assented to Kym joining me.'
'Does that mean that the two of you will stay in the port overnight?'
'We may. I would prefer not to though.'
Jeda smiled and kissed him gently. 'See you later this day then.'
'I hope so, my Jeda. Gods' Guidance.'
'Gods' Guidance, my love.'

Daryo and Kym led their horses to the barn-like structure that was used as a store for the mines. Raw ore was kept there, the smelting work was done nearby and then the iron ingots were kept until they were taken to Zonathor or Baros. Four men were finishing loading the two horse-carts. Ferethor hailed them as they approached. Daryo tied the horses and went to inspect the load. The loads were then covered with cloths and tied down. Daryo and Kym mounted their horses, two men took the seat on the first cart, a single on the second. Ferethor bade them farewell and the carts started forwards, Daryo and Kym taking up the rear. They joined the main road and headed west down the steep hill out of the village, crossing the River Bhaar into Sodidor. On the far side of the bridge they passed between two carved stone chalices the height of a tall man full of carved flames. The road turned northwards briefly to avoid a treacherous marsh and then south-west again towards Zonathor. The road became narrow, barely wide enough for the carts, and crossed the wooden bridge across the wide Galiasth River. On the far bank, a tree was down across the road. The carts stopped. Daryo and Kym reined in their horses.
'This is not right,' he said to his daughter. 'In the ancient scrolls there are plans of an ambush and this is the first plan.' He passed the reins to her and dismounted. The cart

tenders were dismounting too. 'Stay with your cart, Varti, Hisiro! Samradus, help me move the tree. Be on your guard.' Daryo glanced back at Kym. She had dismounted and tied their horses to the rear of the second cart. Under her saddle blanket, she had concealed a bow and a quiver of arrows. He could not avoid smiling. 'Very good, Kym. Keep watch.'

'Yes, father.'

Daryo knew his daughter had never fired at a man, only at animals. He hoped that, if necessary, she would be able to loose. He slid between the front cart and the bridge wall and Samradus, the largest of the three, a man of Daryo's age but much stronger in build, joined him. The tree was a small silver-barked one and had been clearly felled by an axe. Daryo searched the bank of the river with his eyes for any threats. Finally he saw the three figures lying in wait. Samradus had been about to cross the tree trunk.

'Stay there, Samradus!' instructed Daryo. The figures realised they had been seen and they emerged from cover. All three had swords: one had a shield, another bore an axe as well as his sword.

Daryo drew his twin swords: the Horse and the Bear, and spun the Bear so that he held it point-down. Samradus had a stubby, rather rusted blade that he drew. Kym, stood on the second cart, drew back her bowstring. The other two cart drivers had stood up. Varti, the driver of the second, had a broadsword; Hisiro had only a knife. The man with the shield swung his sword threateningly.

'This is a toll bridge!' he announced in gruff tones. 'Pay and pass unharmed!'

Daryo met Samradus' eyes and shook his head slowly. Then he turned towards the attackers and jumped up onto the tree trunk. 'I am no mere traveller. I am no meek merchant,' he declared. 'Stand aside.'

The other two men exchanged worried looks. Their leader scoffed. 'Pay.'

Daryo brought his swords into a guard position. 'Your last opportunity. I have killed many men but none for many years. Do not be the next.' Something in the tone of his voice, the look of his face and the cast of his swords spooked the two subordinates.

'Thelithon! Come on!' one urged his leader, backing away.

'We can stop the next carts,' the other suggested.

Thelithon growled. 'Get back here.' The two men made garbled objections and were soon sprinting up the hill. 'No matter.' He turned back to Daryo and rapped his shield against his sword. 'Come then, Batribi! How good are you?'

Daryo sighed. The would-be thief charged the twenty yards between them. Daryo waited until he was close enough and then leaped off of the tree trunk, his boot smashing into his attacker's shield and knocking him backwards, the shield lost. Daryo used his other knee to drive the thief into the road and impaled the man's sword arm with the Bear. The man screamed in pain and tried to struggle, but he found the blade of the Horse across his throat.

Daryo lowered his face until he could smell the man's breath. 'You have a wound.' His voice was barely a whisper. 'No more. I will not kill a man with my daughter watching. I am going to release you now and take your weapon. Then you will run. If I see your face again, I shall not stay my blade.'

In one motion, Daryo stood, withdrawing the Bear. The thief moaned with agony, scrambled backwards several feet, gained his feet and then ran after his erstwhile friends. Daryo took several long, deep breaths, wiped the small amount of blood from the Bear and sheathed both blades. He turned around and saw the three mine workers looking impressed and Kym looking amazed.

'Relax your bowstring, Kym,' Daryo told her. 'Samradus, help me move this tree.'

They had ridden nearly three miles before Kym spoke.

'You were a warrior.'

'I think I still am,' Daryo admitted.

'You looked like a warrior. That man did not even get his sword up and you were standing on top of him with his life at your will. Where did you learn to fight, father?'

'I went from a winter through ten summers wielding a sword, Kym. I learned from the Order, from the Yashoun army, in the Silver Island, Hajma, Jaboen, Gourmin, Boskinia and Adaca. I have learned many techniques and ways to kill. The Fourth Goddess has gained many servants by my hand.'

'But you do not kill when you do not have to.'

'I try not to.'

'Then you are an honourable warrior. My father is an honourable warrior. At least in his daughter's eyes.'

'My thanks, Kym. But being a warrior is a path, as being a miner, a smith or a woodsman is. I have chosen another path.'

'I understand.'

# Chapter 78

Zonathor was built around the Mitraszona Bay in a sweeping half-circle divided by the Unthaos. It was dominated by two thoroughfares- Dock Street and Wall Street, and the two were connected by a web of smaller streets and alleyways. The walls were high and strong, well-manned and secure. Daryo steered his horse to the side of the road and allowed the carts past, bidding farewell to their drivers. He had seen something that he was more interested in than the docks: a series of conical tents a short distance from the road and close to the walls.

'Kym, this is something you have never seen.'

'I have never seen Zonathor before,' said Kym peering through the gates into the town.

'No, this is much more interesting.'

Daryo kicked his horse on towards the tents. Kym took a long look through the gates and followed her father. Daryo heard an almost-forgotten cry.

'An approach! Are you one?'

Daryo dismounted, spreading his arms wide. 'I am Daryo, kin of Dostan. This is Kym, my daughter.' Kym dismounted.

The Batribi man on watch lowered his sword. 'I am Trauva, kin of Yilarin. Dostan? Of the Lake?'

'He is part of the community by the lake, yes.'

Truava laughed. 'You are not of a clan!'

'I am kin of Dostan but we do not walk as many of our people. We have found peace and acceptance in Adaca. Why?'

'Dostan was chosen leader of the community. There is talk of his being made king!'

Daryo nodded, impressed. 'I am most proud of my kin if that is so. My daughter has not spent any time with our people. May we speak with your Elder?'

Trauva beckoned them forwards. 'You may. Yilarin is aged, very frail.' They passed several other members of the clan until they reached a particular *kaff*. Trauva held up a hand for patience and ducked inside.

'Father, is this truly important?' asked Kym.

'I believe so. You have never had a chance to learn the nature of our people.' He held his arms out. 'This is it. The Batribi are a wandering people, our people walk the roads and live and sleep in the *kaffa*, the tents. We are fortunate that Adaca is a permissive and tolerant land with a benevolent leader. In many places we are shunned, vilified, even hunted.'

'Hunted?'

'Indeed. Not as we once were, and there are places of safety now. The lake has been given to our people by the Jaboen but most of that land is unfriendly. Adaca is safe, Ishter is more welcoming than it was. Yashoun too. But Armynya and Gourmin are not friendly to Batribi, the Kyi Sun Islands are dangerous, Tibilia is not welcoming. Many of our people live in fear.'

Trauva emerged. 'Yilarin is very frail. Her niece Cracha is with her. Go in.'

Daryo held the flap open to allow Kym to precede him and then stepped through himself. A withered old woman was sat on a pile of cushions and bolsters, propped up on them. Her milky eyes were sunken in dark hollows, broken teeth showed behind dry lips above a pointed, wrinkled cheek. She lifted a skeletal hand to indicate cushions facing her. Daryo and Kym sat down, Kym's face betrayed a definite wariness. Seated alongside the old woman was a younger woman, a little older than Kym, dressed in a green hooded jerkin like Daryo's armoured one but without the protective sections, seated cross-legged on a folded rug.

'Daryo and Kym, kin of Dostan, welcome,' said the young woman. 'I am Cracha, kin of Yilarin, with us.'

'Our thanks for your welcome,' said Daryo. 'We no longer travel the roads, my daughter is almost of age and I thought it important for her to see something of the Batribi people as they have always been.'

'Our people walk and walk and walk again,' recited the Elder in a scratchy voice.

'We do, Yilarin,' said Cracha soothingly.

'Many years walking on many roads and through many marshes and in many villages and across many rivers.'

'Where were you last at rest?' Daryo asked.

'Dentithir. We are able to spend nearly a score of days there,' said Cracha. 'Then the city guards came and forced us to move.'

'Why?' asked Kym.

Cracha smiled sadly. 'Because we are Batribi, Kym, daughter of Daryo. We are unwelcome.'

'Why?'

Cracha leaned forwards and held her hand beside Kym's. Kym's skin was the colour of clay, Daryo's that of dark oak bark, Cracha's was even darker than that. 'Because of our skin. People fear difference and what they do not know. Tell me, do you fear the Gods?'

'I do.'

'People fear what they do not understand. They do not understand us, our way of living, our heritage, they do not understand even that our skin is a different colour and that colour is the only difference. Your skin and mine are both skin, we are both the same form of animals. If a cow is brown and another is white, they both give meat, hide and milk, do they not?'

'They do.'

'And that is what many do not understand. We are people as the Yashoun and the Silver Islanders and any others are. So we are forced to move on.'

'Walk and walk again,' said the Elder. 'This fate of ours.'

'It is,' agreed Daryo. 'Those who have settled are few.'

'This fate of ours is each one's bane.'

'To sleep beneath the stars each night, to walk and walk again in flight,' concluded Daryo solemnly.

'That is the Verse,' Cracha told Kym, seeing her confusion. 'Our people are skilled at the use of words and we use the Verse to relate our experience, our lives and our thoughts to others. The refrain is always the same and it is, briefly, the story of our people.'

'The clans are scattered, all over the world. The clans are scattered.' The Elder shook her head.

'The clans gather. At Stannia Lake,' said Daryo. 'Your clansman Trauva said more than ever and that the land has been given in perpetuity. The Batribi have a nation again. A land of our own. The clans are reuniting.'

'Scattered. It is as it should be.' The Elder looked distressed.

Cracha stroked her arm gently. 'Peace, Yilarin. It is as it should be. Yilarin believes that the clans should continue to walk.'

'Walk and walk again,' muttered Yilarin to herself.

'We shall continue as our people have done from long ago,' said Cracha. 'Many are fortunate to settle, as you have, some enjoy the peace that such a life gives them. But we will continue to walk.'

Daryo nodded. 'We have taken too much of your time. If your clan is forced to move on, take the road to Adaca and the village of Ritaro. I am the smith. You will be welcome to stay as long as you wish. The village will welcome you.'

'Our thanks,' said Cracha. Yilarin seemed to have fallen asleep. 'Yilarin would thank you also. You are welcome with this clan to the end of days, Daryo and Kym, kin of Dostan.'

'Gods' Guidance on you and your clan, Cracha.'

'And on you. Walk in safety.'

Daryo and Kym took their horses back to the road and into Zonathor. The warehouses were on the far side of the docks, they followed Wall Street to the Unthaos River and

crossed Wall Bridge. Just across it, Daryo led Kym and the horses down one of the streets leading towards the harbour. They then had to tether their horses to a pillar to allow them to pass down a tiny alley. Daryo reached a certain door, grinned at his daughter and knocked.
'Who is it?' demanded a voice from inside, a woman.
'The Walker.'
The door opened. The woman looked to be slightly older than Daryo, her hair had been dark but was almost grey, she was muscular and compact, wearing a leather bodice that barely covered her breasts and tight leggings that did not reach her knees as well as boots. A short sword, a hammer and a pair of tongs hung from her belt.
'The Fuller,' Daryo greeted her.
'Come inside, Daryo. And...'
'Kym. My daughter.'
'By Dule, you were barely walking when last I saw you!' Siva the Fuller said to Kym as they entered. 'You look scarily like your father. Much prettier though.'
'Warriors and blacksmiths are not known for their looks, Siva.'
'Oh, I am so grateful.' She closed the door.
They were stood in a very small shop, less than six feet square, the walls were lined floor-to-ceiling with shelves, full of grubby boxes and other items, with spaces only for a small fireplace, the door and a small window. It was the mid-afternoon and the sun was bright but the grubby window allowed little light in. Kym saw a shield propped against the side of the fireplace with the image of a shield and sword painted on it with a crossed blade and chain at the pommel of the sword.
Siva was searching through her stock. 'Black rocks?'
'Indeed.'
'Black rocks... black rocks... my supplier has not been for many seasons.' She stood on the lowest shelf and reached up. 'Are you out of them?'
'Not completely but I have had an order for a sword and I would like a surplus.'
Siva hopped down, ushered Kym aside and took a dirty canvas pouch from the shelf. 'I knew I had some.'
Daryo took the pouch and looked inside. The black rocks were crucial for making real and good steel. 'Excellent.'
'Nine silver halves, Walker.'
'Siva... The Calm would have broken his placidity at that price.'
'Rare. Very rare. Perhaps my last ones if my supplier is out of business. Eight.'
'Five.'

'Five! Seven.'
'Six.'
'Six silver, three bronze.'
'Six silver, two.'
'Daryo...'
'Siva, six silver and two bronze.'
'Done.'
Daryo handed over the money and tied the canvas bag to his belt. 'My thanks, Fuller.'
'Any time you are in Zonathor.'
'With your prices, I might be better going to Baros.'
'You may have the last black rocks in all of Sodidor, Walker.'
'Then I have no need to return to Zonathor.' He nodded to Kym and went towards the door.
'Daryo!' barked Siva. She looked desperate for a second and then relaxed. 'I may be able to get more. If I send word to you... and can do them for five halves each.'
'Then it is better to return to Zonathor than to travel to Baros.'
Siva seemed to be close to collapse. 'My thanks.'
Daryo opened the door and ushered Kym through. Then he turned back, drew the Horse and held it up by the hilt, point down. 'My sword and my service.'
Siva drew her blade and raised it the same way. 'My sword and my service.'
Daryo replaced his sword and closed the door behind them. He nudged Kym down the alley back towards their horses.
'Who was that, father?' she asked.
'Siva the Fuller. Siva was a Member of the Order of the Shield and Sword. She was a smith at the Order's home, the Five Towers. I do not know at the time that she survived the battle that destroyed the Order but we met by chance here, just after you were born. Siva has tried many things to make her living in the past few years. She lost the smithy that she gained, she lost the chandlery that she tried to run; that tiny little cupboard of a store is all that she has. Her honour, her spirit, her desire for life has gone. She is trying to scrape a living at the Fourth God's feet.'
'That is why her prices are so high?'
'I could get ten black rocks in Baros for two silver halves and thanked for my custom. Few people have the knowledge to use them so they are not expensive. But because I want them, Siva thinks they are valuable and so she charges me more than she should.'

Kym reached the horses and reached up to untie them. Then she stopped, lowered her hand and turned to look at her father. 'In some way, some manner, that is the saddest thing I have ever been told.'

Daryo smiled weakly and stroked his daughter's cheek. 'I agree. Come, we should check at the warehouses and find somewhere to stay the night. The Precious Cargo inn is probably best. It is on Dock Street.'

They stayed at the Precious Cargo, having a roast duck for dinner, slept in a small room at the back of the inn and then had an uneventful but rain-soaked ride back to Ritaro.

# Chapter 79

Strange riders were not unknown in Ritaro but ones in fine robes and riding alone with minimal baggage was interesting enough that the baker came out of his workplace to see. The rider wheeled around when he saw the baker, an elderly and stout man covered with flour.

'Master Baker, I seek the smithy,' said the rider.

'Horse need shoeing?'

'Not exactly. The smithy?'

'Ride into the centre of the village. The smith is alongside the temple. The smith is a Batribi, name of Daryo.'

'I know.'

The horse was kicked on and cantered forwards, on into Ritaro. The forge was quiet but for a young boy hammering a roughly-made blade.

'Boy, I am looking for the smith,' said the rider.

'He is inside the house,' said the boy. 'He is my father. Who are you?'

'I will speak to your father. Fetch him now.'

The boy put down his sword and hammer and ran inside.


'Father! Father!'

Daryo had been fixing a broken rung in the ladder into the roof. 'Slowly, Stai! Calm, breathe slowly. What is it?'

'A rider, father. Ordered me to fetch you.'

Daryo exchanged looks with Jeda, who had been starting a fire. 'What manner of rider?'

'I do not know.'

'Stay in the house,' Daryo ordered his son. He nodded to Jeda and took the Horse and the Bear from their places hung above the bed. He handed the Bear to Jeda, slid the Horse into his belt and stepped outside. The rider dismounted.

'Daryo,' he stated flatly. 'Daryo the Batribi, kin of Dostan of the Batribi, the Walker of the Order of Shield and Sword, once Lord of Scara of Boskinia, smith of Ritaro.'

'You seem to know as much of me as I do. Who are you?'

The man dismounted and held his cloak aside. On his chest was a crest: blue with a yellow sun and a white bull. 'An emissary of your king.'

Daryo inclined his head respectfully. Jeda lowered her sword. 'My apologies for our caution, we did not know what to expect.'

The rider nodded. 'I understand. My name is Giuglo. I am junior marshal for King Lallano. I come, sir, because Adaca requires your help.'

'In what way?'

Giuglo looked around cautiously. 'I would prefer to discuss such matters in more secure surroundings.'

Daryo invited the man inside. Stai and Vehllal were told to leave by their mother but Daryo insisted that she stay. Giuglo seated himself, lowering his cowl. He was only a few summers older than Kym with a large chin, hooked nose and wire-like brown hair.

'What do you know, sir, of the politics of Armynya?'

'Little. And what I know is most probably old and outdated.' Daryo seated himself opposite the visitor.

'Armynya is a land of tribes. Each tribe had its own lands and ways. They share a language, the last peoples known that do not use the Common Tongue, and some beliefs in old gods but little else. The land was held together by these things only and a belief that one day a mythical being would come forwards and claim the Stone Chair, the ancient seat of the long-dead ruler of the tribes. The myth claims that this person would be neither man nor woman and they would claim the Stone Chair, unite the tribes and lead Armynya against all foes.'

'And this person has come forth?' asked Jeda, standing by the fire pit.

'So it would seem, Madam,' said Giuglo. 'The Twenty-Two Tribes gathered at the Stone Chair in the ancient and abandoned capital of Thamriev and proclaimed a person as their leader. They have ascended to the Stone Chair and the Twenty-Two have sworn fealty and allegiance. This new leader comes from an obscure tribe, the Haustihya, from the very south of Armynya.'

'What makes them think that this is the fabled leader?' Daryo questioned. 'How can one be neither man nor woman?'

Giuglo shook his head. 'A wonder of the Gods. Or an abomination before them. It is said that this person has the anatomy of both man and woman, the organ of a man but stunted, the opening of a woman but not fully formed, the face of a man and the breasts of a woman.'

Daryo swallowed hard. Jeda gasped: 'Is that possible?'

'So it would seem. The Armynyan mind is not easily convinced and the king's advisers and the king himself are in no doubt that this person would not have been permitted to take the Stone Chair unless the Twenty-Two Tribes accepted the claim.'

'Forgive me,' said Daryo. 'But have you truly ridden from Darsux to Ritaro to tell me of Armynyan politics, sir?'

Giuglo laughed humourlessly. 'No, sir, I have not. I have ridden from Scirito. That is where King Lallano has his camp. Tanaab has fallen, Tovbi has fallen, Ensadri is threatened. The One of Two, as the Armynyan leader is called, was prophesied to be a leader that would lead their people to victory over all foes. The first foe that they have chosen is Adaca. We are invaded, Daryo of the Batribi. King Lallano begs that you ride to our aid.'

'You swore to me! You swore that it was over!' Jeda's sobs broke her words. She seized handfuls of Daryo's shirt as she cried.

Daryo embraced her tightly. Giuglo had gone. The children had not returned. 'I did. I swore that the Walker was behind me and that I would hold you and the children in front of me.'

'Then you cannot go!'

'I have been summoned by the king. I cannot refuse.'

'You could. You are not Adacan. You do not answer to the Adacan king! I am not Adacan, I am Yashoun. I do not answer to the Adacan king!'

'Kym, Stai and Vehllal are born Adacan.'

'The offspring of a Batribi and a Yashoun! They are not Adacan!'

'We live in Adaca. We use the money, eat the food, work the iron, live to their codes. The children know no other life.'

Jeda sobbed harder. 'I cannot let you go.'

'I do not want to go.' Daryo spoke slowly to keep his upset in check. 'I want to fulfil my oath to you. But what alternative is there? If I refuse, I could be executed as a traitor.'

'Then we run! We pack what we can carry, load the ponies. Go south into Sodidor. Or west into Yashoun.'

'And live as fugitives.'

'Like Batribi.'

'This has become my home, Jeda. You and Kym and the boys. I am the smith of Ritaro. I am husband to Jeda Siyon of Ossmoss, father to Kym, Stai and Vehllal. I am a bladesmith and a blacksmith and I thank the Gods every day that I breathe that they have permitted be to be so for nearly twenty summers!' He gripped his wife's shoulders and looked her in the eye. 'But I owe a great debt to the Fourth Goddess. I made another promise as a young man to defend those who needed it. And the people of Adaca need it now.'

'We need it now! I need you!'

'I cannot defend you if I am the last man in the village and the hordes of Armynyan tribesmen are swarming up the Baros road. Can you tell Vehllal how much you need me when he is screaming in fear? Can you tell Stai how defenceless we are when it is my blade against a thousand? Can you tell Kym what my oath meant when the Armynyan men pin her to our bed?'

Jeda wailed in fear, hate and anger and pounded Daryo's chest with her fists. 'How can you say that? How can you say that? Your own daughter?'

Daryo seized his wife's wrists. 'I say it because I have to. Jeda, I love you. I love you and no other. I love our children and it because I love them that I must go. If I must fight this war, I choose to do it as far from you and the children as I can.'

Jeda took several shuddering breaths. 'I do not want you to go. But if that is how you can best defend our home and our children…'

'Then you will let me go.'

'I will.'

Daryo kissed her hard through the tears. 'I shall leave with the dawn.'

They told the children that he had to go away on the business of the squire. Stai and Vehllal accepted the tale but Kym looked unconvinced and asked many questions, probing the weaknesses in the story. After the children had retired to bed, Daryo began to pack his things, watched from the bed by a tearful Jeda. Eventually her emotions' drain sent her to sleep. The last things that Daryo assembled were the items he knew he would need in battle- his shield, the Horse and the Bear, his old armoured jerkin and Temma's Sword. He checked each one by the light of the lamps and readied them for the morning.

'Father.'

Daryo turned. Kym had descended the ladder, dressed in her nightshirt, her blanket around her shoulders.

'You should be asleep, Kym.'

'You are packing to leave.'

'Yes.'

'If you are going on smithy business for the squire, why do you pack weapons?'

'It may be a dangerous road.'

'You are leaving us. Forever. You will not return.'

'Kym!' Daryo cupped his daughter's face. 'Never. It is true. I go on the king's business, not the squire's.'

'You go to war.'

'Yes, Kym. I go to war.'
'I want to come.'
'No.'
'I am of age in a matter of weeks. I have no reason to stay here.'
'I could not see you risk your life in battle.'
'I will come with you, father. My horse is fast, I am strong, unless you chain me to the pillars of the temple, I will follow.'
'You cannot use a sword.'
'I can learn. And I am the best with a bow in the village.'
'Kym...'
'Father, you had the chance at little older than I to go off and explore the world and learn to be a warrior. You had no choice. I do, and I choose to take the opportunity.'
Daryo sighed. 'Your mother will be distraught. And angry.'
'She will have Stai and Vehllal to care for.'
'And what of my daughter?' Jeda had sat up in bed. The conversation had woken her. 'Mother, I need to get out. I need to see more of the world than the village. I want adventure.'
'You could be killed.'
'I may not be.'
Jeda took a long, sobbing breath. 'I cannot stop you. Either of you. Kym, go to bed.'
'Yes, mother.'
Kym climbed the ladder. Jeda got out of bed and strode across to her husband by the table. Temma's Sword was bare on the table and Jeda picked it up and put the tip to Daryo's neck. 'Bring her back alive, or I kill you myself. By all the Gods and Goddesses of the Pantheon, I will kill you myself.'
'I will bring her back alive.'
Jeda lowered the sword. 'I could not bear to lose her. Or you.'
'You will not, my love. I swear.'

## Chapter 80

'Father, father! Wait for me!'
Vehllal came running around the house, wearing his pretend armour, brandishing his wooden sword and carrying a bag. 'I can come too!'
Daryo had been just about to mount his horse but stopped. 'I wish that you could come, son. I truly do. But if you come with me and so does Kym, who will defend your mother?'
Vehllal looked at his mother, then the already-mounted Kym, then at Stai. 'Stai is running the forge. Not him.'
'Precisely. You must stay and guard your mother. See that no harm comes to her.'
Vehllal nodded solemnly. 'I will. Gods' Watch, father.'
'Gods' Guidance, Vehllal.' He hugged his son. 'Stai, take care of the forge and your mother.'
'Yes, father.' He embraced his father too.
'My Jeda.'
'My Daryo. Take good care of her. Remember my promise. And yours.'
'I will. Try not to worry. We shall both return.'
'I know.'
'The Fourth Goddess will not be greeting me just yet. I love you.' Daryo the Walker kissed his wife, saluted his sons and mounted his horse. He nodded to Kym and they rode away.

The road followed the cliff top, never more than about a hundred yards from the edge, hugging the contours and curves of the south-west Adacan cliffs. The ride to Baros took two full days with good conditions and the rain was constant and driven in by a stiff wind from the sea. Kym rode behind her father, head down in her waxed cloak, trying to keep as much of herself under its protection as possible. The wind pierced even the best protection and chilled both riders right through. The rain was pervasive and persistent and they reached their first halt soaked and miserable. Daryo insisted they both change for dry clothes before leaving again. The space in a small rocky cave was tight and Daryo tried not to notice the womanly shape of his daughter as she changed with the impunity and innocence of a child with their father. They resumed their ride in the unceasing rain and wind. Daryo hoped that they would reach their first overnight halt without having to spend a night in the open. There were no villages on the cliff road between Ritaro and Baros, just two inns known by their respective distances from Baros as the First Halt and the Second Halt. Thus from Ritaro, the Second Halt would be the first that they came to. Ritaro's inn had once been known as the Third Halt but that name had passed with the growth of the village around the mine and its importance as a settlement in its own name and not just as the outbuildings of an inn.

The land was depressingly featureless and seemed even more so in the dismal weather conditions: scrubby salty grasslands on the cliff top, interrupted only by small rocky outcroppings from ancient movements below the surface, cut only the passage of the old stone road. To their right, below the cliffs and beyond, was the sea but the driving rain from off of the ocean kept them from admiring the waterscape. By late afternoon the road was well below the height of the cliff, reducing the wind but giving no mercy from the rain. The thick clouds were making the light poor, a long time before sundown it was all but dark. Daryo urged his horse onwards and with almost the last light they reached the Inn of the Second Halt: a long building with its own small dairy, a large stable block and a welcoming host. Daryo spent most of the evening with the Horse and the Bear, teaching Kym to wield a sword against an opponent.

The next morning they rode out early towards the First Halt. The road slowly but progressively got further below the level of the cliffs as the rain finally lifted. The wind remained and the clouds remained dense but without the rain it was a much more pleasant journey. The horses were on a better road surface and were able to keep a steadier pace on their journey. They made much better time and Daryo called an early halt to give both riders and mounts an extra rest. Kym insisted on using the time to continue to work on her sword skills. After some practise, they remounted and continued eastwards.

The clouds began to break and clear through the afternoon and the wind died by sundown. By evening, the sky was blue with only small patches of grey and white cloud and the wind was a gently breeze from behind the riders instead of a near-gale from the flank. They were able to hold conversation easily without the shrieking of the wind and the spattering of the rain. Kym questioned her father on his past battles, her questions increasingly on how he had felt and how he had known what to do. Daryo tried to talk more of the consequences of war, the injuries that he had seen and suffered, then tried to talk of the dangers and risks. Kym simply returned to her theme and Daryo relented, trying to remember the events of over twenty summers before. He spoke of the battles at Outros and then Sibiri and some of his experiences on the roads and in the Silver Island. He managed to describe his first meeting with Jeda and how they had moved to

Ritaro, even though Kym knew the tale she allowed him to retell it and even asked for more details at times.

The First Halt Inn was larger than the Second Halt, with a hamlet that had grown around it to house the workers at the inn and supply the guests and staff with everything that they needed. The better conditions had allowed them to arrive well before dark so Daryo again took Kym out for weapons' drill: giving her a sword and shield borrowed from the innkeeper while he used wooden representations of axes, spears and swords to assault her. She learned fast and he was most satisfied by the time they stopped. Another night's sleep at an inn and they resumed the road to Baros.

Giuglo had left instructions that Daryo should report to the King's Steward in Baros, the city's governor at the appointment of the king. Baros was the oldest of Adaca's three great ports; the others, Cali and Ensadri, had grown larger but Baros retained importance due to its proximity to the largest city, Aden, and the capital city, Darsux, and its reputation as a fair, free and safe port. Taverns, brothels, gaming houses and horse races were available for sailors, storage for cargo was plentiful, the anchorage was safe and well-policed and the city itself was welcoming and calm. The Old City and docks were contained by the wall on the western bank of the Wyhr River, which reached the sea at the city. The New City stretched along the higher eastern bank. The road led down from the cliffs to the sea, through the sand dunes that stood between Baros and the sea and in through a towering iron gate near the river bank. The Old City streets were narrow and winding, the buildings built of stone quarried from the nearby cliffs. At the centre of the city was the modestly-named Steward's House: a three-storey house only a little larger than those around it and only clearly distinguished by the blue and gold banner and the armed soldier at the door. Daryo and Kym dismounted and a servant came hurrying from inside.

'I am Daryo the Walker. I have been told to come to the Steward. I believe that I am expected.'

The man bowed low. 'You are, sir.' He turned and called inside. A young boy hurried out. 'The boy will take your mounts to the stable. Please follow me, sir.'

Daryo and Kym followed the servant inside, through a hall, up the stairs and to a grand door. The servant knocked, opened it and announced them before ushering them through. The Steward was a man slightly older than Daryo, of similar build, bald but with a long dark beard.

'Master Batribi,' said the Steward. 'Welcome to Baros. I gather that you are well known at the docks but less so here.'

'The king himself knows that I wished for a peaceful existence somewhere remote and quiet.'

'But also ensured that you were somewhere that he could locate you if you were ever needed, sir. And Adaca needs you.'

'That is why I have come. My daughter comes to fight beside me.'

The Steward bowed deeply to Kym. 'You are both most welcome. There is a carriage ready to leave, sir. I have been given instructions to send you straight away onwards.'

'Where are we required?'

'The king is at Scirito for now so the carriage will take you to Hullava. If the king is forced to withdraw, it will be there. If not, you can continue to Scirito.'

Daryo nodded. 'A carriage?'

'Your horses can be taken in tow.'

'They are not warhorses, they would be best left here in safety. We can collect them on the return.'

'Of course, sir. Allow my marshal to take you to your carriage.'

The carriage was large but simple: a wooden box with a door at the back and windows in the sides. The interior had a padded bench on either side that could double as beds, tapestries along the walls, curtains across the windows, a luggage section at the front of the carriage and oil lamps hung from the ceiling. Kym smiled as a young servant boy of about her age gave her a hand up into the carriage. A team of four horses were already harnessed at the front and a coachman and a man-at-arms climbed on to the front. Daryo climbed in behind his daughter, the young servant smiled shyly at Kym and closed the door. He called to the coachman and the carriage started forwards.

'How far is Hullava?' Kym asked.

'Four hundred miles.'

'Eight days in a wooden box.'

'I am sorry, Kym. Not all travelling is great adventure.'

'No. Some of it is riding through the unending rain in a wind that would blow down a tree.'

Daryo chuckled. 'Some of it.'

'What is the king like?'

'He is a good man. He was a young man when we first met, a Regent for his father. I met his sister as well, Tari.'

'The princess?'

'Indeed. The soldier princess.'

'Is it true that she has pledged never to marry?'
'She did. It is claimed that she had pledged herself to the Second Goddess and the service of Adaca.'
'Will we meet her?'
'Possibly.'
Kym beamed. 'The soldier princess.'
'I do not need one. I have a soldier princess in the carriage with me and another at home caring for my sons.'
Kym laughed. 'You say some things that are remarkably sentimental, father.'
'I am a warrior. I have been walking a long time, fighting for a long time and then I have grown to be a man of peace and family. I am allowed to be sentimental at times.'
'I shall permit you to be sentimental, father.'
'My thanks, Kym.' Daryo removed his boots and swung his feet onto the seat. 'I think it best that we rest and be comfortable.'
Kym kicked off her own boots and mimicked her father. 'I think so.'

The journey was accomplished in seven days. Daryo and his daughter spent the time talking, resting and watching the landscape pass. Kym had done some sewing and spent every opportunity while they were stopped to practise her weapons' drill. The changes of horses had apparently been planned well, every half-day was a new team of horses; the coachman and guard were also replaced at the end of each day. It was very early morning when the carriage came to a halt. Daryo had been sleeping on one of the seats and felt himself being shaken by the shoulder.
'Walker. Time to rise, sir.'
Daryo blinked. The lamps in the carriage had gone out and only a thin, pale light came through the open carriage door. He could see only a fair-haired woman. 'Is this Hullava?'
'We are just a few miles north of Hullava. Sibiri is a long way west.'
'Sibiri? What do you... Princess Tari?'
'It is good to see you, Daryo the Walker.' The Adacan princess stepped back. 'You look no older than you did when last we saw each other.'
'Neither do you, my Lady.' Daryo sat up, rubbing the tiredness from his eyes. 'It is early.'
'It is early in the day but the hour is late. Much of our country is under foreign control. Allow me to be the first to thank you for accepting our call.'
'I could not in good conscience have said no.'
'And I see you brought a comrade. Your daughter, Kym.'

Daryo's daughter had obviously been roused by the light or the conversation and her eyes flickered open. 'Father?'

'It is morning, Kym. We are in Hullava. May I introduce to you Princess Tari, sister of the king, commander of the Adacan armies.'

Kym sat up as if jabbed with a spear. 'Princess...'

'Kym, daughter of the Walker, you are very welcome with the armies of Adaca.' Tari curtsied formally in the close confines of the carriage.

Kym scrambled to her feet and tried to curtsey but almost fell over. Tari grabbed her arm to steady her, laughing, and smiled kindly. 'Come. Let us get out of the carriage. There is much work to do.'

Daryo nodded. 'We are dressed for sleeping on the move, Princess. We shall dress and join you.'

'Of course, Walker.' Tari smiled. 'I shall be in the captains' tent. Please be swift.'

Daryo dressed as he always had in combat: leggings, shirt, boots, his armoured jerkin, Hajma bracers, the twin swords' harness and his sword belt. Carefully he checked the knife he made in Ritaro several summers before, a short and straight blade with a barbed point, Temma's Sword went in its place on his belt and finally the Horse and the Bear in their sheaths on his back. He picked up his shield, attached its leather strap which went over his shoulder like a sash so that the shield hung on his back: the blindfolded girl and the harlequin holding hands across a Yashoun milepost with a sword and shield device where the distance should have been written on the top of the milepost.

Kym had sewn thin steel plates, specially made by Daryo many years before as spares, into the sleeves and back of a brown tunic that matched her father's jerkin, a pair of black leggings with green and gold leaves embroidered on them and her short boots. At a stop on the way, Daryo had found a small round shield that perfectly fitted Kym's arm, and he had found a well-made long dagger that she wore uncovered in her belt.

They climbed down from the carriage and found a white-haired attendant waiting for them and they were led to the captains' tent. A large map was spread across the table in the centre. A dozen other tables were piled with parchments: maps, rosters, lists of supplies, scouting reports and intelligence briefings. Over a score of men thronged the tent and at the heart was Tari, her hair tied behind her head, a chainmail vest just visible beneath her robes.

'Walker, welcome back to the Army of the Adacan nation,' she said, her tone business-like. 'You have been made my personal military lieutenant. Any order given by you is one given by me, on the authority of my brother, the king.' Tari's voice was loud enough that everyone present in the tent heard her clearly.

'As you wish, my Lady.'
'Captain Casilia will give you the situation.'
A young captain stepped forwards, a bow on his back. 'My Lord, this information is vital. It is not for the ears of young girls and civilians.'
Daryo saw that he was looking at Kym. 'I am not in the uniform of the Adacan Army and yet I am privy to this information. As for young girls, the princess was one once and won the Battle of Sibiri. Kym is my daughter, my lieutenant and my counsellor. What I am fit to hear, so am I.'
Tari nodded. 'Continue, Captain.'
Casilia looked suitably chagrined. 'Yes, my Lady. I am sorry, my Lord.' He pointed to Scirito. 'The Armynyan horde took Scirito two days ago. They forced the bridges and were able to send mounted men across in large numbers. We were unable to deploy our reinforcements in time, however we are now able to concentrate our main force, which we were not able to do before.' He pointed to the city on the south coast. 'Ensadri is completely surrounded and has been besieged for almost twenty days now. Our nearest forces are in Trapereri but not in such numbers to break the encirclement of Ensadri.'
'Can Ensadri hold for another twenty days?'
'Perhaps, my Lord. They can still get some ships into the harbour and have stockpiles.'
'What of numbers?'
'The Army of the Centre, the force here, numbers twenty-one and a half thousands. The Army of the South, in front of Ensadri, is of fourteen thousands. The Army of the North, on the North Plain, is ten thousands. A force of the same number is in Darsux, and one half that size in Cali.'
'The Armynyans?'
'At least thirty thousands around Ensadri. The force that took Scirito is of about the same size. There are some reserves but our scouts have not returned. The Armynyan methods have been... barbaric, sir.'
'How so?'
Casilia glanced at Kym again. 'They march into battle behind newborn babes nailed to poles, my Lord. Their conduct of battle is ruthless: waves upon waves of men thrown at our lines with no thought to their own lives. Any prisoners are tortured and killed in the most gruesome fashion. One of our scouts managed to get into Tanaab and he could barely relate what he saw when he returned. The last of our scouts that returned did so horribly mutilated.'
Daryo nodded. 'My thanks, Captain. Is there a small detachment of Armynyan troops within easy reach of here?'

'My Lord?'

'Is there?'

Casilia turned to another officer, who consulted some parchments. 'There is a scouting and forward watch post two miles south-east, my Lord,' he said. 'It would be the direction we had been considering taking the Army of the Centre to relieve Ensadri.'

'That would serve little purpose,' said Daryo. 'Princess, we need to put the army of invasion in fear. I need four dozen of the best men available, ready to leave by sunset.'

Tari inclined her head. 'As you wish. Captain Taliarali, four dozen of the Second Company. Ask their sergeants for the best men.'

'Yes, my Lady.' A weathered and dour-looking soldier bowed formally and left the tent.

'You plan a raid,' Tari said to Daryo.

'Indeed. I want the Armynyan commanders to know that their positions are vulnerable. I assume that no such actions have been launched previously.'

Tari shook her head. 'We have been too busy trying to hold back the tide.'

'No matter. It is done and it will be undone.'

'You mean to push them back?'

'As soon as possible. We will have this raid this night. Then Adaca counter-attacks from its centre. How soon could the Southern Army join us?'

'Two days.'

'Have it done, leaving just a token force behind but making as much of a show as they can. The Armynyans not looking at Ensadri should believe that they are still watched by a potent army.'

Tari signalled to another captain. 'Have it done.' He bowed and hurried away. 'That will leave Ensadri without hope.'

'It may. But if the Armynyan commander has to withdraw his besiegers to aid his main army, then Ensadri will have relief.'

'I understand. What if the Armynyans see the deception?'

'Then we can deploy the new combined army southwards instead.'

Tari nodded slowly as she thought through all of Daryo's proposals. 'I give my assent to your plans, Walker.'

'My thanks, Princess. May I ask, where is the King? I was told he was at Scirito.'

'Thanks to the Good Shepherd's guiding hand, he moved back to Hullava the night before the attack to organise the supplies. Since then, with my counsel and that of others, he is now moving back to Oia and then to Darsux. He has come to the thought that he is best withdrawn to safety.'

'And what of his wife and heirs?'

'Queen Hala and the infant princes have been accepted by the Emperor in Ossmoss. They are in seclusion and safety in the city of Nadakso in Yashoun guarded by a company of White Bulls and a contingent of the Yashoun Imperial Paladins.'
'Good. Your brother is well?'
'In his body, yes. In his mind, he is sick with worry for his country.'
'I will do all I can to alleviate his worry, Princess.' Daryo drew Temma's Sword and raised it, point down in salute. He saw from the corner of his eye Kym draw her dirk and mirror the salute. '*We* offer you our swords and our service.'
'And they are gratefully received, Kym of Ritaro and Daryo the Walker. We have already selected a unit for your personal command, Walker. They are our best soldiers and have been trained for five years before being permitted to join the unit. They are the Vazzeccoes. In the old language of Adaca, it means The Walkers.'

The unit had obviously been drawn up ready for their new commander. Each man wore a straight-sided helmet with nose guard, a slightly domed top and jointed cheek guards that tied under the chin. They wore light armless cuirasses over dark blue beneath, bracers and carried large rectangular shields similar to those of the Boskinian Oaken Guard. Their swords were long and curved in the manner of Temma's Sword.
When Daryo approached, the captain stepped out of the line, drew his sword and raised it in salute, point down. 'Walker, we are at your service,' he announced before dropping his salute.
Daryo nodded. 'My thanks.'
'Four hundred and twenty men of the Vazzeccoes trained to the highest standards in Adaca. We are ready to follow you into battle.'
Daryo nodded. 'What is your name, captain?'
'Captain Avenzi, sir.'
'Captain Avenzi, I want the entire unit ready for battle, drilled and prepared. You will find a sword and other necessary equipment for my daughter and will obey any command from her as a command from me.'
The captain nodded. 'Yes, sir.'
Daryo nodded. 'Is this the unit from which my raiding force will be taken?'
'Yes, sir. The men are already chosen.'
'I want them to meet me at the captains' tent at sundown.'
'Yes, sir.'

One of Tari's aides came to Daryo and showed him and Kym to twin tents immediately beside Tari's. They were almost identical, a folding canvas bed, a leather trunk, a collapsible table and a folding stool. Daryo's had a canvas construction on the wall for the hanging of weapons and the aide promised that one would be produced for Kym before he departed. They were left alone in Kym's tent.

She sat down heavily on the bed. Daryo sat down next to her and put a hand on her knee.

'Overwhelmed?' She could only nod in response. 'If you wish to stay in camp then that is no shame. You have come a long way into a strange place and an alien circumstance. You have shown great commitment to me and to yourself to come this far and I am proud of you, Kym.'

'It gets so real. So many soldiers, so much armour, so many swords. This is a war.'

'It is. Many have died already. Many more will die before the end. You or I may die before the end, Kym. Have you considered that?'

'The Fourth Goddess would not take you from me.'

'She may do. I am much in her debt. She may take you from me.'

'I will resist.'

Daryo smiled and squeezed her knee. 'I am sure that you will. Come, if you are to fight, we need to keep practising.' He stood up, drew the Horse and offered the hilt to Kym. She looked at her father, blinking away the tears that had welled up, and seized the hilt firmly.

The captain of the Vazzeccoes and forty-eight of his men were waiting alongside the captains' tent just before sundown. Kym had been found a short sword but decided instead to go for a larger blade, a hand-and-a-half for a man but easily two-handed for her as well as her bow. Daryo left his shield and Temma's Sword, opting just for his twin blades.

'We need to move quickly so leave your shields,' Daryo told his small force. 'I want the best dozen archers to get longbows and quivers and we shall meet you on the south side of the camp. From when we leave the camp there is to be no unnecessary conversation. Captain Avenzi, you know our destination?' Avenzi nodded. 'You will lead, I will be the last in line. Nobody else here needs to know where we are going or why, only that there will be a short fight at the end. If any man is separated from the others, return here without hesitation. It is better that you return alive than risk capture. Questions?'

'Are we capturing someone, sir?' asked one of the soldiers.

'No.'

'Is this some kind of drill, sir?' asked another.
'No. This is real. There will be Armynyans at the end of our hike. Anyone else? No? Archers, fetch your bows. We shall meet you outside the camp.'

The little force went south-east, Avenzi at the front with a bow, following a narrow creek firstly and then through a small wood. The sun was well down and the light gone by the time they had carefully traversed the trees and another creek. Ahead was a small but steep hill and a fire was burning at the summit. Avenzi brought the force to a halt along the banks of the little waterway, barely two feet wide, and Daryo and Kym joined the captain, gathering the small group around them.
'There is an Armynyan scouting force on that hill,' said Daryo in a whisper. 'I have been told that you are the best soldiers in Adaca: I give you now a chance to prove this. All of the archers remain here. The rest come around the hill with me. My archer will fire a flaming arrow up as a signal. The archers here will then commence firing into the Armynyan camp. Fire a dozen arrows each and then you must stop. My party will attack from the opposite side, you will remain here and only attack if signalled by another arrow. Is all understood?' There was a mutter of assent. 'Good. May the Second God guide you all. Archers, remain here with Captain Avenzi. All others with me.'
Daryo led the thirty-six and Kym around to the right, skirting the base of the lonely hill, through another small wooded patch. Daryo decided that it would make good cover for their assault and stopped his force. Kym took out an arrow, someone produced some oil, dipped some cloth in it and wrapped it around the arrow's tip. A flint and steel were produced, the spark caught the cloth and Kym swiftly notched the arrow, raised the bow and fired it up over the hill. There was brief pause, the Armynyans had not seen the burning arrow, and then Adacan volleys began to land in the Armynyan encampment. Little of the camp was visible from below but the shouts and cries were clear in the darkness. A figure was silhouetted against the fire and then fell. Allowing for a slow count of three per arrow, Daryo counted to twenty-four before waving his men forwards. Kym and her assistant with the fire-making supplies hung back.
Daryo led the charge up the steep slope, drawing his swords as he went. A half-naked Armynyan lurched out of a tent, an Adacan arrow through his bicep. He swung a huge, square-looking blade at Daryo, who ducked under the wild slash, speared the man in the ribs with the Horse and shoved the body aside as he withdrew his blade. By this time, most of the Adacans had passed him and were spreading through the small Armynyan camp, swords reflecting the fire light. Flashes of steel met with cries of surprise and agony. Daryo went towards the centre of the melee and found that the battle was over.

There were a score of tents, two score dead Armynyans. One Adacan soldier had been killed and another had taken a severe wound to his ribs. Daryo sent one man to bring Kym and her assistant to the top and another to bring the archers up. The Adacan soldiers were making a quick check of the Armynyan dead; reports had come through that Armynyans would feign death in order to surprise their enemies later. To counter this, the Adacans were moving around in pairs driving the points of their swords into the throats of the Armynyan dead. Kym joined her father and winced with the noise of each thrust of a sword. There was a lot of blood on the ground and on the Horse in Daryo's hand. She moved around Daryo to take a better look at something and shrieked in dismay. Daryo turned to see what it was. A long pole with a short crossbar at the top lay on the ground as if knocked down. On the ends of the crossbar were purple ribbons. Nailed to the join by the ankles was a baby that looked to be have been barely weeks old when nailed there. The amount of blood on its body suggested that it had also been alive. The brown-green colour of the skin suggested it had been dead for many weeks. Kym sobbed, dropping her bow and hiding her head in her father's chest. Daryo fought down the bile in his throat. Avenzi reached Daryo, saw the grotesque spectacle and closed his eyes tightly.

'A cohort banner,' he said in pained tones. 'Their belief says that the longer the poor infant lives, the stronger and more fortunate the unit will be in combat.'

'Where do the infants come from?'

'Those captured in war and some from slaves or serfs in Armynya.'

Daryo took Kym by the shoulders and moved her away from his body. He sheathed his sword, drew his knife and used it to remove the nail through the dead infant's legs. He ripped the banners from the pole and wrapped the tiny corpse with them. 'Have someone bury the poor child with our man as man and child.'

'Yes, sir.'

Daryo stood up. 'We should search for anything useful and burn the camp. Leave the Armynyan dead where they lay.'

'Yes, sir.'

Daryo moved away, Kym close behind him, her tears still falling silently. He picked up one of the Armynyan weapons. It was crude but deadly, over three feet long, a single piece of iron with a round, leather-wrapped grip, sharpened to a blade on both sides, the top branching out sideways as well as coming to a point at the summit so the sword effectively had three points; a spike in line with the sharp edges of the sword blade and the normal sword point.

'A letian, sir,' said another Adacan soldier. 'Almost every Armynyan soldier carries one. They can be used as axes and swords. Nasty weapons, sir.'

Daryo hefted the weapon. 'Indeed.' He dropped it and turned to Kym as the soldier turned away. 'I am sorry, Kym. This is what you wanted.'

'I know.' She rubbed her eyes furiously. 'I know, father.'

'The first time that you see this is the worst until the next time that you see it. The little child... that is barbaric. I have never seen such a thing before.'

'What kind of man would do such a thing?'

Daryo shook his head. 'I cannot say. Come, we have to be leaving.'

The Vazzeccoes were already burning the tents. Avenzi rallied his men together and they departed as they had arrived: in single file through the darkness with their captain at the front and their commander and his daughter at the rear.

# Chapter 81

The rain started just before the small force returned to the Adacan camp. Daryo left a brief written report in the captains' tent and went to his own rest exhausted, conscious that he had been the oldest man in the raid, maybe two times the age of some of the soldiers in the Adacan army. Before he slept, he knelt and offered a brief prayer to the Fourth Goddess and he slept dreamlessly.

The rain was still falling when dawn broke and the wake and arise was beaten around camp by drums. Daryo found hot pork, butter, bread and apples left for his breakfast and he went to the next tent to breakfast with his daughter. Kym looked tired and depressed.

'Did you sleep poorly?' he asked as they ate. Kym nodded silently. 'I would have been concerned if you had not. You are spending a first night in a strange bed, you have seen your first sight of battle and seen a gruesome display that I have not seen in over thirty summers on the roads. You are a strong woman, Kym, and you will come out of this much stronger.'

Kym managed a smile. The rain was beating down on the roof of the tent and the ground outside. The drums to wake the sleepers were still beating around the camp. A flute was being played nearby, presumably a soldier entertaining his comrades. The tramp of feet, the clinking of mail, the clang of steel, the thud of wood, the noises of thousands of men in camp was a constant noise.

'Sir! Sir!' A young soldier put his head in the tent. 'Sir, there is urgent news for Princess Tari.'

'Then tell her,' said Daryo shortly.

'With respect, sir, you are her lieutenant.'

Daryo sighed. 'Proceed.'

'There is a... delegation approaching. Armynyans, sir. They wish to treat.'

Both Daryo and Kym jumped to their feet. Daryo swiftly pushed the young soldier out of Kym's tent. 'Where are they?'

'There is a ruined building about a third of a mile from the edge of camp, sir. There is a sentry position there and they have consented to stop there.'

'Have the princess and the captains informed.'

'Yes, sir!'

'Hurry!'

The princess, her captains and Daryo swiftly agreed that there was little that could be lost by not talking to the Armynyan delegation. If nothing else, it would buy extra time for the Army of the South to join them. The Armynyan party was reported to number fifty so Tari insisted that an entire half-company of the Vazzeccoes accompany her, her three senior captains and Daryo, who in turn insisted that Kym be included in the party. Horses were provided for the six dignitaries, as Avenzi named them, and the two hundred of the Vazzeccoes. With banners flying, they set off.

'Why now, do you think?' Tari asked as they made their way through the camp.

Daryo considered his response for a moment. 'They may be stalling for time, as we are. They may be hoping to come to a truce, to take what they have gained, to earn tribute or servitude from Adaca. It could be a delaying tactic, or a deception. It may be an attempt to administer victor's justice. Any of those or none of those. I cannot say, my Lady.'

The princess frowned.

Before the spread of the true faith of the Pantheon, there were the older religions- the White Lady, the Good Shepherd, Titheirianism and the Cult of The Orbs, the worship of the everlasting duel between the sun and the moon. The ruins of the temple on the road to Tanaab was the remains of a temple of The Orbs; twenty circular pillars arranged in a twenty-yard circle that once had supported walls and a vaulted ceiling. All but three of the pillars still stood, the three that had collapsed had fallen inwards, taking most of the west and south walls too. The ceiling had collapsed into the centre, leaving the ruin, once of brown stone, to be overrun by weeds, moss and animals. A small tree had taken root and grew from what had once been the western plaza, a paved square on which worshippers congregated at sunset for their devotions. The ruins looked deserted still but Daryo knew that to be untrue. He dismounted first. The Walker had ridden to combat: his jerkin, bracers, three swords, knife and shield. He slid his arms through the shield's straps and drew Temma's Sword, holding it down at his side.

'This is a parley, Walker,' said Tari. 'Not a war.'

'This is a parley in a war,' Daryo said shortly. 'You are the sister of the King of Adaca and the commander of Adaca's army. You are valuable beyond treasure.' The rest of the procession began to dismount. Daryo identified Captain Avenzi. 'Keep three quarters of the men out here.'

'Yes, sir.'

'The rest of the escort with me and the princess.'

'Yes, sir.'

Avenzi gave the necessary orders. As they approached the temple, Kym drew her sword. They passed the tree and went through what had once been the west door of the temple. The south and east walls were still almost complete, the north was intact from the middle downwards, only the arch of the west door remained. Inside the floor was littered with the debris of the fallen ceiling- piles of stone, heaps of rotten wood, growing grasses and shrubbery. In the centre had been twin circular altars, single huge pieces of stone; a brown one on the west side, white on the east with around ten feet between them. The western one had been buried in the collapse but sat on the eastern altar like he was sat on a throne was an Armynyan man- he was tall and broad-shouldered, wearing a leather baldric across his bare chest and leather guards on his forearms, he had on rough trousers with leather and iron reinforcements on the thighs, a letian hung from the baldric and a long oval shield was propped against the altar beside him. A dozen figures were stood at the back of the ruined temple, half of them dressed as the seated man was, the other half in dark brown cloaks with the cowls raised.

The Vazzeccoes fanned out across the west side of the temple in ordered ranks, their commanders in front. Daryo motioned to Kym to remain with the Adacan commanders as he accompanied the princess.

'Princess Tari,' said the Armynyan man in a slow, gravelly, accented voice. 'And your Batribi... companion.'

'My lieutenant, Daryo, kin of Dostan,' said Tari stiffly. 'If you know who I am, then it is politeness that I know who you are.' She stopped in front the rubble-covered western altar.

'I am Tyokyov. I command the army of the One who is Two.'

'You command the soldiers that burn our towns and murder our people,' said Tari, doing her best to keep her voice level.

'The One who is Two is not violent. The One who is Two has a prophecy to fulfil. The One who is Two must lead Armynya against all foes. Adaca is not Armynyan and therefore is a foe of Armynya. But the One who is Two has led our people against Adaca. You can agree to be defeated and the One who is Two will have started towards completing fate's dictation. Persuade your brother to kneel before the One who is Two and Adaca will live on, as a valued servant. Its lands could even expand, when the One who is Two takes Sodidor, Boskinia, Ishter, Vidmaria. You could have your own nation, Princess. You could be a queen. You could be an empress. If you kneel at the feet of the One who is Two.'

Tari looked at Daryo, who tipped his head. Tari shrugged and took half a step back. Daryo inclined his head to the Armynyan. 'You have come a long way, Master Tyokyov.

As that is so, and your comrades have come the same long distance, can we not speak directly to your leader, as he is standing behind you?'
Tyokyov smiled broadly. 'How did you know, Master Daryo, kin of Dostan?'
'The men behind you. Some are cloaked, some are not. All the cloaked men are standing together but for one. All the evident warriors are standing around the other cloaked figure but not within arm's length: a respectful distance for a feared or respected leader.'
'I am both,' said the figure. The hood was lowered and the cloak removed. The One of Both handed the cloak to one of the warriors. The face was of a man, only five or six summers older than Kym, a beard beginning to show, the hair was long and braided, beneath an elaborately-embroidered silver and gold tunic were the rises of small breasts, the legs in tight silver breeches were powerful but lean. The voice was that of a boy but the body was obviously of at least twenty-five summers.
'I am respected and feared, loved and hated, wanted and rejected, adored and despised.' With those words came footsteps until they stopped stood next to Tyokyov, who had stood. 'I am the One who is Two, the foretold leader of my people. I admire your observation and deduction, Daryo the Batribi. Have you not considered what I could offer you? The princess could be translated to being an empress but what of you? You could be a warlord, a king, a tyrant or a benevolent guide. Your wife could be enthroned alongside you. Your sons could be princes. Your daughter... your daughter could be a princess in her own right. Ruler of her own nation.'
Daryo made a conscious decision not to look back at Kym. 'She could.'
'The Batribi have a nation of their own. You could be their leader. The outcasts could be the ruling caste.' The One of Two's arms spread wide. 'Empress Tari of the South, Emperor Daryo of the North. I ask for no lands. Armynya is the first among nations. Kneel at my feet and I shall give you all that I have promised and more.'
Daryo looked at Tari. The Adacan princess's face was unreadable. Very slowly she walked forwards. Daryo felt stuck in his spot, unable to move or to speak. Tari seemed to take a long time to cross the short gap.
'You wish me to kneel,' she said, her voice barely loud enough to hear.
The One of Two smiled benevolently. 'Only to kneel.'
Tari bowed her head. 'Then I have no choice.' She sighed. 'I have mail on beneath my leggings, I cannot bend my knee that far.' With a single rapid motion she drew a dagger, grabbed the half-man half-woman's hair and thrust her dagger point to the throat.
Tyokyov roared in anger and drew his sword but Daryo had crossed the gap and caught the swing at Tari with Temma's Sword. He heard the sound of weapons being readied. Tari pulled hard on the hair in her hand.

'I will not kneel to you and any Adacan who does is a traitor. I am a princess of Adaca, the sister of the king. You have killed my countrymen, killed our children and our women. You have burned our towns and crops. You will leave Adaca or you will be chased from these lands. If ever I see your unnatural face again, I will slay you with my own hands.' She pushed the One of Two back against the altar and retreated a few steps. Daryo knocked Tyokyov's blade aside, covered himself with his shield and stepped back alongside the princess.

The One of Two stood up panting. 'You have been given the chance to take my gifts from my hand and you have refused.' The voice was lower now, more threatening. 'I have destiny guiding me. I will lead Armynya to victory against all foes. And all the world is foe. Your nation shall burn! Your people shall beg for death! Your infants shall be nailed to the banners of the armies that slay their parents and their cries shall be the music to which my army marches across the world.'

Tari took a deep breath and spat at the Armynyan's feet. 'Leave while you still draw breath, filth!' She turned and strode back towards the west door, followed by Daryo. The One of Two looked at Tyokyov and growled something in their native language as they removed themselves. The Vazzeccoes parted to allow their princess and her commanders through and then retreated behind them. Outside, Daryo saw that Tari and Kym were mounted first. He had just taken the reins of his horse when the Armynyan force that had been protecting their leader streamed out of the west door a hundred yards away, letians waving, screaming a battlecry.

'Kym, protect Tari!' shouted Daryo. 'Avenzi, take your men back with them! Princess's Force, shellback!'

The Vazzeccoes were indeed highly trained. They quickly rushed forwards and the fifty men that had been in the temple quickly formed a solid wall, locking their Boskinian-style shields together at the front, the rear ranks lifting their shields to form a roof and, as Tari, Kym and the others galloped away, the charging Armynyans were met with a solid brick of shields, breaking like tide on rocks. Daryo, without a large rectangular shield, had taken refuge in the centre. A screaming Armynyan leaped onto the top of the formation as his fellows attacked with their lethal weapons. The shellback rocked and the leaper fell through a hole in the roof. Daryo ran the Armynyan through with Temma's Sword. A letian found a gap and slashed into the arm of an Adacan. The man fell back from the line but the shellback condensed to close the gap quickly but not before another Armynyan got into the formation. The closest Adacan soldier let go of his shield and drove his sword into the Armynyan. Another pair of Armynyans leaped the wall and landed in the formation. Daryo was closest, smashed one in the face and hacked him down with his sword. Three Adacans broke from the roof but one was slain before his comrades overwhelmed the Armynyan.

'Out!' roared Daryo. 'Push out!'

The Vazzeccoes roared together and shoved outwards with their shields, creating a vital half-yard of space before boiling out of their formation like water from a pot. The letians clashed against rectangular shields and into flesh, swords swung against long oval shields and Armynyan bodies. From the centre came a single Batribi, his curved sword flashing in the light, moving with apparently effortless speed and precision among his enemies, oblivious to the chaos, seeing only a battle that he must win. Countless blows of letians were caught by his old shield, his sword was relentless and lethal. When it was knocked from his grasp by a shield blow, the Batribi's shield was used as a missile against the offender and suddenly the Batribi was wielding two small, straight, narrow blades, one pointed up and the other pointed down and the machine of steel and wooden shield became a vicious storm of steel that carved through all before it. A lethal double-blade cut through the throat of an Armynyan and he turned, looking for his next victim. There was none. All the men around him were Adacan.

'Victory!' shouted one of the Vazzeccoes. 'Victory for Adaca and the Walker!'

Daryo lowered his blades as the others took up the shout. Many Adacans had been killed as well as the Armynyans, all of whom were dead. None seemed to have fled. Daryo counted thirty-one dead Armynyans and sixteen Adacans. He found that he had taken a blow from the spike of a letian, a bloody dent in the side of his left upper arm. Seventy yards from the battle, the horses were still tethered.

'Get the wounded and dead on horses!' he ordered. 'Did anyone see the princess's party leave? Or the Armynyans?'

'The princess got away safely, sir,' said one man. 'They were not pursued.'

Daryo nodded, suddenly aware of the pain in his arm, a soreness in his shoulders and neck and a pain in his right hand. He sheathed the twin blades and found Temma's Sword unharmed. A soldier handed him his shield, which had taken several heavy blows. Daryo picked out five men. 'Check that the temple is empty but be swift. This place will be full of Armynyan soldiers by midday. We need to get back to the camp.'

# Chapter 82

'Walker, I am sorry, it is late.'

Daryo sat on one the stools in the captains' tent. 'Not at all, Princess.' They were alone in the tent, only lit by a series of stout candles along the line of the table.

'You were injured in the battle.'

'Not seriously. The physician has cleaned and bound the wound. It will heal.'

'The One of Two tried to have me assassinated.'

'I believe so. I can think of no other reason for that attack. I imagine that was a major reason for the invitation to treat. If you refused the offer, they could then try to eliminate you.'

'I had my dagger against that thing's throat. I could have killed it.'

'And been no better than they are. You did the right thing.'

'Maybe not for our people.'

'Or perhaps so. If you decapitate the leader of the pack, the rest of the pack may not rest until they have your head alongside it.'

Tari nodded thoughtfully, pacing the tent. 'Walker, what do you think of women?'

'Women, Princess?'

'Women.'

Daryo shrugged. 'I do not know what to say. I love my wife and daughter, I honour and admire you, I respect Wulia Sasi the potter in Ritaro...'

'In common, as a sex.'

Daryo thought. 'I think, commonly, that women are like wolves, Princess. I think most women think of their pack, their family, before they think of themselves. They are family-first, they think of their children and husbands, their homes.'

'And men?'

'If women are wolves, then men are bears- they do their duty by their wife and children but are at heart creatures of solitude, hunting alone, providing. May I ask what purpose your questions have?'

'I have been thinking about the One of Two. A creature that is both man and woman will surely have the weaknesses of both a man and a woman.'

'But the strengths also.'

'One cannot win a war fighting to the enemy's strengths.'

'But one can lose a war if one is not aware of them.'

Tari murmured noncommittally and continued pacing the tent. 'We have to win this war. Defeat would mean the destruction of Adaca.'

'I concur.'
'What would you have me do, Walker?'
'I? It is not for me to say.'
'My brother summoned you to save his kingdom. How do we do that?"
Daryo nodded his understanding. 'Have you asked for aid? Boskinia? Ishter? Gourmin?'
'Boskinia is still occupied with the Vidmarians. Their king is a warrior but has only one sword-arm. He is aware that there is an Armynyan threat but if that is so, he must look to his own borders.'
'Understandable.'
'The Ishteri are a small nation with many challenges. They have only a token militia. They would be of little help but have promised what troops they could spare, if sorely needed, for example to escort the Adacan court to safety.'
'There is a refuge planned?'
'Yes. Ishter would give us sanctuary initially and then we would go to Yashoun.'
Daryo nodded. 'And Gourmin?'
'The Gourmini have had no leader for fifty years. Their council is indecisive. They have a large army and many men at their summons but cannot make a choice as to what to do with them.'
'Perhaps they could be persuaded,' mused Daryo. 'A resource or a treasure that would give them incentive.'
Tari considered this. 'I will suggest it to the king.'
Daryo pulled across a map of the known world. 'If the Gourmini could be persuaded to strike south from Sitak as we attacked to the north-east from Tanaab.'
'First we must retake Tanaab. That will not be easy. Tanaab is a citadel, a high-walled town on the top of a flat mountain. The cliffs to the base of the walls are thirty feet and the walls are another two hundred feet or more. There is a single gate reached by a causeway, overlooked by the Towers of the Presidents.'
'There must be a weakness.'
'Not that I know of.'
'Then we must find one.'
'There is an Armynyan army between us and Tanaab, Walker. Camped around Taletesedro.'
'Then we must find our way past it.'
Tari nodded and yawned. The hour was late, approaching midnight. 'I think I shall retire.'

'Of course, Princess.' Daryo rose from his seat as Tari left and then returned to his stool. He studied the map, fetched the reports on the Armynyan army and reread every one. Afterwards he reread the information on the Adacan army and consulted the maps again. At the conclusion, he rechecked every detail and continued working late into the night.

The Adacan captains were all woken at dawn by a young half-Batribi woman that many vaguely recognised as the daughter of Daryo the Walker. They were asked to report to the captains' tent at the centre of camp before she disappeared into the morning fog. The score of senior commanders, including the princess and Avenzi assembled and seated themselves at the table. Daryo the Walker stood at the head of the table and slowly explained his proposed plan in detail. The captains listened in silence until Daryo had finished.
'How do you know that this will work?' one asked after Daryo had sat down.
'I do not know,' said Daryo simply. 'I read the accounts of the early battles on the eastern frontier, part of the reason for the failure of those early battles was that the defence plans were adhered to as if they were holy orders. The Armynyans did not behave according to the battle plans and therefore the frontier battles were lost. We must have tactical awareness, be willing to adapt.'
Tari nodded. 'Agreed. Does anyone directly oppose the Walker's plan?' She permitted a brief period of silence. 'Then the Captains of the Army of Adaca consent. Captain Tivilio, send a message to the Army of the South and have them divert to Taletesedro.'
'Yes, my Lady.'
'Captain Avenzi, have the Vazzeccoes take the vanguard. Captains Aitir and Galjendro, have the army strike camp and march for Taletesedro.'

The Army of Adaca began to form up and march east. As they left camp, they passed their princess and several of her captains beside the road. The captains were mounted, watching their troops pass. The princess was on foot, talking to passing men, taking some out of the line of march to look at their weapons or discuss their families. Alongside her a lot of the time was the Batribi captain, his distinctive swords and shield about him and his daughter nearby. Many of the passing units hailed the Walker and a few had even composed marching songs around the theme of the heroic Walker and the great deeds that he had done and would do in battle.
Kym sidled up to her father as he saluted another singing, departing unit. 'Father? When did you defeat three hundred Yashoun soldiers with a fruit knife?'

Daryo laughed. 'I do not think I ever have done but they seemed to know more of my reputation than I do.'
'Why do they sing things that are not true?'
'It is not intentional, I am sure, Kym. They may have heard exaggerated stories. You remember the old child's game when you pass a message around from one to the next?'
'It always gets distorted.'
'It always gets distorted. Reports from the battlefield are often distorted the same way. If one person hears a message in a game and passes it on it can be distorted. If a thousand men are on a battlefield and get told a message, the actions of a commander, an atrocity, and the message gets distorted a thousand times. The message gets passed on and further distorted and then different versions of the message get confused.'
'And then they make it into songs?'
'Lots of things become songs. Soldiers are known for singing on the march, it helps pass the time and fight the boredom.'
Kym nodded. 'Why is that I and Princess Tari are the only women in the army?'
Daryo thought. 'War in armies has always been the precinct of men. Women traditionally care for their families and homes while the men go to war. Some nations have women warriors, they are a lot more common in Boskinia, Jaboen and Gourmin than in Adaca or Yashoun.'
'I think perhaps that I could be a warrior.'
'I think perhaps that you could,' said Daryo with a smile. 'We should find our mounts and catch up with the Vazzeccoes.'
'Yes, Walker.'
Daryo smiled and punched his daughter playfully on the arm.

The road was relatively new and had been well-laid, wide enough for ten men to march comfortably shoulder to shoulder, almost straight and closely paved with stone and gravel. The march progressed north-east, the army strung out with the Vazzeccoes in the lead and the cavalry having overtaken other units via the sides of the roads and had taken position behind the vanguard. A small unit had gone ahead has scouts, joined by Avenzi. Tari's bodyguard joined the straggling procession near the rear. It was a full days' march before the Vazzeccoes stopped to make camp. Slowly, as night fell, the rest of the army arrived and the camp grew. The scouts returned just after sundown and reported the Armynyan army camped around Taletesedro.

## Chapter 83

The destroyed village of Taletesedro was on the top of a low hill. Alongside it had been built a wooden bastion, apparently from the very material of the houses that had once been homes. The road ran up the hill from the lowland, up the slope and through the what had once been the village. At the bottom of the hill, joined to the load by a track, was a farm, in slightly better condition than the village but looking as if it had been fired. The Armynyan army was clustering in front of the farm and in front of the village. Daryo led the Vazzeccoes to the brow of a hill across the road from Talatesedro's rise and Tari's bodyguard joined them. Immediately in front of them, the Army of the South that had been before Ensadri formed up in five units, each of more than three thousand men, five ranks deep, with its small mounted party went to the right flank. Behind them, the Army of the Centre formed three units, their archers and cavalry to the left, between the smaller hill and the army from Ensadri. Opposite them the Armynyan army had formed two massive groups, more hordes than formed-up army units. The Adacan army was tensely quiet, the Armynyans were screaming challenges in their own language, waving their weapons.

Daryo wheeled his horse to a position between Tari's guard and the Vazzeccoes. The trumpeters to signal the Adacan army found him and readied themselves. Among the princess's entourage he noticed Kym. He had been able to talk briefly to Tari just after breakfast and the princess had happily agreed to invite Kym to join the Royal Guard as her honorary squire. A messenger came from the princess.

'Sir, my Lady asks if you have noticed that the Armynyan unit on our left is a long way offset from our own forces.'

Daryo reviewed the battlefield once more and nodded. The Armynyan formation on the Adacan left was significantly offset from the Adacans. 'Please tell the princess that I am aware and I believe that this is quite acceptable.'

'Yes, sir.' The messenger retired.

The noise across the valley suddenly stopped. There was a deep, low horn blown and the Armynyans in front of the village, on the Adacan right, charged down the hill.

'Forward line to meet the charge!' Daryo called to a signaller.

The signaller lifted a large metal horn and blew the appropriate signal. The forward units began to move to meet the Armynyan charge. The clash was audible from Daryo's position: wood, steel and flesh colliding at a sprint. The smash of steel blades against wooden shields, the thump of steel hitting bone, the screams of men wounded and dying filled the air. The Armynyan numbers told at first, the force of the men behind pushing

their comrades on into the Adacan lines but the discipline and organisation of the Adacans was superior. The Ensadri Army's archers began firing into the rear of the Armynyan formation. Slowly the Adacan vanguard worked forwards. The Armynyan archers, between and behind the main forces were firing towards the Adacan second line but few were in range and the Adacans sheltered behind their shields. The Armynyan horns sounded again and their second huge horde began to run to the aid of the first.
'Runner!' shouted Daryo and a young man dressed in only short breeches and a vest hurried forwards. 'Tell Captain Avenzi to take the Vazzeccoes to the left flank behind the cavalry. Have the Army of the South's cavalry move behind them.'
'Yes, sir.' The runner raced away.
'Second line, ten paces forwards!' Daryo ordered the trumpeter. The signal was given and the Army of the Centre marched forwards the required distance. As they did so, the Vazzeccoes jogged behind the hill onto the Adacan left, followed by the southern army's cavalry. Daryo was gambling that the cavalry's move would be obvious but not the unhorsed Vazzeccoes. The second Armynyan force smashed into the Adacan foot-soldiers' left flank. The combined pressure of both Armynyan forces began to constrict the Army of the South's position, forcing them backwards.
'Cavalry!' Daryo called to the trumpeter. 'Around left and into the archers.'
The three blasts for the cavalry was blown, two for left movement and two long and a series of six short blasts for archers followed. The signal was repeated and the three units of Adacan cavalry formed a single mass, wheeled around the Armynyan infantry and charged their archers in the rear. The attack was seen late but the Armynyan bows began to fire just as they were hit by the galloping horsemen. The Adacan cavalry was in behind the Armynyan line but the Armynyans had a mounted unit of their own that now began to manoeuvre to attack the Adacan left.
'Second line forwards!' ordered Daryo quickly. He wheeled his horse and galloped across the front of the princess's guard. The only units on the right were the Army of the Centre's archers, and the Vazzeccoes. In the front of the Adacan elite's ranks was Avenzi, his white and red cape evident. He raised his sword and dramatically the Vazzeccoes' line became a spearhead. The Vazzeccoes then dived behind their shields, their curved Batribi-style swords coming out of the wall like spikes on a porcupine. The Armynyan cavalry broke against the Vazzeccoes like waves against a cliff. As the last of the assault broke against Avenzi's shield at the point, the Adacans suddenly turned about and again hid behind their shields as their archers sent barrage after barrage into the stunned and confused Armynyan horsemen. The Armynyan horsemen broke and scattered.

Daryo almost laughed in delight, turned his horse and sprinted it back to the trumpeters. 'Second line push forward!'

The signal was given. The Adacan cavalry had cut off the retreat. The full weight of the Adacan line was now brought to bear on the main force of Armynyan infantry. Again the discipline and organisation of the Adacans paid as the disorganised Armynyans, relying on their numbers, were outmanoeuvred and found their rear attacked by cavalry. Daryo decided to play his final trick.

'First line, disengage! Army of the South to retreat to the hill!'

It was a gamble, but one he intended to win. The signal went out and the remnants of the Adacan force began to pull back, in apparent retreat but in full knowledge of the plan. There were many of their number dead, injured or caught in the crush of the melee. Perhaps less than four thousand withdrew but it was enough. Daryo left his horse and had the final signal given. The royal guard, all but a few left to guard the princess herself, dismounted and followed Daryo down the hill. They joined the battered patch unit of the Army of the South and Daryo was cheered through to the front row. He found himself elbowed aside slightly as he took his place in the line.

'Kym!'

'I had to!' she said breathlessly. She was wielding her two-handed sword with an archer's arm brace on the outside of both forearms.

Daryo cursed under his breath. 'Too late for else now!' He drew Temma's Sword. 'For Adaca!'

'FOR ADACA!' came the answering roar, taken up by the whole unit.

'CHARGE!'

With a collective bellow, the newly-rallied Adacan reserve charged into battle, the mix of royal guard's unused men and the Army of the South's survivors. The force of the charge was exceptional. Daryo found himself cleaving through Armynyan bodies, his daughter at his side. They were fifty, seventy, ninety, over a hundred yards into the fray, two hundred. Daryo ducked a hammer blow from the side of a letian and slashed Temma's Sword into the Armynyan's guts. As he did so, Kym's sword came over his head and took the Armynyan in the face, almost taking the man's skull in two. Daryo followed his daughter into the next clash, Kym's sword stuck in the next Armynyan's chest and Daryo's blow with the bottom edge of his shield knocked the body clear.

'FATHER!'

Daryo could do nothing but throw himself down. A letian cleaved through where his head had been and Kym's sword amputated the attacker's arm and then his head. Daryo scrambled up, ducked under another assault, caught the following blow on his shield and Kym drove the edge of her blade into the man's back. Daryo spun around so he was back to back with his daughter. Together their blades flashed and they moved in concert to protect each other. The Armynyan forces were fleeing. Few were surrendering, many were fighting desperately but the rush of their comrades retreat carried most along like fish in a school. Daryo tripped an Armynyan charging at his daughter and drove Temma's Sword deep into the prone man's back. When he looked up, he saw a very disturbing sight: Princess Tari was wielding a Batribi-style curved blade and a buckler and was duelling an Armynyan larger than Daryo.

'Kym! With me!' he shouted and sprinted to the scene. He slid across the blood-wetted ground and knocked down the princess's opponent. Tari's blade did the remainder of the work. Kym was quickly at the princess's side and on guard but the battle had gone. The cavalry were harassing the Armynyan soldiers as they fled through the ruined village. The Army of the Centre was moving forwards and the forward lines were already assaulting the defences of the all-but abandoned Armynyan camp.

Daryo summoned a nearby soldier. 'Go back to the battlefield trumpeters. Have the signal given to hold position.' The soldier raised his sword in salute and raced away. Daryo sent another man to Captain Avenzi to have the Vazzeccoes rally at the princess.

'We have taken the field, Walker!' said the princess, her tone exhilarated.

'We have. You should not have been on it though, my Lady.'

'Royal prerogative,' said the princess tartly.

Daryo sighed and turned to Kym. 'Well done.'

'My thanks, father.'

'This may mean little to anyone but me but do you remember the promise that I made as a Member of the Order of Shield and Sword?' Kym nodded. 'I took my promise in the face of battle. Hold your sword in salute.'

Kym held her sword by the hilt, point down and repeated without prompting: 'With my heart, my mind and my honour, I promise to do my duty as a Member of the Order of the Shield and Sword. I swear my Shield and Sword to the defence of the just, the righteous, the innocent and the weak. By this oath, I pledge my sword and my service until I am discharged by death.'

Daryo clasped her hand. 'I am immensely proud of you, Kym.'

'As am I,' said Tari. 'Your bravery, your devotion and your loyalty are beyond reproach, Kym, daughter of Daryo. Any reward that you wish to claim is yours.'

Kym looked as if all capacity for thought was drained from her. 'My Lady... my Lady...' she stuttered and Tari laughed.

'You do not have to choose something immediately. Is it not the tradition that Members of the Order took names? May I suggest a name?'
'I have one already,' said Kym. 'The Devoted. To my promise, to my princess and to my family.'

Daryo returned with Kym and Tari to the hill from which they had started and had the captains brought in. Three of them had been killed, including the cavalry commander, so lieutenants were present instead. Daryo gave orders for the cavalry to pursue the Armynyans to Scirito and then form a picket line until the main army had reformed and was able to march again. The baggage train was brought forwards and the wounded tended to. Within five days, the physicians estimated that half of the three thousand wounded would be battle-ready again. Within ten, perhaps another six hundred would be so too. Approximately the same number of wounded had been killed. Daryo's tent was set up behind the hill from which he had commanded. He had parchment and ink delivered and he wrote.

*To my dearest and most loving Jeda,*
*From your loyal and worshipful husband, Daryo the Walker, and in representation of Kym the Devoted, our daughter.*

*I write to you, my love, on the evening after the battle. We have won a victory and no more but it is the first step on a long road. I know that you were unhappy that I chose to come to battle but I feel now more than ever that the best method that I can use to protect you and our family is to remain here.*

*Princess Tari has been most welcoming and has given me the position of her lieutenant. The princess has also given Kym the position of her honorary squire. Kym fought in the battle against my wishes, as did the princess, but both distinguished themselves. Kym has earned the favour and gratitude of the princess and her bravery and skill were quite remarkable. I have always been guided in such matters by the Fourth Goddess but the Second Goddess surely guides our daughter as she fights for our family and the lives that we have built in Adaca.*

*Try not to worry too much, my darling. This long road will have a destination, that destination is Ritaro and the hearth by which my wife is seated with my sons. I love you, my wife, kiss Vehllal and embrace Stai for me. I shall bring Kym home alongside me. I swear.*

*I pray that the Fourth Goddess spares me and the First God guides me to you once more. I remain your devoted and loving husband despite the many hundreds of miles that separate us.*

A royal courier was provided by Tari and Daryo gave strict instructions that the letter was to be taken to the village of Ritaro on the road to Sodidor from Baros and to be delivered only to the hands of the Yashoun woman who lived at the forge. The courier bowed low, took the letter which was placed in a sealed pouch within his robes and he hurried outside to his waiting horse.

Daryo was eating his midday meal the day after the battle when a wounded soldier approached, a bandage wrapped around most of his right arm and another around his neck.
'My Lord Walker, I am in command of the soldiers guarding the prisoners. There is an Armynyan who wishes to speak with you.' There were fewer than four score prisoners. Almost all of the Armynyan army had either fled or fought to their deaths.
'What manner of man?'
'He claims to be a kinsman of their leader, the unnatural animal.'
Daryo was intrigued. 'I need an empty tent.'
'Yes, sir.'
The tent was prepared and the Armynyan was shackled by the wrists to the centre pole. When Daryo arrived the commander of the prisoners' guard and one of the Vazzeccoes were present. Daryo was unarmed but for his knife, both prisoner escorts had curved swords and the Vazzecco had an Armynyan letian slung across his back on an improvised rope sling.
'Step outside,' Daryo told them. They passed their commander and stood immediately outside the door of the tent.
The Armynyan was taller than Daryo, his skin had a sallow tinge, as did his eyes. His body had a withered look, a muscular man who had been ill for a long time, his hair was thin and lank, his beard thin and his hands shook. He had been given a rough sackcloth tunic and trousers and wore reed sandals. 'You are the Batribi captain?' His voice was accented but clear.
'I am. You speak the Common Tongue.'
'Once I traded with Adacans from Ensadri. I learn it there.'
Daryo nodded. 'I am told that you asked to see me.'
'I did. I can help you, Batribi.'
'How?'

'I am kin of our leader, the One who is Two, the One who is Neither.'
'In what way?'
'He is of the tribe Haustihya. I am of the tribe Haustihya. The tribe is small. All the tribe are close kin.'
'And how does this help my cause, Armynyan?'
'I can tell you of his knowledge and his weaknesses.'
'Why? Why would you betray not only your leader and people but your kin too?'
The man shrugged heavily. 'I am sick, Batribi. Many of the army are. We follow the One who is Two because so many believe he is the one prophesied. If this is so, the prophecies are not good. The prophecy says that the One of Two will be the best of the Armynyan people, a benevolent king, a nurturing parent, a great captain. The One who is Two is none of these things. He marches the men on foot while he rides in a carriage. The men starve as he gives no thought to provisions. The men grow sick from tiredness, insects, spoiling meat, and he marches them on with whips at their backs. But he is followed because he is the One of Two.'
Daryo nodded his understanding. 'Is the One of Two both? Have you seen this?'
The Armynyan nodded. 'He is my kin. He is man and woman. The breasts are of a young girl, the orifice is that of a child but the man's organ is fully formed and you see in his face that he is a young man.'
'You call him a man. Is this how he was seen as a child?'
'Yes. The name given to him on his ninth day was Fathrin, after his father's brother. The... differences only became known as he grew.'
'There is no illusion?'
'No.'
Daryo thought for a moment. 'What is your name, Armynyan?'
'Dathrhyn Haustihyana.'
'If you were unaware, I am Daryo, kin of Dostan.'
'I was aware. Rumours of the Batribi hero of Adaca spread.'
'Why do you fight, Dathrhyn Haustihyana?'
'Because I am of Armynya and because I am kin of the One of Two. It gives... status.'
'So why do you know stand before me in shackles? Many of your kin and comrades die rather than live as captives.'
'I am too sick to fight. I know that the King of Adaca is an honourable man. I knew I would be well treated if I gave myself up. I hope that my usefulness to the captain of Adaca will earn me and my countrymen better treatment.'

Daryo smiled. 'I swear on my honour, Dathrhyn Haustihyana. Is there anything else you wish to tell me?'
'I can say only one more thing I believe to be of import to you. Thamriev is empty. He who controls the Stone Chair by force of arms would have much sway over the simpler folk of Armynya, especially over an army that is beginning to despise its own leader.'
'My earnest thanks to you.'
'Use what I have said well.'
'I shall.'

Just the senior commanders were summoned to the captains' tent, set up at Daryo's insistence on the hill from which the Adacan leadership had directed the battle: Daryo, Tari, Avenzi, the new cavalry commander Midlai, the Army of the Centre's captain Passegi and the Army of the South's captain Yatesi. Daryo noticed that Kym had a praying woman within the Fourth Goddess's dead moon and the Second Goddess's flames painted on her left arm guard. He related everything that Dathrhyn had told him about the Armnynyan army and the One of Two.
'Surely we can take an advantage from this,' said Tari when Daryo had finished.
'I concur,' said Daryo. 'Captain Midlai, you said earlier that the Armynyan army did not try to hold Scirito.'
'No, sir. They withdrew through the town and across the river.'
'There is no defensible place on the Sciti Moor,' said Yatesi. 'I was born there and I know that land, my princess. The only defensible place that they could go to is Tanaab.'
'And there may be no more defensible place in Adaca,' said Avenzi.
'For an army, yes,' said Daryo. 'But maybe not for a small group.'
'You are thinking of something like your raid?' asked Tari.
'Not exactly. We move the army to within striking distance of Tanaab but not close enough to lay siege. Then a small team sneak around the rear, into the city, open the gate and the army pours in.'
'You make it sound so simple, Walker,' said Yatesi grimly.
'I may be making it so,' Daryo admitted. 'But theoretically it would work. The Armynyans will be watching for units of men numbering in thousands, not a team of less than a score.'
'Are there any secret ways into the city?' asked Avenzi.
'We would need someone who knows the city better than any other,' said Tari. 'A thief, someone of that nature who would know the secret ways. Ask among your men. A man of Tanaab who knows the hidden doors and secret hiding places. Meanwhile, the army

will march east in pursuit of our would-be conquerors. Midlai, keep your men close on the heels of the Armynyans, Avenzi have the Vazzeccoes keep to the vanguard of the army. If the Armynyans turn and fight, the Vazzeccoes are the best to have in that position.'

'Yes, my Lady.'

## Chapter 84

Five days' unhindered march followed for the Adacan army. Reports from the single Adacan spy outside Tanaab's walls said the One of Two had fled to Tanaab immediately after the battle of Taletesedro and the Armynyan army had followed its leader back to the citadel. After five days' march, the Adacan army made camp just under three miles from the city. On the road, Daryo had made use of the time to talk to the men of the Vazzecco unit and identify the most likely members of his team. Whenever the column, or their part of it, halted he was out training Kym or testing out prospective colleagues for his clandestine work. The expert on Tanaab was produced, he had been the Adacan army's spy in the area until the Armynyan retreat and it was he who had seen the One of Two's return to the city and the Armynyan army's flight inside the walls. Now the Armynyan army was concentrated inside the walls and the gates were securely shut. With the sun setting, Daryo accompanied the spy forwards to survey the city.

From a mile distant, the city looked like a single immense tower. The walls were stone and at least two hundred feet high. They were built within feet of the edges of the cliffs on which they stood, which themselves rose nearly forty feet from the ground around them. The gate was on the south side of the walls, a mighty arch filled by metal-reinforced wooden gates. To reach the gates was a single causeway, a ramp that took the road up to the height of the cliffs. It was barely ten yards wide, not much wider than the road itself and, flanking it as it reached the cliffs were two mighty towers, the one to the right was star-shaped in plan, the left was taller and rounded, both rose all the wall from the ground to taller than the height of the walls, almost three hundred feet in total, Daryo estimated. The walls of each was a patchwork of arrow slits and what appeared to be spouts.

'What are those?' Daryo asked softly.

The little man with him hissed through his teeth. 'Spouts for the tar, my Lord. Below the city, in the caves, hot natural tar comes through the ground like water from a spring. It is stored in the towers. If Tanaab is attacked, the tar can be heated.'

'And poured out of the spouts onto anyone attacking up the causeway,' Daryo finished.

'Yes, my Lord.'

'Why was this not used when the Armynyans attacked?'

'The gates were not closed, my Lord. The Presidents of the City did not believe that the Armynyan army numbered as high as it did and that it was as close as it was. They were inside the city so fast... Do not judge the Presidents too harshly, my Lord. They paid with their lives and they did not die well.'

'And how many others have died and will die for their hesitancy?'
The spy shrugged. 'I cannot say. The gates are not just locked as normal doors are. You must ascend into the gatehouse and released the blocks on the hinges and the bars on the top to open the gate as well as remove the bars across it.'
'Where is your concealed entrance?'
'On the east side, my Lord. You wish to see it?'
'No, if we are seen or caught, we may not be able to use it again. We will come to do our work on the morrow. You will guide us?'
'I will.'
'Can you fight?'
The little man grinned, showing broken teeth below his broken nose. 'I can.'
'Good. Take whatever food and drink you require tonight in camp, on my authority.'
'My thanks, my Lord.'
'Come. We should return to camp.'

Daryo had his team meet just after the midday meal. They numbered twenty-five; two groups of nine each would go to the towers to neutralise them as a threat, one team led by Avenzi, one by a young but exceptionally talented sergeant named Cambrati, the remaining seven included Kym and Daryo and would go to the gatehouse to open the gates. When that had been accomplished they would show a torch from one of two chosen locations and the Adacan cavalry and the Vazzeccoes would charge the gate, followed as swiftly as possible by the Army of the South. Meanwhile a portion of the Army of the Centre would have snuck into position to cause a diversion on the north of the city.
Daryo told his team to wear black or dark only, to bring the weapon that they were most comfortable and able using and to meet back in the same place at sundown. When he dismissed them, he was left alone with his daughter.
'Mother would probably be happier if I stayed in the camp,' said Kym.
'Would you?'
'No. I want to come with you.'
Daryo clasped her hand. 'I am glad. It will be a difficult night. We will be little more than a score against thousands.'
'But they will not see us.'
'That is the plan.'
Kym grinned maliciously and ran her hands over her blue, white and yellow tunic of the princess's squire. 'I should change. Will my jacket be dark enough?'

'The green one? Yes, I should think so.'
'I shall meet you here at sundown, father.'
'Bring only what you need.'
'I shall.'
Kym smiled and retreated to her tent. Daryo turned to go to his own tent and almost collided with Tari.
'My humble apologies, Princess Tari.'
Tari smiled. 'Accidental, I presume, Walker.'
'Indeed, Princess.'
'Your daughter is a fine young woman. She is a credit to you and her mother.'
'Jeda is the moon in the night sky, my children are the stars around her.'
'Does Kym have a sweetheart or a betrothed?'
'She had feelings for the landowner's son but I think she may have all-but forgotten him. I cannot believe that you have come so far without a husband, Princess.'
Tari chuckled. 'I am fifty years old now. What man would have a woman of two hundred seasons who knows little else but leading armies?'
'What man would not have a princess?'
'You would not. You came to Adaca with a lady before and when you returned it was with a wife. I understood that when you met with my brother in Baros when you returned, you asked his equerry on arrival if I was present.'
'Curiosity only, Princess.'
Tari smiled shyly. 'As you say. You are a good man, Daryo the Walker. Jeda is a most fortunate woman. I am glad that you returned, Daryo. Adaca is grateful. And I am most grateful.'

Twenty-four men and a woman assembled just before sundown. Daryo checked each one's clothing and equipment. Most carried the curved swords of the Vazzeccoes but two bore straight swords, two carried one-hand axes, Kym had her two-handed sword that she had christened Devotion and Daryo bought only his twin blades. With the little spy, they left camp silently. He led the group along the road at first and then they diverted to the east. The city loomed out of the gathering dark. Daryo envisioned scores of pairs of hostile eyes watching them as they reached the base of the cliff. The spy reached a certain point and stopped still. Daryo stopped alongside him.
'Here?' he whispered.
'Nearby,' muttered the spy. 'It is difficult to find the entrance. It is a Gods-made thing and concealed.' He ran his hands along the cliff, probed into a cleft into the rock and

then another. 'Here, my Lord. The passage is narrow and there is no light. Tread carefully.'

Daryo turned. Kym was behind him. 'Tell the man behind you to tread carefully, there is no light inside, have him pass the message down the line.'

Kym did so and followed Daryo and the spy into the rocky passage. It was barely two feet wide in some places and only just tall enough to stand up in, the little spy was able to slide through easily, Kym had more trouble, Daryo and some of the larger Vazzeccoes really had difficulty in the narrower places and they had to grope their way along the walls in the utter blackness and also keep their heads low as, in places, the ceiling dropped suddenly. Daryo had hit his head twice by the time the spy stopped.

'We have two options, my Lord,' he hissed. 'The right turn takes us to a drain that comes up in the main square. The left takes us into the cave where the tar comes up. Either are likely to have guards.'

'Your reports said that much of the town was burned,' Daryo confirmed.

'Indeed, my Lord.'

'Then the Armynyan soldiers will be sleeping where they can. A large open square will take many men. The caves will be better, even if guarded.'

'Yes, my Lord.'

The spy groped his way to the left. After a few turns, a flickering light became visible ahead and a bitter smell filled the air. The passage ended abruptly and gave into a cave, very large but no higher than the passage. The air scalded the back of the throat and choked the breath. Small bowls containing candles lined the edges of wooden walkways hung from the cave walls above a black, shiny cave floor. Many of the candles had gone out but there remained light to see by.

'Do not step on the ground,' the spy warned. 'You will sink into the tar and you cannot escape. You will die choking in agony.'

Just to the right of the passage outlet, one of the wooden walkways was anchored to the cave wall. Carefully, the spy used the wall of the cave for support and stepped out onto the walkway. It bounced slightly with his weight and then stabilised. One by one the rest of the group joined him. The walkway stretched for nearly three hundred yards across the immense cave, joined in places to others but the spy kept on a straight course. The walkway reached the exit, a passage wider than the one that they had used to get in, the floor sloped upwards sharply and soon became steps hewn out of the rock. At the top of the steps was a metal grille door, held open by a macabre doorstop: a naked female corpse. The spy hissed a warning and pointed. Two Armynyan soldiers were playing dice on a table nearby, their weapons forgotten. Daryo eased the little man aside and slowly

drew his swords. He slipped past the spy and said a silent apology to the Fourth Goddess before driving both blades into the exposed and defenceless backs of the two men. The Vazzeccoes poured into the space behind him. It was another cave, the size of a large room, furnished as a guard room with racks for weapons, benches, tables and a hammock.
'Take the bodies and throw them in the tar,' Daryo instructed. Two men seized each body and dragged them away down the stairs. Kym had stopped and was staring at the dead woman holding open the grille. She looked to be about Kym's age, she was bruised all over her bare skin and her groin and face were bloodied, her dark hair had been roughly shorn short and she appeared to have died from a blow to the back of her skull. Her body had then been propped against the door in a slumped sitting position to hold the door in place.
'Why?' asked Kym.
Daryo shook his head. 'Barbarity. A complete lack of normalcy and decency.'
Kym went to the hammock slung in one corner, cut it down with her knife and, with Avenzi's help, wrapped the young woman in it and they carried it down to the tar. When the impromptu burial party had returned from their grisly work, the infiltrators silently proceeded up the next passage of steps, this one well lit by tallow candles in recesses, to a wooden door at the top.
'This is the door into the tar stores,' said the spy. 'There may be men in here, I do not know.'
Daryo checked behind but found no need to ensure his group had their weapons ready. Every one had their weapon in hand and ready. Even the little spy drew a long, narrow dagger. Daryo reached passed their guide and opened the door slowly. The tar store was a square stone building, with a tiled roof. Row after row of barrels, some stacked eight or nine high, filled the room. The stores were deserted. Daryo held the door opened and beckoned his followers on. They streamed past him and spread out, checking the room, Avenzi and Kym going directly to the door. Daryo closed the door carefully to avoid noise.
'Where to next?' he asked the spy.
The spy had apparently been considering this. 'The stores are against the city wall between our entrance down below and the gate. One entrance to the towers is immediately beside us and leads through the passages in the walls through which the tar would be taken to the towers. The captain is best to take his teams in there. The gatehouse entrance is immediately beside the gate itself. That is more difficult. I advise going a longer but clandestine route. I shall guide you.'

Daryo nodded and beckoned to Avenzi and Cambrati. 'Your way in is immediately beside us; the route the tar is taken to the spouts. Go in that way. You both know what to do.' Avenzi nodded firmly, Cambrati whispered 'Yes, my Lord'. 'The guide will come with us, he knows a safer way into the gatehouse.'
The little spy got Avenzi's attention. 'Take your left hand out of the door. The first door you come to is the correct one. It is less than twenty yards from this door.'
Avenzi and Cambrati both acknowledged and gathered their teams. Slowly, carefully, Kym opened the door to the outside. A rush of cold, fresh air came in, a relief from the overpowering tar. She checked outside and waved Avenzi forwards. The nine-man team hurried past her, led by their captain. The door to the towers was where the spy had said, Avenzi shouldered it open and his men dived inside. Avenzi waved a safe signal and Cambrati's group ran past Kym and in the next door. Avenzi waved farewell to Kym and closed the door behind him. Kym closed the door to the tar store quickly.
'They all got there,' said Kym.
Daryo checked his team were ready and nodded to the spy. 'Where are we going to?'
'There is a drain to the right,' said the little man. 'That leads into the vaults below the Chapel of the White Lady. Opposite the chapel door is that of the gatehouse.'
Daryo waved the signal to Kym. The little man was the first out of the door then Kym, the other five soldiers and Daryo last. The air had been fresh at first but now stank of death, rot and smoke. The wooden buildings along the street had been burned leaving blackened skeletons. Several rotting corpses were littered across the street. The drain was an iron grille in the street, the spy tried to get a grip and lift it but was not strong enough. Quickly two of the soldiers helped him to lift it and Kym was the first down the square hole, landing heavily. The team slid down after her into the low tunnel. Daryo ensured that the spy went before he did and he slid the grate back into position behind them. The tunnel got briefly narrower and lower. The team had to crawl in the dark until Kym reached another grille. The youngest soldier squeezed past her, apologising profusely, and managed to the lift the cover far enough for Kym to escape. The chapel vault was a low, plastered room lined with shelves laden with small boxes, containing the ashes of those who had been burned after death and their remains kept. As well as the normal remains, several shrouded bodies had been laid against the walls, more recent deaths. By the door were a dozen naked corpses, much more recent deaths. Kym found a broom in a corner and pushed it under the drain grille and she and the Vazzecco were able to use it as a roller to move it aside. The team scrambled into the vault as Kym checked the way ahead. Two more vaults, all nearly full of the bare bodies of the dead,

gave onto the door to the chapel itself. Kym waited for the team to reach her before opening it.

The chapel was horrific. The space was about the same as in the smith's house in Ritaro and lit by burning torches. The wooden floor was almost completely carpeted by Adacan girls, most barely old enough to be moving into womanhood, most of them were exposed from the waist down and most had been nailed crucified to the ground by the arms. Faces had been viciously beaten, clothes ripped asunder, their genitals mutilated. Kym was violently sick against the wall. Daryo gripped her shoulder.

'Spread out, see if any of them still live, release the ones that you can,' he murmured to the nearest Vazzecco. The soldiers started moving among the defiled females, prising the nails from their limbs and trying to put the bodies into dignified positions. They counted fifteen bodies, all dead. All of the soldiers had been wearing cloaks, they removed them and cut them in half to form shrouds, Daryo and Kym volunteered theirs as well. A strip of tapestry was left hanging from a wall and this was used as well. Kym recovered herself and accepted a brief embrace from her father. The young Vazzecco handed Kym her sword with a supportive smile.

'My thanks.'

The group gathered behind the spy at the door and Daryo eased the door open. A shape on the outside of the door made him jump and then turned his stomach. A girl child, no more than seven or eight summers old, had been nailed to the door by her feet and a letian driven into her chest. Daryo quickly averted his eyes past the disgusting display and sought the entrance to the gatehouse. This was guarded, three Armynyans were passing around a jug and talking in low voices, their backs to the chapel and Daryo. He beckoned Kym forwards and pointed at the Armynyan on the right of the three.

'Can you manage him?' he whispered and got an affirmative noise in response. 'Go.'

Kym slid past him and ran silently across the space, Daryo on her heels. As she ran, she levelled her blade like a lance. The Armynyan must have heard something at the last moment as he turned just in time for Devotion to be driven through his stomach. His comrades turned and reached for their weapons, shouting an alarm. One had his throat opened by the Horse, the second turned to flee and Devotion cleaved into his chest.

'Move, quickly!' Daryo pushed the gatehouse door open and his small force streamed across the lane and inside, taking the bodies with them and dumping them in the gatehouse. Kym pulled her blade free and preceded Daryo through. Immediately inside the door were stairs and the Adacans led the way up the spiralling flight almost to the very top of the wall. The gateroom spanned more than the width of the gates below. At either end of the room, the titanic pins of the hinges protruded from the floor, turned by capstans that were locked in place by wooden bars. In the centre what appeared to be a small portcullis protruded through the room floor to block the gates below from opening. The room was also full of Armynyan soldiers in the midst of a riotous party. The arrival of eight Adacans and two Batribi caused more noise and confusion as letians were found to be out of reach and jars of wine, brooms and knives were the majority weapons used in a makeshift defence that was soon overwhelmed by the concerted attack.

'Clear the bodies from the gears,' ordered Daryo, sheathing his swords and starting to unblock one of the capstans. 'Kym, the other winder. Satoro, get those bars raised. Grambera, go down to the door and keep watch.' The Adacans hurried into action, the sentry disappearing back down the stairs. Another door that Daryo thought may be another exit turned out to be a store room for spare chains, ropes and other parts for the machinery. Within heartbeats, the young soldier Satoro and a comrade had the small wedging portcullis lifted. Daryo went to the open window hole overlooking the causeway. All seemed quiet. He hoped that Avenzi and Cambrati had done their work as effectively. He took a torch from a bracket and held it out of the window on the right hand side. After a few heartbeats there, he dropped it to the causeway dozens of feet below. In answer, a torch was lit out in the blackness.

'They are coming,' he announced. 'Satoro, go down and help Grambera remove the bars.' The young man ran down the stairs. Daryo switched to the gateroom's rear window, looking onto the darkened town. There were some scuffles and crashes from below and then a high-pitched whistle.

'Open the gates!' Daryo commanded and threw himself against the nearest capstan. With half the team on each, the gates of Tanaab slowly opened. When they were fully so, Daryo ran back to the causeway-side window and listened intently. Very faintly was the sound he had hoped for. The sound of hoof beats grew as the Adacan cavalry charged up the causeway with the Vazzeccoes mounted behind them. The Adacan infantry would be running behind. Daryo turned to Kym and drew his swords again. 'Ready to retake Tanaab, Devoted?'

Kym had laid Devotion down by the door and retrieved it quickly. 'I am ready, Walker.'
'For Jeda, Stai and Vehllal?'
'For Jeda, Stai and Vehllal.'

## Chapter 85

The Adacan war council had to meet in a tent outside the city as there was no standing building in Tanaab that had not been used as a forced brothel or a slaughter house or both. Hundreds if not thousands had evidently been burned alive in locked buildings, the dead had been piled in cellars and dark corners. A stack of partially-burned bodies had been found in a well and Tari had ordered the city emptied completely until there was sufficient organisation to clear the dead. Less than a hundred people had been found alive either as tortured captives or in hiding, meaning that the Armynyans had killed over a thousand score in the city.
'The One of Two escaped,' said Avenzi, who had led the search of the city.
'I doubt it stayed here for long,' Daryo offered. 'There is little to keep anyone in this city. We found little food in store and the well was fouled. The prisoners we took are badly ill. That so many submitted suggests that they were simply too ill or tired or dispirited to fight.'
Tari nodded. 'I agree. I have sent a bird to the king but I think it may be prudent to rest on what we have: our nation whole again.'
Daryo smiled tiredly. 'That may be very wise, my Lady.'
'You have done sterling service, Walker. And you, Kym the Devoted.'
Kym smiled. 'My thanks, Princess.'
'Rest, both of you. We are safe for now.'

Daryo found himself awake in the early hours of the morning. Dawn was a long time away and the watchfires were the only light. He decided that a visit to the latrine pit was in order, picked up Temma's Sword and put on his cloak. The air was chill and the night still. The soft tones of voices, snoring and the crackle of fires were a low background noise. Daryo went to the latrine and returned, noticing there was still a candle burning in Kym's tent. He assumed that she had either gone to bed and left the candle alight or she was unable to sleep. He crossed the stretch of grass between their tents and eased the tent flap open. Kym was laid on her cot with the young Vazzecco Satoro, their lips pressed passionately together, his hands on her hips, hers grasping his fair hair. Their eyes were closed in the pleasure of the moment and Daryo was able to withdraw unnoticed. He felt an odd anger towards the young soldier but also a joy that Kym was able to attract a young man and divert herself from thoughts of the war. He returned to his tent smiling.

'Good morning, father.' Kym sat on the stool next to Daryo in the captains' tent. Daryo looked up from his oatmeal.
'Gods' Watch, Kym.'
'Gods' Watch.' She picked up a handful of dried grapes from a bowl and started to eat.
'I saw young Satoro this morning,' said Daryo.
'Satoro?'
'Yes. Did you know he is from very close to Ishter? His father owns a large farm there.'
'Yes, I did. How do you know?'
'I am his commander. It is my duty to know. How do you?'
Kym flushed. 'Oh. Well I...'
Daryo smiled at her embarrassment. 'No worry necessary, Kym.'
Kym sighed. 'How did you know?'
'I am your father as well as his commander. It is my duty as both to know. Will he treat you well?'
'I pray that he will.'
'Then enjoy it.' Daryo reached across and squeezed her hand. 'I should go and see to the clearing of the city. I gave the Vazzeccoes the day to rest. The princess's agent tells me that there is a beautiful waterfall south of the city. I will have a groom ready horses for you.'
'My thanks, father.'

Daryo found a covert location to watch Kym and Satoro leave. Afterwards he relieved Avenzi in supervising the clearing of the Armynyan bodies from Tanaab and the decent removal of the Adacan bodies. The Armynyan bodies were piled in a large pit by their surrendered comrades that had been excavated by the concealed entrance to the caves and burned. The Adacans were interred in smaller excavations along the length of the causeway, no more than ten in each grave. The work was nauseating, repellent and foul. Many bodies had been in situ since the town had fallen, over thirty days' decomposition. If a person had enough about them to be identified as a follower of a particularly faith, they were put in graves with the appropriate honours where possible. A particular effort was made for those women and girls who had been abused by the Armynyan troops, a team of women from the baggage train- laundrywomen, cooks, provisioners and others- washed the bodies and ensured that the women were dressed before being buried. Many children had been inexplicably and hideously mutilated. Many soldiers that had their own children were unable to handle the small corpses and a small group of the younger soldiers banded together to try to inter the murdered young whole in body and with an adult to escort them across the bridge to the next kingdom. The army's blacksmiths were kept busy making grave markers, using hot metal to sear the symbols of the Pantheon, the White Lady and the Good Shepherd on flat stones with the number of the buried on it. Tari came into the city dressed in a plain black tunic and assisted in the burying of the children. The Vazzeccoes and the cavalry had taken the main brunt of the battle and the horrors of the city and had been given the day to rest but the Vazzeccoes supplied water and cloth to the burial parties from soon after noon until sundown.

At sundown Daryo made his way away from the camp and into solitude and quiet to pray. For the first time in his memory, he could not think of what thoughts to offer the Fourth Goddess. She would be presiding over the affair with great relish and Daryo decided that she was best left undisturbed by an ageing warrior who she may want to join her while she had the opportunity. He instead prayed to Dravin, the First God, granter of health, giver of strength and bulwark of the spirit, that he and the others at work in Tanaab would keep the resolve to finish their grisly work and that justice would be done on those responsible either in life or death and asked for the First God's intercession with the Third Goddess, Spinel, in bringing the war to peace and reason. He prayed for a long time and was only roused when two Vazzeccoes came to find him.

'We are sorry to disturb you, Walker,' said one. 'Something has been found that the Princess Tari believes you should see.'

Daryo stood. 'Of course. The First God and I were near finishing.'

'You follow the Pantheon, sir?'

'Most of my people do.'

'I do too. I was dedicated to the Second Goddess as a child. It is why I became a soldier.'

'Unusual for an Adacan.'

'Yes, sir. But I am proud of my faith.'

'As am I.'

The Vazzeccoes, the Walkers, led Daryo the Walker up the causeway and into the town, taking a torch from a bundle near the guarded gates, lighting it from the guard's brazier and they continued into the city, through the town streets and to the Merchant Hall, the base of the town's banking and commerce and the seat of the City Presidents. The stone-built building had escaped the incineration that had affected most of Tanaab and two soldiers were guarding the elaborate, silver-ornamented door. Daryo was told that Princess Tari was inside. The Merchant Hall was a single large space, the tables, chairs and counters that Daryo assumed normally filled the room had been smashed and piled in a corner. One of the seats that he guessed were for the Presidents on a dais near the

far end was almost buried in a pile of letians. The other had a body in it, its hands still on the hilt of the sword in its chest. It bore a striking resemblance to the One of Two.
'Avenzi found it. It is not the One of Two,' said Tari, who was standing near the body with Avenzi, holding a torch, and another captain.
'I would have been startled if it had been,' said Daryo, examining the body himself. The clothing, hair and face were good matches for the Armynyan leader but, under the clothes, the breasts were simply those of a fat man and there was a crude clay imitation of female genitals stuck beneath the man's own.
'This is a poor imitation meant to fool us,' said Daryo.'
'Indeed. Why?'
'The Armynyans wish us to believe their leader is dead,' said Avenzi. 'This was a double, to impersonate the One of Two. Maybe the One of Two was never really here.'
'This is a poor fake,' said Daryo. 'Perhaps readied in a rush. Or never finished properly. That suggests it was... made, if that is the word, at short notice.'
Tari assented. 'If that is so, my question remains.'
'I think Captain Avenzi may be right,' said Daryo. 'A fraud to persuade us that the One of Two killed itself as we attacked. But our actual assault came before they were ready and the half-finished fake was left behind, perhaps in the hope that we would be fooled anyway.'
'Why try to make us believe that the One of Two is dead?'
'To end the war, my Lady,' said Avenzi. 'We see the instigator and the aggressor of the war dead at its own hand and therefore have no reason to invade Armynya.'
Tari looked at Daryo, who nodded in agreement. 'This needs to be considered. The One of Two is still alive but we have taken back what we lost. Perhaps it should be thought of in our sleep.'
Daryo and Avenzi nodded and bade the princess a peaceful rest as she departed. Avenzi studied the strange corpse for a moment.
'Walker, I believe that this is desperation.'
'How so?' asked Daryo.
'Lakheti and I found the body.' He indicated the other captain with them. 'The Armynyan wish to show us a way out of the war. Having been a vicious invasion force, they are now fleeing before our response and trying drastically poor methods to make us think that we have been victorious. A confident army with a strong leadership does not do so.'
'I agree.'

'This suggests therefore that the Armynyan army before us may be an army close to collapse.'

'That is the theme of what I was told by the prisoner,' mused Daryo. 'I was disinclined to following the advice of a desperate captive but this is additional evidence.'

'May I ask where that road of thought leads you, Walker?'

'I am unsure myself. The clouds are thick and the rain is heavy. Perhaps the princess is correct, a sleep and the thoughts of dreams may bring the sunlight.'

Avenzi and Lakheti bowed shortly and Daryo left the Merchant's Hall. The light was gone outside and the darkened city, inhabited by phantoms and soldiers only, was unwelcoming. Daryo felt a strange fear that he had no shield and only Temma's Sword with him. He strode quickly back to the gate. The gates had been closed for the night and only the wicket gate, a pair of guards either side, was open. All four saluted the Walker as he passed through and followed the causeway back down to the ground and the Adacan camp. As usual by night, sentries randomly patrolled the perimeter, weapons drawn, but all recognised the Batribi captain. Daryo found his tent and Kym, who was lighting a candle in the lantern on his table.

'Gods' Watch, Kym.'

'Gods' Watch, father.'

'Did you have a pleasant day?'

'Yes. We rode out and found the waterfall that you mentioned. We talked and then I hunted and caught a wild pig which we cooked.'

'That does sound very pleasant.'

'But not for you. Selvana told me that you were helping bury the dead.'

Daryo smiled kindly and sat down on his bed to remove his boots. 'And by so doing, I spared you and Satoro having to and allowed you to have a pleasant day by the river. I performed my duty as a leader and a father. The Second Goddess is flowing through me,' he finished grandiosely.

Kym laughed. 'And the Second God is banished to the other kingdoms.'

'For at least one more day.'

'Rumours in the Vazzeccoes' refectory tent is that the army will be moving east within three days.'

'Soldiers talk about any subject that they can find,' Daryo warned her. 'Trust very little of what you hear.'

'So the army does not march?'

'There has been no decision.' He pulled off his second boot and unbuckled his sword belt. He described the discovery of the mocked-up body in the Merchant's Hall.

'So we may have won the war.'

'May have but that is not a certainty.'

'Surely if the Armynyans have retreated in chaos and are trying to make us believe that their leader is dead, then victory has been reached and we can go home.'

Daryo sighed. 'Perhaps not. If we stop now, it may be that in some months, the Armynyans will retake Tanaab and we will be facing the same circumstances once more. Conversely a campaign into Armynya may be a waste of lives against a defeated, broken army. We cannot say. That decision has to be made with careful consideration and judgement.'

Kym nodded her understanding. 'I should sleep.'

'Sleep well, Kym.'

'And you, father.'

She slipped out of the tent and Daryo listened to her footsteps cross to her tent. He picked up a scouting report from the cavalry reconnaissance force but decided that he was too tired to stay awake and read so he put it back down, put on his nightclothes, blew out the lantern and got into bed. Again the feeling that he was insufficiently armed came to him. He sat up, reached for his knife and slid it through the canvas of the cot so that the handle was immediately beside his hand.

*Fourth and Darkest Goddess, in the presence of so many of your new acolytes, I beg that you free my mind from your torments. I pledge my blade, as ever, to your service. My life is yours but I ask your mercy to allow me to sleep peacefully, take my body if this is the night that it is due but release my mind so that I may meet you in tranquillity.*

Daryo kept his eyes closed and eased his hand gently around the hilt of his knife. He could tell by the soft noises of clothing and breathing where the intruder was. A slow movement to bring the knife blade free of the cot canvas and then Daryo threw his legs sideways into the intruder and flung himself on top of the figure, his knife at the throat.

'My Lord! My Lord Walker! Please!' gasped the figure, apparently an older man. 'I am sorry to disturb you, my Lord! I was asked to wake you!'

Daryo relaxed his grip slightly. 'By whom?'

'The king, my Lord! I am Zuccataro, the king's chamberlain!'

Daryo released his erstwhile captive. 'I am sorry, Zuccataro. I am somewhat battle-weary and rather oversensitive at this point after a battle.'

There was a panting period of recovery from the shock from the king's official. 'I am most apologetic, my Lord Walker.'

'You are new to the king's service?'

'Not that new, my Lord.'
'Within eighteen summers?'
'Yes, my Lord.'
'Then you will know that I dislike being named as a lord when I am a blacksmith. Daryo or Walker is quite acceptable.'
'As you wish, Walker.'
Daryo got his lantern lit. The chamberlain was older than Daryo but not enough to be his father, somewhat stout with a grey beard and bald scalp, bearing the yellow sun and white bull of the Adacan king on the breast of his robe. Daryo quickly pulled on trousers over his nightclothes and a green tunic from his bag, cinched by his sword belt, and then grabbed his boots. 'In the tent alongside is a young woman, my daughter. Wake her please.'
'I was asked to wake only you and the princess, Walker.'
'And I am telling you to wake my daughter. Do not fear, she will not sleep with a knife.'
'As you wish, Walker.' The chamberlain bowed stiffly and left. Daryo fastened his boots and stepped out into the chill night. He heard the chamberlain apologising profusely to Kym and he left her tent at a near-run. Daryo waited for a few moments and his daughter emerged, pulling on a jerkin as she did so.
'The king?' she asked her father sleepily.
'The king,' he replied. As they followed the still-hurrying chamberlain, Daryo glanced back and a nearly bare figure slipped out of Kym's tent and vanished into the night. *Fare well, Satoro*, he thought to himself. That was evidently the cause of the chamberlain's embarrassment.
The captains' tent was well lit by lanterns. A pair of the Adacan Royal Guard were on post outside. They saluted Daryo as he passed inside, Kym trailing uncharacteristically shyly behind. King Lallano the Eighth was over fifty summers and was starting to show the strain of a life on the throne: his face was lined, his once thick hair was thin and almost white, his left hand was shaking slightly, he sat looking tired on a folding high-backed chair at the captains' table flanked by the chamberlain and another official. Tari was sat at the table at her brother's right hand. Daryo drew his sword and raised it in salute.
'My Liege, my sword and my service are yours.'
'Thank you, Walker,' said the king. 'They are gratefully received and greatly appreciated. It has been too long since we met. You bring with you...?'
'Kym the Devoted of Ritaro, daughter of Jeda, my daughter and honorary squire to Princess Tari.'

Kym curtsied deeply and the king waved her up. 'Well met, Kym, daughter of Daryo. Any member of my sister's escort is an honoured ally and the daughter of the Walker is doubly honoured in my court. Please, both, be seated.'

Daryo went around the table and sat at the monarch's left hand. Kym sat almost three yards from Daryo, almost using her father's figure to hide behind.

'Firstly I must congratulate you on your retaking of Tanaab, Walker. You are an inspiration to the Adacan people.'

'My thanks, my Liege. I had some very good assistance. I would in particular have Captain Avenzi and Sergeant Cambrati noted for their performance and bravery.'

Lallano nodded. 'Of course. Are either nobles?' he asked Tari. Tari shook her head. 'I shall grant them both lands and titles. Now, this fraudulent corpse. What do you think of it, Walker?'

'Several people have already said that they think this is a sign of desperation. An attempt by our enemy to make us think that we have killed their leader. It may have been a better attempt had we been later in arrival.'

'So you think the Armynyans wish peace?'

'Possibly, my Liege.'

'I believe you are correct.' Lallano nodded to his official and was handed a small but ornate scroll. 'The Gourmini have not consented to come to our aid but the Gourmini do still have contact with Armynyans in their own land. There is dissent, growing dissent within the Armynyan people. Their prophesied leader is not the great one that was foretold. The army is being led to ruin.'

'Then we should take advantage of that,' said Tari. 'Strike swiftly and in numbers.'

Lallano shook his head. 'Not yet. On this scroll is an invitation.' He unrolled it and passed it to Tari.

'I cannot read these words,' she said.

'Nor can I. The words are the language of the northern tribes of Armynya. As well as his lack of military skill and leadership, the One who is Both is not from one of the leading tribes of the north, he is from a small, obscure tribe from the south and this is not... welcomed by the majority of those in power in Armynya. Some believe it contradicts the prophecy, some believe it is an attempt by the small tribes of the south to take leadership from the larger ones in the north. So we are invited to talks with the northern tribes. According to the translation of this scroll by the Gourmini experts, they wish us to aid them in removing the One of Both.' He handed another, plainer scroll to his sister.

Tari unrolled it and read it twice. Then she passed it on to Daryo. 'How well-versed in the language is the translator?' she asked.

'I cannot say but we have some people who read the language after a fashion and they concur with the meanings.'
'Sutiv,' said Daryo, when he had read the text. 'They wish to meet us in the marshes.'
'They do.'
'Why?'
'I cannot say.'
'It may be a trap,' said Tari.
'It is also an opportunity,' said Kym. It was the first words that she had said. Everyone present looked at her. 'My Lord, this is a chance for us to finish this war.'
Lallano pointed at Kym as if indicating something obvious. 'The best argument that I could possibly give. Well spoken, Kym.'
'You flatter me, my Lord.'
'The condition of the invitation is that the king attends so I must do so,' said Lallano flatly. 'Tari, you will remain here as regent in my absence. If there is treachery, if anything should go amiss and I do not return then I name my first son, Koman, as my heir and king in my stead as Koman the First of Adaca.' He looked at his chamberlain, who bowed deeply.
'My king... brother... I think...'
'There is no alternative, Tari. The Walker and his daughter and a guard of the Vazzeccoes will accompany me.' Tari looked mutinous but stayed silent. The king surveyed the tent. 'We must leave at dawn.'

## Chapter 86

The small party had proceeded due north from Tanaab to a clandestine meeting. The king was mounted and accompanied by his squire and the other official that had been in the captains' tent at Tanaab with him, his equerry. Daryo had chosen Cambrati to command the sixteen Vazzeccoes, which included Satoro, and Kym brought the delegation's number to twenty-two people, twenty-two mounts and a single pack horse. A day and a half's ride through formerly Armynyan-occupied land was a sober and macabre one. Every farm, hamlet or village that they passed had been destroyed and their former inhabitants left disfigured and without dignity outside their homes. Every woman and girl aged over twelve summers had been used as a plaything by the soldiers, often staked out on the ground and left there. The king was forced to give the order to simply ride on. They camped overnight in a field among ripening wheat with nobody to harvest it when it was ready. As soon as there was light to see by, the Vazzecco on watch woke the others and they rode on to the point that the king had been told to reach by the bank of the River Vlenti.

At the side of the river was a small camp, three low tents, a small camp fire and a few men. One came forwards as the Adacan party approached, lowering the cowl of his cloak. Lallano halted his horse and dismounted, Daryo alongside him. The Armynyan approached and bowed shortly.

'King Lallano of Adaca. Daryo, Captain of Adaca and Walker of Batribi.' His voice was heavily accented, his Common Speech slow and carefully pronounced. 'I, Takhlin, clan Kithmonsyna. To the Sutiv I take you.'

Lallano nodded. 'As agreed.' He motioned his equerry forwards. 'Tell our host that we have come in small numbers and trust him to guide us safely.'

The equerry translated into the slurred, breathy Armynyan language for Takhlin who bowed shortly again and replied.

'He states that we must cross the river quickly and proceed, sire.'

'Then let us do so.'

The Armynyans had evidently crossed in a couple of small canoes but had manufactured a ferry from trees they had cut down and the Adacans were able to cross in fours with their horses. Daryo and Kym were last to cross with Takhlin and the other Armynyans struck their camp and paddled across in the canoes to meet a single comrade waiting on the Armynyan side with their horses. There were five of them in total, Takhlin evidently their leader, all in the simple baldric and trousers of Armynyan soldiers but carrying short swords instead of letians. Takhlin had both letian and a small bow. One of his men was a boy no older than Daryo's son Stai and as well as his sword he had a pole with a ferret's pelt hung from the top.

'No poor infant,' Kym observed to her father. Daryo got the equerry's attention.

'Ask the banner-bearer about his standard.'

The equerry did so and the boy replied cautiously.

'He says that it is the standard of the Kithmonsyna.'

'What about the children used in the One of Two's army?'

'That is the standard of the One who is Both's tribe,' was the reply. 'Armies carry the banner of their commander. If a Kithmonsyna and not a Haustihya was the One who is Both, they would carry this standard.'

Takhlin spoke to the equerry in the Armynyan language and the equerry translated: 'The barbarity of some of the southern tribes is one reason that the northern tribes seek this alliance. But he says all will be explained by his... *shurtrussh*?' He repeated the Armynyan word to Takhlin who affirmed it.

'What does that mean?' asked Kym.

'I was taught that it means *companion*, my Lady. But companion can have many meanings. You are your father's companion, the Queen is the King's companion, at court my dog is my companion.' He looked back at Takhlin and asked a question. Takhlin simply repeated: '*Shurtrussh*.'

'How did you learn their tongue?' Kym asked the equerry.

'At the king's behest, several years ago,' the equerry said proudly. 'The king thought that one day it may prove useful. I was sent to Tanaab to work with the Armynyan expatriot merchants there. They taught me.'

They rode until nightfall and stopped on the banks of a small stream. The Armynyans had their small tents, the Adacans had several waxed linen sheets as shelters that were perfectly acceptable in the late spring weather. The king had a small tent that had been carried by the baggage horse but declined it, putting his blanket roll under the same shelter as Daryo's, and gave the tent to Kym. Lallano insisted to Takhlin that the Vazzeccoes would share the watches with the Armynyans and Daryo and Satoro took the first watch with a sullen-looking Armynyan who sat by their small fire in silence.

Daryo walked the perimeter a couple of times, Temma's Sword in his hand from habit. He returned to the fire where Satoro was stood a short distance from the Armynyan. The young soldier snapped his sword arm across his chest in salute.

'I am not a captain, Satoro.'

'You are our commander, Walker. You have led the armies many times. You are more than a captain, sir, you are a hero.'

Daryo sighed and smiled. 'I will not start a dispute over semantics.' He surveyed as far as he could across the gently rolling grassland and returned Temma's Sword to his belt. 'I understand that you invited my daughter to your parents' land in the north.' Satoro swallowed hard and stuttered the start of a response and Daryo chuckled softly. 'Be calm. I would not stand in the face of my daughter's wishes. She is an accomplished young woman and has a mind and will of her own. I respect her choice. If this relationship is one that lasts for a week or for a season, I ask that you treat her correctly. Not for my sake but for your own. I would not wanted to be the man that wronged Kym.'
Satoro chuckled nervously. 'My thanks, Walker.'
Daryo squeezed the young man's shoulder. 'Is there any of the salt pork left?'
Satoro chuckled louder. 'Yes, Walker. The provisions are alongside Kym's tent.'

The dawn came and Kym and Cambrati woke the Adacans. The Armynyans were all awake and clearing the camp. The Adacans had to eat as they packed and were soon in the saddle. The horses were easily able to ford the stream and the party headed almost due north. They were forced to skirt a cluster of villages and proceeded through lush flat country. The peaks of the Armynyan Mountains, known as the Shivering Mountains in Adacan due to the fog that rose around them, were just visible in the distance.
'Whose land are we on?' Daryo asked Takhlin and the equerry translated.
'These are lands of the Kasshuti,' he was told. 'The Kasshuti are the tribe of the marsh. They are known to the northern Armynyans as the last northmen as they act as the northern tribes do. Their customs and beliefs are the same as the northern tribes. The Kasshuti agreed to hold the meeting here as their lands are hard to travel across.'
Just after noon they crossed a wider, slower but shallower river. They turned east and joined a roadway made of a halved tree trunks laid centre-up to form a rough causeway across the increasingly swampy ground. On the causeway was a hide tent erected, cleverly nailed to the causeway and a cluster of men were stood around it. The standard above the tent was a snake wrapped around a wooden pole. Takhlin dismounted and exchanged words with a small man that had a letian hung from his shoulder. They had a short conversation that the equerry did his best to translate. It seemed to be an interrogation on Takhlin's identity. They were eventually allowed to pass but one of the sentries took off on foot ahead of them. The causeway crossed innumerable streams and ponds, getting closer to the feet of the mountains, the spring sunshine reflecting off of the water around them. Daryo felt exposed but safe on the causeway: the roadway rose, in places, over eight feet above the ground but there was not shelter or opportunity for concealment on either side. The vegetation was sparse and low and, unless one was

submerged in the water, there was nowhere to hide to set an ambush. The roadway crossed a grey-brown lake and at the far bank, sloped down to rejoin the ground on a rocky shelf among the waters; an island of stone enclosed by a marshy sea.
At the foot of the causeway was a large reception party- nearly fifty men and women on foot with a selection of tribal standards around them including the snake and the ferret but also an oak branch, a polecat and string of dried lacy seaweed. Lallano was the first to get down from his horse. The Vazzeccoes dismounted in a cascade, instinctively supporting their king, their hands on their weapons. Daryo and Kym stayed back slightly. An elder stepped out of the small mob of Armynyans and made a short speech of welcome and a promise of safe passage. Lallano's equerry introduced his king and thanked the Armynyans for their invitation. The elder then turned about and led his people into the swamps, the Adacan party close behind.

The assembly point was another rocky island reached just after dark by another, much shorter causeway, less than two hundred yards long but much lower to the ground. In places it was covered by an inch of water. The island was fringed with the largest trees around, several lines of large willows that looked to have been planted decades before specifically to screen the rocky plateau from view. The forty-yard island was surrounded by thick willows and the Armynyans had erected their shelters and tents against the trees and along the edge of the island. In the centre was a stone basin on a short pillar that stood less than two feet high. Fourteen ornate wooden chairs had been placed in a close circle around the basin. A team of Armynyans bearing torches stood around the outside of the circle and as the council assembled, the standard-bearers of each tribe took position behind their assigned chair. Cambrati had surreptitiously brought an Adacan banner, a blue-red-blue pennant fringed with white, the size of a man, which he attached to a borrowed spear and he stood in the only available position behind a chair. The Armynyan leaders took their seats in front of their respective banners, most with one or two in attendance. Lallano signalled Daryo and his equerry to join him as he took his seat. All were gathered and silence fell. Most of the seated were men, mostly of Daryo's age or older, some wore the warrior's dress, others wore skin coats or cloaks. Two were women, including in the seat beside which Takhlin was stood opposite the Adacans, and one of the men looked old enough to crumble under a slight breeze like a tower of dry sand.
The Kithmonsyna woman, presumably Takhlin's companion, stood and lowered the hood of her cloak. She made a short announcement in her own language. The equerry translated quickly and quietly for Lallano and Daryo.

'This council is called under the ancient rites. The council is sworn to speak of this to nobody outside the council. What is sworn in council is an oath in blood and water.' The Armynyans all raised their hands as if voting. The woman said something to Lallano and the equerry translated: 'My Lord is asked to raise his hand if this is acceptable.' Lallano did so and then all hands were lowered. The Kithmonsyna continued.

'Thia Kithmonsyna called this council to agree action against the so-proclaimed One who is Two in answer of the ancient prophecy. The prophecy speaks of one who will lead Armynya to victory over all its foes and this leader's road leads only to defeat. The great master is a tyrant who leads the army with no counsel, takes provisions from the starving and leaves those who require mercy desecrated and...' The equerry struggled with the last word. 'That may be said to be abandoned or broken, sire.' There was a wave of assent from around the circle. She went on: 'The One who is Two brings the savage ways of the south and spoils the name of Armynya. The One who is Two has taken the harvests before they were ripe and the stored food as well. The One who is Two has led the army not to victory but to utter defeat and humiliation. This is not what was prophesied and therefore this leader is not worthy of our loyalty.' The sound of the response was guarded agreement.

Another stood, possibly the youngest man present, in front of a banner of three dead rabbits. 'Haust Shutitessnya calls on the Gagrichti, those of memory and records, Drahk Gagrichti must speak on this.' He sat down again and raised his arm. Over half of the others did so. After a moment's consideration, the Adacan king raised his arm.

The painfully elderly man stood and muttered an order. A great scroll, over four feet wide, was brought forth and two young boys unfurled it in front of their elder. He withdrew a long, thin wooden rod from his cloak and traced it across the densely-packed words on the scroll, looking for the passage that he wanted. He looked at Lallano and bowed shortly and said slowly and quietly in the Common Speech: 'The One of Two, the greatest of leaders, the leader of Armynya to victory over all foes, the kind master but the mistress, the heir son but the favoured daughter, the farmer but the milkmaid, the smith but the weaver, the strong father but loving mother. The One of Two, neither man nor woman, the one who shall lead Armynya as no other, none shall be wiser as they should not have the wisdom of both he and she.' He then repeated the passage in his native tongue and dismissed the scroll and its bearers before returning to his seat.

Thia Kithmonsyna stood again and Lallano's equerry translated once more. 'The One of Two is neither man nor woman but is no farmer and no loving mother or strong father. It is our belief that the Haustihya have indeed found one of their kin that is both man and woman but that this One is not the One foretold. Thus the Vow of Thamriev is annulled.' She sat and raised her arm. This time, every hand around the circle was raised immediately. Lallano abstained from this purely Armynyan vote. Thia stood again. 'The Kithmonsyna have fulfilled their part of this council. The Vow is annulled. Who calls for these here to join as united tribes against the false One?'

A strongly-built man with a dense beard sat beside the king, dressed in warrior's garb and with a letian over his shoulder stood, his banner the polecat. 'Yevirsh Vushtih calls for the thirteen tribes here assembled to stand together to rid us of this parasite who names itself our leader.' He was seated and the vote was unanimous again. He stood and turned to Lallano. 'I call that the thirteen tribes request the aid of the King of Adaca to aid us and that this aid be peace between us thereafter.' He sat and all thirteen assented. There was a few moment's silence and stillness before Lallano decided that they were waiting for him to speak. The Adacan monarch stood and spoke as the Armynyans had. 'I am Lallano, King of Adaca, I agree that Adaca shall aid this council in its efforts to defeat the One of Two on the firm condition that this is peace. If the Armynyan people invade the realm of Adaca again, this agreement shall be broken and we stand once more opposed.' He sat and raised his arm. One by one, the other arms in the circle were raised.

Yevirsh Vushtih stood up and grinned broadly, showing broken teeth. 'We shall fight together.' He stepped up to the basin in the centre of the circle, drew a knife, cut the palm of his hand and pressed his hand to the basin, leaving a bloody smear behind. In turn around the circle, each one rose and did the same, Lallano being the last to do so. Yevirsh poured a silver jug of water into the basin and spoke. The equerry translated: 'This vow is made in blood and water. Let he who breaks it perish.'

The remainder of the council was to decide strategy. This was much slower and more complicated. There were disagreements, sometimes several stood together and refused to give way. The elderly Gagrichti acted as arbiter and chairman. The consensus was that a strike should be made quickly and from more than one direction. The One of Two's army was still large and, since they had retreated completely from Adaca, half of his army had escaped the crushing of Tanaab having been in the south of the realm at the time. They had retreated around the mountains at Tethpriv and set up camp. Eventually the Armynyan army would be divided into forces led by the Kithmonsyna and the Vushtih while the Adacan army would act from the south. The timings agreed, the council dissolved late in the night.

## Chapter 87

There were two ways of reaching the planned ambush of the One of Two's army. One was a long and circuitous route down towards the coast; the other crossing a ford and skirting the massif. The drawback of the route was a fortification. South of the mountains was a deep and foul marsh, between the two features a single road had been built to the river bank protected by four towers- three of hide-covered wood, less than a hundred yards apart, on the south side and one of stone on the north side. All four were nearly a hundred feet high and the Armynynans kept them well-guarded.

Nine days after the meeting in the marshes, a small force crossed the River Vienti opposite the Armynyan road in small boats. Two score and seven of the Vazzeccoes, each carrying only their sword, Avenzi, Cambrati, Kym and Daryo slipped ashore on the east bank. Without words, they followed the edge of the road, facing the rising sun. Two patrolling Armynyans did not see their killers- Kym and Avenzi approached soundlessly, eliminated the guards and shoved the bodies into the marsh. The attack force then moved forwards to within striking distance of the towers. In sight of the fortifications, Daryo slipped in behind a large bush and becokoned his men around.

'This is the time,' he said in a bare whisper. 'Cambati, the closest tower. Kym, the centre. Avenzi, the furthest. My men, the stone tower. Satoro, you and your archers go now. Past the back of the wooden towers and watch the road.'

The young man and his four companions, the best with bows, scurried away across the road.

'We wait until they are in position, then go,' said Daryo. The force had needed to travel quickly and lightly so he had only his twin swords.

The sun had gone and darkness was coming. The Adacans wore dark blue and their armour was dark. In the shadows, they became almost like phantoms in the gloom. The darkness deepened and eventually Daryo gave the order to move. The stone tower was the largest of the four and where most of the towers' garrison were quartered, therefore Daryo led the largest group: a score of men followed the Walker along the roadside. The tower was surrounded by a curtain wall the height of a man. The gate was of iron-banded wood, strong and thick but open. Two men stood watch beneath the battle standard of a crucified owl. Daryo drew his twin swords slowly, ducked low and scuttled along the wall to the gate. The Armynyans were looking into the tower's confines. Daryo reversed both blades and drove them through the sentries' backs. As he withdrew them, his force streamed past him. The tower door was open and the Adacan's streamed through the waiting portal, drawing their curved swords. Daryo rotated the Horse in his right hand to point up again and rushed after his men quickly. The ground level of the tower was a large dining hall, busy with Armynyan soldiers. The Adacans fell upon them ruthlessly. Most of the Armynyans had their weapons to hand and the fight was fierce. Confident that his men had the advantage in the hall, Daryo saw the stairs and made for them, cutting down a large, almost naked man wielding a letian. Daryo ducked a swipe from a rough axe and then charged up the stairs. An Armynyan reacting to the cries and screams from below impaled himself on the Horse's perfect point. Daryo lurched to his left, withdrawing his sword, and allowed the body to fall down the rest of the steps. He continued up to the first level, a room packed with straw mattresses, a makeshift dormitory. Several Armynyan soldiers were struggling awake, reaching for clothes and weapons. Daryo took a deep breath and said a heartbeat-long prayer in his head to the Fourth Goddess before moving into the room properly. There was a dozen Armynyans but most were barely awake and they were taken completely with surprise. The Horse and the Bear flashed in the light of the candles. One young Armynyan was able to defend himself with a letian but Daryo kicked his opponent in the midriff, drove his right fist into the man's face and slashed the youngster across the chest with the Bear. Another door led only into a privy so Daryo continued upstairs. The sound of the battle in the hall below was dying and two of the Vazzeccoes came up the stairs, blood staining their swords. Daryo led them up on up the stairs. Three more floors had but one Armynyan soldier, sleeping, between them. Daryo considered binding him but decided that the risk was too great. He reluctantly drove the point of the Bear through the sleeping man's throat and then continued up the stairs towards the top. A few late-wakers stumbled down the stairs onto the swords of the Batribi commander and his Adacan soldiers, only to be quickly despatched. Daryo continued upwards to the anteroom at the top of the stairs. He pushed the door open. A broad-shouldered, powerful, bear-like man had just pulled his baldric over his head and grabbed a letian. He already had a sword in his left hand and he turned to meet Daryo's first swing with both weapons in hand. Daryo's comrades rushed in and the huge Armynyan opened the throat of the first with his letian, kicked Daryo back and drove his sword through the second Vazzecco, almost to the hilt. Daryo ran forwards again, trying to catch the big man with his sword stuck in the dead man. The Armynyan simply released his sword and swung the letian at Daryo's head. Daryo blocked the blow with the Bear but was nearly thrown sideways by the force of the swing. Another incredibly hard slash came at his head. Daryo ducked underneath it and slashed the near-giant across the stomach. The Armynyan laughed derisively and hacked downwards. Daryo threw himself to the right, lashing out with the Bear as he dived. The blade caught the titan across the legs and the letian swung down again. Daryo barely got his swords up in time to block. The letian swung down a third time but its target had rolled away and was on its feet against one wall.

The Armynyan laughed triumphantly and spat something in his own language. Daryo took a gasp of breath and brought his blades up to guard again. The Armynyan took a two-handed grip on his letian, bellowed a war cry and chopped downwards. Daryo waited until the last moment and stepped inside the Armynyan's swing, driving the Horse through his enemy's chest and deflecting the letian with the Bear. The Armynyan weapon grazed his shoulder, just above the armoured slats on his upper arm, before the Arymynyan was too dead to continue his assault. Daryo shoved with his other shoulder, knocking the Armynyan backwards. The huge dead man fell backwards and Daryo pulled the Horse free. He hurried back down the stairs and almost collided with an Adacan bowman.

'Walker! Your daughter needs reinforcements! There is an encampment beyond the towers!'

'Is this tower secure?' asked Daryo, following the man down the stairs.

'Almost, my Lord! We can spare some men!'

'Send all you can after me!' Daryo jogged out of the door, increasingly aware of the pain in his shoulder and another in his hip. Several Vazzeccoes joined him. The central wooden tower was starting to burn; something had apparently gone awry with Kym's assault. But the sounds of battle were coming from the left, beyond the towers. Daryo hurried in that direction, his men behind him. Behind the last tower was a spreading Armynyan camp, hidden from the road by the towers themselves and a depression in the ground. Fires burned across the camp, lighting the chaos of battle.

'Move in,' ordered Daryo. 'Find our men and reinforce them before anything.'

The Vazzeccoes raced down the incline to the camp, their commander in their midst. The Armynyan camp was obviously more prepared than the towers- the noise of the assault on the forts had woken many of the sleepers. A clear skirmish line was visible and Daryo almost physically leaped into it, his twin swords reflecting the firelight. Daryo ducked a blow from a letian, spinning to his left and driving the Bear into the wielder's middle. He withdrew the blade, straightened up, blocked another swing with the Horse and shoved his assailant back. An advancing Vazzecco almost decapitated the man. It was only as the Armynyan fell that he saw Kym. She was wielding Devotion, both hands and the blade covered in blood, pirouetting in place and holding nearly a dozen at bay with only her one blade. A Vazzecco tried to break through the cordon around the Batribi girl but was cut down. For some unapparent purpose, the Armynyans seemed focussed on

killing the warrior woman in their midst. A slash narrowly missed Kym's head but grazed her arm. She cried out and swung Devotion in a lethal horizontal arc that almost bisected the culprit. The sight of his daughter's blood sparked something primal and furious within Daryo. Despite his wounded shoulder and aching hip, he unleashed a barrage with the Horse and the Bear, driving through the Armynyan ranks without pause. He drove both blades through the last man between him and Kym and was then fighting back to back with his daughter, two Batribi and three swords working in unison.
'Why did you take so long?' Kym demanded of her father.
'There was a few score Armynyans in the road!' Daryo replied, reversing the Horse as well to block a strike and shunt it sideways onto Devotion's tip.
'Down!'
Daryo ducked and Devotion whistled over his head as Kym turned full circle and sent two Armynyans leaping out of range and cut down two more. As Daryo stood up again, the Armynyan force broke. Cambrati's force had subdued their tower and were rushing into the fray. Satoro's small group of archers were picking out targets and shooting them down from the safety of the top of the rise. Outnumbering their enemies but surprised, confused and apparently leaderless, the Armynyan were fleeing south. Daryo spotted the young sergeant in the chaos.
'Cambrati! Make sure the retreat goes south!'
'Yes, sir!' Cambrati made a charging gesture with his sword and a dozen men followed. Satoro's archers fired the last of their arrows, drew their swords and joined the pursuit. The battle moved away and Daryo allowed himself to relax. Kym cleaned the blade of Devotion on an Armynyan tent canvas and sheathed it before examining the cut just above her left elbow.
'Is it serious?' asked her father, coming to inspect the wound.
Kym produced her knife and cut her left sleeve away at the shoulder to allow a clearer inspection. The wound was the side of her hand and a large piece of skin hung loose.
'Kym!' Satoro had appeared and put his hand on her lower arm lightly. 'Is it serious? Do you have any other wounds?'
'No, just this.'
The young soldier produced a bandage and carefully wrapped it around the wound, holding the flap of skin to the arm firmly. Kym winced as he tied it but smiled.
'My thanks.'
Daryo decided that his daughter was well-tended. He cleaned the Horse and the Bear and returned them to their sheaths on his back. He asked men coming past him if they had seen Captain Avenzi and was pointed back towards the towers. A small group of

Vazzeccoes were outside the burning tower, herding a group of nearly thirty Armynyans, mostly youths and elders. Avenzi was supervising, his sword in one hand and a captured letian in the other.

'Walker, we have twenty-nine prisoners accounted. We have lost three men and several are wounded. Including yourself, I see.'

Daryo looked at his left shoulder. There was a nick beside his neck and some blood on his jerkin. 'Marginal. Kym is wounded too, more severely than I but not too severely.'

Avenzi nodded. 'I shall make sure someone attends her.'

'Satoro is already. She is quite content and I believe he is also.'

'Your orders for the prisoners, Walker?'

'The vanguard of the king's army will cross the river before midday. Confine them in a shed or outbuilding and the army can take responsibility when they arrive.'

'Yes, sir.'

'I have sent Cambrati to herd the Armynyans southwards and prevent them from warning the main army. They should return soon. If you can manage the prisoners, I will have a watch set further west on the road in case we are disturbed and then we can only await the King's force.

## Chapter 88

The Vazzeccoes moved slowly and quietly through the trees at the foot of the peaks. The force was ready for battle, swords drawn, shields on their arms. Daryo had Temma's Sword drawn, his old shield in hand, twin swords sheathed on his back and a white cloth tied around his upper arm; at his side was Kym and Devotion, alongside her was Satoro like a bodyguard with his charge. Behind the Vazzeccoes, also sneaking through the trees in the predawn, was the rest of the Army of Adaca: nearly twenty thousand infantry, three thousand archers and three thousand cavalry. Somewhere to the north and to the north-east were Armynyan forces led respectively by the Kithmonsyna and the Vushtih, wearing white identification cloths on their arms too, also creeping up on the One of Two's slumbering army. It would be trapped: the Adacans to the south, the mountain to the west, the Kithmonsyna's force to the north holding one bridge across the impassably deep and fast river and the Vushtih to the east and holding the other bridge, thus using the river itself to complete the encirclement. At the council, some had argued vehemently for a secretive approach and to slay the sleeping army quickly by the other Armynyans pretending to be still friendly. This was eventually and acrimoniously out-voted in favour of King Lallano's proposal that the One of Two be given a chance to surrender and spare the need for battle. As the army crept through the woods, Lallano and a guard of his White Bulls was with Yevirsh Vushtih and the northern tribes' deputation approaching from the north-east. They would enter the camp and offer the ultimatum. Signals had been agreed to tell the encircling armies the result swiftly, even if nobody from the parleying party returned. Initially, Daryo had suggested that he accompany the king but was overruled so that he and Tari would both be at liberty to command the Adacan army with or without the sovereign's return. They reached the edge of the treeline and Daryo held up a hand to stop them advancing any further. Less than two hundred yards away was the first of the Armynyan troops, most sleeping without shelter and the perimeter poorly guarded. Only one sentry was visible and he wore a just-visible white cloth belt. He was an infiltrator from the Kasshuti tribe, there to give signals to the armies. He was patrolling back and forth on a short beat, the signal to stay concealed and wait. Each approaching army had their own signaller. The Vushtih's army would be approaching and the Kithmonsyna were supposed to arrive slightly later to demoralise the One of Two's army and to close the trap.

A warning was sounded from the east side of the camp; a real sentry had sighted the Vushtih-led army. It was not an alarm, they were fellow countrymen. The Adacan's signaller stopped his beat, turned defiantly away from the camp and took half a dozen slow steps before turning back.

Daryo raised his arm. 'Be ready.' A small mounted party separated from the Vushtih-led army and approached the camp. Lallano, his equerry and Captain Avenzi were among the Armynyans in the group.

The surrender offer was simple and, in accordance with the council's agreement, comprised a written document and would be made verbally in both Armynyan and the Common Speech. It announced the decision of the thirteen tribes that had attended Sutiv to renounce the One of Two, offered them amnesty on the condition that they step down from the leadership and return to their tribe. The army would be disbanded and free to return home. In return, the Armynyans would pledge to leave a neutral space of ten miles from the Adacan border into which no Armynyan army would enter.

The signaller walked back to his previous position and resumed his short patrol. To the casual observer a sentry a little more diligent and professional than most had simply varied his patrol route slightly. There was a long wait. Kym found a tree stump and perched on it. The signaller kept looking out towards the other army; Daryo assumed that he was a Vustih and was drawn towards his kin. The camp was beginning to stir, Daryo took a few steps back into the trees to lessen the chance of a hawk-eyed observer seeing him. A skeletal, near-naked Armynyan tottered into view and exchanged a few words with the signaller as he went to relieve himself. His ribs stood out and his legs looked barely strong enough to support him. Daryo turned and got Kym's attention. She had been talking in a whisper with Satoro.

'Do not kill unless you have no choice,' Daryo told them firmly. He beckoned Cambrati forwards. 'Spread the word, Captain. Do not kill unless there is no option.'

The newly-promoted captain nodded. 'Yes, sir.'

The spindly figure had gone back into the camp. The signaller stretched his arms. A small bird of prey swooped at something in the yellowy grass between the woods and the camp. The dawn came and yellow light bathed the Armynyan camp like warm water. A cluster of horses emerged from the Armynyan camp at a brisk trot. Daryo strained to see them but the distance was too large. The signaller saw them too. The standards were being flown by bearers on the horses and they abruptly were lowered together and raised again. The signaller drew his sword and ran into the Armynyan camp. Daryo sighed.

'Standby to engage the enemy! Vazzeccoes on me! Form up!'

The Vazzeccoes led the rest of the Adacan army out of the woods at a run and began to form ranks. The deputation had divided and half a dozen horses were galloping across the ground to where the Vazzeccoes had emerged from concealment. The king rode the lead animal and stopped his horse in front of Daryo.

'They refused,' he said simply. 'The One of Two made a decision. None of his attendants would speak against him.'

To Daryo's right, the Adacan infantry were forming up, the cavalry was assembling behind and to the left. Daryo knew that to the Adacan infantry's right would be the friendly Armynyan's entire cavalry assembly and two formations of infantry. Somewhere to the north, one large infantry formation would be approaching the northern bridge and the river in its shallow gorge would be used to protect the archers. The Adacan archers were protected by their infantry. Alarm bells and horns were being sounded in the Armynyan camp.

'This is needless,' said Lallano sadly. 'I had just ridden through my enemy's army. Most of those men are sleeping without shelter and some look near death from illness and starvation. This is a massacre.'

'I have given orders not to kill unless there is no other option.'

Lallano nodded his assent. 'I shall have the White Bulls close behind the advance. No prisoner will be killed and all shall be permitted to go home after this is concluded.'

'Yes, sir.'

Lallano drew his sword and raised it high, raising his voice to the Vazzeccoes. 'Follow the Walker! Be swift and sure in what you do! Show mercy but only to those who deserve it! Fight for your king, for your homes and your families! Fight for Adaca!'

'For Adaca!' roared every soldier that had heard.

'For Adaca!'

'For Adaca!' Even louder than the first shout, Kym raised her sword and voice.

'For Adaca!'

'For Adaca!'

The king reared his horse and cantered through his troop's lines to a chorus of cheers and battle cries. Avenzi, the new commander of the king's White Bulls bodyguard raised his sword in salute to Daryo and followed his monarch to the rear. The war drums were beating in the One of Two's camp calling the soldiers to battle but few were visible. A high pitched whistle came from the right, followed by another. A signal being passed by the Vushtih force. The Kithmonsyna were in their blocking position. King Lallano was directing the Adacan force, Daryo leading it from the front. The king must have given the order as a horn from the rear blew a single long note. The advance.

Two battalions of Adacan infantry, one on the right and one in the centre, and the Vazzeccoes on the left began to move forwards. The archers would follow at a distance,

escorted by the cavalry. As they approached the camp, the smell of filthy humanity became almost overwhelming. The One of Two's call to arms had apparently called the soldiers to the centre of camp as the only bodies that they came to were already dead or near death. Cambrati gave orders for Vazzeccoes to stop and tend to them as they passed by. The camp was carpeted in gritty mud and there was filth and decay everywhere. Ahead a shaky line of Armynyan troops had formed. Daryo raised his hand to stop the Adacan advance. He stepped out of the line and waved his hand across the line.
'Armynyans, lay down your weapons!' he called, doing so himself. 'You will be safe!'
There was no movement, one Armynyan soldiers shouted something that sounded insulting. Daryo picked up his sword again. A drum began to beat. There was a hesitation in the Armynyan ranks. The drum was joined by others and the pace increased. The Armynyans began to advance. Daryo took a deep breath and raised his sword. Cambrati did the same.
'Vazzeccoes of Adaca!' the young captain shouted. 'Follow the Walker! For Adaca! Charge!'
'For Adaca!' was the battlecry as the Adacans beat the Armynyans to the charge. Daryo swung his shield viciously laterally. The Armynyan in front of him ducked but was caught across the face by Cambrati's blade. Daryo was already into the second rank of Armynyans. He blocked a blow from a letian with his shield and stabbed the attacker through the midriff. Kym's swinging blade took off the man's head. The Vazzeccoes were easily pushing through the Armynyan lines. One in just a loincloth dropped to his knees as Daryo approached, dropping his sword. Daryo shoved the man aside in haste and raced onwards. There were only four rough lines of Armynyan soldiers and they were quickly dispatched by the Vazzeccoes. Daryo saw a group of Armynyans approaching with white cloths around their arms and raised his sword in salute.
'Adaca! Adaca!' shouted one of them.
Daryo ignored him as a letian-wielding man came running forwards, screaming in anger. Daryo blocked the first slash with his shield, shoved the blade aside and found Kym leap between them, kicking the Armynyan in the crotch, smacking him with the back of her lower sword hand and cleaving into his chest with the backslash. Daryo managed to give his daughter a quick smile before bashing another Armynyan in the face with his shield and he found Satoro there to finish the man. There seemed to be sudden quiet. Dozens of Armynyans barely strong enough to stand had been rounded up by the Adacan infantry. An Armynyan from the Vushtih's force hurried up to Daryo.
'*Hutassh munyush khurin stusth tha.*'
Daryo spread his arms and shook his head in ignorance. The Armynyan pointed north.

'*Shumu! Shumu! Munyush khurin tha! Shumu!*' He seized Daryo's arm and pulled urgently.
'I think he wants us to head that way, father,' said Kym. She came alongside him and got the Armynyan's attention. '*Thurma?*' she pronounced carefully and the Armynyan laughed.
'*Shumu! Thurma!*'
'Enemy,' said Kym. 'I think the enemy are the way he is pointing.'
'Where did you learn Armynyan speech?'
'I had the king's equerry teach me a few basic words on the ride back to Tanaab.'
Daryo nodded. 'Vazzeccoes form on me!' he called.
Quickly, his unit rallied around, only very slightly depleted by those with Armynyan prisoners or wounded. The Armynyan kept repeating '*Shumu*' and waved Daryo and his force forwards. They passed through a more formal part of the camp, more tents and shelters. A wooden-walled, canvas-roofed structure sat in a circle of emptiness with one of the gruesome infant tribal battle standards erected outside. This was apparently the vacated residence of the One of Two. A grand wooden bed, a number of chests, one nearly full of silver and a large table were inside the single-roomed structure. Daryo spent little time inside as his guide was still urging them northwards. The camp degenerated into small sleeping holes and patches of mud again and it was only on the open ground to the north of the camp that an army became apparent. On the higher ground beyond was the Kithmonsyna's army. Daryo estimated that there were twenty thousand Armynyan troops in the One of Two's army still, pinned between high ground and river to east and west and between the two forces north and south. On the right of the Adacan force, an Armynyan cavalry company came galloping through between the two sets of infantry. The Vushtih command was not giving any further opportunities for the One of Two's men to submit. From across the narrow but deep gorge that carried the young river from the mountains, the Kithmonsyna's archers began their deadly rain. The Adacan battle horns blew and the Adacan archers began to fire over their infantry's heads in support. Daryo held his men as the arrows rained down on the Armynyans. Many did not seem to have shields and were helpless. The Armynyan archers stopped firing and the Vushtih cavalry charged. This was seen and the Adacan archers held their fire too.
'For Adaca! Charge!' called Cambrati.
The Vazzeccoes, supported by the Adacan infantry to their left and the Vushtih cavalry, supported by their infantry, charged to be the hammer against the Kithmonsyna's anvil. Daryo found himself several yards behind the leading Vazzeccoes as they engaged the enemy. Kym was alongside Satoro and Cambrati in the front line of the vanguard. The

Armynyans of the One of Two's army resisted desperately. Daryo tried to keep Kym in sight but was soon too involved in his own personal battles. A particularly large Armynyan wielding both letian and hand axe drove the Batribi backwards under a barrage of blows. Daryo took a bad blow to his shoulder before being able to counterattack and finish the duel. He sensed danger and ducked. A spear haft swung through the air where his head had been, he reversed Temma's Sword and stabbed back and upwards into the body of his assailant. He rolled sideways to avoid the falling body and struck out with his sword. On his feet again, he found himself some way behind the battle. The One of Two's army were falling back against the Kithmonsyna's lines and many were surrendering as they were separated from the main force. Daryo jogged to catch up with the advance but the battle seemed done. The Armynyans were throwing down their weapons in large numbers and being thrust through the Adacan lines. The Adacan cavalry were following their infantry now and corralling the prisoners. There was a great shout from the front and something of a scrum around the Adacan left. A group of Vazzeccoes had formed an outward-facing circle, shields raised in the midst of the greatest concentration of their foes. A number of the Vazzeccoes' comrades were hurrying to their aid and Daryo managed a sprint to reach his unit's circle. He faced little opposition to reach the circle and was permitted through the perimeter. Kym, Satoro, Cambrati and a dozen other Vazzeccoes had taken a score of prisoners. One of them was the One of Two, another seemed to be another poor attempt to duplicate the leader. All the prisoners were on their knees with blades at their throats. The shout was going up that the One of Two was captured. Daryo gave orders to summon the king. The defeated Armynyan leader was sobbing pitifully and begging for clemency. Daryo did his best to ignore the whining.

'Are you hurt?' he asked Kym.

'I do not think so. You are.'

Daryo looked down and found some blood on his shoulder. 'A graze, nothing more.'
The One of Two wailed something in Armynyan as Yevirsh Vushtih shouldered his way through the Vazzeccoes' circle. The clan leader spat something harsh and then looked at Daryo.

'*Thurma dnasin tashsti.*'

'I wish that I understood,' said Daryo obligingly.

'*Thurma dnasin tashsti.*' The Armynyan pointed to Daryo's wound and then at a deep gash across his own arm. '*Tashti asbursh asih mustha.*' He gripped Daryo's uninjured shoulder in a brotherly gesture.

Daryo could think only to raise his sword, point down, in salute. 'My sword and my service, my friend.'

The circle of Adacan soldiers parted to allow Lallano, Avenzi, the king's equerry and two guards through. The group dismounted. The One of Two ducked away from Satoro's blade at his neck and lay prostrate at Lallano's feet.

'Please, merciful king! I did only what was required! I did only what the prophecy said that I must! Attacking your people, only what I must!'

Lallano looked down disdainfully. 'That is not for me to judge. Adaca has been greatly wronged by you. But your own people have been starved and exhausted even more so. I decline my victor's rights to your life and give you to what mercy you may find among your people.' He looked at Yevirsh Vushtih. 'I give this one to his people. Do with him as you will.'

The equerry translated and Yevirsh Vushih bowed respectfully, thanking the Adacan king and promising that the One of Two would face justice. Lallano nodded and looked to Avenzi. 'Commander, have the wounded seen to and the prisoners given to the guard of the Armynyan armies. Have the army prepare to return to Tanaab.'

'Yes, sire.'

A victory procession seemed unsuitable and the Adacan army's return to the near-abandoned city of Tanaab was sedate and unspectacular. The sextet of guards at the gates came to attention as the king's party passed and made its way to the Merchant's Hall but the king then immediately turned about and returned to the camp outside the city walls. A symbolic re-entry into an uninhabitable Adacan city followed by an instant return to the pragmatism of the camp. The king, despite five days' travel, a battle and another six days' travel, called an assembly at dusk of a select group: his sister, his equerry and chamberlain, Avenzi and the three most senior commanders, Kym the Devoted and Daryo the Walker. The captains' tent was lit by lamps, empty but for the king's canvas chair and a dozen canvas stools. When everyone was seated, the king looked from face to face in turn and finally announced: 'We have won.' There was a collective exhale around the room. 'Our nation has been raped and violated and whole communities destroyed but we can now start to repair the damage. I wish to commend all of you here for your efforts. Daryo the Walker and Captain Gallo have both been wounded in this war. The Walker and his daughter, Kym, have been taken away from their life. This is the second time that the Walker has come to the aid of Adaca and, Walker, we thank you most humbly for your assistance and your daughter's assistance.' Daryo inclined his head. Kym blushed. 'I intend to dismiss all units as soon as possible but the much of the brunt of this war, the bloodiest of the battles, has been born by the Vazzeccoes so I hereby disband them. The men are free to return home and may return to service on the first day of autumn. Walker, Kym, you have a home and a life in Ritaro. You should return to Ritaro with my gratitude and that of all Adacans. Captain Avenzi, I promote you to the Walker's position as Princess Tari's lieutenant and deputy commander of all Adaca's armies.'

The remainder of the meeting was the arrangement of the armies and ideas for reviving the towns and villages destroyed by the Armynyan invasion. The meeting was dismissed late in the night and in the morning, Daryo and Kym along with Satoro, Cambrati and a dozen other Vazzeccoes rode westwards for home.

Some of the party left them almost immediately, joining the road south towards Tovbi and the Sandy Coast. Another small group left at Scirito for Ensadri and Cambrati parted from them when they reached Hullava, hoping that his parents' farm had survived the nearby Armynyans. The group stopped for its eighth night just west of the small town of Kyiti. The weather had been hot and sunny during the day and it remained warm after dark, so they slept outside under a small stand of trees. Daryo, conscious of how busy he had been, took the time to walk away from the company and pray. When he rose to return, he saw Kym watching him. He smiled at his daughter.
'Here?'
She looked puzzled. 'What do you mean?'
'You have been trying to find a time to tell me you are leaving. You have been wanting to since we left Tanaab and since it is here that it is most logical that you and Satoro turn north, this is your last opportunity.'
Kym blushed. 'I did not think that we had been so obvious.'
Daryo embraced his daughter. 'You are my daughter, Kym. If I do not know what is in your mind, I am no father. Have you at least penned a letter for your mother?'
'I have. And it is not forever, father. I will come back to Ritaro. I will want to see Stai and Vehllal and mother. Satoro and I do not have any plans to marry or anything like that yet. It is a romance. Many girls my age have them.'
Daryo chuckled. 'Of course. Your mother will be furious; I promised to bring you home.'
'And you will. Just a little delayed.'
'Bruszo is a lovely part of Adaca. Visit Ishter and Boskinia too.'
'I will, father.'

## Chapter 89
### Midsummer's Day

'Vehllal!'
'I am fighting bad robbers!' The little wooden sword swung through the air as he ran around his parents' bed. 'I am saving the princess.'
Jeda reached out and got hold of a fire poker. When next her youngest son ran past her, she locked fake blades with him and used a hard twist to lever the wooden sword out of his hand. 'Vehllal. Last chance. Bed. Now. Or I throw that sword in the fire.'
Vehllal stared wide-eyed at his mother. She stretched down and picked up the sword. The fire was small, for cooking rather than heat; Vehllal was naked from the waist up and Jeda herself wore only a light linen tunic. But the wooden sword would have burned. He decided that his mother was not bluffing and scrambled quickly up the ladder. Stai was already abed. Jeda put the wooden sword against the wall and replaced the poker before returning to her usual evening activity of needlework. Having no clothes to make or repair she was embroidering a decorative hanging for Stai's bedside, depicting a hammer, anvil and the fires of a forge. There was a heavy knock on the door, harsh and demanding. After less than two heartbeats, it came again. Jeda looked up sharply. The knock came a third time, louder and more insistent.
'Mother?' called Stai from upstairs.
'Quiet,' she commanded as the knock came a fourth time. Worried by the situation, she opened the chest beside the bed and brought out the short-bladed sword that Daryo had made for her. She took a firm grip on the hilt, seized the bolt of the door, yanked it back and pulled the door hard inwards, bringing the sword up to guard. A curved blade flashed out of the dark, parried her blade aside and both swords fell to the floor. A hand came out and gripped her arm. A dark-skinned hand.
'Daryo!' she squealed and threw herself forwards, seizing her husband around the neck and planting her lips against his. 'Daryo! Daryo!'
'Father?' came Vehllal's voice. 'Father!' He slid down the ladder and threw himself into the embrace, closely followed by an equally-delighted Stai.
'You came back! You are well! You are well!' she stepped back and her face looked anguished. 'Gods, no! Where is Kym?'
Daryo took his wife by the shoulders. 'Safe. Well. She has fallen for a young man and has gone to his home in Bruszo. She promises to come home soon.'
Jeda frowned. 'You promised to bring her home.'
'I was not responsible for her decision. It was hers. She will come home, Jeda. I promise.'

Jeda sighed and embraced her husband again. 'If that is her wish...'

'It is. And she will do as she said.'

The family moved back far enough to allow Daryo back into his home and Stai closed the door.

'Did you fight many robbers?' asked Vehllal.

'Was it difficult?' asked Stai.

'How are you feeling?' asked Jeda.

Daryo smiled and sat down on the nearest chair. Jeda stood behind him and started rubbing his shoulders. Stai perched next to him on the table and Vehllal crouched on the floor in front of him. 'I have been riding for nearly twelve days. At the moment I am just tired. It is late. Stai, Vehllal, go to bed. We shall talk in the morning.'

Both looked disappointed but they obediently hugged their father and clattered up the ladder talking excitedly. Jeda squeezed a little harder, bent forward and kissed the side of Daryo's neck.

'Was it bad?'

'Barbaric but Kym was exceptional. She is a natural warrior.'

'She takes after her father.'

'And her mother.'

Jeda came around and sat sideways on Daryo's lap, kissing him hard.

'I missed you,' he said.

'Were you gone?' she asked playfully.

'How were the boys?'

'The same. Stai did his best to run the forge but he is not big or strong enough for many of the tasks. He made a few horseshoes for the farm and repaired some pots and pans. Vehllal seems to be spending most of his time rescuing princesses and fighting evildoers. His father's son.'

Daryo reached up and opened the top of his jerkin. Jeda slid her hand into the gap but he took hold of it and removed it.

'No?' She looked hurt.

'I am very tired, Jeda. I love you, my beautiful wife but I have had no rest for many weeks.'

Jeda smiled and stood up. 'No?'

'No.'

She took a knife from her belt and slit her tunic down the front, undid her belt and let the lot drop to the floor. 'No?'

Daryo found it difficult to readjust to family life. Early on his first morning at home, he had Stai put the rope across the forge entry to signal that it was closed. He had helped Jeda with some household tasks, given in and shown Stai some basic sword skills and then had taken Vehllal hunting, although they had only a knife and Vehllal spent most of his time climbing trees and ambushing his father. He spent the next day resting, then on the third he walked to the home of the landowner two miles away. Squire Lirani was welcoming. He knew Daryo's history and that he had been fighting in the east with the king. He offered a large mug of beer and prompted Daryo to describe the campaign. His horses had had to be done by a smith in Zonathor but he promised that he would immediately resume using the forge on his own land. Daryo reopened the forge the next day. There was an immediate tide of people from the village that required jobs doing. Halidir came and asked after the progress of the sword he had ordered. Daryo had been unable even to start before being called away but the farmer was content that it could be done for the end of the summer and gave Daryo clearance to proceed with the blade. Two days were taken up by the jobs of the village and then Daryo was ready to make the sword. He took Stai and Vehllal to Zonathor for some high-quality imported Jaboen iron and started work on the sword with his eldest son watching closely and assisting where he could. The result was slightly shorter than Daryo had initially intended but the blade was perfectly honed, a delicate engraving of flames and fire-drakes on the blade itself and the pommel was shaped as a fir cone. Halidir was delighted. Daryo had offered to reduce the price because of the massive delay but the farmer refused to pay less than the agreed amount and took the blade gratefully. Instead Daryo spent the remainder of that day using some leather and a small amount of bronze that he had to make a scabbard that Stai delivered to the farmer on his father's behalf with strict instructions to refuse any payment and return.

\* \* \*

It was the last day of summer when Kym returned. Satoro came with her to meet her brothers and mother. The confident, capable young soldier seemed a little overawed by meeting his paramour's family. He seemed uncomfortable around Jeda and slightly embarrassed by the innocent questions of Vehllal and Stai. Daryo alleviated his discomfort by taking a couple of bows and taking the young man hunting for boars. Satoro staying in the forge house would have been somewhat awkward so they made arrangements to stay at the village inn while Daryo roast the boar over the forge fire. Over the dinner, Kym announced that they intended to stay in Bruszo. Jeda's tears subsided and Vehllal was finally persuaded to release his grip on his sister when he understood that she was not going to leave immediately or forever. Daryo gave them his blessing.

# Book 7 - Legacy of a Hero
## Chapter 90
### Midspring Day in the Twenty-Fifth Year of the Reign of King Lallano the Eighth of Adaca

Bruszo had grown from its humble state as a mining village into a flourishing trading town. On the south edge of the village was an elegant two-storey house belonging to the local landowner with a smaller house behind it- stone walled, a thatched roof large enough to accommodate a garret room. Four horses were reined in outside the smaller house and a stable boy ran out from the stable-building to take the horses.
Daryo the Walker handed the reins to the boy and looked around, taking in the scene. He was somewhat heavier than once he had been but not overly-so. His once totally black hair was starting to turn the colour of steel. He turned to help his wife dismount. Jeda removed the Sodidoron headscarf that she had worn to travel and allowed her husband to help her down. Behind her, her sons were dismounting. Stai had grown to be a powerfully-built young man, in his eighteenth spring, he had the start of a short beard like Daryo's, the last two fingers of his left hand were slightly misshaped having been struck in an accident with a hammer but facially was more like his mother, his skin was paler than his father's too. Vehllal, in his twelfth spring, was almost a copy of his father, a similar shape and hair, the same face, even his voice sounded akin to Daryo's. To that end, he had even recently been given a horse by his parents that was the same as his father's.
The door of the little house opened and Satoro emerged. 'Hail, Daryo and Jeda, Stai and Vehllal! You are most welcome!'
Daryo grasped his daughter's husband's hand. 'We are most glad to be here, Satoro. It has been many seasons since last I came to Bruszo. It is much more than I remember.'
'My parents and their foremen at the mine have been doing much work, especially since the war ended. The town is growing and prosperous.'
'And my daughter?' asked Jeda.
'Kym has gone to the market. She should return any time now.' He looked at the stable boy. 'Terrazzi, stable the horses, make sure they are well-watered and fed.'
'Yes, sir.'
'Come inside,' said Satoro, holding the door to the house open.
The interior was almost the same as Ritaro's smithy; the hearth was rather larger, the windows too. The ceiling was lower all the way across the building and the upper level was reached by stairs rather than a ladder. There was no bed downstairs and there was a

small workshop next to the steps. Satoro took down a large flagon from the shelves and poured some light wine for the travellers.

'Kym's last letter said that you were continuing to learn the mining work,' said Jeda, accepting a cup of wine.

'Yes but I also have been teaching myself carpentry,' said Satoro. 'I had to mend one of the stairs to the bedroom and I enjoyed doing so. I have thus far managed to build three acceptable stools and a table that we were able to sell at the market. We got five bronze halves for them. The chair that Stai is sat on is also mine.'

Stai looked down, rocking backwards and forwards slightly. 'It seems adequate to me.'

Satoro laughed. 'That is very kind, Stai. The highest praise my work has received to date.'

The door opened and Kym stepped in, carrying a basket and with a canvas sling across her body. 'Mother! Father!'

'Do we not exist?' Stai asked Vehllal.

'Kym! And Haziko?'

Kym handed her basket to Satoro. 'I got duck eggs.' She loosened the sling and lifted out her two-season-old baby girl. 'Haziko, meet your grandmother.' She passed the little girl to Jeda. The baby was much lighter-skinned than her mother, her wisps of hair completely black, her chubby hand tapped against her grandmother's cheek as Jeda kissed her cheek.

'She is beautiful,' said Jeda, laying the baby comfortably into her arm as Stai and Vehllal crowded around for a closer look at their niece.

'She looks uncomfortably like her father,' suggested Daryo.

'Is there something wrong with her mouth?' asked Vehllal.

Kym looked. 'No. She sucks on her top lip.'

Daryo reached down and ran his finger lightly across the baby's cheek. 'She is beautiful, Kym.'

'It makes thirteen days on the back of a horse well worth it,' said Stai.

Satoro had hunted and shot a deer and roast the venison over an outdoor pit that night. His parents had their staff move the table and seats outside so that they could dine outdoors. Satoro's older brother, a meat merchant who lived in Oia, was also visiting with his wife and twin sons and the entire family dined together. The night was warm and still and the atmosphere was relaxed, convivial and familiar.

'This wine is exceptional,' said Jeda, raising her cup to Satoro's mother.

'It is the same one that we served after Satoro and Kym's marriage. That is the last bottle, we were saving it for their first child.'

'Kym, did you have a naming ceremony?' Jeda asked. 'Your letter did not say.'
'We did, mother. We felt it best to do so the same way that we did the wedding. On the eighth day we had a naming ceremony at the Temple of the First Goddess in Sovenna. After forty-two days, we took her to Olanyi for a blessing at the Good Shepherd's chapel.'
'We think Haziko should choose the faith that she feels comfortable in,' Satoro added.
'That is a very permissive attitude,' said Daryo.
'It is the only fair and reasonable thing to do for Haziko,' said Kym. 'I was given the choice to be Yashoun, Batribi or Adacan. It was only that both of you believe in the Pantheon that I was raised the same way.'
'All people should be able to choose their own beliefs,' said Satoro's mother. 'It is a key part of who a person is. Their beliefs in gods or qualities are the key to what makes one alive as much as who their parents are and how they are taught and what they learn as they grow. And the best people are those that continue to grow until they die.'
'I agree,' said Daryo. 'If one stops learning, one stops exploring life.'
'Kym tells us you were not raised a Batribi, Daryo.'
'I was not. I was raised in the School of the Temple in Jaboen. I was taught to be Jaboen in every way. The only Batribi thing that I was permitted was my skin and face. I was almost thirty summers before I was able to really live with my people for any time.'
'And you keep some of their ways?'
'Not many. I live in a solid building, I do not walk the roads as I once did, I cannot sing and use rhyme and verse as they do.'
Satoro asked: 'Would you like Haziko to learn Batribi ways?'
'That is not my decision,' said Daryo. 'That is to you and Kym. I think it would be good for her to one day understand something of where she comes from but that means that she also needs to learn of Yashoun and its history and customs too.'
'And she will,' promised Satoro. 'I want our daughter to know everything that we can teach her and for her to grow proud of who she is and who her parents and grandparents and ancestors were.'

After five days at Bruszo, Daryo and Jeda and their sons bade their daughter and her new family a fond and emotional farewell and rode away south. The journey was less than three days old when Daryo's horse stumbled crossing a stream and jarred his rider viciously. Unable to remain in the saddle due to the pain in his back, Daryo was forced to walk painfully to Olanyi and the physician was called by the innkeeper. The physician prescribed strong spirits for the pain and implored Daryo to spend at least three days in bed before trying to ride again. Jeda thanked the physician and paid him as he left. Stai and Vehllal had gone seeking entertainment and their parents were alone.

'A poor rider will blame his horse for this,' said Jeda in tones of mock-warning.

Daryo sniffed in derision. 'A poor horse is poor with or without a rider. It was not his doing, it was a treacherous stream and he is an ageing beast. Like the rider.'

'You are not so old yet, my Daryo,' said Jeda, seating herself beside the bed.

'I do not in truth know my age. I know from the number of summers that I have seen that I have passed fifty-five of them. Perhaps sixty if the priests at the Temple School were not skilled at guessing such matters. It is old enough.'

'For what?'

'For what indeed. I think it time to stop. I will see out perhaps this summer and Stai will be the smith of Ritaro.'

'Truly, Daryo?' Jeda leaned forwards earnestly.

'Truly. Every ache is a little keener, every injury takes a little longer to heal, each burn lasts longer on my skin.'

Jeda smiled supportively. 'If that is your wish, I would not stand against you, my husband.'

'I think it is as much the Third Goddess's wish as mine. She would have me show compassion to my own body.'

'And you will sit out your dotage looking over the cliffs of Ritaro with my hand in yours.'

'I did not say that.'

'Oh?'

Daryo sighed. It had been a thought in his mind for several seasons, one that he had not wanted to divulge to Jeda in case she disagreed with it but the first meeting with his granddaughter had solidified the notion in his mind. 'The Fourth Goddess comes for all of us some day. I do not wish to meet her in Ritaro. I know it is our family's home but it is not where I believe my home to truly be.'

'Where is your home?'

'With my people.' Daryo held up his hand for Jeda's inspection. 'I am Batribi, Jeda. In my heart, in my mind and on my skin, I am Batribi. For all the things that have happened, I have not been able to live as a Batribi. But it is my wish to die as one. Among others.'

'Ru'uatan.' Jeda spoke the name that the Batribi had given to their settled land.

'Ru'uatan,' agreed Daryo, lifting himself up slightly, ignoring the spikes of pain. 'But I know what it would mean. It would mean our uprooting from our home. Kym is settled with a loving husband and a precious child. Stai would be welcome to keep the forge if he wished. Vehllal would be welcomed by either, I am sure, or he could accompany us, as Stai could.'

Jeda sighed. 'It is such a great change, Daryo. We have been very happy in Ritaro for many years.'

'I will not ask you to do something with which you disagree.'

'I do not disagree outright but you ask much.'

'I know. And I respect if you wish to stay in Ritaro. I appreciate that it is our home.' Daryo laid his head back, letting his aching back rest. 'Do we know where Stai and Vehllal went?'

'No. Let them go, they are old enough to cope.' Jeda stroked his forehead. 'I think Haziko looks like Satoro too.'

# Chapter 91

The last day of the summer was unusually damp. The rain of the week before had passed but left the earth sodden, the roads unfriendly and the air moist. A cart made its way across the bridge from Adaca in Sodidor. It was driven by Daryo, the former smith of Ritaro having passed on the assignment, the forge and the house to his elder son. Behind the cart, Jeda and Vehllal rode on their own mounts. Jeda looked back frequently, as if looking for another glimpse of Stai stood outside waving farewell. The decision had been a collective one after many weeks of discussion, arguments at times, tears and quarrels and rationality had all played equal roles. Stai would remain in Ritaro. He was skilled enough to run the forge and would only learn more as he worked. He was happy to have the independence and opportunity to progress alone in the world. Vehllal was too young and unready to be so and was accompanying his parents to the port. They had passage booked on a ship bound for Paloss in Yashoun. The three would then take the river road west to the Batribi land of Ru'uatan. Daryo had sent notice that he was leaving Adaca to the king and Lallano had offered a royal courier and even an escort. Daryo had accepted the courier but declined the escort. The courier had carried a letter to Kym in Bruszo and then gone on into Ishter and Boskinia, bound for Ru'uatan to notify Daryo's clan that he was coming.

The port was busy and Daryo steered the cart through the traffic to a large two-mast ship near the centre of the port. The *East Wanderer* was owned and mastered by a Sodidoron, Salithen, the brother of Ritaro's mine foreman. He greeted Daryo warmly, bowed with extravagant courtesy to Jeda and hailed Vehllal like a lost son. While their possessions and the two riding horses were loaded, Daryo excused himself and walked into the town, through the maze of alleyways and lanes that connected Dock Street to Wall Street. He reached the door he had sought and knocked. When there was no answer, he knocked harder. He stepped away from the door, looked around and knocked once more. A window above opened.

'What do you want, Batribi?' demanded the elderly man. 'That knocking would awake the dead.'

'I seek the woman who lived in the room here,' Daryo told him. 'A Yashoun woman named Siva. Sometimes known as the Fuller.'

'Oh the dirty woman! Not sad that she is gone!'

'Gone?'

'Died. Pestilence. Starved maybe. Never did see her with food. Last winter.'

Daryo bowed his head. 'Fourth Goddess guide you, Siva.' He looked up to the man at the window. 'My thanks, sir. I am sorry to have disturbed you.'
'Were you a friend of hers?'
'An old comrade.'
'She decayed like a piece of old fruit. I think her mind was broken.'
'I think so.'
'I am... sorry for your loss.'
'My thanks, sir. And again, I am sorry for the disturbance.'
Daryo returned to the port slowly, not consciously but overwhelmed with thought. He almost collided with Vehllal.
'Father! Our things are on the ship. We are almost ready to leave. Where did you go?'
'To look for an old friend who used to live nearby. She is no longer there.'
'She moved?'
Daryo sighed. 'She passed. In a poor way, near the nadir that a person can reach.'
'I am very sorry, father,' said Vehllal.
'It is a fact that we all face,' said Daryo. 'Remember what I told you.'
'The Fourth Goddess is both friend and foe?'
'Just that. My friend Siva faced her foe with little defence. She stripped herself of them. It is not the way to go. One should choose a dignified or justified way to greet the Fourth Goddess.'
'So we will not drown on the ship?' Vehllal smiled. Several of his peers had been trying to scare him with the perils of sea travel.
'Not at all.'
'Then we should board. Salithen says that we have to sail when the tide is fully in and that he will teach me to steer the ship when we are in the open sea.'
Daryo smiled at his son's enthusiasm. 'You are not sad to leave?'
Vehllal thought for a moment. 'I am sad. But this is what you always used to do, I thought. Adventures, travelling to new places, learning new things.'
'It was.'
'Then you should come aboard for one more adventure, father.'
Daryo laughed. 'As you wish.'

The ship made its way out of the bay of Zonathor, caught the wind and began to sail swiftly south-westwards. Daryo stood at the stern rail with Jeda watching the coast recede. He reached up to scratch his neck and felt the absence of his twin swords on his back. With such a long distance being put between him and his elder son, he had gifted them to Stai, as he had been given them by his son's namesake, he felt it most fitting to leave them with a man that bore the same name. His son had tried to refuse them but Daryo told him something that the elder Stai had told him many seasons before that it was the height of rudeness to refuse a given gift and his son had relented, drawing the swords in turn and pledging to use them only if needed and only as his father would have used them. Daryo's shield was on his back and Temma's sword still hung by his side alongside his parting gift from his son, a broad-bladed knife, but his old knife had also gone. He had sent it with the royal courier to be given to Kym, a gift for his granddaughter when she was old enough to need such a tool.

He heard his son's voice, asking one of the deck hands if they might meet sea pirates on their journey. The deck hand laughed and said no. Daryo knew that the seas off Yashoun's coast was well-watched by the ships of the Emperor. The northern coast, along from Yashoun's Northern Ports along the shores of Jaboen, Gourmin and Armynya were less secure, which was why he and Jeda had decided to travel only as far as Paloss and then take the road east instead of sailing on to Nalb in Jaboen or Spiert in Gourmin. Both of them felt much more confident with their feet on the ground and a sword in their hand than on a ship reliant on the bows and slingshots of the crew.

The ship was due to sail into Denithir, Sodidor's first city penned in by precipitous cliffs, then to negotiate the difficult Obsidian Channel to the Island City, Haniten. They would then round Black Point, berth at Durat in the Black Bay and then sail north along Yashoun's Long Cliff Shore stopping at Nudakso, Kalimoss and finally Paloss in twenty-three days' time. The only other options were the long and torturous route through Yashoun's interior via Denithir in Sodidor and then Hampimoss, Vendor, Jundan, Veritimoss, Nudakso and Paloss, a complicated but unavoidable route that would take nearly twice the time; or the inland route up through Aden and Darsux through Ishter, into Boskinia through Psephana and Sataos, into Armynya, cross into Gourmin at Sitak and then the Gourmin road through Spiert, Allesbury, Aslon and across the Tember Pass, a journey that Daryo estimated would take over ninety days. The ship and the Dithithindil road from Ossmoss was the only viable route.

Denithir was a depressing city. It was built on a sea-lashed shelf of sand and rock at the foot of towering grey cliffs nearly five hundred feet high. The squat little houses below the natural walls were battered and crumbling under the weight of the ocean that sometimes filled the city at high tides. A forbidding fortress was built on a rock at the end of the fragile harbour wall and it offered no strident banners or welcoming beacon. The port area against the wall was clogged by weed and salt. The *Eastern Wanderer* was the largest ship in dock and was soon on its way, unloading some iron ore from the Ritaro mines and taking on just a few barrels of salt fish. The crew took to the oars to take the ship through the maze of islands, reefs, sandbars and spits that littered the Obsidian Channel to Haniten. The Island City was more protected than their previous stop. The harbour was a natural inlet, the bay lined by warehouses, taverns and gaming houses, the town beyond spread up a gentle hill with wide avenues and an impressive Temple of the Fourth God; Dule as bringer of security and safety was a favourite of mariners. The ship was staying in port overnight as the tide had dropped, so Daryo, Jeda and Vehllal gladly went ashore. The family prayed together at the temple, ate at one of the inns that offered incredibly large lobsters with hot parsley butter and slept at another inn, where Salithen had arranged beds for them as part of their passage.

They were woken before dawn so that the ship could sail with the tide and the *Eastern Wanderer* slid down the western side of the Obsidian Channel, slipped between the Black Spur and the bird-covered island of Tobis and then headed west to round Black Point. Durat was a tiny port that was squeezed by the cliffs of Black Bay. It was simply a stop for provisions for any ship larger than a fishing smack and the *Wanderer* was soon under sail again.

The Long Cliff Shore of Yashoun was also known as the Empty Shore. Over six hundred miles of high cliffs, uninhabited by any person, impossible to approach due to submerged and half-submerged rocks at the foot of the cliffs and without shelter for any ship. Captains with experience of the shore knew that the safest method to negotiate the Empty Shore was to sail wide of the northern claw of Black Bay and head north towards the cluster of islands known as Dule's Boon and allow the prevailing wind and current to gradually guide the ship into the port of Nudakso. The ten days of sailing gave the captain the opportunity to teach Vehllal to steer the ship. Vehllal approached the task with the same enthusiasm that he approached anything that he wished to accomplish or master. He spent most of each day with his hands on the ship's tiller at the stern of the ship alongside either Captain Salithen or Guci, the Silver Islander lieutenant. Jeda had embroidery and was trying to teach herself to play the Adacan flute, which was appreciated by the sailors as they had some music, albeit slow, to work to. Daryo helped the sailors fish for food and assisted when some of the side walls of the ship required some patching. When one of the on-deck braziers got particularly hot, he used it to do some metal work for the captain- a metal brace for the tiller bar, a few score of arrowheads and some metal frames for the anchor cable hole.

Nudakso was a busy commercial port, ten miles along the Sjok River. It was the main stop for ships before heading south along the Long Cliff Shore and those like the *Eastern Wanderer* that had just traversed it. Nudakso was also the main point for Yashoun's farming country to bring its goods for export and the coal and silver from Hajmachia. The *Eastern Wanderer* then continued on north to the fishing port of Kalimoss and then into the Dithithindil estuary and docking at Paloss just before sunset on the twenty-second day of the voyage. Daryo and his family stayed on board that night before helping Guci unload their horses, possessions and cart the next morning. The horses were rather skittish and unhappy after their long confinement but were much more content when taken out and allowed a long rope on the thin grass by the dock side. Daryo walked into Ossmoss and found a hostel with a large stable and they relayed the horses and the cart to the stables for some hay and fresh water. With profuse thanks to Captain Salithen, they started to walk to the inn.

'Daryo, the Nightside Bridge!' said Jeda, pointing to the westernmost bridge between the twin cities. 'We had our first kiss on that bridge,' she told Vehllal, who rolled his eyes. 'I cannot see any future where that knowledge will help me, mother.'

Daryo chuckled. 'Maybe we should show our son everywhere we kissed in the city.'

'Perhaps!'

Vehllal covered his eyes with his hands. 'Please no!'

'We should go to the Temple at some time before we leave,' said Jeda.

Daryo nodded. 'That is a sight worth seeing, Vehllal. The Great Temple.' He pointed through the crowd of buildings to the immense dome of the temple, just visible through a gap.

'Can we go now?' asked Vehllal, his excitement replacing his previous horror.

Daryo and Jeda exchanged a glance and Daryo nodded. 'Of course.'

They made their way through the port area of Paloss, across the Noon Bridge onto the Noon Avenue that led straight to the main door of the Great Temple. Vehlllal gazed in awe, it was by a long distance the largest building that he had ever seen. The doors were open and Daryo led the way inside. Vehllal still looked amazed as Daryo offered him as long as he wished to spend in the temple. He spent a long time wandering around, looking at the architecture and he questioned a priest on the building's history and the significance of some of the features. Then he found his parents again.

'Where do you want to pray, Vehllal?' asked Jeda. 'Any of the Eight of the Pantheon.'

Vehllal looked around. 'Who is your guardian, mother?'

'I was named in this temple. The whole Pantheon.'

'Father?'

'I was named and raised by the School of the Temple of Dule. But I have devoted much of my life to the Fourth Goddess and the rest to Brokea.'
'That does not help. My guardian is... the Third Goddess?'
'We chose Spinel because Kym's was the First as our first child and Stai was the second so the Second Goddess. You as the third...'
Vehllal thought for a moment. 'I want to pray at all three. Mother, you have to choose.'
They went first to the sept of the Third Goddess. Vehllal prayed that Spinel would guide him to be a good son, Jeda that reason and understanding would guide her as a wife and mother, Daryo prayed for compassion from the Third Goddess for his actions in his life. Jeda chose the Third God, Spellis and prayed that her family would continue to be blessed with good health. Daryo prayed that Spellis would protect Haziko and Vehllal added his prayers.
Daryo had been tempted to pray at the altar of the Second God but inevitably was swayed and it meant that they were the only three knelt in the sept of the Fourth Goddess. Vehllal asked for long life, Jeda asked for long life for her family. Daryo was silent for a long time.
'Darkest Goddess, mistress of all, constant companion. You have leant power to my sword and strength to my shield for many seasons. You have allowed me to be your instrument and never your subject. As I approach, as all of us must, the day when I join you, I ask that you watch over those that continue to walk this world and grant them the same kindness that you have granted me.'

The overland journey took sixteen days. They followed the Dithithindil road to Stimoss and took the little ferry upriver to Sictan. The road then followed the Dithithindil into Jaboen and branched north to follow the fork through Thiel and Three Rivers and then the road went northwards around Lalbi and as it climbed towards the Tember Pass there was a small wooden building with a Batribi stood at the door and a white pennant hung from a pole alongside. Daryo halted the cart as the grey-robed Batribi stepped forwards. A familiar style of curved sword hung from his belt.
'Are you one?' he challenged.
Daryo bowed shortly. 'I am Daryo, kin of Dostan. My wife, Jeda, and my son, Vehllal. I believe our arrival is anticipated.'
'It is, sir,' said the Batribi with a wide grin. 'I am Burun, son of Dostan. You are most welcome, clan-uncle.' He copied Daryo's short bow. 'Welcome to Ru'uatan, land of the Batribi. Welcome home.'

# Chapter 92

From an encampment of canvas the settlement alongside Lake Stannia the fledgling Batribi nation had grown to one of wood and thatch. The homes were mostly round in plan with conical thatched roofs to mimic the shape of the *kaff* tents. Broad streets were laid out between the houses that grouped in clusters of about a dozen. Some of the old *kaffa* remained, often in groups like the houses. A few clans apparently still preferred their traditional accommodation. Some had stables, some small dairies and bakeries adjacent, Daryo saw a carpenter, a whitesmith and a fletcher at work. A small temple had been constructed with a tiled dome immediately alongside the lake, roughly where Daryo remembered long ago attending an assembly of clan leaders. Burun had handed over sentry duty to another and had climbed aboard Daryo's wagon to direct them through the little town. Everywhere flew the same white pennant- a radiant golden sun emerging from behind a silver mountain above blue waves. Often a smaller pennant flew beneath bearing the clan's symbol. Burun identified a plain green pennant with a broad white border as that of their clan.

Vehllal rode up alongside. 'How many live here?'

'Nearly four thousand now,' Burun told him. 'No one person could say how many of our people still walk the roads but it is thought that maybe one in four of all Batribi now live in Ru'uatan. And mostly inspired by my father. He has been the leader of Ru'uatan for much of its time.'

'He is no longer?' asked Daryo.

'Not now. Every fourth spring, the clan leaders elect one of their own to lead until the next time of choosing. Father was the first leader chosen, the third and fifth. He is now too old to lead, Dasre of her clan leads our people until the next spring. That is the flag of Dasre's clan.' He pointed out a white and blue pennant.

The concentration of flags suddenly went completely green and white and Burun suggested a place to stop the wagon. Daryo stopped the horse and Vehllal immediately got down from his mount. A young girl looked out of the nearest house.

'Father!'

'Yurra, come and take the horses to the stable.'

The young girl emerged. She was a little older than Vehllal and took the reins of his horse with a friendly smile. 'Yes, father.'

'Is your grandfather at home?'

'Yes, he is.'

'Come inside, clan-uncle,' said Burun.

Daryo got down from the cart and helped Jeda down from her horse. The house was simply furnished. On a canvas cot, high off the ground for a bed, an elderly man was laid under a thin blanket. He looked up as the visitors entered.
'Daryo, my brother. Welcome,' he said in a strained voice.
'Dostan.' Daryo knelt beside the bed. 'You look not a day older.'
'You lie, brother.' He chuckled weakly. 'You came as you said. Two days earlier as well.'
'Indeed. The tides and roads were kind to us. I bring with me my wife, Jeda, and my youngest son, Vehllal.'
Dostan raised his head a little higher. 'A sight of great beauty and radiance. And your wife is very attractive too, Daryo.'
Daryo laughed. 'You seem well to me, Dostan. How fares your brother?'
'Laulra is well. He is at Halmia speaking with the Lords of Jaboen. He bids you welcome in his absence. He arranged with the procurator a house for you built with a *kaff* alongside. They are popular with small families such as yours. It is across the street, the home with the clan pennant alone. Come for evening meal with us, Daryo.'
'We would be honoured.'
Dostan laid back and closed his eyes, sighing painfully. Daryo exchanged concern looks with Burun and withdrew.
'He is near,' said Daryo quietly when outside.
Burun nodded gravely, his eyes wet with tears. 'Very. He hoped to see you come.'
'Maybe now it will allow him to rest. But it may yet quicken his heart.'
'It may.' Burun pointed to the home across the way. It was the same as the others but for a *kaff* built alongside and with its sides buttressed by wooden walls to make one unit. 'That is the house that my blood-uncle Laulra had given to you.'
'My thanks, Burun.'

The house was divided into two, a living area to the front with table and fire, the main bed behind the partition. A curtained doorway in the right wall led in the *kaff*, which had another smaller bed and some elementary house stores. Jeda inspected the house and declared it acceptable. Vehllal tried to claim the larger bed by dropping his bag on it but Daryo picked it up and returned it to him. Vehllal trotted into the *kaff* room. Burun and his daughter, Yurra, assisted them in moving their possessions from the wagon and then left the family alone.
'Is it what you wished for?' Jeda asked Daryo, removing her headscarf and freeing her hair.
'I believe so,' Daryo replied, kissing her gently. 'Among my people.'

'And Vehllal's.'
'And Stai, Kym and Haziko's.'
'Then I am content too. I think Vehllal will gain much from being here.'
'We should unpack our things and find ourselves.'

The evening meal was no intimate meal between family members. It was an assembly of the entire clan of Dostan that could be summoned, over seventy people met on the edge of the township. A large fire had been used to roast three entire sheep and the clan dined together, all but Dostan sat on the ground as equals, the elder sat on a small chair near the fire. Good beer and good meat were excellent welcome gifts for Daryo, Jeda and Vehllal. The warmth of welcome and familiarity was great from all around the fire. After the meal, the clan was sat around the fire talking and laughing together when a steady beating noise began to cut through the voices. Dostan had begun to tap his hands on his knees and the action spread until everyone present was doing so. Dostan went to speak but shook his head and nodded to Burun. Burun's voice was strident.

*'Our people walk and walk again,*
*This fate of ours is each one's bane.*
*To sleep beneath the stars each night,*
*To walk and walk again in flight.'*

The whole clan spoke together:

*'Our people walk and walk again,*
*This fate of ours is each one's bane.*
*To sleep beneath the stars each night,*
*To walk and walk again in flight.'*

Burun continued:

*'Our kin have come, their light we greet,*
*New faces seen, new brothers to meet.*
*The light has gone but fire burns,*
*From they and us, the both shall learn.'*

*'Our people walk and walk again,*
*This fate of ours is each one's bane.*
*To sleep beneath the stars each night,*
*To walk and walk again in flight.'*

A woman's continued, Daryo recognised her as a niece of Dostan.

*'The walking fades, the town must grow,*
*The ways we know, our sons forgo.*

*Our life has changed, our hearts are strong,*
*Batribi hearts beat loud and LONG!'* This was greeted by a cheer as the clan recited.
*'Our people walk and walk again,*
*This fate of ours is each one's bane.*
*To sleep beneath the stars each night,*
*To walk and walk again in flight.'*
*'The road was long, the road was hard,*
*The horses fade but our spirit unmarred,*
*To sit with kin is bliss indeed,*
*Our love and bond will only breed.'*
Daryo listened with amazement at his son's confident words. Jeda wiped a tear from her eyes swiftly. The Verse continued for a score more speakers before it faded. A united clan began to drift back to their homes. Dostan died that night.

A young woman proposed at the clan assembly eight days after Dostan's death that Daryo be chosen as the new leader of the clan but Daryo declined. Laulra had been summoned home on his brother's death and likewise declined. He was older than Daryo and felt it unwise to have another aged leader. He proposed Burun but he also declined. Instead, after most a day's debate, Tella, daughter of Temma niece of Stai, was chosen as the new leader of the clan and the clan's messengers went forth to proclaim themselves kin of Tella. Daryo had found the town's smithy and offered his services as an occasional assistant, which was gratefully accepted as there was a shortage of smiths within the town. The only other fully-experienced smith was also of Daryo's clan and was glad for the help even if only one day in eight or sixteen. Vehllal had got to know Burun's daughter Yurra and the group of her cousins that she was close to, all between eleven and fifteen summers old. They were all keen to join the town's watch and were often practising with bows and wooden swords. Jeda worked with the town's quartermasters, particularly responsible for the distribution of food, four days of eight. Daryo spent one day of eight at the forge and one with the town watch, being named a titular captain of the watch by Dasre, the town's leader, when they met on the third day in Ru'uatan.

# Chapter 93

The Batribi courier was a remarkable sight in Bruszo and even more so when he reached Ritaro. He bore two messages only, identical in wording. One was given to the wife of the squire of Bruszo, the second was handed to the wife of the smith of Ritaro to be given to her husband when he returned from Zonathor. The wording was stark:

*Come as quickly as you can. He is near death. His heart grows weak. Please come swiftly, father will not last. Gods' Guidance, Vehllal.*

Stai, the smith of Ritaro, immediately packed a bag, knowing it may take him forty days to reach Ru'uatan. He left his young wife and just-walking son and rode hard for the Zonathor docks, hoping for a swift boat to Paloss.

Kym, the squiress of Bruszo, had her daughter of ten springs' life and her son of six winters, and her husband insisted on accompanying them. They loaded a carriage and left the next dawn to take the road route through Boskinia, Armynya and Gourmin and through the Tember Pass to Ru'uatan. Kym arrived after twenty-nine days on the road, having used three teams of horses.

Three days later, having exhausted four individual mounts, a lone man rode up to the gate of Ru'uatan. A man carrying a sword lazily in her hand stepped out of the guardhouse.

'Are you one?'

The rider thought for a moment. 'I am Stai, kin of Daryo the Walker, kin of Tella.'

The young man nodded. 'I am Srai, kin of Tella. You arrived most timely, cousin. Alongside the temple is a house. Your father is there. Look for the blue banner outside.'

Stai kicked his weary horse on. The house alongside the wooden-built temple was half-timber with plastered walls, two floors tall with a well-thatched roof. He threw the reins of his horse to a startled passing woman and raced into the building with the blue banner by the door. He almost collided with a woman in blue robes just inside the door.

'Sir, this is a place of healing and peace,' she said, scandalised.

'Daryo the Walker? Where is he? I am his son.'

'Oh.' The woman pointed up the stairs. 'The room to your right hand, sir.'

Stai took the steps three at a time. On the landing at the top of the stairs, he recognised among a small group of Batribi, Satoro, his sister's husband, and guessed the girl and young boy with him were his niece Haziko and his nephew Toroli. Satoro stood up quickly.

'Stai.'
'Satoro. Inside?'
'Yes. Be prepared.'
'I have had a long journey to prepare myself.'
He took a long breath and opened the door. Daryo the Walker was laid in a bed, he had apparently thrown off his coverings and wore just a long shirt. His once black hair was steel grey and thin almost to disappearance like snow in warm sunlight. The hand that did not grip his wife's was shaking. His eyes looked milky and moist but his lips were dry. He blinked slowly.
'Who is that?'
Jeda, almost totally grey-haired herself but still with a shade of her old self, squeezed the withered hand in hers gently. 'It is Stai, Daryo,' she said slowly and clearly.
'Stai? Stai? He is long dead.'
'No, your son. Your eldest son.'
'Stai! Yes of course, I knew that. I may be blind but not foolish.'
Stai stepped into the room and closed the door behind him. His brother Vehllal was sat beside his mother and had stood up when his older brother entered. His sister Kym was stood on the other side of the bed, the right, by the open window. Tears were flowing unchecked down her face. Stai extended his hand to his brother and Vehllal tapped it familiarly. Stai then embraced his sister, who sobbed heavily.
'Stai! Stai!'
Stai knelt by his father's bedside and gripped his free hand. 'I am here, father.'
'Vehllal said you were coming. He said it. I remember that now.'
'He sent me a message. I came as quickly as I could. I had to leave Salyan and Darothir in Ritaro. He would have loved to have met you, father.'
'Of course he has met his father.'
Jeda met her son's eyes and shook her head, starting to cry. Stai exhaled slowly and gripped his father's hand tighter. He spoke slower next time. 'He has talent with a hammer, father. He will be a great smith as you were.'
Daryo laughed, a wheezing sound soon overtaken by a cough. When the cough subsided he said: 'I am no smith. A warrior. A warrior. Always. The Walker of the Order of the Shield and Sword. The first Batribi Member of the Order. The very first. Remember, Jeda?'
'I remember, Daryo.'
'The first. The very first. The Walker. I never was going to be a smith. A warrior. A walker. The Batribi warrior who walked the roads fighting the unjust. Ha!' He coughed

again, a wetter cough. 'Ha! Now look here. A blind swordsman. I could fight a mouse and loose the fight! Ha!' He coughed harder and struggled for breath. Kym sobbed again and Vehllal came around the bed to comfort her. Daryo tried to manage a word through his coughing. 'Sword,' he managed. 'Sword.'

'Daryo, you should rest,' said Jeda earnestly.

'I will meet death with a sword in my hand!' snapped Daryo angrily, his voice suddenly firm.

Kym waved a hand at the door, unable to speak. Vehllal opened it and Jeda saw a clansman that would suffice. 'Lorda, run back to the house. Above the bed will be a sword. Bring it. Run. For all the Gods, run.' The young man almost somersaulted down the stairs and his receding footsteps went out of the door. 'Lorda is fetching your sword, Daryo.'

'She is a good girl.'

'Lorda, Daryo. Tella's son.'

'Jenni? She died at the Five Towers. I think. I remember that. I fought there. I fought the army of Sevant the Stone in Gourmin at the Five Towers and slayed him in Adaca years later. Drove my sword into him. I have killed many people. Many people. Never the slain, always the slayer. The Fourth Goddess has guided me. I fought at the Five Towers. I fought at Outros. I fought in Adaca and the Silver Island. Jeda, we should have gone to the Silver Island. You would have loved the Silver Island. Stai! Stai! Take that son you had to the Silver Island.'

'I will, father.'

'The Silver Island! Animals you cannot think can live, live on the Silver Island. Animals that look like no others! Kym, take your children to the Silver Island.'

Kym nodded keenly but could not make words. Vehllal said: 'She will, father.'

'The Silver Island. Unimaginable creatures at every turn of the head! I fought many seasons on the Silver Island. And in Boskinia. A beautiful country. Beautiful. Like Jaboen. Even Hajmachia. The mountains in Hajmachia! Towering mountains.... Towers.' He coughed again, each one shaking his whole body.

Kym sobbed again and Vehllal clutched his sister tightly, murmuring reassurance in her ear. Stai tried to look at the wall; to look at his father or mother would have broken his composure.

The door opened and Lorda presented Temma's Sword formally on his wrists. Stai took it by the hilt, thanked him and Lorda closed the door behind him as he left.

'I have your sword, father.' He carefully guided his father's skeletal hand to the hilt and Daryo gripped it tightly, bringing the pommel to his chest. 'Better. That feels better. Like a part of my body. I had almost forgotten what it is to hold it.'

'You look every inch the warrior, Daryo,' said Jeda.

'Maybe a duel. A fight. Someone find me a foe!' he cried, shaking his sword.

'Father! Peace,' said Stai, laying a hand on his father's chest.

Daryo gave another wheezing laugh and choked. 'I joke, I joke.' He relaxed. 'I have no strength to rise out of bed, I cannot fight. I had that sword with me when I first fought someone. On the road south from Salifa. Vilya the Ranger stopped me from killing a man. *Hold your blade, Batribi*, she shouted. I did. A blade is nothing if not tempered by water and wisdom. Stai, temper every blade you make with water. The wisdom must be left to the wielder, I fear.' He coughed again and groped in the air. Jeda took his hand and he relaxed again. 'Who is that?'

'It is Jeda, Daryo.'

'Jeda?'

'Yes.'

'Jeda? My Jeda? My wife?'

'Yes, Daryo.'

'Have I been a good man, Jeda?'

Jeda sobbed. 'Yes, Daryo.'

'I have?'

'Yes, Daryo.'

'I swore to protect you, Jeda. I cannot do that now.'

'The clan has promised to do so. Remember? The clan swore on its honour to care for me.'

'They did?'

'Yes, Daryo.'

'And what of the children?'

'They have their own families to protect.'

'They are just children.'

Jeda laughed despite herself. 'Oh, Daryo, Stai is bigger than you ever were. Vehllal must stoop through doorways. Kym is a fine woman. They are children no more.'

'Children? My children?'

'We are here, father,' said Stai.

'Which are you? I cannot see you.'

'Stai, father. I am Stai.'

'Stai? Stai! Oh no, he is long dead!' Daryo's laugh became another body-wracking cough. 'Dava. Fayd. Kym. Leroyfa. Horuz. Jenni. Stai. Laulra. Dostan. Temma. All dead.' He redoubled his grip on Jeda's hand. 'I swore to defend the just, Jeda. The righteous, the innocent, the weak. Did I do that?' His cough grew still worse.

'Yes, my love. You did. In every country that you visited, you did good. You helped the cause of justice and righteousness. Everywhere you went, they remember your name.'

'I swore you my sword and service, Jeda. I swore that I would give you both until I was discharged by death. I swore an oath.'

'Yes you did, Daryo. You gave me love, devotion, care and service with honour, Daryo. I cannot put my gratitude in words. You gave your sword and service.'

'Until I am discharged by death.'


'Vashine.'

'You know me.'

'How could I not?'

'You have walked my path many times, Daryo the Walker.'

'But never at your side. I have avoided that fate.'

'It is the fate of all. Each one's bane as your people say.'

'A bane and a boon. It is a release.'

'You have done a mighty service for me, Daryo. You have sent me more disciples than most do. I have legions of followers that would never have joined me without your blades' work. You are most welcome in my halls.'

'Are they as dark as their reputation?'

'No. They are halls of light. Halls of the valiant, the worthy and the righteous. Those who have died well and in my service.'

'And your worship. I feel I have owed much of my life to you.'

'Not your life. That was your own deeds, your own work. Only this is my doing.'

'I am ready.'

'You have already passed.'

'I suspected seeing you and speaking your name were signs to that effect. My children? My Jeda?'

'Will not see me for many, many seasons. Your grandchildren will flourish and grow and for many more seasons beyond that.'

'And... will I see them again?'

'You will. You have my word.'

'My thanks.'

'I ask only one thing of you now, Daryo.'
'You are a Goddess, ask it.'
'Lay down your sword and walk to my halls with me.'
'Then I can pledge only my service.'
'And I accept. Come. There is a most magnificent road that you have yet to walk.'

## Chapter 94

Vehllal had sent but two messages but word that Daryo the Walker was dying had seemed to spread, perhaps at the mouths of the Batribi themselves. Not long after the flags above the physician's hostel were lowered to signal the death, a party flying the banners of the Adacan monarchy reached the gate of Ru'uatan, led by a silver-haired woman who identified herself as Princess Tari, sister of the king. With the next dawn, another group of mounted soldiers arrived bearing the Oak Tree of Boskinia's Oaken Guards and escorting a mail-clad elderly woman who was unable to speak and a barely-alive elderly man in a carriage who gave his name as Carbreo. Later in the day, Avenzi of Adaca arrived with a party of the unit known as Vazzeccoes. An old woman arrived on foot, wearing a battered olive-green tabard with a sword and shield device on the front, wearing a yellow canvas hood with a matching band around her arm, escorted by a small group of like-attired people. Another small group arrived, stating only that they had been comrades of the Walkers, that he had saved their lives flying from a nest on a harsh night once long ago and that they wished to show their respect.

The body had immediately been washed and embalmed by experts from among the Batribi community and laid on a bier in front of the altar in the Ru'uatan temple with his shield on his chest. For eight days, from dawn until dusk, his children stood vigil over the body in the Batribi custom, swords ceremonially drawn to repel predators. Kym wielded Devotion, Stai held both twin swords, Vehllal held his father's blade known as Temma's Sword. From dusk until dawn, the siblings were replaced by an Adacan Vazzecco, an Oaken Guard of Boskinia, one of the group from the Nest and a Batribi watchman. On the eighth day, the body was placed on a litter and, covered in a black shroud, bourn by Daryo's clan and they processed from the temple towards the Batribi burial ground south of the township, the way led again by his children with drawn swords, his wife behind the litter comforted and guided by the Adacan princess Tari and her daughter's husband, Satoro. Hundreds followed in procession. A priest and the leader of Ru'uatan, a clansman of Daryo named Sotyo, were waiting by the ready grave. The bier was laid alongside it.

The priest lead prayers to each of the Pantheon in turn: praying for health for those who remained, good years of harvest, a life of peace, an adherence to oaths, swift relief for those who suffered, compassion and love between friends, safety and prosperity and finally for the Fourth Goddess to guide their lost loved one into her halls. Sotyo spoke of what death and loss was to the Batribi as a people: a transition for those remaining but a chance for great new adventure in the next kingdom for those who died. He then invited anyone present to speak of their memories of Daryo and their wishes for his spirit or his family. He looked first at Jeda, who simply shook her head tearfully. Kym and Stai declined but Vehllal stepped forwards.

'When I was a child, I was an adventurer. My father made me armour and a sword of wood and I went fighting bandits, bears and monsters in the land around Ritaro. I did not realise until I was older that in my own way I was emulating my father's adventures. He walked the land to learn, to discover. Some of his last words to us were to take our children to new places to see new landscapes and new creatures. That is why he walked. That is why he walked abroad. Not just out of a sense of duty, which was irresistibly strong, but out of a sense of curiosity. I take both of those from my father. And I swear my sword and service to the pursuit of new discoveries.' There was a widespread murmur of approval.

Tella, daughter of Temma, stepped forth. 'My mother's name was forever attached to the blade that Daryo wielded. His name and hers are forever linked and I am thankful for that honour. She played but a small part in his life and was of no blood with him but Stai joined them as kin within our clan. The bond of clan is stronger than that of blood. I like to believe that the bond called Daryo here for his final seasons. In the old speech of our people: *Kaff yan tayar, to hun lurus tu, Daryo.*'

Princess Tari of Adaca spoke. 'Daryo the Walker was the saviour of many nations. He would not acknowledge this himself. He declined lordship, title and position. He led the Silver Islanders against the Nar Silver, he commanded the Boskinians in defence of their own land, he fought alongside the Adacan army against the Vidmarians and then led our army against the Armynyan invasion. The numbers that he killed are pathetically small compared to the number that he saved. When his soul is examined, I pray that the weight of this salvation is judged rightly. Thank you, Vazzecco. Our people will speak your name forever.'

A man stepped forwards. 'My name is Boukus. I was a child of the Order of the Shield and Sword. My father, Dumar the Vale, died at the Five Towers. I was taken with the other children to the safety of Sinsebil. Before that, I was at the facility known as the Nest in Allesbury. Daryo the Walker saved the lives of dozens of children, many of whom have accompanied me to show our gratitude. I never before now had a chance to thank the Walker and I am shamed that I have waited until his graveside to do so. Our most humble and heartfelt thanks, Walker.' He and his companions drew their swords and raised them in the Order salute. Kym raised Devotion in acknowledgement of the salute.

Silence fell, each person lost in their own thoughts. The priest caught Stai's eye and received an imperceptible nod.

'We commit Daryo's body to the ground,' the priest intoned. As he spoke, six Batribi lifted the bier onto slings across the grave, placed Daryo's shield on his chest again and began to lower the body into its grave. 'We commit his spirit to the care of the Fourth Goddess. We commit his honour to the pages of history. We commit his memory to our minds. From the First God, we ask health. From the First Goddess, we ask bounty. From the Second God, we ask resolve. From the Second Goddess, we ask loyalty. From the Third God, we ask recovery. From the Third Goddess, we ask compassion. From the Fourth God, we ask security. From the Fourth Goddes, we ask that we shall one day stand alongside Daryo in her kingdom.'

The attendants began to gently shovel the earth onto the body. Everyone present remained until the grave was filled and a stake was hammered into the ground at the foot, a clan pennant on it and *Daryo the Walker* was engraved on the bronze plaque below. Sotyo knelt beside the grave.

'*Daryo the Walker, a man so great,*
*The orphan who rose to hero state.*
*His children thrive, his clan will sing,*
*His name throughout the ages rings.*'
'*Our people walk and walk again,*
*This fate of ours is each one's bane.*
*To sleep beneath the stars each night.*
*To walk and walk again in flight.*'

He stood and stepped back, bowing deeply to Jeda before withdrawing. The mourners gradually drifted away. Jeda waited for the privacy of her children and nobody else around before allowing herself to cry.

The attendees of the funeral took their leave over the next few days. Each one visited Jeda and her children before their departure, offering their sympathies and their support for the family if they ever were required. Ten days after the funeral, Stai departed, hugging his mother tightly and swearing that if he was needed, he would return to Ru'uatan with all speed. Unhappily, Jeda bade farewell to her older son. The next dawn, Kym and her family left Ru'uatan. The children found the Batribi land strange and daunting and Satoro and Kym both had duties in Bruszo that would require attention. Kym struggled to release her mother from her embrace and, with both weeping copiously, climbed into the carriage and Satoro cracked the whip to start the horses walking forwards. Jeda retreated inside the house, Vehllal following her closely. She sank onto the bed, sobbing. Vehllal sat beside her and held her until the tears receded. Finally Jeda looked up at her son. 'You are leaving too, aren't you?'

Vehllal took a sharp breath. 'Why... how... how did you know?' he conceded.

'I am your mother, Vehllal. I have seen you almost every day of your life. I know. You really are going to leave you aged mother here?'

'Mother...'

'I am sorry, Vehllal. That was unfair. I am sorry.' Jeda hung her head. 'I am. The clan will care for me. I feel at home among them and I know that Tella will make sure that I am well provided for.' She stood up and took Temma's Sword down from its place back on the wall. 'Take this. You may need it.'

'This is father's sword,' said Vehllal, standing up too.

Jeda shook her head. 'Father is dead, Vehllal. Nobody can take any possession with them to the next kingdom. I have a sword that I have not touched in seven summers and not used in three times seven summers. I have no need for this. You may.'

Vehllal reluctantly took the sword. He had not wielded it before and had only held it a few times; it was his father's blade. 'I am not leaving immediately. It will be harvest soon. I shall stay though the winter and leave with the spring.'

## Epilogue

The road was quiet. A small bird pecking at a dead animal took off at the approach of the traveller. The Tiverta Pass seemed tranquil. In a heartbeat it changed as three armed men emerged from the trees. The travelling priest raised his hands defencelessly as two swords and a club menaced him.

'Hand us any valuables that you carry,' demanded one of the ambushers.

'I have no valuables,' said the young priest fearfully. 'I am a scholar. I travel to the Archive in Allesbury to study.'

'All priests carry valuables!' growled the man. 'Alms for the poor, chalices, something of that nature!'

'No, no! Nothing!'

'Priests should not lie!' growled the man with the club, shoving the priest hard.

'I do not lie! I have nothing!' shrieked the priest.

'Unhand him!' commanded a voice from behind. The ambushers and priest all turned. Walking north, the same way as the priest had been, was a young man in a cloak. The thieves looked at each other and scoffed.

'On your way, boy!' said the first. 'But not until we take what you have as well.'

The young man removed his cloak in a swift movement. He had on an old-fashioned armoured jerkin with the hood raised, elaborately-carved metal arm guards and a curved sword hung at his side. He lowered his hood. He was a Batribi, his hair a tightly-curled fuzz of black, a wide nose and full lips that were frowning in anger. His appearance seemed to anger the third thief.

'Run away, dog! This is none of your concern!'

'On the contrary. Release the priest, allow him and I to pass and I shall do you no harm.'

The thieves laughed. 'One of you against three?'

The man with the club bludgeoned the priest suddenly, knocking the slight man to the ground. The Batribi reached down and with a flick, his sword came free and was in his hand. The angry thief ran at the Batribi, who ducked low and used his body and free arm to hurl the man over his head, crashing to the road with an awful noise. The man with the club lashed out. The Batribi's blade drove into the wooden cudgel and stuck. The Batribi swordsman used this to yank the club from its owner's hand and he used the edge of the club to smack its owner across the side of the head, knocking him to the ground. He put the sword down, stepped on the club, freed his blade and parried the last thief's blow. A quick twist of his curved blade and the thief's blade spiralled through the air. The Batribi drove the thief back against a tree with his hand in the man's chest and the point of the sword at the man's throat.

The thief garbled a plea for mercy. The Batribi glared in the man's eyes.

'If I give you your excuse of a life, I will never see you in this world again. If ever you lay a finger on any man ever again, I will find you and kill you very slowly.' Every syllable of each word was dripping with menace.

'I understand.'

The Batribi stepped back and turned away. As the man moved away, the thief looked for his sword. He went to grab it and the Batribi's fist caught him across the jaw.

'No more chances,' said the Batribi. 'Run.'

The thief scrambled up the bank into the trees, leaving his two battered comrades in the road. The Batribi helped the priest back to his feet.

'How is your head, sir?'

'Just an ache. I trust the Third God.'

'As do I. Would you like me to escort you as far as Tiverta?'

'My thanks but I prefer to travel alone.'

The Batribi nodded. 'As you wish. Gods' Guidance.'

'I am sorry,' called the priest. 'I would at least know your name.'

The young Batribi retrieved his cloak, put it on and raised his hood. 'My name is Vehllal Vazzecco, the new Walker of the Batribi.' He raised his sword by the hilt, point down, in salute. 'My sword and my service, sir.'

He returned his sword to his belt and turned north.

## The End

# Addendum

These notes taken from the Imperial Records in the Vaults of Records in Ossmoss, in the year 493 of the Empire Age of Yashoun, the 4th year of the reign of King Koman the First of Adaca, the 8th year of the reign of King Suhmuz the Fourth of Jaboen and offered with the wish of Guidance from the Third Goddess in your comprehension

## Contents
- A note on dates
- The recognised realms, their rulers, ranks and nobility
- The Known History of the Batribi People
- Geographical features of the world
- The Gods and Goddesses of the Pantheon and other recognised faiths\

## A note on dates

There are somewhat different systems of dating in the world. Most ordinary people have little concept of a year. Instead they think in terms of cycles of seasons. If a child is born in the summer and have lived through ten cycles of seasons and reached the tenth anniversary of their birth, they are thus said to be ten summers old. Some may add the extra seasons, thus by the First Day of Spring, they may be said to be ten summers, ten winters. This is most common in the north and west- Jaboen, Gourmin, Armynya, Boskinia and the Kyi Sun Islands. With this system, events are dated according to when they happen in relation to other events. Thus, Daryo was born in the third summer before the Yashoun withdrawal.

Adaca and Yashoun date in years. Adaca dates years according to their current king. Thus, Daryo was born in the Thirty-second Year of the Reign of King Benini the Eighth. Yashoun has three dating periods- the Separate Age, before Yashoun became one realm, which ended in 800SA; the Pre-Imperial Age, before the united nation began to conquer, which ended in 771PA; and the Empire Age, as an imperial power. Thus, Daryo was born in 342EA, or 1913SA by the old reckoning. This can be compared to the modern BC/AD system and 342EA in Ossmoss and Nudakso is 1188AD in London and Jerusalem.

All following dates are in the Yashoun style.

## The recognised realms, their rulers, ranks and nobility

### Adaca

Adaca is a kingdom ruled by a hereditary monarchy, the House of the White Bull, since 761PA. Three years previously the seven provinces had united to repel the only recorded Yashoun invasion of Adaca. The first leader of the united army, Lallano the White Bull of Darsux, was proclaimed king following the battle of Kershaya and made his capital at his seat in Darsux. King Lallano VIII, son of Kyomi X, son of Mattiori XXI, ascended to the throne in 368EA. Adaca has no law mandating that sons take precedence in succession over daughters but no woman has sat the Adacan throne. The kingdom is ruled from Darsux, a small walled citadel on a branch of the Wyhr River, but the largest city is the sprawling agrarian town of Aden, downriver.

Adaca's land is ruled and led by lords, sometimes called squires, on behalf of the king. The land is divided into manors by the king and lords, some hereditary, some granted by royal favour, administer their manor on the authority of and on behalf of the king. Adaca also has captains, a rank of nobility as well as a military position, below the lords, who may be a lieutenant of the lord or in the direct service of the king. Squires, the formal title, are also official positions ranking below a captain. Squire is a minor rank and the holder tends to be young, a servant of a higher noble or an aspirant military leader.

Its people are probably the fairest known, the palest skin and the lightest hair. Adaca has little influence from Yashoun, the people are known for their skills as archers, the Pantheon of Gods is not strong, many Adacans follow older religions and Adaca cares little for the Empire's customs, politics and fashions.

### Armynya

Armynya is a tribal nation that has little in common but an ancient language, a shared tradition and similar customs. There are traditions and prophecies of a leader who will come forth, unite the nation and lead it to victory. The prophecy states that the leader will be neither man nor woman. The One who is Both, who came forwards in 387EA and led Armynya against Adaca, was ruled by the Council of Tribes in 390EA to be illegitimate and not the fulfilment of the prophecy. In the absence of the foretold leader, the nation's loose national government is the Council of Tribes.

Armynya's tribes are divided into northern and southern, roughly demarcated by the Sutiv Marshes. Traditionally, the northern tribes are more peaceful and more willing to trade; even other Armynyans see the southernmost tribes as barbaric and backwards. Armynyan tribes follow their inherited faiths and their tribal beliefs. Most fight with the traditional *letian*, a triple-spiked sword-like weapon, and long oval shields. Southern tribes are often semi-nomadic and hunt and forage for food while the northern tribes are more sedentary and farm. Many of the larger northern tribes have their own towns and villages. The national first city is Thamriev but the old customs state that it may only be occupied by the prophesied leader. The Council of Tribes, made of the chosen leaders of each tribe, meets where it is required. If a flood occurs in the west, the Council meets close to the flood to show its concern and so that is as close as possible to the scene to render aid quickly.

The Yashoun Empire is a distant and irrelevant thing to those Armynyans aware of it. Its language, known as the Common Speech, has not reached Armynya. They retain their ancient language although those who deal with other realms often learn the Common Speech. Armynya has closest ties with Gourmin, as it the nation adjacent to the most progressive and permissive of the northern tribes. The Kyi Sun Islands off of the north coast of Armynya were once an Armynyan tribal seat but fell under Yashoun control in 66EA. As Armynyans are poor seaman at best, they have remained securely so.

## Boskinia

Ruled by the House of Oak, Boskinia is ruled from Hamlakia but it is a recent change. The old city of Hivamakia was once the capital of the lost land of Crimir and the first city of Boskinia. The largest cities have long been one of Hypsios, Iannakia, Psephana or Thetri, the thriving Lake Cities. Boskinia is a land of ancient trees, water and horses. The realm's king, Gorero IX, is the eightieth ruler of his kingdom. Boskinia is the oldest nation known to exist. The Halfwood Palace is the seat of power of the House of Oak, who took power in 510SA in a war that is almost forgotten, even by students of such things. In this war, the River Towns were also taken from Vidmaria.

The nation is divided into lordships. Some lords rule entire cities, some small manors based on villages or even tiny hamlets. The precedence of lords among the court is that of the size of their manor. The highest lords rule the largest cities. They have captains and lieutenants to serve them and squires to educate and to be served by. Some lords, even small ones, have strong forts, others have grand houses.

Boskinia has a small following of the Pantheon but the older religions of the White Lady and the Good Shepherd are more common. The people are known for their fierce loyalties to their homes and their families but also to their lords.

## Gourmin

A strange and sparse land, Gourmin is a land without a king. The last Gourmini king, Trison IV, died without an heir in 639PA and there was little enthusiasm among the lords of the land to replace him. Consequently the lords treated and Gourmin became a nation of large manors that existed almost completely harmoniously alongside each other- Allesbury, Aslon, Sinsebil, Sitak, Spiert and Tiverta. The people speak the

Common Speech and have a freedom of faith, belief and following that few others possess. Gourmin is covered in deep forests, coastal plains and deep, marshy grasslands. It sends much timber to other nations; it is even rumoured that the famous Halfwood Palace in Hamlakia was built of Gourmini timber.

## Hajmachia

Hajmachia is bound south and east by the mountains, to the north by the mighty Dithithindil River and to the west by the smaller Rith River. It has a history as a single realm that is almost as long as that of Boskinia. The nation's last ruler, a Queen Joun, was killed by the invading Yashoun forces in 12EA as Yashoun took the first of its imperial provinces. In 310EA, the Emperor granted the Hajma Council authority to rule its land under him, with a set number of its members appointed at Imperial command. Hajmachia was, before invasion, a small and homogenous realm with the unique custom of sigils and awards being worn as patterns on the skin. It became tradition over time that men had these designs permanently inked into their skin and that women had them redrawn as they faded. The Hajma had small but productive mines of gold, copper and tin, which are often quoted as the reason for the Yashoun invasion. The little kingdom fought against the invaders but was eventually forced into surrender. The occupation of Hajmachia started brutally but quickly became one of acceptance on both sides, which led to the eventual reinstatement of the Hajma Council. Since the acceptance of Hajmachia as an Imperial Province, there have been some rebellions, most notably in 362EA.

Hajmachia's old capital, named Hajma after its people, was razed in 15EA but the Emperor permitted rebuilding in 61EA. Before invasion, the Hajma had a temple of the old faith in the centre but the Pantheon was imposed by the Empire and its dissolution spread totally. The Hajma people granted designs wear them proudly but few travel far from their homes except within Yashoun.

## Ishter

The Mountain Keep. Ishter is a tiny nation riven in two- the Ishteri who occupy the mountain city and the small tribes that roam the vale between the mountains. The city-dwellers were the most powerful tribe of the nation around the building and formation of the city between 233 and 250PA. It is accessed by only two roads- the Northern Gateway to Boskinia, the Southern Gateway to Adaca. It is led by the Senate, a group chosen by vote from the populace. This development was akin to the Gourmini loss of royalty- the Ishteri lord died naturally and there was no immediate successor. The elders chose from their number a small group to rule until one could be found. A successor was never found and the senate remained as the power in Ishter. The mines of the mountain keep the city in silver with more than sufficient to trade with Adaca and Boskinia for other needs. In matters of state and feuds, Ishter is known to favour siding with its neighbours.

## Jaboen

Jaboen is a land that has been riven by conflict. United by a lord of Halmia as the first king, it was divided between Gourmin, Yashoun and Vidmaria in 11EA. The Gourmini withdrew in 79EA after conflict with Armynya and the Yashoun Imperial army sacked the Vidmarian post of Three Rivers in 310EA and the Vidmarians withdrew. In 349, the new Emperor decided that the province was not bearing any real profit or benefit for the Empire and the Yashouns withdrew. As a result of other three centuries as a Yashoun rule, Jaboen is in essence a copy of Yashoun in religion, customs and practice. A scion of the last Halmian king was discovered living in exile in Boskinia and returned to his ancestor's throne somewhat reluctantly. As a result, the monarchy of Jaboen is weak and the king is mostly reliant on the eight Lords of the Council for power. Jaboen is a mostly mercantile nation and trades freely with Yashoun and its provinces, and with Gourmin and Boskinia as well. It requires a strong defensive presence due to the length of its border with Vidmaria along the Dithithindil River.

## Silver Island

The Silver Island is approximately two hundred miles from the coast of Yashoun and has been an imperial possession since 99EA. The island has been divided between two different civilisations since at least 100PA- the Silver Islanders living in the south of the island and with Suxin their major town; and the Nar Silver tribe, semi-nomadic and xenophobic, confined to the north of the island following the Yashoun arrival. Before 99EA, the Silver Islanders were a maritime people with a rich heritage of their own, a panoply of gods and an expressive if complex native language. The Yashoun conquest, achieved with overwhelming force and the near-destruction of Suxin, replaced the Silver Islander language with the Common Speech of the Empire, the native gods with the Pantheon and the culture of the Silver Islanders with the Yashoun way. The Nar Silver resisted and retreated into the mountains and preserved their way of life, especially after the Yashoun withdrew leaving just a small garrison under a Viceroy.

## Sodidor

The little nation of Sodidor was, before 757PA, a province of Adaca. When Yashoun invaded Adaca that year, Sodidor declined to join the resistance in return for Yashoun respecting the independence of the little corner of Adaca. The wide peninsula and associated islands had little resource other than the sea and a small population.

Although a small nation, the Sodidoron people were proud and determined and the little state maintained itself.

## Tibilia

Less than 100 miles south of the Adacan port of Baros is the island of Tibilia. Tibilia was a province of Adaca until 114EA when it was invaded by the Yashoun Empire. Tibilia is the most distant province of the Empire from the capital of Ossmoss and thus the most independent. Imperial oversight was all but ended in 301EA when the last Imperial garrison was withdrawn, leaving only a viceroy. There has been talk of Tibilians starting a movement to evict the last remnants of the Empire and either be independent or look to Adaca for protection.

## Vidmaria

Dominated by mountains, Vidmaria has a long history of belligerence and aggression. Vidmaria has little by way of natural resources other than stone and wood and thus tends to take what it wishes from Boskinian and Jaboen lands. The land is densely populated for its size, the capital city of Verdeeleon is reputed to be the largest city in the world and also the best-defended. Unlike most nations that have small standing armies supplemented by men commanded by their lords, Vidmaria has a large standing army and often employs mercenaries from wherever they can be found. The Vidmarian kingdom is almost as old as Boskinia, the first King was Sreon and he led a large invasion of Boskinian territory in 539SA retaliation for Boskinia's seizure of the River Towns. The land was not retaken until 700SA. Vidmaria launched a wave of raids and conflicts continued all through the Yashoun Pre-Imperial Age and Vidmaria eventually held a long strip of Jaboen, south of the forward base of Three Rivers, which was retained from 709PA until the Yashoun army destroyed Three Rivers in 310EA.

## Yashoun

Before 800SA, Yashoun was separate provinces and often mutually hostile. The unifying forces were King Ossmoss and his new bride Queen Nudakso. Their union brought the two largest provinces together. The major cities of the new nation were later named for them and the twin city of the new capital, Paloss, for their son. A Vidmarian incursion into Yashoun in 740PA first created the notion in the Yashoun royalty's consciousness that Yashoun was large enough and powerful enough to dominate. The first imperial excursion was into Adaca but it was repulsed. The invasion of Jaboen and Hajmachia came first, followed by Kyi Sun Islands, the Silver Island and finally Tibilia formed the Yashoun Empire by 114EA. Although Jaboen was allowed secede from the Empire in 349EA, the remainder of the Empire has been held together by a combination of force, trade and inertia. Emperor Lisadako III was crowned in 381EA and launched an impressive series of efforts to bring the Empire closer.

Yashoun's size, influence and spread has meant that it is perhaps the dominant realm and its customs, manners and even its language are all but universal. The vast majority of people have faith in the Pantheon of Gods, the Great Temple of whom is sited in Ossmoss and is the grandest building in the Twin Ports. The Yashoun assignment of the week into eight days, a rest on the eighth, is used even in the most distant corners of the world. The wheel-and-spears symbol of Yashoun appears on much of the currency used in trade and the best ships come from the Yashoun shipyards on the Silver Island.

## The Known History of the Batribi

There are little written records of the Batribi people. The Batribi themselves prefer stories and poems to making written records, mostly as their lifestyle would mean that storage and transportation of the records would be difficult. Most written accounts of their history come either from the Imperial Records in Ossmoss, Yashoun, or the ancient Archive in Allesbury, Gourmin.

The Batribi arrived in the area of what is now the Northern Ports in Yashoun around 760PA in a series of ships in various states of wreckage. Some were barely afloat. Some did not make the shore and sank, killing scores or even hundreds. What drove them to leave their home across the seas remains unclear but it is presumed to be some form of natural catastrophe or plague. Batribi were and are a clan-based society, extended families led by an elder or, sometimes, simply a strong leader. It is estimated that between two and three hundred individuals landed safely and most chronicles of the time suggest that there were more women than men and few children. The Batribi did not speak the Common Speech, they used their own language. They were an oddity to the Yashoun people: the Batribi had dark skin, tight curly black hair, wide noses, large eyes and were tall in general. The Batribi were at the mercy of their new neighbours. The Yashouns barred their gates against these newcomers and sent to Ossmoss for aid. The Batribi were not violent but the arrival of such a large group of such alien people must have been startling. The Batribi made camps, one believed to be south of the town of Dumoss, the other further east. Shovomoss, now a Yashoun port, was no more than a fishing village and is believed to have been almost taken over by the Batribi seeking more shelter than their tents made of sail canvas and shacks built from the ruins of their ships. An Imperial deputation and a large number of troops arrived, making their base at the waterside castle in Dumoss. Negotiations and liaison was difficult as neither side spoke the other's language. The Batribi were forced away from Dumoss and congregated around Shovomoss. The remaining residents fled east to Tanduldo and thence got a ship to Dumoss. They pleaded their case directly to the leader of the Emperor's representatives, believed to have been a Lord Famoshi. Famoshi, a landowner from the Dithithindil River, ordered his troops to remove the Batribi. Somehow the Batribi were warned of the impending assault and came to the decision to leave before they were evicted. The records do not suggest how many groups the Batribi divided into but it is guessed to be seven due to reports from elsewhere of their arrival. They used whatever they could to manufacture carts and goods sleds and then divided. Reports have been found from Ossmoss, Rotir, Ninato, Taam, Sictan, Thiel in Jaboen and Lichon in Vidmaria reporting these wandering people arriving outside the city within the next few seasons. Jaboen was a more welcoming place than most. The group that reached Lichon were massacred by the town garrison. The groups that arrived in Rotir and Ossmoss were accused of thefts and other crimes, united on the Dithithindil and made their way into Hajmachia. By 66EA, Batribi clans had travelled as far south as Veritimoss, as far east as the Jaboen town of Lalbi and south-east to Hivamakia in Boskinia. Adaca, northern Jaboen towns and Hajmachia were particularly known for their tolerance of the wanderers. The Vidmarian King Brenot XVI passed a law literally making it a crime punishable by death to be a Batribi in Vidmarian lands in 91EA. Few Batribi made it to Sodidor, Boskinia's eastern regions or Gourmin simply due to the distance involved, even as late as 300EA.

Much of the Batribi way was and remains different from Yashoun and the lands around it, even before they were forced into a nomadic lifestyle. Their loyalty to clan was not a loyalty to state that a Yashoun lord would expect, or the loyalty just to one's own immediate family that a Yashoun villager would know. Their dense hair was strange, often in elaborate braided patterns, and the women used colour to enhance their features. Many Batribi men, particularly the elders, shaved their skulls completely, anathema to many of the faith of the Pantheon. They came with their own faith in different deities and sat around large fires in the night, speaking poems and stories in their language that many ordinary folk that heard them took as witchcraft. They wielded broad curved swords and short spears to defend themselves, all made with excellent steel, better than any the Yashoun army could produce. Children, boys included, were encouraged to form a deep emotional connection to their parents and to mutually rely on them even into old age. Clans divided only when there was no other course but new clans formed and the Batribi spread from the north of Yashoun over the years. Some settled where they were permitted, some yearned to do so permanently, but many quickly adapted to their life as walkers, travelling constantly, never staying for more than the space of a few days. This leant the community a somewhat ethereal and mystical reputation. One Batribi was indistinguishable from another. A clan left a town's vicinity one day and within a few weeks, another clan would appear, make camp and leave again. One Batribi was all Batribi, one clan was any clan. A Batribi thief in the summer in Lalbi could be the next boy of about the same age that arrived in the autumn. A Batribi beggar woman in Paloss was the woman with a like braid in her hair that was seen the next week. The Batribi soon learned to use this to their advantage as they could easily leave an area if there was trouble and the local people would be unable to distinguish the clan they sought from the others that walked the roads.

The Batribi numbers declined sharply between 760PA and 5EA but the population recovered slowly. An Imperial estimate in 280EA suggested that there were approximately 3000 Batribi, about one third in Yashoun, a quarter spread between Jaboen and Gourmin, one fifth in Boskinia and the remainder scattered in Hajmachia, Adaca, Sodidor and Tibilia. No Batribi are known to have been able to make a life in Armynya and clans rarely make the difficult trek through the mountains to Ishter.

In 358EA, in response to a diplomatic approach and to solve local tensions, the Lake Stannia glen was given by King Suhmuz II of Jaboen to the Batribi people in perpetuity. The settlement on the lake's east bank, named Ru'uatan for the Batribi's near-forgotten homeland, grew to a town of some 1900 by 390EA, perhaps by then half of the Batribi population. By 440EA, the town was nearly 4000 strong. The community was led at first by an Assembly of Clan Leaders but they soon elected a leader from among their number, the first being a man named Dostan.

## Geographical features of the world
## Mach

The tallest mountain, a spiked peak standing thousands of feet above its neighbours, a giant of rock south-east of Hajma and west-north-west from Verdeeleon between the nations of Hajmachia and Vidmaria. No man has ever climbed any distance up Mach, as the peaks around it are impenetrable

## Dithithindil

The longest river, stretching 1139 miles from its source in the Boar Mountains between Armynya and Boskinia, along the northern fringes of Boskinia, Vidmaria and Hajmachia and cutting through Yashoun to its mouth at the Twin Ports, Ossmoss and Paloss. Large ships can proceed up the river as far as Sictan in Yashoun, nearly three hundred miles, and large river craft ply the waters between Hivamakia and Hypsios in Boskinia, the broad river Hypsios joining the Dithithindil in its early reaches. Historically, the Dithithindil has formed the northern borders of Hajmachia, Vidmaria and Boskinia for as long as any records exist. Control of river traffic in certain areas has decided battles and the fate of cities and states.

## Great Cities

The largest city known to either the Imperial Records or the Archive of Allesbury is officially the Twin Ports, Ossmoss and Paloss. Either is bigger than the nearest rivals for size- Aden in Adaca and Allesbury in Gourmin. Unofficially, it is said that largest city in the world is Verdeeleon but there is no verification of this. By population, the largest cities of each state are: Adaca- Aden; Armynya- Unknown, probably Shtumov; Boskinia- Psephana; Gourmin- Allesbury; Hajmachia- Hajma; Ishter- Ishter; Jaboen- Halmia; Silver Island- Suxin; Sodidor- Zonathor; Tibilia- Sonitimino; Vidmaria- Verdeeleon; Yashoun- The Twin Ports, Paloss is the larger by population although Ossmoss covers a larger area.

## Natural Occurences

Yashoun's Northern Wastes are the driest place in the world. No rain falls at all for most of spring, summer and autumn. The only natural water sources are some very rare wells and the lethally saline Salt River. The temperature is also very high for much of the year although late summer in the Silver Island is known to be hotter.
Adaca is the wettest nation and has the coolest climate. Tibilia is also known for its particularly cold and foul winters. Some parts of Tibilia's highland has snow for eight tenths of most years and Ishter has snow from mid-autumn to early spring. Verdeeleon's name among its residents is the Frozen City, it is high in the mountains and often snow-covered too.

## People

Yashoun has the largest population as a single state, believed to be in the region of 4,600,000 in 350EA. It is possible that the population of Armynya is greater but it is difficult to ascertain. Adaca follows with approximately 2,100,000, Boskinia about 1,900,000 people and Vidmaria guessed to be about the same, Jaboen and Gourmin less than 800,000, Sodidor around 300,000, Hajmachia 220,000 and Ishter and Tibilia both less than 40,000. The Silver Islanders number approximately 11,000, the Nar Silver are estimated to be about 2,000 and the Kyi Sun approximately the same.
For area of land, Adaca and Armynya are close in size but sparsely populated. Yashoun is the next largest and its cities and towns are larger by average. If islands and provinces are included, Yashoun is the larger although Hajmachia, Tibilia and the Silver Island are imperial provinces and not part of the nation of Yashoun itself.

## The Gods and Goddesses of the Pantheon and other religions
## The Pantheon

The Pantheon of Gods and Goddesses is the recognised religion of the Empire of Yashoun, officially declared as early as 40PA, and is the predominant religion in the Empire, Jaboen, Sodidor and Gourmin. It has also been adopted by the Batribi, who are particularly fervent believers.

The Great Temple is at the exact centre of Ossmoss. The Great Temple has an immense dome at its centre surrounded by eight smaller domes that contain the septs of the deities. The chosen leader of the faith, the Reverend Apostle, has his seat in the Great Temple and is spiritual servant of the Emperor directly. The circular central altar sits directly beneath the centre of the great dome and the Reverend Apostle's chair is on the south side, facing the Grand North Door, the entrance to the Temple. Most temples of the Pantheon are domed to reflect the Great Temple and altars are traditionally circular. Priest and priestesses serve the Pantheon individually, a priest is sworn to a particularly deity as are individual temples. Prayers are normally said to each of the Pantheon in turn when outside a temple but to the patron of the temple only when inside. Children are normally given a Guardian at birth, one of the Pantheon as their patron and protector, normally the deity on whose day the child is born but sometimes for other reasons. The faith teaches that the dead proceed to an afterlife known as the Next Kingdom although there are many different interpretations of the Kingdom's nature. The Gods and Goddesses are ranked in precedence, the First Goddess is considered equal to the First God in all things.

- o Dravin, the First God. Symbolised by a spreading tree. Bringer of health and strength, protector of kings and commanders, venerated on the first day of the eight. Offerings are often of steel or wood and prayers may be addressed to 'Mightiest of the Mighty'.
- o Tahili, the First Goddess. Symbolised by a bound wheatsheaf. Patron of farming, harvesting, hunting and giver of plenty. Guardian of farmers, hunters, fishermen and miners. Venerated on the fifth day offerings are always edible and are given as gifts to her priests.
- o Thiney, the Second God. Symbolised by a spear, sometimes burning. Giver and taker of war, conflict, strife, struggle and adversity. Venerated by soldiers, particularly on the second day. Offerings are usually armour but also symbols of peace such as broken blades. The Second God is said to intervene both for and against conflicts, depending on the circumstances and the wishes of the supplicant.
- o Brokea, the Second Goddess. Tutor of duty and loyalty, guide of parents, symbolised by a burning fire of passion and devotion. Soldiers and lords also

worship her. Offerings must be precious to the giver and burned on the altar and on the sixth day.
- Spellis, the Third God. The patron of healing, medicine, potions and witchcraft and magic symbolised by a ten-pointed star representing the elements but sometimes as an old man. The Third God asks for herbs and healers' tools such as bandages to be given, especially on the third day of the eight. Healers, alchemists and those who produce products such as wine pray to the Third God.
- Spinel, the Third Goddess. A kindly guide in the ways of compassion, reason, thought and mercy. Mothers and soldiers are both frequent devotees of her ways, many wearing her crystal symbol or carrying one with them. Her day is the seventh and her offerings are often books or gems.
- Dule, the Fourth God. Symbolised by an anvil, the patron of merchants, shopkeepers, smiths and builders, bringer of wealth, prosperity and mercantile security. The fourth day is devoted to the Fourth God and is often a market day. Offerings can be items produced or sold by the worshipper, gold or any other material possession. Dule is the most commonly invoked God in curses and oaths.
- The Fourth Goddess is named but her name is never spoken as speaking it is said to provoke her to act on the speaker. The dead moon is the unchallenged symbol of death and demise. The Fourth Goddess goes by many other names and by many guises: often called the Darkest Goddess, a cruel trickster, a manipulator, a whisperer in the ears, she is believed to be a predator of the living, taking the souls of those who die to be her acolytes in the Next Kingdom. Many of those who have killed, soldiers and warriors, believe that the Fourth Goddess most desires the souls of those who kill as her most valuable servants and some believe that in their prayers they can bargain with the Darkest Goddess to keep their own life in return for sending more souls to her charge. Many fear the Fourth Goddess but some court her as an inevitability and a capricious but powerful mistress. Unlike the other deities, the Fourth Goddess demands no offerings but souls and has no day as people die each day. The eighth day is one for the entire Pantheon. The name Vashine is said to be only safely spoken by the dead.

## The Cult of the White Lady

An older religion than the Pantheon, the cult of the White Lady is based on a feminine deity with various guises. Its earliest chapels were said to be built in about 470SA. The White Lady is depicted in many forms- a mother with her child, a virginal daughter, a bride, a huntress and her prey, a queen enthroned and scores more. The White Lady is particularly prevalent in Boskinia and Gourmin but also in Ishter and Adaca. The faith is based on the writings of the White Lady herself, a legendary woman said to be from beside the Dithithindil. The writings are a guide to how life should be lived, emphasising the role of women in the world, the need to respect and accept others and to cooperate as communities and families. Whereas the worship of the Pantheon is often the duty and choice of the individual, the White Lady's chapels hold worships on alternate days and have a set litany of prayers and exhortations.

The White Lady's female priests also conduct certain rites- a girl prays for the whole day on her tenth name-day and again on her twentieth. As a sign of devotion, a bride is shut in a purpose-made cubicle in the chapel the night before her wedding, bares her entire body to the White Lady as she prays and does not emerge until she is to be married the next day. It is said that for every recitation of the full bridal litany, the bride is given a year of harmonious marriage. Men undergo a similar ceremony when they come of age, but at home, and after the birth of their first child.

Some cities have retreats where women who wish to may go to live as servants and acolytes of the White Lady. They give up all they have and spend the vast majority of their time in seclusion due to their nakedness and renunciation of possessions. Such institutions exist in Aslon and Spiert in Gourmin; Hypsios, Topakia and Vhamsia in Boskinia; and Kyusi in Adaca.

### The Good Shepherd's Flock

As with the White Lady's following, that of the Good or Great Shepherd is older than the Pantheon's faith. The Good Shepherd's Chapel in Aden is said to date to 399 or 409SA. The Good Shepherd's followers are mainly concentrated in Adaca and Sodidor but there is some representation in the far south of Yashoun, the only place in the Imperial heartland where there is religious dissent, and in certain parts of Gourmin. The Good Shepherd is said to be just as his title suggests, a loving and attentive father figure caring for people as a shepherd cares for lambs. The small shrines to the Shepherd are normally richly decorated with pastoral and ovine scenes and each altar has a shepherd's crook embedded in the centre, some of which protrude like masts and some of these are engraved with similar scenes to the wall paintings. Unlike the faith of the Pantheon or the White Lady, the Good Shepherd's priesthood are known for having their own families and for welcoming the followers of other religions to their shrines. The Shepherd's Flock are a peaceable, caring and welcoming community and some Batribi have been known to prefer the Shepherd's teachings to those of the Pantheon.

## Other faiths

There are as many faiths, a revered and blessed Reverend Apostle wrote in 1EA, as there are clouds in the sky. Different states and different monarchs, different communities and different individuals are known to trust their own beliefs on assigned religions and on their interpretations. Some may outwardly follow one faith but believe another. Some may eschew any faith. Gourmin is known as a place of particularly freedom for those with different faiths, Boskinia to a lesser extent. Yashoun, as home of the Pantheon's Great Temple, is not permissive of other faiths and followers of these faiths are persecuted.

The Old God is a now forgotten deity although the ruins of temples are found as far apart as western Jaboen, eastern Adaca and southern Yashoun. Nothing is now known of the veneration or beliefs of the faithful or the dictations of the faith although offerings of fabric and metal have been found in the temple ruins.

There is a state faith in Vidmaria, as in Yashoun, but not the same. The god of Vidmaria, as it is known outside Vidmaria itself, is a god that has its followers wear pottery and bronze amulets and have a score of feasts through the year, concentrated around the harvest period. The temples have steeply-pitched roofs and ring bells before each service, which are held twice daily and four times every five days.

The Silver Island faith, before it was supplanted by the Pantheon's, was based on the elements- water, ice, fire, wind, calm, earth, sand, rock, flesh and blood. The old faith of the Batribi was based on a similar principle. The Armynyan faiths are varied. Some northern tribes follow the Good Shepherd but old tribal religions survive and thrive, especially in the south. Some have gruesome customs and rituals, others venerate nature or animals.

Printed in Great Britain
by Amazon